Translated from the German by
M. L. WINITSKY

a novel

A fly on the Wall

The Discovered Journals of Heinz Linge, Valet to Adolf Hitler - Volume I

Waldaur Price Simons
Stuttgart - London - New York

Waldaur Price Simons
Stuttgart·London·New York

First Edition, 2019

Editing and book design by The Artful Editor

ISBN: 978-0-578-54274-4 (paperback)
Published in the United States of America

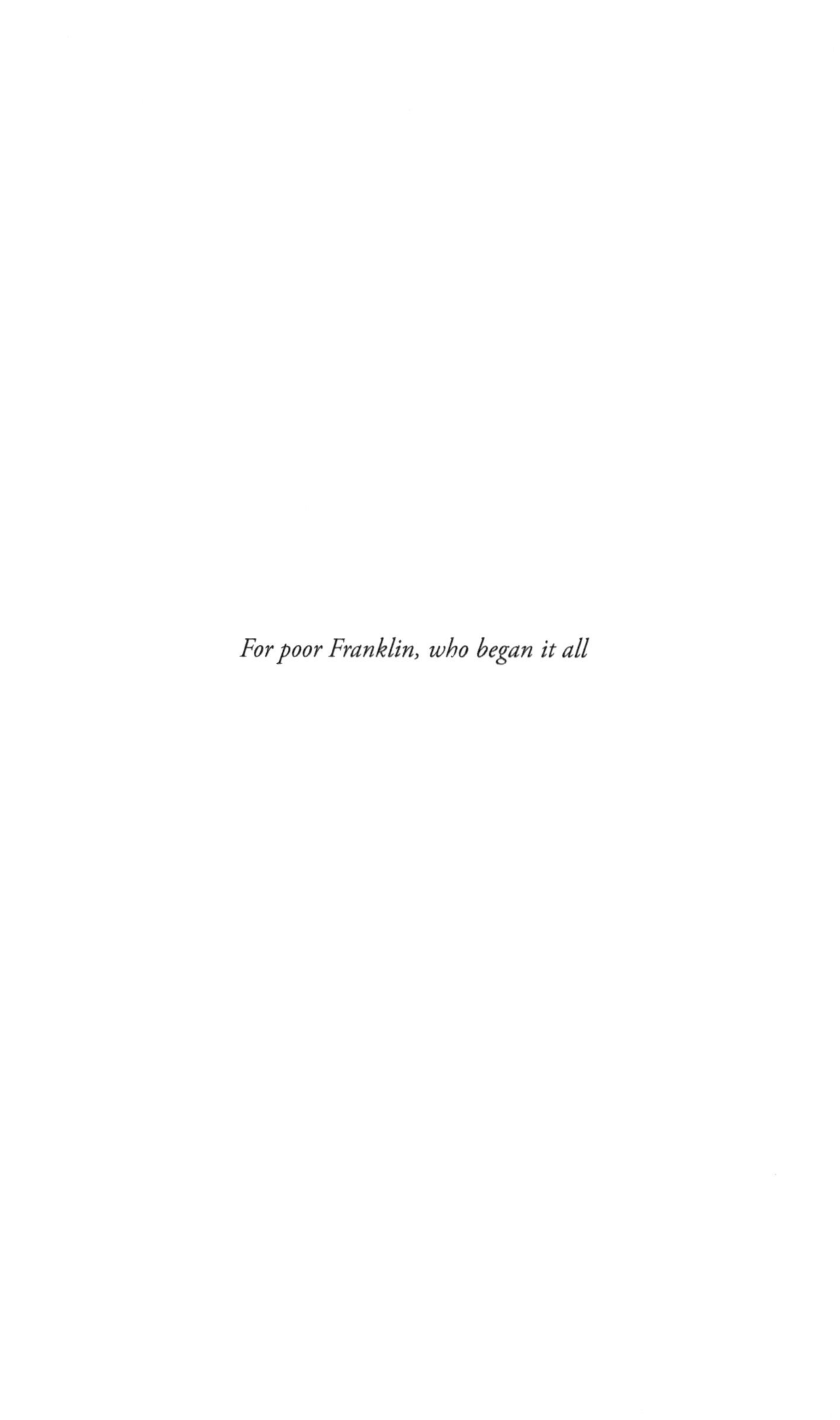

For poor Franklin, who began it all

Translator's Note

FEW WOULD KNOW his name, but it is impossible for those with even a passing interest in that most consequential decade in world history from 1935 to 1945 not to have observed the tall man with a dimpled chin and receding hairline, resplendently malevolent in the black and silver SS officer's uniform, always just behind Adolf Hitler, whether the latter was alone or surrounded by important personages from within Germany or without. At the very least, his figure might generate mild interest, if not curiosity. Some might well guess him to be an important, high-ranking member of the Führer's security staff, or an adjutant of the race-obsessed monster Reichsführer-SS Heinrich Himmler. However, they would be as wrong as could be, for the man was only a servant, Hitler's personal valet, Heinz Linge.

Knowing this, they might then dismiss him with a finger snap as a mere SS-liveried servant, one of the multitude of nameless, faceless people "below stairs" who cared for the Führer. And yet this, too, would be entirely wrong, for Heinz Linge was, despite his station—or perhaps because of it—one of the most important and influential figures in Hitler's inner circle.

He was born in Bremen in 1913. His father, Klaus Linge, was an itinerant, drunken, brutish labourer, and his mother, Beata, a hapless, browbeaten *hausfrau* who was obliged to perform menial tasks to make ends nearly meet. Though an inordinately bright child, with the death of his parents, Heinz was forced to leave home and school at the age of ten to fend for himself. He spent his adolescence foraging, pilfering, and scrapping on the streets even while residing unwillingly in a few orphanages and detention facilities. Ultimately weary of such a dead-end existence, he managed, in his late teens, to apprentice as a bricklayer. Not a political man by any standard, but unable to visualize a future in bricklaying, in 1933, at the urging of a coworker, he joined the SS, where his size, strength, and apparent lack of guile secured him a position with the elite SS Leibstandarte, Hitler's personal bodyguard. In 1934, while part of Number 1 Guard at Hitler's residence on the Obersalzberg near Berchtesgaden, Linge was selected to serve at the Reich Chancellery.

However, this is only a superficially minuscule part of the story now fully realized through his journal, sent to me by a source close to Linge whose identity, by her express wish (and a written agreement on my part), cannot be divulged.

When I accepted the task of translating and editing the recently unearthed multivolume journal of Heinz Linge, I was immediately confronted with a number of challenges, not the least of which was the existence of two other accounts of the man's role in the Hitler saga: a tiny volume entitled *With Hitler to the End: The Memoirs of Adolf Hitler's Valet,* published in 1980; and *The Hitler Book: The Secret Dossiers, Prepared for Stalin from the Interrogations of Hitler's Personal Aides,* a 413-page report of daily Soviet interrogations of Linge over a ten-year period (published in 2005), both differing significantly from each other and radically so from my own source material in tone, form, and substance. This alone raised significant questions concerning authenticity, accuracy, and even veracity. In addition, and not surprisingly, it evoked serious questions about motivation, that is to say, the *why* of these extraordinary disparities.

After even the most assiduous reading, Linge's truncated anecdotes in *With Hitler to the End*, already well known to most readers of Hitler's rise, rule, and downfall, are easily dismissible, both as serious historical work and as a legitimate memoir. For the most part, the work is an apologia for Hitler (as are all the several servants' memoirs). Far more troublesome is the irony that, in this as in all the other ostensible memoirs, we learn virtually nothing about their authors, their personalities, interests, and attitudes, or the significance (to them) of their interactions with those above and below stairs. But one can carry selflessness to excess, and, as a result, their accounts add little or nothing to the virtual libraries of works on Hitler and less than nothing to accounts of those retainers who were reputed to have served his every whim on a moment-by-moment basis.

Given all this, I contend that the importance of Linge's personal Journals cannot be overstated. Unlike the slobbering hagiographies of Hitler's other servants (perhaps with the minor exception of Christa Schroeder's), in Linge's Journals we gain a truly unique glimpse into the secret innermost thoughts and feelings of the man who, it turns out, was the Führer's most constant and intimate companion for ten years, despite the universally accepted historical accounts of Hitler's bohemian solitariness, lack of trust in anyone, mania for monologues, visceral decision making, and not infrequent domestic purges.

And, finally, a brief word on authorial methodology and the translator's challenge. Heinz Linge was far from a professional writer and had very little formal education. This Linge himself admits repeatedly in his Journals. However, he was a voracious and eclectic reader from his earliest years and was possessed of a photographic memory. As a consequence, I venture to suggest that he made authors his teachers and so, in his own writings, achieved a remarkable sense of proper style (perhaps, at times, too proper) and a highly developed and sophisticated use of grammar and punctuation.

Fortunately, Linge kept to a reasonably strict routine and a fairly consistent methodology in his journal writing, so his dates are chronological and match the events they describe. I saw to it that names were set out in full and that sufficient background was provided for most individuals and events (I tried my best to provide the missing items in Translator's Notes, set as footnotes). Since these are contemporaneous daily journals, and not a professionally considered history composed after years of research and analysis, there are many spontaneous thoughts and remarks, day-to-day musings, scenes, and opinions concerning daily life in a household as filled with trivia as it was with historical events. I chose to include them all to maintain the integrity of the Journals and to illustrate the life of a man who, daily, was forced to negotiate the perilous tightrope between power and servitude without the aid of any balance bar other than his own native intelligence and adroitness.

Initially, his Journals consisted of a series of handwritten notes that he photographed and then destroyed. He mailed the photographic negatives to an address he did not divulge in his writings. Unfortunately, not all journal entries were included, some because, even in Germany, small-negative photography was not yet the perfected medium it would become in the 1960s and 1970s. Moreover, Linge had to use a standard (though high-wattage) bulb for illumination, and film has just so much shelf life before deterioration sets in. Some supposed entries may never have existed, perhaps because of conscious omission for reasons never provided. Regardless, I (with the invaluable assistance of Sir Arnold Batts, a veritable magician in a darkroom) was able to glean a remarkable amount of detail from even the lesser quality negatives.

I conclude with something William Gladstone is said to have told a young member of Parliament: "The truly powerful of this world are not necessarily those the public knows."

Even more so can this be said of their servants.

VOLUME ONE

22 February 1935 to 31 August 1939

1935

I FACE A blank page.

How do I speak to you?

What do I reveal?

How does a man truly alone turn to perhaps the only person in the world he can trust and confide in him in the days and perhaps even years to come what will most certainly be both the momentous and trivial events of his life and the times? Does this to you sound like two identities? It is conceivable, but is not such an existence the only one vouchsafed to me in my new life? I imagine that this is for you to judge. I record this not as a writer but as a reader, not merely of books but of people. As a result, you may detect the influences of those far more highly qualified than I to set this down.

By this decision, you might reasonably ask whether I, lowly and unlettered as I am, have merely substituted literary masturbation for the anatomical—certainly not an unreasonable question if asked by a stranger. But my answer then is a simple one: to my journal, I am no stranger. Although I may mystify you from time to time, may contradict you from time to time, may dispute and even quarrel with you from time to time, I never lie to you or withhold from you. Ever. For in a solitary life of repression, there must be someone to whom I can confide, divulge, confess, render dangerous opinions without risking dire consequences, keep my

emotions in check, sort through the mental and emotional clut-
ter of my daily life to gain insight, entrust my troubles, and,
perhaps, even grow from the effort to set it all down.

And so, I begin.

I am Heinz Linge, born into dire poverty to a feeble, masochistic, and indifferent mother and a brutal, violent, drunken
father. Having had a short and negligible formal education, I
became a hooligan and roustabout until I wised up and became
an apprentice bricklayer. I am of over-average height, possess no
excess fat and even less hair—all in all, an entirely ordinary fellow,
you would say, save for one quality: a photographic memory. As
a consequence, as the saying goes: while a person like that may
remember everything, he understands nothing—a dubious gift at
best. However, once I became aware of my curious mental abnor-
mality, I made three far-reaching decisions that would direct my
life from that time forward: first, that I would read anything and
everything I could lay my hands on; second, that no one would
know of it; and third, the devil with understanding. It would be
only natural to inquire as to my motive.

You ask what has saved me from the justifiable and dangerous suspicion of others, and I can only answer that one sees what
one expects, and with my history and "attainments," a dullard
is expected, and so a dullard is seen—and so interpreted. But I
leave all that for another time, as I fear I may have confessed too
much on a first attempt at revelation.

Those others? you may ask. I will provide one example. Once
arrested in my sixteenth year, for a petty survival theft not unlike
that of Jean Valjean, I was taken by the police, who, after a series
of fruitless but mysterious interrogations, quickly gave me over
to a clinic in which the doctors placed me under an equally
fruitless and no less mysterious scrutiny, and then released me

without a word of explanation. Giving that experience no more thought, and requiring a means of subsistence, I concentrated on and took whatever menial labour I could obtain, until, ultimately, I secured a position as an apprentice bricklayer. Only when I was recruited by the SS[1] did I consider the consequences of my mysterious attributes and record.

And yet, in all the interviews and examinations I underwent with SS-Personnel, nothing of my arrest and inspection ever arose, even by inference, and I passed with no adverse comment whatever—or any comment, to be entirely accurate. And if they did know, what would they know? What could they ask? What could I tell them? That I function with a superordinate brain I cannot predict or control? That in a few unguarded moments, I speak a language I have only encountered in books? That, without the repression born of fear, necessity, and pure will, my memory of what I read would intrude into my nightmares as well as my everyday thoughts and human exchanges? Is that what I tell the mediocrities, both high and low, who surround me and rule my existence? And even were I to make the attempt, to none of these questions do I have any answers. What never leaves me is the knowledge that others will find me incomprehensible and, in an age of authoritarian simplicity, dangerous, since ordinary people, especially at this moment, require safety, that is to say, a consonance between what they see and know and what they think they see and know. Therefore, in this world, I navigate precariously.

Even now, it is difficult to believe my good fortune. Until

---

[1] The Schutzstaffel (SS), or "Protection Squadron," started out as the *Saal-Schutz* (Hall Security) to provide protection for the Nazi Party members and grew to become the Nazi regime's premier paramilitary security organization that also dealt in surveillance and terror. [All footnotes are translator's notes.]

today, I had encountered Adolf Hitler only twice. The first time was in 1933. I met him at a boisterous beer-hall political rally; yet at the time, I could say that he never met me. This puzzles you? It ought not, as I am not speaking of an ordinary encounter with an ordinary man. There, I was not a person but merely a hand, one of the thousands of anonymous hands he had grasped that day, my hand in his, a tiny drop of rain touching the ocean. So, you can see that at the time, any consideration of one day actually having the most intimate and personal relationship with him was as alien to my mind as to imagine a flying pig.

Yet not long after joining the Party and the SS[2], and for no reason I could discern, I was detached from my unit with about a dozen others to the Obersalzberg[3] as No. 1 Guard. However, during my entire time there, I saw the Führer only once, when he appeared on his immense balcony and shook hands perfunctorily with all assembled—until he came to me. Then he stopped, tilted his head slightly back to look me squarely in the face, and asked me what my sign was and if I had visions. I, of course, was too much in thrall to speak, and he appeared to know the answers in spite of my stricken silence. All I saw were his lips pursing and a cursory nod as he continued down the line.

People invariably ask me about his eyes. This I have been told. But I will inform you now that I was not among those who were impressed. This makes me—how is it said?—a majority of one. However, as with everyone else, I too was instantly transfixed by him. But it was his hands. My own hand was, of course, sweaty and trembling, and my embarrassment at it almost overcame me. But then he took my trembling hand and held it fast in his

---

[2] Linge provided no immediate explanation of his decision to join the Nazi Party or the SS.

[3] The county seat of Chancellor Adolf Hitler.

own. Though my intellect instantly recorded the coldness of his palm, I only felt a curious warmth, like a womb, enfolding me in its wordless embrace. Yes, I was looking into his eyes—how could one not? But I saw only a void, a vast nothingness, yet I was comforted. I was at peace. Hands are underrated.

Again, for no reason I could make out at the time, I was selected from a list of fifty, sent to a course in hotel training, and afterward served in a variety of menial capacities in an assortment of Reich Chancellery departments under SA General Wilhelm Brückner, the Führer's chief adjutant.[4]

But you wish to know of today, yes? And I think rightly so, for it was the most remarkable day of my life.

It began with an unexplained, urgent, eleventh-hour summons from Reichsführer-SS Himmler's headquarters. Nursing the remnants of a bout of influenza, I sat for three hours in the sterile Chancellery hallway of interminable marble and glass alongside a seemingly infinite row of rigid, eyes-front, black-and-silver-clad male bodies, their utter silence punctuated by the occasional oily creak of gleaming boot leather. And there was the odour of sweat, but not the sort of sweat you could see, the kind popping to the surface of faces, necks, armpits, and the smalls of backs, but the sweat of ambition, the kind you glimpse in a facial twitch, a fluttering of the eyes, a trembling of the lips, in the fixed stares of the desperate. I looked and acted no different from the rest, save that I'd been late, and yet it was I who was commanded to sit directly before the polished mahogany double doors to the Führer's quarters. For how long I sat there I have no knowledge, for I was benumbed with anxiety.

So benumbed that, without even noticing it, Brückner was

---

[4] SA stands for Sturmabteilung, or "Storm Detachment," the original paramilitary organization of the Nazi Party.

standing before me. At first, I failed to acknowledge him, for he was wearing in place of his resplendent SA General's uniform a brown, double-breasted business suit, off-white dress shirt, striped tie, and highly polished brogues, elegant but anonymous, save for a black eye patch. However, once my conscious mind placed him, I shot up from my chair at full attention and presented the Hitler salute, perhaps a bit more stridently than the occasion called for, the sound thundering through the hallway as if we were in a deep canyon. Brückner returned my salute perfunctorily, curved his thin, pale lips into something resembling a grin, and told me to stand at parade rest.

Brückner, a head shorter than I and considerably thinner, scanned me up and down, swinging his head like a metronome on its side. "Well, then, let's see if we can expedite this so you can recuperate fully, yes?" and without waiting for a response, he took me by the elbow and guided me to the massive doors. "Go in, Linge."

"But, Herr General, the others were ahead of me," I demurred.

Brückner chuckled mirthlessly. "Ah, you are quite the sentimentalist, Linge. Perfect. But you needn't concern yourself. Just go in," he repeated. "There are no others. There never were."

I shut the doors silently and passed through an uninhabited reception salon crammed with repulsive and ungainly furniture that was not intended for comfort or aesthetics and into the Führer's actual living room. It was approximately a thousand square feet in area and, unlike the salon, clearly designed for ease and even a certain exotic cosiness, despite its size. There was a beamed ceiling, old-fashioned chalet-style, wood wainscoting, and, suddenly, an immense fireplace facing me like the terrifying entrance to a forbidden cave. At the first sight of it, I could feel all the blood rush to my brain, my hands trembled uncontrollably, and I almost passed out right there, hoping that I'd throw myself in as in my dreams and swirl endlessly downward, downward, on fire, to . . . However, for reasons beyond my poor powers, I was able to collect myself sufficiently to narrowly escape the igneous maw and complete my tour. Around the fireplace were grouped a sofa and chairs upholstered in dark leather, all save one, which was turned away toward the far wall, its back to me. Beside the immense sofa stood an equally large table topped with swirled marble on which several newspapers lay. A large desk stood before a wall-length tapestry and two paintings I could not recognize. There must have been a colossal window, but it was completely shrouded by thick, heavy, dark-burgundy draperies. The only light was provided by a small green glass-shaded desk lamp, which did less to illuminate than to throw sinister shadows throughout the vast space.

As with the foyer, the living room seemed also uninhabited. To be frank, I had no idea what to do, for I also had no idea why I was summoned in the first place. As a consequence, I merely stood in the centre of the room and tried to banish all thought from my mind with little success, because I'd learned long before that the less you know, the more you imagine. Almost hysterical with curiosity, I decided to keep occupied by wandering with apparent aimlessness over to peer through the draperies. I had just reached them when his voice emerged from behind me and I spun round.

A welder I once worked with in my former life, who had lost several toes and one ear in the war, told me that in the face of danger, there are only three possible responses: fight, flee, or freeze. Fight, he said, was risky, flight was reasonable if conditions permitted, but freeze was suicide. I froze.

A voice is information, like anything written down or seen, so my memory needed no prompting to recognize his. But he was speaking to me in the sort of tone one assumes when having known a person for years. I saluted with panicked abandon and was about to shout *Heil* when the Führer whispered: "Linge, you look terrible. Are you ill?"

"No, my Führer," I lied. "That is, I . . . was laid up with the influenza for a time, but I am definitely on the mend. But, my Führer, I—"

He quickly raised his index finger to his lips. "No ceremony, Linge," he said. "You know, I had a . . . call it a vision, during the night, as I lay sleepless in my bed, of a man quite uncommon. Not truly extraordinary, mind you, but possessed of the singular ability to elicit the extraordinary from those capable of it, do you follow me?"

I was both transfixed and flummoxed. I could feel drops of sweat cascading down my armpits and back. "I . . . I . . . am afraid I do not, my Führer."

His little moustache rose as he smiled, something I had never seen before. "Naturally," he said, mirthfully, "this must appear to you to be quite irrational, for you have, to this point, dealt only with the rational, the humdrum, the ordinary. It is to be expected. But there is quite another reality. I have always known this, a reality that only the exceptional can perceive and make manifest. And we will make it known to each other."

There was silence, save the pounding of blood in my ears. I was confounded. Lack of formal schooling aside, I understood nothing of his monologue, but that did not appear to matter, for he merely gazed down at the floor, then began pacing round the room, seemingly oblivious to my presence, head bent, hands clasped behind his back like an ice skater. My own back felt like a waterfall. I was close to panic. Should I speak? Was he waiting for a response? I had no way of telling—or how perilous it would be in my breaking the silence. After his third circuit, he turned and moved toward me, stopping close enough for me to smell his breath. It was unutterably foul.

"Are you a spiritual man, Linge?" he asked, almost in a whisper.

"You mean, am I religious, my Führer?" I queried back.

"Not necessarily, but do you believe in fortune?"

Once I was reasonably certain that I was not to be subjected to a reprimand over something I knew not what, I answered: "I . . . I am standing before you now, my Führer. Is that not fortune?"

"No, Linge," he replied, "that is destiny, and you will be the final link in the chain that binds me to it."

I was utterly out of my depth, and so I remained silent as he turned round as if to walk away, but suddenly turned back, came up to me, glanced up for a moment, then grabbed me tightly by the shoulders, his eyes piercing through me like swords. "Don't speak, Linge; the expression of mystification on your face is sufficiently eloquent." He released his hands and stepped back, then, as if weighted down with a terrible burden of which he could not speak, moved slowly to his desk, and eased himself into his chair. "Linge," he began, his voice exhibiting a strength I had not expected, "those officers lining the hallway outside are but a façade, a stage set, if you will, a ruse to convince those who surround me that I was seeking merely one more valet. Of course—there is some truth to that, for I learned long ago, that for a lie to succeed, not unlike bread, one must surround it with a crust of truth."

For reasons that baffle me still, instinct overrode judgment and I blurted out: "But, my Führer, I was not born, educated, or trained to personal service. I am an ignorant labourer." Of course, I knew I didn't sound like one, though, in my untutored brain, the how was conveniently separated from the what.

The Führer smiled indulgently, his hands splayed, palms down, on his desk. "I expected that very reaction. In my position, Linge, I must see beyond the obvious and consider matters that elude others, even those most highly placed. It is only natural for you to wonder why I raised you above all the others, whom you consider far more qualified. I will disabuse you of this at once. You come with the highest recommendations from men whose knowledge of certain matters is both unique and essential to my purpose. I, of course, had to witness this for myself, and I tell you that I concur completely."

"If . . . if you say so, my Führer." I couldn't imagine that he was unable to see me sweating and shaking, but if he did, he gave no sign.

He eased himself up and came toward me again, then stopped. He was looking at me, and yet looking past me, a thing difficult to describe but easily seen. He was completely silent, not even the sound of breathing, and all I could hear was my racing pulse. Then he spoke, almost in a whisper, to that space beyond me. "Linge, do you believe that there is genius among the animal kingdom?"

"I . . . I have no idea, my Führer."

"I, for one, cannot believe it, because he would not have survived. And even among the early humans, any sign of deviance would have meant death or banishment—even worse than death for such creatures, don't you agree? Not even here, now, in this mere sand grain in the vast ocean of time, could someone with my unique gifts survive, much less become the saviour of the Aryan race, who is poised to place Germany at the very centre of

Western civilization. And yet, I have survived and will continue to do so, of this I am convinced. However, even I cannot accomplish this alone, and so you have become quite irreplaceable."

Stunned, I uttered: "B . . . but, my Führer, how can I of all people be irreplaceable?"

He nodded knowingly. "There is much I cannot divulge to you now," he replied. "Perhaps one day . . ." his voice faded to a murmur, then gained volume as he said: "There is a story, perhaps apocryphal, of a time when Henry Ford the automobile genius was walking down a hallway with his subordinate, and he stopped to ask him what time it was, and the subordinate replied: 'What time do you want it to be, Mr. Ford?' I am no less beset by such sycophancy, I'm afraid. The problem, Linge, is that a man in my position hears only what those round him think he wishes to hear."

It must have been because of the panic I could not express, for again, curiosity trumped prudence. "But, my Führer," I asked, "what if they were to tell you what you didn't wish to hear?"

He nodded slyly and his lips curved into a mischievous grin: "You must never lose that sense of humour, Linge; it is a most beguiling quality." He returned to his desk. "In any event, you will assume the duties of a personal valet. Realize that there will be many who will make demands upon you, including my inner circle and visiting dignitaries, but especially Krause, my ostensible chief valet, an efficient but unpleasant fellow—and for appearances, you must be seen to comply. But never forget, Linge, that there is only one to whom you answer. And when all are gone from my sight and your mundane duties and the attendant abuses are done, I will, increasingly often, call for you, and you will undertake your destined role."

Every part of me was screaming for an explanation of that

role, but I said nothing. Frau Linge, from fear or inclination, could not express any human warmth or feeling towards me, but she had not born an idiot. I knew to keep silent, but from that moment, if not before, my previous existence ended. I was reborn and nothing could ever be the same, that is, assuming it ever was.

Once dismissed, I emerged into a hallway now completely free of "applicants" and encountered Greta Hoffln, one of the many maids who tended to the Führer's domestic needs. A plain-looking peasant type: cheerful, short, overweight, red pockmarked cheeks, and bad teeth. She offered to show me round the Chancellery and to my new quarters and had begun doing so when we were suddenly blocked by the presence of the Führer's formidable chief secretary, Christa Schroeder, who informed Greta that her function was to clean toilets, not to be a tour guide. Without a word, Greta executed a short, quick bow and hotfooted it away.

Schroeder was a large, homely woman with a braided bun of hair so thick, dark, and dull, it looked as if a layer of coal ash had settled on it. She wore a drab grey dress that ended not far from the sort of sensible (that is to say, hideous) high-top laced shoes you find on aged nuns.

"You are staring at my shoes, Herr Linge." It wasn't a question and I did not treat it as one, and so remained silent, since she seemed rather put out by her task, in any event. "I select my shoes for comfort and utility, not for glamour and allure," she announced with an icy sneer. "This is the Reich Chancellery, not a dance hall."

"But I had no intention of—" I began, as if I would find anything about her even remotely glamorous or alluring, but she cut me off with a shrug of indifference.

She handed me the suitcase I'd left at the last guard station. "Normally, Herr Linge," she continued, "you would be directed to your quarters by your superior, Lieutenant Krause, but since he is unavailable at the moment, the task was thrust upon me. However, you will discover, I am not one to deal in idle chatter, gossip, or other frivolities, do you understand?" And without waiting for a reply she clearly didn't want, with the very tips of her long, chunky fingers, she then pincered my elbow with a grimace of distaste, as if I were a particularly disgusting discovery in a garbage bin, and began moving me to a short hallway that led to a set of steep stairs that we descended into another hallway that was far narrower and more dimly lit. There were only the two of us, and I wondered at the lack of activity but chose to keep my curiosity to myself. The institutional-green walls were lined with an endless row of identical cream-coloured doors, each with a number stencilled in the centre. She aimed me toward a door marked "5" and released my elbow. "This is your room. It contains a phone directly connected to the Führer, General Brückner, and your direct superior, Lieutenant Krause, should they require your services. Calling out is by permission only." Without another word, she pivoted on her comfortable and utilitarian shoes and returned upstairs.

Receiving no key, I assumed there was no lock, so I turned the knob and entered and shut the door behind me. I was right—there was no lock. The room was a small, narrow rectangle. There was no window. The light-green walls, like the hall outside, empty of decoration. A garish 150-watt bulb hung naked from a ceiling cord with a short on/off chain attached. An army cot graced one corner, and in another, a small, unfinished table. In the third corner stood a short chest of drawers inside a narrow, scruffy armoire. A door opened onto a tiny lavatory with a pull-chain

toilet, a tiny sink with a stained mirror above it, and a narrow
stall shower. All that was missing from my "cell" was a Bible and
a rosary.

I was just opening my valise when I heard a muffled scratching at my door, so muffled I wasn't sure I even heard it until it
happened again. Before I could open the door, a folded piece
of paper slid underneath it toward me, which I picked up and
unfolded. The typewritten note was most explicit:

> Herr Linge, you are not new to us. Realize that no move
> you make here will go without intensive scrutiny and
> analysis. While you help tend to the Führer, you labour
> under the likes of Krause, Günsche, Himmler, Goebbels,
> and Heydrich, and so you exist in a grossly malevolent
> and competitive goldfish bowl. You must never forget
> this. There are no locks on your door for a reason, so
> you must exercise caution. However, as consolation,
> you also have friends, even though you do not—or may
> never—know them. Incinerate this note immediately,
> for your sake and for all our sakes, for even typewriters
> can be traced.

There was no signature. I tore up the note, tossed the shreds in
the sink, set a match to them, and washed the resulting ashes
down the drain.

All that happened today, my friend, caused me to make five
major decisions:

1. Never ask a question of anyone if I can discover the
   answer for myself.
2. Never answer a question if it can be avoided, and if it
   can't, be as insipidly ingenuous as possible.

3. Be as invisible as those around me will permit.
4. Never display authority, intelligence, cleverness, or imagination.

And, most important,

5. Never, ever, commit anything personal to paper for more time than it takes to photograph it with my new Leica camera, utterly destroy the paper, and develop and conceal the film.

Of course, decision number five may well prove to be the most important, and so may also prove to be the most dangerous and complicated. And yet, as such, it must be executed fully.

I am fortunate in having that otherwise unbearable naked bulb, but I know nothing about photography, save that I open the back of the camera, insert a film cartridge, push a button, wind the film to the next empty space, finish the roll, wind it all back into the container, deliver it to a camera shop for development, and pick up the prints. Clearly, that impersonal and indolent procedure might no longer be suitable for my purposes.

I sat on my cot morosely considering the dilemma facing me and, after a time, concluded that even I can take pictures, but somehow I would need to quickly be schooled in the basic techniques of development and, somehow, gain access to a darkroom that is secure from the eyes of others. Until then, I would have to photograph my day, open the back in the dark, remove the cartridge, open it, place the exposed film into an envelope, and keep it there until I was able to develop in safety. But where would I store them? I pondered this as someone unschooled in techniques of object concealment and faced with a virtual monastic cell of a room without a lock on my door.

To refresh my brain, I concentrated only on things over which I had immediate control, namely, all the steps prior to hiding the film. I would grab the small chair and shove it under the doorknob (a risk, but it must be tried at least once), then lift the bedside table onto my cot, remove from my valise my Leica II 35mm camera I'd bought for sightseeing with the last of my money, place a film cartridge inside, close it, wind the film into place, get back onto the cot, move the sheets of paper that contain my conversation with you under the bright, naked bulb, photograph each sheet, go into my bathroom and tear the sheets into small pieces, burn them, then flush the ashes down the toilet, take a blank envelope from my valise, unspool the film in the dark, place the exposed film into the envelope, seal it carefully, place it under my pillow until the next morning when I could transfer it to my inside jacket pocket and seek out a secure hiding place in the Chancellery itself, far removed in space and suspicion from my own quarters.

And so, a quite amazing first day with you ends: was it a miracle wrapped in a puzzle?

Or a curse?

I AWAKENED, DETERMINED to employ a hide-in-plain-sight plan of procedure for my photography: Yes, let all see me with a camera; yes, let all see me taking pictures of the Chancellery grounds, Chancellery personnel, visiting dignitaries, Chancellery interiors, even the Führer. The ultimate enthusiastic amateur photographer, in aesthetic—and, of course, ingenuous—thrall to everything connected to his surroundings. The only caveat, and this was absolute, was never, ever to cause even the slightest friction with the arrogant and surly Hoffmann, the Führer's official photographer![5]

So much was Hoffmann a favourite of the Führer, that I went to him, once I knew I'd be photographing you, and told him—in the most general terms, of course—of my poor interest, despite my inexperience and calculated lack of talent, and begged him to permit me to roam around and take pictures of life in and around the Chancellery. Because I did not appear to be the remotest threat, he was most gracious and told me I could make use of his darkroom. Of course, I thanked him with almost a lover's ardour but steadfastly refused to burden his personnel and equipment

---

[5] Heinrich Hoffmann joined the Nazi Party in 1920 and was chosen by its new leader, Hitler, as his official photographer. Hitler and Hoffmann became close friends—so close, in fact, that when Hitler became the ruler of Germany, Hoffmann was the only man authorized to take official photographs of him. Hoffmann's photographs were published as postage stamps, postcards, posters, and picture books.

with my inadequate and amateurish efforts and remarked that I felt it would be much more fitting (and convenient for him) if I located some accommodating small shop in Berlin to develop my shitty negatives. He shrugged, claimed it would have been his pleasure and most certainly not a burden, but acceded to my stubbornness, thank God.

And I actually found one, ideally, owned by a Jew named Adolf (of all names!) Adelsheimer, a modest, neat,[6] inconspicuous little shop, well off the Kurfurstendamm. Here, no awkward questions would be asked, and my needs would be met without complaint. I no longer possessed a civilian suit, so when I entered his shop in full SS regalia for the first time, the colour instantly drained from the poor man's face. I was so overwhelmed with self-consciousness that I made a special effort not to appear as if I'd just come from Heydrich with an arrest warrant. It bothered me that the mere sight of my uniform could cause such terror, but I imagined that it had been designed for that very purpose.

"Good afternoon," I chirped in the cheeriest tone I could muster, but from his expression, and the Chancellery conversations I'd overheard, I imagined that, in his mind, cheeriness was a standard SS and Gestapo tactic to lull the subject before the forcible removal and rigorous interrogation. About what? What possible harm could this miserable creature cause? It was a situation I had no stomach for and longed for the kind of escape that Chancellery life afforded me, despite my occasional grousing at the hermetic isolation. Was creating this racial climate of dread and suffering truly a national necessity?

"Good afternoon, sir," he replied in a slightly uneasy voice. "And . . . how may I help you?"

---

[6] By 1936, most Jewish-owned businesses were covered in anti-Semitic graffiti painted on their outer walls, windows, and doors.

At that point, my instinct told me that no pleasantries would work until a relationship was established, so I would need to get to the point quickly. But first came security. I knew he'd misunderstand, and that would only add to his unease, but I couldn't risk being overheard.

"Please be so good as to place your 'closed' sign in the window and lock the door so we can speak more freely, yes?"

He splayed his hands anxiously, then bowed his head—as if my pulling out his fingernails with pliers was to be the next agenda item—reached under his counter, grabbed the sign, almost dropping it, ran to the window, and placed it on the narrow sill. Then he secured the door and came back to me, more agitated than ever.

"Please, Herr Adelsheimer," I said, "I'm here on a purely personal matter, and I require your assistance."

Adelsheimer squinted. "My assistance?"

"Yes. I wish you to grant me uninterrupted use of your darkroom from time to time. What I develop is my own affair and will not in the least burden you, that is a solemn promise. On the other hand, who I am and what I do here must be between the two of us and no one else, you understand?"

"B . . . but I don't know who you are and what you wish to do."

"Exactly right. I knew I could rely on your ignorance."

He shook his head and shrugged, as if he were holding the weight of the world on his meagre shoulders and had no idea why. "But, your honour," he replied, "you must know that I am a Jew, and so under constant surveillance."

I glanced at the yellow *Jude* armband just above his elbow and puffed some air from my nostrils. "So much the better, so to speak. It would be perfectly natural, then, for an SS man to be visiting you from time to time, yes?"

"Yes," he replied with a shrug of resignation. "I agree. It would be perfectly natural."

I knew he wished to add "now," but thought better of it. "Surveillance may continue, but I seriously doubt that you will be bothered once they've seen me. By the way, my name is Linge, Heinz Linge. So, we have an arrangement?" I suspected he'd consider this some sort of trap, but what choice did he have? I didn't even bother to employ a pseudonym.

"Herr Linge," he said, "you, of course, will have unlimited use of my humble shop and its facilities. When do you wish to begin?"

"Now," I told him. "This minute."

"Yes, of course. Do you have some film?"

"Yes, but I wish to do it entirely on my own. I only require rudimentary instruction in developing, some peace, and much privacy."

"Of course, Herr Linge."

"In private, you would call me Heinz. May I call you Adolf? I don't get many opportunities." I would have expected anyone to miss the irony.

His hands stopped moving. "Of course . . . Heinz. Please consider this shop your own. Before long, it probably will be."

I chuckled awkwardly and, in my mind, sadly at Adolf's black-humour prediction of the inevitable.

S**TARTLED AWAKE BY** a pounding on the door. I jumped from my cot, shrugged into my woollen robe, and raced to the door. When I swung it open, standing before me was a fat, middle-aged, fully uniformed SS-Second Lieutenant. A layer of perspiration covered his florid face like a gleaming veneer, his plump neck bulged from his collar, his eyes were narrowed menacingly, and his fists were jammed into his ample waist. His entire being indicated that he was less than pleased. Since I was a mere sergeant, and knew nothing of his obvious problem with me, I merely clicked to attention, heil-Hitlered expressionlessly, and awaited his next move.

"You are Linge?" he spat out. I didn't respond, assuming he required no confirmation from me. "I am Lieutenant Krebs. You were not told to report to SS-Regimental Sergeant-Major Huber at zero six hundred hours? Hmmm?" he continued. "Well?"

"Herr Lieutenant," I stammered, "my abject apologies if I erred, but I was not aware that I was to report to anyone. After meeting with the Führer, I was shown to my quarters by Fräulein Schroeder, who said nothing to me of it, and left immediately. The Lieutenant is the first person I have seen since then." I assumed the redness of his face and neck, not to mention the perspiration and protrusion, was due to the strangulating tightness of his uniform collar. A tailor could have solved the problem in minutes, but I assumed the lieutenant preferred to endure distress in order to produce distress—a typical SS characteristic I do my best to avoid.

Without addressing my defence, he said: "Within the hour, Linge, you will have in your possession an alarm clock with an illuminated dial for your table. You will need it, for your immediate superiors, not to mention the Führer himself, may call upon you without warning, and I need not tell you that you must be available at all times."

I remained silent, electing not to point out the contradiction in his statement.

"I am quite a good judge of men, Linge," he went on, "and I must say that you do not appear particularly energetic or intelligent. But perhaps I am wrong. We shall see. For the present, Sergeant-Major Huber has been deputed to act as your tour guide and show you through every part of the Chancellery. Take copious notes, for from that moment on, you shall be expected to know where you are and where you need to be, without any explanation or excuses, am I clear?"

"The lieutenant is most clear," I replied. Then I determined on a strategy that I would continue to employ if successful. "With your permission, of course," I told him, "I will be glad to report the Lieutenant's dedication, generosity, and diligence to the Führer at our next encounter."

Even as a humble bricklayer, I learned that when dealing with an arrogant and hostile superior, mollification was infinitely preferable to confrontation. At that, the lieutenant's features softened slightly, though no smile was forthcoming.

"At ease, Linge," he commanded. "This isn't a parade. I say, do you happen to have a clean handkerchief?" he asked, his tone considerably subdued. "Mine is soaking wet."

I stared for a moment at the lieutenant's collar and the raw ring of glistening skin squeezed over the top. "If the Lieutenant will permit," I ventured, then pivoted round and moved to the chest of drawers, removed two fresh linen handkerchiefs, took them into the bathroom, dusted one with talcum powder and returned to find that he had stepped into my room. I shut the door and went over to him. "Sir," I said, "while I am far from an expert in such matters, I believe that if you would wipe your face with the plain one, then loosen your collar and apply this talcum-coated handkerchief, you will feel considerably better. If you are so disposed, when you can spare a moment, I can adjust the buttons on your collar sufficiently to ease the pressure on your neck."

You will ask why I took this risk, and I answer that sometimes, one must take one's wisdom from untried sources. In this case, it came from a story I had read years before, in a book I "borrowed" from the city library and still have, entitled *Androcles and the Lion*. Androcles is a runaway slave of a former Roman consul administering a part of Africa. He takes shelter in a cave, which turns out to be the den of a wounded lion. He removes a large thorn from the animal's foot pad, forces pus from the infected wound, and bandages it. As a result, the lion recovers and becomes tame toward him, acting like a domesticated dog, including wagging its tail and bringing home game that it shares with him.

After several years, the slave eventually craves a return to civilization, resulting in his imprisonment as a fugitive slave, and he is condemned to be devoured by wild animals in the Circus Maximus of Rome. In the presence of the unnamed emperor, the most imposing of these beasts turns out to be the same lion, which again displays its affection toward the slave. The emperor pardons the slave on the spot, in recognition of this testimony to the power of friendship, and he is left in possession of the lion.

Afterwards we see Androcles with the lion attached to a slender leash, making the rounds of the city. Androcles was given money, the lion was sprinkled with flowers, and everyone who met them anywhere exclaimed: "This is the lion, a man's friend; this is the man, a lion's doctor." I will tell you, even with my mere suggestion, I was moderately surprised at the lieutenant's reaction.

"I am mightily impressed, Linge," he said, while he unbuttoned his collar and wiped his face. "You are not quite the pudding-head I'd first thought." Then he unbuttoned his tunic, removed it, handed the sodden garment to me, and began dabbing his inflamed neck with the talcum. "All right then, you will be my tailor, since Sergeant-Major Huber has not yet arrived. But understand that I would prefer that we keep this matter between us. In that regard, place your chair under the doorknob. Should anyone come in upon us, the situation could well be misinterpreted, yes?"

"If the lieutenant will demonstrate," I requested ingenuously, which he proceeded to do, and then, handed back the chair. I had to stifle a laugh. I took the chair and jammed it—again—under the doorknob, this time making certain to do it badly so he would think me inept at furtiveness. After the second—and more successful—attempt, I returned to him, said, "Not to worry, sir; it will only take a moment," then went over to the chest of drawers, removed a small military sewing kit from the top drawer, sat down on the cot next to the lieutenant, and proceeded to move the button right to the collar's edge.

I was about to return the altered garment when suddenly there was a vigorous knocking at the door.

Lieutenant Krebs jumped up as if a bolt of electricity had passed through him. "It's Huber," he whispered in panic.

I handed him the repaired garment. "Hide in the bathroom," I advised, "and close the door. I'll take care of it."

The lieutenant whispered, this time more calmly: "Excellent, Linge. Yes. The bathroom. Try to delay him while I dress."

I went to the door and opened it to find a tall, well-built, youngish man in an impeccable SS sergeant-major's uniform. He had narrow-set blue eyes, a perfect Aryan nose, a thin thatch of straw-coloured hair, thinner, even, than mine, and a mocking sneer on his lips. A sergeant-major at his age, was someone to keep in mind. Without a word yet exchanged between us, I knew him to be far more dangerous than the older, unpolished superior, Krebs. I also understood the latter's panic. "Yes, Sergeant-Major?" I began, with a heel-click and salute, forcing myself to play the naif while betraying no apprehension.

"You are still in your bedclothes," he remarked icily. He didn't blink. With little mental effort, I knew to expect very little blinking from Sergeant-Major Huber. And there would be no thorn in this lion's paw.

Keep playing the greenhorn, I told myself. "And you are Sergeant-Major . . . ?"

"Huber, Sergeant Linge. Huber. You were told to expect me?"

Clearly not meant as a question. "Ah, yes, Sergeant-Major," I replied. "Lieutenant Krebs came by a few minutes ago to tell me you were to provide orientation to the Chancellery. However, he didn't say when you might arrive. I was just beginning to dress when you knocked."

He checked me over slowly, up and down, as he would an unsavoury prostitute introduced to him at a questionable brothel. "I have been informed," he said with obvious distaste, "that the Führer has taken a fancy to you, and that, of course, puts an unfortunate end to whatever consequences your laziness and sloth would have received from me," but then added the ominous: "for the present."

Normally, it requires enormous efforts of will to constantly appear to others as stupider than you are; nevertheless, I've had to do it often enough that it had become virtually second nature. "I'm afraid that I am unable to follow the Sergeant-Major's train of thought," I responded, accompanying my words with a quizzical expression. *Perhaps,* I thought, *if I wear him down with inanities, he'll get to the point.* It appeared to work.

"You have half an hour, Linge," he snarled, "to get yourself into a presentable state. You will then meet me in the Grand Foyer, and our tour will begin. Bring pencil and paper, for you will, from that moment on, be expected to know, as if it is your own body, every nook and cranny of the Chancellery. Have I made myself clear?"

Not being the idiot he took me for, I could discern that this was not a show he was putting on for my benefit but a clue to his character. In short, he was an asshole. I clicked my bootless heels again and saluted smartly. "At your command, Herr Sergeant-Major," I replied.

Without a word, Huber heel-clicked and saluted, pivoted, and marched down the hallway. I quickly closed the door, replaced the chair, dashed to the bathroom, and knocked gently. From behind the door I could hear the lieutenant's muffled whimper: "He is gone?"

This, if nothing else, confirmed my opinion of the sergeant-major: he was not only an asshole but also a dangerous asshole. I wondered how many of these malignant types hovered like a constellation round the Führer. "Yes, Herr Lieutenant," I answered. "You can come out." There were more things I wish I had time to consider, but they would have to wait.

The door eased open and Lieutenant Krebs stood there all outfitted again, buttoned collar and all. Much of the swollen redness had deflated and paled, and the sweat had all but dissipated. "I thank you, Herr Sergeant," he effused. "I feel like a new man." He came toward me and extended his short, pudgy hand, which I took in my own, giving it one pump.

"It was my great pleasure, Herr Lieutenant," I replied, risking a slight smile.

"But I would strongly advise, Herr Linge, that you take Sergeant-Major Huber with utmost seriousness, as he reports directly to Obergruppenführer[7] Heydrich, who is Reichsführer Himmler's chief deputy—and a great deal more. Along those lines, get fitted up quickly and go to him without delay. I'll wait a few minutes after you leave before also leaving. Remember, Linge: 'He who sups with the Devil should have a long spoon.'"

Actually, it was "He must have a long spoon that must eat with the devil," from Shakespeare's *Comedy of Errors*, but I had no intention of correcting him. But I also understood what it meant and would follow that advice to the letter.

Not surprisingly, SS-Sergeant-Major Huber turned out to be a far more adept tour guide than humanist. The Chancellery was an enormous city unto itself, and the officiously inhospitable bastard did know every millimetre as well as all the hordes of personnel we happened to meet along the way (secretaries, sentries, kitchen staff, maids, communications workers, department officials and their assistants, adjutants, liaisons, and so forth), all greeting me with slightly varying degrees of the sergeant-major's frigid punctiliousness—a response I attributed to Huber's

---

[7] The rank of full general, second only to field marshal.

particular influence, not to me. My first thought was that avoiding him in future would be impossible. My second thought was that attempting the impossible was definitely worth the effort. My third was that by memorizing all I was shown, I would ultimately discover a hiding place for my exposed film. I'd brought a pad and pencil as "advised," but, as it was unnecessary, I merely doodled at appropriate times, for later incineration. And, as to be expected, Huber reserved Lieutenant Karl Wilhelm Krause, the Führer's chief valet—and my immediate superior—for last.

Only one door down from the Führer's quarters was a cavernous, sterile antechamber containing a green metal army desk and swivel chair behind it, no other chairs, no windows, three bare walls, and the fourth decorated with an enormous portrait of the Führer, dazzlingly imperious in his Party brown shirt with swastika armband, his face stern, and his head facing obliquely left, his piercing blue eyes gazing slightly upward toward a space over the heads of adoring viewers: the purposeful visionary pose I'd seen so often in public buildings and private homes. A uniformed SS corporal[8] was seated behind the desk and popped up with a click and salute to greet Sergeant-Major Huber. His eyes, fixed only on my guide, told me I didn't yet exist.

The corporal was not quite as tall or as young as Huber but was considerably more muscular, as could be seen even through his impeccably tailored SS uniform. His almost-white blond hair was pomaded into lacquered, centre-parted submission, save for the sides, which were shaved to the skull, a hairstyle favoured by the more rabidly partisan. His features could have graced any Nazi recruiting poster but for one thing: he had no discernible chin; instead, a hideous, jagged, horizontal scar filled its space.

---

[8] Rottenführer.

"As ordered, Corporal," announced Huber. "I have delivered Linge."

Face still rigidly facing forward, the corporal swivelled his eyes to the right to acknowledge me, then back to Huber. "He is late, Sergeant-Major," the corporal slurped, as if he were eating soup directly from the plate, clearly the result of his affliction. "Lieutenant Krause will not be pleased."

"I have no doubt," said Huber tonelessly. "Though there may have been some misunderstanding. But in any event, I've given him the grand tour of the Chancellery, and so my responsibilities are at an end; you and Krause are to take over from here."

"Quite, Sergeant-Major." The corporal's words writhed and flailed liquidly in his mouth as he spoke. "Thank you." They heel-clicked and saluted in unison; Huber pivoted and left the room. Finally, the corporal turned to me.

"I am Corporal Albrecht. Before [*slurp*] we proceed, Sergeant Linge," the corporal garbled, "I will explain something [*slurp*] of which you would not speak but about [*slurp*] which you are obviously curious."

I had no idea what the corporal was referring to, but obviously he did, so I said nothing and waited.

"In the [*slurp*] War," he began, with me straining to understand him, "I'm serving with the [*slurp*] Führer's platoon in France, and also as a courier. One day, he asks me if I would [*slurp*] relieve him of a mission so he could look at some building of historical significance to him. We was comrades, and so I says it would be fine with me. [*slurp*] So he went off to see his building, and I got my [*slurp*] fuckin' chin blowed off. You can imagine [*slurp*], this got him real upset and he blames himself. But even then, I'm already [*slurp*] seeing in him, what all see, and so's I told him [*slurp*] 'Better my chin than yours.' At that, he starts bawling. Bawling, Sergeant, and [*slurp*] he promises me that if he has anything to do with it, I would never want for nothing. So here I be: no chin, but a grateful Führer. Now which [*slurp*] would you like better?"

As questions went, that one, I prayed, was entirely rhetorical and was merely part of the standard speech he gave to all he felt might be repelled by his gross disfigurement, which would include all but surgeons, the blind, and the deaf. Unfortunately, his frozen stare told me an answer was expected, and so I reverted to my standard response: "I would say, Corporal, that the answer is obvious," and left it at that, and, as usual, it worked, because people have already answered the question for themselves and merely seek confirmation.

"Of course [*slurp*], Herr Sergeant, who could do less?" he asked, while a thin, yellowish ooze dribbled from each corner of his distorted mouth. Then a red light in a wooden console on top of the corporal's desk began blinking. "That will be Herr [*slurp*] Krause summoning you," he said, as he came round from behind his desk, ramrod straight, and accompanied me to the double doors, knocked once perfunctorily, opened them, ushered me in, left, and closed the doors behind me.

I was in a room that made my meagre quarters look like the Adlon Hotel ballroom. There was only space for a tiny metal desk, a vertical metal filing cabinet, and a short, narrow army cot similar to mine. As with my room, there were no windows, and each wall but one contained a thorough coating of tacked-up hand-scribbled notes. The fourth wall contained a painting of the Führer, identical in all but size to the one in the antechamber. There was a door to the side that I imagined—hoped?—opened onto a bathroom. On the desktop stood a metal console with several coloured lights and accompanying buttons. Otherwise, it was vacant of furnishings, save for Krause, standing where a desk chair would have been. In a moment of facetious commiseration, I considered offering to exchange rooms. I left the offer unspoken.

I already knew that Karl Wilhelm Krause was born in West Prussia and had studied cabinetmaking and architecture before joining the navy in 1931. In 1934, the Führer chose Krause from a line-up of sailors to be his personal orderly and bodyguard under his personal command and gave him the rank of Second Lieutenant. More important, I also discovered that the Führer called Krause his "shadow," as he was always behind him at public appearances and followed him everywhere. There was something obscenely comic when he came round his desk to greet me and I had to coerce myself into not making conspicuous the tilting of my neck downward.

As I heel-clicked and Hitler-saluted, my brain brought up what John of Salisbury said: "We are like dwarfs on the shoulders of giants, so that we can see more than they, and things at a greater distance, not by virtue of any sharpness of sight on our part, or any physical distinction, but because we are carried high and raised up by their giant size." I never thought of the Führer as a physical giant, but after seeing his "shadow," I was compelled to revise my entire opinion of stature. Aside from Krause's height, which was barely above the border of midgetry (perfectly complemented by the diminutive proportions of his limbs), aside from a pushed-in nose, such as a seasoned prize-fighter might sport, his facial features possessed the eerily sandpapered smoothness one associates with the work of a skilled surgeon on a burn victim. Between the corporal and now Krause, I felt as though I were more in a military hospital than the Reich Chancellery.

Without a greeting or even an introduction, Krause got right down to the business at hand—his business. "It appears, Herr Linge," he said in a voice far deeper than one would have predicted from his size, "that you have a problem with punctuality."

I wanted to respond: With all due respect, Herr Lieutenant, it could be said that Chancellery officials have a problem with communication, and I do not yet appear to be in their chain of delivery, but my instinct informed me that Herr Krause had in mind a stern lecture, not a comradely mentor's chat, and so I merely stood there at attention and gazed—quite uneasily—over Krause's SS cap.

"At ease, Linge," he commanded. "And you can look at me as if you were not uncomfortable about our physical differences, yes?" He then moved behind his desk, as if to deny his previous magnanimity. "I will be honest with you: a man needs two feet, two hands, two eyes, two ears, yes? But he does not need two valets. That is to say, I will confess that I strenuously advised the Führer against hiring you, since I believe I alone have served him both well and faithfully, without even the merest hint of complaint, and so it would be both unduly awkward and completely unnecessary to employ an additional valet. However, the Führer is a man of extraordinary insight, knowledge, vision, and instinct, as all Germany knows, and soon the world will know. But he is also—and this is for your ears only, for I will utterly deny that I said it—a man of extraordinary whimsy and caprice, and I attribute his desire for your services as a supreme example of that. So, he overruled me and here you are. No more will be said on that score.

"Now, since Sergeant-Major Huber was good enough to provide you with the 'grand tour,' I'll get straight to your duties and responsibilities," he said, curling his thin lips into a faint, clearly seldom-employed smile. "First, I must confess that you were, to some degree, misled," he began, "when you were, ah, selected to be a secondary valet to the Führer, that is to say, my assistant. Therefore, it is only proper that I introduce you to your superior: me, his primary valet. First, you must realize that I have a completely unique position, which calls upon me to exist solely to serve one man, to the total exclusion of any other concern, personal or otherwise.

"To prepare for my role, after a particularly energetic orientation," he related expressionlessly, "I wiped the sweat from the Führer's naked body and spent the entire evening licking the cloth. I collected and swallowed the pus that oozed from a boil on the Führer's buttocks. After a particularly arduous bowel movement, I sampled the foul-smelling shit that he had deposited. When he sneezed, I took and kept his snot-filled handkerchief in my mouth for hours. I have it still. When I failed to fulfil my duties to my satisfaction, I raced to my quarters and smashed my nose against my wall. This, of course, establishes a bond that is unbreakable, Linge. The Führer's valet is, first and foremost, pure anticipation, and second, mindless obedience. A valet that fails to anticipate dilutes that obedience and may even nullify it. The valet is not a person in the traditional sense. He is the polish for the Führer's shoes, the toilet paper to wipe himself, do you understand, Linge? The Führer's valet's only reason for existence is to always unquestioningly and immediately serve him, to be a mere implement in the meeting of his needs, an extension of . . ." His voice drifted away in my brain as I refused to listen further to this maniac.

As with his voice, I, too, was drifting farther and farther away, as if I were an intoxicated orderly sitting at the bedside of a severely shell-shocked soldier. From my associations thus far, I could never rationally explain the Führer's rise to pre-eminence.

There had to be people of both sanity and extraordinary qualities to advise and assist him in implementing his vision. I fervently hoped I'd meet them soon. But with Krause, I wanted to tell him that, at best, he appeared to be one of those pathetic circus clowns who dress and make up as important people and take pratfalls for laughs, even—perhaps especially—from the people they are imitating, not unlike a court jester. I wanted to tell him that he was, without question, a lunatic, a sadomasochistic freak. Instead, I continued to stand at perfect ease, a window mannequin whose ceramic ear was pressed to the ceramic mouth of another window dummy.

I had no sense of time, but it seemed that after an endless recounting of self-mutilations that would repel even Martin Luther, I began to detect actual duties that made some sense to a normal human being. "The Führer," he related, "despite his historical significance, is a man of simple tastes and habits, and yet, those tastes and habits must be seen to with fanatical zeal. I make sure that his clothing and private rooms are in perfect order. Though I have several chambermaids at my disposal, I entrust this task to no one but myself to ensure perfection. I also handle all the business arrangements in the Führer's household. I must be in constant attendance, even beyond the usual beck and call. I accompany him on his travels, no matter where or for how long or short. Except for Herr Kannenberg, all the servants, officers' mess orderlies, caterers, and everybody whose duties are, in some way, concerned with the Führer's care are subordinated to me. I deliver all messages to him and escort people in to meet with him. And no less important, nothing said or done by anyone, high or low, concerning the Führer goes unheard and unreported. And for all that, nobody but the Führer is ever permitted to give me orders," he crowed. The multicoloured lights on Krause's console blinked hysterically, perhaps a summons or the like. Krause appeared not to notice them. Perhaps irony was his point, but I had no way of telling.

"And *my* duties and responsibilities?" I interjected in desperation.

"You have none," Krause replied matter-of-factly, "except to serve me, and only when I express the need. Nothing more, nothing less. Am I clear, Linge?"

"Most clear, Herr Lieutenant," I replied mechanically. "I do nothing but wait for your instructions."

"Exactly," he confirmed. "You are dismissed."

I clicked and saluted again, pivoted, and marched out past the chinless sergeant-major and into the vast, bustling marble hallway, now a place of business, no longer a stage set for my bewildering audition.

What is real and what is contrived? I asked myself as I made my way back to my quarters. What, if any, was the connexion between my perplexing conversation with the Führer and the bizarre lecture by Krause? While composing this soon-to-be-photographed-then-incinerated written record, I consider the possibly brilliant, subtle, even covert meaning behind Krause's maniacal lecture. The power the man had! It reminded me of a book I'd read about the American president Woodrow Wilson, who had suffered a mental stroke and who was allowed no visitors but his wife and who could only receive and send messages through her. What actually got through? In actual fact, she, and not her elected husband, could well have been governing the United States. What power! Did she use it? No one will probably ever really know. How different from her was the Führer's valet?

Incidentally, while on my tour, I'd located a promising hiding place for you.

Taking Krause seriously (no small feat, I can assure you), I intended to perform no official service until he (or the Führer, I prayed) expressly ordered it. That being the case, I decided to use my "freedom" from official duties to hide my film, virtually in plain sight, but, as such, ignored by prying eyes, even the most paranoid. I experienced a shudder of relief and satisfaction.

Once accomplished, I employed the remaining moments to acquaint myself, as inconspicuously as possible, with those of the household staff who could and would accommodate me. One such was a maid named Hannelore Böchner whom I met as I passed a room adjacent to the enormous kitchen. She looked like a picture I'd seen in a book of paintings of farm women by the Dutch painter Vincent van Gogh. Her face was like a smiling potato, and her shape like a cabbage. She told me she would be happy to chat so long as I assisted her in polishing the silver. I asked whether that might not get us both into trouble, but she was quite casual about the entire matter, claiming that she could use the help, for her lowly status caused her to be given more menial duties than she could possibly handle, and that only when there was a special occasion like a formal state visit or invited dignitaries did strict supervision and surveillance occur, and then, woe betide the poor slave exhibiting any slacking or casualness.

She remarked on my height, saying that except for Lieutenant Krause, all SS men seemed to be tall. She asked if I was married, engaged, or at least keeping company with someone.

"Unfortunately, I have no time for social matters," I lied, "at least until I receive a fixed set of duties and a routine."

This appeared to cheer her up. She did tell me, even from her lowly position she could see that the Führer was a man of no fixed set of duties or routine; his unpredictability was his only consistency—an insight that made me wonder about her position relative to her intelligence, something I consistently do with women, no less than myself. Then she placed a banana peel under my feet. "You aren't a Gestapo spy, are you?" she asked, then added, "Well, it doesn't really matter, does it? We all are, in one way or another, aren't we?"

Frankly, I didn't know how to answer her. Was she a plant to trap unwary innocents? Was she the ingenue? "I am new to the Führer's service," I weaselled. "I'm merely getting my sea legs."

Suddenly, the potato became a prune of rumpled perplexity. "Sea legs? What is a sea leg?"

Mistake. Never assume anyone knows more than you, for they will interpret anything they don't know as dangerous erudition. "I meant, get used to a new situation," an answer that seemed to satisfy her.

"That will take time," she cautioned.

"It will, you bet," I answered with prole-like grammar and honesty. "This is . . ."

I could not finish my sentence, for just then, an enormous woman wearing an SS-sergeant's uniform with an apron affixed to the front marched in and snapped: "You may leave us now, Fräulein Böchner, and finish the silver later. Entertainment is not among your duties, I believe."

Upon which Fräulein Böchner withdrew so quickly that I was reminded of those American cartoons in which a terrified animal races from danger, its feet a blur, leaving a circular cloud with a vapour trail of dust behind. I would have smiled at the imagery but for the tight-lipped expression on the Amazon's face.

"You are Sergeant Heinz Linge."

Sensing correctly that she did not intend an answer, I merely stood there.

"You perhaps have a watch? You will remove it and hand it to me, yes?"

I unbuckled my Nova Ancre aviator's watch with its enlarged face, illuminated dial, and oversize numbers that I'd won in a beer hall bet. I handed it to her. She looked at it, compared it to her own, held it to her ear, and handed it back. "It appears to be working properly, Herr Linge. You should use it."

Taking her actions and remark as her notion of a joke, I said, while replacing the watch on my wrist, "I truly appreciate your advice, Fräulein Sergeant. However, I generally employ such a precision instrument when provided with a schedule. Is there one I perhaps overlooked?" At the time, I considered my flippant remark relatively harmless, but I quickly altered my strategy when the loathsome virago removed a notepad from her inside tunic pocket and scribbled something before returning it to its original location.

"Herr Linge," she said emotionlessly, "I have been instructed to inform you that the Führer wishes to see you at precisely fifteen hundred hours. You will notice, on that fine watch of yours, that it is now fourteen fifty hours. You would do well to proceed to the Führer's rooms without delay."

Without delay? I must confess that punctuality appears to be highly overrated by the Chancellery staff at Führer Headquarters.

After breaching a moat of three armed SS guard checkpoints and a humiliatingly painstaking screening of my papers at each, I was eventually shown into the Führer's spacious study, a full forty-five minutes later than I was "advised" to be there. The room was startlingly cosy for its size. A large window dominated one entire wall, floor-to-ceiling glass-door bookcases covered two, and the fourth supported an enormous old-fashioned portrait of some obviously historical figure above an oversized fireplace. There was a large desk with a high-backed swivel chair, the desk containing the same panel of lights and buttons as Krause's, and a long, creased leather sofa and two matching armchairs completed the arrangement.

Normally, I would have wandered over to the bookcases and studied the titles, but a man was sitting on the sofa. I was convinced that he'd chosen the sofa because his bulk was far too massive for the armchair. He looked like a blond version of those illustrations in children's books of Humpty-Dumpty. From what I remembered when I'd seen him at rallies and in the newspaper, Göring was above average height, and his face was bright red, as many highly strung, corpulent blondes seemed to be. He was wearing a button-straining powder-blue uniform with row upon row of ornate medals, worthy of a particularly megalomaniacal African potentate.

He did not acknowledge my presence, as he was studying his perfectly manicured fingernails, seemingly lost in thought. I can say now that it is doubtful that he even saw me. After a few minutes—I cannot say how many—the Führer, still in his bedclothes, emerged from what I presumed was his bathroom, also ignored me, though I know that he saw me, went over to an armchair facing the general, and eased himself into it. I took a chance and stood at parade rest before one of the bookcases. After a time, Göring slapped his ample thigh and chuckled.

"I have to tell you, I was at a cabaret the other night and

there was this so-called comic performing, but—please hear me out—not all his stuff was bad. After a bunch of typical Jew jokes, there was an amusing one about you."

The Führer's face was totally impassive.

"It seems that you visit a lunatic asylum, and the patients all give the Hitler salute. As you pass down the line, you come across a man who isn't saluting. 'Why aren't you saluting like the others?' you shout. 'My Führer,' he answers, 'I'm the nurse, I'm not crazy.'"

They faced each other in total silence, then the Führer shrugged. "Not terrible, Hermann. I've heard worse. A few months ago, Canaris[9] informed me of one he'd heard, one that had been told by some staff member about both of us. It seems that you and I are standing on top of Berlin's radio tower. I say that I want to do something to inspire the people, and you say, 'Why don't you jump?'"

Göring's red face began to sprout beads of perspiration.

"What, Hermann?" the Führer inquired. "You do not find that amusing?" Göring just sat there, apparently stupefied. "Please, Hermann, don't look so abject. The culprit was quickly identified, taken out and strangled with piano wire. Rather harsh, I would say, but it appears that the admiral is far thinner-skinned than I am."

I had to keep telling myself that this exchange between the two most powerful men in Germany was occurring while I stood in the room. Then, as if none of this depraved levity had taken place, the Führer rose and began pacing. "I will have the announcement made within the month, Hermann, you under-stand. Are all preparations in order?"

"All is as you directed, my Führer. The announcement can be made at your discretion."

---

9 Admiral Wilhelm Canaris was Hitler's chief of the German Military Intelligence Service, the Abwehr, from 1935 to 1944.

"Discretion has little to do with this, my friend. As I've told you many times, the first steps of any significant act must be bold, even audacious," he announced, gazing up at the painting, "but when all the deluded weak sisters who surround us have finished mulling and dithering, we will have our Air Force.[10] I will inform our guests at dinner and make the formal announcement personally to the nation before the month is out, naming you as commander in chief. Before long, you'll require a special brace to support all your medals."

At that, Göring burst into a fat-flailing coughing fit of laughter, which only subsided when the Führer said: "You see, Hermann, I can be as funny as any cabaret comedian. Just don't tell Canaris. I prefer my piano wire in pianos."

The Führer then stopped his pacing as he neared the couch, and he faced the general. "And please convey my fondest regards to your lovely wife."

Göring took that to be a dismissal, for he grabbed the arms of the couch with both hands and, with a mighty grunt, pushed his bulk up to a standing position, turned, and left without a salute or even a goodbye. I can tell that he and the Führer have a special relationship which I must never overlook.

The Führer then motioned me over to one of the armchairs. "Come, Linge." I raced to the chair. "Sit," he bade me, then took the other armchair, where we just sat without a sound between us, until he broke the silence:

---

[10] Under the terms of the Treaty of Versailles (1919), Germany was prohibited from having an air force. German pilots were secretly trained for military aviation, first in the Soviet Union during the late 1920s, and then in Germany in the early 1930s. In Germany, the training was done under the guise of the German Air Sports Association at the Central Commercial Pilots School.

"So, Linge, what is your opinion of my second in command, my chosen successor?"

I plunged into a flaming cauldron of numb panic. What to say? Who was I even to be asked? Was the Führer baiting me? What was I expected to do? To say? I experienced no physical pain, but I couldn't speak; I could barely breathe. *Focus on something else,* I commanded myself. *Anything else.* I've done it once before and it allowed me to survive. I must do it again! Göring. Yes, that distended bladder in uniform. *Focus! It's not the Führer before you but that dirigible in thigh-boots, Puss in Boots, yes, but this "puss" was a hippopotamus! Yes, visualize him that way and survive,* I told myself, until unseen, powerful hands began shaking me violently as if I were imprisoned in a demented centrifuge. And a voice . . .

"Linge! Linge!" the voice insisted. "Are you all right? Are you having a fit? Shall I call for someone?"

And as quickly, I was again facing the Führer and his question—and the dilemma it posed: What did I truly know of the general? What could my opinion of such a man be, after overhearing a five-minute conversation with the undisputed master of the Third Reich? Despite that, I sensed that the next words from my mouth would mark our relationship from that moment on—for good or ill.

"My Führer," I said haltingly, "I know little, if anything, about the general, short of his war record and physical dimensions, but I humbly ask you: Would a man such as yourself place anyone in such a position without having great confidence, a master strategy, and a full arsenal of alternatives?"

The Führer's face was a death mask until it broke open with laughter, and truly, I did not know what to do. But after a time, the laughter subsided into what I can only describe as a playful smirk. "Yes, I chose well, Linge, at least in you," he said. "Göring succeed *me*? As you intimated, it beggars the imagination. Can you see that corpulent martinet, resplendent in one of those South American dictator uniforms, or Roman emperor tunics of his, waddling to the balcony or podium to deliver a serious address to the German people? Only a Leni Riefenstahl could do it full justice. After the raucous guffawing ceased, the crowd would begin throwing assorted spoiled fruits and vegetables, then, exhausted, they would issue a collectively dismissive wave, turn, and empty the square. Hermann is an old and valued comrade, as is Hess, for that matter, but most certainly neither is a fit successor. More important than that, you refrained from slobbering the usual sycophantic dribble I constantly receive—that no one could possibly succeed me—though I must say that the whole notion of succession is one that troubles me constantly."

I was still suffering from shock but, amazingly, had the presence of mind to also refrain from asking the Führer why he had named Göring as his successor in the first place if he harboured such views. My assumption, held by me to be absolute, is that the Führer has good reasons for doing anything and everything, though I vowed never to tell him that. I'd read that instinct and intuition can inform strategy successfully but that they can seldom, if ever, replace it successfully. I wanted to tell him that, but that would be a different person than the valet I thought he'd selected and, more important, the one I wanted him to know. That was instinct and intuition informing *my* strategy, I imagine.

"I told Krause to contact you as soon as possible, so I assume that you've had the pleasure of meeting the little Napoleon?" he remarked with what I took to be a mischievous twinkle. He tilted his head forward slightly and placed his hands together under his chin like a church steeple.

I felt trapped, but I took a chance. "Yes, my Führer, I met him, but for only a few moments. However," I added, "I believe the pleasure was all mine, I'm afraid." I was beginning to gain a new respect for bricklaying.

The Führer removed his hands from his chin and chuckled. "He was born in Prussia, you know, and so he has none of the charm you find in Bavarians or even in the rest of the Reich. As a valet, Krause is efficient and dedicated. Unfortunately, he is typical of the diminutive Prussian: authoritarian and humourless, unctuous to those above, aloof to those beside, and arrogant to those below."

At this point, I had heard nothing I did not already know, but was gratified at the confirmation.

"I imagine he already despises you for your height alone, and even more so for your position. You see, he is almost obsessively attached to me—frankly, I'm amazed he didn't manage to insinuate his way in here while we spoke. Unfortunately, he will become apoplectic when I inform him that he is to assume other duties while *you* are to be with me at all times."

That, I didn't know.

"Why I wish it this way," he said, "will become clear as time passes." The Führer then stood up, and I immediately shot to attention.

The Führer raised both his hands, palms forward, in what I took to be a peace gesture. "Relax, Linge. You're among friends." He chuckled. "In any event, I am having a few guests join me for dinner tomorrow night, to suffer through my vegetarianism, but mainly to receive my decision on the Luftwaffe. They will wish to discuss it, even debate it, but the matter is settled and will proceed as I have already planned. You will assist in the serving, so you'll need to coordinate with your friend Krause, and 'Emperor' Kannenberg, my 'House Manager.' I'm reasonably certain, though, that—"

He never finished, for suddenly his face turned purple-red and puckered with pain, and he doubled over, hands pressing in hard upon his stomach, followed by a long, loud *pfishing* sound from behind him and an abominable stench I could barely tolerate. It took all my will to remain passive yet concerned.

"My Führer!" I exclaimed, "What—?"

"Bloch . . . g . . . get me . . . Bloch!" He screamed through his anguish. "*Bloch!*"

"But . . . how, my Führer?"

"Button on . . . desk . . . yellow. *Press!*" he groaned.

I raced to the massive desk, went for the yellow button on the console, and pressed it repeatedly. It couldn't have been more than a half minute before Krause and a middle-aged portly man of medium height, pre-War moustache, and closely cropped receding hair, donned in a long, white laboratory coat, raced into the room, the latter carrying a doctor's satchel. Without a word, the latter rushed to the Führer, placed his arm around the bent shoulders, and guided him to the bathroom without shutting the door. I have no proof, but I don't believe Dr. Bloch even saw me standing there. However, Krause did, and his tiny face twisted in rage.

"*Get out of here, Linge!*" he shouted. "I will deal with this. We'll discuss your presence here later."

I knew at that moment that words would only make things worse. I turned and left, vowing not to refer to the incident if Krause didn't, though I had little faith in Krause's forgetfulness or restraint. I went back to my room and read until it was time to write to you.

I LIFTED OFF my cot at 0500 hours, courtesy of my new alarm clock. I already understood that today was to be my . . . debut, so to speak, by helping to attend the Führer and his guests at dinner. My phone jarred me with its brassy clanging at 0530 hours with Karl "Herr Humanist" Krause informing me that he was utterly opposed to my presence at such an important occasion, but, since it was the Führer's wishes—"God knows why," he emphasized—I was to report to him at 0645 hours for a "thorough briefing."

Thus far, most of my short time at the Chancellery had been a boring chaos of hostile negativity, punctuated only by the warm-but-mystifying comments of the Führer. I pulled my suitcase out from beneath my cot to unearth several photographs I'd taken, with which to decorate my empty walls and, also, to lay a foundation for possessing and using a camera, and discovered that someone had already searched all my belongings—and was not terribly tidy about it, indicating to me that I was to take sur-veillance (whether random or scheduled) as standard operating procedure. Nothing appeared to be taken, but all I could think of was that, though I possessed some control over my surroundings when inhabiting them, I was at their mercy when away.

I also remain perplexed about the persona of callow, unin-formed innocence I'd chosen to display. I don't think that will change, if at all, even after I become more familiar with the people with whom I must daily interact. I had been told by a retired actor acquaintance that going onstage without a script or direction is a dangerous business, but no other way appears open to me. I must learn onstage, all alone with my audience.

❧

I was waiting at ease in full SS raiment in Krause's anteroom by 0640, so as to not add more to the list of malfeasances with which he would surely present me and the Führer. I tried smiling at my superior's dreary secretary, who appeared intent on shuffling and reshuffling the papers on his desk, but only a cursory glance, a frozen stare, and back to his papers were returned. Convinced that his behaviour reflected a personality rather than a mood, I fixed my gaze on Krause's closed door.

At precisely 0645, a buzzer sounded, presumably to indicate that the exalted Krause was ready to see me. I imagine he hoped I'd be late, but I also imagine that his sentinel had furtively notified him that I was there and waiting. Expecting a sandstorm of invective, I braced myself as I marched to his door, knocked once, opened it, entered, shut the door behind me, stood before the sitting Lilliputian,[11] and saluted smartly. With agonizing deliberation, Krause looked up from his papers and white-knuckle-clasped his tiny hands in front of him—a model of theatrical tolerance.

"All right, Linge," he began, "would you be so good as to tell me why you were in the Führer's private quarters?"

---

[11] From *Liliputaner*, the name of a diminutive character from a fictional island called Lilliput in the novel *Gulliver's Travels* by Jonathan Swift. Clearly, Linge had read the novel.

I decided to present a maximum of calm and a minimum of information and see how far that got me.

"I was instructed by a woman who came to my room, Herr Lieutenant, that the Führer wished to see me. I obeyed her instructions."

Krause's eyes narrowed. "A woman, you say? What woman?"

"Regrettably, I cannot say, Herr Lieutenant. A female in SS garb. She omitted to give me her name, but she gave me no reason to doubt her words."

His tone rose a notch on the stridency scale. "And you, of course, did not see fit to notify your superior before you went?"

Instead of subjecting this piece of shit to a suicidal barrage of justifiable invective, I determined on the much safer course of benevolent discretion. "Herr Lieutenant," I said, "I naturally assumed that she was sent by you, and so I chose not to cause her to think for one moment that I doubted your wishes or her instructions, and thus require confirmation. Did I err?" Judging from his obvious frustration, I believed that if he had a revolver on him, he would have reached for it. I knew that somehow, since I had no hope of winning him over, I might at least neutralize him, or my time at the Chancellery would be hellish, but I had no idea how.

"Herr Linge," he finally said, his voice smoothing out and lowering, "I can appreciate your inexperience and ineptitude. However, you would do well to make no further assumptions. In future, you will notify my adjutant of every move you make outside your quarters, omitting nothing. Am I sufficiently clear on this point?"

I ached to flay the fucking bastard. "Quite sufficiently, Herr Lieutenant. Does the Lieutenant have any further matters to discuss with me?"

"Yes, actually: What did the Führer want with you? What went on in there?"

I shook my head subtly. "What do you mean, Herr Lieutenant? You yourself dismissed me and remained. I don't see how—"

"Yes, well," he cut me off, "the Führer had some important duties for me, and so I had to leave right after you."

Then why ask me, you moron? Was he daft? Be careful, I cautioned myself. "So, it would appear that we're both in the dark, then. You might wish to ask Dr. Bloch."

Krause's normally florid face turned a particularly unbecoming shade of purple. "You're not in the least funny, Linge," he snapped. *"That fucking Jew-bastard quack!"* he shouted. "How the Führer permits such degenerate filth to violate his person is beyond me." After Krause took a few moments to calm himself with an amateurish display of theatricality, his eye slits widened somewhat. "All right, Linge, sit," he commanded, waving a short arm towards one of the chairs before his desk. I eased myself onto the hard, wooden seat.

"Have you ever waited table?" he asked.

"Never, Herr Lieutenant," I admitted.

"As I suspected," he sniffed derisively. "Bricklayer, were you?" and before I could answer him, Krause proceeded to inform me of the Führer's dinner plans (excluding his purpose, of course, which I already knew) and announced the guest list: Reichsminister Joseph Goebbels and his wife, Magda; Lieutenant-General Walther Wever; Admiral Wilhelm Canaris; Joachim von Ribbentrop; and Ernst Hanfstaengl. I must confess that up to that moment, I'd never heard of Wever, or Hanfstaengl, and, considering my earlier meeting with the Führer and the purpose of the dinner that I knew, I was rather surprised that Göring would not be present.

"I will, of course, train you personally," Krause announced, "and well before the appointed time. As even you would imagine, the Führer will accept nothing less than complete competence and total efficiency, and he will get both, you understand me, Linge?"

Careful! I warned myself. "Completely, Herr Lieutenant," I responded. "I will, of course, rely totally on your expertise and guidance." I imagined that even a creature like Krause could find nothing to carp at after such treacly diplomacy.

After a longish pause that I assumed was to consider whether there was anything remotely snide or insubordinate in my response, Krause appeared to capitulate. "All right, then, we begin now. You will want to take notes, since even the slightest error is not permitted." He reached forward and nudged a pad and pencil towards me. I didn't need to take notes, but I saw only peril in doing otherwise, so I reached over, took the offering, and poised the pencil over the pad, as expected.

"First," he began, "you are to realize that at every moment, you are in one of the most important and responsible positions in all the Reich: the direct personal service of the Führer. Others can only dream of being in his presence. They savour every moment they hear his voice or see him in a parade or read of him in the newspapers. They save his used paper napkins and frame them. They'd even bottle and sell his piss if they had access. But you and I, Linge, we have such access. We attend to him daily, sometimes minute by minute, ministering to his every need, protecting him at the closest range. Does this not give you a thrill?"

Listening to Krause rhapsodize, I was reminded of stories I had read of the Knights Templar, whose sole mission was to guard the Holy Grail, whatever that was. This is not to say that the Führer was not, in great measure, precious, but I could not bring myself to consider him holy. "Words fail me, Herr Lieutenant," I answered.

"As they should, Herr Bricklayer," he snitted. "So, you see," he continued, his tiny face glistening with perspiration, "there can never, ever, be a margin for error. We are of the SS, Linge, the elite of the Reich. And what is our motto?"

"*Mein Ehre heißt Treue,*[12] Herr Lieutenant."

Krause nodded and placed his hands out, palms upward, in a gesture of obviousness. "Quite right. And understand further that the loyalty you extend unconditionally to the Führer, you also extend to me."

I didn't recall that as being part of the SS oath, even by implication, but I let him ramble.

"Tonight is a night of crucial importance for the Führer and so, naturally, for the Reich. There will be a number of dignitaries. Therefore, you are to stand at ease, doing nothing, saying nothing, unless addressed directly. Moreover—"

His inspirational oration was disrupted by a loud buzz and a green light flashing on his console. He pressed the accompanying button to hear his chinless adjutant announce that Arthur Kannenberg had arrived, and a blink of an eye later, a rotund, energetic chap of moderate height and small moustache virtually bounced into the room and immediately took the other chair facing Krause. I was surprised by his energy and agility, considering his girth. He was wearing a double-breasted suit of impeccable tailoring and costly accessories to complement it. Clearly, he had money to burn, or a sturdy line of credit. He did

---

[12] "My honour is loyalty."

not even look at me, even though I was seated less than a foot from him. Krause began to speak, but Kannenberg beat him to it.

"Krause, my good fellow," he said. "Listen. I heard a really good one the other day, I have to tell you: the Führer, Stalin, and the Pope are discussing in heaven who is the most important leader. Stalin says, 'I ruled absolutely over the biggest of all countries.' The Pope laughs and says: 'That's nothing. My orders come directly from God,' and the Führer just purses his lips and says: 'What did I order?'" At that, Kannenberg bounced up and down with laughter, followed by a bout of phlegmy coughing. When it subsided, he looked at Krause, who hadn't moved a facial muscle during the joke. "You don't get it?" he asked incredulously.

Krause admitted it was clever but that he would hesitate to tell it to the Führer.

Kannenberg chuckled, coughed, unbuttoned his jacket, and said: "Krause, my lad, I would never dream of you joking with the Führer. However, I have no hesitation. I may even bring it up before dinner tonight, which is presumably why you asked me here, yes?"

Krause nodded, glanced down at a typed list, and raised his little head. "Yes, Herr Kannenberg, in part. I wanted to give you the guest—"

"No need," Kannenberg interrupted. "The Führer has already told me who would be attending. Not a big deal, I assure you. They'll eat what's put in front of them and be grateful."

He began to push himself up when Krause said: "I am also obliged to introduce you to my . . . adjutant, for want of a better term. He will attend the Führer only if and when I am unable. As you can see, he looks the part—like a particularly insensible store-window mannequin, I dare say—and presumably as useful.

But the Führer wants him, for some reason I cannot possibly imagine, and," he shrugged helplessly, "who am I to argue?"

Kannenberg slowly turned his round head towards me, without the rest of his body following, a movement I'd always assumed that fat men adopt as economical. With Kannenberg, I also had to add dismissive, since, without a word of greeting, he swivelled his head back to Krause. "Right," he said. "It's a relatively small gathering, so Freda will take care of the details, menu and settings at a minimum, and so forth. Considering Magda, only a decent corsage will be necessary, which Freda will supply. You, your . . . adjutant, and all other male staff will be in standard livery, in this case, short, white dinner jackets with SS-embroidered neck collars and black trousers. The maids will be in their standard dress. Right, then. Anything else? If not, I must be off to see to the arrangements." Without waiting for a reply, Kannenberg rose with some effort, said, "Despite your misgivings, I wager the Führer will love my joke," and waddled out.

"Is there anything else, Herr Lieutenant?" I asked Krause once the door closed.

"No," he replied impassively, "except that you must be thoroughly prepared at all times, because the Führer is notoriously unpredictable. In any event, be in the dining room from eighteen hundred hours on, attired as Herr Kannenberg specified, without a stitch out of place, do you understand me?"

Prepared for what? "You are most clear, Herr Lieutenant." I wanted to add a witticism, such as: *and you can bring a microscope to check that every stitch will be in place as ordered,* but feared the consequences if, by accident, Krause actually understood it.

Krause then reached to the side, slid open a drawer, fished out a series of sealed manila folders, and handed them to me. "What you now have is a dossier on each of the Führer's guests. Study them carefully, and commit as much as possible to memory . . . to the extent your bricklayer's brain can. It will be useful for you to know who may, without warning or reason, wish to have any needs met by you—even though it is purely academic in your case."

I longed to step out of character for a moment to test the extent of my persona. *Herr Lieutenant,* I wanted to say, *it would seem as if my only role is to be a smartly dressed SS recruiting poster, but I'm certain the Herr Reichsführer has no shortage of them. Perhaps, then, it would probably not alter the event significantly if I didn't bother to attend at all, yes?* But there was also the Führer's wish, so instead I replied: "Yes, Herr Lieutenant, it will be as you wish."

Krause sniffed derisively. "You may be thinking—that is, if you think—that you have no place at such an event, considering your background and the understandable role I have chosen for you, but we must always remember that the Führer was once a corporal and even I was trained briefly as a cabinetmaker. Does that surprise you? In a land once dominated by Jews and other degenerates, that is the beauty of National Socialism, is it not?"

All I could think of was: *And you're sniffing farts, wiping up vomit, cleaning toilets, and waiting tables,* but instead answered: "I never thought of it quite that way, Herr Lieutenant."

"Well, there you are," said Krause with an awkward nod. "You, I'm afraid, are not a thinker. You must leave the weighty matters to the Führer and me. But so long as you follow my every instruction to the last detail, one day, I might actually give you something to do. Now go and study that dossier; that shouldn't tax you too much. And, Linge, be in the dining room not one second past eighteen hundred hours, you understand me?"

Clearly, the malignant dwarf was both a megalomaniac and

an idiot, a truly dangerous combination, since one can never predict such creatures' interpretations or reactions. I said: "Of course, Herr Lieutenant," saluted smartly, pivoted, went right past the chinless adjutant without a word, and finally reached the long hallway where I truly breathed for the first time since I'd arrived at Krause's office.

I had wished to secure my film but instead proceeded directly to my room. Even though for me memorization was automatic, I still needed to read the dossier—in the certain knowledge that Krause would quiz me thoroughly before dinner.

At 1700 hours, I gazed in my bathroom mirror to confirm that I looked every bit the appropriate window dummy that Kannenberg and Krause demanded. I'd done some photo research on the proper dinner livery and found the clothing waiting for me in my armoire when I returned to read the dossier. Not being a complete imbecile, I checked it thoroughly for accuracy, just in case Krause wished to use it as an excuse to give me a . . . dressing-down, so to speak. Once investigated, I had to consider what I had discovered: the top collar button was missing. Unwilling to suffer any more slings and arrows, I hurried discretely to the staff lunchroom, cornered the first SS orderly I saw who looked even remotely humane, in this case, a captain, told him my story, and asked most humbly if he could spare a collar button. He laughed heartily and said that when he first arrived as one of the Führer's multitude of guards, the same prank was pulled on him by Kannenberg, who was notorious for such antics. He said that Krause was far too unimaginative to ever think of such a thing. I made a mental note of it as he took me to his quarters, which were even smaller than mine. He was good enough even to sew the button on himself. No words were exchanged between us during the process.

"How can I thank you?" I asked him with ostentatious sincerity once he'd finished.

He merely asked back: "You are Heinz Linge, are you not?" When I told him I was, he shrugged, smiled enigmatically, and said: "You are caring for the Führer."

I nodded and shook his hand warmly, since no salute seemed proper or adequate under the circumstances. I turned and left, closing the door behind me. I never asked him his name and he never gave it. I made a mental note of that too.

For the rest of the afternoon I pored over the dossier and considered at length the backgrounds and character of those who held my fate in their hands, and once done and all buttons secured, I left my room at 1750 and headed up the stairs and down the hallway, ultimately joined by a massive throng of service personnel, male and female, through all the SS checkpoints, toward the Führer's chosen dining room.

Looking more like my notion of a posh restaurant than a governmental dining hall, the medium-sized space contained several circular tables, all stripped, save for the centre one, which was opulently set with fine china plates, crystal glasses, and sterling silver utensils. A single, moderately sized ornate chandelier adorned the ceiling, and the walls contained widely spaced, single-bulb wall sconces. No special chair appeared to mark the place where the Führer would sit, and I wondered absently whether this arrangement was by intent or inheritance. I considered that in my earlier reading of the story of Camelot, that with the Round Table, King Arthur wanted nothing to set him apart from the rest of his knights, so perhaps the Führer felt the same way, though I could not imagine the Führer entertaining visiting foreign dignitaries in such a manner.

Aside from the traffic jam of carpet sweepers and the cyclone of feather dusters, there was a highly disciplined, silent flurry of activity surrounding the finishing touches on the table. Three housemaids were intensely involved in completing the final settings, with their male superiors ensuring uniformity and symmetry with rulers—and all under the relentlessly intolerant eye of Lieutenant Krause. Years before, I had read about the daily routines in English manor houses—which the National Socialists continually excoriated as decadent—and found the situation here curiously similar.

I marched directly to Krause and click-saluted smartly. His response was a half-hearted returned salute and an ostentatious glance at his watch. "I see that you can tell the time. I'm encouraged. Your next assignment will be simpler: you are to do precisely nothing. When Obergruppenführer[13] Brückner or Gruppenführer[14] Schaub announces the Führer and his guests, you are to do nothing but stand at attention until they are all seated. Then you are to do nothing but stand at ease. Now, do you feel that these duties are beyond your capabilities?"

I was about to explain to Krause that I felt confident in my native ability to be silent and shift from attention to at ease, when Brückner[15] approached us. Krause and I sprang to

---

[13] Lieutenant General.

[14] Major General.

[15] Wilhelm Brückner was, until 1940, Adolf Hitler's chief adjutant. By the next year, Brückner had become Adolf Hitler's adjutant and bodyguard, later rising to chief adjutant. On 9 November 1934, Brückner was appointed SA General by Hitler. It was through a car accident later that same year when

attention, heel-clicked, and saluted with great vigour. It was the general who spoke first.

"Good afternoon, Herr Krause. I trust all arrangements are proceeding on schedule."

In a tone that even a rabid sycophant would shrink from employing, Krause said: "Of course, Herr General, as you can see."

Personally, I would have avoided all references to vision when speaking to a man wearing an eye patch, but Krause then said in a somewhat quavering tone: "Please forgive me. Have you, ah, spoken to Herr Kannenberg?"

"Krause, my dear fellow," the general replied with a chuckle, "Kannenberg is the final stop on my journey. You are the first. And as for the Führer, you know that he comes when he comes. This isn't an affair of state, so just be ready, yes?"

Krause's entire cellular structure slammed to attention. "Consider it done, Herr General! I personally guarantee that the Führer will have nothing with which to express displeasure."

"I'm certain the Führer will be relieved to know that," the general replied sardonically. Then he turned to me. "How are you, Herr Linge? Adjusting well?"

Miraculously, I was able to collect myself enough to stammer: "Y . . . yes, Herr General."

The general's brow wrinkled with concern. "You are all right, Linge?" he asked.

"Yes, Herr General. I am entirely fit, thank you."

"Good," he replied. "The Führer would like a word with you before tonight's festivities." Then he turned to Krause. "I do hope you can spare him for a short while."

---

he lost an eye and damaged one leg that Brückner managed to procure for Hitler his personal doctor, Karl Brandt, who stayed with Hitler for years.

Inside, I was shuddering with joy over Krause's obvious misery. "Of course I can spare him, Herr General," he lied brightly. "I am honoured that the Führer would even wish to speak with my untested underling. I am certain that Sergeant Linge will gain immeasurably from the encounter."

"I entirely agree with you, Krause, so we'll be off." As Krause click-saluted as if his limbs were propelled by some superhuman force, General Brückner, without returning the salute, took my arm gently at the elbow and guided me to the Führer's quarters. As we walked, there was a seemingly endless series of salutes all round, and we glided through every checkpoint without a flutter of concern. I concluded that General Brückner was no small potatoes in the Chancellery. Without any ceremony, he led me to the Führer's door, knocked once, pushed open the door slightly, announced my presence, nudged me into the room, and shut the door behind him.

In the near dark, the Führer was a mere featureless silhouette facing his enormous floor-to-ceiling window, hands clasped behind his back. "Close the drapes further, would you, Linge?" he asked in barely a whisper. He seemed ill. "My eyes can take just so much light. Gassed in the War, you know."

"Of course, my Führer, but how?"

"Button on right side of the draperies."

I rushed to where he told me and pushed the button, sliding the room into total darkness.

"Thank you, Linge. Now go to my desk and turn on the lamp."

Remembering its location, I did as he bade me, and the darkness was instantly replaced with shadows. He was wearing the uniform I'd seen so often: a tan double-breasted jacket with the Swastika armband, black trousers, and black tie.

The Führer moved slowly from the window to his desk and eased himself into his high-backed leather chair. "I regret having to place you at the feet of an unpleasant character like Krause," he began, "but I have found it necessary to camouflage change in familiar garments. Krause is a good man, as far as it goes, and an assiduous valet. Of course, his personality falls regrettably short of amiable, but there you are. No matter, for you know the truth of it: that he is, to some degree, useful, but you are, to all degrees, indispensable, a difference beyond rational explanation."

Beyond rational explanation? Yes, no disagreement there, since there was none and I had no idea what the Führer was talking about. I hadn't one since I first met him in this very room at my interview. It didn't appear as if I were meant to engage with him, so I remained at ease and totally silent, save for the pounding throb in my ears. In what manner could I possibly be considered indispensable by anyone, including myself? I pushed such useless considerations well to the side of my brain.

"You know, Linge," he went on, "when I was in the army, I began to have these recurring dreams that each morning I would sit at the head of a large, weathered oaken table with members of the general's staff and would be asked to predict to them what would occur that day, and each evening, to recount to them what actually did occur. I still have those dreams. They never matched, that is to say, my predictions and the actual events. Never. I was invariably wrong, and yet they continued to ask me. Do you see any significance in these dreams?"

"I . . . I don't know, my Führer," I stammered, completely ignorant of how to answer. "I know nothing of such things." A lame reply, I must admit, but what else could I have said?

The Führer leaned forward slightly. "You are not alone, Linge," he responded with a certain resigned weariness. "You know, I will miss the Jews, but for only one reason: there will no longer be creatures with the power and skill to interpret dreams accurately."

The Führer then glanced down at what appeared to be a military map of the British Isles. "A historic moment, Linge. It begins tonight with my announcement. The Luftwaffe will be a major step towards the fulfilment of my grand vision. One day, there will be those who call me cruel, Linge. But I ask you to consider the words of Antonin Artaud, who wrote that cruelty in art 'signifies rigour, implacable intention and decision, irreversible and absolute determination.' So, you can readily see that I am, and always have been, at heart, a true artist, especially in politics, my most efficacious medium.

"Now, Linge, I am reasonably certain that tonight Krause will want nothing from you but invisibility in plain sight. His mindless jealousy fits my plans to perfection, for you will have only one job while we meet: to listen; that is all. Listen—and later, you will speak of what you heard, not merely to me, but, from time to time, to certain others as well. Who they are is of no importance to you. This will be your sole responsibility. You understand what I'm saying?"

"Of course, my Führer," I lied, for I was utterly confounded. Could he not sense this, or did he actually care?

"And, Linge," he continued, "this is of critical importance: you are to reveal absolutely nothing to anyone of your special situation, or what is said within these walls. I won't require your word on this, for we have a special bond, you and I."

Suddenly, that ear-cracking *PPFFFFFT* and stench arose again to saturate the room with noxious fumes. "I have always had a delicate belly, Linge," the Führer confessed, "and it taunts and vexes me constantly. It is something of which even my Jew doctor cannot rid me."

"Is there anything I can do for you, my Führer?" I said while breathing through my mouth.

"I'm afraid not," he replied with a pained smile and shrug. And with that, he pressed a button on his console and within less than two seconds Brückner swung open the door and came in. "Yes, my Führer," he chimed, seemingly oblivious to the stench. Clearly, he had endured many encounters with the toxic vapours.

"Brückner, would you be so good as to take Linge back to his quarters and brief him on tonight's event, such as the guests, the purpose, and so forth? I fear that Krause may have neglected such matters and we do want Linge to feel as a welcome member of our family, yes?"

"Of course, my Führer. May I ask when you will be arriving?"

The Führer shrugged. "I have several delicate matters to attend to, as well as dealing with my confounded intestinal infirmity. I will be there when I arrive; that is sufficient. Just make sure to have everyone ready by twenty hundred hours."

"They will be ready, my Führer," Brückner answered quickly and saluted. He then turned to me, his one blue eye bright. "After you, Linge," he said, indicating my time to go. He followed close behind into the grand hallway, stopped me, and said: "Why not avoid Krause for as long as we can, yes? A walk in the gardens might be a refreshing experience . . . considering," he suggested with a pucker of his nose, and led me through enormous double doors.

As we strolled, Brückner spoke rather frankly, a complete surprise since he had never met me before. "You know, Linge," he said, "speaking of flatulence, the Führer once joked—he has quite a playful sense of humour—that he was so adored by his people that if he could get his scientists to bottle that odour in liquid form, it would sell in Germany like Chanel No. 5 does in France and America."

I strained to imagine an elegant Nazi matron or debutante, much less the women of other nations, spritzing "Hitler No. 2" on herself before going out on the town, but stopped myself before I lost control entirely and had to explain my hysterical laughter.

The evening proceeded exactly as Brückner outlined to me in the Chancellery gardens earlier. Fat and fastidious Kannenberg and his wife had seen to every detail of the dinner, and the loathsome, ever-efficient Krause had gotten the Führer ready to meet his guests. I merely stood mute in the corner at attention while Brückner announced the guests and told them where the Führer wished them to sit. Frau Goebbels was to sit on the Führer's right, and the rest would sit according to rank. Once the dinner began, I and three other male "waiters" shifted to at ease. The three were to serve; I was to stand, as per Krause's instructions. There were also several female staff, whose sole task, according to Brückner, was to clear away dishes, silverware, and glasses to make ready for the next course that the males would deliver. Krause appeared to be absorbed in periodically checking on the top button of my server's tunic, which was perfectly in place—as if he expected (hoped?) it to pop off at any moment. It didn't, much to his displeasure, I surmised. Since Kannenberg was, as usual, at the Berghof and so nowhere near my clothing, I finally dismissed him as the original culprit, except perhaps as the mastermind who may have suggested it to the unimaginative lackey.

All shot up and heiled when the Führer arrived at 2130

hours with the matronly Frau Goebbels on his arm. She was staring up at him with what I could only interpret as reverential awe and longing, something I could only wonder at, since she looked remarkably like an aging chief administrator at a particularly drab hospice, futilely attempting to counteract the effect with circus makeup. I sensed that Reichsminister Dr. Goebbels watched his wife with a similar sentiment, and not a little envy. I say *watched*, not *seen*, for it was as if he were no more than a street beggar, gazing at her through a smart restaurant window as the bizarre creature sat adoringly with her lover. Dr. Goebbels's almost pristine ugliness, compounded by his feebleness from infantile paralysis, his club foot, and his drab brown uniform, belied, according to Brückner, the cunning brilliance of his undisputed propagandist's art, and the extent to which women are prone to overlook such impediments in the powerful.

Though I knew of him, of course, and had actually seen him with the Führer at various times before joining the latter's household, I possessed very little specific information. I gleaned from the dossier that, as with many talented, rootless, and ambitious losers, he found a home in the Nazi Party, which he joined in 1924. He also despised capitalism, viewing it (from afar, of course) as having a loathsome Jewish core. He rose to power in 1933 along with the Führer and the Party and, ultimately, was appointed Propaganda Minister, in which position he exerted totalitarian control over the media, arts, and information.

Beside the Reichsminister sat the austere and expressionless Lieutenant-General Walther Wever, ramrod-straight, and the presumptive subject of the evening's festivities. Whether he was aware of this or not, I had no way of knowing. Being an archetypal Prussian military man, he placed his total allegiance at the service of whichever government was in power, whether

Kaiser, Weimar, or Nazi. As such, he had become commander of the Ministry of Aviation in 1933.

Beside General Wever sat Captain Wilhelm Canaris, chief of military intelligence, no less austere and expressionless.

Next to Canaris sat the deceptively regal Joachim von Ribbentrop, who, I imagine, considers me so completely and thoroughly inconsequential that I pose no possible threat. A former teacher recalled that von Ribbentrop "was the most stupid in his class, full of vanity and very pushy." In 1925 his aunt, Gertrud von Ribbentrop, adopted him, which allowed him to add the aristocratic "von" to his name.

But von Ribbentrop appeared to be less than popular with the Nazi Party's Alten Kämpfer.[16] According to Brückner, Goebbels expressed a common view when he confided that "von Ribbentrop bought his name, he married his money, and he swindled his way into office." Despite that—or perhaps because of it, said Brückner—von Ribbentrop became the Führer's favourite foreign policy adviser, partly by dint of his familiarity with the world outside Germany, but more so by his unabashed flattery and sycophancy. According to Brückner's source, von Ribbentrop acquired the habit of listening carefully to what the Führer was saying, memorizing his pet ideas, and then later presenting the latter's ideas as his own—a practice that as much impressed his boss as it proved von Ribbentrop was an ideal National Socialist diplomat. According to Brückner, von Ribbentrop quickly learned that the Führer always favoured the most radical solution to any problem and, accordingly, always tended his advice in that direction.

Brückner also remarked that another and more important

---

[16] Old Fighters.

factor aided von Ribbentrop's rise: the Führer's distrust and disdain for Germany's professional diplomats, suspecting that they were all reactionary toffs who did not fully support his revolution, and so he was on the lookout for someone to carry out his foreign policy goals.

For all this, the Führer rewarded von Ribbentrop by appointing him Reich Minister, Ambassador-Plenipotentiary at Large. As Brückner put it, he humphed at the "Large" in the title, which he said exemplified von Ribbentrop's arrogance more than his position. At all this, I remained utterly indifferent but attentive.

And finally, next to von Ribbentrop—and, logistically fascinating, being next to the Führer—sat the ugly giant Ernst Franz Sedgwick Hanfstaengl. If I knew little if anything about the others, I knew absolutely nothing about Hanfstaengl, save for hearing him at the piano. The dossier entry was left virtually blank except for the entry: "called 'Putzi' by his intimates, he is a favourite of the Führer," so I needed to rely on the audacious, witty, and cynical Brückner for the proper perspective on this "Putzi."

Much of his influence was due to his friendship with the Führer, who enjoyed listening to "Putzi" play the piano. More important to Brückner—and to me—as the Party consolidated its power, several disputes arose between Hanfstaengl and Germany's propaganda minister, Joseph Goebbels. As a consequence, the latter appeared to glare at Hanfstaengl almost as much as he did his wife, though with different motives.

In my role of Sphinx, I learned that while dinner is the main meal, it is as simple as one could imagine. The Führer's repast consisted of some vegetable stew followed by stewed fruit as dessert. This he topped with one or two glasses of beer (seemingly the extent of his alcoholic indulgence and, from what I learned, seldom done). The Führer ate rapidly, mechanically. Because of his earlier, poverty-fuelled bohemian existence, Brückner informed me, food is, for him, merely a means of subsistence. In the course of a few minutes, he was finished, but the entire dinner lasted two hours.

For most of the meal, little actually centred on the Führer, whose table manners were as bohemian as his history: he abstractedly bit his fingernails, he ran his index finger back and forth under his nose, and, as in his quarters, he emitted an occasional cacophonous fart, which all, including the sender, knowingly pretended to ignore as they did the inescapable fact of his complete dominance—all punctuated by chatty inanities with Mrs. Goebbels or Hanfstaengl, or he just sat there, engrossed in his own thoughts, seemingly without listening to the talk going on around him. However, though I had no personal knowledge or outside guidance, from my vantage point, I had the pronounced sensation that he followed each conversation vaguely, for the effect that music has on others: to both stimulate his thoughts and relax him. For all intents and purposes, in that room, I did not exist.

Eventually, the Führer signalled to Brückner with a slight turn of his head, and the latter called the guests to order.

"Gentlemen and lady," Brückner declared in a more formal tone than I'd seen him use up to that time, "the Führer wishes to make a momentous announcement." He turned to their host. "My Führer?"

Not rising, he spoke in a mellow baritone, forsaking the raucous, histrionic, gesticulating stridency of his public speeches.

"To all of you present tonight, and without a lengthy and tiresome introduction—or the necessity of a discussion afterward—I have instructed General Göring to formally establish the Luftwaffe, the German Air Force, in complete and utter defiance of the accursed Treaty of Versailles, and I have decided upon General Wever as its chief of staff. I wish Reichsminister Goebbels to ensure that all who will soon learn of the Luftwaffe's existence, especially abroad, will feel secure in the knowledge that no military use will ever be contemplated. I am entrusting Admiral Canaris to use every resource at his disposal to learn the true and accurate reactions to my announcement. In actual fact, by my estimation, my decision will not create a single substantive ripple of concern among our enemies."

After the cheers and applause had subsided, the Führer turned to Hanfstaengl. "Now, Putzi, play some Wagner for me while dessert is being served. You can do without the calories."

Hanfstaengl chuckled mirthlessly at the remark, lifted his considerable bulk, and moved his giant frame to the upright piano in the corner and began pounding out some bombastic horror that I assumed was Wagner, which appeared to be the signal for dessert to be served while the guests murmured animatedly among themselves about the Führer's announcement.

Once the table had been cleared, Brückner announced that the Führer was "understandably weary" and so would retire to his private chambers alone. At that, the Führer leaned over, kissed Frau Goebbels's hand, rose (as did everyone), turned, and left the room, followed closely behind by Brückner. Krause stayed on, presumably to make certain that I remained a meaningless mannequin to the end. I hoped that one day soon he'd answer to the Führer for his treatment of me, but it did teach me about Krause's priorities. I prayed that I'd be able to employ that knowledge to my own advantage one day.

When all had left, I made my way to my quarters and related my day to you.

ALTHOUGH I'VE BEEN at the Chancellery for only a few days, I concluded that putting the flesh of insight onto the bones of fact would be up to me alone. Nevertheless, I felt the need at every moment, not only to consider my situation but also, once considered, to discover, with a minimum of risk, an ally in the midst of filth like Krause, Schroeder, and those like them I had yet to encounter—but most assuredly would.

I ruled out any active member of the SS as far too perilous (perhaps save the one who affixed my tunic button—I wish I'd gotten his name, but I expect that I'd run into him sooner or later in the relatively cloistered environment of the Chancellery). Who, then? Brückner? Too exalted, I decided. Also, I didn't really know him at all, and so his loquacity could well be more a tactic than a trait. Unfortunately, I knew virtually no one, mostly thanks to Krause, who provided no introductions, even though I had been selected personally by the Führer. Nevertheless, I had to proceed, despite Krause's obvious desire that I suddenly disappear forever.

For most of the morning (in which I was, again probably due to Krause, alone and without instructions), I pondered the risks and benefits, the number of alternatives, and the hazards associated with each. However, after far less mulling than I anticipated, an instinct I'd kept chained in the deepest recesses of my brain suddenly burst out: it had to be a female! Yes, a female, potentially more treacherous, but tempered by training to be sentimental, understanding, and compliant, that is, once the cynicism underlying it all is neutralized by loneliness and hope, and, if sufficiently cultivated, infinitely more reliable. Despite the Party's strictures on the role of women in the Third Reich, the Chancellery was teeming with females, granted, secretaries aside, invariably on the lowest menial levels, but, after reading several novels about servants in nineteenth- and early-twentieth-century England, who better to know the actual inner workings of the higher orders than the lower orders?

To make certain I'd have the necessary freedom, I shaved, dressed, and made for Krause's office, only to be told that I must be exhausted from last night's dinner and should spend the rest of the day recuperating. The tiny bastard was as predictable as I'd thought. How the Führer could stand intimate contact with such a malignant nonentity was beyond my limited analytical powers. But Krause wanted my recuperation, and, acting on that piece of practical wisdom, I thanked him profusely, withdrew quickly, and strolled down the hallway past two armed SS checkpoints to the secretaries' office.

Taking what I believed to be a minor gamble, I entered without knocking and closed the door, to find a miniature, barracks-like room studded with bunks strung along military-grey walls and, in the centre, running the length of the room, sat wooden desks, each one supporting a typewriter and short, three-sided wooden typing-paper trays. At the desks sat young to middle-aged females in slightly varying degrees of drab homeliness. There were no males in such roles that I could discern. Did the Führer actually prefer such creatures round him so not to be tempted or even distracted? Another mystery, and a personally frustrating one at that. A few were typing furiously, most, mechanically. I apologized for not knocking and claimed that I was searching for the kitchen. All gazed at me with speechless wonder until the door opened and the redoubtable Christa Schroeder stood there, heavy legs straddling the linoleum floor combatively, pad and pencil in both hands resting menacingly against her abdomen. Her eyes were slits of disapproval; her thin bare lips pursed similarly. After a few pregnant moments, she spoke.

"What are you doing here, Herr Linge?" she asked in a tone I could only describe as barely controlled viciousness. When I hesitated, she said: "All right, ardent defender of the Reich, please state your business and leave. My girls have actual work to do."

I apologized with stammering abjectness, told her that I had no intention of disrupting her routine but that I was merely seeking the kitchen. I knew my apology and excuse would have no effect except to stall for the time I needed to generate sufficient nurturing instincts in the others, which was my goal.

Fräulein Schroeder's mouth twisted into a grimace of utter detestation. "Then obviously, Herr Linge, and not surprisingly," she spat, while waving one arm round the room, "you entered the wrong area. If anyone here is keeping you, I have not detected it."

There are many ways of dismissing someone, and this was probably the most diplomatic in her repertoire. I wanted to ask her if she was related to Krause, even sexually, but the image of any possible coupling between them kept me civil. "Again, Fräulein Schroeder, my apologies. Perhaps you might direct me to the kitchen so I don't disrupt another office."

She lifted her bony shoulders and puffed out her meagre chest dismissively. "Herr Linge, I am a secretary, the Führer's *chief* secretary, to be precise. I am not a concierge. There are many in the hallway who have precious little else to do, who can direct you. I suggest you ask them."

Gratefully, I took her hint and brushed past her (making sure of the distance of the brush) and out the door. In the hallway, I was greeted by the usual "March Hare"–style bustle of uniformed people going about things about which I had no idea. I decided to move a discrete number of yards down the hall and sit on one of the marble benches to wait. Since it was near lunchtime, the wait was relatively brief, as the women I'd seen in the secretaries' room filed out the door—all but Fräulein Schroeder, that is, who I assumed would do nothing so human and congenial as to eat with her subordinates.

I could almost touch the sighs of relief issuing from their mouths as they made their way down the hall towards me. All passed without even the slightest sideward glance, save one, at the back of the line, who furtively dropped a folded piece of paper and moved on, rather more swiftly than before. She was of medium height, her dull-brown hair was tortured back into a bun, her forehead was low and narrow, her eyebrows were heavy, her lips were thick, and a wide, flat nose provided that final touch of hereditary peasantry, one who'd risen against all odds.

Obviously, the paper was for me. But how did she know I'd be there? An intriguing but useless question at the moment. I waited until all had gone down the second set of stairs to the lunchroom before barely beating a janitor to the paper. I took it back to my room and set it unopened on my night table. The kitchen would have to wait. I unfolded the typewritten note and read it:

> For reasons that should be obvious to you, I omitted
> your name, and did not sign it, as Herr Himmler and his

numberless lackeys are everywhere. First, be assured that I harbour no illusions about myself or your intentions. I am short, dreary, unlovely, and low, the first of my family to rise above slopping hogs. Second, I know that you were definitely not looking for the kitchen when you entered our office. I also entertain a suspicion that you were there to seek out someone like me, even if it was not me. Fortunately for you, I know my officemates, and I can tell you that there *is* only me. There may well be others, but not where I toil. You have probably surmised by now that I am the one who placed that note under your door, and I advise you once more to trust no one—not even the Führer, who claims incessantly—and disingenuously—that we are his family. This is a self-serving fabrication, for we are truly alone here. I tell you this as a friend, not as a "family member." If you wish to have further contact, you will find a way to let me know. If not, I wish you safety and so urge upon you a precious commodity: strategic discretion.

Trust, I thought to myself. Years before, I'd read in a book of essays that trust is more important than love, because one can trust without love, but one cannot love without trust. I'd never given the matter any thought until now. Was that true? The note writer seemed to think so, and yet so many people behaved as if the necessity of trust for love was a cliché that dissolved when a person—or even a nation—was smitten. Clearly, the note writer was not smitten by anyone at the Chancellery, not even the Führer. *Remarkable,* I thought. Did I believe it? An entire nation both adored and trusted him completely. Her bitter and articulate cynicism was breathtaking. And yet, was there substance to her claim, beyond mere disillusionment and envy? I'd sought information, yet after reading her note I was more befuddled than ever. Was she truly a benevolent friend or a dangerous provocateur? In any event, how could I possibly heed her advice? And how could I "establish contact" with a woman so secretive and anonymous, even if I dared risk it? More questions than answers, which was certainly not my goal.

A knock on the door jolted me out of my frustrating ruminations. It was Brückner, who stayed just long enough to commiserate with me concerning dinner duty the previous night; to inform me that the Führer required my presence at 2200 hours in his quarters; and that he would come back to fetch me at 2130. Then he tapped the brim of his cap in a friendly salute and left. Again, more questions than answers.

I decided that in the intervening hours, I would make a quick visit to the university library.[17] It originally contained a massive collection of books, rendered considerably less massive after the Führer took power. For I'd learned that it was from the university's library that some twenty thousand books by "degenerates" and opponents of the regime were taken to be burned on 10 May 1933 in the Opera Square,[18] for a demonstration protected by the SA that also featured a speech by Reichsminister Goebbels. Books have always been my salvation, even the ones not considered kindling by the Reichsminister. For me, books create life from death, something that Mary Wollstonecraft Shelley might have appreciated. The fact that, for the most part, I had to learn to read on my own made me necessarily halting and inefficient but far more appreciative and assiduous. However,

---

[17] Humboldt-Universität zu Berlin.

[18] Opernplatz.

I knew long before it became a necessity that I must confine my reading to furtive forays into libraries, that ignorance is a form of innocence that enhances invisibility. That is to say, a village idiot is more easily ignored than a professor.

I located what I considered to be a reasonably safe location for you (until I had access to a secure darkroom) and used it for the first time. As I strolled back into the Chancellery, I lamented that there was no one with whom to share my joy of reading, to rethink my—at times, inevitable—misinterpretations (or to even know that they were misinterpretations).

Brückner is SA, not SS. I need more time to figure him out and, in the process, learn what truly distinguishes the SS from the SA, and, if there is a real difference, is it significant? But my research would have to wait, because Brückner came when he said he would, efficient as ever. He came in and closed the door behind him, then motioned for me to accompany him into the bathroom, whereupon he closed that door and turned on the cold water tap to maximum. Over the noise he said, "Can't be too careful, my friend. I'm glad to see that you've recovered sufficiently from all that frenetic activity last night," he jested amiably. "The Führer certainly knows how to moderate a debate, and Krause certainly knows how to keep someone hopping in place, yes?"

Was Brückner jesting further? Was he testing me? Both? Something else? I thought I knew what he was saying but didn't dare venture a response beyond: "I'm too new to judge, I'm afraid." Aside from the effect of the faucet's din, my brain was in turmoil. What to say? How much could I afford to show this man I hardly knew? Trust no one, the note had warned. "I don't think Krause likes me, Herr General," I replied blandly.

"You have a remarkable flair for the understatement, Linge," he remarked, with the merest hint of a grin. "Yes, while Krause worships the Führer and would gladly throw himself upon a grenade to protect him, he is a man truly nasty by nature, and he is also intensely jealous of you, an unfortunate and potentially dangerous combination. However, and far more important, the Führer has the highest regard—and, from what I gather, rather grandiose plans—for you, so perhaps Krause can somehow be neutralized, yes?"

Be careful, I commanded myself. What I say next could well colour all future communication with the Führer's chief adjutant. "Herr General," I said. "I wish only to serve the Führer to the fullest. Anything that can be done to make my wish a reality would, of course, be most welcome." I held my breath.

Brückner stood looking at me without expression, perhaps assessing the genuineness and, far more hazardous to me, the degree of sophistication of my reply. I wanted to tell him that my reply was also a test of *his* genuineness and sophistication, but remained silent and waited, while the water gushed cacophonously.

Finally, Brückner broke the silence. "Yes, Linge. I completely agree. We certainly cannot have anyone standing in the way of you properly serving the Führer, can we? The only question, then, is methodology—a mere matter of tactics, eh?" In my reading, not really a question, confirmed by his moving to the sink and turning off the tap. "I think we should leave now for your appointment, don't you?" I had the same reading on that one as well. I began to understand that for Brückner, a question mark was merely a period. But for how many was this also true?

When Brückner shepherded me into the study, I was greeted

by the bizarre sight of the Führer attired only in an ill-fitting nightshirt perched precariously on the seat of a small, straight-back chair. He appeared to be screwing a lightbulb into one of the higher wall sconces. As he reached up, his nightshirt lifted to show neon-white shins.

Being the person I am, I started to rush over to assist, but Brückner took hold of me by the shoulder, his grip gentle but determined, held me back, turned me toward him, and lowered his only eyelid conspiratorially, presumably to send the message that no help was necessary or requested. Then, message delivered, he released his grip.

"Thank you, Linge," the Führer said, as he finished threading the bulb into the socket. "But, as you can see, I am perfectly capable of putting in a simple light bulb. What is quite impossible for a Russian or a Pole is quite simple for the average German," he chuckled to himself. "Thank you for delivering him, Brückner," he added. "I'll buzz for you when you're needed."

Brückner instantly saluted, said, "Yes, my Führer," and left me with the nightshirted supreme leader of Germany, still standing on his perch.

"Linge," said the Führer as the door shut behind Brückner, "do be so good as to help me down." A short show of teeth under a barely raised moustache. "I didn't wish to have my chief adjutant tattling all over the place that I was too feeble to alight from a chair."

I went over to him and held the chair with one hand and took the Führer's outstretched hand with the other, thus ensuring his balance as he lowered himself to the floor, whereupon he went to his desk and sat down with a puff of breath. "My gratitude, Linge," he murmured. "Your first physical act as valet, yes? Do sit."

I grabbed the chair that once supported the Führer's feet, placed it before his desk, and sat.

"I understand," the Führer began, "that we have a personnel problem." He then shrugged and raised his hands, palms up, resignedly. "I must confess that I anticipated this. Having had to rely on my own poor resources for most of my life, I've been forced to radically adjust to being attended to, on both the grandest and the most minute levels—not an easy task for someone with my monastic inclinations."

Then the Führer rose and began pacing, in the speed-skater style, as I'd seen him do before. I assumed that such movement was important to his thought process. "Do not misunderstand me. Krause is an excellent valet," the Führer continued, "but a little too proprietorial and overprotective, no doubt about that. Also, I must confess, a bit too full of himself. I require and expect loyalty from those close to me, and loyalty, as you know, is absolute, or it is nothing. In this, I harbour no doubts about Krause whatsoever."

He ceased his pacing and pivoted to face me, swinging his arms round to the front and clasping his hands. "However," he declared, "this rivalry must cease. Therefore, I've decided to employ a battle-tested strategy: divide and conquer. That is to say, Krause will handle all my business arrangements and all matters concerning my internal and external travel, and you, Linge, I wish to have you with me constantly. You are to ensure that my clothing and private rooms are in good order, and to assist you, I will assign a chambermaid. But far more important, we will, from time to time, discuss with you a variety of matters in which I am involved and will become even more so with time, which means that of the two, you alone will be on call, and so will need to have quarters close to my own. Of course, Krause will grouse," the Führer japed, chuckling at his witticism, "but he will do as instructed. Have you any questions for me?"

The Führer's selecting me to be his constant companion and asking me whether I had any questions for him was even more comical than his statement about Krause. Was I Moses, a prince of Egypt and the Hebrew God's chosen liberator? God might ask *him* if he had any questions? But that the supreme leader of the entire German nation would ask the same of an utterly insignificant callow menial seemed as preposterous as it was undeniable. My brain was rendered insensible with it.

"I . . . am truly . . . overwhelmed, my Führer," I stammered back.

"No need, Linge," the Führer reassured with an accompanying chuckle. "It's only in the natural order of things, as you will soon see. Krause is useful, and so will be kept occupied to exhaustion, of that, I can assure you. On the other hand, you are essential, but—and this is critical—before all but me, you must always 'hide your light under a bushel,'[19] do you understand?"

Some years before, while a winter storm raged outside, I'd read that exact phrase in *Ivanhoe* in the dry, musty comfort of the university library but had no idea what it meant, much less what it might have to do with me. But the context of experience provided me with the reasonable guess, and by that, I realized that I had always hidden my "light," such as it was, and fully intended to continue. But now I was beset with the question: How did the Führer mean it?

"I . . . think I do, my Führer. But . . . I pray that you'll guide me."

He let loose a hearty laugh. "It's quite the opposite, Linge. In

---

[19] To conceal one's good ideas or talents.

any event, Brückner is already presenting my wishes to Krause, and he'll begin his new duties at once. I completely understand that you might feel inadequate to a most critical role of which you have no knowledge. Having been a roustabout and labourer is no disgrace and certainly no impediment, I can assure you. I, of course, can appreciate this as few can. It's monstrous that a man's entire life should depend on a stupid piece of parchment that he either receives or doesn't. I ached to go to the School of Fine Arts, but the first question from the moronic examiner to whom I'd submitted my work was: 'Which school of arts and crafts do you come from?' This cretin found it difficult to believe me when I replied that I hadn't been to any, for even he could see that I had an indisputable talent for art and, especially, architecture. But, so what, in his stupid, myopic, class-obsessed eyes?

"My disappointment was all the greater," he expanded, "since my original idea had been to paint. It was obvious to anyone with even a simian's sensibilities that, painting aside, I had a true artistic gift, but I learnt that it was impossible for me to enter a specialised school, because I hadn't a matriculation certificate. I therefore resigned myself to continuing my efforts as a self-taught man and decided to escape Austria and settle in Germany, arriving in Munich, full of great enthusiasm, enormous talent, and little else.

"I intended to study for another three years. I entered a competition, telling myself that I'd show them what I could do! That was why, when the short-listed plans for the new opera house at Berlin were published, and I saw that my own project was less bad than those which had been printed, my heart beat high, for I had specialised in that sort of architecture. Of course, it was rejected," he said, with what I considered to be a well-practised nonchalance. "But now, it no longer matters. Having always considered myself in the avant-garde, I possessed a laughably limited view of art and architecture, not nearly comprehending their true nature and scope."

His voice suddenly rose to an almost oratorical pitch. "Now, I create nations! Not the future, as we know it, but *timelessness, Linge. Timelessness*, not a future of Jew-infested office buildings, petit-bourgeois opera houses, and vainglorious statues and fountains. *And you will insure that I succeed!*"

I was, once again, utterly flummoxed as his voice dropped back to its normal timbre. He was staring at a middle distance between us, instead of at me, and his words suddenly had become officious—as if he hadn't been speaking to me as before: "Your duties, Herr Linge, will consist of two kinds: the mundane tasks that will be explained to you by Brückner and will begin this evening. The critical tasks will be explained to you later by me personally, and only when the need arises." He pressed one of his coloured buttons and within seconds Brückner entered. I leapt from my chair to attention. Brückner and I saluted with fervour, while the Führer raised his upper arm languidly, elbow bent, palm sluggishly forward, his traditional return salute. Then Brückner and I both pivoted round and exited.

When we reached the main hallway, Brückner stopped abruptly, grasped my elbow, and turned me to him. "Alas, Linge," he said, "when I told you that dealing with the Führer was a mere matter of tactics, I confess that I may have grossly understated the matter." Then he let go of my elbow and we continued walking to my room, where he said at the doorway: "Incidentally, the Führer has promoted you to lieutenant, a rank making you coequal with Krause, so no toadying necessary. I'll return later to help supervise the move to your new quarters and brief you on your household duties, now that Krause has been given his." Then he gave a mock heel-click and salute, turned, and walked away.

⁂

I sat in the dark, on the edge of my cot, waiting to be shepherded to my new quarters—or were they really new? Could this have been arranged from the beginning, and who knows when that beginning began? Perhaps only the Führer really knew. I only hoped that there would be a bulb powerful enough to photograph you, for I felt that I would have so much more to report, now that my situation was moving swiftly from the illusion of transparency to completely opaque. By my judgment, it could only get clearer, unless that, too, turned out to be an illusion. Dare I say this: the Führer was the most complicated man I had ever met, or even read about. Even in our few cursory encounters, I truly believe that his power resides, not in his speeches, his appearance, his gestures, or his ideas but in the degree of enigmatic complexity that defines the real essence of the man.

⁂

At 1400 hours, there was a barely audible knock. Expecting Brückner, I moved to the door and swung it open only to see a small, exotically attired middle-aged woman. She was wearing the ornate silken robe of a gypsy fortune-teller, though she had none of the swarthy skin colour of a Southern European, South American, or North African. For a few pregnant moments, she studied me as if I were a particularly intriguing laboratory specimen.

"Can I help you?" I asked. She stopped her staring and said, "You are Heinz Linge." Not a question. Her German was flawless but possessed no accent I could associate with any native Germans. Her voice was mellow and low in register. Almost hypnotic.

"Yes," I replied, somewhat befuddled. "And who are you?"

"Give me your hand," she demanded mildly. "Please."

Not sensing anything threatening, I held out my hand.

"No, the other one," she requested. "My apologies for not specifying."

I held out my other hand, which she clasped with her tiny, perfectly manicured fingers, and a strange warmth flowed through me. She held my hand only for a few seconds, but it felt far longer before she released her grip. "I am Savitri Devi Mukherji," she told me. "Your Führer chose well."

With that, she turned and disappeared down the hallway, leaving me shaking my head in bewilderment. I was about to close the door when I spotted Brückner coming towards me from the stairway. I began to salute when he raised his hands, palms outward.

"Linge," he said, "we both serve the Führer as best we can. But when we're alone, I recommend that we deal with each other as comrades, not as impersonal links in the chain of command, don't you agree?"

Trust no one, the note had said, not even the Führer, but what was I to do? "If you say so, Herr Gen—"

"Wilhelm," he rejoined, "or even Willie, if you prefer, and you shall be Heinz. I'm weary of formalities. So that's settled, yes? Now, to your new duties, you—"

"Herr . . . Wilhelm," I corrected, sensing no way out, "did you see a woman leaving before you arrived?"

"A woman? Who?"

"I have no idea. Just before you arrived, I was visited by a woman—not German, I'm reasonably sure—dressed as a gypsy fortune-teller, who grasped my hand, and then left."

"I'll assume you were sober at the time. Did she say why she sought you out?"

"All she said, after much staring at me and hand holding, was that the Führer had chosen well."

"Chosen what?"

"I . . . have no idea. Maybe herself. Maybe anything. She took my hand. Maybe me. Do you know anyone with that name?"

His one eye swivelled to the ceiling in thought. "No, the name means nothing. I think I'd remember the name and the person you described. So would the Gestapo, I dare say. Why do you think she sought you out?"

Trust no one! "No matter," I replied with a dismissive shrug, deciding that no reason was better than a weak one. "You were going to discuss my new duties?"

"Yes, of course," he began as he guided me back into the room, closed the door, nudged me into the bathroom, and turned on the tap again. "But please realize, Heinz, that these are only your official duties, which, considering the Führer, might be very mundane but subject to modest or radical adjustment at a moment's notice. The Führer is, at his Bohemian core, a person of the night, so in the morning, you will awaken him at eleven hundred hours by a knock on his door, at which time he rises. You enter, hand him the newspapers, foreign dispatches, and the post, and he reads them in bed—beside which there needs to be a tea trolley for them, as well as for his spectacles and a box of coloured pencils. While the Führer reads, you prepare his bath and set out his clothing for the day."

"His spectacles?"

Brückner chuckled. "Yes, Heinz. Spectacles. You understand,

he never likes to be seen wearing them in public, for he believes it to be a sign of weakness. Gassed in the War, you know. Moreover, you must always carry at least two spare pairs of glasses when you travel with him, which, I predict, will be rather frequent in the days to come. He tends to break them often while toying with them in his hand as he ruminates over a problem. Incidentally, you will also be responsible for keeping him stocked with other writing materials.

"In any event, after his morning reading session, the Führer generally follows the same routine: he shaves, removes his white nightshirt, lays it on the bed, bathes, takes the clothing that you've made ready on the clothes stand, and dresses. Very important now," he added, wagging his index finger like a schoolmaster: "Unlike his counterparts, the Führer will not permit anyone to dress him, but you must attend when he dresses himself. Also, he dresses to a stopwatch, so your role will be as a sort of referee. According to your good friend Krause, at his command '*Los!*' he sets the watch going and the dressing race begins. The quicker he finishes, the better his temper. I wish something like that worked as well on Krause." We both chuckled at that.

"Now, in the evening, you wait with me for any instructions concerning the guests who will attend, and whom he will escort, the seating arrangements, and any other matters that involve the evening's events, then report to him, once all his guests are assembled for dinner. After all the festivities—if any—have ended, you follow the Führer to his quarters and stand by, while he changes into his night clothes, and issues whatever instructions he may have for you for the next day."

Brückner permitted himself a mischievous smile. "Sounds simple, almost quotidian, Heinz, yes? But, unfortunately, what I've just given you is merely a small notch above pure theory. In a real sense, even in the official realm, you must be whatever the

Führer wishes you to be, regardless of your official job description. The Führer, in addition to possessing a superior intellect, is also a man of instinct, whimsy, and impulse. As a consequence, infinite flexibility must be the major attribute that you bring to the task." His smile then faded. "You understand me?"

Brückner's briefing reminded me of a novel I'd read in which a reputedly learned professor told his class: "There are two rules you must always follow: look before you leap, but he who hesitates is lost."

"Of course . . . Wilhelm, I understand completely," I lied. "But you said these were my 'official' duties. What of my unofficial ones?"

His smile returned. "Ah, yes, those. Well, my friend, only the Führer can brief you there. Just concern yourself with the official ones and leave the rest to circumstance."

After Brückner left, it struck me, I suppose, from the back of my mind, that I couldn't imagine Brückner—or the battalion of Chancellery guards, for that matter—overlooking that creature who'd called on me.

Seventeen days since Brückner's briefing.

Regarding my official duties, I'm reasonably certain that he did the best he could by me, theory being what it is. However, the everyday reality of adjusting to the surrealism of the Führer's idiosyncrasies rendered me exhausted by the end of the day, too weak to do more than stumble into my new quarters, crawl onto my cot, and steal as much sleep as possible before the Führer's sporadically unremitting buzzer summoned me. Regardless, I fear that I've ignored you far too long, and so, despite being severely enervated, I take my pen—and camera—in hand.

I told you—it seems like a lifetime ago—that I was attempting to seek allies among the other menials. In the moments spared me, I first wandered the Chancellery to get my bearings, and, especially downstairs, I came across a labyrinth of rooms, from humble to grand, many in total disrepair, some in different stages of repair, and a few completely refurbished.

Through the grudging acquiescence of a Gestapo brute who, I suspect (with the indispensable assistance of my identity card), had finally convinced himself that he was actually assisting the Führer's valet, rather than a Jew, a cultural or sexual degenerate, a spy, or merely a curious nonentity (I'll spare you the dismaying interaction), I finally located the kitchen I'd claimed to be seeking at the time when I ran into the detestable Fräulein Schroeder in the secretaries' office.

Since, through strategic invisibility, I had heard much about the deceptively jolly, rotund house manager, I waited until I knew that he and his wife were away on temporary loan from the Führer to the Italian embassy before daring to enter their domain. There, I discovered a mammoth room containing several sinks, ovens, wooden preparation tables, and one large rectangular, window-topped door facing an outside passageway, presumably used for bringing in supplies for the Führer's vegetarian concoctions as well as conventional items for his guests who didn't share the Führer's abhorrence of meat and disdain for those who ate it. Four kitchen maids appeared to be scurrying about active cauldrons and ovens, making ready for luncheon, which I was obliged to attend, albeit standing in a corner.

As I stood in the doorway, one of the maids looked up from some carrots she was dicing:

"Yes, Herr Lieutenant? We have made you perhaps hungry?" She was the least plain of the four, the only one who glanced away from her duties, and appeared to have a certain affability, seemingly unknown or well hidden by the other household staff. Her hair was done up into a bun atop her head with a small net pressing it down into a thick wad.

"Not particularly, thank you," I answered, as if she'd invited me for a snack. "I just came to acquaint myself with all the others who care for the Führer." Since that didn't appear to animate the other kitchen help into even uttering a word of greeting, I concentrated on the one who had responded. "You certainly keep busy," I said, silently embarrassed by the banality of it.

"Oh, yes, never a dull moment with the Kannen—" She stopped dead in her tracks when suddenly one of the other kitchen maids, presumably her superior, turned to her with as sharp a glance as I'd seen since my last meeting with Krause. "I'm sorry, Herr Lieutenant, but as you can see, we are on a tight schedule."

I was desperate to spare the poor creature any repercussions from her superior and "their majesties," who would invariably be informed of her indiscretion the moment they returned. "Actually," I said, "it was the Führer himself who asked me, as his personal valet, to look in on you all and tell you how pleased he is that life goes on without constant managerial oversight. I will, of course, report back to him that the Kannenbergs have things well in hand, even when they are absent."

It worked. This time "the glancer" turned to me, bowed, and begged me to convey their utmost gratitude to the Führer for his gracious compliment. Before I was inundated with more sycophantic slobber, I nodded and left with no further ceremony.

My thinking took me only as far as the buzzer that sounded in my room as soon as I entered. I grabbed my cap, raced out the door, and made for the Führer's study, where he appeared to be staring at a row of identically bound books, shelved at eye level on his wall-to-wall, floor-to-ceiling bookcases.

"Are you a reader, Linge," he said without turning round. He was standing before the twenty-volume *Brockhaus Enzyklopädie*.[20] Since he couldn't see me at the moment, I took the opportunity to study one wall, which contained an enormous pull-down theatre screen with several columns of numbers and geometric figures and a map on which these numbers and figures were displayed. I had no idea what they represented, nor did I have any intention of asking.

---

[20] *Brockhaus Enzyklopädie.* This *Lexikon* included geography, history, and in part biography as well as mythology, philosophy, natural history, and so on.

"Are you a reader, Linge?" he repeated.

"Whenever . . . possible, my Führer," I squeezed out while holding my breath. "As you must know, I've had little formal schooling, but felt the lack, and so I taught myself to read."

"Many wouldn't have bothered. Why have you?"

Brückner's allusion to the Führer's "instinct, whimsy, and impulse" was certainly in evidence. I had to deal with this question somehow, stumble though I might. "I imagine, my Führer," I replied, "so that I could interpret my experiences with some perspective, clumsy and perhaps inaccurate though it might be."

"An intriguing answer," he responded. "So, you realized, as did I, that reading is not an end in itself, but the means to an end."

I feared I'd given away too much light from under my bushel, and so needed to regress. "I never thought of it that way, my Führer," I replied. What else could I say?

He turned from his books and faced me. "It's quite simple, Linge," he began. "Literary reading is an ennobling enterprise, of course, but more than that, if you are to truly serve me, I must know that you not only understand what I say but also understand what I mean, and what those who surround me are saying and meaning. I appreciate that your knowledge would be of a most superficial and disconnected sort, but just the same, the information would be there for the taking, and our discussions, which will be several, can be of great assistance." The Führer then waved back toward the bookshelves. "Therefore, I encourage you to take books freely from my library, especially the *Enzyklopädie* volumes, for general knowledge, but not limited to them, of course. There are even books here that our good Dr. Goebbels had ordered burnt or banned elsewhere. But what is harmful to the masses cannot hurt us, yes? What did you think of my announcement about the Luftwaffe?"[21]

This was presumably what Brückner meant by "unofficial duties." My brain was in turmoil. My opinion of the Luftwaffe announcement? Does the Führer really wish to know that from the likes of me? I knew that the Luftwaffe was never intended to be a banal passenger service and, more, that the Führer's Reich was never intended to be a stodgy bourgeois centre of commerce—another Switzerland. "I'm afraid, my Führer, that, without other orders, I was following Lieutenant Krause's directive and merely stood at ease the entire time."

"Without listening?" the Führer inquired, a mask of incredulity spread over his face.

"I'm afraid I did no listening, since my entire duty was to obey Lieutenant Krause's order to stand at ease and do nothing. I followed his command to the letter."

The Führer smiled, spreading his narrow little moustache across his upper lip. "Linge, you carry out orders a bit far. In the War, loyal soldier that I was, even I stopped short of complete literalness, if only to retain my humanity. In future, my friend, always remember that one of your principal duties—to me—is to listen, listen well, and for that, you must read as much as you can."

My friend? My friend, the Führer? A figure of speech only, I reminded myself. *Trust no one.* "Of course, my Führer," I replied. "I will begin at once."

The Führer nodded. "Good lad. You'll need all the

---

[21] On 26 February 1935, Nazi leader Adolf Hitler announced to his inner circle and signed a secret decree authorizing the founding of the Luftwaffe as a third German military service to join the Reich army and navy. In the same decree, Hitler appointed Hermann Göring as commander in chief of the new German air force.

information you can get, as quickly as possible, for soon, I will have another major announcement to make, and I must benefit from your involvement, though no one but you and I must know of it."

"But what shall I read, my Führer?"

He pointed to his bookcase. "For now, read as much as you can about Frederick the Great. My *Enzyklopädie* will do for a start. I still look to old Frederick for wisdom, guidance, and inspiration. It will be of use in the days to come for us both."

I assumed that was all the Führer had to say, but there was no sign of dismissal.

"So," he said, with a grin, "what's this I hear about you pestering my kitchen staff?"

At that very moment, I burnt into my brain that not even the merest trifle goes unnoticed by the Führer—or unreported to him. I relied on the grin—and the truth. "I . . . I was just getting acquainted with my new surroundings, and a maid was kind enough to begin telling me about Herr Kannenberg, when—"

The Führer snorted jovially and farted with gusto. "Ah, Linge. Still the labourer, I fear. You must learn quickly that there are Krauses in every organization. They made life a living hell for me during The Struggle, but they also were enormously useful, once identified and manipulated. Himmler is a master manipulator of such types, so I leave such matters to him. Unfortunately—or fortunately for me, at least—you are no Himmler. But you must always be on guard. Trust no one, and so you must discover more, ah, ingenuous means of gaining such information."

Trust no one. Apparently a covert mantra in the Chancellery, and not merely a survival strategy for me. But did the Führer mean *ingenuous* or *ingenious*? "Yes, my Führer," I assured him, "I will definitely employ more discretion in future." I was almost reeling from the stench of his accumulated vapours. *Had to get out!* "Is there anything I can do for you at the moment?"

"Not now, Linge. I'll be entertaining some old comrades this evening, so you'll be on your own. Brückner and Kannenberg will handle the details. Just avoid the kitchen for a while," he joked. "I'll buzz if I need you. And take one of the encyclopaedia volumes with you and begin your education."

With that, I rose, saluted, went to the bookcase, slid out a volume at random, and left. I would never tell the Führer that I had memorized all the volumes years before.

Once in the hallway, I dared to breathe, but some of the reek must have crept into my nostrils unannounced, and I almost gagged. Every time the Führer breaks wind—which is often and repugnant—I'm jolted back in time to my days with a particular foreman in the brick yard where I apprenticed, who had a particular fondness for every food and beverage that guaranteed prolonged bouts of stomach-turning farts. The other men appeared able to ignore them, but I couldn't bear being near him. One day, I spotted him behind a row of bricks, cupping his hand to his posterior, emitting a thunderous burst, then quickly cupping the same hand over his nose. I never asked him what particular pleasure he received from the manoeuvre, but I'm eternally grateful that the Führer appeared to have no such need. At least in my presence.

AFTER A FITFUL night and a miserable waking, I splashed cold water on my face, then sat numbly in my new quarters, staring blankly at my bare walls, waiting for the inevitable buzzer. The Führer's encyclopaedia was permanently closed and sitting uselessly on my bedside table like a broken lamp, redundant to me as much of the Führer's library was. I promised myself that soon I would pore carefully over his entire collection, hoping to discover the one volume that explained the incremental absurdity of my situation.

I haven't the experience or knowledge to fully place or fully examine my feelings, but all round me, in all the incessant bustle in which I play no role, I sense something—but what? If I dare give it a name, I would call it a kind of overarching, pervasive violence, yet not actually seen or experienced by me. I have no explanation for it, but it is as palpable as an aching muscle, or an itch I cannot scratch. And, oddly, at the same time, I feel a strange detachment from it, as if I were visiting a stranger with that affliction instead of myself.

A crisp knock on my door shook me out of my depressive torpor. It was Brückner in full dress, standing in the doorway, a narrow, expensive, shiny leather attaché case under his arm. "Good morning, Heinz," the general greeted with a light-hearted lilt in his voice, a bit too light-hearted to be genuine, in my opinion. "My apologies if I awakened you," he said. "I imagine your 'Führerbuzzer,' as I call it—and you—must be fairly worn ragged by now. I've been, ah, blessed with one of my own for quite some time, so I can appreciate your situation."

Meet artificiality with artificiality, I decided. "I'm just fine, Wilhelm, truly. Even though it goes from frenetic to nothing and back again without warning, but one adjusts, yes?"

Brückner came in, shut the door, again motioned me into the bathroom, and opened the tap. Such care, and for what? "Yes," he sighed, "that's how it is. You were never in the military, am I right?"

"Yes. I was born in 1913, much too young to serve, and once I came of military age, it was well into Weimar."

"Lucky you," he said. "In war, the soldier's life alternates between chaotic horror and numbing boredom without warning or let-up. Even with all its many idiosyncrasies, life here is a distinct improvement, I can tell you. Well, in any event, we must have all things prepared and perfect for this evening, so—"

I pursed my lips. "This evening?"

"Ah, yes, big doings. There will be a stellar guest list, including Himmler, Goebbels and his wife, even Göring, also Hjalmar Schacht, General Beck, Admiral Canaris, and the two 'vons': Neurath and Ribbentrop (at least one von being authentic). Oh, yes, and there will also be the film actress Renate Müller—why, I couldn't say. Kannenberg and his wife are making certain that all dinner arrangements are in consummate order."

Yes, that definitely was a stellar list of dignitaries, even though I had never heard of Schacht or seen Müller off-screen. "And my role?"

Brückner laughed heartily. "Well, aside from getting the Führer ready for the evening, not a great deal different from the mornings, actually. You are to stand at ease in a corner, inert, while others perform the actual physical labour. However, this time, you will not be a window dummy answering to Krause, but a . . . how shall I say? . . . listening device (so long as we're discussing inanimate objects). This is the Führer's express wish."

A wave of pettiness then spread over me like a malicious salve. "And what of Krause? What will his role be?"

Brückner pursed his lips and shrugged his shoulders so high, his epaulets almost reached his ears. "Grunt work. Despite his new duties, he'll help to serve and remove, run errands as requested, that sort of thing. I dare say that, despite his menial tasks, it will make his day to imagine you assuming the position and role he'd originally marked out for you. However, you should be magnanimous and give no clue as to your true function, yes?"

A clue to my true function? No problem there, since I didn't know what it was. "It would help, Wilhelm," I answered, "if I perhaps knew a bit more about the guests I've never met or even heard of. I imagine the more I know, the better I can listen."

A wry smile sneaked across Brückner's lips. "You have a splendid imagination, Heinz." He lifted the flap on his case, extracted a clump of typed papers, and handed them to me. "The Führer anticipated your need, and so had me prepare these. Should you need more, let me know. Despite his bohemian manner, you must never underestimate the Führer's attention to detail. Nothing here is by accident, so pay particular attention, even to the seating arrangement. Burn and flush these papers after reading, and try to remember as much as you can. Now, I must go. The Führer expects you to join him at nineteen hundred hours." Brückner lowered the case flap, rose, patted me hard on the shoulder, comrade style, and left.

I sighed wearily, leaned over and closed the tap, ending the roar with a single clank, but I stayed seated on the toilet lid and began to pore over the papers Brückner had given me. As a game to hold my attention through the multitude of pages, I endeavoured to guess the nature and purpose of the dinner by the positions and histories of the guests. However, when I'd finished, incinerated, and flushed the dossier, I sat there marvelling at my initial lack of crucial knowledge and a dangerous artlessness concerning political matters and those intimately involved with them on the very highest levels. I had always possessed little or no interest in such things, but, as I read, I came to the crushing realization that, as the sole, day-to-day personal valet to the most powerful man in Germany, this state of affairs had to change radically.

And so, after seeing to the Führer's immediate needs, I made my way to one of the less modest dining rooms chosen for the occasion, and waited. And perspired.

As I stood there, pressed against the wall in full SS servant's livery, my armpits a tropical lagoon, my starched white dress shirt clinging to my back as if glued, I had ample time to consider the many causes of perspiration: the first, from physical exertion; the second, from illness; the third, from fear. As a reasonably healthy man, accustomed by nature and circumstance to hard manual labour and physical mobility, constantly standing mute and sweating as if I were a marble fountain would soon become burdensome in the extreme. However, this enforced inactivity was mitigated by the third kind: the knowledge that I was entirely alone, inhabiting an alien and hazardous environment, without any suggestion of what might happen at any moment. So, if my new duty provided the information I needed to function—perhaps even survive—then there I was: the weight of bricks was to be exchanged for the far heavier burden of suspense.

As fat, coarse, and short as Kannenberg was, he and his wife had no peers in dinner preparation. He clearly ran his kitchen like a gifted, ruthless field marshal, capable of obtaining extraordinary obedience, efficiency, and quality from his "troops." I couldn't imagine even the king of England boasting better service from his own chief of household. So, I stood silently at ease, as Brückner had instructed me, and observed with wonder as they and their subordinates converted a drab dining room into a Pasha's fantasy.

As with other dinners, the arrivals were late, due to the Führer's legendary lack of punctuality. Finally, the double doors swung open, Brückner entered, moved to the side next to me, winked in my direction, and began announcing the host and his guests as they came through. First, of course, was the beaming Führer, sporting Magda Goebbels on one arm and Renate Müller, the famous film actress, on the other, the Führer standing at the head of the rectangular table with the ladies standing on either side. Müller, held up as the ideal Aryan female (according to Brückner's dossier entry), was even more glamourous in person than on the screen. I had seen her films for several years, and she never failed to display allure, even when her part required a certain measure of drabness. It was difficult to turn my concentration away from such a beguiling creature, but I had my instructions.

After them limped the repulsive, pock-marked, stick figure Reichsminister Goebbels, who, in his inevitable plain, shit-brown uniform, took his place next to his wife, who appeared to be staring at Fräulein Müller, who, in turn, appeared to be staring back at her. The Reichsminister stood stiffly by his wife.

Brückner's dossier had mentioned several extramarital affairs by both parties in the couple over the years. Did their posture signal some meaning useful to me? I would have to wait, I concluded.

Next entered my nominal boss, Reichsführer-SS, Heinrich Himmler, whom I'd seen, but never met, and of whom I knew virtually nothing, aside from gossip, rumours, and reputation, none of which filled me with joy or calm. He moved to the other side of the table, directly facing Goebbels. A typed note had been affixed to the front sheet of the dossier in bold letters: "READ COPIOUSLY AND BE CAREFUL, MY FRIEND. THIS MAN IS NEVER TO BE UNDERESTIMATED!" So, with this one, I had taken special care in my reading.

He looked to me like a particularly fastidious elementary schoolteacher, and I could not for the life of me see anything outstanding or extraordinary about this middle-sized, round-faced man. Under a brow of average height, two grey-blue eyes peered out into some middle distance behind a glittering pince-nez, with an air of stern, emotionless judgment, despite the ambiguous upturn of his mouth. The neatly trimmed moustache, not entirely unlike the Führer's, below the straight, well-shaped nose traced a dark line on his unhealthy, pale features. Only the receding chin surprised me. The skin of his neck was flaccid and wrinkled. Two almost invisible rows of excellent white teeth, peeked out between his thin, colourless lips.

After him came Hjalmar Schacht, minister of economics, who moved by instruction to a chair next to Himmler.

And, as if on cue, immediately afterwards, Göring marched in behind Schacht, resplendent in one of his apparently number-less garish military uniforms worthy of the most extravagant African military dictator, and stood as directed and, as I'd pre-dicted, immediately across from Schacht. Of course I'd seen him before with the Führer, but this particularly astounding getup was totally unfamiliar to me and perhaps to everyone there.

According to Brückner's dossier, when Hitler was named chancellor of Germany, Göring on 30 November 1933 established a Prussian police force, the Gestapo. Göring, not a man to overwork himself, handed over control to a more-than-willing Himmler on 20 April 1934. By this time the SA numbered over two million men.

As the creator of the secret police, Göring, together with Himmler and his enthusiastic immediate subordinate, Reinhard Heydrich, exterminated the SA leadership in 1934 and established the early concentration camps for political opponents, showing formidable energy in terrorizing and crushing all resistance. According to Brückner, the flamboyant Göring and the ascetic Himmler, while not friendly by any means, were content to allow ambition, mutual interests, and closeness to the Führer make them strange bedfellows—but bedfellows just the same. I wondered how many official beds in Berlin boasted such arrangements, how much of that I might discover tonight—and whether, perhaps, that was even my purpose.

But there was no time to ruminate, for General Ludwig Beck came in close on Göring's heels and apparently was assigned to sit next to Schacht and opposite Göring. I tucked away, temporarily, the question of purpose. Ramrod-straight as a marble statue—and as expressive—Beck had all the characteristics associated with his class and breeding, but an enigma for all that. All I knew was that by 1935, Beck had been selected chief of the General Staff. A definite big shot. A note was appended to the last sheet: "WATCH HIM AND GÖRING CLOSELY; THEY ARE NOT FRIENDS."

Admiral Canaris and von Ribbentrop stood next to each

other at the table. I'd already read about and seen both at the Luftwaffe dinner, so I skimmed through their dossier entries. Now, I cared only for their actions, not their biographies. At this point, neither was looking at the other—I felt, studiously so.

And, finally, Foreign Minister Konstantin Freiherr von Neurath made his entrance. His name alone would intimidate an ordinary human being, and I was well below that. According to my information, he was the scion of a dynasty of barons. Another scribbled note had been attached to the end sheet advising me to read this in conjunction the material on von Ribbentrop, emphasizing his relationship—or lack thereof—with Von Neurath. Having read the dossiers on both, I could see very little basis for any relationship, short of awe for the one and contempt for the other.

Once all had entered and taken their prearranged places, the Führer nodded, the two ladies sat, then he sat, and the rest followed suit. Brückner leaned out the door, clapped his hands once, then left the room as the all-male servers entered. The dinner had begun.

I'd been instructed to listen, and I discovered early on that the Führer appeared to have no problem with all members of the table engaging in private topics of conversation. Perhaps in such cases, that was to be my role: the Führer relaxes while I mentally transcribe the chatter. But to what purpose? Was I to interpret as well as relate? And, to me, a more alarming question than any of those: Who was I to be doing any of it?

Despite this, I noticed that, initially, there was utter silence, which I assumed to be the guests waiting to see if the Führer had any pre-dinner pronouncements to make. Once satisfied that he hadn't, tiny clusters of conversation sprouted like new, freshly watered plants, occurring simultaneously so that full coherence was denied me. I could make out the Führer telling those in immediate proximity how much he admired Müller and telling her specifically that "during the time of struggle, when the skies hung low and dark for me and our cause, I would invariably shrug off some of my burdens by watching one of your films. I particularly enjoyed *The Son of the White Mountain*." Müller merely smiled politely, thanked him, and said no more. If there is such a thing as a language of the body, it was speaking of extreme discomfort.

Then the Führer asked Goebbels why such an excellent and ideally representative leading actress of the New Order hadn't appeared in some of his commissioned films, and Goebbels replied that she should probably answer for herself, that he had been endeavouring for a long time to talk her into making films for the ministry that promoted National Socialist ideals but that she had consistently demurred.

Magda Goebbels sniffed with more than just a hint of derision. "My Führer," Magda said, "should this surprise you? She is not even a Party member. Dietrich fled to America and this one remained. One could say that not knowing English is the extent of her patriotism." Then, sliding her eyes slightly toward the Reichsminister, "Is that not true, my husband?"

The Reichsminister, who appeared highly uncomfortable up to then, lost all colour in his already pallid face. "My Führer," he rejoined, "Fräulein Müller is, first and foremost, an artist, and one who upholds our finest Aryan ideals, even though not in a . . . how shall I put it? . . . formal way."

At that, Magda Goebbels emitted one withering laugh and said, "Yes, my Führer, quite informal, considering." By their expressions, it appeared that both the Führer and the Reichsminister understood what she meant, but said nothing. I had a vague idea, since Brückner had earlier noted that Müller's lover, whom she steadfastly refused to abandon, was a Jew.

Then through the door came a cadre of liveried servers, followed by that tiny motherfucker, my arch nemesis, Krause, lugging a ponderous mahogany drink trolley, and making bloody certain to avoid any toothy smile I would have loved to have given him but didn't. He was sweating profusely, but I dismissed exertion and assumed conclusively the true cause of his perspiration: rage.

Since the Führer was a virtual teetotaller and a complete vegetarian, serving him was rather complex, because every effort needed to be made to visually approximate his guests' meal without including what the Führer considered to be the "body-destroying properties" the others round him were ingesting to their peril. For this, Kannenberg, with the creative assistance of the cook and the Führer's personal photographer, Heinrich Hoffmann, created wonderments of approximation. Even so, the Führer, as usual, ate rapidly, mechanically. For him, food appeared to be merely an inconvenient means of subsistence, and so, in the course of a few minutes he was finished. Not so the others, who appeared to view food from a more hedonistic perspective.

Since Himmler was completely silent, I slid over to where Göring and Goebbels were sitting. The former was asking the latter if it were true that he'd been spreading rumours that he, Göring, went to bed wearing medals on his pyjamas. Before Goebbels could answer, the Führer leaned forward and said loudly enough for all to hear: "Now don't waste our time denying it, Hermann," he joked. "I've even ordered Hoffmann to design some special medals of gold and silver foil as well as a bombastic citation for bravery, all designed to match your bedclothes."

At that, Göring hesitated a fraction, then exploded into raucous guffaws, while patting Goebbels on his bony shoulder. "Well, Joseph," Göring blurted, bubbly lines of spittle seeping from the corners of his flabby lips, "obviously you were right on the button, and the rumours have been proven fact. Unfortunately, though, I can no longer lie about all the bruises on Emmy's body every morning." All laughed heartily at that rather tasteless response to a rather tasteless remark.

Out of the corner of my eye, I noticed Himmler move his hand furtively, slide a small notepad and pencil from his inside jacket pocket and scribble something, then replace the items. No one else appeared to notice.

From my reading, I expected to overhear some hostile repartee between Göring and Schacht, but Göring was still belly-laughing over his medals and the latter was staring intently at his food and appeared not to notice the loud, coarse behemoth opposite him. In fact, Schacht looked as if he'd rather have been in a particularly vile section of Hades than at that table. Sensing futility, I moved closer to Canaris and Beck. It was difficult to learn anything, since, according to Brückner, Canaris was a spymaster, and the aristocratic Beck was far too discrete to even raise his voice. However, I did manage to overhear the following:

> Beck: So what do you know of this?
>
> Canaris: You mean the dinner?
>
> Beck: Of course, Willie, the dinner. I'm reasonably certain this is not some manufactured opportunity to try out a new vegetable recipe. The

Führer has a wizard's sleeves; what does he have up them?

Canaris: You'll see soon enough, Ludwig. You know as well as I that, while the Führer loves suspense, he is far too impatient to prolong it.

Beck: So you do know. Is there anything you can tell me now?

Canaris: Well, unless you imbibe too much of the Führer's inferior wine, I can predict that from this dinner, you'll not receive any heartburn. Stay sober and listen, my friend.

I wondered how many others actually knew of the dinner's purpose. Toward that end, I edged closer to the "two vons," but the conversation was decidedly one-sided, since von Neurath, his face a study in barely forbearing repugnance, never uttered a word throughout. "You must admit, Konstantin," von Ribbentrop said, "that the Führer is always the perfect host."

As if on cue, the Führer then put forth one of his legendary "wind-breakers," which all assiduously ignored while opening their mouths for more congenial breathing.

"Yes, the perfect host," von Ribbentrop repeated ironically to the silent von Neurath. "Pity that the purpose of this dinner is a state secret, even from you, but the Führer wishes to present his fait accompli[22] at his own place and time, and too many ears have a habit of running off at the mouth." I didn't quite follow that particular line of insult, but Admiral Canaris appeared to know, and so I waited for a response from von Neurath, which

---

[22] A thing that has already happened or been decided before those affected hear about it, leaving them with no option but to accept.

did not come to pass, but also which did not appear to bother von Ribbentrop in the slightest.

I moved stealthily back to where the Führer and his two female guests were just finishing their coffee. He was waxing euphorically on the progress of the Reich's highway system, which interested me not at all, and I just let the sound drift like smoke from a freshly doused campfire.

My attention returned when Müller attempted a response, but the Führer had already turned to the front and began pinging his spoon on his water glass to gain attention. The attention was both instantaneous and rapt, and I began to carefully watch all the assembled for reactions. Initially, there were none that I could discern.

"Some of you already know what I am about to say," he began. "Some of you have guessed; and some know little or nothing. To all of you, I now tell you formally of a decision of justifiably profound proportions and implications. No one who has read *Mein Kampf* should be surprised to learn that as soon as I deemed it strategically sound, I would deal decisively with that abomination, the Treaty of Versailles, that the basis of my foreign policy would be to utterly undo what had been imposed on Germany, that I would reunite all Germans into one nation and completely rearm the Reich. And all that, as radical as it may sound, I planned as merely a feeble beginning."

I noticed that his voice began to assume a muscular stridency I'd encountered only in his public speeches.

"I needn't remind you," he reminded, "that Germany, that is to say, the Third Reich, is the centre of Europe and potentially the greatest power in Europe—and far, far beyond. As such, the Fatherland must possess an all-powerful, even, dare I say, invincible, military. Throughout the 1920s, Germany . . . technically kept to the terms of the Treaty, but in reality, she had been bending the rules regarding training. For example, the treaty did not state that Germany could not train submarine crews abroad or that pilots for the banned German Air Force could train on civilian planes. Therefore, while on paper I inherited a weak military, this was not in reality the case."

As I studied the guests, their faces, their surface inertia, I sensed a seething internal exhilaration—and something else as well. It was similar to the sensation of violence I'd experienced since my arrival in all who surrounded the Führer—perhaps also a breathless anticipation that had no name. Only Fräulein Müller appeared immune—either she cared not at all, or she cared too much.

"As early as 1933," he continued, "as soon as I was able, I ordered my army generals to treble the size of the army to three hundred thousand men and commanded the Air Ministry to build a thousand war planes. Military buildings such as barracks and shelters were built. This was not done whimsically, since I anticipated a certain measure of external hostility. However, even then, I knew that even greater audacity was required, and so I withdrew from the ridiculous Geneva Disarmament Conference when the French refused to accept my plan that the French should disarm to the level of the Germans, or that the Germans should rearm to the level of the French. Either way, the two main powers of Europe would be balanced. Of course I knew that the French would not accept my plan and, therefore, when I indignantly withdrew from the conference, it was pure strategic and tactical artifice." At that, his lips curved into a sinister smirk, spreading his tiny moustache almost to the limit.

Then, without warning, his voice rose even higher, and the volume increased accordingly; his clenched fist smashed into the table, setting all the objects on it bouncing and shifting noisily. And yet, from the assembled, there was complete immobility and silence. "So, for two years," he ranted, "I had the German military expand in secret. Yes, even though some of my own comrades, some even sitting here tonight, advised strongly against it. Regardless, I followed my instincts, knowing that other nations either would not care, or would place a pillow over their heads. And, as always, my instincts were proven correct!"

Suddenly, he shifted to conversational mode, effortlessly, as I had seen him do on several occasions: a master of mood.

"So now, we come to the present, and one more step in what all my ideas, plans, and efforts have been leading to. Tonight, I tell you, and tomorrow," glancing at Goebbels, "all the world will know: that the Luftwaffe has twenty-five hundred war planes and the Wehrmacht, three hundred thousand trained men. And this, my friends, is only the bare beginning. I will also publicly announce tomorrow, that there will be compulsory military conscription in order to increase the Wehrmacht to five hundred fifty thousand men. What does this signify, you are asking yourselves? That quite soon, my friends, I will take all necessary steps to create a new Europe, one in which our beloved Fatherland is the centre, its values and might, radiating out in all directions. Invincible. Unstoppable."

At that, all the assembled but the Führer shot up, issued the Hitler salute, and applauded thunderously. After a theatrical while, the Führer nodded benignly and raised his arm slowly in his traditional bent-arm return salute, then swung it across his chest for order, and all resumed their seats, and instant silence descended on the room once more.

"Eventually," he resumed, "the entire nation shall play a vital part in this act of creation, but for now, the initial tasks must be performed by a select few, some here now, some not. In the coming days, I will brief selected members of this gathering individually concerning details, but tonight I address you all with some general outlines." He turned to Goebbels. "Joseph, you and I will arrange the widest and most suitable and effective domestic and foreign dissemination of what I have just announced tonight. I needn't tell you what I mean by suitable."

"No, my Führer," Goebbels replied. "It will be done exactly as you require." I could swear that his eyes were moist.

Then Hitler looked down the table at Göring and Schacht. "Hermann, Hjalmar, your task will be to properly staff and coordinate all activities connected with the most efficacious implementation of my directive and all those that follow from it." I had no idea what that meant, but Göring and Schacht appeared unfazed. Did they already know and had they already planned for it, whatever it was? The two immediately formed a loud chorus of "Yes, my Führer!"

Then the Führer turned his eyes to Beck. "As chief of the General Staff, you will take immediate command of my newly created armed forces and ensure their complete readiness for any and all . . . contingencies."

By the look on their faces, Beck's elevation appeared to be a surprise to all the guests, except Beck.[23] He merely responded: "At your command, my Führer."

---

[23] Despite Linge's observation, few, if any, should have been surprised. It was well known in the higher circles that in Beck's conception of power politics, it was crucial to have German military power restored to its pre-1919 levels, and from the latter half of 1933, he advocated a level of military spending beyond even those considered by Hitler. In Beck's opinion, once Germany was sufficiently rearmed, the Reich should wage a series of wars that would establish Germany as Europe's foremost power and place all of Central and Eastern Europe into the German sphere of influence.

The Führer's attention then turned to the "two vons." "Your task, gentlemen, will be to visit all the major capitals and gain an official sense of how they regard my decision and the actions taken to implement it. Ribbentrop, you will concentrate on Great Britain, and Neurath, the others."[24]

Both accepted the assignment wholeheartedly, von Ribbentrop, far more passionately, even thanking the Führer profusely for the honour.

Finally, the Führer addressed Canaris and Himmler. "And now, Wilhelm," he said, "now that I've announced my decision and given my directives, I need you to turn all your energies and resources to making certain that I know the *true* feelings of these other governments, regardless of what they say formally to Neurath and Ribbentrop. While I am confident that they will do absolutely nothing, regardless of their attitudes, I must know what those attitudes are." Then he turned to Himmler. "Heinrich, while I have every confidence that my people in general will do gladly whatever I require of them, I am not so naive as to think that all will be equally enthusiastic, especially concerning conscription. I daresay there will be a few misguided and even traitorous dissidents who do not share my vision or fervour. They must be discovered and crushed."

Himmler again removed his little pad and pencil, jotted

---

[24] Von Ribbentrop was concerned with German foreign relations with every part of the world, but especially Anglo-German relations, because von Ribbentrop knew that Hitler favoured an alliance with Britain. In November 1934, von Ribbentrop visited Britain, where he met with George Bernard Shaw, Sir Austen Chamberlain, Lord Cecil, and Lord Lothian. On the basis of Lothian's praise for the natural friendship between Germany and Britain, von Ribbentrop informed Hitler that all elements of British society wished for closer ties with Germany. His report delighted Hitler, causing him to remark that von Ribbentrop was the only person who told him "the truth about the world abroad."

down something I couldn't make out, replaced them, and replied, "Of course, my Führer, no one will defy your will, even in their thoughts."

Up to then, the Führer had been sitting, but now he stood, and with his two arms extended and palms pushing down, indicating that all should remain seated. "Now I am weary and so I will retire. However, there is no need for the festivities to retire with me. My servants will still be at your disposal and you may stay or go as you wish."

The Führer did look exhausted, even more so than after a major balcony address. His eyes were bloodshot and his face, never a study in tan, was even paler than usual. His hands appeared to tremble slightly. I assumed that the Führer intended me to remain until the last guest left, which was confirmed when Brückner came in and whispered as much in my ear. Then all saluted the Führer, but he merely turned and exited with Brückner, but not before murmuring to him out of their hearing: "Get me my Jew." By the look of him, I guessed that he was referring to his "secret" physician, Dr. Bloch.

TOO EXHAUSTED TO relate all that took place yesterday, so I tell you now.

I possess no knowledge of military matters, for I am not a military man, a descendant of military men, or even one who, out of an outsider's curiosity, ever investigated the subject. And so, once I gathered my senses for the day ahead, I dressed and sat on my cot, utterly failing to comprehend in any regard what good my inert and mute "observations" would do for the Führer, a decorated soldier himself—albeit a corporal—surrounded and advised by the most eminent and outstanding military leaders in the entire Reich, if not the world.

Once the Führer and Brückner had left, I remained at my post while the festivities continued, unabated and unhindered by the Führer's absence. I considered that, perhaps, this is what I was meant to do: transcribe the *real* attitudes of the guests through their various reactions, rather than the invariable "yes-my-Führer" responses that would follow any in-person pronouncement by the supreme leader of the Reich. However, much to my disappointment and boredom, little of the evening's event ventured beyond "decision-long-overdue" comments. Eventually, those who spoke before the Führer's announcement continued along the same trivial lines, and the silent guests maintained their silence. My ignorance and naïveté prevented me from divining the meaning of this phenomenon, or even that it might have meaning.

Therefore, this morning, once the "Führerbuzzer" sounded, I jumped up and raced to his quarters, joyous yet apprehensive at the diversion. However, once there, I was confronted by the same dilemma that plagued me in my room. You must understand that, though the Führer publicly—and even to a certain degree towards his most intimate entourage—was ultimately unapproachable and inscrutable, he appeared to abandon that persona with me, even from the beginning of my service. Why, I didn't know and would never ask, but I was no more comfortable for all that, the inevitable question nagging at me: why?

I entered his bedroom, laid out all his clothes; the Führer emerged from the bathroom freshly shaved and commanded, *Los!*[25] I pushed the timer, and the race commenced. The importance of this ritual had been told to me by Brückner, who advised that the quicker he dressed, the better his temper. Of course, he advised me—off the record—to always begin the count a few seconds late to ensure victory and a reasonable disposition. Today was no exception, though I suspected that the Führer has always been wise to my ploy. I'd determined that it wasn't his dressing speed but whether he sucked on his little moustache or not that signalled his mood. Today, his moustache was bone dry.

"Keep the drapes drawn," he told me when we entered his darkened study, then went over and pulled the chain on his green-glass desk lamp.

"So, Linge," he said. He pressed his famous diagonal slash of hair into its proper place across his forehead and I saw to his tie, the only item of clothing that occasionally vexed him. "I regret

---

[25] *Off!*

that you had to perform such a tiresome duty, but it was necessary to test you and, I hope, benefit from your interpretive powers, a talent I discovered in myself when I was not much older than you, and we believe you also to possess. I will enlighten you."

Again, the enigmatic "we."

"Even from my earliest years," he said, "I was aware in me of a power which I was far too young and inexperienced to name that set me apart from all others. Aside from my only friend in whom I confided only the periphery of my awareness,[26] I thought little about it. Then, in 1915, while I was on military leave in Munich, having no interest in beer halls or brothels, I happened upon a lecture by some fellow from America, who had conducted some puzzle experiments concerning what he called 'creative thinking.'

"There were few in the audience, but apparently enough to satisfy the experiment. The first thing he did was to give us each a pen and a sheet of paper upon which there were three rows of three dots, and then he told us that our challenge was to link all nine dots using four straight lines or fewer, without lifting the pen and without tracing the same line more than once.

"Immediately, I dismissed him as a charlatan or a fool. No stupid carnival tricks for me, I said to myself. But a force, something I still cannot name, impelled me to continue, and so I returned to the paper and the dots, but, while others appeared transfixed by the shape of the configuration, I, being a naturally creative sort and cursed with impatience, concluded that the configuration was meaningless and had nothing to do with the instructions—that the configuration was the trick, not the experiment. As a result, I immediately connected the dots, but

---

[26] Anton Kubizek.

only by going outside the configuration—and it worked! Others dismissed and derided my solution as incorrect, duplicity, or at the very least, a breaking of the rules, but the lecturer said that what I had done was exactly what the experiment was designed to achieve: to see if people were able go beyond current and often unnoticed assumptions about a situation, which the configuration represented. Naturally, everyone else saw it as a trivial, frustrating game; I saw it as a critical test of a special mental acuity. Do you follow me, Linge?"

I'd been listening intently but simultaneously remembering a time when I was apprenticing as a bricklayer and confronted by a structural problem that had completely stymied the foreman. For reasons I still can't explain, I saw the problem differently from him and dared to suggest a solution, but the foreman glared at me as if I had declared black as white and dismissed my suggestion as the babblings of a backward child. Later, his boss made the same suggestion, and it came to pass. As usual, position trumped perception. "I . . . think so, my Führer," I ventured with some caution, still unsure of his point or the consequences of my response.

The Führer smiled. "Of course you do," he said, "even if you do not know why. It's far better that way, actually." All the exhaustion I'd seen the night before had vanished and, even in the dim light, had been replaced with a supernal glow of vigour and purpose. "I will tell you what I have told only those in the shadows who share a dimension with me that no one else could even imagine." Then he moved toward me with a suddenness and swiftness I never anticipated, grasped me by the shoulders, stared fixedly into my eyes, and said, "Tell me your thoughts. Now, Linge, no censorship, no deference, no ceremony."

I had planned to tell him that, from my vantage point, his

announcement appeared to be of no surprise to any of the guests, perhaps with the exception of Renate Müller, who couldn't have cared less, that everyone but von Neurath would benefit from it, and that it really didn't matter so long as von Ribbentrop was happy, that when a decision benefits virtually everyone, universal agreement, obedience, and even adulation are assured.

This is what I had planned to say, right or wrong, perhaps even willing to risk, come what may. He released his grip, moved to his desk, and pulled once again on the lamp chain, and suddenly, there was no Führer or valet, just the sound of breathing in the dark.

Many times in the past, my brain flooded with insights I was unable to relate. What I'd felt last night and wanted to say were the consequences of the slender and subjective differences in the guests' self-interest. All less important by far than what he represents; that people obey power, but they worship God. God is the figure standing on a stage in the meeting hall, shouting and gesticulating on the balcony, and saluting from an open car. Power from any other source is extrinsic, acquired, super-imposed—subjective, so that the power derives from inferior and temporary sources, whether through elections, force, wealth, fear, ambition . . . even love. I could not place the source of these thoughts.

Despite this, all I could say was: "From what I saw, my Führer, your announcement will be obeyed completely and enthusiastically by all assembled." I thought I'd add: "But they will obey it for their own reasons, not for yours, for they do not worship you. Such men are to be used, but never trusted." However, I let the matter rest with that anaemic utterance.

I felt psychically and physically enervated. The voice in my head urged me to continue but was now no more than a croaking mutter, and the darkness had become even blacker and I could hear—or thought I heard—a raspy, disembodied voice say: "It is as we hoped. He has the gift, but it is far too early."

⁂

I must have been sitting there, in some sort of trance, for it is as if I'd come awake from a dream I couldn't have had. The dim, directed light from the desk lamp was casting the familiar shadows. It was Führer and valet again, but now, they had been joined by a third man. Had he been there all along? What had he heard? In any event, the Führer was slumped at his desk, his elbow held rigid at an angle, his right sleeve rolled up, and the third man, wearing his white laboratory coat, was aiming a syringe at the crook of the arm, then injecting him with some fluid. It was Dr. Eduard Bloch, "Hitler's Jew," as he was called, a short, stocky man with an Edwardian moustache and a hairline that had receded almost to the top of his head, the remaining hair being parted in the middle as if it were full. He wore a three-piece, striped, brown suit with a prominent bow tie. A professional man of another, more tolerant century trapped in the present.

I had seen the man several times tending to the Führer, and, despite the utter illogic and ideological contradictions of such a relationship, I had discovered from Brückner, without explanation, that Dr. Bloch held a unique position, independent of and insulated from the Führer's inner circle.

After the doctor administered the serum, the Führer nodded weakly, the doctor turned, glanced at me—or rather, it seemed, my uniform—bowed his head slightly, and left. I don't believe he even saw my face. Once the door closed, I went over to the Führer and asked him if he was all right, and whether there was anything he needed.

He rolled down his sleeve. "You can fetch me my jacket," he said, which I promptly did, and he stood up unsteadily and shrugged into it.

"How are *you* feeling, Linge?" he asked me, once he'd buttoned up.

"But, my Führer, it is you who received the injection." I had witnessed him receive innumerable pills and injections at all hours, ever since I began serving him.

"Yes, but that shot was for my everlasting blasted constipation. I wasn't unconscious for two days, as you were."

The force of his words sent a lightning bolt of anxiety through me as if I'd been given a fatal diagnosis. My face must have told the story because he added: "Yes, Linge, two days. We were all quite concerned, but of course, a hospital was out of the question. My Jew tended to you personally and, by my order, hadn't left your side until you came to."

I sprawled akimbo on the Führer's plush sofa, merely sitting there, mouth agape, as would a cretin, totally speechless, so the Führer filled the vacuum. "Do close your mouth and listen to me. Don't be alarmed. You should be gratified to know that you exceeded all my needs and expectations. My apologies for any discomfort you were caused, but it was essential."

Altogether flummoxed and pouring sweat like an exhausted hog in a Turkish bath, I could only stammer: "I'm . . . of course overjoyed to have been of . . . such great service, though I must confess that I am . . . completely unaware of what that service was."

The Führer laughed heartily, whether from his satisfaction, my predicament, or the injection, his tiny moustache bobbing up and down in merriment. "Yes, yes, Linge, I understand as no one else can. You are not now in a position to ask questions. It is only natural. But, believe me, the time will come, and I will happily satisfy your curiosity. Now, I—"

A gentle tap on the door and Brückner entered with the news that the delegation from the major industrial firms had arrived for a meeting, as per the Führer's summons. He glanced at me, turned back, and said: "My Führer, have you been preparing Linge for the upcoming Olympic Games?"

The Führer grinned mischievously. "Yes, Brückner, for the 'Valet Event': the 50-yard bow-tie-tying contest. He has yet to master it." He glanced at me and winked. "The English, as always, believe they have the advantage, but we'll show them what for, eh?"

With no prior preparation for this topic, I could only pretend I'd known all along. "They can consider themselves done for, my Führer," I declared, ecstatic to be at least temporarily removed from our prior discussion, even by way of such infantile foolishness.

The Führer turned back to Brückner. "Now, once you and the Kannenbergs have done your work, only a minimal staff will be necessary, so you and Linge will be free until tomorrow. These avaricious fat cats will be happy merely to hear that the additional military production will make them even richer, and I have only to inspire them with tales of future glory and even greater profits to come. And, anyhow, the two of you have been stuck with me here far too long. You need to get out and taste of the delights Berlin has to offer. Use Kempka[27] if you need to, and also have him and Baur[28] join you. 'Go and sin no more,' as those infernal Papist confessors say."

And we did, at least the former.

---

[27] Hitler's chauffeur.

[28] Hitler's pilot.

ANOTHER CURSED MIGRAINE became my alarm clock this morning. As always, I strive to ignore them as well as I can, but I achieve only limited success, and so this entry may be somewhat helter-skelter.

After the Führer's rearmament announcement, things for me settled into the maddening routine that Brückner had described: prolonged periods of numbing boredom punctuated by moments of frenetic bustle. Yet, even the boring moments possessed a, how shall I say, an ominous quality I had not the insight or language to explain. As a result, I could not, much less dare, discuss it with anyone but you. Of course, there was no more of that frightening isolation of my first days, for by now, I had made several casual acquaintances whom I considered safe enough to engage in innocuous chatter, and especially one female secretary named Hannelore, who claimed to see in me more than I saw.

Despite the size of the Chancellery, and the multitude of personnel working there in all capacities, the tiny cloistered world I inhabited was akin to a tiny home containing several extended families, and so very little, if anything, whether fact or rumour, was a secret for long. Every movement or word out of the unremarkable routine was the subject of closed-door, hallway, or corner dissection, discussion, and speculation, and so, for me, discretion had to be both absolute and undetectable.

I had, in one of the furtive moments of our association, asked Hanne (as she liked to be called) what that special quality of mine was, but she would only curl her lips coyly and say that she wouldn't tell me, for once I knew, she claimed, I would lose it. It all seemed like a chapter from a child's fairy tale, and so, to a great extent, I believed it.

She was far from a great beauty like Renate Müller or the other cinema stars the Führer frequently invited to dinner or tea, but Hanne was comparatively pleasant-looking for a Chancellery secretary, for whom a speedy hand and decent spelling counted for much more than long eyelashes, high cheekbones, a model's torso, and provocative attire. And even more important, she seemed to like and trust me, though I hadn't done anything to deserve it, save appearing good-natured and not exhibiting an exaggerated sense of my own importance or abilities.

To everyone else, I was Herr Linge, Lieutenant Linge, or just Linge; to her, I was Heinz. Since I was in and out of the Führer's company much of each day and evening, our paths crossed several times per week, though such conversations were strictly forbidden by the unwritten laws of prudence—and of course, Schroeder's fiat.

Even though she and I had become conversationally comradely, I never confided in her anything that occurred on the night after the Führer's "rearmament announcement." Since I had no idea what had happened, and so had no explanation, any discussion would have been as decidedly inarticulate and meaningless to her as it was to me, not to mention potentially perilous in ways I had no way of knowing. However, that certainly didn't prevent our commiseration on other matters. Today, for example, as we sat at a small, relatively secluded Ratskeller on a less-travelled Berlin byway.

"You look exhausted," I said, alarmed at seeing the dark circles under her bloodshot blue eyes and the unhealthy pallor of her skin. "Don't bother with me today. Get some rest. Later, we'll both have a better conversation for all that, yes?"

She shook her head, I felt, far more vehemently than honesty would indicate. While I could only smell her perfume, the degree of pungency seemed to me her way of masking liquor. It wasn't the first time. "I'm fine, Heinz. Truly," demurring, I thought. "You've looked better yourself, if I may say so. You, more than anyone, should know what being on call to the Führer is like. Especially now."

"Up to a point, yes," I agreed. "But adjusting a bow tie isn't quite the same as transcribing, re-transcribing, waiting, then re-re-transcribing the Boss's inspirational rambles." She was on her fourth shot of whiskey, while I hadn't even finished my first beer.

She chuckled at my foolish audacity, and it appeared to me that the dark circles lightened. "See? You've made me feel better already. But I must confess that he was in rare form last night, even for him, you know."

I knew what she was referring to, but I wanted her to confirm, or better yet, expand, without detecting any undue knowledge, curiosity, or savvy on my part. "Rare form? Hmm," I murmured, "I hadn't noticed anything special when I took my leave of him."

"Heinz, Heinz," she chided gently, smiling her coy smile. Then she placed her hand on my forearm and whispered with her other hand cupping the side of her mouth like a single bracket, conspiratorially: "I think that perhaps part of you is the perfect valet, hearing nothing, saying nothing, remembering nothing. But—" she stopped herself.

"And the other part?" I queried cautiously. What did she think she knew? "Actually, Hanne, I'm far from a perfect anything. I must confess that I'm not even a terribly interesting fellow, just one ignorant spoke in the Führer's wheel of menials."

Ignoring my attempt at humility, she said: "You think that, do you? Well, I, on the other hand, Heinz, am not the perfect secretary," she sidestepped, "not even part of me. I'm much more than an appendage to a typewriter or steno pad. I hear, and I remember, and, unfortunately for me, I also imagine. Why, just tonight, for the Boss's Rally speech, I waited, hands cramping over my keyboard, three full hours I tell you, between the salutation and the first sentence. But once he began, he rattled on forever, pacing, staring into space, altering, and realtering constantly. For most of the time, I had the distinct feeling that he was . . . oh, how can I put it—?"

"Somewhere else?" It was another risk, but I could no longer resist.

She removed her hand from my arm and downed her drink. "Yes, that's it. Absent. Quite the analyst." Her eyes narrowed slightly, then she laughed. "Are you sure you were a bricklayer?"

Risk taken, I attempted to recoup with feeble levity. "Not really. I never made it to quite that exalted a level. I came in as a lowly apprentice and never rose above it."

"There, maybe, but not so lowly here," she countered. "The Boss, I can tell you, is elated that he finally discovered your perfect calling."

"*He* discovered it? He told you that?"

She shrugged. "I meant you, of course. But maybe you shouldn't be so perfect, yes?"

I didn't know what she meant, or where this was leading, if anywhere.

"Not so perfect," she repeated, forcing me to see beyond the liquor she'd gulped down. My headache and her perfume were beginning to render me light-headed. I felt a dull ache of confusion and guilt. God, if she were even the least bit sexually alluring! She was everything I'd want in a sister, but I was no different from other men, and so required some form of physical beauty. And now this "my calling" business.

"The Führer has spoken to you of me?"

Her thick, painted lips curved into that beguilingly homely smile of hers, and she returned her hand to my arm, this time, pressing a little harder, and said: "Well, Heinz, not to me. Not directly. But you know the Boss. He has conversations with others, with himself, and . . . you know, with no one in particular."

I wasn't sure where this streetcar was going, but something I couldn't explain told me not to jump off. Not quite yet. "And in which one of these conversations was I mentioned?"

Her entire body became inert, save for some barely perceptible fidgeting of her hand. "Well," she replied hesitatingly, "I'm honestly not sure. Now that you press me, perhaps none of those. At any rate, it made no sense, but there you are, but I mean . . . aren't, because you weren't there. What I'm saying—"

Enough flailing; enough gibberish! "All right," I cut her off, "let's forget about what you're saying. What was the Führer saying?"

"Well, naturally I can't remember his exact words, because I wrote nothing down, you understand."

"Okay," I said. "No harm done. You said you listen and remember. All right. The best you can, yes?"

Another nervous shrug and smile. "That's right, the best I can. While I was waiting, seemingly forever, hands poised for his next inspiration, he was facing his portrait of Frederick the Great, as he always does when deep in thought. After a few moments of this, I think I heard him mutter under his breath that you and some Otto will allow him to render all diplomatic manoeuvring—even his most inspired—to be meaningless absurdities, and that the Reich, as we know it, will be transformed forever, and replaced with . . . something 'unreconcilable and timeless,' or something sounding like that. I couldn't truly make it out because he began to mumble incoherently, slap his sides vigorously, then rushed from the room, leaving me alone with my typewriter and a virtually blank paper. I waited another hour, and when he didn't return, I sneaked out. It's actually funny. Crazy-funny, you know. Even Fräulein Schroeder laughed, and you know she never laughs at anything."

I blew out a puff of air. "You told Schroeder?" I asked in jest. "And she actually laughed? I wish I'd been there, if only to hear what it sounded like." The Chancellery, a gossiper's Valhalla.

She giggled like a child, a most disconcerting sound, considering her age and appearance. Then she ordered another drink, against my urging. "She doesn't like you, Heinz, that's true." She suddenly paused, the wrinkles in her forehead deepening. "I'm sorry if I'm making you uncomfortable," she finally said. "I can see it in your face. But please understand, I don't get many opportunities to chance upon a kindred spirit these days."

Kindred spirit? What was she intimating? Was she merely engaging in reckless small talk, or attempting to draw me even further into the piranha pool of political revelation? How could I answer her innocently?

"What did she say when you told her what you just told me?"

"Nothing really. She just said that I must have been daydreaming, and that I needed to exercise more discipline."

"That sounds like Schroeder, no doubt about it," I kidded, but had to confess (only to myself, of course) an incipient uneasiness about the whole business. "Well," I asked, "do you think you might have been daydreaming?"

She just finished her drink, smiled again, this time, sadly, and said that we should probably be getting back.

∾

When I returned, the first thing I saw was Krause standing erect, expressionless, and mute in front of the massive wall of books, not even the flicker of an eye to acknowledge my presence. There was nothing extraordinary in that, but the Führer was screaming at someone through the mouthpiece of his phone. I assumed it was about the Party Rally, and that he'd been at it for a while, because I merely heard him shout with an hysterical finality that he'd better not be disappointed in such an important event. The Führer had been extremely agitated about the Party Rally ever since a wave of anti-Jewish violence had begun in summer, for not the least of reasons that he had always looked forward to them, the public and Party adoration, and his eloquent and emotional speeches invariably bringing out his star quality.

But I could tell that he'd been dreading this one. His dressing time plummeted, and he appeared oblivious to my attempts to substitute a better score. After reports of the first wave of assaults came in, he plopped down in his massive desk chair and sighed loudly. "Let's go for a walk," he said, wearily, though the day had just begun for him. "Some fresh air might be just the ticket." But there was little conviction in his voice, and my head felt as if a jackhammer were trying to pound its way through my skull.

Once in the gardens, with its seemingly infinite cadres of heavily armed SS guards and security checkpoints, I walked slowly to keep behind him, but he waved in a curved motion to bid me walk beside him. "Linge," he finally said, "have you ever faced a situation in which you desperately wanted something to happen, and when it does, you would rather it not?"

I wanted to tell him that these . . . situations happen to everybody, and certainly to me, who both relished and abhorred my status as an officer of the dreaded SS, but I would never use the word *ambivalence* with him, lest my mask of unlettered innocence instantly vanish. "My Führer," I replied carefully, "a chap once told me of an old saying that a person should be careful what he wishes for, because he might get it. Is that what you meant?"

He slapped his fist down on his thigh with suddenly renewed vigour. "*Yes*, Linge, that is *exactly* what I meant! You are as perceptive as ever. It's called *ambivalence*, but I wouldn't expect you to know that."

As a lover of irony, I let the remark go. "But, my Führer, what had you wished for?" I asked honestly, since I actually didn't know.

The Führer took a deep, shuddering breath. "There are certain things I was cautioned to keep to myself, in order to receive from you a more . . . how shall I say . . . asymmetrical perspective, so to speak. But for us to converse on that level, Linge, I must first provide you with a brief history lesson of our movement."

My brain was cracking like an egg, but what could I do but attempt to listen? Appearances.

"When we began our movement," he began, "my supporters were nothing but a ragtag bunch of violent malcontents. However, I discovered early on that when you need shit to cultivate a garden, you use it and ignore the stench.

"Yes, Linge, these thugs and hooligans served a worthy and essential purpose. Later on, of course, we managed to secure an infinitely broader—and higher—level of supporter, and so our initial group had become a public embarrassment. And yet, from time to time, they were still of some value when contending with those who would turn back or impede our revolution. So, you can see, there was, from the beginning, a tension between needing them and employing them."

See? I could hardly see beyond the agonizing shifting kaleidoscope of flashing lights before me.

"All this," the Führer continued, oblivious to my condition, "took on a larger and much more troublesome turn after the Party finally seized power. Many of these gutter extremists, led by Ernst Röhm, motivated by envy and greed as well as by a feeling that they had been excluded from attractive positions within the higher civil service, grew even more determined to act decisively and independently on the 'Jewish Question.'

"This was intolerable to me. I wished to deal with this from the very top, at the most advantageous time, under the most optimal conditions, and certainly without brutality. The time had long passed for public displays of mindless savagery. Legitimacy demanded it. I had thought that eliminating Röhm and his mob of hooligans and degenerates had ended the problem.

"But then, in the spring, I received a Gestapo report stating that the rank and file of the Party would, in fact, set in motion a barbaric solution to the 'Jewish Problem' from below that the government would then have to follow. As you can imagine . . ."

My headache was increasing in virulence. His voice began to drift as I forced myself to consider his words. I believe myself to be, right through, a reconciler, a peacemaker. My father was a drunken, merciless brute, exactly the sort of ignorant savage the Führer had been describing, though I don't recall any particularly political, racial, or religious animus in his incessant and violent rants and ravings. For him, all, both high and low (including my invalid mother and me), were *shit*, pure and simple. To me, Jews were just ordinary Germans who didn't worship Jesus—that is, save those who wore odd, dusty-black, ill-fitting suits and sported long, tight curls, snaking out from tall, wide-brim hats. I found these insular characters to be truly strange, but hardly dangerous.

My attention snapped to when we were approached by a breathless Brückner, who, after apologizing profusely for the interruption, reminded the Führer that he had an appointment with a Cardinal Pacelli.[29]

"Let him wait," the Führer replied with a sneer. "Did you know that I have never seen the bloody man perspire. Eventually, he'll drown in his own juices, but so far, he'll do as he's told, to protect his precious German flock. So, give him my sincerest expressions of regret, and tell him that I was unavoidably delayed by urgent matters of state, and will see him once they are resolved, that's all."

Brückner smiled, saluted, and left. The Führer continued as if there hadn't been a suspension.

"As you can imagine, Linge, I was justifiably furious. Even though I cautioned strongly against any anti-Jewish violence, considering my own—I must say, ingenious—plan for settling the 'Jewish Question,' as well as my desire to have absolutely nothing interfere with Germany hosting the Olympic Games next year, I was powerless to act decisively at the time. The

---

[29] Before his election to the papacy, Pacelli served as secretary of the Department of Extraordinary Ecclesiastical Affairs, papal nuncio to Germany (1917–1929), and Cardinal Secretary of State, in which capacity he worked to conclude treaties with European and Latin American nations, most notably the Reichskonkordat with Nazi Germany, with which the Vatican sought to protect the church in Germany from Adolf Hitler, who sought the destruction of "political Catholicism."

ensuing wave of assaults, vandalism, and boycotts by the Alten Kämpfer and SA thugs in the spring and summer was far more violent than the anti-Semitic campaigns of the two previous years. As a result, and as I predicted, the matter was raised to the forefront of the state agenda, and so, with extreme reluctance, I'm obliged to become involved directly.

"In any event, before I take any action, I will call for you after this evening's tea, and we will speak further on this. Now I must be off to deal with that Papist weasel Pacelli."

With that, he scurried off before I could even salute. For a moment, I merely stood there, dumbfounded. What did he possibly think I could contribute to the issue of Jews? They were fine with me, and so, as meaningless as any other Germans. I'd read *Mein Kampf*, and a few of Streicher's newspaper screeds, but could, in my experience, discern nothing sinister, dangerous, or harmful in them. Yet, who was I to question the opinions of men such as the Führer, Göring, Himmler, Goebbels, and the rest?

∾

Some years ago, when I'd gotten to the *P* volume of the encyclopaedia, I read of something called "parallel universes," defined as "the hypothetical set of infinite or finite possible universes (including the historical universe we consistently experience) that together comprise everything that exists and can exist: the entirety of space, time, matter, and energy as well as the physical laws and constants that describe them." The term was attributed to the American philosopher and psychologist William James in 1895.

As Braille is to a sighted man, I understood absolutely nothing of it at the time, but now, sitting as if anaesthetized in my room, waiting for the Führer's summons, I actually felt as if I not only finally understood the phenomenon but actually was in one of them—and not necessarily by myself. But I still hadn't a clue as to what any of it signified, or why I, an unsophisticated, uneducated, twenty-two-year-old nothing appeared to be the centre of that universe. Was that suddenly mysterious Hannelore actually onto something in her drunken chatter? Or perhaps there is only one universe: me, and the one of my own making.

A sharp knock tore me away from such fruitless speculations. It was one of the Führer's chauffeurs, Kempka,[30] and from his florid face and precarious posture, he seemed as if he had barely survived a visit to his favourite ratskeller. A cheerful, hail-fellow-well-met sort of chap who tipples to excess when off-duty (which is mostly by day, since the Führer loves to roam anonymously in the night). Though he outranks me considerably, Kempka is no man to flaunt it. He's rough-cut but genuine. I truly like the man.

"You look like shit, Linge. Is this a bad time?" he muttered, dried spittle caking the sides of his mouth like hardened clay, and his breath, of an intensity that could melt steel.

"That's something I should be asking *you*. Come in, if you can make it."

Kempka stumbled in, wobbly but intact, uniform askew, and flopped down on my cot. Finally, he mustered the energy, if not the sobriety, to say: "I love you, Linge." Fresh drool oozed over the crust. "I love you, my friend. No matter the crisis, you are totally fucking unflappable, like the goddamned pastor in the church in my village when I was a child. My God, us kids

___
[30] SS-Obersturmbannführer (Lieutenant Colonel) Erich Kempka, on 29 February 1932, was tasked as a reserve driver for Hitler's personal entourage. In 1934, he was present at the arrest of Ernst Röhm. By 1935, he was Hitler's principal chauffeur.

did everything to rattle the old gent, but he'd just yawn and say: 'Enjoy yourself now. When you grow up, you'll see how serious life really is.' Well, Linge, by that standard, I've avoided life to the best of my ability—and all the seriousness with it."

I took him by the shoulder, walked him into the bathroom, and turned on the tap. "That's admirable, Erich, but I need something to be unflappable about, so what's the crisis?"

He fumbled about his pockets searching for something, ultimately in vain. "Say, my friend, do you have a cigarette?"

I shrugged helplessly. "Erich, you know I don't smoke."

"Yeah." He coughed out a laugh. "I remember. Just like the Boss. What did you say?"

He was in even worse shape than I, so I was careful. "I asked you if there was any crisis I could flap about."

His bloodshot eyes swivelled painfully upward in thought. "A crisis, a crisis, yeah, right, a crisis. Yeah, now I remember: that old fucker Schreck is trying to do me in."

"Kill you?" I asked incredulously.

"No, no, Linge, I mean get rid of me, get my ass canned, take my place." He'd finally found a crumpled package of cigarettes and a lighter. He pulled out a bent cigarette, and without straightening it, lit it and inhaled extravagantly. "Sees me gaining on him. He's old-school Nazi, Heinz, like that fucking faggot Röhm. Even headed the original SS. Him and the Boss go back to the beginning, moustache and all, and you know how that goes. I'm ten times the driver he is, and the Boss knows it, and that's the problem. Loyalty on his part, and ambition on mine, pure and simple. Say, do you have a drink around here?" His hands had begun to tremble. "He's a sick old fucker, but like all those types, he'll last forever and I'll remain a spare part."

I nodded, leaned down, retrieved a "hospitality" bottle of

schnapps from the tiny cupboard below the sink, grabbed a glass on top, opened it, poured a sizeable shot, returned to Kempka, and handed it to him. "Be careful," I warned, "if the Führer calls for you—"

He held up a quavering hand. "Yeah, yeah, I know. Don't fret. I'll be okay. Metabolism, you know—and Sen-Sen, right?[31] He won't ever suspect a thing."

Somehow, I doubted that, but kept silent, as he gulped the drink down and began to weep. Once he'd worn that out, he murmured: "Damn, how I wish I could be like the fuckin' English, who could go through an amputation without anaesthetic and keep their stiff upper lip. Us Germans, true Germans, we wear our feelings on our sleeves. That'll be our undoing, I can tell you."

Who were the false Germans? I asked myself, mostly in jest. "Then I imagine you'll just have to kill him," I advised jokingly.

Suddenly, he sobered up, with sweat glistening on his face, as if he'd just awakened from a horrible dream. "*Linge!*" he exclaimed. "I was thinking more along the lines of you putting in a good word for me with the Boss."

"Erich," I replied, hands up, palms outward, "as for putting in a good word? Who am I? I'm a twenty-two-year-old uneducated servant who's been with his employer less than a year. What would my word be as against an old comrade from the years of struggle? Even if I weren't instantly fired or arrested, you'd be able to hear the Führer's laughter for miles. No, you need to go to someone with a history, like Krause, for a good word, not to me."

At that, Kempka began laughing hysterically. "Linge, you *are* new. Krause? I'd do better approaching a fucking rabbi, or

---

[31] Sen-Sen was a type of breath freshener originally marketed as a "breath perfume" in the late nineteenth century.

worse, Fräulein Schroeder. If I approached Krause as I did you, I'd be in front of Heydrich a minute later, and the rest, I leave to your imagination."

I had never met Heydrich, but his reputation was more than enough. But what was I to do, I asked myself. If I did what Kempka asked, I couldn't imagine the Führer even listening to me, much less acting favourably. "Mind my own damn business" would probably be his most charitable response. Also, if word got out—and I'd learnt quickly that in such a hermetically cloistered society, it always does—how would Schreck respond? As the first head of the SS, he certainly wouldn't congratulate me on my loyalty to Kempka. I knew enough about the real SS, and especially the old-timers, to know that I would have a target nailed to my back from that moment on—with a real nail! Then was there someone, anyone I could recommend to him, who might be able to help? I needed little time to consider that. And yet, how could I disappoint Kempka, a man who far outranked me, whose goodwill I might need someday, and whose animosity could place me in serious jeopardy?

"Erich," I finally said, "I'll speak with the Führer at the earliest opportunity," I lied. "In the meantime, I'll try to learn something about his current relationship with Schreck." That was only a half-lie. "Perhaps they are not now so cordial as their beginnings would suggest."

Kempka leaned over and shook my shoulders warmly, causing my aching head to erupt with pain. "That's all I ask, and I thank you. One day, I hope to be able to demonstrate my appreciation in a more tangible way. Incidentally, you're not married or otherwise attached, yes? So how are you fixed for female companionship? I seen you on occasion with that undersecretary, Hannelore, but she's hardly even a female. I tell you, being stuck in the Chancellery can be like taking a vow of chastity, considering the talent at hand and the opportunities, if you know what I mean."

His assumption was crass, blatant, and correct, but I didn't wish to become involved in the sexual politics of the Führer's inner circle, and he had me pinned to the wall like a butterfly-collector's specimen.

"By the way," he said, "where did you learn that bathroom trick?"

"Just common sense," I lied again. "The people here are like a bunch of human radios, listening to each other's programs."

"Sly for a mere lad, so new to these surroundings. You're wise beyond your years, as they say. It will be interesting to see how perceptive you become by the time you're my age. Anyways, now I gotta go." He grabbed my hand with both of his and shook it exuberantly and raced from my quarters, leaving me alone with my throbbing head, his request, and the Jewish Question.

The Führer appeared quite agitated when I answered his summons: perspiring, trembling, screaming, stomping, farting, contemplating: his entire repertoire of responses to problems. I assumed that he'd had a troublesome meeting with Cardinal Pacelli, or the matter he began to discuss with me on our stroll, but it could have been anything—or nothing.

"Naturally," the Führer said, while pacing manically, "I possess no sympathy toward the Jews; all know this. From the beginning, I have made my position abundantly clear that the Reich must be rid of the pestilence. But the solution must be coldly rational: *strategic, not emotional!*" he screamed with no little irony. "*Never emotional!* I have always—"

He stopped abruptly at the enormous portrait of Frederick the Great on his wall, hardly visible in the meagre illumination, and stood there gazing up at it. I'd seen him do this several times in moments of extreme stress. Without turning, he said:

"There are many occasions when I feel like a person divided into two, Linge. Has that happened to you?"

"I'm not sure, my Führer," I responded. My true answer would have been an unequivocal yes, but as with many occasions, I had no sense of where he was headed, so I let him ramble.

"Conflicting sentiments, Linge. That bloody ambivalence again." He chuckled. "That word you must commit to memory, if you can. A great part of me is still the poverty-stricken, struggling artist, the solitary, friendless bohemian, wandering the streets of Vienna and Berlin, receiving rejection and scorn at every turn. Did you know, Linge, there was a time when I had nothing, *nothing!*" he shouted, still fixed on the painting. "No family, no friends, no job, no support, no place to lay my weary head? For days I slept—*slept*—in doorways, alleyways, underneath bridges, forced to sneak the greasy scraps left by others on plates in beer halls. But all to serve my independence, my freedom, my art."

I'd done the same thing, of course, but for brute survival, hardly art.

"I must say," he continued, "and not with the soppy romanticism that accompanies nostalgia, that a part of me truly misses those carefree days of failure. I owed no one and no one owed me. Freedom, Linge. Now I ask you: What freedom do I possess? None. I am at an entire nation's beck and call. I am at the service and disposal of all. The solitary artist in me is repelled, even at the idea. And yet, this other part of me, the supreme leader, no longer hidden under the surface, the man surrounded by and relied upon by multitudes, the creator of worlds, the now successful artist who discovered his true medium and who must have more and more canvas on which to paint his ultimate masterpiece. These two sides are fighting within me constantly. Do you understand me?"

Without waiting for an answer I had no way of giving, he again went over to his desk and turned off the lamp. "Now, what are we to do about the Jews? Your true opinion, Linge, and damn all other considerations," he asked me, as if his disquisition on his two warring personalities had never occurred.

For how long we sat in the darkness, I cannot say, but gradually, I could feel the migraine ebb, and the voice I'd heard since I first became aware of thinking began in my brain, and flowed from my mouth, unbidden, to counsel the Führer:

My Führer, the voice declared, *I advise you to follow your own unassailable instincts: leave the Jews be. At their best, they add to the coffers and culture of the Reich, and at their worst, they're completely harmless and can only lead you and Germany to disaster by considering them more important and dangerous than they actually are. I fear, however, that you will be compelled to ignore this, and so, that said, were it not for the drooling anti-Semites in the Party, I would caution you to do nothing save absolutely forbid further organized physical attacks. You are beset by a Cardinal who clearly feels nothing one way or another for the Jews but who is terrified that whatever you do to them will eventually be visited upon his own flock, and in this, he is not mistaken. Therefore, I would mollify him to buy both image and time. Moreover, the Olympic Games are to be held soon in Germany. Is it your wish to antagonize a world not yet ready to deal with Judaism? To see the host nation exercising overt aggression toward selected citizens of your Reich?*

As you are aware, my Führer, the voice continued, *you have been placed in an untenable position. As a consequence, only three* imperfect solutions present themselves: first, forbid, with no exceptions or mercy, violence against anything even remotely Jewish for the time being, and you have already done this; second, enact race laws that will satisfy and thus keep the vulgar and violent members of your Party at bay and, at the same time, illustrate unmistakably to the Jews in Germany that they are not Germans, and so things will never be as they thought they were and would be, and, infinitely more important, take race matters out of all hands but yours and those of whom you specifically designate; finally, place the obstructionists—and anyone else in disagreement with your master plan—in a position where they can do you no more harm.

Then, just as suddenly, the voice vanished, the crushing pain resumed, and I saw myself hanging by my bloody fingertips over a deep, fiery maw that slowly closed in on me, becoming hotter and hotter as it became smaller and smaller. In panic, I tried to move but couldn't, then searched for escape routes but was inextricably trapped within it, only my head and shoulders now remaining above the flames. I could see a featureless naked man on the ledge in front of me, bent over, back to me, excrement oozing from his scrotum. Then he was suddenly next to me, attempting to push my head down into the abyss. I could feel him shaking me by the shoulders violently, and then the desk light snapped on, and the Führer in his pyjamas was standing over me, shaking my shoulders.

"*Linge! Wake up, Linge!*" he urged loudly, his little moustache rising mischievously. "I can't have my principal valet fall asleep for hours while I'm speaking to him, now, can I? How would it look?"

Then he let go of my shoulders and his smile disappeared as he returned to his pacing, this time screaming, red-faced and spittle-spewing: "*Yes, Linge, you're right! In you, we chose well indeed! Those appeasing, finance-obsessed swine and their race-addled allies have placed me in a position I won't be placed in again, I can tell you!* All right, this time, I must comply, but, to make a virtue of necessity, I have another motive as well: to clarify—and codify, once and for all—my racial policy. I already ordered an immediate halt to 'individual actions' against German Jews, and now, I will inform my ministers that we will quickly establish some harsh, new, anti-Semitic laws, as a consoling gesture to those coarser party members who were disappointed with my order—and whose support I still need."

After the Führer's philippic, he returned to the portrait and murmured with a seamlessly eerie, solicitous calm: "Nothing special on my agenda, so says Brückner, and you appear completely run through. So, no need to remain. I'll have Krause attend me tonight."

Good bloody God! I thought with an internal quake. Had I actually uttered those words to the Führer? He was acting as if I had, but I had no awareness of it and was totally contrary to the persona I had taken such pains to establish and maintain. Was I losing control of my thoughts as well as my body?

I ONCE READ that most human activity deals with drawing conclusions, which some later discard or keep building on. The latter, unfortunately, twist all they see to merely justify their conclusions and, so, make their conclusions into an impregnable personal reality. Therefore, I decided, as I lay on my cot this morning, that when there is a chaos of confusion in one's life to accept it as best one can, swim with whatever current one can discern, and allow circumstances to play themselves out and hope that they suggest courses of action. One can second-guess oneself into oblivion or the madhouse, which, to me, is the same thing.

Today, the Chancellery staff were seething with "information," both real and imagined, about the Rally and the Führer's new race laws that he would soon present to the Reichstag through General Göring.[32] I'd attended the Rally, and I can tell

---

[32] On September 14, the night before the Reichstag's special session, Nazi legal officials presented Hitler with four drafts of the new laws. Hitler chose the fourth version, which happened to be the least militant. Around midnight, Hitler told the same legal officials he also wanted an accompanying law concerning Reich citizenship. The officials, scrawling on the back of a hotel food menu, hastily drafted a vaguely worded law which designated Jews as subjects of the Reich. Hitler approved the draft around 2:30 a.m. The Nuremberg Laws classified people with four German grandparents as "German or kindred blood," while people were classified as Jews if they descended from three or four Jewish grandparents. A person with one or two Jewish grandparents was a *Mischling*, a crossbreed, of "mixed blood." The Nuremberg Laws classified all non-Jewish white Europeans as Aryans. These laws deprived Jews and other non-Aryans of German citizenship and

you that the announcement created a sensation: all through the massive crowd, it was as if Zeus's lightning had struck them—a fraction of stunned silence, followed by an explosion of cheers, applause, chants, and patriotic songs. The Führer was stern-faced, arms crossed pugnaciously with conviction, but I knew that internally he was of two minds on his actions. I'd learned that much in his presence.

Today, I was almost as much in demand as the Führer, since I was infinitely more accessible and considered to possess the sort of personal information that only an intimate eye witness could relate. The checkpoints came first, because they were everywhere and the sentries were virtually erupting with curiosity and envy: "So, Herr Major (I'd been promoted, along with the Führer's other valets, to prevent fraternal friction), you were actually present at the beginning of a new era for the Reich. So how does it make you feel?" Obviously, a guard of high rank. Another: "Now the Jew swine will learn what being vermin gets you in the New Germany, yes?" And another: "The Führer has finally given the Reich what it's needed: an end to Jew contamination of pure German blood."

My response was the same for all: "As you can imagine, I was in too much thrall to the Führer's words to even think clearly. His voice was enough." Meaningless, yet effective. All consoled me on my inability to put my true Nazi sentiments into words, but

---

prohibited racially mixed sexual relations and marriages between Germans and Jews. On 26 November 1935, the laws were extended to "Negroes or their bastard offspring." The Nuremberg Laws also included a ban on sexual relations and marriages between persons classified as Aryan and non-Aryan. They ultimately prevented Jews from participating in German civic life. These laws were both an attempt to return the Jews of twentieth-century Germany to the position that Jews had held before their emancipation in the nineteenth century; whereas in the nineteenth century, Jews could have evaded restrictions by converting, this was no longer possible.

they, of course, fully understood my feelings, and that seemed to make their ignorance and distance more palatable to them.

Then came the secretaries, wide-eyed, gossipy, curious—all but Schroeder, of course. "Who was there?" they asked. "Anyone exciting? You just needed to stand there, you tall, fine-looking lump. You must have seen all the important people. Come on, Linge, you can tell me. I won't breathe it to a soul. On my parents' life." On their parents' lives yet. Yes, eager, they certainly were. And I actually considered giving them all they asked for—and more, even though it would be utterly false, since a simple, meaningless too-overwhelmed-to-remember would have been enough, should it ricochet later.

My only concern was Schroeder, since she was the only one who didn't ask me anything, and somehow, I suspected that she'd know the truth of things and instantly race to the Führer—or worse, Himmler—with it. So, my reply had to be fraught with significance, yet signify nothing. "Leni Riefenstahl," I told them truthfully and jocularly, "filmed the entire affair, and I'm certain she will be asked to present it to you all at one of the Führer's evenings. I refuse to spoil it for you, so you'll just have to suffer until then."

I suppose I betray my age. I was both proud and ashamed of myself for being so successfully duplicitous, but I was the Führer's principal valet, so there you are.

The Chancellery consensus, to no one's surprise, was that the race laws were long overdue and not nearly harsh or comprehensive enough. Disturbing. Who would be next?

As I passed the salon, I could hear Hanfstaengl playing a melody I couldn't recognize. I'd learned from Brückner that he was once the Führer's close confidant, and even had him as godfather to his son Egon, but Hanfstaengl's arrogant manner and strong opinions had alienated Goebbels and other high officials, and so the Führer was gradually keeping him at arm's length. In the old days, so I was told, he would be playing for the Führer alone, or for his elite guests; now he mostly played to himself in empty rooms.

When I arrived at the Führer's quarters with the newspapers that been laid on the table by his door, he was already engaged in a typically "vigorous" discussion with von Neurath. Neither appeared to notice my entrance, so I padded discretely to the bookshelves and began to arrange the already-rearranged volumes. Neurath was speaking in the deep, measured tones of the aristocrat, while the Führer was screaming, stomping, and spewing spittle.

"*Complete and utter nonsense!*" the Führer harangued. "The foreign dogs will bark to satisfy their Jews, but their bite will succumb to their need for German goodwill."

"But, my Führer," von Neurath countered, "'their Jews,' as you put it, have much influence outside the Reich, and their . . . bark can frighten the neighbours. With your permission, you ignore them at your peril."

"Neurath," the Führer replied, having calmed himself with astonishing speed and shifted to theatrical forbearance: "have you actually read the foreign press?"

"Yes, my Führer," he said. "Copiously."

"And what reaction did you discern from them?"

Neurath took a deep breath. "I cannot make an accurate accounting, so soon in the game."

"All right," the Führer fumed, "you cannot—why does this not surprise me?—but it would appear that Ribbentrop can. Just this morning, he informed me that while some foreign visitors, even some political opponents within Germany itself, harboured negative views, most appeared beguiled into believing it was merely a phase, and that I, in the words of former British prime minister Lloyd George, was 'a great man.' And, more important, Neurath, the foreign press and embassies have been either supportive or silent on the matter. So much for world Jewish influence."

The Führer then virtually leaped up from his desk and spread his arms wide. "*Must I constantly teach you so-called experts?*" he bellowed, causing me to almost drop a book I was needlessly reshelving. "You, *you*, in your cloistered world of embassies and manor houses, see nothing but aristocratic ostriches in their evening dress, with their anachronistically simple-minded heads buried in the sand, while their numberless servants measure the correct distance between table settings. Coming not from that world, I see everything, and what I see is a world only too happy to be rid of Jews, if only they can get the benefits before they disappear. Even if the world criticize us, they envy us in their innermost desires. We have shown the way, and soon, mark my words, all will follow."

"But not immediately, my Führer," von Neurath ventured.

"No," he said, his tone returning to normal. "In that, at least, you are correct. For us now, it is necessary to refrain from any further actions against the Jews that would serve to undermine my credibility on the world stage. I must present myself as someone who can and must be taken seriously, not as the leader of an anti-Semitic mob."

The Führer then sat down, farted vigorously, stretched out his arms, and clasped his hands in prayer. "Go now, Neurath, and play billiards and cricket with your kind. I will continue to deal realistically with the Jewish Question. Their turn will come soon. Now, my principal goal is to rebuild the German Army and exploit any opportunity to expand the Reich."

Once von Neurath left, I asked him whether he wished to get dressed, but he whisked it away with a wave of his hand. "Linge, Linge," he moaned theatrically, "what am I to do with these monocle-brained 'vons' who consider even the eighteenth-century corrupted by progress?"

"But what about Herr von Ribbentrop, my Führer?" I replied. "You agree with his assessment of events, yes?"

The Führer chuckled. "*Von* Ribbentrop, Linge? Herr Exalted von Ribbentrop is no more a von than I. Some relative bequeathed the title to him in her will, like a pocket watch or a dog. But, thank heavens, he is a realist with no silly illusions about our allies and enemies. He leaves wishful thinking to the fox hunters."

I noted that he never said *friends*.

After preparing the Führer for the day's events, which were to be much later in the evening, I bumped into Brückner in the grand hall.

"No tap to turn on here, Heinz, but hiding in plain sight also has its virtues, don't you agree?"

I smiled, as much for effect as for the wit behind Brückner's remark. "Anything that will provide privacy in a beehive is welcome," I answered.

"True, my friend, only too true. Then you should salute, yes?"

I snapped to and saluted smartly. "The whole place is buzzing with questions and opinions about—"

"The Rally. I know. Military expansion and Jews. The old

story. I got the same thing. The devil with the Rally. We need to get you away from here. This place can become a world unto itself, with nothing outside. Like a convalescent hospital—or lunatic asylum. I know exactly what you need, and I'm ordering you to take the cure. I'll get Krause to care for the Führer in your absence. You just follow Kempka's lead and have a good time, German-style, yes?"

I couldn't wait! It had been months since I'd even ventured outside the Chancellery with anyone but Hanne, who I hadn't seen since that time in the *ratskellar*. I was told that she'd been obliged to resign, due to the onset of an undisclosed illness, and that her whereabouts were unknown. "If that is an order, Herr Obergruppenführer."

"It is, Herr Captain, and then some," he replied with a smirk. "Even the Führer has expressed concern for your social well-being."

"Then I shall follow your order without reservation," I replied in the same spirit.

I located Kempka in the Chancellery garage, which was justifiably enormous. It appeared to be a garage, repair station, and storage facility all in one. It smelled of sweat, oil, and metal: garage smells; mechanics' smells. I easily located tiny Kempka, who was in a corner, standing over a tool table, appearing to be making some entries in a ledger. He was wearing a filthy white jumpsuit over his SS uniform. I was just standing there wondering why an item of clothing that was destined to become black wasn't constructed of black cloth in the first place when I heard: "*Linge!* So, you finally climbed down from your exalted mountaintop to visit the trenches."

"Brückner steered me to you. He said I needed a diversion from the Führer."

Kempka laughed heartily. "Brückner should know. Okay, my needy friend. I ain't Baur, but then, who the fuck else is? Okay, let me see." He turned and scurried to his tiny glass-enclosed office and soon returned with a torn-off slip of grease-stained paper, which he handed to me as if it were a particularly reliable treasure map. "Okay, try this bird," he offered with a lascivious sneer and wink. "Katrin's her name. A few glasses and she'll gladly spread her . . . wings, eh?"

When I arrived at her opulent apartment building just off the Kurfürstendamm, I had the sensation that I would be out of my depth in ways I wouldn't even understand, and I wasn't wrong. Katrin was . . . in a word, magnificent. Statuesque, slender, rather than the prevailing Rhine-Maiden-like full figure that most German men seemed to prefer, and dressed impeccably—and expensively—in the latest fashion: silk, satin, and fur, though I assumed it rather than knew it, since my knowledge of fashion was second only to my knowledge of calculus. She was of that indeterminate age that some women seem to master with no apparent effort. Her face, even her full lips, boasting a minimum of makeup—or so it seemed—was a model of perfect sensuality: angles and curves that would have had a painter arrested for degeneracy had she been his model, but not before the arresting officer confiscated the painting for his personal collection. In my former life, my idea of a date was a plain-featured shop girl, a coworker's ordinary sister, or some unexceptional female I might chance upon in an adjoining seat on a tram: coarse but willing. This creature was certainly not coarse, and I never even gave a fleeting thought to willing. The Chancellery did nothing to alter my expectations.

After giving her time to glance me up and down, I imagined, to see if I passed, I asked her where she wished to go, and her answer appeared to be calculatedly spontaneous: "*Anna Karenina*. It's playing at the Titania.[33] A long, weepy melodrama, but I've heard that it's quite well done. You can call me Katrin." And without more, she took my gloved hand in her gloved hand and led me to the posh motorcar I'd borrowed from Kempka, had me open the front passenger door, and slid in gracefully and effortlessly.

Of course she was right. It was a long, well-done, weepy melodrama about a class of people of whom I had no conception. Afterwards, she suggested that we go to the elegant theatre café for convenience. I assumed that she considered a cabaret far too uncivilized for the likes of her. Despite the crowds of people waiting for a table, we were seated instantly and sat in silence until our order of Turkish coffee and Viennese pastries arrived.

"I know this may not sound terribly demure," she remarked, "but when Erich called and asked me if I would consent to a date with you, I couldn't believe my good fortune."

Astonishment was too feeble a word for how I felt hearing that, but I played along. "Being a gentleman," I answered, "I refuse to comment on the height of your standards."

Her perfect lips curled up at the corners. "I say, you're rather droll for such a young man."

"Whatever droll is, I imagine that age is not an absolute

---

[33] The Titania-Palace was an extravagant movie theatre in the Berlin district of Steglitz-Zehlendorf and was known until the 1960s far beyond the borders of Berlin.

requirement." *Watch your sophistication!* I warned myself. "What do you do?" I asked, to shift the conversation to her.

"You mean work?" She laughed. "Well, not a great deal, I must confess. On occasion, I do the odd job for the Reich Security Main Office." That was Himmler's empire. I noticed she said "for," not "at" or "in." But what it signified, if anything, I had no idea, but it troubled me.

"So, you work for Reichsführer Himmler?" I asked.

Her lips pressed into a pout and she shrugged her highly-but-perfectly-padded shoulders. "In any event," she deflected, "it must be thrilling, being so close to the Führer day and night."

Farts and all? I wanted to ask. "Actually," I replied, "I came with you to escape my thrilling job. I'd like to think you were with Heinz Linge the man, not the Führer's valet."

"But in such a position, how can you separate the two?"

It was a good question, and I had no little difficulty in answering it. "Well," I struggled, "I was myself long before I was a valet, and I have qualities that go beyond preparing baths, delivering mail and newspapers, timing him while he puts on ties, and standing mute at parade rest behind him during dinners and meetings." Then, to lighten what was quickly becoming burdensome: "Instead, would you like to hear stories of my time as a bricklayer's apprentice? Now *that* was thrilling."

She chuckled gaily and her entire amazing face opened up. "Not especially," she said. "I'm afraid that my interest in bricks and those who lay them is regrettably limited. What would you really like to talk about?"

"How about the movie?" I ventured. It didn't seem a stretch.

Another shrug. "If you like," she conceded. "Would it be the kind of film one would play for the Führer?"

I laughed at that one, despite the fact that she'd adroitly

shifted from the movie to my job again. "I doubt it," I said. "In fact, I'm surprised your ministry permitted it to play in Germany. Aside from it taking place in Russia, even as a monarchy, it goes against the Party's view of the role of women."

"Do go on," she prodded. "And what role might that be?"

"The female as devoted housekeeper and proud bearer of Aryan children, the more children, the better. I've heard the Führer go on and on about this at dinner and tea, to universal agreement among his guests."

"Their agreement is understandable. But then he would disapprove of me, I think," she said.

"Not really," I countered gently. "The Führer has a soft spot for the female worker as well, though it might seem a contradiction. All his secretaries, for example, are female, and I've never heard him complain that they would be better off in the home. A secret which all appear to know, but never speak of. I'm sure you know that in Germany today, despite the official declarations, women occupy many positions, perhaps even ones like yours," *whatever they were,* I thought uneasily. "There are exceptions to everything, I've discovered." I didn't tell her that the Führer even has a Jewish physician. "On the other hand, I think he would object to Anna Karenina, not because of her lack of nurturing instincts but because of her infidelity. On that subject, the Führer is adamant. And, anyway, he likes American cartoons far more than even the best heavy domestic drama."

"So, the Führer is hardly a *cinéaste.*"

"A *cinéaste?*" I knew what it meant, but that wasn't for her to know.

"French. 'A lover of film.'"

"No, not true. The Führer is definitely a . . . what? *cinéaste?*

It's just that his taste runs to the more, ah, cheerful. Yes, that's it. Cheerful."

"And what does Heinz Linge prefer?"

The question threw me off balance, though I should have been prepared for it. After a contrived pause to sip my coffee, I said: "Having no formal education to speak of, I prefer books, especially nonfiction. Of course, understanding them is quite another matter entirely."

She placed a gloved hand on my arm. "Admirable," she said, without an apparent trace of irony. "But, then, it would be rather awkward, the two of us going out to read a book, wouldn't it?"

I laughed. "Not really," I said. "At least not for old married couples, I suppose." Though she would have been hard-pressed to have discovered that activity going on in my parents' house—or even a book, for that matter, I wanted to say, but I let my inanity stand.

Then *she* laughed. "How old are you, Heinz?"

"Twenty-two . . . as of March."

Her ice-blue eyes widened. "You are remarkably sophisticated for your years and education, if I may say so. I am not exactly twenty-two, something I'm sure you must realize."

"One thing I've learnt while attending those who visit the Führer is that women like you seem ageless, or perhaps, make age irrelevant."

"You've also learnt flattery, I see. I've heard that there's no better man at flattery than the Führer." She finished her coffee. "I say, being in such constant and close proximity to him, does he ever confide in you things that he shares with no one else?"

Something had been troubling me ever since we sat down at the café. I struggled to say something diplomatically sappy, but, after her question, diplomacy lost out to audacity. "I'll answer you," I said, "providing you tell me what 'odd jobs' you do for the RSHA."

At that, her expression instantly shifted from engaged to detached. "Yes," she said, "despite everything, you *are* quite the sophisticate," she observed, glacially. "I keep an apartment at the Adlon.[34] I was about to ask you if you wished to see it, but I can see that you're tired, and concerned that the Führer may require your attentions at any time, so I think that you should merely take me home, yes?" Since, by her manner, I discerned no question in her question, take her home I did—entirely in silence.

As I conclude this reflection upon my evening with Katrin, I cannot help but wonder whether I may have been one of her "odd jobs." Questions tugged at my brain: Who was she, and what was she? With her two residences (and how many more?), was she highly paid or independently wealthy? What was she after with her probing and evasions? I have no answers to any of these, but I do know at least one thing: there was far more to our date than a movie.

---

[34] The Hotel Adlon was one of Berlin's premier hotels. In the years of political and economic upheaval, the hotel became a location of political and diplomatic decisions. The SS preferred the Hotel Kaiserhof on Wilhelmstrasse.

I ENDURED A tumultuously sleepless night after returning Kempka's car, sneaking—I hoped, unnoticed—to my quarters, and writing to you. Not even a nightmare dared intrude upon my insomnia. I sat on the edge of my cot, as usual, of two minds, and waited anxiously for the distraction of the Führerbuzzer, but also desperate for time to think without extraneous responsibilities. Yes, extraneous. I say it, for I remain convinced that last night was infinitely more than an ordinary date gone awry. I was physically debilitated but mentally seething with questions that I could not articulate but that persisted as virulent phantoms tormenting me. Who? Why?

As if by subconscious command, a knock on the door brought Kempka into my room, all his usual hail-fellow-well-met.

"So, you young stud," he began, "I'm surprised I'm not catching you sneaking along the hallway with your shirttails out, zipper unfastened, and your boots in your hands."

Sensing confidentiality to come, I motioned him to the bathroom and we performed our conversational ritual. "I had to drive the Führer to his apartment—and wait," he confessed, "and envying you all the while."

Kempka meant the Führer's *other* apartment, the one he reserved for female "guests" he preferred his circle not to know about. They all did, of course, but for obvious reasons, they were the souls of discretion. However, given his attitude toward women, and certain peculiarities I'd noticed since I arrived, I couldn't imagine what he did there. "I feel sorry for you, Erich," I said.

"It was worse than that," he complained. "All he did during our ride was to alternately bemoan and praise Mussolini's decision to invade Ethiopia next month, to which the Boss swore me to absolute secrecy. Il Duce this, Il Duce that, he went on and on. I know nothing of politics or world affairs, and so I was forced to guess when to nod my agreement and utter the 'yes, my Führer,' 'of course, my Führer.' My neck was really stiff by the time we arrived, you bet."

So much for even considering swearing Kempka to absolute secrecy, I thought, as the comforting roar of the tap soothed my anxieties. "I imagine you couldn't go anywhere in the meantime."

Kempka let out a bitter laugh. "Right you are. With the Boss, there is no meantime."

Being a man who reveres order, I knew that unpredictability is the enemy of one who waits.

"True," I said. "But you had the radio at least, yes?"

"Ah," he sighed wistfully, "I had the radio, but you had Katrin. The radio is a shitty substitute, my friend."

Not necessarily, I wanted to tell him. I agonized over what—or even whether—to tell him about the evening, since I didn't fully understand the evening in general, and especially the part in the café. I had to be careful—but how careful? I needed more information, that was certain, but how to get it discretely? "She was quite a fascinating creature, Erich," I told him, "without a doubt. Do you know her last name?"

Kempka smiled lecherously. "Ah, so it was that sort of

evening. No time for names, eh? To be twenty-two again. *Shit!* You *are* a fast worker."

"It was quick, no arguing that," I obfuscated. "I never even got her name beyond Katrin, just that she . . . had some connection with Reichsführer Himmler's domain. She appeared far too highbrow to be interested in a valet. Just how did you manage to get me a date with the likes of her?"

Kempka shrugged. "Well, to be frank, I confess that I had little to do with it. It seems that Himmler spoke with the Boss and told him she wanted to meet you, and they brought Brückner in, then me, and said that I was just the guy to set it up, and was I gonna say no?"

Of all people, Himmler and the Führer—*the Führer!*—had a chauffeur arrange a date for me without discussing it with me—and doing it personally? My cynicism, not to mention paranoia, escalated precipitously. "You were going to tell me her name, yes?" I asked, sidestepping the issue for the time being.

"Ah, so you wanna, ah, get maybe a longer date this time? I'm surprised she didn't tell you. All I know is that she's a von something-or-other."

My eyes couldn't help but narrow at that. "And a 'von something-or-other' wished to date a valet?"

"Heinz," he said with a weary tilt of his head, "who the fuck knows what's going on in a woman's head?"

He was right, of course, but not quite right enough. "So now I'm suddenly worthy of an aristo?"

He thought for a few seconds, index finger pushing against his lower lip. "Yeah, sure, Heinz, I guess it was the day you became principal valet to the Führer."

I let the issue of rank go for the time being. "Any idea what she does for Himmler?"

More pursed lips. "If she didn't tell you, how the hell would I know? I was just ordered to get you two together. That's it. You think I'm gonna quiz the Führer, Himmler, or Brückner? I keep my curiosity for matters of advancement, not affairs of the heart, yes? Which reminds me: Have you had a chance to discuss me with the Boss? About . . . you know . . . ?"

I nodded with simulated verve. "As a matter of fact, Erich, no reasonable opportunity has come up yet," I lied flagrantly. "You know the Führer. The timing must be perfectly calculated. I think I can bring it up with him when I relate my evening with Katrin, if he asks." Kempka didn't appear to catch the fact that before he told me of the Führer's interest, I had no idea of his involvement. Kempka was an excellent driver and apparently efficient go-between, but not exactly a model of guile.

Kempka buffed his tiny hands together. "That's great, Heinz; I appreciate it. The sooner, the better, naturally. You'll let me know what's what, yes?"

"Naturally," I said, in keeping with the lie. "Naturally." I glanced at my watch. The Führerbuzzer hadn't sounded, but I had many things to do, since Kempka proved to be of limited assistance. "Now, as the Reich's chief valet, at least according to you and Katrin, I must live up to my exalted status and see to the Führer."

Kempka laughed. "Sure, Heinz. And don't forget about me." His eyebrows lifted.

"Aside from the Führer timing me while I fix his bow tie, I will make it my top priority."

Kempka laughed again and banged my shoulder like we were old comrades. "Hey, I expect nothing less," he effused. Then he turned round and exited, again rubbing his hands in what I took to be anticipatory triumph. I shut off the tap, and, despite the fact that I was experiencing again one of my brain-crushing headaches, I prepared myself as decently as possible to attend the Führer and then negotiate round the rest of the small cloistered world beyond my room.

⌇

When I entered the Führer's chambers, he was telling Brückner to invite Goebbels again for lunch (with the late-rising Führer, lunch was generally held when ordinary beings would be belching from their supper). He had the Reichsminister to lunch often, primarily because, with the Führer, Goebbels was invariably cheerful and highly entertaining. When they saw me, both appeared alarmed.

"*My God, Linge,*" the Führer exclaimed, "*you look terrible!* Brückner, fetch my Jew. He'll have you tip-top in minutes."

But before Brückner could act on the command, I intervened. "My Führer," I entreated, "I'm most grateful, but Dr. Bloch is hardly necessary. I merely had a long night. Some strong coffee later, and I'll be right as rain."

"Ah, yes, your female encounter. Kempka told me. Himmler, despite his demeanour, has quite the eye for the ladies—once he's investigated them, that is. Göring and Goebbels would normally keep the best ones for themselves. So? Was she up to snuff?"

What could I honestly say? "My Führer, I can honestly say that I've never met anyone quite like her."

"Good," he replied, rubbing his hands together excitedly, just as Kempka had done. "I could recognize that just by looking at you. It's good to escape the Chancellery, as I do from time to time. Confinement in one space reminds me too often of my time in Landsberg Prison, and for a confirmed bohemian like me, two hundred and sixty-four days was an eternity." Brückner chuckled, so I followed suit. "All right then," he said, "since you'll live, let's do our business quickly. I have a mass of documents to review and decrees to sign."

Brückner had readied the Führer's desk, so I only had to prepare his bath and watch him dress, and later, stand in the corner of the smaller dining room while the Führer and his guest or guests ate.

After an endless hour, I'd completed my chores and left, searching eagerly for Brückner to discuss the Katrin matter with him, but after a thorough scouring of those areas of the Chancellery where I might locate him, I conceded defeat. I stood in the Great Hallway, inert with frustration. I was impatient; that, I dared admit to myself. But then, a quote from Samuel Johnson sprang to my rescue: "In all evils which admit a remedy, impatience should be avoided, because it wastes that time and attention in complaints which, if properly applied, might remove the cause." Easily understood, and I considered it with all seriousness. Too vigorous and tenacious an inquiry, I concluded, creates suspicion, and even more so in a palace of paranoia like the Chancellery.

I headed toward my quarters for some reading until the Führer's lunch demanded my presence, when I heard an unfamiliar female voice behind me: "You dropped this." I turned quickly, but by then, she seemed to have vanished through one of the myriad of doors lining the hallway. I looked down, stealthily, to discover a folded piece of copy paper. I gazed around me, saw nothing suspect, leaned over, casually picked it up, and placed it in my tunic pocket. I'd learned quickly to read as little as possible in plain view. An ally, an enemy, or, more likely, another enigma. On my way back through the servants' hallway, I was greeted by someone at my door I'd only heard of by reputation in guarded whispers but had never actually met, either through the Führer's lunches, dinners, and teas or even through my nominal boss, Reichsführer-SS Himmler.

He was unmistakable, and much of what I'd heard of his appearance was borne out the instant I saw him. At one of the Führer's teas, I'd overheard Walter Schellenberg, his protégée in the Reich Main Security office, whisper a description of him to a female companion, that SS-General Reinhard Heydrich was a "tall, imperiously impressive figure of a man with a broad, unusually high forehead, small restless eyes as crafty as an animal's and of uncanny power, and a wide full-lipped mouth. His hands were slender and rather too long—as they made one think of the legs of a spider. His splendid figure was marred by the breadth of his hips, a disturbingly feminine effect which made him appear even more sinister. But," he'd added, "whatever the reality of his physical appearance, Heydrich was, by all accounts, brilliant, ruthless, sadistic, and profoundly anti-Semitic."

From this description, I'd discovered no contradictions, only consistent embellishments. For example, I'd heard that, unlike so many of the top Nazi leaders, Heydrich actually fit the "Aryan" stereotype in physical appearance: tall, blond, slender, and athletic. He was also reputed to be a gifted musician with the ability to bring rivals to tears with his cello. Aggravated since childhood by rumours that his grandmother was Jewish, Heydrich had ordered SS ancestry researchers to establish beyond contradiction that he had no Jewish forebears. He was also an intensely competitive sportsman and daring aeroplane pilot.[35]

---

[35] When Himmler's SS became independent of the SA after the purge of SA chief of staff Ernst Röhm and the top SA leadership on 30 June–2 July 1934, Heydrich took command of the Gestapo while remaining chief of the SD. Nine days after his appointment as Reichsführer-SS and chief of German Police on 17 June 1936, Himmler appointed Heydrich chief of the newly

All of this, and all the things I didn't know, was standing almost too erect before my door as I approached. I began to tremble but somehow managed to control any outward appearance of it. At least I hoped I'd done. Men like that can sense weakness like a tiger senses prey.

"You are Linge," he said.

"Yes, Herr General," I replied, desperately trying to remain calm, not exactly a recipe for success.

Without moving his head, he looked me up and down with theatrical deliberation, not unlike Katrin had done. "You appear to know who I am," he said, "even though we've never met. I now return the compliment: I've heard much about you, as you would expect."

I must confess that I was at a complete loss in dealing with such a creature. "Is this an official visit, Herr General?" was all I could say.

His lips spread slightly into a slit of a smile. "Of course not, Linge," he said. "If this were official, you would be visiting me and not the other way round. No, as deputy to Reichsführer Himmler, I considered it my duty for us to become acquainted, and to make certain that you are well and content in your situation, wouldn't you agree?"

I'd read where Napoleon once remarked that "the inevitable must be accepted and turned to advantage." Why would someone of Heydrich's stature and position visit the likes of me at my quarters as if he were room service in a grand hotel? Naturally, I didn't believe a word he said after his first sentence,

established Security Police Main Office (*Hauptamt Sicherheitspolizei*), which brought together into one agency the Gestapo and the Criminal Police detective forces.

but, possessing no alternative explanation, I let him lead, as he would have done anyway.

"Shall we go in?" he remarked with hooded eyes, a formality only. "A hallway is a poor place to do anything but gossip, yes?"

"Of course . . . Herr General," I answered, trying with desperation not to stammer. A pause can be ambiguous, but a stammer is a confession. As we entered, Heydrich peeled off his black leather gloves with agonizing slowness, laid them on top of my stack of books, eased himself down on my cot, and crossed his long, booted legs. "It seems that we are both above average height," he began. "Pity your cot cannot accommodate your full length."

He should have seen my original quarters. I was about to tell him that I sleep curled up, so there was no problem, but he continued before I had the opportunity. "I imagine that you're forced into a foetal position. Not a bad position, actually, if you're an infant or a prisoner, but for the Führer's principal valet, we must see to it that you receive a cot that provides more congenial alternatives."

I looked into his eyes, but there was nothing there—a vacuum. Then I concentrated on every line and crag of his long, expressionless face and detected not one shred of humanity. As he spoke, he studied my room with the meticulousness I always associated, through my reading, with a forensic scientist at a murder scene. He leaned over to see the spines of my books on the small night table, then righted himself.

"I see you are quite the reader, Linge, and your choice of authors is nothing short of ideologically impeccable, though, I'm afraid, terribly pedestrian: Werner Bumelburg, Hans Grimm, Agnes Miegel, Rudolf Binding, Börries von Münchhausen, and even Gottfried Benn. *Oy!* as the Jews would say. We in the

Security Service call such authors 'above the bed.' Do you know why?"

I guessed but said nothing.

"Because," he explained, "what people really read is beneath their beds, where they are presumably invisible from ordinary view. Shall I look under your bed, Linge?"

"If you wish, Herr General," I said. What choice did I have?

That malevolent crease of his lips appeared again, accompanied by an almost imperceptible shrug. "No need. I only jest. I'm certain you would be incapable of comprehending more challenging and dangerous fare, even if you possessed it. By the bye, I'm to have tea with the Führer this afternoon, along with Reichsführer Himmler, Reichsminister Goebbels, and some other dignitaries. You will be there too?"

"Herr General," I replied, "as the Führer's valet, I will be standing in the corner behind him, ready to do his merest bidding," I replied honestly. I hoped it sounded sufficiently humble as well.

Heydrich tilted his head forward in a single nod and stood, whereupon I snapped to attention. He held out a hand with fingers so elongated they appeared prehensile. "Good to finally meet you. I imagine we will be encountering each other from time to time." He replaced his gloves and moved gracefully to the door. I was about to emit a deep sigh of relief when he turned slowly toward me from the doorway.

"Incidentally," he remarked, "it's come to my attention that you have a problem with your bathroom plumbing. Of course, you would not be expected to complain, since I've heard that you are especially accommodating and modest. However, as the Reichsführer never wearies of telling us, no difficulty regarding the Führer's immediate staff is too insignificant to be remedied with dispatch and thoroughness. I trust I am not misunderstood."

My stomach heaved. First the books and now the plumbing. Would the note be next on the general's agenda? Why was he issuing an elegant warning and not conducting an inelegant interrogation? I had no answer, so I just stood there with a waterfall of sweat cascading down my back.

Then, without waiting for an answer, he merely turned and left, without a heel-clicking, arm-raised *Heil Hitler*.

Once he'd gone, despite my exploding brain, I heaved a shuddering sigh of relief, then raced into my bathroom, gulped down a handful of aspirin, reached into my tunic and retrieved the note I'd picked up from the hall floor, moved to the cot that just held Himmler's chief deputy, sat down, and read the infantile script, clearly and carefully scrawled with the opposite hand:

Heinz, Katrin is not what you might wish to think. I could tell that even you sensed this. Understandably, you are a political babe in the woods, but she and those with whom she associates are definitely not. Using the Führer, they will ultimately cause the utter destruction of the Reich. You must not seek her out, and should she seek *you* out, resist.

It was signed "A Concerned Comrade."

I disposed of the note with no comprehension of its message or knowledge of its sender but with a feeling of extreme dread in its wake.

The lunch went well, especially for the Führer, so much so that it went on long enough to replace dinner. As expected, Himmler, Heydrich, and Goebbels were there. In addition, there was von Ribbentrop and an actress I'd never heard of named Marika Rökk.[36] I assumed she was there at the invitation of Goebbels, since his wife was absent. Even though General Heydrich had been with me only a few hours before, neither he nor anyone else appeared to notice me standing in the corner at parade rest.

Initially, the Führer spent quite a long time—even for him—on the subject of education, since Goebbels had mentioned a lecture series he was sponsoring for the high schools, extolling the historic virtues of "National Socialist values." Completely ignoring Goebbels's specific topic, the Führer explained that "it's all wrong that a man's whole life should depend on a diploma that he either receives or doesn't at the age of seventeen. I was a victim of that system myself . . ."

I confess to you that I listened to the Führer's often-told story with only the smallest portion of my brain and envied myself for not having to listen with rapturous attention as did the dinner guests, save Rökk, who, from her vacant expression, had apparently also heard these same words far more than once. I was concentrating on the note I'd retrieved from the hall floor and burnt immediately after reading. But the more I considered the words, the more perplexed I became: Who was the writer? How did the writer know so much? What was the writer attempting to say? Who, in fact, was Katrin, and why was she (and her associates, whomever they were) so dangerous? Why me? Save myself from what? In what peril was the Reich? From what? What did all

---

[36] Marika Rökk's German film debut was *Leichte Kavallerie* (*Light Cavalry*) with Heinz von Cleve. The film made her a sensation overnight. It was the first of a series of modern escapist, lightweight operettas and glittering revue-style entertainments that quickly made Rökk one of Germany's most popular actresses.

this have to do with me? These questions were like darts, jabbing me from a weapon I couldn't see, and held by someone whose identity I didn't know and whose motives I couldn't penetrate.

The greater masochist in me forced my attention away to Heydrich's visit. The inevitable questions came first: Why him and not one of his legion of subordinates? I knew—or thought I knew—his purpose, but why the remark about "above-the-bed" books, and his "offer" to look under it? Or had the chief deputy of the Reich Main Security Office already looked? If he had, he would have seen works by Schopenhauer, Nietzsche, Kant, Goethe, and Schiller, among others, ironically, all lent to me by the Führer from his vast personal library. I understood a bit of each, but the entirety of none, but was beguiled by the elegant flow of words. I wondered whether the Führer understood them but would never, in a million years, dream of asking him. And one other question intruded from where I'd consigned it: Did Katrin have anything to do with the visit?

Fortunately, the Führer, always the perfect gentleman at table, appeared quite taken with Fräulein Rökk and directed many questions to her.

"Fräulein," he inquired, "I was told by Dr. Goebbels that you are Hungarian but were born in Egypt?"

Her eyes had never left the Führer, and she answered unhesitatingly. "Cairo, my Führer," she replied. "My father was an architect and contractor, so we travelled extensively."

The Führer's eyes glittered at the sound of the word *architect*, something he fancied he was as well.

"However," she went on, "I spent most of my pre-War years in Budapest and, afterward, in Paris, where I learned to dance and eventually starred with the Hoffmann Girls at the Moulin Rouge Cabaret. And after that—"

"Ah," the Führer interrupted, "you clearly are quite the woman of the world. I envy you. Perhaps, one day, I will travel to even more places, though I would hesitate to dance in cabaret."

All erupted into raucous laughter, except for Himmler, who grinned thinly, and Heydrich, whose elongated face and predatory eyes remained no less impassive than they had been in my quarters, slit smile notwithstanding.

Ever the one for seizing the moment to his own advantage, the Führer then threw down his napkin, saying: "Alas, I have many pressing duties facing me this evening and tomorrow, so I will leave you all in Dr. Goebbels's, ah, more-than-capable hands." Then he smiled, rose (as did everyone), kissed Marika Rökk's hand, whereupon salutes were given, and he walked out, with me, thankfully, close behind him.

3 October 1935

AFTER THE EVENTS of 17 September, life for me settled into a somnambulistic routine.

No surreptitiously delivered sinister notes or encounters occurred during this period. Obeying the last note's cautionary advice, I made no attempt to seek out Katrin or attempt to discover who had dropped the note. You wonder why. Perhaps it's as simple as something my old foreman at the brickyard said: "Most things come around or go away, if you just leave them alone." Perhaps it was an even simpler matter: cowardice. I prefer to think that if, as Sir Thomas More said: "I do none harm, I say none harm, I think none harm," I will be spared (even though More was not).[37]

To relieve the tedium, I made discreet attempts to become acquainted with the people "below the salt," as the Führer had called them. You may ask what the term means. I must admit that I'd never encountered it until it arose in a discussion with the Führer. While attending him, I became lost in thought but was jarred away when he said:

"Are you feeling all right, Linge?"

Even considering my seemingly unbidden lapses into unconsciousness in the Führer's presence, I began to sweat with the

---

[37] Sir Thomas More was beheaded by Royal command.

embarrassment of again being found inattentive to one who required constant attention.

"Uh . . . why . . . uh . . . nothing, my Führer," I stammered. "I can't imagine how anything . . . should anything be wrong?"

"Linge, Linge, calm yourself. The 'why' of things I leave to the so-called experts, but I pride myself on my judgment of people and situations. And I sense in you some considerable unease."

"With all that you must contend with, my Führer, I regret that your . . . judgment should be so engaged." Who was I to have problems in the presence of someone with the most exceptional responsibilities?

The Führer lowered his head for a moment in silence, then raised it slowly. "Linge, those I choose to surround me are my family. All know this. Their difficulties are my difficulties. They know this too. I am never too occupied to attend to such matters."

For some inexplicable reason, I couldn't let it go. "But, my Führer, the concerns of such as myself must be laughably trivial to someone who is responsible for—"

"Can you be truly German?" he interrupted with mock displeasure. "The English, in their poisonous snobbery, had a term for those of their household who were, by their class, unworthy even to be noticed. 'Below the salt' is what they were called."

"'Below the salt'? But what does that mean, my Führer?" Oddly, I wasn't expecting a lecture, but, considering the Führer, it was inevitable.

"Ah, Linge," he began, "your ignorance of history is shameful. 'Below the salt' or 'beneath the salt' is one of the many English phrases that refer to salt, for example, 'worth one's salt,' 'take with a grain of salt,' 'the salt of the earth,' and so forth. This is an indication of the long-standing importance given to salt in society. In mediaeval England, salt was expensive and only affordable to the higher ranks of society. Its value rested on its scarcity. Salt was extracted from seawater by evaporation and was less easily obtainable in northern Europe than in countries with warmer climates, where the evaporation could be brought about by the action of the sun rather than by boiling over a fire.

"This method was abandoned in England in the mid-1600s, when natural rock salt began to be mined commercially in Cheshire. Prior to that date, the high value of salt was the source of the high symbolic status given to it in the day-to-day language that originated from England in the Middle Ages. At that time the nobility sat at the 'high table' and their commoner servants at lower trestle tables. Salt was placed in the centre of the high table, and only those of rank had access to it. Those less favoured on the lower tables were below (or beneath) the salt. Now you know. Is this how you truly see yourself?"

I decided to be truthful, though not necessarily accurate. "My Führer, I possess no reliable picture of myself in my current circumstances." I didn't tell him that when I was an apprentice bricklayer, my foreman remarked that he found it difficult to be, what I interpreted from his horribly ungrammatical German, neither fish nor fowl; that the men above him considered him a labourer, and the ones below thought of him as a boss. The fish and fowl remark dated from the sixteenth century. So much for my "shameful" lack of historical knowledge. But at least I'd kept my intended intellectual innocence intact.

"As my principal valet," he continued, "you inhabit both the world above *and* the world below. I appreciate that this can be a perplexing position, but hardly one worthy of anxiety. Before long, those above will seek you out for information about which they would be too timid or uncertain to ask me, and those below will come to appreciate your modesty, humility, and good nature and also seek you out. Mark my words, Linge, you will be quite the popular fellow."

As with most of what the Führer said, I took his prophesy with all seriousness and, as a consequence, became even more apprehensive. I craved invisibility and the Führer promised popularity—a tightrope from which I was certain I would plummet.

⬧

After seeing to the Führer's quotidian needs, I attempted to visit one of the new Chancellery secretaries whom I'd passed often in the hall to a wave and a smile and had stood by as she occasionally took dictation from the Führer when the "Wicked Witch of the West"[38] or the other more-seasoned secretaries were otherwise engaged or ill. Her name is Gerda Daranowski and nicknamed "Dara." She is a young Berliner, not only very capable but rather attractive in an irregular sort of way, and always good-humoured.

According to Brückner, no mean judge of pulchritude, "Dara knows how to give her face just the right look to excite a man." Even the Führer expressed delight in her skill with cosmetics and would pay her the most unfettered compliments, though he never discussed her skill with a pencil. I was not as excited by her beauty *or* stenographic attainments as I was by her apparent friendliness and inoffensive humour, qualities, on the whole, I found woefully absent in typical SS and SA functionaries, regardless of sex.

So, today, before most out-of-Chancellery personnel would have arrived, and well before the Führer would summon me, I positioned myself behind one of the enormous columns lining the Grand Hallway in hopes that she would come my way and

---

[38] The malign crone in L. Frank Baum's *The Wonderful Wizard of Oz.*

I could "accidentally" bump in to her, thus having a pretext for conversation. However, as with most "best laid schemes of mice and men," this one went "awry,"[39] for as I stood there craning my neck around the column, I heard a gentle voice behind me, say: "Herr Linge, are you hiding from someone?" I turned round so quickly that I must have startled her, since she jerked back a pace or two and put her hand to her face.

"I . . . I'm sorry if I alarmed you," I stuttered feebly. "I wasn't hiding, I was, uh, waiting."

She closed one blue eye and raised the other. For a split second I thought she was imitating Popeye of the cartoon. "But wouldn't it be more seemly," she replied, "not to say more efficient, if you waited in plain sight?"

I scraped my brain for an excuse that wouldn't strain her credulity. "I totally agree," I finally said, "but you see, Fräulein . . . Daranowski, I wished to meet this particular person without necessarily meeting anyone else."

She nodded as if my excuse had worked, but her intelligent eyes told a different story. She was no great beauty like Katrin, but she had a kind and generous face, one that would only lie if the truth might hurt. "Please call me Dara," she entreated. "All my friends do. Well, then," she said, in the absence of my reply, "I'll let you get on with your . . . strategy, and wish it success."

Believing her response to be indicative of a tongue in cheek, I smiled at her wit and took a chance. "Actually, it *was* successful," I told her, and then she smiled broadly.

---

[39] "The best laid schemes of mice and men / Often go awry" is a shortened form of Scots, "The best laid schemes o' Mice an' Men, / Gang aft agley," from "To a Mouse, on Turning Her up in Her Nest with the Plough" by Robert Burns. Scots is the Germanic language variety spoken in lowland Scotland.

"This is rather like a scene from one of those British drawing-room comedies, isn't it?" she said.

Of course it was. "I'm just pleased that we did finally meet."

Her entire face brightened. "Yes, I'm pleased too. I've heard such good things from my Erich, that I even asked him to arrange a foursome so we could get acquainted."

"Your Erich?"

"Yes, Erich Kempka, you know, one of the Führer's chauffeurs. My fiancée."

My gut experienced a massive chill of disappointment. I'd had no opportunity to develop a romantic interest even if I wanted to, but I was disappointed all the same, for reasons I didn't even know. "Kempka!" I exclaimed. "I see him all the time, and he never told me. I must congratulate him at my first opportunity."

"I'm seeing him tonight and I'll tell him we finally met, that is, providing the Führer doesn't capture him first. He makes quite a formidable rival for Erich's attentions."

I wanted to escape as quickly as I could, so I merely said, "For mine too. In any event, I hope that we can all get together sometime, away from this exalted anthill."

She placed her gloved hand on my arm. "Yes, I hope so too." Then she turned and went back in the direction from which she must have come. After she left, I wondered, even in my misery, how she had arrived ahead of me, and why.

⁓

On the way back to my quarters, I encountered Brückner, who guided me to the gardens and told me that the Führer would be occupied most of the day and evening, working with his secretaries to draft a reply to Mussolini's invasion of Abyssinia.

I'd heard nothing of this until now, nor did I have any idea about or, frankly, any interest in Italy's relations with Abyssinia, wherever that was, since it had little if anything to do with tying the Führer's bow tie or preparing him for his bath. Since I said nothing, Brückner began to regale me with a pedantic spewing of what he called "background." I cut him off before he could continue.

"Wilhelm, it's certainly not that I'm in the least disinterested," I lied blatantly, "but is there any reason why the Führer's valet needs to be briefed about this matter? I'm hardly his adviser."

"Heinz, Heinz," he replied with a mock *tsk-tsk* in his tone, "you must promise me never to lose that wonderfully dry sense of humour. Now, about Abyssinia, yes?" and without waiting for my obvious permission, he said: "Now there are some things you must understand. On the sixth of August in 1928, Italy and Abyssinia signed the Italo–Abyssinian Treaty of Friendship."

At that point, I'd stopped listening. I didn't mind the Führer lecturing me on a variety of subjects about which I knew nothing and had even less interest, because I knew he was off in a world all his own, and didn't care who was in the room when he decided to play schoolmaster, but Brückner was another animal altogether. He'd test me, and I'd had enough of school even before I reached puberty and, so, would abide no more. In actual fact, Brückner, while beside me physically, was not beside me in my mind. Dara was. I was struggling to find flaws in her to justify my brutal disappointment in her utterly misguided interest in that covetous mouse with a steering wheel.

"All good so far, yes? But the matter goes deeper."

To hell with "deeper," I thought guiltily, for I truly liked Brückner. But at this moment, he was insufferable, so I forced my thoughts away. If not a dalliance with Dara, then who? I'm a red-blooded twenty-two-year-old male in good health. However, being on call in a cloistered gossip factory and needing to guard my privacy have, thus far, caused me to be lacking in female companionship. The Führer has several secretaries, there are innumerable housekeepers, and the kitchens are full to bursting with females. I feel now that I must take a chance and get among their circle—but without appearing desperate, of course, since the sort of female who'd respond favourably to a desperate male is certainly not anyone I'd desire.

"From our sources," Brückner was prattling on, "we learned that in private, however, Mussolini was disdainful of the Führer and the Party—even from the beginning. He actually described him as boring, and *Mein Kampf* as 'even more boring,' and thought his ideas and theories 'coarse' and 'simplistic.'"

Out of the corner of my eye, I spotted a cluster of SS uniforms about to pass us. I spotted Hans Baur, the Führer's personal pilot, among them. Baur had been with the Führer well before the latter had assumed supreme power. I'd met Baur several times and found him to be even more affable than Kempka and, since he had Hitler's willing ear on every flight, was far less self-consciously needy and ambitious. I considered whether I should approach him later and see if he could find me suitable female company.

"Another important point of difference between the two," Brückner went on, "is their racial views. Mussolini was always scornful of the Führer's writings and speeches about Aryan supremacy. A strutting, arrogant pig, Il Duce, but he could be vital to the Reich. The Führer realizes that . . ."

As he spoke, reality shifted again—this time in broad daylight. The straight lines of the building corners and railings, curved and then dissolved, but I said nothing. I began to panic but managed to hold on by staring at the ground as if in deep concentration on Brückner's blathering. I've had to utilize the technique many times, and it's never failed me. Then, without warning, the original contours returned as they had before, though I wondered whether I would finally end up imprisoned in a world with vague shapeless masses and shadows forever.

"And today," he concluded, "this same Mussolini invades Abyssinia. You see, Heinz, the . . . delicate position in which he has placed the Führer."

I didn't see at all but didn't share this with Brückner. Instead, I said, "To the extent I understand the situation, which is an unschooled valet's groping, it does seem rather awkward."

"At the very least," he replied, with a mirthless chuckle, a tilt of his head, and a shrug, "but just so you have the general outline, should the Führer bring it up."

I had the general outline, and I doubted that the Führer would bring it up, but I only cared about how I would find someone to erase Dara from my consciousness. "I truly appreciate this briefing," I told Brückner, "and I'll keep it well in mind, should the Führer decide to involve me in some way," *even though thoroughly absurd,* I told myself.

Just then, I saw Kempka heading into the Chancellery from the garage and I suffered a caustic, stomach-churning envy. It was entirely irrational and ungenerous, since we were never really in competition for Dara's attentions.

"You should probably check in with the Führer," Brückner concluded. "You won't be disturbing him in the slightest, and he might welcome a break from his ruminations." Without waiting for an answer, he saluted (which I returned in perfect, plain-sight style), turned, and left for the Führer's quarters.

As had become the custom, when I arrived at his door with his newspapers and mail, I knocked once and entered without waiting for a reply. As usual, the room was enveloped in darkness, save for the desk-lamp glow and a sliver of light from minutely parted drapes. He was not alone, for in one armchair sat von Neurath, and in another, von Ribbentrop. The Führer was standing, fists dug into his hips, his face a study in barely controlled rage. Von Neurath's face was parallel to his lap, and von Ribbentrop's face was aimed squarely at the Führer's, a study in relationships.

With these three, this was not an unusual tableau, and for that, I repeated my almost comic personal routine, beginning with the re-re-arrangement of books on the Führer's shelves that I'd already rearranged, in the certain knowledge that his guests would completely ignore me, and so not wonder how I could perform such a visual task with hardly any light. Once I'd begun my charade, the talking resumed.

"So, Neurath," the Führer began, "do you still clutch onto your position that I should do nothing? You needn't feel obliged to look at me when you answer," he japed—maliciously (I thought).

Out of the corner of my eye, I could see von Neurath slowly lift his magisterial head. "If, my Führer, you mean that I still feel that it is none of Germany's business to meddle in a foolish war between a buffoon and a cartoon, then, yes, I . . . grasp onto that position. And especially so when they are performing this ridiculousness in full view of the League of Nations."

Von Neurath went on, but for me, having no particular interest or opinion on the matter, I was concentrating on whether to seek out the company of Johanna Wolf, another of the Führer's secretaries. From what I could gather from the side lines, she was friendlier than Schroeder, but not as much so as Dara. Unfortunately, like the housekeeper Greta, she was unconscionably homely and thirteen years my senior. I was about to turn my attention to the maids and kitchen staff, when I was startled by a loud hand clap. It was the Führer.

"*YES!*" he shouted. "You see, Neurath? Do you? While I sometimes admire your patrician principles, perfectly calibrated for another century, I cannot abide your obstinate adherence to outdated notions that are no longer of any value. You, I'm afraid, are utterly lacking in imagination and perspective. You see an incident; I see an opportunity. Ribbentrop captured the situation perfectly, since he, no less than I, appreciates the unorthodox approach, audacity, the long view."

Von Ribbentrop's expression remained impassive, since a smile of triumph would have been needlessly unseemly, even for him. I wasn't surprised by this, for as I've said, von Ribbentrop was a master at serving a man who makes irrevocable decisions first and asks for advice afterwards. I could learn much from such a splendidly vile parasite.

Von Neurath then stood up slowly and with theatrical precision, his eyelids at half-mast, and said, "My Führer, now that you have made your decision, is there anything further that you require of me?"

The Führer crossed his arms. "No," he said icily, "our meeting is done."

At that, von Ribbentrop also rose from his chair and both saluted, turned, and left the room.

"My Führer," I said, "is there anything I can do for you?"

He laughed. "Not yet, Linge. I'll be fine until you prepare me for dinner—I don't mean as the entrée—as Neurath would like," he joked. "By the bye, Goebbels is screening *Anna Karenina* after dinner. It takes place in Russia, of all places, but you might want to see it. I've heard some good things."

Not being a stranger to irony, all I could say was: "Thank you, my Führer. I'm certain it will be most entertaining."

AGAIN, ANOTHER STRANGE and sinister day ends; but this one deviated from the rest—for a year ended as well, and for me, almost a year since I first spoke to you as a freshly minted valet. I refuse to burden you with a summary, for you've accompanied me all along my seemingly formless and spectral journey. Of course, saying this, I am assuming that a journey is, in fact, what I am on, with an actual destination to be reached at the end. And yet, I cannot be certain of this, or of anything else, for that matter. And, despite this apparent formlessness, I cannot escape the sensation that I'm being manipulated to follow someone's well-thought-out plan, not against my will, but utterly unknowing of it.

Today was marked by unbounded celebration. The first festivity was an intimate one in the banquet room, held by the Führer for his inner circle (Goebbels, Göring, Himmler, Hess, Canaris, von Ribbentrop, Brückner—and me, of course). I made a mental note that von Neurath was not present. What it meant, I didn't know, but I could guess. After the Führer thanked the assembled for their "energy, loyalty, dedication, and enthusiasm" in helping to make his genius manifest, most of the vocal air was sucked from the room by Goebbels, who proposed so many long-winded toasts that I was amazed that anyone, save the Führer and I (who didn't drink), could stand erect by the end. Naturally, one of the longest toasts was to the Führer for his "magisterial vision and sublime mastery of events," by which he meant rearmament, conscription, autobahn construction progress, and support of Mussolini in the conflict with Abyssinia. The second longest was directed at Himmler for his recently established Lebensborn program.[40] Himmler, for his part, accepted the toast and the accompanying applause with his usual expressionless aplomb, merely thanking Goebbels and the Führer for their support, and promising to raise, "for the Reich and for mankind, untold new generations of Aryan perfection."

Then the Führer announced that he had to attend to other celebrants, namely, the secretaries, housekeeping, and kitchen staff, and finally, the enormous mass of general Chancellery personnel and other lesser officials. But before we left, he promised that 1936 would be a "year to remember," that he would personally make it so, and that "generations to come will mark it as the critical turning point in my creation of a Thousand-Year Reich." Again, my head was splitting open with pain, but I suppressed my craving to claim illness and race back to my quarters, for this was a heaven-sent opportunity to begin the process of finally securing the female companionship that had eluded me so far.

Unsurprisingly, when we arrived at the "Staircase Room,"[41]

---

[40] Lebensborn e.V. (literally: Fount of Life) was established by Himmler and run by the SS to raise the birth rate of "Aryan" children from extramarital relations of "racially pure and healthy" parents on the basis of Nazi racial hygiene and health ideology. Lebensborn aimed to do this by encouraging anonymous births and mediating adoption to likewise "racially pure and healthy" parents, particularly families of SS members.

[41] Directly opposite the door of Hitler's study, a few steps led to a long passage with the rooms of his entourage opening off it. The first room, at the foot of some steps, was called the "Staircase Room." It was a sitting room

the Führer was greeted with salutes, cheers, and applause. For a fleeting moment, I wondered what it would be like to receive such complete, heartfelt adoration but quickly dismissed the insane notion. The Führer gave the same speech he'd made earlier, made the same promise, kissed the hands of the ladies, shook the hands of the gentlemen, made his apologies for needing to attend the largest gathering, graciously accepted further salutes and applause, and left—with me trailing behind. Not once, during the ceremony—for that's what it was—could I detect any eyes aimed in my direction. I'd hoped to make some kind of social contact with the females, but I hadn't anticipated the formality and swiftness of the event. My head was being crushed in a vice, I could hardly breathe, and no one gave a bloody damn.

I was also struggling to avoid, or at least delay, the hallucinations that invariably accompany my headaches by disappearing into the most populated and, I imagined correctly, the most raucous gathering. When we entered the main reception room, there was a virtual explosion of salutes, heel-clicking, and hand clapping, and a stunning array of uniforms and party dresses, not to mention a mammoth quantity of food and drink. *Maybe, just maybe,* I thought.

I despaired when the Führer made the same speech he'd delivered twice before (how he could stand to do it three times with equal conviction was a marvel), for I could easily picture a scene not dissimilar to the one in the staircase room, just noisier. But this time, as soon as he finished and the expected thunderous response had subsided, he turned his head to me and whispered, "Linge, you've had to endure my speech three times. It's only right that *you* celebrate the year we've shared. I can see myself

---

for the secretaries, the adjutants' waiting-room, and was sometimes used as a bedroom by some unexpected visitor.

out and Brückner or Krause can attend me. Stay and enjoy the sense of freedom that inevitably follows my departures."

Then he said farewell to all and walked out to a stunned hush of astonishment, followed moments later by an uncontrolled cacophony of singing, shouting, dancing, cross talking, food gorging, and liquor swilling. It was a Teutonic interpretation of what I'd seen referred to in literature as a *bacchanalia*. When I was laying bricks, my "colleagues," at the end of our shift, would all repair to the local beer hall and spend the entire night slopping lager, shouting, and roughhousing, before stumbling home to beat their wives and children, fall into a drunken stupor, and work like horses the next day as if they'd just come from a spa. I never joined them, and I didn't intend to now.

A perfect time to insinuate myself into the narrow female enclave of the Chancellery was spoiled by the hammering in my head. Defeated by my own body, I was about to make a stealthy and rapid exit, when a hand slammed my shoulder and a voice shouted: "*Linge! Can this be my good friend, Linge!* No," Kempka said, clearly on the way to stumbling drunkenness. "My good friend Linge would have sought me out and personally wished me a happy new year—and then seen to it that I would have one."

Clearly, the dwarf wasn't that drunk yet. I turned to face him and ended up facing him and Dara. Seen in the coarse light of their relationship, I wondered why I'd been obsessed with her. Katrin made her appear no more glamourous than a medieval etching of a peasant drudge. To her, I raised a stiffened hand to my cap, said, "Happy New Year," and when she sweetly and humorously returned the salutation, I turned to little Kempka. "You do me wrong, Erich. I certainly wish you—and Dara—the very best of the new year. I'm feeling poorly and feared that I would certainly not add more merriment to the festivities."

Kempka pursed his lips in mock disappointment. "I'm truly sorry to hear that, Linge. To miss such a chance to escape the pose we have to assume with the Führer and his high-powered cronies. But I get it, I get it. Don't you get it, Dara?"

"Of course, Erich, I do . . . get it," she said, clearly uncomfortable, then turned her head to me. "I'm just sorry you aren't feeling well on such a happy occasion."

"I know you do," I replied, "and I thank you for it. And, as for you, Erich, I haven't forgotten our conversation. As the Führer said, next year will be only the beginning for the Reich—and for you, as well, I think." I winked. My head was on fire, the revelry was deafening, Kempka was with Dara, I had to escape!

"Well, that *is* good tidings," he said with a mischievous smirk. "But maybe none of that is necessary, since I decided to take your sage advice about resolving the Schreck matter, so as to insure a splendid year." Then he turned to Dara: "We should allow poor Linge, here, to go and recuperate, don't you think?"

"Of course we should," she said with that solicitous, Florence Nightingale-like concern that had originally flung me into the abyss of desire. Even though I'd suddenly lost interest, I wanted to damage her, yet she'd done nothing, and I experienced a guilt that stood on a false foundation. Regardless, I never understood the nature of women, and I feared I never would. And what was my "sage advice" he was going to take?

However, the next few minutes I find almost impossible to fully capture, but I'll try now. While Kempka and Dara were speaking to my physical body, my brain had conjured another me, to my senses, no less corporeal, wedged into the sweating, cacophonous festivities surrounding me, and I could see myself, as if viewing a stranger from a distance, oozing through the mob. The din had become a vague, echoing hum, the individual bodies of the throng had lost all definition and morphed into inchoate shadows that coalesced into a dark, shapeless, viscous mass.

I shook my head to clear it, but failed. I had to get out, so again, I bade Kempka and Dara a feigned friendly farewell, and they obligingly moved away toward the revellers. Suddenly, from the side, a long, pale female hand slipped something into my outside jacket pocket. I thought at that moment that she must have been somewhat tipsy or she wouldn't have dared. I didn't recognize her and assumed that she must have been a guest of one of the invitees. I had no idea, but in a fraction of an instant, the hammering in my brain vanished, along with any further thoughts of Dara. I assumed that she was a part of my hallucination, and I was being pulled into it.

"If you're leaving," she purred, "I won't keep you. But I do hope you're not."

Hallucination or no, I was not leaving—anymore. I was transfixed, and she knew it, for even as young as I was, I knew that women like that know from birth that they're women like that. Not all men recognize this truth, and it inevitably dooms them. Literature made this quite clear to me. From her long veil of red hair framing deep, luminescent green eyes, precipitous cheekbones, perfect nose, and full, barely painted lips, down her tall, sylphlike body, encased in a skin-tight green silk gown, to the pointed toes of her satin pumps, she was far beyond what I'd ever imagined as seductive. Dumbfounded and desperate, I decided to attempt a cynical version of the truth, for what it would be worth, and be done with it.

"I'm merely a valet," I told her. "You've undoubtedly mistaken me for someone of stature."

"I seldom make mistakes," she replied, with a sly suggestion of a smile. "And you're not 'merely a valet.' You're the Führer's valet. I know more about you than you think."

Of that I had no doubt, and it disquieted me, as I imagined it was meant to do, and so I risked disquieting her. "I'm both honoured and gratified that, to you, my status is as exalted as my life appears to be transparent."

I could see by her perfect face that she was not in the least taken aback by irony or erudition, and that disturbed me more than the mysteriousness of her interest in me. I was more concerned that she might not even be real, just one more hallucination among the uncountable ones I've had over the years since that night of horror of which I do not speak, even to you. In any event, for habit and my own safety's sake, rather than from mere curiosity, I decided to emphasize the gull over the prodigy, and see how that would fare.

"May I ask how you happened to be here tonight?" I inquired, if only to get her talking. There's just so much someone can glean from a few cryptic remarks.

"I say," she deflected deftly, with just the right trace of concern. "Are you feeling all right? Are you ill?"

"N . . . no," I lied. "I'm fine. I'm merely tired. A long day, you know. And all this noise and so many people."

She pointed to her ear with a long, perfectly manicured green fingernail. "Yes, it is rather like the orgiastically inebriated spectator section at a British football match. Perhaps we could go somewhere a bit more sedate . . . and more private?"

Unlike my encounter with Katrin, where I'd had some time to prepare, I had no response to her dazzling display of suggestive cultivation, but who cared what I said if it were truly a hallucination? But I responded, nevertheless. "You'll receive no argument from me there," I replied. For a cheap laugh, I would have suggested my quarters, and then, recalling Heydrich's "casual visit," laughter took on additional value.

"You find something amusing?" she said, her arched carmine eyebrows raised slightly.

"No . . . P . . . please," I stammered, "I was just reminded of something. I meant no disrespect."

"Nothing was interpreted as such," she replied. "But the fact remains: where shall we go?"

I considered the matter with that small portion of my brain that was able to ignore the splendid phantom before me. "Ah, the gardens, perhaps," I finally ventured. "The snow has been cleared from the walkway after the storm." That had to be real, I told myself, remembering all the effort I'd seen expended in making it so. Then I considered that it would be freezing there and she had no wrap. "But it—"

"I'll be fine," she said, anticipating my concern. No reality there, I convinced myself. On our way, she would have had to show her papers at least three times, and she didn't even have a handbag, but, since she was with me, and all the sentries knew who I was, we passed all the checkpoints without incident. "You see?" she remarked, once we were outside and she appeared not the least bit uncomfortable from the cold. "You are no 'merely.' In fact, far from it, wouldn't you say?"

"I hate to disabuse you," I replied, "but what we experienced was familiarity, not status."

She stopped me and we stood against the waist-high wall along the terrace winding along a serpentine walkway down to the once-spectacular Chancellery gardens, now a thick blanket of snow and ice. The air was cold, but she didn't appear to care about the temperature. "Before we left," I ventured again, "I'd asked how you came to be here tonight. Was that presumptuous of me?"

"Not at all," she replied. "It was perfectly natural, since I don't work here. Though might it have been even more natural for you to have asked me my name first? Not terribly imaginative, I'm afraid. My name is Emerald, and I came as the guest of General Weisthor."

"Of course you are," I jested. She was right, of course; I should have asked her name, but I'd been far too flustered to think in a straight line. I imagined she knew that. As practised as I was in the art of innocence, I felt my control could easily slip with her, and I imagined she knew that too. As a consequence, I resolved to speak as little as possible and get her to do more than ask questions and issue clever, cryptic quips. "General Weisthor," I replied, with my index finger pressing my lower lip. "The name isn't familiar. What branch of the military does he belong to?"

She smiled. "He's not in the military, per se."

I was struck with unease. A part of me needed to pursue the matter, but I was dumbstruck.

"He maintains an office in Reichsführer Himmler's headquarters."

My blood turned to powder. Himmler again. Did she know Katrin? Did she know Heydrich? What was Himmler's interest in me, and why? Did the Führer know?

She must have sensed at least some of my unasked questions, for she said, "Herr Linge, you needn't be alarmed. I'm not with the police—and neither is Weisthor. He heads Section VII, Archives. He only investigates paper, and only certain kinds of that. By your uniform, you too are SS, and yet, how many enemies of the Reich have you encountered, interrogated, and eliminated in the course of your duties?"

As she smiled, her perfect face opened up. No one like her could ever hold a sensible conversation with any male still breathing.

"And in any event," she continued, "he didn't accompany me here. He is an extraordinarily private person and so shuns gatherings. He graciously gave me his invitation so I wouldn't be bound by his predilections."

Innocence, always innocence. I squinted. "Predilections?"

Her lips formed a pout. "My apologies. I'd forgotten that you lack formal education. I meant a predisposition, an idiosyncrasy, if you will."

She said it with such sincerity, I almost ignored how she would know such a thing about me. What more did she know? What more *was* there to know? "Shall we walk?" I asked. "You may be part polar bear, but I'm freezing."

"Oh, my apologies. I'm never cold, and I always assume everyone feels as I do. A very self-centred attitude, I'm afraid. Yes, of course, let's walk."

Remaining on the terrace, we circled the ice that covered much of the gardens. "Inside," I said, "you mentioned that you knew much about me. Flattering, even though coming from someone from the Archives Section of the RSHA."

"But I'm not a member of the SS. I'm not even a Party member. I'm a political innocent for all that. Weisthor gives me the odd job, just to keep me close."

I recalled Katrin's "job description" and wondered how many of these stunning odd-jobbers haunted the ministry halls. More mystery, to be sure, but this one was somehow even more so, and it gave me a bone-cracking chill, far colder than the outside air. "The general is no fool," I replied, with a touch of forced jocularity.

"No," she said expressionlessly, "that he is not. You've been with the Führer almost a year, yes?"

Careful, Heinz! "Yes, but why did you seek me out?" I asked, wary of any answer she might give.

"Would my being bored and you being alone do?"

When I didn't respond, she said: "No, I didn't think it would. Not with you. I wasn't bored. I'm never bored. But I'm always curious. Better?"

"Curiosity? Much better," I said, once committed, "but what about?"

Her full lips curled up at the edges provocatively. "You," she said, "the sort of knowledge that goes beyond dossiers, gossip, and a superficial chat on a balcony. But for later, I think."

I also ached to know more about *her*. "But one can know too much, yes?" I said. "And then boredom sets in."

"Not to worry," she assured me. "I told you I'm never bored. But realize, Heinz, that you need to understand, truly understand, that being more important than you think is not nearly as important as being more important than you know. So, you need to know—before it's too late. Now, shall we go back in? I've kept you in the cold far too long, I fear."

"Of course," I said, reluctantly, without a thought of the ambiguities in her mystifying remark, and guided her back to the thunderously boisterous celebration that hadn't shown any sign of lessening. Back in the brightly lit room, she was even more dazzlingly alluring, and I hoped that what I thought she'd said was merely a part of my hallucination, because I'd understood none of it. "So, I am to see you again," I managed to say—at that moment, more from pure lust than from inquisitiveness.

"Of course," she said, with what I thought was a touch of theatrical surprise. "I most certainly wish to continue what we've begun. Until then," she said, "though it's rather early in the day, I would ask you to read *Julius Caesar*." Then she placed her hand on the edge of my sleeve, slid it down to my hand, grasped it, pressed gently, smiled, turned, and melted into the crowd.

Praying she'd been real, and that I'd see her again, I raced from the room, my headache having returned with a ferocious resolve.

Now, I sit here with you, considering what she'd said about limbo. You derive a unique perspective from limbo, I should have told her, but didn't, since I didn't know what that perspective was. I thought of the Führer, and it reminded me of the time I'd read Tolstoy's memoirs, in which he claimed that in his last years, he felt as Jesus must have felt—that a human being, surrounded by worshippers, can never permit himself to forget his humanity. In fact, he must keep his sense of humanity at all costs, else he becomes one of the worshippers himself. Tolstoy believed that the only real purity is to truly know and be oneself but also it is the most difficult thing to realize and maintain. Yes, the Führer. I considered how impossible it is to be one's true human self in a place like the Chancellery; how easily one's actual purity—if ever it existed—can be lost—or transformed—into a burlesque of purity.

"Happy New Year," I said aloud to my bleak cell, in the absolute certainty of it being overheard. Burlesque, indeed.

1936

ANOTHER BRAIN-CLEAVING HEADACHE and a dark foreboding. Not liquor, but a far too large dose of the night before. I had read that "men are not prisoners of fate but only prisoners of their own minds," but what control over my own mind did I truly have? I woke up from my nightmare, longing for the simplicity of bricks and mortar—and those uncomplicated hard-asses who wielded them. Too late, I feared. You can never truly go back, because even if time could be reversed, you're no longer the same as you were. Yes, far too late.

When I arrived at the Führer's quarters for the late-morning preparation, he was in the lavatory, moaning savagely, with a particularly horrific case of constipation and gastritis. I instantaneously shifted into open-mouth breathing but even that couldn't prevent some of the ungodly stench from invading my senses. He was being attended by Dr. Bloch. What remedies beyond a military-grade enema he was providing, I knew not, but they—and he—appeared to be impotent in the face of the pain and the reek. The fermentation of a rotting corpse in summer swelter would have been preferable.

I laid the mail and newspapers that Brückner had given me on the desk and stood as far away from the odious wafting as I could, until the heavenly sound of shit plummeting into the toilet gave me hope of an end to the torture for us all. I felt bad for the Führer, but that was, according to Dr. Bloch, the price of his history and his diet. My price was mouth breathing, intermittent nausea, having to shower twice after meeting with the Führer on days like these, and changing my uniform twice to rid myself of the olfactory memory and be presentable to others. Even so, everyone I encountered knew where I'd been.

While I waited, Brückner entered, instantly understood why I was standing in the farthest corner of the room, and, nose pinched tightly between thumb and forefinger, came quickly over to me.

"The new year begins," he mumbled, with no trace of irony in his voice. It was difficult to speak with your nose clamped.

I merely shrugged and squeezed my eyes shut.

"Poor Heinz," he went on, "I should have warned you from the beginning that the Führer is the victim of uncontrollable and skin-flaying flatulence. You've no idea how many times I have had to calm a foreign diplomat or even head of state after enduring a gas attack, which the Führer claims to me jokingly is no worse than the sort he suffered during the Great War. 'If I can withstand it,' he would say, 'they can.'"

However, gas attacks were not the only problem for me. At least the others didn't have to accompany the Führer as he gazed into the bowl to examine his faeces and administered chamomile enemas himself. Masochist that I must be, and to speed the process, I even offered to perform the stomach-churning "ceremony" when he'd suffered a cramp in his arm, but he wouldn't permit me to touch him. He would say that agony only made him stronger.

"It's that damn vegetarianism of his," Brückner whispered. "The Führer decided to swear off meat completely in 1931, when his niece, Geli Raubal, committed suicide. When presented with a plate of breakfast ham the next morning, he pushed it away muttering, 'It's like eating a corpse.' And, Heinz," Brückner warned me, "never mention that name to anyone, especially to the Führer. In any event, from that squeamish moment on, great piles of vegetables, raw or pulped into a baby mulch, have been his daily staple, since he claimed that all cooked foods were carcinogenic." Brückner lifted his arms resignedly. "The Boss was utterly unfazed by the fact that this roughage was having the opposite effect on his digestion than he had intended, but there you are."

I had never heard of Raubal before, and so I tucked the name into a cramped crevice in my brain for later consideration, for at the moment my only interest, perhaps even obsession, was learning more about Katrin and Emerald and seeing them again. As a consequence, waiting for Dr. Bloch to finish his disgusting task and then preparing the Führer were just distracting necessities, best performed quickly and done with, until the next episode.

All Emerald had told me was that she wasn't a member of the SS or even of the Party. "I'm a political innocent for all that," she'd added, which I did not believe for one second. She might be many things, but innocent was not one of them. "Weisthor gives me odd jobs," she claimed, "just to keep me close." That I did believe, and I couldn't blame him, but just who was this Weisthor? What did he have to do with the SS? Katrin did "odd jobs" too. Who the hell were these "odd-jobbers"? How many of them were there? What exactly were these "odd jobs"?

" . . . but my guess is that the Führer wishes us now to share a responsibility," Brückner was saying, just as a loud, shuddering moan issued from the bathroom, and a few moments later, the Führer emerged, dressed loosely in a bathrobe (with a sizeable gap displaying his entire frontal anatomy), backless leather bedroom slippers slapping against his heels as he moved, his face ashen, his hands trembling.

Once near us, he began gesticulating wildly, screaming. *"IT'S THAT FUCKING NEURATH AGAIN! HE CAUSED THIS, GODDAMN HIM!"*

At that, Brückner raced over and moved his face within an inch of the Führer's, saying, "My Führer, please listen. The arrogant swine is not worth a moment of your time, much less your health. Please let me handle this."

After a pregnant pause and total silence, the Führer shook his head, as if to clear it, then grasped Brückner by the shoulders. "Yes, Brückner, well done. You handle this. I don't wish to see him again. He meets with you or no one, am I clear?"

"Yes, my Führer," Brückner replied, "perfectly clear. You won't see him until you wish to."

The Führer then released his grip and began pacing, as I'd seen him do so often when his thoughts were solidified but he still wished to consider his words.

"That fatuous bastard actually had the temerity to scold me—*ME!*—for ignoring the actions of those two weak sisters.[42] Calmly, I informed the 'esteemed diplomat' that, according to von Ribbentrop, in Britain, public opinion against my methods and attitude toward the Jews had recently subsided, and there had been a swing toward some sympathy for our ignominious treatment at Versailles. I also told him that the only thing the English cared about was their London, and the French, their precious Paris, and if I had the means to eradicate both cities, the Reich would have ports from the English Channel to the

---

[42] Britain and France. Great Britain had announced an increase in armaments, and the French increased conscripted military service from one to two years because of a shortage of young men of draft age.

Atlantic Ocean. But, of course, that reactionary fucking prig Neurath . . ."

I was straining to concentrate, but failing, because, at the moment, I was suddenly more concerned about the piece of paper that had been placed in the pocket of the jacket I'd worn during the New Year's Eve celebration. Thus far, I'd been too afraid to check, so it might or might not be there. Anyone could have entered my room and seen it. Of course. If it was real and accessible, who put it there and what did it say? If not, how might I continue to function in reality, half in and half out (and, more important: how would I be able to know which is which at a critical moment)?

"Linge." A voice nudged in from the void. It was the Führer's.

"You as much as I," he said, his voice clearly weak from his recent ordeal and more recent screaming, "know the extent of mail I receive each day. Most of it comprises passionate love notes from adoring females and hero-worshipping letters from venerating males—all to be expected, of course. But some, unfortunately, are less-than-complimentary scribbles from those who would obstruct, if not destroy, what I am striving to accomplish—Jews, Communists, political rivals, homosexuals, mental defectives, and the like. I also get innumerable packages, most bearing gifts, but a few containing items somewhat more lethal. Regardless, all mail must be inspected, and only the safest, most immediate, relevant, and important can reach my desk, the rest, taken care of in ways appropriate to the material. Up to now, this daunting task has fallen primarily on poor Brückner, here, but now, I wish for you to divide the labour between the two of you so as to free him for other duties. Brückner will instruct you in his sorting technique."

I was dumbstruck. How could the Führer feel I would do

justice to such a complex and subtle use of personal judgment? It would also make me privy to things I wished not to know—for my own safety's sake. "But, my Führer, I—"

The Führer laughed loudly, bringing some colour back to his cheeks. "*I KNEW IT!*" he shouted at Brückner. "Did I not tell you that Linge would try to hide from responsibility with his usual humility? I keep telling him that I am no mean evaluator of one's abilities, but Linge refuses to take me seriously. How can we convince him of my goodwill and even better judgment?"

Brückner shrugged. "He is very young, my Führer," he said. "And not used to such great responsibilities. Time and experience will rid him out of his modesty, don't you agree?"

I wanted to appeal to Brückner's sense of proportion, or just plain sense, but I could see that the decision had been made, and with the Führer, the matter was closed. "Whatever you command, my Führer," I replied. "I'll do my best to be worthy of your trust."

The Führer shook his head slowly. "Not trust, Linge. That, I take for granted. It's instinct. You can begin today, eh, Brückner?"

"Of course, my Führer," he replied, then turned to me. "I'll be by this afternoon for your . . . tutorial," he informed me, turned back, saluted the Führer, and left.

"Brückner's a good man," the Führer said when the door had closed behind him, "and is well liked. That's important. Not just in a leader—but also in his valet, for you too, I'm informed, are well liked."

I began the ritual of timing the Führer's dressing. "I am gratified, my Führer," I told him, "but by any females?" I asked, partly in jest.

He laughed at that, and more colour returned to his cheeks. He was almost himself again. Just then, Dr. Bloch emerged from the bathroom, his face awash with sweat, his tie askew. "Is there anything further I can do for you, my Führer?" he asked shakily.

"No, Bloch," the Führer responded expressionlessly. "You are the undisputed master of shit. But I believe I can function adequately for the rest of the day. But," he added, "keep yourself handy—and invisible. The SS are all around me, even in this room," he added, with a slight nod to me, "and so you must be, shall we say, even more than discreet. I've had to explain you far too often to Reichsführer Himmler, who would love to have you to himself—and not for enemas, I can assure you."

The Führer meant "defend," not "explain." This I knew.

Dr. Bloch nodded vigorously while adjusting his tie and wiping his glistening face with his pocket handkerchief. "I . . . ah . . . fully understand . . . my Führer," he stammered. "I appreciate your dilemma, and, ah, will strive mightily to not cause you further . . . dis . . . ah, awkwardness." With that, he withdrew quickly without saluting.

I brought the Führer his gleaming black shoes. "About those women, my Führer," I persisted.

He sighed deeply. "Women, Linge," he said, "one day we must have a long talk about them. But now, you must finish with me and meet with Brückner. This mail situation is becoming increasingly burdensome, but no less important for that. If you're feeling amorous and it can't wait, seek out Baur. I'm told he's the ladies' man here, and," he added with a wink, "I don't mean merely for himself. Now, Linge, my other shoe. We have a historic new year to mould."

As usual, the Führer was right: Baur was definitely the man to see about meeting the opposite sex. As the Führer's chief pilot,

I'd encountered him on several occasions, both inside and outside various aircraft, but we never exchanged more than banal
pleasantries. He must have been quite the handsome and dashing
devil in his youth, but what I saw, when I called upon him at
his quarters, was an endomorphic egoist with several unsightly
facial blemishes and hair even thinner than mine. He reminded
me of a bargain-basement replica of Göring. However, I'd heard
rumours that his "black book" was voluminous and his appetites,
insatiable. Moreover, employing his services wouldn't preclude
a search for Katrin.

When we met, Baur was extremely cordial and more than
eager to assist me, since I made certain to have him instantly take
pity on my (calculated) shyness and (natural) social ineptitude.
When I asked him if he might suggest a decent female companion, he laughed mightily at the word *decent*, then reached for
a large, thick, ledger-like volume, each page containing carnal
photos of women, accompanied by their names, addresses, phone
numbers, and "vital statistics" about their particular sexual proclivities and varying degrees of skill in exercising them.

"Here you go, my young Heinz," he offered. "Volume One.
Sit down and take a gander. If you haven't had some in a while,
you can, ah, 'scan' it in my bathroom if you need to. Being
trapped here so often, I do it all the time, even in the plane, but
that's between us, yes? Doesn't beat the real thing, of course, but
there you are, eh?"

I sat down in his chair and began perusing the pages. Good
God, the man is vulgar! The pictures reminded me of the ones
in the brickyard locker room. Pure porn, and the "vital statistics"
and "proclivities" made me want to vomit. After a few moments,
I slammed the volume shut.

"Nothing there excites you, Heinz?" Baur kidded. "You're the first, I must tell you. If I manage to get that priggish Goebbels to allow it to be published, I would be named the Führer's Minister of Sex that very day." Then he slapped his thigh. "I know what it is: they're not refined enough for the Führer's valet's delicate sensibilities, yes?"

I'd made a fool of myself and needed to recoup quickly, so I said: "No, Hans, that isn't it at all. Your collection is more than enough to adequately exhaust the entire Wehrmacht and make you richer than Krupp." I hoped that my allusion to Baur as a super-pimp would sail right over his head, and it did, as he merely shrugged and beamed with pride.

"Actually," I continued, "I was wondering if you knew of two particular women I'm interested in."

"Ah," Baur replied with a crafty grin. "A man who knows what he wants. Well, why didn't you say so? My little volume here is only the beginning. Okay, who are they?"

I considered my response: Did I really want this disgusting ponce knowing of my interest in Katrin and Emerald? And what of my interest in them: What if their pictures actually emerged from another Baur volume? I had another idea, and made a decision about Baur immediately. "Hans, I do appreciate you trying to assist me, but I just remembered that I must run an important errand for the Führer. May I come back later?"

Baur shrugged. "Naturally, Heinz. We mustn't ever keep the Boss waiting. You know where to find me—that is, if I'm not in the air, and in the meantime, you can find a juicy landing site for your hand, eh?" he snickered.

From that disgusting event, I mentally dismissed Baur. From what I'd learned during my brief encounters with Katrin and Emerald, they would hardly be obvious candidates for his catalogue. And even if they were, I doubted that I would ever wish to see either one through such means. I needed another avenue.

⁊

I made for Kempka's quarters, but only silence answered my knock. I discovered later that he'd been told to drive Schroeder to visit her sick sister. Considering that a train would have taken her virtually to her sister's doorstep, I had to admire her exalted status, almost as much as I loathed her as a person. On my way back, it occurred to me with an icy jolt, that I needed to check for that note in my jacket pocket, just in case I was of an even remotely sound mind when I'd felt that hand place it there in the ballroom.

As I reached my quarters, I almost bumped heads with one of the regiment of housekeepers who was struggling under a bundle of my dirty clothing and linen. I'd never seen her before, and, after giving her my apologies, I asked her to leave the bundle with me. She laughingly disabused me of such a silly notion, informing me that she was a paragon of thoroughness (she put it far more ungrammatically), had rummaged with a watchmaker's precision, and had removed "absolutely everything" not needing cleaning before creating her bundle. While admiring her diligence, I felt a shudder of unease about someone like that going through my pockets, even with the most benign motives, and I was definitely not confident of that. And yet, after what she said, how could I take back the ungainly heap? So, I thanked her, apologized again for my clumsiness, and she saluted Heil Hitler with excessive zeal and marched off.

Normally, such a situation wouldn't have bothered me, but there was no *normally* here: this was the first time that my laundry had been taken by another, the unvarying procedure up to now

being that I would carry my own items to the housekeeping staff
for transfer to the appropriate cleaning personnel. Someone else,
somewhat less schooled in Chancellery life than I was by now,
might well pass it off as a compliment and a convenience. But,
after almost a year of no locks on the doors, bathroom faucets
as foreground music to accompany background conversations,
and Heydrich's "casual" getting-acquainted visit, I was far from
a babe in the woods, and it scared the shit out of me. But what
to do was another matter.

I entered my quarters and immediately went to my tiny
armoire, ignoring the small stack of paper scraps and other
pocket detritus my clothes had accumulated, arranged by the
housekeeper with surgical precision on my night table. In it,
hung one uniform jacket next to a couple of liveries. I reached
into a pocket of the former, extracted the folded sheet from
the envelope, but out of cowardice decided to read it later, just
before transferring you to film and so, returned it to its envelope,
slid it into my inside jacket pocket. Had she read it? No way of
knowing, so I headed for the main garage. Perhaps Kempka had
returned.

As I strode through the Chancellery, past the seemingly
endless, narrow-eyed checkpoint sentinels, the numerous clusters of conversation, the echoing din of well-shod boot heels
and women's pumps on marble, I wondered how to keep to
my contrivance: Can the principal valet to the Führer ever be
truly invisible? A servant in an aristocrat's manor house can
melt (almost literally) into the walls and be casually unseen
by those who are trained from birth to consider those, as the
Führer put it, "below the salt" as mere sentient appliances. Not
here, where even the appliances are suspect. Here, I can trust no
one—including myself—and that, my friend, is the horrendous

dilemma I face: I worry less about them than I do about me and the increase in my waking "spells," especially in a world where sheep are assigned to guard wolves.

When I finally arrived at the massive underground garage that housed a legion of black open-air four-door Mercedes, I asked the first of an army of white-overalled mechanics where I might locate Kempka. After three failures that I attributed to Kempka's desire to avoid his hated superior, Schreck, I eventually found him in the very back, shielded behind some crates of spare parts. He was gaping with salivary abandon at some proscribed pornographic material. I announced myself as I approached so as to assure him that the situation was harmless.

"Ah, Heinz," he declared effusively, "you found my little retreat. I trust you won't reveal it." His smile told me he had no excessive fear of disclosure.

"Your secret is safe with me," I assured him. "I've been looking for you."

"To again wish me a happy new year as the Boss's future chief chauffeur?"

The man was monomaniacal, and I couldn't blame him. I had to admire Kempka's relentless ambition, even though I had none of my own.

"Yes," I told him, "I wished one for you last night, and to help make my wish a reality, I intend to regale the Führer with amazing tales of your driving prowess, to nudge him toward you in this new year, as well as make certain he knows of my deep concern for the Führer's automotive safety, considering Schreck's advanced age and delicate health."

Kempka nodded slyly and slid his magazine into a small space between two boxes of spare parts. "Heinz, my friend, he already knows about my . . . prowess, since I've been driving him whenever that bloody invalid wasn't able to, which is more and more," he said, his thin lips spread in frustration, "but go right ahead. It certainly can't hurt."

"But these are things he cannot deny."

"Well, I think that maybe you need to be with him a bit longer, my friend. The Boss is the world's expert at denial. You'll have your work cut out for you."

"I'm not lazy, Erich, and from my former life, I learned how to lay foundations and build from there."

He sniffed, shrugged, and raised his tiny hands to ear height, palms facing outward in mock surrender. "All right, bricklayer," he conceded, "go about it, but I can tell you that you've already been extremely helpful, and I'm most appreciative."

My eyes narrowed. "I have? How?"

"Never mind," was all he said, and then changed the subject. "You said you wanted something from me, yes?"

I shifted to a whisper, barely audible over the noise of the mechanics at work. "I need to know as much as you can discover about two females, one, with whom I believe you're already acquainted."

He pursed his lips. "I'd love to oblige, Heinz, but for female matters, you should try Baur. He's got a monopoly. Trapped in this fucking monastery, I don't know what I'd do without that master procurer."

I shook my head. "I already tried Baur, but I merely want information, not intercourse, and certainly not with his posse of pussy."

Kempka laughed heartily. "The Boss has made a monk out of you, Heinz. The last time I wanted . . . 'information' about some bimbo, it was whether she was a virgin or not. Virgins are popular, God knows why, but for me, they're a total loss, lacking both experience and imagination. They can stay virgins, for all I care. I want my women raw, experienced, and eager, and able to leave their meagre brains at home."

Instantly, I thought of Dara.

"All right, my friend," he said, "so what is this information business about, and why me?"

"Okay, to business," I said. "I want as much information as you can dredge up, through whatever means you have, for two women: one is that Katrin you'd put me on to. And the other calls herself Emerald. You said that Katrin's a von something or other, but I have no last names for either one. Both claim to do odd jobs at the RSHA, the latter for Himmler, and the former for some character named Weisthor."

Kempka flicked his cigarette at the floor, ground it out, and began biting his lower lip. Anxiety. "Heinz, do you realize what you're asking?" he exclaimed in a raspy whisper. "You want me nosing around Himmler's little empire! You've lost your senses, or you must think I've lost mine."

"'Nosing' is entirely your affair. I imagine that you have several acquaintances who have connexions with the organization, and some entirely discreet inquiries might well bear fruit."

"Or cart me away to a KZ."[43] His face had blossomed into a tropical garden of sweat droplets. "You ask too much, Heinz. Far too much."

I took a deep breath and merely stared at him.

Kempka dragged out a soggy, wrinkled handkerchief from his back pocket, scrubbed his face, and returned it.

"Erich," I said, "you get me the information I'm after, and, with my sales campaign, before summer, I guarantee that you

---

[43] Konzentrationslager, or KZ, for short; concentration camp.

will be the Führer's principal driver. You'll never answer to Schreck again."

Kempka's eyes bulged wide. "But do you think he will choose me, once Schreck's out of the picture, that is?"

"I wipe the Führer's behind." Untrue but suggestive. Of course, I knew that my promise was entirely dependent on my untested influence with the Führer, especially as it concerned an old and trusted comrade from the "days of struggle."

Kempka performed a second ritual with his handkerchief and I was, for a moment, deeply concerned that he might say "you first," but luckily, aspiration trumped caution and he didn't. "*Shit!*" he declared. "This request of yours could be ruin and disaster for me, but I'll do what you ask—or at least give it the old try."

"I cannot reasonably ask for more," I responded gracefully.

"You hit the nail right on the head there," he said, then paused for an interminable period, staring down at the greasy floor while tapping his right toe. "Okay," he finally conceded, and I left.

Brückner never got back to me for my tutorial, and, for a reason not disclosed to me, it seemed that the Führer asked for Krause to attend him at dinner and beyond, so I remained in my quarters. Deciding to wait no longer, I reached into my jacket pocket for the note, but it was empty of all but some lint and a child's metal top etched with foreign characters I took to be Hebraic, since I'd seen many of them in the residences of Jews who'd taken pity on a hungry, homeless street urchin. Was there ever a note? How did such a dangerous "toy" end up in my pocket, and why? Who would do such a thing? And what did it mean?

Unable to answer any of these questions, and the top being far too hazardous to keep, I decided to package the object with my film and, the next day, mail it to my place of safety.

I'm beginning to wish I could mail myself there too.

2 *January* 1936

Brückner finally came to explain and divide the task of explaining the final stage of mail sorting. His "special technique," as the Führer called it, consisted of taking two heaping canvas bags and giving me one of them. "Here," he said, "now pour all the contents on the floor, open every package to determine if it's worthy of the Führer's personal attention. The same with the letters."

When I responded that I was hardly a judge of worthiness, Brückner laughed and asked me: "Who is?" However, he went on to tell me that I should develop some rules of thumb. For example, he said, "toss away anything from people you know the Führer to dislike. The same with negative mail. However, with those, if you can detect who the sender is, or anything about him, inform me immediately. Another would be to keep anything sent directly by a head of state—not that he'll necessarily read it, but at least he can present it if asked whether or not he received it. Of course, answering them is another matter." He cautioned me that under no circumstances should the Führer be denied communications from his *alten kampfer*, his old comrades in arms from his "time of struggle," for "they were with me at the darkest hours," he would say over and over. And "When in doubt, come to me and I'll give you my best advice." With that, he left me with the mountain of mail on the floor. I decided to delay this ridiculous task as long as possible.

More important, I'd learned, while overhearing a conversation between some underlings in the Abwehr,[44] at the New Year's Eve celebration, that a subminiature camera was about to be introduced, perfect for spying, they'd said. In theory, it was no less perfect for me. But theory, I've discovered, stops at the Chancellery steps, and a very special reality takes over, and reality, for my purposes, doesn't favour such a gadget. If it were ever noticed, how could I explain why a valet would possess one?

---

[44] The Abwehr was an intelligence-gathering agency and dealt exclusively with human intelligence, especially raw intelligence reports from field agents and other sources. The chief of the Abwehr reported directly to the High Command of the Armed Forces (Oberkommando der Wehrmacht, or OKW).

I MUST WATCH myself with even greater care and sensitivity. The Führer informed me this morning that he just approved Himmler's plan to unify all police and security agencies under the latter and his SS. Of course, I'd known of this plan earlier, and, though I didn't dare tell the Führer, I harboured serious reservations about anyone but him consolidating governmental power of any kind, much less police powers. If nothing else, with Himmler and Heydrich in sole charge, all Germans, especially the Jews, would be in for it now.

All that aside, what I cared about most was that Kempka said he "might have" some information about Katrin or Emerald for me soon, and had I taken any steps to fulfil my portion of the bargain? I hadn't. I was most grateful that he had not the wits to ask me why I needed him, and not perform the detective work myself. In all truth, I didn't believe that he would risk such an effort, but I felt I had to ask. Also, to be frank, I couldn't blame him. All I could do for him was to occasionally and discreetly mention Kempka's qualities to the Führer as well as insinuate Schreck's current and increasing infirmities. I knew that the Führer prized loyalty above pedigree, knowledge, physical condition, and skill, and so I would have to be both subtle and measured.

Tonight, as I stood mute behind the Führer, the dining room resembled what I'd imagined to be a supreme military headquarters (to the extent I had any idea of what one looked like). It had spilled over from a late-afternoon meeting of the Führer's top uniformed leaders. There were no women present, or even civilian males.

They were arguing animatedly among themselves about the nature and potential of the Reich's current and future fighting forces. I found the subject far too intricate and irrelevant to bother myself about. However, the Führer clearly did not share my view, as he sat, tapping his fingers with scowling impatience at every word and implication. Unusually—and unfortunately—Krause was there, too, standing at ease in the opposite corner, glaring daggers at me with his beady, jealous eyes. Brückner was nowhere to be found.

General Beck was describing the Reich's rearmament program in which he sought to provide the basis for fighting a "defensive war on several fronts with some prospect of success."

The Führer broke in with a jolting slam of his fist on the table. "'*Defensive*'? Did I hear you say 'defensive,' Beck?"

"Yes, my Führer," Beck replied without emotion. "However," he added, "despite the term which you appear to find so odious, the addition of three armoured divisions, fought for by several of my officers, to convince the Army leadership of the need to compensate for the numerical restrictions of Versailles by increasing the Army's mobility, necessarily shifts the emphasis away from defence even if described as 'offensively conducted defence.'"

"So, General," the Führer declared, "you are now bandying words with me? I wish to hear facts, not technical military gibberish. I heard enough of that in the Great War to last a lifetime."

"Yes, my Führer, as you wish," answered Beck. "In a

memorandum I will present to you later, I contend that the present plan for building up the Army and its present organization were determined by the requirement to provide the Army initially with the necessary defensive capability for a war on several fronts, and by *defensive*, I mean what I described earlier, gibberish, notwithstanding."

As for me, I was more concerned about Krause and his reason for being there. I also had several reels of exposed film I needed to develop and, somehow, I would have to arrange time tomorrow to take care of that, before Heydrich became my darkroom assistant.

"So, General," said the Führer, "rather than concern ourselves with nomenclature, you would say that we will soon be prepared for major offensive military activity, yes?"

"Yes, my Führer, we should."

"*Should?*" shouted the Führer. "*Again, linguistic evasion!* General, are you constitutionally incapable of a definitive response to a simple question? A simple yes or no will do for this lowly corporal here."

Beck turned his head to his right. "What is your opinion, Fritsch?"

Fritsch shrugged, glanced at the Führer, then leaned forward and turned his head toward Blomberg. "Regardless of what General Blomberg may choose to call it," he remarked, "I would contend that any accelerated pace of rearmament would far outdistance our ability to pay for it. It would seem—"

Eyes bulging with rage, the Führer again slammed his fist on the table, this time with such force that several water and wine glasses fell over, spilling plum-coloured contents all over the once pristine white tablecloth.

Since I was no part of the housekeeping staff, all I could

focus on was why all this talk of war, when Germany was still weighted down by the worldwide economic collapse and the harsh restrictions of the Versailles Treaty. How could the Führer, who had seen—and experienced—the horrors of war as I hadn't, be so eager to fight again? But, of course, what did I know of any of this? Did Krause know more, and so that was his purpose here? Would it ever be revealed to me?

The Führer merely turned to Admiral Raeder: "And you, Raeder, you've managed to maintain some degree of independence. What have you to say?"

The only military man in full-dress uniform, he was a luminescent vision in gold and black, with an immense mosaic of medals covering most of his left breast. The admiral cleared his throat and took a sip of what remained of his water. "My Führer, in this most sensitive and important matter, I must confess to having two minds. As you recall, you became Führer while I was chief of the German Navy, at which time, I . . . advised you to authorize the immediate building of a German battle fleet, with the intention of surpassing even the power of the British Royal Navy. However, now I believe that our navy is, as yet, unprepared for any serious armed conflict by about five years."

"Five years, you say, Raeder," the Führer replied with an eerie calm. "Do you agree with him, Dönitz?"

"In my professional opinion," answered the admiral, "I believe that any war with Britain in the near future would doom it to uselessness, and all the Germans could hope to do would be to die valiantly."

The Führer merely nodded perfunctorily, told Admiral Canaris to have his department consider all that had been said, then asked Krause to call for the next course and more wine for his guests before he left the room, with me trailing behind him.

War? All this talk of war? I, of course, possessed absolutely none of the experience and expertise of the exalted military gentlemen round the table, or even the lowly experience of the Führer, but I shuddered at such talk, considering such an overwhelming and degrading defeat for Germany. Even with my ignorance, I could only see disaster emerging from such a discussion. Was the Führer so hellbent on reversing the viciousness of Versailles that he would risk another calamity, even when his top military leaders were divided?

Despite all this, I forced myself to consider the entire discussion hypothetical, even though it failed to appease my anxiety about the subject itself, and the need for its being raised at such a time. However, a voice inside my brain told me that the Führer had already made up his mind, so the entire discussion was a mere formality, and not the first time, by any means. He would have his war.

I WAS OBLIGED to hold further action on the Katrin/Emerald matter in abeyance due to a flurry of Chancellery activity concerning the remilitarization of the Rhineland.[45] For some time, I'd been aware of the Führer's eagerness to remilitarize, for he had said as much to anyone within earshot. This afternoon, I was summoned again to alphabetise his library (which I had done several times before, merely sliding them out and sliding them back). I surmised (for reasons I was, at the moment, incapable of penetrating) that he wished me to overhear the exchanges among von Neurath, von Ribbentrop, chief of staff General Beck, Army head General von Fritsch, and war minister Field Marshal von Blomberg.

The "conversation" shifted continually and without warning, from nods, to grunts, to murmurs, to normal speech, to fist-pounding shrieks of rage, and back, all in no particular order—all issuing from the Führer, of course. The rest sat at rigid attention and spoke in deferential tones, whether genuine or contrived.

---

[45] Under Articles 42, 43, and 44 of the 1919 Treaty of Versailles, imposed on Germany by the Allies after the Great War, Germany was forbidden to "maintain or construct any fortification either on the Left Bank of the Rhine or on the Right Bank to the west of a line drawn fifty kilometres to the east of the Rhine." On 12 February 1936, Hitler met with Neurath and his ambassador-at-large Joachim von Ribbentrop to ask their opinion of the likely foreign reaction to remilitarization.

Only von Ribbentrop, always predatorily alert, appeared even remotely at ease.

"I asked for opinions, gentlemen," said the Führer. "Am I to receive any?" He was drumming his fingers on his desk as he sat back in his luxurious, high-backed leather swivel chair.

I knew better: he'd made up his mind, and merely wished to gauge the degree and kind of enthusiasm his underlings would demonstrate to the fait accompli.

"My Führer," von Neurath said, his face and tone a model of expressionlessness, "you know I have supported and still support remilitarization. However—"

The Führer slammed his fist down, knocking his collection of coloured pencils and several papers to the floor. I had no intention of picking them up at the moment.

"*THAT'S YOU!*" he screamed. "However this, however that. You give with one hand and you take with the other. And where are we left, eh, *EH?* Where we began: *NOWHERE!*"

Anyone else would have sat at attention and allowed the insulting tirade to roll off his back, but not the hyperaristocratic von Neurath. "My Führer," he continued in measured and even tones, "as I was saying, I am in complete agreement with rearmament. I was merely going to point out that it would be the better part of wisdom to negotiate more before—"

"Negotiate, Neurath?" the Führer interrupted again. "Is that what you're recommending? With whom? Britain and France have not seen eye to eye from the Battle of Hastings in 1066 to Versailles, so who is left, Venezuela?"

Von Neurath apparently chose to ignore the Führer's snideness and, this time, kept silent. On the other hand, von Ribbentrop, ever true to form, and with his natural affinity for exploiting the inevitable, said: "The Führer has again hit the nail on its proverbial head. German integrity requires swift, unilateral action. As to my esteemed colleague's concern, I would point out that both countries are occupied with internal problems and are also watching Italy and Ethiopia. Most important, if France went to war in response to German remilitarization, then Britain would go to war with France, and that would be that." Not once did the two vons look at each other.

"And what of you, General Beck?" asked the Führer.

"My Führer," he said, "unilateral action is sound, I believe, but—"

The Führer slammed his desk again, sending all the writing materials yet remaining on it to the floor. *"But? BUT?"* he shouted. *"Here are my best advisers and I'm surrounded by howevers and buts! Is there no one decisive in this room besides Ribbentrop here?"* Then, his eyelids lowered slightly and his voice took on a more placid quality. "All right, Beck, I'm listening. Just what is your 'but' about?"

"Thank you, my Führer," he began, while the Führer muttered unintelligibly under his breath. "I was merely going to point out that the German Army would be unable to successfully defend Germany against a possible retaliatory French attack."

The Führer laughed derisively, then spread his lips and pressed them together as a response that invariably meant disdain of a high order. "'Retaliatory French attack,' eh? And what of you, General Fritsch? Are prospects that gloomy for you too?"

Von Fritsch, shifted uneasily in his chair and took a deep breath. "My Führer," he said, "my assessment is that at this exact moment, with all due respect to von Ribbentrop here, the German Army is in no state for armed combat with the French."

"So," the Führer replied, "my top military commanders are

in agreement that we must all shudder at the prospect of French retaliation, am I right?"

Silence.

"So, then," the Führer continued, "it would appear that only von Ribbentrop has any faith in me and my decisions." He spread his hands out in an offering position. "Well, then, I will soothe your furrowed brows: I personally guarantee that the German forces will retreat at once if the terrifying French intervene militarily to halt our advance. Does that not satisfy all the Nervous Nellies in the room? In fact," he added, "we shall keep the number of troops sent into the Rhineland very small so as to allow us to claim that we had not committed a 'flagrant violation' of Locarno,[46] that our move was forced upon us with the greatest reluctance by ratification of the Franco-Soviet pact, and that Germany might—*might*, mind you—even return to that shit pile of a League of Nations if remilitarization is accepted. Moreover, for your information, I happen to have the utmost support of Il Duce[47] in this, not in small part due to my actions concerning their idiotic war with Ethiopia. Of course, as you should well know, I was advised against it at the time, but we now see that, once again, my instincts proved correct. Now, my stalwart comrades," he murmured with undisguised facetiousness, "have I sufficiently alleviated your hysteria?"

Having done as much shelving and reshelving and re-re-shelving as I could bear, and having dusted and redusted to mental and physical insensibility, I just turned and stood there at parade rest, facing the group, knowing that I would be regarded, if at all, as just another empty chair. This provided me

---

[46] Both Britain and Italy were committed to offering a military response only to a "flagrant violation."

[47] Benito Mussolini.

the opportunity to consider whether I should receive Kempka's information before dealing with the Führer about Schreck or afterward. Knowing something of human nature, especially that of the SS, the decision was a simple one: Kempka first, and with plenty of information.

I then took a moment to consider the French. I'd never known a Frenchman, nor had I ever been to France. My only connection was through a grizzled old Berlin bench-sitter who had fought them in the Great War. He had little good to say regarding French military courage and skill, except to grumble that if only America had stayed out, "the Frenchies" would be speaking German. The Führer was clearly of that stripe, and, I might even speculate that he despised the French even more than he did the Jews.

"Well? Do any of you have something to add?" the Führer then asked the assembled, I believe, rhetorically. "No? All right then. Neurath, for the sake of diplomatic decorum, I wish you to have your staff draft legal briefs justifying the remilitarization of the Rhineland, on the grounds that the Franco-Soviet pact violated Locarno. If pressed, you will say that it was done on your own initiative, irrespective of my orders, but that you expected my complete concurrence."

Von Neurath sniffed audibly. "Yes, my Führer," he conceded. "I'll have them initiate it immediately."

I believe I was still watching the group, when suddenly a thick, lava-like stream, grey-black in the centre and edged with glowing red and white, surrounded my brain like a river coursing round a boulder, accompanied by a horrible pressure behind my eyes, as if the stream were straining to push them out. All in the room were now enveloped in a viscous-like pudding with distorted limbs protruding, and the voices appeared to be emanating from the centre, then stopped abruptly. Then it ebbed slightly.

Now I could hear the Führer slap the table gently. "All right," he said (or I think he said), "so there you are." Then he rose, thus causing the guests to shoot up, heil, and leave. Now I believed I was alone with him, as he walked quickly to the light switch, pitched the room into darkness, moved back to his desk, and sat down heavily. "Those books in top shape, Linge?" he asked me, I assumed, in jest, but I couldn't be sure because I was watching myself from another place, as I had done on New Year's Eve. As an onlooker, I was amused by it all, as before, but not afraid, even though I could see nothing but myself.

The Führer chuckled. "You see what I have to deal with, Linge? Linge?" I could hear him calling my name.

Then I heard myself say: "All right, you can come in."

"Sit, Heinz. Please," a sensual female voice requested, but I thought I was already seated. Her voice was familiar, but I couldn't place it. The room was lit, but I could make out nothing but vague, amorphous shapes in the distance, excepting my own. Her voice travelled like a warm, gentle breeze passing through me, as if I'd ceased to be solid. A part of my brain knew that voice; it had heard it before. But whose?

"I'm here. For you, just for you. Now," the voice murmured seductively, "did you see my message?"

"What message?" I heard myself asking. "There was no message."

"In the envelope. The one I slipped into your jacket pocket at the New Year's celebration."

"I . . . I didn't know who put it there."

"I know you didn't. You weren't supposed to. But did you see it?" the voice persisted gently.

"I . . . saw it, but there was no paper. There was only—"

"No need to say it," she cut in. "Conceal it and tell no one. You heard him. Your Führer's only beginning and must be stopped. Heinz, if you don't act, and act now, what can the future hold for us?"

The voice was so consoling, no alarms sounded in my brain. I needed only to respond. "The future for *us*?" I asked the voice. "Who is 'us'?"

"The Reich. You. Me."

From a distorted distance, I saw myself answer, still in a voice not my own: "Only one person has the other. It is not yet the Führer. It is not you or me. I have no name for him."

Then, nothing more, just a welcome blackness devoid of sensation.

∾

Somehow, I found myself in my quarters. I had no idea how I'd gotten there. Had it been merely another hallucination, another nightmare, or only portions? My terror is that it all had been real—or worse. Now, sitting on my metal chair, explanations elude me, as they always have. I end this entry early, my friend. I'm too terrified to sleep, and yet, I cannot write to you any more tonight.

I WAS COMPELLED to rise early to prepare myself and the Führer for a hastily announced train trip to the Berghof.[48] His penchant for whimsy continually throws all connected with him into a flurry of conflicting activities. With Schaub still recuperating, poor Brückner alone had the unfortunate task of coordinating the chaos and making it appear orderly. The Führer's habit of keeping his schedule secret to the last possible moment, even from those closest to him, intensified the problem in the extreme. This is not to say that he didn't have a plan or that the details were not excruciatingly arranged well ahead of time, but the departure date and time would be withheld until the last possible moment, and then be expected to go off without a hitch. And, amazingly, for the most part, they did.

Since this was to be a train trip, Kempka would play a minor role until we arrived, thus giving me the opportunity to receive an update on our arrangement. I'd intended to wait until we

---

[48] In 1933, as Reich chancellor, Hitler ordered a special train built for him and his entourage. It initially had ten coaches. No. 1 saloon coach (the *Führerwagen*) consisted of a wood-panelled saloon with bed compartments, bathroom, and far smaller compartments for his valet and adjutants. There was a coach for dining, and there were also coaches for the *Begleitkommando*, the Criminal Police, the Führer's staff, and guests. It was formed on 29 February 1932 to protect Hitler while he travelled outside Munich and the borders of Bavaria in Germany. The *Begleitkommando* was replaced by the *Führerschutzkommando* after Hitler became Führer in 1934. Erich Kempka was a member.

were onboard, but I couldn't be certain that he'd be there and not Schreck, and I harboured the suspicion that he was avoiding me. So, after ensuring that Brückner was satisfied, I raced over to the main garage. The place was a bursting clamour of Grand Prix gabble and much boisterous toasting. Having no interest in auto racing whatsoever, even when Germany wins, I returned to the Chancellery and began wading through my share of mail. Nothing of consequence, as usual, but it still had to be thoroughly vetted nonetheless. Afterwards, I headed for the Führer's rooms to check for any last-minute necessities, when I rounded a corner and literally bumped into Fräulein Schroeder, who couldn't resist the opportunity my "invasion" represented to her.

"I have just finished taking dictation from the Führer," she announced needlessly, since she was clearly coming from his quarters, clutching a stenographer's pad in her prehensile paw. "It appears, Herr Linge, that we will obliged to share a train ride, in far-too-close proximity to each other. I merely wish to inform you of this unpleasant fact and advise you to keep as much distance from me as you are able."

I never understood the reason behind her virulent hostility towards me. However, being a virtual newborn, desirous only of acceptance and invisibility, and she, a poisonous harridan and, amazingly, a favourite of the Führer, I maintained the greatest (while odious) cordiality towards her when I couldn't be completely silent. After almost a year as the Führer's principal valet, and, I hoped, even wiser in the ways of this most singular environment, a part of me still considered delivering a devastatingly witty rejoinder, determined as I was not to let this particular bit of bile pass. I had read enough of Oscar Wilde (before Goebbels banned his works) to make a valiant attempt. So, in the privacy of my mind, I replied: *My dear Fräulein Schroeder, of course I will do my level best to accommodate you. And to demonstrate my good faith, should fate conspire to have us pass each other in the narrow corridor, and should a sudden lurch by the train fling you into my unsuspecting embrace, I solemnly pledge not to bring the opportunity to its logical conclusion—unless requested, of course.*

However, after balancing a temporary feeling of self-satisfaction against the permanent negative consequences of displaying precocity (and in so doing, extinguishing my carefully drawn persona of untutored, harmless innocence), instead, I told her: "Fräulein Schroeder, of course I will do my level best to accommodate you."

Yet, even with that humiliating sacrifice, all she could do was to stare at me with such utter loathing, I could almost feel it as a searing blast of dry ice. A masochistic part of me longed for at least a brief glacial tirade, but, after a moment, she merely nodded once and continued on her "merry" way.

The Führer was in one of his contemplative moods as we boarded Number 1 Coach,[49] and he immediately made for his wood-panelled saloon car containing a small office, sleeping compartment, and bathroom and, next door, smaller compartments for Brückner and me. He told us that he would ring if he required anything before dinner. Brückner told me he had some business to take care of, which left me time to search out Kempka, who had driven us to the station because Schreck was too ill to drive. I moved from car to car, past the conference

---

[49] Führerwagen.

room, armed checkpoints, SS Begleitkommando,[50] KRIPO,[51] secretaries, favour-seekers, Dr. Bloch, guests, hangers-on, and other assorted Chancellery types, until I arrived at Number 3 Coach, which housed the diner. As I'd expected, there he was, clutching a hefty snifter of schnapps and regaling a group of sodden orderlies and kitchen help with a choice sampler of "Jew jokes."

"Hey, if you liked that one," he said, once the raucous guffaws had subsided, "well, I have an even better one: okay, what is the worst stain on a Jew's underwear?" then paused for effect: "Lipstick from a Jewess." More boisterous guffaws and table pounding with their empty glasses, which they quickly refilled.

I decided that this might not be the most opportune moment to steal Kempka away from his adoring public for a serious chat, and so, clearly not having been noticed, I stole away and went to my quarters to wait out his recovery. My compartment was far smaller and sparer than my quarters at the Chancellery, containing only a small, narrow folding cot, an even narrower armoire, and a tiny, straight-back metal "guest chair." But it did have one thing normally denied me: *a window!* Yes, my friend, a window; now my loneliness had a place through which to escape, instead of ricocheting back to me from four blank walls.

I had just gotten settled when a hesitant tap brought me to the door. I knew it couldn't be Kempka, or there would have been drunken pounding and shouting, even though I was within a few feet of the Führer's quarters. When I opened the door, I could only see an enormous torso, for his height and girth permitted nothing more in such compressed and miniaturised

---

[50] The *SS-Begleitkommando des Führers* protected Hitler as he travelled around Germany.

[51] Criminal Police.

surroundings. He bent his knees so I could tell it was Hanfstaengl. Used to seeing him seated at a piano or dinner table, I hardly realized what a true giant of a man he was.

"May I come in?" he asked, with not a small hint of anxiety in his tone. For such a large man, he possessed considerable grace and a disconcertingly high voice. Despite having resided so many years in America, his German was still perfect, though his Munich accent had been roundly corrupted. "Of course, Herr Hanfstaengl," I offered, and he stooped in as I motioned him to the chair, which he proceeded to overwhelm as he sat with a weary exhalation.

"I appreciate your courtesy," he began, "and I won't abuse it by long-windedness."

I was initially confounded by his subdued deference, even though I harboured a suspicion about it. I had no idea why he would seek me out, so I needed to let him make the first move. When I first encountered him, it was in the presence of the Führer, and he appeared to be a merry and amusing companion, full of charm and vitality. He had a mocking, teasing way about him, an enviable capacity for anecdotal embroidery, and a complete lack of inhibition in his remarks and comments.

I learned through below-stairs gossip that Hanfstaengl had attended one of America's most distinguished universities and, being well connected through his wealthy family to the social elite of Europe, served as a major cultural link with the world beyond the national borders. Moreover, and probably no less important, he possessed a channel to the Führer with which no one could compete, for, when exhaustion would overtake the Führer, he would turn to the form of relaxation that only Hanfstaengl could provide: hours-long sessions on the piano that would ease his overwrought nerves and often make him relatively receptive to the pianist's constant counsels of moderation.

However, over time, I detected a serious breach growing between them, which I, no longer a complete innocent, attributed to two things: the first, a severe lessening by the Führer of a tolerance for moderation, as witnessed by his treatment of von Neurath and others of his persuasion; and second, and no less important, Hanfstaengl's continual disagreements with Goebbels on virtually every cultural and political issue, thus making an ultra-powerful enemy who possessed the unchecked trust and confidence of the Führer. In truth, I wondered how he'd even gotten onto the train.

"This is not a problem," I told him. "I'm completely free until the Führer summons me. What can I do for you?"

His bulk fidgeted in the little metal chair, as if testing its endurance, his hands in perfect accompaniment with the rest of him—clearly a man who understood rhythm by instinct. "You . . ." he hesitated, utterly unlike him, "you are, ah, close to the Führer." A statement fraught with implications—and pitfalls.

"I hope I am as close as any valet can be," I replied cautiously, "but then again, I have no other examples to go by." *Innocence, my friend, always innocence.*

"I'm certain it will do," he assured me, then hesitated with his words held in an odd abeyance. "You have heard me play, several times," he finally said. "I believe that I was never great, but I was good. Of course I aspired to greatness, but it eluded me. I believe that it is better to be a great raconteur than a good pianist, since *great* is to *good* as *genius* is to *intelligence*, a cosmic leap, don't you agree?"

Great is to good? Cosmic leap? What the devil was he prattling about? I couldn't even follow his words, much less divine their meaning. Perhaps he was saying in his own pompous way what I'd always believed about my own brain, that, as cosmic leaps go, memory is to comprehension.

"If you say so, Herr Hanfstaengl," I answered with a shrug. "I merely strive to do my job as well as I can. It is for the Führer alone to judge its quality."

His fidgeting ceased, he crossed his legs, and cracked a small, sad smile. "Ah, to be as simple as you are," he stated with more than a touch of condescension, "and to occupy a role that demands nothing more. I truly envy you, Herr Linge."

"I never thought much about it, Herr Hanfstaengl," I lied, for I continually thought about it. Since I'd joined the Führer's household, Hanfstaengl never appeared to even notice me, much less utter even one word. Now, he was sitting with me in my little train compartment. This alone recommended caution. "So, is there anything I can do for you?" I repeated, if only to prod him to some kind of point.

He uncrossed his long legs and straightened himself as best he could, along the metal chair back, his ape-like forearms resting lengthwise atop his heavy thighs. "Yes, of course. To the point. Herr Linge, I require your assistance in a rather delicate matter."

"Delicate?"

"Yes—most delicate. You see, at one time, the Führer and I were quite close, you might say, even friends. I was one of his most sought-after advisers as well as . . . court musician, if you will. But unfortunately, for reasons totally unfathomable to me, relations between myself and the Führer have become somewhat strained of late."

I ached for him to leave so I could stare out the window at the passing countryside. "Please go on," I said.

"Well, you know the old saying: 'no man is a hero to his

valet.' By the same token, no one is closer—literally—to the Führer than you, and so I would ask you to inquire, in the most discreet manner and opportune moment, as to the cause of my exclusion from his inner circle and, perhaps, discern from his answer, should he provide one, how I might regain entry. Naturally, for this service, I would not be ungrateful."

I perked up. "Grateful?"

"I mean a quid pro quo."

"You have lost me, Herr Hanfstaengl, a . . . what?"

Another condescending smile. "A quid pro quo, Herr Linge, an exchange: a favour for a favour."

Of course I knew what it meant. I'd come across many Latin and Greek words in my travels through the dictionary and encyclopaedia, but the pronunciations generally eluded me until I heard someone use them. Yes, a favour for a favour, though I seriously questioned what sort of favour he could deliver, short of free piano lessons, and then it struck me, so I said: "I appreciate your dilemma, Herr Hanfstaengl. I can only promise that I will be on high alert for such an opportunity and seize it with the utmost discretion. However, should one not occur, I cannot jeopardise my position, you understand."

He buffed his surprisingly dextrous paws together with apparent satisfaction. "Of course, of course," he replied. "It is a most delicate task, as I pointed out, and I would never ask you to risk anything. But for any effort, no matter its result, I—"

"Would be most grateful," I interrupted, suddenly emboldened. "Your . . . quid pro quo, yes?"

"Absolutely," he affirmed with a nod.

"All right then, Herr Hanfstaengl," I said. "I'll try my best to do what you ask, to the degree I can, and on your part—which, I'm afraid, must come first—I wish to have extensive information on two women: the first is named Katrin von something-or-other. I don't know her last name. And the second is a woman who calls herself Emerald, also without a last name. Both claim to do 'odd jobs' for the RSHA."

He began to fidget again. "Herr Linge," he replied, "there was a time when I could have gotten you such information through one strategic lunch or well-placed phone call. However, as you can see from my own request, my credit with the top of the Party pyramid is depressingly minimal, and so inquiries by me into employees of Himmler's sinister empire can lead only to disaster for me, you understand."

Having been ignored by him up to this moment as a miserable menial, one of those the Führer termed "below the salt," I had no sympathy for this mammoth sycophant sitting before me. "I can appreciate that, Herr Hanfstaengl," I answered. "Naturally, it will not be a simple matter, and could cause you no little . . . inconvenience. But you also ask much, considering the Führer, and so those, I'm afraid, must remain the terms of my part of the bargain. It is only for you to accept or reject them."

I sat there, watching a range of emotions wash over the giant's face. Of course, I had no intention of ever bringing up the matter with the Führer, for I knew enough of the circumstances to cause me to keep a safe distance. That, of course, was not for the piano player to know or even guess. Once I had whatever information this waning social lion[52] could provide, I could stretch him out as if he were on a torturer's rack. In so thinking, I was briefly concerned that I'd taken on some of the characteristics of the Führer, but I attributed this to concentrated proximity and a newly discovered gift of political mimicry.

---

[52] A celebrity who is lionized (much sought after).

"Yes," he finally conceded, "what you ask will be difficult, indeed, but still and all, even now, I count some friends who also count." He grinned at his witty play on words. "I will, of course, do my best."

"From someone of your stature, Herr Hanfstaengl, I would expect no less. Now, to more immediate matters, for I may be called at any time. Do Brückner or the Führer know you're on this train?"

"No. The guards were so used to seeing me with the Führer, that it took very little guile to march right past them as if it was perfectly natural. Humiliating but effective."

"Then I would urge you to stay out of sight until all have disembarked, then secure an inconspicuous transport back to Berlin." How such a character could hide or be inconspicuous was his problem to solve, not mine.

He pursed his lips in thought. "Unfortunately, Herr Linge, a splendidly practical idea. Who would have thought, even a year ago, that we would be having this conversation?"

Or any conversation, I ached to add, but kept silent. He'd been brought low enough, and I needed anything he could learn.

"Do you know of a safe place to be until then?" I studiously avoided the degrading word *hide.*

The giant piano player nodded grimly. "I'm nothing if not resourceful, Herr Linge," he said as we both stood. "I thank you, and I hope to have some good news for you soon, as I hope you will have some for me." He extended his enormous hand, I pumped it once, and he left.

I had little hope that either he or Kempka would produce results, but having them on both sides of the case was infinitely safer than exposing myself—to no greater effect.

After distributing the no-excuses invitations to his staff, most of the afternoon and evening was spent with the Führer in the saloon coach. Both Brückner and I were in attendance, as well as Kempka and that accursed Schroeder. Dara was also there, and I could tell that the Führer's compliments to her infuriated her senior and delighted her suitor. I loved every minute of it, for, while I had lost any amorous interest in Dara once her relationship to Kempka was known to me, I harboured a burning hatred for Schroeder, and so luxuriated in her agonized envy.

The coach was panelled with the finest mahogany and contained a large, rectangular table, red leather chairs, thick curtains (always drawn), and indirect lighting. As with his rooms at the Chancellery, dimness was the rule, as the Führer's war-damaged eyes disdained bright lights. As usual, and not a little ironic, he would regale the assembled with stories of his ceaseless travels by car during the time of struggle, and how he loved the auto and revered his drivers as the instruments that helped him become the saviour of Germany. I could see that Kempka, somewhat recovered from his earlier inebriation, was gleaming with gratitude and, as he swivelled his eyes toward me, not with impatient anticipation but with something else, what, I didn't know. Another mystery to dog my trail.

ASIDE FROM THE din created by the seemingly never-ending construction, the mobs of hysterical acolytes that surround the Berghof's[53] perimeter, screaming and cheering at their god and saviour round the clock, and the steady stream of Party dignitaries begging Brückner for an audience and special favours and me for hints as to the Führer's mood, there is my personal dilemma—and peril—of requiring Heinrich Hoffmann's Berghof darkroom to process my film, as well as the torture of having had to ask him, after refusing his spuriously effusive offer at the Chancellery. I didn't tell you of this yesterday, so I tell you now.

---

[53] The Berghof began as a much smaller chalet called Haus Wachenfeld, a holiday home built in 1916 by businessman Otto Winter. By 1933, Hitler had purchased Haus Wachenfeld with funds he received from the sale of his political manifesto, *Mein Kampf.* The small chalet-style building was refurbished and much expanded during 1935–36, when it was renamed The Berghof. A large terrace was built. A dining room was panelled with very costly cembra pine. Hitler's large study had a telephone switchboard room. The library contained books on history, painting, architecture, and music. A great hall was furnished with expensive Teutonic furniture, a large globe, and an expansive red marble fireplace mantel. Behind one wall was a projection booth for evening screenings of films (often, Hollywood productions that were otherwise banned). A sprawling picture window provided a sweeping, open-air view of the snow-capped mountains in Hitler's native Austria. Visitors gathered at the end of the driveway or on nearby public paths in hopes of catching a glimpse of Hitler. This led to the introduction of severe restrictions on access to the area and other security measures. A large contingent of the SS Leibstandarte Adolf Hitler were housed in barracks adjacent to the Berghof, and they patrolled an extensive cordoned security zone that encompassed the nearby homes of the other Nazi leaders.

"Herr Hoffmann," I said to him after another of his interminable photo sessions with the Führer (alone in repose, staring mystically into a future Aryan dawn, or chatting, or strolling with his inner circle and with any guests who were significant enough to shoot), "may I have a word?"

Hoffmann smiled coyly, as if he knew what I had in mind. "Of course, my boy," he patronized. "What can I do for you?"

"Well, Herr Hoffmann, you see . . . I need to ask you—"

"Herr Linge," he interrupted, "let me guess. In this setting, clearly worthy of the best photographer's art and skill, you, unfortunately, have no access to a commercial darkroom as you do in Berlin, and so now you wish to use mine, yes?"

I could only shrug at his accuracy.

"That is what I thought," he filled in with an arrogant smirk. "So now, my humble facilities are worthy of you, eh?"

"You misunderstand me, Herr Hoffmann," I replied. "I would be truly honoured to have such an opportunity," I answered without expression (knowing not what expression would suffice).

"Honoured, eh," he said. "You realize that I now have to swallow my own pride to allow this."

I joked to myself that not even a starving rhinoceros could swallow Hoffmann's pride. Not fully certain of his actual attitude, I considered my options and decided that I had no way out of this morass of theatrically wounded ego except a dubious resort to rank. "Herr Hoffmann," I said, with all the humility I could muster, "truly, I had no idea that I'd insulted you. Perhaps if I asked the Führer to intercede on my behalf?"

Suddenly, as if by magic (a magic that only the mere mention of the Führer could conjure), he shifted to a far different vocal posture.

"Now, now, Herr Linge," he simpered, "I don't believe we need involve the Führer in such trivial matters. I was merely teasing, and you should not take me so seriously. It is I who would be honoured to have you share my . . . as I call it . . . 'palace of miracles,' where, in the darkness, I convert humanity into divinity."

I'd been trembling inside, for the "court photographer" was a particular favourite of the "king," and for me to invoke the latter's name for such a commonplace cause might well have created a dangerous collision of loyalties. But I'd felt like a cornered beggar with no other option. I'll admit—but only to you—that in truth, it was anger, not fear that drove me, anger at this sycophantic hack's arrogance towards me—not that I wasn't deeply disturbed by my need to risk emerging, even for a brief moment, from the shadows. I also filed his humanity/divinity reference away for possible use, if and when necessary.

"Yes, Herr Hoffmann, I'm so grateful for your generosity. I promise I won't get in your way."

"At ease, Major Linge," he joked, now freed from my "suggestion." "Just let me know when you need it, and I'll make every reasonable accommodation. I will even provide one of my assistants."

A magnanimous gesture, Führer-driven, of course, but not terribly practical for my purpose. "A truly generous offer, Herr Hoffmann," I scrambled, "but it would not be proper. You see, I have nowhere near the volume you have, and, moreover, if I am to grow as a photographer, even though I could never dream of aspiring to your level, I must do what I can by myself, from beginning to completion, and without any assistance, don't you see?"

His shoulders straightened slightly in response to my abject grovelling (he was no less a slave to flattery than the rest of the Führer's circle). I was then certain I'd pressed the proper nerve on this bloodless suck-up.

"Admirable, Herr Linge," he replied as I suspected he would. "You will be left to your own devices, I can assure you. Merely let me know of your needs and I will strive to accommodate them."

"You are much too kind," I slobbered. "I will be as unobtrusive as a mouse in a room filled with felines." I expected my remark to be ignored, and it was.

"Not to worry. You will be most welcome," he offered, but then added an innocent touch of irony: "Herr Linge, have you heard of a new subminiature camera called the Minox, invented and produced in . . . good God, Latvia, of all places? Its product has nowhere near the quality of our Leica or the larger-format cameras, but it has, I believe, enormous potential as a tool for spying, something I personally pointed out to Admiral Canaris just yesterday, and he consented to investigate its possibilities. No good for you, of course, since the tiny format is not designed for landscapes or portraits. *Latvia!*" he spat. "A pity our own inventors and Intelligence Services couldn't see the possibilities first."

I agreed with him, for reasons I had no intention of sharing, and tendered a speedy farewell, for much time had been taken up, and I had to report to the Führer and prepare him to greet his dinner guests.

Once I announced the guests and the Führer bade them sit, Brückner and I had little to do but stand invisibly at the door, since Kannenberg and his personally trained and supervised staff ran the complete show here, as well as at the Chancellery, and even more so.

All were seated according to the Führer's wishes: the celebrated filmmaker Riefenstahl at the foot of the table, Eva Braun on his right, Unity Mitford[54] on his left, and the rest wherever Brückner cared to seat them, since the occasion was relatively intimate and the group relatively small.

As usual (and unofficially mandatory), the Führer was the first to speak. He spent much time telling Riefenstahl of his admiration for her cinematic genius and her beauty, and Mitford for her loyalty and dedication to the cause of National Socialism. Goebbels smiled at the profusion of Aryan femininity (though I could feel some tension between him and Riefenstahl), while Himmler sat in his usual manner: motionless and expressionless, as if he were a chief magistrate on the high court, judging—and condemning—all.

Braun was utterly silent, staring into a middle distance, as if in a coma, but I could sense that she had to be seething internally. Some personal experience and much household gossip had provided me with some glimpse into the luckless Fräulein's state of affairs. At the Führer's first dinner upon arriving, I heard him say while Braun sat right beside him that "a highly intelligent man should always choose a primitive and stupid woman, the greater the intelligence, the stupider the woman." None of this particularly surprised me, for, throughout the many times women were present at the Führer's dinners, he'd orate incessantly on the nature and role of women in his life and in the life of the Reich. It was no different when we visited the Führer's mountain retreat. I'd overheard one housekeeper say to another

---

[54] Unity Mitford was an aristocratic English socialite who was a devotee of Adolf Hitler. In Britain and in Germany, she was a prominent and public supporter of Nazism and fascism. From 1936–1940, she was a part of Hitler's inner circle of friends and confidants.

in cupped-mouth stage whispers that even when vacationing, the Führer has little time for Braun and only truly loves her when it suited him. Another said that she's forbidden to smoke, dance, or enjoy the company of other men, even when the Führer's away, so she spends much time exercising, brooding, and reading novelettes. What bothered me slightly was the Führer blithely uttering such misogynistic claptrap in front of women. I'd never even heard such from that lout Kempka.

"Many women find me appealing, Fräulein Riefenstahl," the Führer continued, as the food courses began arriving, "because I am unmarried. It's the same thing with a film actor: when he marries, he loses a certain something among the women who worship him, and they no longer idolize him quite as much anymore. However, considering the obvious cinematic genius you displayed in *Triumph of the Will*, as well as your charm and beauty, I am truly surprised that *you* have not seen fit to marry."

"My Führer," Riefenstahl replied coyly, "my art requires the fullest attention I can provide. Marriage, under such circumstances, would prove a needless and unwanted distraction, as well as an unjust burden on any potential spouse. Is it not the same with you?"

The Führer smiled, raised his right shoulder toward his ear, and the lecture began. "Up to a point, yes, but with me, it is even more important that I never marry. For me, marriage would have been a disaster. There's a point at which misunderstanding is bound to arise between man and wife. It's when the husband cannot give his wife all the time she feels entitled to demand. Every woman is unreasonable to the same degree. One must understand this demandingness. A woman who loves her husband lives only for his sake. That's why, in her turn, she expects her spouse to behave likewise for her sake. It's only after maternity that the woman discovers that other realities exist in life for her.

"The man, on the other hand," he went on, "is a slave to his thoughts. The idea of his duties rules him, and for me, obviously, even more so. He has moments when he wants to throw the whole thing overboard, wife and children too. When I think of it, I realize that during the critical election year of 1932, if I'd been married, I'd scarcely have spent a few days in my own home. And even during those few days, I'd have not been my own master. The wife does not complain only of her husband's absence. She also resents his being preoccupied, having his mind somewhere else. In a woman, the grief of separation is associated with a certain delight. After the separation, the joy of meeting again! When a sailor returns home, after a long voyage, he has something like a new marriage. After months of absence, he enjoys some weeks of complete liberty. That would never have been the case with me, and my wife would justly have been bored to death. I'd have had nothing of marriage but the sullen face of a neglected wife, or else I'd have skimped my duties. That's why it's better not to get married. The bad side of marriage is that it creates rights. In that case, it's far better to have a mistress. The burden is lightened, and everything is placed on the level of a gift." Adding: "What I've said applies only to men of a higher type, of course."

It occurred to me as I half-listened: Did the Führer realize Braun's agony at hearing this? Did he care? Or was it a game to him, to create an internal war among his female worshippers, although I had my doubts about Riefenstahl's ardour when she spread her lips in a Cheshire Cat–like grin. "Of course I see your point, my Führer, but you need only witness the marriage of Joseph and Magda Goebbels to illustrate at the very least a significant *exception* to the rule, yes?"

Though Goebbels appeared radiant with pride, and Fräulein Braun ended her forward stare and turned slightly towards him with eyes hooded, I had seen the Führer at close enough quarters to know that he was upset at Riefenstahl's rejoinder, even though she, no fool, had emphasized the exceptionalness of the matter. And how do I know this? Simple: he instantly changed the subject. A lesson not lost on the filmmaker: whereas the Führer has little tolerance for exceptions, he always allowed himself specific indulgences.

"And may I know what plans you have for our Olympic Games, Fräulein Riefenstahl?"

From previously overheard conversations, I learned that the Führer had given Riefensthal permission to film the games in any way she chose, but Goebbels (who, I also learned, had been previously spurned by her in his romantic advances) was far from sympathetic to her artistic vision. But more appeared to be involved than being dismissed romantically. Goebbels wanted her to take a totally pro-German, even National Socialist, pro-Aryan view. But I'd learned through Chancellery household murmurs that Riefenstahl had remained firm in her intent to film otherwise racially unacceptable competitors with the same degree of professionalism and care as she did the German competitors.

So, before she could answer, Goebbels responded: "I don't wish to burden you with petty details, my Führer, but nothing firm has been established," and turning without expression to Riefenstahl, "Don't you agree?"

"By 'petty details,' Herr Goebbels," she replied blandly, "are you referring to the inclusion of Negroes and Jews?"

Visibly uncomfortable, Goebbels replied: "To a certain extent, Fräulein Riefenstahl, but not entirely."

"Well, regarding Negroes and Jews, at least," she retorted, "would an artist be content to paint a portrait without including all the facial features?"

Probably sensing a potential rupture in *gemütlichkeit*,[55] the Führer intervened. "Joseph, Joseph," he mollified, "as an artist myself, I can appreciate the need for a great deal of freedom of expression, and so must you. But much more important, as a national leader, I must present a side of Germany that will achieve worldwide approbation—and even acclaim. Is this not so?"

It was one of the Führer's famous *have-I-made-myself-clear?* statements, and, as always, he had done: the subject was closed. The only jarring note lay in the inconspicuous but incessant jottings by Himmler onto his little tablet.

As for me, I harboured no interest whatsoever in Riefenstahl's cinematic vision, Goebbels's racial/sexual politics, or even the Führer's desire for beneficent appearances and world admiration. I only cared that in the early morning, I had managed to corner Kempka for a brief moment, during which he assured me of some progress, but that it was still sketchy, tentative, and problematic. He informed me that he had a reasonably reliable source in the Reichsführer's personal chauffeur, who agreed (with some considerable monetary inducement that I was obliged to reimburse) to investigate the matter and provide him with the full name and current location of my two female phantoms. I had no reason to doubt his word, but I was getting increasingly impatient and made this known to him gently, since I hadn't kept any of my part of the bargain. I told him to forget Katrin for the

---

[55] Friendliness, kindness, pleasantness, cheerfulness. I determined to retain the German word in the text due to its universality.

moment and at least get me the information on Emerald, and I would set my part in motion. He agreed, visibly relieved that I'd permitted him to cut his task in half, at least for the present.

"And what is your view of the matter?" Goebbels asked Unity Mitford, who, up to then had merely been staring longingly at the Führer while theatrically ignoring Eva Braun, who was primarily gazing down at her plate morosely, carving designs in the dregs of her pea soup with her spoon.

"Hmmm," she began, savouring the moment. "Well, you know what a devotee of Fräulein Riefenstahl's *Triumph of the Will* I am. Despite the disgusting presence of Jews and Negroes, I trust her judgment in artistic matters. But I also agree with the Führer, that it would be strategically unseemly to film a completely Aryan Olympic Games, in a world that, thus far, stupidly tolerates degenerates, inferiors, and mongrels." Her German was typical of the English, who, I'd read, possessed the singular gift of mangling all languages save their own.

"Well and astutely said, Fräulein Mitford," the Führer concurred, nodding vigorously. "Naturally, I, of all people, am sympathetic to the concerns of all who cherish racial purity, but I'm afraid we will just have to bide our time for its fruition. However," he added, "along those lines, we will be showing a film after dinner, personally selected by our Culture Minister, called . . . called," he faltered.

"*The Little Colonel*, my Führer," informed Goebbels, "a film about the Southern region of America in their post–Civil War period, in which Negroes are, at least, properly servants, even though, unfortunately, no longer slaves and, in this film, serve a charming Aryan infant and her family."

All agreed they'd be delighted to see it, save Fräulein Riefenstahl, who stated flatly that she would rather not. When the Führer asked her why, she replied: "My Führer, I never view other peoples' films. If, by sheer chance, they should be marginally better than mine, I become depressed or angry, and if they are, as usual, worse, I become bored. My way is to maintain the integrity of my personal vision and morale by isolating myself from all corrupting distractions. Please do enjoy your film, but I would prefer ending this wonderful evening on a high note. I will not be missed, I think."

Surreptitiously, I glanced at the Führer's face and could sense, not a sexual desire for her, which I quixotically had, but a trace of bitter nostalgia for what he felt he might have become, instead of the struggling, anonymous, failed artist in Vienna he'd told me about innumerable times. But I was jarred out of my musings by the Führer, who turned to me.

"I say, Linge, would you kindly escort Fräulein Riefenstahl to her car? Brückner will see to the film."

"Of course, my Führer," I replied instantly. Noting that her ivory silk gown had escaped her shoulders and left her back, alabaster bare, I asked: "Shall I fetch Fräulein Riefenstahl's coat or wrap?"

"I came with none," she interjected, "Herr . . . Herr . . ."

"Linge, Fräulein Riefenstahl."

"Yes . . . Linge. I remember now," she said. "However, as an inveterate worshipper of the outdoors in all seasons, I require very little coverage. An escort, though, would be welcome."

I thought I detected the barest speck of seduction but dismissed it immediately as the most preposterous wishful thinking. Even I couldn't recall my last sexual encounter, and, if I could, it certainly wouldn't have been with anyone in her league. I quickly moved over to her, but she'd already pushed out her chair and stood. She was quite *petit*, but her figure, vigour, and poise added untold stature. All the men shot up as we exited the room and made for the entrance, and I assumed all the men were desolate and the females, relieved.

As we walked towards the waiting cars, I tried my utmost to be as professionally business-like as possible, but it didn't last long.

"I really do appreciate the escort. All these damn checkpoints. You'd think I was a political assassin or a vengeful Jew. Good God, a flea couldn't sneak past this number of . . . protectors. I must remember to hire them for my next film. I do so hate curious mobs and hangers-on. I say, Herr Linge, do you, perhaps, have a first name?" She slid her arm through mine and took my hand in hers. It was warm, despite the temperature.

"Heinz, Fräulein Riefenstahl."

"You are losing your hair," she remarked. "Not that I care, you understand. Actually, it gives you an aura of maturity so sorely lacking in someone so young. I'm thirty-four, you know."

"I didn't know, Fräulein Riefenstahl." Somehow, to me, she seemed ageless.

"Leni, if you please. Ah, but you also have that adorable dimple in your chin. Very cinematic."

When, finally, we arrived at her limousine and I swung open the door, before entering, she said: "Many, Heinz, consider me a femme fatale, I'm afraid, even a monster. I pride myself on being an excellent judge of people, and so I feel I can trust you to be discreet—don't ask me why. This is my fate, I fear: to be admired, even worshipped, but to no avail. Many men have succumbed to a charm that was there, I'm afraid, only for display and advantage."

In the harsh bright lights of the parking area, I thought I saw a moistness well up in her blue eyes.

"You see the tears, yes? A purely theatrical contrivance." She again took my hand. "Given all I've said, you may be asking yourself why I am revealing myself to anyone, much less a valet. I have no rational answer, beyond sensing something in you more than a mere valet. Call it artistic insight."

Having no response handy, even a lame one, I remained silent.

Her shoulders began trembling. "You know, Heinz, I have become somewhat cold in this spring night air. I'd be grateful if you would escort me into my back seat."

I, too, was trembling, but not from the night air. "But what of your driver?" I inquired.

"I'm the driver, Heinz, since I came alone," was all she said, as I opened the back door, followed her beckoning finger in, and closed it behind us.

3 *May 1936*

Since the Führer has no pressing affairs in Berlin, we remain at the Berghof. My nightmares have not abated, and though I am as swamped as ever with quotidian tasks, the fresh, crisp, mountain air, the glorious scenery, and the Führer's increased periods of light-heartedness make me eager never to leave this splendidly tranquil setting.

Today, as I happened to round a corner, I stopped abruptly and hid behind it to observe Kempka in a hushed conversation with Dr. Bloch. I could overhear nothing, but the animation of their arms and hands betrayed its seriousness, and so I decided to turn back and go to my destination by another route. In any event, Dr. Bloch's days as the Führer's personal physician are probably numbered.

During a party, the Führer was introduced to a physician named Morell, who boasted that he could cure him of his stomach ailments within a year. He came highly recommended by "court photographer" Hoffmann (not exactly an exemplar of National Socialist moral rectitude), who was treated successfully for gonorrhoea. Franziska Braun, Eva's mother, was also treated with success for her numerous (some actually real) ailments by Morell.

Through the gossip factory, I learned that, to his patients, he appeared to be a miracle worker, and that sobriquet always intrigued the Führer. However, whether a miracle worker or gifted charlatan, if somehow he manages to deliver on his boast, the Führer's "Jew" will have outlived his usefulness and could well be placed at the "mercy" of Himmler and Heydrich, who, unsurprisingly, have always harboured a virulent racial antipathy towards him, which they'd kept discreetly in check up to now.

At the Führer's door, I encountered an exiting Brückner and asked: "Is all well with the Führer?"

Brückner shrugged, resignedly. "He seems to be fine now," said Brückner, "though a bit weary from his bout with his bowels."

"I trust the Führer won."

His one eye shone with impish merriment. "All I know, Heinz, is that if I sinned greatly enough in life, after death, I would be forced to return as the Führer's toilet. But how are you feeling, my friend?"

"Oh, you know I hardly ever get sick, Wilhelm," carefully omitting my hallucinations, migraines, and nightmares, "except for the torpor I develop when sifting through the Führer's fan mail. I'm amazed I haven't gotten diabetes by now."

He laughed heartily at that. "Doubtless. It's the same with me. Except for his official mail, of course. That just gives me heartburn." He paused. "Don't tell anyone, Heinz, but I feel truly sorry for Dr. Bloch. I know a thing or two about this character Morell, and I can tell you that once this arrogant quack gets his pseudo-medical clutches into you, there is no escape. And he never brooks rivals, especially if they're Jews."

"From what you say, you should feel even sorrier for the Führer."

Brückner smiled. "In truth, not so much. A great many of the Führer's ailments are psychological, and the rest, no physician has been able to fully eliminate, so there's little to lose by bringing in some new blood, even if it's tainted. In any event, I didn't come to discuss Morell. I came to tell you that you received a phone call."

I never received phone calls, except from the Führer or Brückner.

"Did it seem important?"

"I wouldn't know," he said, "but she sounded serious. A relative, perhaps?"

Something froze within me. "I have no relatives, Wilhelm."

A smirk. "Ah, then an admirer? Even better. She did sound quite seductive, come to think of it."

"Did she leave a number where she could be reached?"

"No, but she said she would try to contact you again. By her tone of voice, I believed her, you devil."

"And she said nothing more?"

"Mmmmm," he pondered, thumb and forefinger pinching his lower lip. "I do remember something about . . . whether you'd read . . . Shakespeare, I think. *Julius Caesar* comes to mind for some reason. I think she said *Julius Caesar*. Of course, I could be wrong."

"Did she know she was speaking with you?"

"I imagine so, since she referred to me as General."

"And she didn't give a reason for her call?"

"Nothing more than what I told you. I'm not even certain I'm accurate about that."

So, one of them had finally surfaced. It had to be Emerald, from the Shakespeare reference. But for what purpose? Clearly, she knew she was speaking with Brückner and was aware of the extreme disparity in our backgrounds and rank.

"She sounded quite intelligent, and not a little sophisticated.

Have you read any Shakespeare?" Brückner asked with no small amount of gentle scepticism in his tone.

Before my current job, I'd pored through all the Shakespeare plays I could lay my hands on, though I confess to possessing nothing beyond a complete memory of all his convoluted and obscure words, phrases, sentence structures, and speeches, their meaning or meanings utterly eluding me.

"Wilhelm," I lied, "I only came across the name while over-hearing some of the Führer's boasts that only Germans could truly appreciate him. Then I glanced quickly through some volumes carrying his name that occupied considerable space on the Führer's shelves. I'll be frank: even if I'd read him at an ear-lier time, and actually understood what I was reading, it would have been rather comical to discuss Shakespeare with my former associates: bricklayers, barflies, coppers, cell mates, hooligans, petty thieves, and tramps."

Brückner smiled. "Doubtless. He's not easy going, I can tell you. Of course, the Führer's right as always—he's far better in German." He chuckled. "At least that's what we're supposed to say, isn't it? Even so, you should try one. The old boy possessed enormous insight. Might broaden you."

After we parted, and before I began to attend the Führer, I considered the new development: contact at long last, my friend.

But why would she tell all this to Brückner and not wait to contact me?

Trust no one.

Regardless, I spent the night reciting *Julius Caesar* in my mind before writing to you.

WE HAVE BEEN back in Berlin for a time, and, in my Chancellery cell, all I have of the bucolic Berghof are my memories, vivid, but no longer personal; just one more file in the cabinet of my brain.

Continued sleeplessness. It's truly fortunate that my daily duties are substantially quotidian and so require precious little concentration or physical labour. It's becoming increasingly clear that introspection is a treacherous activity, and visibility, a treacherous characteristic. I have always held to the principle that there is no better advantage than others' underestimation. However, against my better judgment, I have slowly, minutely—though sporadically—yielded to the perilous temptation to alter my persona upwards, a disaster for anyone who wishes to operate clandestinely.

But I ask you, my friend, what would I have become—or even be—if I'd contented myself with serving merely as a deferential, mindless menial? Over the years, I've discovered a void in me that must be filled. With what? With vanity? The need to control, to dominate? I claim to you that I am nothing, and yet, I admit, but only to you, in my own way I, too, pursue power. But what sort of power? Like the Führer's? Like those of his inner circle? Never. But what, then? Am I no more than a product, a creation? A vessel?

My mind refuses to rest. Is power an end in itself? For some, yes, and when they achieve it, they know not what to do with it, and so the power lays fallow. For others, the pursuit is merely a tedious, frustrating, and vexing process, the ultimate attainment of power—and its exercise—being everything, as with the likes of Himmler, Goebbels, Göring, and those below them (the more power, the more savoured, and the more brutal the exercise). And then there's the Führer, for whom the pursuit, the attainment, and the exercise of power are of a piece, a mundane yet mystical journey. For example, only this morning, while I tidied his office, he told me:

"Do you know, Linge, a journalist once asked me what was the most enjoyable—yes, enjoyable—thing about being the absolute and undisputed leader of Germany, and do you know what I told him? I told him that it was being able to fart in company and no one would smell it."

"Don't you mean hear it, my Führer?" I countered.

"No, Linge, smell it. That is what is being the Führer. They hear music and smell nothing."

Having both heard—and smelled—the Führer's farts for over a year, I wanted to say: *Unfortunately, my Führer, I have not your capacity to manipulate the senses of others.* I didn't, of course. Instead, I said: "My Führer, you magically possess a quality that few in any position have. I must admit, however, that I confront a challenge, in dealing with Il Duce's after-dinner flatulence, whose vapours know no moderation, schedule, or boundaries." I omitted any discussion of the Führer's inner circle—no less foul-smelling, but infinitely more trusted by the Führer and, to that extent, that much more treacherous.

He laughed. "Naturally. The Italians have no capacity for authority or discipline. Aside from my unique gifts, I laboured long and hard for this 'magical' quality, Linge. It comes with the office."

Before I took my leave, the Führer informed me that Kempka would now be his principal chauffeur, since his "old comrade in arms" had just passed away. Alas, so much for Kempka continuing his detective work for me.

All told, a desolate morning.

❧

The afternoon was barely better, save for my determination to avoid further self-examination. I'd received no call or message from Emerald since her previous attempt. I intended to corner Kempka—once his "period of mourning" over Schreck's recent demise had passed—and try to learn how to reach her on my own initiative, since my part of our bargain had been rendered moot with his elevation through inheritance. I resolved to give it one more day.

I did receive a phone message from Hanfstaengl, inquiring as to my progress in helping to bring him back from exile. I agreed to meet him at a certain café tomorrow, for speaking of such matters in the Chancellery was problematic at best for him, and for me, out of the question.

Once the debate over the inclusion of "inferior" races from other nations into Olympic competition had been resolved by Führer fiat, the matter of homegrown Jews still remained. Much of the afternoon and even into the evening was taken up with this matter by the Führer, Himmler, Heydrich, Goebbels, and the head of the Reich Sports Office, Hans von Tschammer und Osten, expressing a variety of opinions.

Naturally, the Führer, Goebbels, and Osten wished to show a peaceful and tolerant side of Germany and temporarily silence those who were intransigent concerning "Aryan supremacy" and who argued that Jews were not "true athletes" in the Teutonic sense, and so would put up a poor showing anyway (Himmler expressed that such a case actually warranted complete exclusion so that no contestant would weaken Germany's image). In this, as in all things, the Führer took the broader view.

The result was a faux compromise, which barely camouflaged Germany's anti-Semitic and militaristic image while the participating nations were present. They decided that they would hide any signs of anti-Semitic campaigns or plans of territorial expansion. The government would remove signs that stated "Jews not wanted" and other racist slogans, especially in major tourist areas. The Führer would also "clean up" Berlin by authorising the Interior Ministry to have the chief of the Berlin Police arrest all gypsies and place them in concentration camps. But most important for the purpose of the meeting, and as a concession to Himmler, the Führer agreed to initially welcome all potential participants, Aryan and Jew, but ultimately ban all Jews from participation, not by publicised racial decree but by covert bureaucratic and physical barriers, leading to performance disqualification. That appeared to satisfy everyone, and all left on a triumphant note.

Of course, no one took notice of me, much less asked for my opinion, not that I didn't have one. Growing up the way I did, my contact with Jews was both infrequent and coincidental. I believe that my landlady was Jewish, but she seemed no different than any other landlady I'd encountered, Jew or Gentile: greedy and demanding. I may have worked beside them but had no idea. Occasionally, I would see some, called Orthodox, who set themselves apart by their odd clothing and hair, but I never encountered the ones constantly vilified in Goebbels's propaganda films, posters, cartoons, and jokes. Moreover, I had no religion and, frankly, didn't much care if the Jews had killed Christ or kissed him. I have no special knowledge of the Jews' physical prowess, but the ban I believe to be both meanspirited and unnecessary, for what that's worth.

THIS MORNING, AS I was tending to the Führer's immediate needs, Fräulein Schroeder entered with her pad and pencil and waited for instructions, all the while assuming an awkward position that allowed her to avoid all eye contact with me. Since this had been going on since I'd come to the Chancellery, the Führer (no disinterested party in the gossip factory that flourished about him) finally took decisive action to end the nonsense once and for all.

"Ah," he began, "I see I must exercise my formidable diplomatic skills. Fräulein Schroeder, Herr Linge, you must know that I hold both of you in the very highest regard and wish, while fulfilling my historic mission with all its untold burdens and conflicts, to at least have harmony in my own home. So, now that I have you both together, in my chosen role as peacemaker, I declare that you must establish a truce—nothing like the accursed Treaty of Versailles, mind you, but one in which all benefit." He turned to Schroeder. "Fräulein, I pride myself on being no inferior judge of character, and I utterly fail to see what you could possibly have against young Linge here. I have received no reports that he has caused you harm or been anything but courteous and considerate towards you. Am I right?"

Schroeder's stood stiffly, her arms pressed so tightly into her body that she appeared like an unwrapped department-store mannequin, and her face would have made a prune run for its life. "Yes, my Führer," she spewed, "I cannot dispute what you say."

Ignoring (or missing) the contrived ambiguity of her response, he continued, turning to me. "Linge, do you harbour any grudge or grievance towards Fräulein Schroeder here?"

"No, my Führer," I lied, "absolutely not." I just hated her bloody guts.

"As I thought," said the Führer with a slender smile. "All right then, since all this appears to be a matter of misunderstanding and conflicting personalities, I would ask you both to, as the Americans say, 'bury the hatchet' and work together harmoniously for the sake of efficiency, not to mention, morale—for my sake. Can you now shake hands and end the hostilities?"

"Of course, my Führer," we both answered at the same time.

The Führer's smile broadened, then he nodded and pursed his lips with satisfaction. "Well, then," he said, "let me see you do it. Amorous advances are purely optional," he added, to lighten the moment. It reminded me of my "lost" moment on the train.

I, of course, moved first toward her and held out my hand, since she maintained her rigidity. Agony in her eyes, she eventually took it and pumped it once, like a farm wife pushing down on a recalcitrant pump handle, then I moved back.

"All right, then, having resolved another diplomatic crisis," the Führer beamed, "let us move on. Fräulein Schroeder, I will be requiring you for some dictation, and Linge, I won't need you until this afternoon's lunch."

With that, I saluted both of them, turned, and left to go find Kempka, with my morale in the toilet.

⁂

As expected, I discovered him presiding over the Main Garage. He had (no great surprise) quickly made it his own little kingdom, even to the nameplate that had suddenly changed from merely "Julius Schreck" to "SS-Obersturmbannführer[56] Erich Kempka, Principal Chauffeur to the Führer, Adolf Hitler."

He was seated at his desk, now an executive model rather than the small, rough-wood office desk that Schreck had favoured, as befitting a grizzled old soldier of the Party. Since I had also been recently promoted to the same rank, I knocked and entered in one motion, needing to exhibit no sign of deference.

"Ah, come in, Heinz," he said, swinging his tiny feet off the desk. "Come to admire my new domain?"

"Of course," I replied, shaking his hand. "And so quickly, beyond even my expectations. I expect that Schreck's recent passing ends our bargain, yes?"

Kempka tilted his head and pursed his lips. "Not necessarily so, Heinz. True, I could have used that prick's passing as an excuse, but as a man of honour, well, I feel obliged to keep my part of the bargain, since, in a way, you did keep to yours."

I squinted in barely controlled scepticism. "I did? To tell you, in truth, I had just begun to make some tentative progress with the Führer, but far more needed to be done. In fact," I fibbed, "I had planned—"

"No, no, Heinz," he interrupted, "action on your part might have done the job . . . might, mind you . . . eventually. But your suggestion about what to do with the bastard, well, the hell with might. That definitely did the trick, and no delays too."

I shook my head internally. What suggestion? I had made no suggestion. "What suggestion?" I asked him.

---

[56] Lieutenant Colonel.

He lowered his voice by half. "Your suggestion. Have you no memory? When I'd despaired to you of ever replacing Schreck, even through your best efforts with the Führer, you said, and these, I believe, were your very words, as I remember them: 'Then I imagine you'll just have to kill him.' Right?"

I experienced a seismic shudder in my bowels. He was quite right; I did say that, and in those very words. But I'd only been pulling his leg. My God, the covetous maniac had taken me seriously! "But how—"

The chauffeur raised his palms. "Better you don't know, my friend. Can't blab what you don't know, is my philosophy."

The looney had a point, but curiosity was bursting my brain. "I can appreciate that, Erich," I persisted, "but you know you can trust me. Have we not established that by now?" It was a feeble argument, but true, for all that.

More hesitation and pursing of lips. "Well," he finally said, drawing the word out to agonizing length. "I suppose I can give you some of the details, since I can always deny it, and my, ah, former superior is in no position to say otherwise: I had the Führer's Jew doctor slip Schreck some meningitis bacteria. How? Who gives a shit? Schreck was already feeble, and according to the Jew, the disease is natural and can't be traced to any specific source."

So that was, in all probability, the subject of the animated exchange I'd happened upon between Kempka and Bloch. The man was truly diabolical. At the moment, all I could think of was: To what extent could I hold myself responsible for this? I quickly determined that what one person said figuratively bore no direct relation to the actions of another, who took things literally. However, with that understanding, I also vowed to always take that into consideration when dealing with anyone—especially with any member of the SS.

"In any case," I said, suddenly clear of conscience, "you said something about keeping your word."

"Hey, absolutely," he cut in. "I always keep my word. As a matter of fact, I did get something from a reliable pal in Himmler's motor pool. He nosed around real careful, as you'd expect, and told me that there are no records of any Katrin or Emerald, either by name or description, and shit, you know how Himmler and his flunky Eichmann like to keep records. So that's it. I did my best, but it looks like those two females—like all females—led you by the prick down a dark alley and into a stone wall."

I believed him, and so, on this avenue, I was utterly thwarted. At the beginning, Kempka had asked me why I hadn't gone to Katrin's residence to check. Since I'd actually been to her residence (at least one of them), I told him that I *had* gone there, but the person who answered the bell was a seventy-seven-year-old retired Deutsche Bank executive who had never heard of Katrin, at least the Katrin I described to him (but all the while, wishing he had). Now, all that remained was the long-shot Hanfstaengl, and the even longer-shot hope that one or both women would somehow contact me.

Another half-sleep awaits me.

No one, my friend, even his mortal enemies, can sensibly deny that the Führer is a superior human being. However, in my opinion, there are times when he can be too superior.

After our session with the Führer, as if by divine revelation, Schroeder, that poisonous pitchfork, converted from mortal enemy to intimate confidant in a virtual instant. At most, I would have preferred basic civility, but, ever the authoritarian malcontent, she suddenly made it her sacred duty to corner me at every opportunity to "confide," which, in her case, was to bitch and moan about . . . everything!

This morning, she accosted me again in the hallway, whining and complaining again about her claustrophobia and boredom, how the same walls, the same floors, the same useless incessantly humming air-vents, the same people, the same "routineless routine every bloody airless day," all pressed in on her, as she put it, "punctuated by a few hysterically frenetic moments when the Führer decides to dictate." I merely nodded to be agreeable. Again, she asked me how I could stand it.

I told her that I was an apprentice bricklayer, and so boredom and mindless routine (not to mention the coarseness and derision) were the job, and besides, my current duties required far more of me than merely waiting for the Boss's signals. I added that the smaller—she would say confined—spaces actually made for easier access to people and things and so made my endless errands and anticipations more efficient, and actually left me more time for myself. What I didn't tell her was that I actually cherished the austerity, the aseptic womb of it. Among other things, to some extent, it mitigated my incessant headaches and nightmares.

Once she'd vented her seemingly endless miseries, she took her leave as if I didn't exist. Clearly, she was a mental case, but at least she was no longer an enemy.

Once the Führer awoke and was in the midst of his dressing regimen, he began railing against the intelligentsia, a favourite target of his wrath. Perhaps he was practising for his dinner with Himmler, Goebbels, Leni Riefenstahl, Göring, and Dr. Karl Brandt,[57] but, as usual, he provided no motive.

"Are you reading the books I provide you?" he asked.

"Of course, my Führer," I lied, since I'd read them long before in the city and university libraries and knew every word. "I try to read whenever I get the opportunity, despite the difficulty."

"Good, Linge, good," he replied absently, clearly having an agenda that employed me as no more than a human diving board from which he could leap headlong into the pool of his subject. "It is from the basic education of the ordinary citizen," he continued, "that we will ultimately achieve our objectives. I must tell you that the intellectual elite of Europe—whether professors of faculty, high officials, or whatever else—never understood anything of this problem. The elite have been stuffed with false ideas, and on these they live. It propagates a science that causes the greatest possible damage. Stunted men have the philosophy

---

[57] Hitler's chief administrator of the Reich's Euthanasia Programme.

of stunted men. They love neither strength nor health, and they regard weakness and sickness as supreme values."

He puffed some air. "Since it's the function that creates the organ, entrust the world for a few centuries to a German professor—and you'll soon have a mankind of cretins, made up of men with big heads set upon meagre bodies."

Clearly, he savoured that image, for he laughed heartily, slapping his thigh with vigour. I was only half-listening, because I knew I'd be half-listening to the same thing that night at dinner.

As I stood, occasionally assisting in the serving at my request (primarily to keep from dozing off), most of the dinner conversation centred again on the upcoming Olympic Games and the steps required to make visitors from all nations welcome, regardless of their political system or racial position. Having no interest in sports and being assigned no part in the conception, preparation, or execution, I merely strived to maintain my expected—and desired—invisibility. I was also doing everything reasonably possible to avoid Riefenstahl's face, though I could sense that she was, from time to time, furtively glancing at me with a lewd smirk. I could even imagine a sly wink.

When the going got a bit thick, the Führer would throw in a current joke, usually at the expense of Göring. At one point, the Führer glanced at the corpulent general, his enormous garish uniform bedecked with medals, ribbons, and decorations, and said to the group: "Did you hear that Emmy Göring found our Hermann here waving a baton over his underwear in the bedroom and asked him what he was doing, and he replied: 'I am promoting my underpants to OVERpants.'"

All gasped with hilarity, especially Göring, who appeared

to relish jokes about himself, I imagined, as one more mark of importance. All, that is, save Himmler, who merely turned up his thin lips in miserly amusement.

Once dinner had been completed and the table cleared, Riefenstahl excused herself, saying that she had to contend with a myriad of preparations for her commanding role in the Olympic saga. All stood, including the Führer, who kissed her hand and told her that not just the Reich but all nations will be her audience and that he had every confidence in her brilliance and skill in making his Germany the model and envy of the world. She, of course, did not disagree.

Most of the Führer's guests stayed on to watch the American horror film *Werewolf of London*. However, Himmler stayed only for a few minutes, muttering cryptically to Göring as he rose that one day the people of London will wish for werewolves to protect them.

Halfway through the movie, the always-impatient Führer had also seen enough and bade me accompany him to arrange his desk for some special late-night work. As I was preparing to follow, he turned, reached into his inside pocket and drew out a letter-sized envelope and held it up.

"You know, Linge," he said, "Brückner must learn to be more careful. Leaving this tucked in with my own mail merely adds to my burdens, for now he adds postman to all my other duties." He chuckled for a moment, then handed me the envelope. "This appears to be for you," he said simply. "From a female admirer, perhaps?" he added with a repeated raising and lowering of his eyebrows, not unlike Groucho Marx. "Read it later, once you're done with me."

It took every drop of willpower I possessed to appear composed. Was this an accident on Brückner's part, or intentional?

Had the Führer—or anyone else—read it? It appeared unopened, though at the Chancellery, it was virtually impossible to tell. "Of course, my Führer," I replied, quickly slid the envelope into my tunic pocket, and followed him out the door.

⁖

Once free, I made for my quarters with very deliberate speed, closed and locked my door (for what it was worth), and sat down on my chair, breathing raggedly. Finally alone, I allowed my hands to shake, almost tearing the contents while opening the envelope. With animals, all is instinct, but humans must obey the dictates of sentience, and so I finally opened the envelope and read the brief, typed contents:

My Dear Heinz—

If you are reading this, please thank General Brückner for me. I'm most gratified that you've attempted in so many ways to seek me out. I too have desired to be with you again, but the current circumstances are less than opportune, perhaps even impetuous. At any rate, I know that you received the "trinket" I sent you, and hope you secreted it securely. When the time is right for us to meet, I'll contact you to arrange a suitable time and place. All I can express now is my fervent hope that it will be soon, and that I have not misjudged you. With my fondest hopes and best wishes for us all.

— E.

Once the adrenalin rush of elation and bewilderment had subsided, I flushed the note, dressed for the inevitable summons from the Führer, unlocked the door, and returned to my chair, utterly confounded and exhausted with frustration. Yes, I had followed instructions and "secreted" the "trinket," as she put it—to the same place as I did my negatives. Like all the notes I've received by unconventional means, this latest one was both cryptic and suggestive and provided no means by which to decipher its meaning or act further on its contents. And yet, I thought, could *that* have been its meaning: to refrain from acting? I had to admit to myself that, in great measure, inertia was welcome, since, for a person heavily invested in invisibility, all impulses are treacherous.

Thankfully, any possibility of further thought vanished with a perfunctory tap on my door and Brückner's jocular entry.

"Well, Heinz," he chirped, "did you like the movie? Afraid to venture out at night now, I imagine, yes?"

My thoughts instantly turned to the Jews, but I kept that notion well to myself.

I laughed. "Wilhelm, I wouldn't be a bit concerned. It was London, after all," I told him, "not Berlin. And anyway, I never got to see the entire film, since the Führer had some work for me."

"Pity," he commiserated. "But don't be too complacent, my friend. Berlin has its share of werewolves—and they even venture out by day."

It sounded vaguely sinister, but I had no idea what he was referring to, and so had no intention of pursuing it.

"To what do I owe the honour?" I asked instead.

"Hardly an honour," he replied with a sideward nod of his head. "Just avoiding duty for a little while. The Führer's been on the telephone with Mussolini for three numbing hours, and he finally took pity on me and waved me out.

"Yes, even though Mussolini seems to be of two minds on the subject, he's still interested in persuading the Führer to enter into a formal alliance. Personally, I'm convinced the alliance will happen, but not until the Games are well over. But you know how these things are."

"So, you think that the Führer and Mussolini will sign an agreement?"

Brückner smiled thinly. "Oh yes. No doubt about it. Aside from actually liking Mussolini, God knows why, the Führer, the supreme realist, harbours no illusions about the world's good-will when it comes to a fully restored and powerful Germany. On the other hand, he also harbours no illusions about Italian resolve and military competence. Where we all go from there is as much a mystery to me as it is to you. You have, perhaps, some schnapps?"

"You're in luck, Wilhelm," I informed him. "I just happen to have a fresh supply." I moved quickly to my armoire and retrieved a bottle, brought two glasses from my bathroom, and set them down on my night table. Brückner took the bottle, opened it with practised ease, poured two glasses, handed me one, and we both sat and sipped, until he said the magic words.

"By the way, did you ever get that letter? I'd intended to give it to you personally, but mistakenly placed it with the Führer's mail through haste, and then forgot."

"Yes. Many thanks," I said truthfully. "The Führer actually handed it to me himself, then chided you playfully for adding 'postman' to his other duties."

"So, my error caused no damage. Good. When am I to meet this erudite mystery woman of yours?" he asked, relieving me of further wondering whether or not he'd read my mail or desired to further discuss Il Duce. And for that matter, whether I'd know the meaning of *erudite*. Just how much of my persona had he pierced?

"Wilhelm," I explained truthfully, since to lie would only

pull me further into more lies, like quicksand, "she's as much a mystery to me as she is to you. I met two remarkable women, both only once for the briefest of times, and I've no idea who they are."

"I'm truly intrigued," admitted Brückner, with pursed lips. "But, since you also seem to be, let us hope she surfaces quickly, and that I get to meet her. You will introduce us, yes?"

How to reply? "It will be my pleasure—and my relief," I told him, for what it was worth, since she'd actually referred to him in her letter and included him in the chain of delivery, for reasons I couldn't fathom. "As I said, I only met her once, briefly."

"Well, my friend," he said, lifting his glass, "you must have made quite an impression. Here's to a second meeting."

We both drank to that. And yet, I wondered whether he'd made anything of her expression of hope that she had not misjudged me. But misjudged me as what?

TODAY, I LEARNED that my unfettered run of the photo lab was coming to an end, since, under Himmler's increasing strictures, "my Jew" had been replaced by an SS-approved Aryan proprietor who knew nothing about photography and who possessed the intractable surly stubbornness of the truly ignorant. A short, stocky man in a brown double-breasted suit with pugnacious beer hall–brawler features, unruly eyebrows, an oil slick of black pomaded hair on top.

My mistake was in wearing a civilian suit instead of my uniform.

"Where is Herr Adelsheimer?" I asked on arriving to find this lout behind the counter. Other than the two of us, the shop was empty.

"You mean the *Jew* Adelsheimer," he sneered. "Who knows where they go—and who cares, so long as they're gone?"

"You mean gone, as in no longer running this shop?"

He gaped at me as if I were the village idiot. "You have eyes, yes? You see me, not the Jew, yes? That's your answer." His eyes narrowed. "Now, what is it you want? I run a business here."

I trusted such a creature not one bit, and so I would have to approach Hoffmann, as I did at the Berghof, and make some sort of arrangement. This, of course, would be far more awkward, due to the Führer's greatly increased need of Hoffmann's services at the Chancellery. Moreover, how many more pictures could I take of the buildings, grounds, and personnel before it generated annoyance or suspicion? And yet, it had to be done.

"I'll come back when you aren't so busy," I said, and left.

⇛

While having lunch in the Servants' Quarters, I chanced to overhear another idiotic debate among some household staff and a messenger from Reichsminister Goebbels's ministry, regarding the nature of intelligence. One was saying that in a world without Jews, the entire question would have to be considered differently. Differently from what? asked another, and received a shrug for a response. One particularly zealous SS-sergeant said, laughingly, that once the Führer rids Germany—and eventually the world—of the "Jewish Pestilence," there will be a pure form of intelligence, an "Aryan intelligence," not one based on who can better cheat decent Aryans of their money, who can better sneak around blood-sacrificing Aryan babies to their "filthy Jew God," or who can better hide behind Aryans while the latter believe they control their own destinies. One hapless temporary secretary who'd been recruited to replace Hannelore dared to suggest that, if Aryans were so weak and gullible that Jews can do all this, perhaps intelligence is not the problem. The sergeant jotted down her name, and I knew that she would soon become far more temporary.

Once the messenger had left, I immediately told the sergeant to forget what he'd heard, since it was merely kitchen blather, and when he bridled, I pulled rank and told him that the woman was just joking, and that knowing the Führer as I do as his principal valet, he would be sorely disappointed at what was clearly a misguided and meanspirited attack on one of his personal household. "If I were you," I advised with no little menace in my voice, "I would leave such matters to General Heydrich. You must have other, more pressing duties."

That shut the bastard's mouth for a time, and he reluctantly handed me the paper on which he'd written her name. I gave it to the secretary, who smiled in sweaty relief and shook my hand vigorously. Pity she was homely (I'm being charitable) and engaged (God knows how).

I must confess that, personally, I had no interest whatsoever in such things but considered what the sergeant was spewing to be utter idiocy and, perhaps, even a refutation of his own argument. If pressed, I would have had to agree with the secretary: that perhaps heredity, sophistication, training, education, and tradition had more to do with intelligence than race, but always maintained the strictest discretion in such dangerous company. So, when one of the cooks asked me in all politeness what I thought, I answered that, being thoroughly unschooled and in an isolated position, I rely completely on the Führer and his closest advisers to deal with such weighty questions, and left, quickly.

After breakfast, Brückner and I had very few official duties to perform, save stay awake and at hand, since Goebbels, Göring, Himmler, and von Ribbentrop were conferring with the Führer concerning ways in which the Reich could make the most favourable impression in its role as host of the Olympic Games, to begin in less than a fortnight. Von Neurath was conspicuously absent, indicating to me that the Führer had already made up his mind and wished as little disputation as possible. Himmler and Göring expressed half-hearted concern, contending that, purely accidentally of course, should Jews and Negroes from other nations outdo Aryans, it might cast serious doubt on all that the true Germans had been told since the dawn of the Party.

The Führer, all the while pacing as the discussion proceeded, finally moved to his desk, sat down heavily, and clasped his hands in front of him, as if in prayer. The rest remained standing.

"There can be no denying the Jewish problem," he began, "both in general and specifically, as regards the Games. However, gentlemen, at the moment, a far greater problem—our international reputation. You all have the luxury of ignoring it, but I, unfortunately, do not. Already, I have been asked again by . . . by . . . who, Brückner?"

"Count Henri Baillet-Latour, my Führer, the Belgian president of the International Olympic Committee."

"Right," said the Führer. "This Latour fellow informed me almost a year ago, before the Winter Games, that all race-based signs and other such formulations, should be eliminated prior to the Games. And he was right to do so. If we're to receive the respect we amply deserve as a major player on the international scene, we must rein in all our well-meaning anti-Semitic zealots, both before and during the Games. None of you has ever enjoyed the 'hospitality' of our prison system. I have, and I can tell you that one thing you learn is patience. They too must be made to understand that they must now be patient, for their time will come, as mine did. This is *your* job, Heinrich, and you too, Hermann, distasteful though it may be."

Göring merely nodded, then heaved his bulk onto a guest chair to a clanging and jangling of his seemingly endless rows of medals, like an obese bell tower.

For his part, Himmler's eyelids lowered slightly with what I'd read as a schoolmaster's tolerance of a gifted-but-wilful pupil.

"Yes, my Führer," he said, with his usual lack of expression, "you're right, as always. The German people can wait."

Wait for what? I thought absently, but all appeared to know what he meant, and so nothing further was said about that.

"In any event," the Führer continued, "this Latour also informed me that it would violate protocol for me to congratulate the winners, and so, if, by some miracle, a Jew or Negro should win a medal, I would not be obliged to congratulate the person, so a little sunshine in the gloom, yes?"

This appeared to satisfy Himmler and Göring sufficiently.

"And you, Joseph," said the Führer, "along with Ribbentrop here, will see to our important and, I expect, impressionable guests. Incidentally," he said to all, "in case you were unaware, I've named Ribbentrop to be our new ambassador in London. Perhaps he can bring those pig-headed Britishers to a proper appreciation of our common heritage and interests."

There were shouts of "hear-hear!" all round, as von Ribbentrop stretched himself to the breaking point to appear grateful and humble. I assumed that von Neurath's days were numbered.

"All right, then," the Führer concluded, "as you would imagine, I have much to prepare, so if you gentlemen will excuse me." The signal to leave had been given and all but I saluted and left.

I'd noticed that during the meeting, the Führer had been sweating profusely, his face red and pinched, and now he grasped his midsection in apparent torment. "Get Morell," he groaned loudly. "*Morell now!*"

"My Führer," I replied, "Dr. Brandt is closer at hand. Shall I—?"

"*No, NO, Linge!*" he shouted in agony. "I'm not a defective infant or its mother.[58] I require sound medical treatment, not a premature death. *Quickly now!*"

"At once, my Führer," I answered crisply, phoned for some household staff to keep watch, and raced from the room to locate Brückner, who was in the kitchen swilling brandy from the bottle. "Wilhelm," I asked breathlessly, "where can I find Dr. Morell? The Führer is suffering and will only accept Morell."

Brückner moved his bottle away and shook his head. "That bloody quack?" he asserted. "What about Bloch?"

"He's in Linz on vacation," I informed him, "and he won't accept Brandt. The Führer's screaming for Morell."

He sighed. "I fear that Bloch's 'vacation' will be a long one. All right, Morell it is then. He's in one of the guest rooms. I'll go and fetch him while you try to calm the patient."

Grossly obese, with frog-like features, sulphurous body odour, and venomous halitosis, Morell was truly a repulsive character. But when he'd cured a painful case of eczema on Hitler's legs and provided temporary relief for his stomach cramps, the Führer was won over. To the irritation of his other doctors, the Führer then proceeded to (literally) swallow any of Morell's advice, no matter how hair-brained. For example, to combat recurrences of the volcanic stomach problems, Morell plied him with a remedy called "Dr. Küster's Anti-Gas pills," which contained significant amounts of strychnine—and his patient often took

---

[58] In the context of the 1933 Nazi law *Gesetz zur Verhütung erbkranken Nachwuchses* (Law for the Prevention of Hereditarily Diseased Offspring), Karl Brandt was one of the medical scientists who performed abortions in great numbers on women deemed genetically disordered, mentally or physically handicapped, or racially deficient or whose unborn foetuses were expected to develop such genetic "defects." These abortions had been legalized—as long as no healthy Aryan foetuses were aborted. On 1 September 1939, Brandt was appointed by Hitler co-head of the T-4 Euthanasia Programme.

as many as sixteen of the little black pills a day. The sallow skin, glaucous eyes, and attention lapses noted by observers appear to be consistent with strychnine poisoning. Another ingredient in the pills, atropine, causes mood wings from euphoria to violent anger. All this, in my poor, untutored opinion, did not auger well for domestic and international relations, not to mention relations with his personal staff, for all I could think of was that a man with the Führer's pre-existing temperament needed no enhancements.

I raced back to the Führer to tell him that help was on its way, but by the time I arrived, the entire quarters were enveloped in a toxic fog of flatulence, and I could hear the Führer moaning loudly from his bathroom. The servants were standing guard just outside, trembling with fear and nausea, as if their nervous systems were unsure of which negative sensation to attend to. After thanking them for "holding the fort," I dismissed them and stood watch alone.

Within what seemed only a matter of seconds, a short, fat, smelly, bald, ugly, heavily pockmarked creature carrying a large doctor's satchel entered. If he had a shell, he would have resembled a particularly hideous snail. "Where is the patient?" he demanded.

"In the bathroom, Doctor," I answered needlessly, since the horrific groans and stench were emanating directly from there, as if they were struggling to escape the Führer.

Without a word, Morell hurried into the bathroom, and Brückner took me by the shoulder and pulled me into the hall-way and shut the door. "No need for the two of us to endure more radiation than we have to, eh, Heinz?" he joked. "That's what Morell gets paid for." Nothing seemed to faze him. "Now what would your adoring femme fatale write if she could see what you actually do here?" he joked with a knavish wink.

"Even shorter notes for you to read, I imagine," I jested back, and he smiled, I felt, benignly. I'd once read a novel in which an interrogator said that "anyone who tell me everything, must have something to hide." I knew that my joking so carried with it a certain amount of risk, but I had to give a strategic amount of calculated trust to someone, or I would surely explode, like a container being constantly filled but containing no safety valve to expel the excess. Of all the people I'd met since my arrival, Brückner appeared to be just the safety valve I needed, and just how much to contain, the only question—and not a small one, for he might well be a far better undercover agent than I, so there you are.

Within only a matter of minutes, our ears were pummelled by a scream, a mammoth gas explosion, and silence. A moment later, Morell came out, his white lab coat drenched in shit, removed the garment, and with thumb and forefinger handed the foul thing to me by the collar, stretching his arm to the side, all the while gazing placidly at Brückner. He bade us carry the unconscious Führer to his bed and make him comfortable until he awakened.

"He'll be right as rain," Morell assured us. "However," he cautioned, "the effects of my injections may be only temporary, I'm afraid, so you must call me at a moment's notice should the symptoms return, yes?"

"Of course, Herr Doctor," Brückner said, and I nodded in complete agreement, even though he hadn't even glanced at me since he'd entered.

After we had tucked the Führer in, and I had tossed the reeking coat into the bathtub and cleansed my hands thoroughly,

Brückner turned to face Morell. "So, you intend to remain at the Chancellery?" he asked, I believed, rhetorically.

He reached into his pocket, drew out a card containing his telephone number, and handed it to me. "I've already been provided sufficient quarters close by. The Führer wishes me to be his primary physician, and so I shall remain virtually at his side. A year under my special care, and he shall be a new man, mark my words."

"Think Morell can deliver?" I asked Brückner later.

Brückner's shoulders lifted. "Who can say—except Morell, of course. From what I've heard from Hoffmann, he's highly unorthodox—and highly successful. Since those attributes characterize the Führer as well, they may be a perfect match."

I remained after Brückner left. I tucked Morell's card into my pocket, and, after phoning for a cleaning crew for the bathroom and arranging for my old boss Krause to "babysit" for a while, I left for a few minutes to shower, then confide in you.

But even as I write, I can still smell the Führer on me.

A DAY OF celebration for the Führer, for his circle, and for Germany. As for me, I cared not at all, but nevertheless had to adopt facial expressions implying though not showing a barely controlled hysteria.

The Führer, accompanied by all the top-ranking Reich officials, their virtual regiments of SS Guard, and the great majority of the Chancellery household staff, including myself, attended the opening ceremony of the XI Olympiad. Musical fanfares, directed by Richard Strauss, announced the Führer's arrival to a sustained explosion of *heils* and salutes from the natives! The immense stadium was jammed to overflowing—primarily with Germans. Hundreds of athletes in opening-day regalia marched into the stadium, team by team in alphabetical order.

Not being a sports enthusiast, notwithstanding that these were the Olympic Games, the only thing that interested me in the slightest was that a lone runner would arrive bearing a torch carried by relay from the site of the ancient Games in Olympia, Greece, inaugurating a new Olympic ritual, and why I even cared about that eluded me.

Accordingly, my brain glazed over at the entire business, since in the very early morning, I had a humiliating-but-essential meeting with Hoffmann concerning my photographic activities. I encountered him in his studio, preparing his assistants and equipment for the day's events—namely, photographing the Führer and his entourage, since Leni Riefenstahl would take care of the rest and would brook no associates or interference.

"Historic day, Linge," Hoffmann chirped impatiently. "Nothing less than historic. And since I am vital to the process, I have little time to spare, so be quick about it then."

I had no wish to agitate the arrogant bastard, but it had to be done. "Herr Hoffmann," I said, "I'll be quick. The photo shop I'd been using is no longer . . . available."

His eyes widened with a melodramatic flourish. "Ah, let me see if I understand this: And now you wish to use my own humble facilities here, as you did at the Berghof? Now, I'm good enough for all your photographic needs wherever you happen to be, am I right?"

I ached to rip out his throat with my teeth, but of far more importance, I didn't want to draw any attention to my perilous clandestine darkroom activities. "Herr Hoffman," I continued, "please appreciate that never for a moment did I consider your facilities to be anything but of the finest and highest quality. I merely felt that my awkward and amateur efforts were worthy only of a Jewish establishment, and now that it's no longer possible, I beg for your indulgence. I promise I will never interfere with your truly extraordinary endeavours for the Führer and the Reich." I wanted to vomit but forced the bile down with a plunger of pure necessity. I knew well the risks of close and repeated association with Hoffmann's sacred domain, but attempting to replace Adelsheimer at this stage of the Reich's Aryanisation policy would be no less perilous than manipulating that bilious egomaniac. In point of fact, it would be merely an extension of my hide-in-plain-sight stratagem.

Hoffmann slowly drew a discoloured thumbnail to his

pouting lower lip as if in mortal turmoil while considering the matter, then, after an ostentatious exhalation, said: "You understand, Linge, that I was quite prepared to tell you to make tracks, but your plight has truly touched me, especially the Jew part. I would never have wished that alternative on anyone, even you. And now that such a loathsome avenue is closed, I would be less than generous to deny my facilities to one who also serves the Führer, though as a menial. So, yes, you may utilize my darkroom—in off hours, of course, provided that, otherwise, you keep completely out of the way."

I was a study in sweaty degradation, doing everything but kissing his ring, but that almost medieval degree of grovelling was spared me, for he merely told me not to concern myself, for he was notorious for his generosity. Then he scraped me off, as if I were a smudge of shit, coating the bottom of his shoe.

As I fled, I remembered what Brückner had told me when I first arrived at the Chancellery: "Always remember, Linge," he'd said, "in your job, you may need to constantly humble yourself, for there are many who lack the breeding or self-confidence to be good-hearted. Even the Führer had to grovel before swine to obtain the funds and influence necessary to reach the pinnacle of power. Later, he informed me that grovelling was merely a tool like any other, and that one must be judged, not on the need for its use, but on how well one uses it."

I imagine I used it well enough this morning.

While the mob continued to burst into a nationalist frenzy at every German victory, and the Führer and his acolytes reacted similarly, though with somewhat less frenzy—as befitting their station—I was shaken from my recollection of Hoffmann savouring his morning triumph and godlike benevolence by a light tap on my shoulder and a voice whispering in my left ear: "Look straight ahead, Herr Linge, say nothing, and accept this envelope with your opposing hand." I reached over with my right hand and took the envelope. By the time I swung my head toward the voice, he'd gone.

Since no one was paying me the least mind, and the envelope had my name typed on the front, I decided to open it then and there. It read:

> My Dear Heinz, I see I have a rival for your affections—a dangerous rival. This is not in the least surprising, in light of your inestimable value. I'm painfully aware that our last encounter was less than fulfilling for you and no less so for me. You were too inquisitive and I was too sensitive. A mistake on both our parts, don't you agree? Therefore, I would have us begin again, this time, without questions or judgments. In spite of the awkwardness of our parting, you've attempted to contact me, so I believe that what I propose should not be anathema to you.

It added that I would have been contacted, "regardless of Kempka's and Hanfstaengl's less-than-discreet inquiries," and concluded with the statement: "Please believe that my impatience is as considerable as yours." At the bottom was a Berlin phone number that "will respond only to you."

Something rattling round in my subconscious sounded an alarm that had no rational explanation, but the subconscious never provides reasons, does it? My headache now returned with a vengeance, so I quickly replaced the note in its envelope and slid it furtively into my jacket pocket for later incineration. I must tell you that my reaction was quite irrational, for despite the business-like language and mechanical tone of the letter, I was euphoric with anticipation and desire.

I moved several metres over from my position directly behind the Führer to where Kempka was standing with Baur, a veritable tableau of transportation, and, during an intermission, implored the former to accompany me to a relatively quieter and definitely more private place. Once there, I thanked him heartily for his efforts in getting Katrin to contact me, not mentioning her reference to his method of inquiry since Kempka bore no blame (for I never felt I had subtler means at my disposal). He accepted my thanks with aplomb but was visibly eager to watch more Aryans trounce the inferior races.

Before departing, I thanked him once again, hoped there would be no repercussions, apologized for spiriting him away from his Olympic Valhalla, and returned to my position behind the Führer. As I stood there at ease, staring sightlessly into the middle distance between myself and the hollow nonsense on the field, I considered, in an unbidden moment of clarity, whether I should ever dial that number. But, suddenly, the Führer's quote from Frederick the Great nudged clarity aside: *"l'audace l'audace toujours l'audace."*[59]

I knew then, that I shouldn't, but that I would, just the same.

---

[59] "Audacity audacity always audacity."

BEDEVILLED BY KATRIN'S note, I slept not at all last night. By morning, bleary with mental and physical exhaustion, I was left with more questions than answers. And it wasn't just Emerald. Within a relatively short period, I'd been "approached" by *two* stunning enigmas who appeared to find in me an importance of which I was entirely unaware.

There was nothing in my past or present that suggested personal significance—quite the contrary if I'm honest. And yet . . . and yet, what to make of all this attention.

Sir Isaac Newton wrote, "I do not know what I may appear to the world; but to myself, I seem to have been only like a boy playing on the seashore, and diverting myself now and then in finding a smoother pebble or prettier shell than ordinary, while the great ocean of truth lay all undiscovered before me." Even when I read it in my adolescent years, I intuited in that statement, genius simulating humility, as if the Führer claiming to be merely a mediocre politician who got lucky. I was as distant from them as a parrot from a philosopher.

But, be that as it may, I knew, without actually knowing, that contacting Emerald would entail risk, if only for the reason that there would be action on my part rather than inaction—for my chosen persona, risk was a fearsome enemy. Of course, that should have ended the matter then and there: the path of least risk. And yet, against all reason, I still considered taking the other path; the why of it I couldn't possibly fathom. My brain, like a ball spinning around a roulette wheel, had raced through several references to risk that I'd encountered through my reading, finally landing on one by Kierkegaard: "To dare is to lose one's footing momentarily. Not to dare is to lose oneself." It wasn't that I was a stranger to hazard. After all, since I'd arrived, I'd already experienced my fair share, through my photographic exploits and my dealings with Hoffmann, Schreck, Hanfstaengl, and Kempka. It was that I didn't wish to be a human snowball rolling down a mountainside, picking up bulk and velocity as I plummeted to a shatteringly destructive end, and not even know why.

Fortunately, at that very moment, there was a harsh knock at my door, followed by the entry of Fräulein Schroeder with a sealed envelope and mock scowl.

"Fräulein Schroeder," I exclaimed, "this is the first time you've come to my quarters. To what do I owe the pleasure?"

She pushed her arm forward and I took the envelope. "A pleasure for you, but a chore for me. I'm too accommodating for my own good, and pay for it. On my way to the Führer, I was accosted in the Great Hall by that disgraced piano-playing mammoth Hanfstaengl who gave me that," nodding at the envelope in my hand, "and asked me if I would be so good as to deliver it to you. Why I agreed, escapes me."

"I'm truly at a loss. Why would he give it to you of all people, and not to a mail-room clerk or one of the legion of guards?"

She shrugged her padded shoulders, lifting them almost to her ears. "Perhaps he was on his way to do just that, but my beauty cast a spell over him," she grumped. "How should I know? He did, and that's that. Surprised he would even show his ugly face, I was too taken aback to ask questions, and once he'd given me the envelope, he thanked me and left without a backward glance, his mission accomplished—and mine just beginning."

Then she smiled, two rows of small yellow teeth, as if to illustrate the tender goodwill behind the theatrical grouchiness. "Mission done," she said, almost wistfully, I thought, "now I'll go where I'm needed and finish transcribing all the Führer's dictation by myself, Wolf being indisposed for the fourth time this month."

"What about Dara?" I asked. "She's never sick."

"She doesn't have to be," Schroeder said, acid oozing from her words. "All she has to do is moan to the Führer that she desperately needs some time with her fiancé Kempka, and that's that. I'm not complaining, mind you. The Führer deserves only the best, and so I abide and endure."

"I know how much he appreciates your selfless dedication, and well, maybe one day, he'll actually break down and hire another secretary."

She smiled again, a vision in yellow. "I'm not holding my breath. You know once the Führer is used to someone, well, you know how that is. You're the last valet he's taken on, and he probably wouldn't have done *that* if you weren't so unique, or so he claims."

I suddenly recalled Katrin's cryptic letter, referring to my "inestimable value."

"'Unique'? He actually said that?"

"Yes, a few times, in fact. But he's never said why, and," looking me up and down, "I couldn't possibly guess." Then she grinned in a way that a hyena would envy, perhaps to have me believe that she meant well with her insult.

"Isn't it obvious?" I joked. "Who can time the Führer's toilette as I can?"

Her teeth disappeared into pursed lips. "Well, I've done my duty," she said. I thanked her again for her sacrifice, and she said, "Save that blarney for one of your lady friends," then nodded and left.

I immediately tore open the envelope. In the message, the male Medusa inquired (I could tell, with no small measure of anxiety) as to whether I had yet spoken of him with the Führer since our encounter on the train and, finally, ardently requested (begging, I imagined, would have appeared unseemly) a meeting to discuss possible strategies if I hadn't.

With not a little guilt (since I had done nothing about the piano player's request up to now), I still hoped he'd learned something about Emerald and Katrin, at least more than what I'd gotten from their notes, and so I composed a short response, giving my apologies and agreeing to meet him, specifying the popular and so always-crowded Café Kranzler for our chat, since it was also situated on Unter den Linden, so little time and justification would be required (again, a matter of hiding in plain sight). I would mail it during one of my frequent diversionary photo strolls outside the Chancellery. One stone, two birds.

I made my way to the Führer's rooms, only to find him emerging from the bathroom, sporting a broad smile.

"Ah, Linge," he sang, "that Morell is a true miracle worker. Bloch was a decent chap and well meant, but, being traditional— and a Jew—he was far too conservative and unimaginative in his treatments. This Morell, though dismissed and disparaged by the medical mossbacks, has worked wonders on my bowels.

He actually told me that, under his care, within a year I would be cured of *all* my ailments, and I tend to believe him. I only wish that I could find a Morell for my military, instead of a creaky pack of stiff-necked, arrogant, and reactionary 'von thisses and thats.'"

What could I possibly reply to that? I began readying him for the day ahead. But suddenly, in the midst of timing him, he stepped back.

"So, Linge, how goes it with your mystery woman—or is it women?" he asked, I first thought, completely out of the blue. "Two stunning women fighting over you. In my time, I was also fought over, as you can imagine, but nothing could come of it, I saw to that. You, on the other hand, are far freer than I, so who shall win?"

"But . . . how—?"

The Führer let out a jocular laugh. "Linge, Linge, do you think I am ignorant or oblivious to the goings-on of my family?"

"Obviously not, my Führer," I responded feebly. "I just find it difficult to imagine that a man like yourself would be even the least interested in such mundane matters."

After shaking his head in mock disappointment, he said, "For a man like myself, as you put it, no matter is too mundane for the father of his children, especially as regards their problems and their affairs of the heart."

Clearly, my mail is never delivered to me at the Chancellery directly, so to deny anything he probably already knew would be both useless and fraught with peril. "I have little time for such pursuits, my Führer. If and when I do, I hope that my efforts will bear fruit."

"I have great faith in your industriousness, Linge. I, of course, have no time for such things, as you've heard me say on several occasions. Have you ever read any Shakespeare?" he asked, I imagined, based on the note he'd obviously seen.

"No, my Führer," I lied, "only a mere mention of *Julius Caesar* in an anonymous note I received."

He nodded slowly. "Yes, *Julius Caesar*," he repeated. "I'm especially fond of that play. Did you know that in 1926, I drew a detailed stage set for the first act, with sinister façades enclosing the forum where Caesar is cut down? Even now, you notice that I reserve the Ides of March[60] for fateful decisions. The English never understood him, but Germans do, instinctively."

"Truly," I said, "I had no awareness of your interest, my Führer."

I, too, had read all the plays, but of course without the Führer's understanding and insights. To the extent I possessed any comprehension of the arcane and convoluted stories and language, the common denominator seemed to me to be the heavy price one pays for ambition and power. Given the numerous failed attempts on his life, did the Führer see himself as Caesar but as Caesar having escaped the murderous conspiracy of his intimates? Even so, I couldn't imagine why the Führer would possess any great enthusiasm for that theme, and so I dismissed my interpretation immediately.

"Oh, yes, Linge, my interest is both ardent and long-standing. In truth, I possess all of Shakespeare's plays and keep them in my second-floor study at the Berghof. When we're there, you're welcome to borrow and read any or all of them, that is, unless Bormann has appropriated them."

"That's most generous, my Führer," I said. The reference to Bormann was not inaccurate. At the Berghof, I encountered

---

[60] March 15th.

Bormann frequently. Without deviation, he would arrive, just as I was about to take my leave, but he visited with the Führer at all hours and attended every meeting. A stocky figure in Party uniform, his briefcase always at hand, listening, weighing situations, diligent, calculating, ever supportive of the Führer, not unlike von Ribbentrop. I once overheard Major-General Schellenberg describe Bormann as "one of the most dangerous men in the Reich."

For my part, I saw only a thickset functionary with square shoulders and a bull neck, his eyes like those of a boxer advancing on his opponent. His appearance was utterly proletarian, coarse, conventional, and unassuming, and, as a consequence, according to Brückner, those who were rivals and even enemies always underestimated his abilities. Of course, this skill I could readily appreciate. While the more conspicuous leaders strutted before the people and paraded for the news media of the world, Brückner cautioned me that Bormann was unobtrusively gaining control of those points of power that counted. And, most dangerously, not unlike a talented toad like Morell, he had gained the total trust of the Führer. Brückner loathed him. I wondered what someone like Himmler might think of him, but, in a million years, I would never dream of asking.

"My pleasure entirely, Linge," the Führer said. "To be frank, I'm quite determined to further your education by any means necessary. Just look out," he admonished, "that you don't begin to put on airs. Always remember that regardless of our outward attainments, we are still of common stock, for it is the likes of us that will guarantee the Thousand-Year Reich."

Little chance of me forgetting. "Yes, my Führer," I said, resetting my stopwatch. "I won't forget. Would you care to finish dressing now?"

I WAS JOLTED awake to confront a waterfall of sweat cascading down my cheeks and my pyjama top glued to my back. Fire as usual, but this time, I wasn't in that decrepit stairwell but in the Führer's study. The enormous fireplace I manage to avoid looking at when awake, I saw nothing else in my nightmare. In it, the immense fire is expanding, contracting, pulsating, radiating, and even screaming its intense heat, as if corporeal, sentient. I force myself to look away, and when I do, I see the Führer, lying on his plush sofa in a woman's ragged nightdress, sticky with ashes and blood, with only a tiny patch of filthy white having escaped. He doesn't speak, but I can see his eyes pleading with me, but I don't know what the pleading is for. Then I see that he's trying to speak, but the words are not audible. When I lean down to hear, he suddenly raises his arm in his traditionally languid manner, then grabs my arm and whispers: "Now, Heinz. Can't take any more. There's nothing left. I beg you. Please." I reach down and lift the Führer into my arms as if he were an infant, carry him to the roaring fireplace, and toss him into the flames.

I read once that certain people are actually able to control their dreams, and even direct them, much as in the cinema, but, I am not one of them. I asked Dr. Bloch about this some time ago, but he merely shrugged and told me that these were "grandmothers' tales" and that the subconscious is called that for a reason.

I found the Führer in a foul mood, still in his robe (for I'd been slightly late), but not angry with me. His anger was reserved for General Wever's successor, Field Marshal Kesselring, as well as General Udet,[61] obviously allowed in by Brückner, who was also there, wisely standing at a safe remove. When the latter saw me, his eyes rolled quickly to the ceiling and back, out of view of all but me. I joined him.

The Führer was standing behind his desk, fists pressing white knuckles into the desktop blotter. Then he lifted his hands and unclenched his fists, for Kesselring was saying, "My Führer, I understand and appreciate your position entirely, so much so that I expressly told General Göring that, while I was honoured and humbled, he should clear the matter with you before proceeding, for I had no idea what your own preferences might be."

The Führer nodded with a few bobs of his head. "You were right to do that, Kesselring. Was it the same with you, Udet?"

"Yes, my Führer, exactly so."

Brückner's eyes again travelled to the ceiling.

"Yes," the Führer said, "too often the corpulent Hermann fails to see where he leaves off and I begin. In this case, I happen to agree with his choices, so I will brief you now. You both know the situation in Spain, yes?"

Both replied, "Yes, my Führer," in unison.

"All right, then," he continued. "I promised Generalissimo

---

[61] Walther Wever was chief of the Luftwaffe General Staff. His participation in the construction of the Luftwaffe came to an abrupt end on 3 June 1936, when he was killed along with his engineer in a Heinkel He70 blitz. After Wever's death, Göring began taking more of an interest in the appointment of Luftwaffe staff officers, not necessarily conferring with Hitler first. Göring appointed Wever's successor, Albert Kesselring, as CS and Ernst Udet as head of the Reich's Air Ministry Technical Office (*Technisches Amt*).

Franco that I would render some military assistance in his attempt to bring order to that chaotic country, smash their Communist menace, and, not so incidentally, provide badly needed training for our pilots, navigators, and bombardiers. Two days from now, Kesselring, you will order the Luftwaffe arm of the Condor Legion[62] to assist Franco. I have already given instructions to the commander of the ground units."

General Kesselring stirred visibly in his chair.

"Yes, Kesselring?" the Führer asked. "You have something to add?"

"Yes, my Führer," he answered, cautious. "I know that you must have considered the international reaction to what might be viewed by other nations as a provocative—"

"Naturally, Field Marshal," the Führer interrupted, his voice slightly raised. "You can always rely on me to consider the implications of everything I decide. Now, are you sufficiently relieved, or do you require me to call for Morell?"

I could tell from Kesselring's face that the Führer's snideness had registered. "Of course not, my Führer. I am completely satisfied, and we will proceed on the fifth, as you instructed."

The Führer nodded. "And you, Udet?"

"I'm in complete accord with you and Field Marshal Kesselring, my Führer," he said, fawning blatantly, not unlike von Ribbentrop. "We are prepared for any eventuality."

"I see no . . . 'eventuality,' as you put it, but complete success.

---

[62] The Condor Legion was a unit composed of "volunteers" from the German Air Force (Luftwaffe) and from the German Army (Wehrmacht Heer) that served with the Nationalists during the Spanish Civil War of July 1936 to March 1939. The Condor Legion developed methods of terror bombing that were used widely in the Second World War shortly afterwards. The bombing of Guernica was the most infamous atrocity carried out by the Condor Legion during this period.

Good," the Führer concluded. "Both of you keep me informed through Brückner here, yes?"

Both agreed enthusiastically, shot up, clicked, saluted, and Heiled, then marched out when Brückner swung open the door and followed them out.

As I began to prepare the Führer, he shouted: "Do you *believe it*, Linge? *Timidity on all sides!* Von Neurath, Kesselring, and the rest of the so-called professional classes. All they know is caution, delay, discretion, implications, endless discussion. You wish to know why we lost the War? *THIS IS WHY!*" he screamed, smashing his fist down on the desktop, sending several pencils and papers to the floor.

I didn't ask or wish to know, but I assumed by his tone that the Führer's question was entirely rhetorical. I also noted that, for once, the Führer had left out the Jews, but I was confident that they would not be absent for long.

"It's nothing short of ignominious," he ranted on, "that so many who have sworn to serve me and the Reich without hesitation believe that I am flexing muscles I don't possess or, no better, that though I possess the muscles, I should not flex them publicly."

To be frank, I'd read a bit about Spain but cared no more about it than I did about Ethiopia. The Führer had been discussing Franco with his diplomats, industrialists, and military men for weeks, but I wasn't listening. With a memory like mine, I've trained myself to tuck away irrelevancies, or my consciousness would become a tidal wave.

"But they seem to be necessary, do they not, my Führer?" I replied, as blandly as possible.

After a moment of silence: "Yes, I suppose you are right, Linge—for the present, at least, until you . . ." His voice trailed off and his face took on a glazed expression that I had seen very infrequently. It was similar to the one I saw while he was interviewing me for my position. *Until I what?* My brain writhed with curiosity, but I would never ask.

THROUGH BRÜCKNER, I was able to get the swine Krause to attend the Führer in order to make my way to the Café Kranzler to meet with Hanfstaengl. I was not a little apprehensive about this, assuming that the place would be virtually deserted since the Games were still in progress and most Germans would be either at the stadium or at their radios, few, if any, daring to demonstrate their disinterest in public. While I desired no undue attention, I needed information, and I had no idea how long the hapless Hanfstaengl would be available.

I was right. Germans had been replaced with foreigners who were unable to obtain passes—or had sold them. Whether this was good or bad for me I had no way of knowing, since not all "foreigners" were necessarily foreigners. I'd learned from experts that certain Gestapo agents, as a matter of routine, dress as ordinary citizens to make certain that ordinary citizens were, in fact, truly ordinary. As a consequence, it would have been fruitless for me to study the crowd, and so it came down to doing it or not doing it. Dressed in full SS finery, I at least felt less like a daredevil.

The ugly giant was already seated amidst the mob, looming over a tiny cup containing the dregs of what had once been an espresso. However, he wasn't alone, for with him was seated an elegantly dressed and coiffed brunette, daintily embracing a multicoloured drink and appearing to look past him as he spoke. When I arrived, he didn't stand or introduce her but instead waved me to a chair across from him. I imagined it was all a gesture to impress the lady and to underscore the social, cultural, and intellectual distance between us, despite his need of my help. As it turned out, I was only half right.

"I say, you don't speak English, do you?" he asked in his Munich drawl, not unlike the Führer's, but without the latter's lilt.

"I'm afraid not, Herr Hanfstaengl," I replied truthfully. "My formal schooling was quite limited, as were my contacts with English speakers. To be frank, I can hardly even speak proper German."

I thought I could see the lady stifle a laugh.

"No matter," he said indulgently, while raising his shoulders. "I was merely curious. Would you care for an espresso or," with lifted eyebrows, "perhaps something a bit stronger?"

"No, thank you, Herr Hanfstaengl," I said. "The one will render me jumpy and the other will do me in."

"Not even a compromise, like our fine German beer?" he persisted.

He waxed pompous enough to be compensating for his long association with America. "No, thank you," I replied. "I leave that to fine Germans. I'm merely a valet."

The woman said nothing, merely stirring her already well-stirred drink and studying me (I felt). "Since Herr Hanfstaengl omitted to introduce us," the lady finally said with a beguiling smile, avoiding Hanfstaengl's indifferent gaze, "I'm Bella Fromm,[63] Herr Linge. You can call me Bella, or Frau Bella, which

____

[63] As a Jew and an outspoken liberal, Bella Fromm found her social and journalistic position increasingly precarious after the Nazis came to power in

is what I'm generally called in polite company. Herr Hanfstaengl
was good enough to satisfy my insistent journalistic sensibilities
by arranging this meeting. I assume you had no warning, am
I right?"

What could I say? "You're right," I said. "Did you wish an
interview with me?"

"I'd kill for it, but that's not my reason for coming."

"Which is? I'm merely a valet."

"Ah, blessed humility," Hanfstaengl interrupted. "But what
a valet! On such a day, how did you possibly manage to pry
yourself loose from the Führer?"

"Not difficult, actually. I arranged for Krause to take my
place—the process isn't important, save that the Führer was
agreeable." I despised the arrogant swine.

"Well, then, Herr Linge, I regret that I must take my leave
for a few moments to place some important phone calls. I'm
certain that Frau Bella can adequately substitute for me in the
meantime. She's a Jew, incidentally, in case you didn't know."

The ugly behemoth then pushed himself up, bowed his head

1933. She was protected to some extent by her friendship with leading foreign diplomats and with conservative members of Hitler's government, such
as Schacht and von Neurath. In 1934, she sent her daughter to the United
States. After 1934, she was no longer able to write under her own name,
but her journalism continued to appear anonymously, and she continued to
be invited to diplomatic and social events. Deprived of most of her income
from journalism, Fromm returned to her family's trade as a wine merchant,
exploiting her contacts with foreign embassies and wealthy Berliners.
According to her account, she also used her contacts to secure visas for many
German Jews desperate to emigrate. For this reason, she wrote, she refused
to heed the advice of her friends that she should leave Germany before it
was too late. In 1938, however, Jews were excluded from the wine trade.
Left with no income, and in the face of increasing anti-Semitic persecution,
Fromm emigrated to the United States in September 1938.

slightly, proffered the Hitler salute, and lumbered towards the lobby. I had no idea what this was all about, so I waited.

Frau Bella took a sip of her drink and put it down daintily. "He's a detestable prig, don't you think?" she said.

I shrugged. "I've encountered worse," I replied.

"Ah, yes, of course. You're Hitler's valet. I almost forgot."

I was not a little put off by her remark, but I let it pass. I needed to see what she was up to. "I suppose that him telling me you're a Jew," I remarked, "was intended to clear the air between us, which, I must say, was a needless insult to us both since he invited you and you agreed to come."

She smiled enigmatically, displaying teeth so perfect they would have any yellow running for its life. "My apologies for that last comment. A pilot isn't a passenger." She took a sip and lowered her glass delicately. "I'm told you have no vices," she remarked.

"You make me sound like a pious dullard."

"Not intended, especially to someone who, given your age and . . . background, says 'pious dullard.' But I'd very much like to tempt you into one minor vice."

"Yes?"

"You said you didn't drink, but I do wish you'd break your vows this once," she offered, raising her glass. "It won't do any more than relax someone I sense is a bit apprehensive. It's called a Zombie.[64] Quite the thing. American, you know. Served heated. Legend has it that a fellow named Donn Beach originally

---

[64] A Zombie contains ¾ oz 90-proof rum, 1½ oz gold rum, ¾ oz light or white rum, 1 oz pineapple, 3 tablespoons lime juice, 1 teaspoon super-fine sugar, 1 tablespoon 151-proof rum. Mix all the ingredients except the 151 rum in a shaker with cracked ice. Shake till cold and pour it all into a tall (hopefully, Halloween-appropriate) glass or mug. Float the 151 rum on top by softly pouring it over the back of a spoon slightly above the drink. Dust

concocted the Zombie to help a hungover customer get through a business meeting. He returned several days later to complain that he had been turned into a zombie for his entire trip, then ordered another, so being rendered a zombie seems to have had little dissuasive powers. But fear not. Legends are just that. In any event, I can assure you that, despite my occupation, I can be the soul of discretion. I solemnly promise, even as a devious Jew, that your reputation and your honour will remain intact. What do you say, Herr Captain?"

Trust no one.

"My name is Heinz, Frau Bella," I replied. "All right, one Zombie," I conceded. After all, how much control could I surrender after one drink? "If that'll make you happy."

She laughed. "It's to make *you* happy, my wary friend, not me." Then she motioned to one of the waiters, who rushed right over, presumably to my uniform, took her order for two Zombies, and withdrew.

What she failed to tell me, and what I should have known, was that any alcoholic drink, no matter how weak, will be exponentially more potent if it's one's first.

"Like it?" she asked.

"Rather like a warm fruit punch laced with a delayed-fuse grenade," I answered.

Her laughter was cut short by the approach of two men in identical suits, wide-brim hats, and long leather coats, one man, short, the other, tall. They were studiously nondescript, and so I was able to instantly identify them.

"Heil Hitler," both intoned. "Is everything all right, Herr

---

the drink with powdered sugar. The fruit serves as a mask for the potency of the high levels of alcohol.

Captain?" the short one said. No expression; narrowed eyelids; all business.

"Of course," I replied without returning the greeting. "Does anything look wrong?"

"Just routine," the shorter one said. "You have your papers?"

"Naturally." For effect, I slowly slid out my identity card, personally signed by the Führer and Himmler, and handed it to him.

The shorter one glanced at it and passed it to the tall one. Both gaped at the signatures. The tall one handed it back to me with dispatch and clicked his heels smartly. "And . . . the lady?" the short one stammered.

"She's my personal guest," I replied nonchalantly. "Is there anything else you require, to justify your intrusion?"

Both sweated profusely, and I was enjoying every moment of their discomfort.

"No . . . Herr Captain," the short one stammered.

"Good. I'll give your regards to the Führer," I stabbed.

They both saluted smartly and fled.

"I'm mightily impressed," Frau Bella remarked, her perfect eyebrows raised. She was olive-complected and elegant, an exotic type I'd never encountered before.

"They don't know what I really do," I remarked, "but in truth, why did Hanfstaengl bother to tell me you were a Jew?"

"Believe me, for him, it was no bother. But as to why, I have no idea," she said. "To humiliate me? To cause you to doubt my sincerity? To assure you of my willingness to help—or else? Or to just be Hanfstaengl. I leave the final analysis to you."

"To doubt your sincerity? Sincerity about what?"

"About whether I would agree to work to locate your mystery women. Actually, I haven't the foggiest notion, except that the whole bloody business has a scent I wouldn't wish even my worst enemy to wear."

"A scent? What sort of scent?"

"That's unimportant," she said. "All I want to know is whether you're SS by position or by inclination."

"That's a bit too highbrow for this untutored menial. Just what are you asking?"

"Do you actually mean it?"

"Mean what?"

She took another sip, set her drink down, leaned forward on her elbows, and whispered: "All right, I'll say it: Do you, Heinz Linge, truly believe in the National Socialist dogma and the SS creed? Yes, and I'm gone, no harm, no foul, as they say. No, and we might have something to talk about."

"A heavy couple of questions, Frau Bella. But how can you trust any answer I might give? Wouldn't you be taking quite a chance?" I took a sip of my Zombie.

She gazed silently at me for a long moment. She was not in the least unattractive, but it was the remarkably audacious intelligence behind her eyes that defined her allure, as it did with the stunning Emerald and Katrin, women I'd never hoped to encounter in my former life, save on a movie screen.

"Jews," she answered with a shrug, "have been taking chances for thousands of years, some fruitful, most disastrous. This will merely be one more."

What could someone like me say to someone like her?

"I was an uneducated vagabond and later an uneducated bricklayer's apprentice. That's about as close to ideology as I ever got. And now, I'm an uneducated valet. I leave things like dogma and creed to those above stairs."

She smiled again. "'Above stairs.' You haven't finished your Zombie," she said. "Still wary?"

"No," I replied a little tipsily. "My position provides a certain . . . immunity?"

"I dare say," she replied with a nod and pursed lips. "Unfortunately, my position doesn't. But I'll do my best to look into that matter for you. Despite my . . . situation, I still count some associates—even friends—in high places. Thus far, that is, but please realize that my condition is rather precarious under the current regime."

Interesting. I never thought of the "current regime" as "current." Did she mean temporary? Transitory? "Of course I'm most appreciative, but why would you agree to assist me?"

"You don't think that a 'Jewess,' as you people like to call me, is capable of a grand, selfless gesture?"

I issued no reply, waiting.

She laughed. "I was only pulling your leg. Naturally, I thought that someone in a position such as yours might prove helpful in case of an emergency. Was I wrong?"

For a flash, I could see desperation in her eyes.

"No," I replied, "you weren't wrong."

I was about to shift into more chit-chat, when Hanfstaengl returned without apology or explanation. He merely nodded, then signalled for the waiter, and ordered another double espresso for himself and nothing for us. Once it arrived, he lifted it with his surprisingly nimble bear's paw and gently sucked the foam from the top, then turned to Frau Bella.

"I say, I have some rather confidential matters to discuss with Herr Linge here. Would you be so good as to excuse us?"

Frau Bella's lips edged up slightly and her eyebrows rose

again. "Confidential, eh? My stock in trade, and you would deprive me of a few juicy tidbits?"

Hanfstaengl just stared at her solicitously. "Be patient, pet," he said. "Soon, I should have an even better morsel for your rag."

She shrugged. "In the words of my people, *vos vet zeyn di tog.*"[65]

"Meaning?" Hanfstaengl asked snidely.

"Ask another Jew—if you can find one," she tossed off, and stood.

This time, both Hanfstaengl and I rose when she did. I walked her a few paces away, hoping I didn't betray my tipsiness. "Shall I escort you to the door so you won't be unnecessarily . . . inconvenienced?" I offered.

She placed her flawlessly manicured hand gently on mine, then removed it just as gently. "Thank you, Heinz, but from what I've seen, this small gesture of mine will assure that, I think. To the point: I promise you that I'll be in touch when I know something." She pivoted and walked away to the stares of many, but not to our two Gestapo men, who appeared to find their beers suddenly fascinating.

"Well, Herr Linge," Hanfstaengl began, gazing at my drink, "I see that you've been roundly seduced. Not surprising, though, seeing that Frau Bella has that effect even on the most virulent Jew haters in the Reich. Well, perhaps then you'll speak to me now about the Führer, that is, as to whether you'd made any progress since we last spoke on the Führerwagen."

I hadn't spoken a single word to the Führer about Hanfstaengl, since I'd been warned by Brückner and others

---

[65] Yiddish for "That will be the day"; *das wird der Tag sein*, in German.

that such intercessions even from top officials were risky and seldom successful with a man whose convictions about people were tightly held and highly intractable. Moreover, who was I to become involved in such matters, and why? What did I owe to this mammoth in both body and ego? Yes, he'd gotten me Frau Bella, but still . . .

"It's been on my mind constantly since then," I lied, exerting all my willpower to keep from showing the effects of the Zombie. "It would appear that you may have run afoul of Reichsminister Goebbels, and even of General Göring, and one does that to even one of them at his peril." According to Brückner, that part was true, so I proceeded. "Aside from the Kurt Lüdecke affair,[66]

---

[66] It has been claimed that Hanfstaengl's final break with the regime can be traced to a day in October 1934, at his usual lunch with Hitler and his aides at the Chancellery. The conversation turned to Kurt Lüdecke, and the anti-Nazi radio broadcasts he had started making from America. Lüdecke was already a member of Hitler's inner circle when "Putzi" (Hanfstaengl's nickname) joined the movement. However, Lüdecke had drifted away from Hitler as early as 1925 and moved to the United States, where he married an American woman. However, as popular support for the Nazis grew, he tried to find a way back into Hitler's good graces, assisted by his patron, the rabid Nazi Alfred Rosenberg. A few months after Hitler took power, Lüdecke was back in Berlin, demanding to be made press attaché at the German embassy in Washington. Hanfstaengl watched all this with dismay, especially because of Lüdecke's relationship with the fanatic Rosenberg, and so he began collecting compromising material on both to discredit them. With the assistance of the head of the security police, he discovered that Rosenberg, a virulent anti-Semite, was having an affair with the daughter of a Jewish publisher, and that Lüdecke had fabricated much of his own history. Putzi passed on all his information to the authorities and, shortly afterwards, Göring had both Rosenberg's mistress and Lüdecke jailed. However, Hitler himself intervened and ordered Lüdecke's release, and probably because he knew where certain skeletons were buried, he was taken into "protective custody," also on Hitler's orders. He escaped to Switzerland, and from there returned to America, where he began making broadcasts denouncing Hitler and his regime. Hanfstaengl crowed about this directly to Hitler, saying: "There you are, Herr Hitler. I have warned you for the last ten years against

I've been informed by a highly placed source that Goebbels had complained to the Führer that you had referred to him as 'that poisonous dwarf' and that you were constantly trespassing on his jurisdiction.[67] And as for Göring, mainly from kitchen gossip, it may have been the birthday party at Karinhall, at which you rebuked him for displaying artworks you claim he plundered from various German galleries."

I found it virtually incomprehensible that a man of such sophistication could make mortal enemies of two of the Führer's oldest and closest associates and still expect a warm reception at the Chancellery. But such seems to be the myopia of arrogance. All the while, Hanfstaengl's lips were pursed in grim concentration. Aside from the initial slurp, he hadn't touched his espresso.

"As I hoped, you appear to be only too well informed, Herr Linge," he admitted, "even though what you say is not entirely unknown to me and, also, not a little discouraging. However, I will confess to you that I acted only out of my regard for the Reich and my love for the Führer, and may have, in my zeal, gone beyond the bounds of propriety and discretion. The only questions that remain are: Can my reputation and relationship with the Führer be restored? And if so, how?"

I had no respect or regard for the haughty swine, although it confirmed my belief that a formal education only made a fool more articulate, but no less a fool. "I have some ideas along those lines, Herr Hanfstaengl," I said, stalling. "Please give me some time to experiment, yes?"

---

having people of this type around." But, instead of agreeing, Hitler was livid, screaming: "*It's all your fault, Hanfstaengl!* You should have handled him much more diplomatically." From then on, relations were never the same between them.

[67] His dealings with the foreign press.

"What ideas?" he pursued.

"I'd rather not say until I know more, but I'll tell you if and when I have anything tangible. Will that suit?"

His huge shoulders rose. "Unfortunately, I am in no position to disagree. That was not always the case, but there you are."

I'd wearied of this meaningless exercise and I needed to get back to the Chancellery to send Krause on his way, check the Führer's mail, and prepare the Führer for a celebratory Olympic evening. Germany had been doing quite well.

"I do appreciate your bringing Frau Bella. She might be able to deliver what others couldn't. As I said, I'll be in touch the moment I've gained anything of value for you," I repeated for reinforcement. Then I rose, saluted ostentatiously, and left him to his double espresso.

5 August 1936

DESPITE HAVING TO be present at an intimate celebratory luncheon for vR,[68] the "master salesman" (as the Führer liked to call
him), on the occasion of his appointment as ambassador to the
United Kingdom of Great Britain and Northern Ireland, I was
still able to concoct an excuse to leave the Chancellery, stroll
casually to the most innocently visible public phone in Berlin,
and dial the number I'd been provided in the note.

However, before I could even execute phase one, I was accosted
in the hallway by my new, Führer-commanded "comrade
in arms" Fräulein Schroeder, who tugged me into the empty
Staircase Room.

"Herr Linge," she whispered: "You are, I believe, close with
General Brückner."

On her pinched face I could see the strain just to speak
normally to me. "To some extent, Fräulein Schroeder," I admitted with no great anxiety, since it was common knowledge from
the Führer on down, though even I didn't know to what degree.
"He was," I replied, "and, to a great extent, still is my mentor
and even, if I may be so bold, my friend." *What was the devious
shrew cooking up?*

"Yes, I thought that. And, since you regard him as a friend,

---

[68] Von Ribbentrop.

and, by Führer fiat, I now am obliged to so regard you, I must confide that I came into possession of information that Reichsleiter Bormann, for whom I have the utmost respect and admiration, is, I believe, somehow determined to have the general removed from his position as chief adjutant."

I was amazed she still had breath after such a recitation. I had only met Bormann under official circumstances, and only at the Berghof, the renovations of which he'd been put in sole charge. He seemed to be a particularly nondescript but indefatigable functionary, hysterically loyal to the Führer, and utterly humourless (even more so than Hess, if that can possibly be imagined). In other words, totally unlike Brückner.

"Fräulein Schroeder," I asked, "may I ask how you came into possession of this information?"

She nibbled on her lower lip for a moment. "Herr Linge, my source would prefer to remain anonymous, but I can assure you of its honesty."

Honesty, perhaps, but what of its accuracy? Something was afoot, of that I was certain.

"Did your source explain the why and how of it?" I asked her.

"No. But my personal opinion is that the Führer's . . . disenchantment began with the Sophie Storck matter."

"And what might that be?"

"He hasn't told you?" she asked, with bushy eyebrows lifted, incredulous. "She was his fiancée. You are of course aware of General Brückner's severe injuries from his accident. Well, Sophie Storck was a passenger in the car and also suffered several injuries."

I was aware of that—and more. Yes, Storck was a talented artist who was a frequent guest at the Berghof and had received many commissions for her hand-crafted ceramics from the

Führer and Fräulein Braun. After the general broke off their engagement, the Führer took quite a dim view of the matter. Her answer didn't really matter to me, since I already knew of Schroeder's antipathy towards Brückner, but I could detect no discernible distance between the Führer and him. It was the Bormann connexion that puzzled me, but I dared not broach the subject. Her story could be factual or, due to a claustrophobic boredom, with which she continually claimed to be afflicted, she'd made a decision to stir the cauldron of rumour to make some entertaining mischief.

"In any event," Schroeder concluded, "the Führer took a dim view of the breakup and, I'm told, even provided considerable compensation to her." She shrugged and turned to leave, then turned back. "Well, I've told you all I know. Duty done, I certainly hope that you and the Führer are satisfied with my congeniality." A final snipe.

I didn't know whether to laugh at that or cry. News of his romantic inconstancy was well known to me and not a few others in the Chancellery, even though I never knew the particulars and never inquired of them with him.

I grovelled gratitude to Schroeder for her "comradely generosity and thoughtfulness" in coming to me with this and not keeping it to herself. I promised that I would treat and pursue the matter with utmost discretion, and inform her of anything I learned (of course, promises I had no intention whatsoever of keeping). But all that could wait.

❧

After she left, I was about to search for a public phone booth that was both entirely visible, yet, for that reason alone, entirely private, when I opened the door and was greeted by my old nemesis, Krause the malignant mouse. It had turned out to be quite a morning.

"Ah, Herr Linge, I hope I'm not disturbing you?" he simpered, quite a change from the hostility, snideness, and avoidance of the past, even outdoing Schroeder.

"Not at all," I fibbed, "what can I do for you?"

"Well, first, to congratulate you on your promotion to major—as was I." He handed over my new badge of rank.

Major, I thought. I had no idea I'd been promoted. More money I had no means of spending, and a rank that meant nothing to me as a valet. "Well, Herr Major," I replied, "please accept my congratulations as well. It would appear that we are being groomed for greatness," I kidded, but it fell on deaf ears and a blank mind.

"I wholeheartedly agree, and so I thought, as the senior valet, that I'd make the initial approach towards a . . . a . . ."

I noted that he didn't refer to himself as *my* senior. "Truce?" I assisted.

"Exactly so," he responded with grudging gratefulness. "A truce, indeed. We both serve the saviour of Germany in our own way. The Führer has made it perfectly clear to me that, while our roles may differ, we are both quite indispensable."

The Führer is truly the most brilliant diplomat. "Indispensable, eh?" I said. "Well, that's far better than any promotion, don't you agree?"

He pulled himself all the way up to his full five-feet-four inches.[69] "Of course . . . uh, may I call you Heinz?"

"Naturally . . . Karl. We're colleagues engaged in a great and

---

[69] Linge was six-foot-three inches.

historic enterprise, are we not?" I had no idea what I was saying, but whatever it was, it seemed to satisfy the obsequious toad.

"Yes, yes," he said, his face suddenly flush. "Absolutely, despite our relative ages and years of service. Of that, there can be no doubt."

Relative ages and years of service, indeed! Even with the Führer's obvious prompting, it was still killing him.

"Agreed," I said. "I see no reason why we can't be congenial colleagues, am I right?"

"Absolutely no reason at all," he said, and held out his tiny hand, which I shook with gusto to illustrate my goodwill, after which, we exchanged the Hitler salute with some verve, and he trotted away. Hardly.

After Krause, I managed to locate Brückner, who was just emerging from the Führer's quarters. He was shaking his head, but his face presented no clue to the reason.

"Am I disturbing you?" I asked timorously as I approached him.

His grimace curved upwards into a smile. "No, Heinz, not at all. What's cooking?"

"I just had a visit from Krause, who now seems as eager as Schroeder to patch things up—with the Führer's prompting, of course."

Brückner's lips pressed together into a half-hearted grin sitting above a slight raising of his shoulders. "My philosophy is simple, my friend: take what you can get. If the little man wants to play comrade, there's no harm in indulging him, since, at the very least, you satisfy the Führer, and isn't that what all the play-acting here is all about? Everyone benefits. Oh, and congratulations on your promotion. I predict that, one day, you may come to outrank me."

I laughed. "Well, if so, I promise to issue my orders to you as delicately as possible."

And so we parted on a note of levity.

※

Finally disentangled from unanticipated obligations and encounters, both occupational and personal, I quickly affixed my major's insignia for authority, grabbed my Leica for appearances, and left the Chancellery in search of a suitable telephone kiosk. As I strolled with theatrical nonchalance into the centre of Berlin's teeming commercial district, I arrived at the corner of Möckernstraße and Hallestraße, adjacent to the Anhalter Bahnhof,[70] where stood an enormous red-brick post office and letter distribution centre. There would be a row of public phones there. Unfortunately, with a row, the stress would be on public and I also needed private. Next, I considered the single, glass-enclosed, public-telephone kiosk, only a few metres away, marked Oeffentlicher Fernsprecher,[71] but dismissed it as unsuitable for a major of the SS. A restaurant? Too noisy, and I might be recognized. But was I making too much of a stupid call that would signify nothing to anyone else, even a spy? Probably, I concluded. A part of me was stalling, and that was the key: you can't use what you can't find.

And so I kept walking, camera slung round my neck, until I reached Leipziger Platz. I was standing before the mammoth Wertheim department store,[72] and it struck me. I recall reading

---

[70] Railway station.

[71] Pay station, a vertical booth containing both a public telephone within and vending machines for postage stamps on the outside.

[72] The chain's most famous store featured eighty-three elevators and a glass-roofed atrium and was one of the three largest department stores in Berlin.

Jonathan Swift, the Anglo-Irish satirist, who wrote: "Discovery consists of seeing what everybody has seen and thinking what nobody else has thought." With that, I walked into the huge space with its vertiginous glass ceiling and seemingly endless rows of goods. Hands behind my back browsing-style, I strolled the aisles until I came to a luggage counter, studied the leather toiletries containers, purchased a quite decent one, and had it gift wrapped, paying full price even though the salesman offered it gratis to the SS major standing at parade rest in front of him. From there, I proceeded to the perfume counter, had the salesgirl pick out an especially alluring but subtle fragrance, had it gift wrapped as well, and again, as with the leather container, refused to take it without paying, causing me to consider whether the SS ever paid for anything. However, this time, I asked the girl where I might find a pay phone, and she directed me to an upstairs lounge containing couches, armchairs, coffee tables covered with magazines and newspapers, and a wall containing three phones. Since all were being used, I sat down in one of the chairs and pretended to read the day's *Volkischer Beobachter* until all three phones were vacant.

After almost forty-five minutes, I was alone. I laid down my unread magazine and went to the end phone farthest from the window, inserted a coin, and dialled the number I was given.

"Yes?" It was a male voice.

For a moment I was unable to speak, and there was total silence on the other end, waiting for me.

"I was told . . ." I struggled to say the right thing, "that only *my* voice would be responded to."

"You will wait, please," the man instructed. More silence.

Then a sultry female voice came on the line. "Anna Karenina here," the voice greeted. It was unmistakably Katrin. "I'm so pleased you decided to respond to my note so quickly. I can imagine how difficult it must have been to escape the suffocating insularity of the Chancellery."

"You sound like the Führer's chief secretary."

"Do I? But I'll wager that despite her grousing, she couldn't live without it. Not like you."

"You know me that well?"

"I hope so. In any event, you mustn't be on the phone so long. Someone might want one or both of the other phones."

Both of the other phones? I glanced all round me with agonizing subtlety and saw nothing that might provide a clue. "But how—?"

"Nothing to concern yourself about. I've so missed you, especially after the awkwardness of our parting. We should remedy that, don't you think?" And then, without asking for my agreement, she said: "You'll receive word of a suitable time and place, and then we can take up where we left off when we first met."

Look before you leap, but he who hesitates is lost, I told myself with a silent laugh. "I'd like very much," I said, choosing to leap, but not fully trusting in a safe landing.

"Then it's decided. Good," she said, followed by a click of the receiver, then silence.

I AWOKE WITH a sense of profound unease, determined to push the phone call from my mind for as long as possible. That required a surrogate matter with sufficient powers to preoccupy. As if to answer my need, a voice instructed me: "Concentrate on those around you; jettison the solitary observer, and engage; involve yourself in the stupidity, the pettiness, the below-stairs politics and gossip; no more avoidance, self-destructive superiority; become one with them, for they are your mental salvation from oppressive thoughts and feelings. They all have a purpose. They are not uncomfortable furniture in the living room of your mind but valuable allies in your escape from perilous thoughts. Immerse yourself in their imbecilities, intrigues, petty jealousies, and rivalries. Drown yourself in their ordinariness, their stupidity, their inferiority, their coarseness."

A brief knock, the door swung open, and Brückner entered, lugging a large leather sack. Where does he fit? I have no proof, save my instinct, but I truly feel that he, unlike the others above stairs, is doomed and he knows it. Perhaps that raises him above the rest.

"Rank aside, Herr Major," he said, "I thought I'd work on my fitness and personally deliver your share of the mail. Are you not gratified?"

I glanced down at the bag filled with verbal confections,

requests, and proposals. "Gratification is hardly the word to describe my feelings, Herr General," I kidded back. Brückner was a man difficult to dislike.

"It's a bit early to rouse the Führer," I said. "You were right about fitness, Wilhelm. Perhaps we might walk around a bit in the good old outdoors before immersing ourselves in our critical sorting task." I leaned my head towards the bathroom sink, useless since Heydrich's visit.

"Splendid idea," he replied, with a knowing nod.

We headed for the Chancellery Gardens, and once there, we stood gazing at all the foliage and statuary that too soon would be battered by rain, then covered in snow.

"Pity Heydrich is so fastidious about plumbing, eh? But the weather's good, for a change," he remarked. "Come winter, we'll get two days of decent weather and then the rain and snow begins."

"Wilhelm," I said jokingly, "I'll wager you hardly ever had to huddle and sleep in garbage-filled doorways to avoid the rain and snow as I did—for years."

He laughed. "You're right. I'm partial to actual bedrooms, even in good weather—with the right companion, of course." He pushed his lips out. "You had it pretty rough growing up, I imagine, having no parents, home, training, or education."

"You can add no orphanage as well. I refused to submit to a children's prison."

"So just how did you survive, before the panacea of the brickyard beckoned?"

"Between us, for the most part, I sneaked into whatever unguarded or empty buildings I could find, stole rotten food from vendors without them noticing or caring, and engaged in unsavoury but necessary physical culture exercises towards my competitors." I didn't mention the libraries I continually inhabited from opening to closing. Better to be thought an urchin than a prodigy.

"And then the Führer rescued you from choking your lungs away on brick dust. But enough fond youthful memories of maggots and mayhem, yes? I sense there's more to this walk than exercise and reminiscences."

"What do you mean?" I asked, a look of puzzlement creasing my face.

"Well?" Brückner asked, "what's really on your mind, this fine morning? "

After a pause, "I . . . was visited by Schroeder, and—"

"You're in love," he kidded. "Shall I ask the Führer to be best man at your wedding?"

"A bit short of love, I'd say, and so any wedding announcement would be premature. Actually, she said she came to tell me something I'm certain she wanted me to run and tell you."

Brückner pursed his lips, his one eye bright with curiosity. "Yes? Intrigue in the Chancellery? Novel notion. So now I'm the subject. All right, then, you might as well tell me—or I can return to hearing tedious stories of your hapless youth."

"She told me—in the strictest confidence, of course," I smiled snidely, "that Bormann was set upon getting you removed from your post."

"Which one?"

"Which one what?" I asked.

"Martin or Albert?"

I slapped my forehead hard with the palm of my hand. "You know, she didn't say, and I didn't think to ask. She just said 'Bormann.'"

Brückner nodded. "Well, then," he said, "until one of us

learns which brother, both will bear watching, though I would place my money on Albert, because he's right here among us, while indefatigable Martin is stuck at the Berghof, seeing to its renovation. Also, and more important, Albert is a favourite of that evil, slimy, ambitious *apparatchik* Bouhler.[73] We get our mail sacks from his office, in case you didn't know. Hmm, so Schroeder told you that at least one Bormann wants me gone. Well, in a sense, the situation, if true—and which I have no reason to doubt—confers on me a stature I never knew I possessed and, at the same time, presents me with a new sense of occupational mortality. What is that I see on your face, Heinz?"

I struggled to reply, but no words emerged.

"You needn't say what you cannot say, my friend. You're clearly upset, and soon, it will turn into depression. But don't let it be so. I would have felt no different from you had not my physical infirmities brought home to me, rather starkly, the temporariness of all things. There's a sort of freedom in that."

"But . . . the Führer—" I struggled.

"Heinz," he interrupted, "despite appearances, nothing was the same between the Führer and me since the Storck matter, but that's neither here nor there. As we both know, the Führer can be an award-winning actor when it suits him, and for now, it suits him, God knows why. You have no family, so I wouldn't expect you to understand this, but while all siblings are assumed to be equal, there are rankings in all households, despite even the best of intentions, and there are precious few best of intentions here. Moreover, understand that there is no difference between

---

[73] In 1934, Bouhler became police chairman of Munich and only a month later was appointed chief of Adolf Hitler's Chancellery, a post specially created on 17 November 1934 that was, first and foremost, set aside for Nazi Party business. Bouhler's office was responsible for all correspondence for Hitler.

the political and the personal, no matter what you may have heard or wish to believe. Politics is akin to a fatal disease: the end is inevitable, and while it cannot be cured, with care, it can be prolonged. In any event, we'd best be getting on to our duties. There'll be little of interest—routine meetings with a few industrial leaders, Speer, of course, and Ley, so nothing fancy, I should think, for either of us."

"Of course, Wilhelm," I answered feebly. Even then, I felt I understood what lay behind Brückner's feigned blitheness. But as I turned to go back inside, Brückner took me gently by the shoulder.

"Heinz, my young friend, after this, I will say no more, but you might take a few leisure moments and consider this: Why did Fräulein Schroeder want me to know—and, no less important, why did she choose you as her messenger?"

My apologies for again neglecting you, but I hadn't sufficiently come to terms with my phone conversation with Katrin—if it can be accurately called a conversation. Though I still haven't adjusted to it, I could no longer keep my turmoil to myself. As always, I was left with more questions than answers, but I won't bother you with those here. Years ago, I read that "the only true wisdom is in knowing you know nothing." And yet, I know so much, it almost bursts through my brain. But what do I understand of all that knowledge? Really understand? The Englishman George Bernard Shaw said that we must "beware of false knowledge; it is more dangerous than ignorance." But how can I know what is false if I have too little understanding? It's not unlike what the American Henry David Thoreau said: "It's not what you look at that matters, it's what you see." And what do I see? What is there to see? And how will I know it when I see it? In any event, Katrin hasn't contacted me since my call. Why?

My brain is splitting into a million puzzle pieces that I cannot assemble, for they are all from different puzzles, with no pictures to guide me. All I really gained from the call is that, despite everything—especially if I hear no further from either mystery woman—I must establish some sort of normal relationship with a decent-looking *ordinary* female!

But first, I needed to stop at Brückner's quarters on my way to the Führer, to collect my share of the meaningless mail. When he answered his door, while in full uniform, he hadn't yet affixed his eye patch, and so I was greeted with a hideously gaping crater, with jagged inflamed red lines radiating from the centre to a zipper-like scar to the side.

"Ah, Heinz," he greeted. "I'm afraid that you caught me somewhat undressed. I can assure you that it feels far worse than it appears." He chuckled darkly at that. "Come in while I finish."

I followed him into his "living room," which was merely a small cube containing a Formica and chrome kitchen table, two chairs of the same design, and a worn leather couch. "Sit anywhere," he said, "while I complete my toilette. And you needn't time me," he added, I imagined, to lighten the mood. He repaired to his bathroom and quickly emerged fully dressed. "I say, it's early yet. Shall we take a brief stroll before attending the Führer?" he suggested—with my heartfelt concurrence, as if he knew of my discomfort.

As we circled the grounds, Brückner said: "Big day today, my friend. If you chance to see any sallow-looking chaps with slanted eyes, exotic uniforms, and exorbitantly meaningless courtesies, know that we are to be graced by the Emperor of Japan—in the form of his most esteemed representatives, of course. But then, you knew what was in the works, eh? Ribbentrop wouldn't stop his fait accompli sales-pitch to the Führer for love or money, and it worked. Suddenly, the 'Yellow Peril' is a major bulwark against the 'Red Menace.'"

"But wasn't such an alliance proposed at least a year ago?" I ventured. "But I don't know where it went."

"Ah, Heinz, you mean to say that you were actually listening in those idiotic meetings with Ribbentrop and Neurath?" he kidded. "True, it had come up, as you say, but you need also remember that both von Neurath and Marshal Blomberg cautioned strongly against damaging traditional Chinese-German relations, and so it was postponed."

Naturally, I remembered. It was one of the few times the Führer actually listened to those two, but I had no idea why.

"They can caution all they want," Brückner continued, "but you know as well as I the Führer's attitude towards the Soviet Union. For him, China could hang, despite our traditional alliances, provided he's able to stifle Soviet ambitions, if not destroy them altogether. Of course, Ribbentrop was drooling with glee at the thought of anticipating the Führer again, and also checkmating the Soviets, with no real harm done to their precious British. So, finally, with the jabbering of Ribbentrop in his willing ear and, for once, an actual agreement from von Neurath, as well having signed the recent pact with Italy and his formal recognition of the Franco regime, the Führer sees such an accord with Japan as a way to bring about an Anglo-German alliance against the Soviets."

I was confounded by it all. "But what of Aryan supremacy?" I asked him, my eyebrows raised.

Brückner laughed heartily, causing no little attention from the myriad of guards, military, and civilian functionaries populating the grounds. "Aryan supremacy, my friend, is a political tool, not a reality. Did you know that, by scientific standards, Indians are Aryans? In Calcutta and Bombay, there is a thriving Nazi Party. Now, do you truly believe that Himmler, Goebbels, and Göring, much less the Führer, would hesitate for one moment to solve that inconvenient problem, once the time is right?"

I knew nothing of such things, so I merely shrugged. "So, there will be complete formality governing the evening?"

"Complete, yes, but we can leave it to Kannenberg to deal with that. Moreover, if you'd like, I can probably get your new bosom comrade Krause assigned to act as statue for the evening. In any event, at least, vegetarianism will not pose any insuperable difficulties."

Brückner's articulate generosity was typical and timely, since I'd banged my toe against the frame of my cot and, so, consumed the night soaking it gingerly in Epsom salts and writing to you.

12 *December 1936*

WHILE EATING BREAKFAST in the commissary, a certain Sergeant-Major Hüber was discussing that evening's visit with the Führer by his boss, Baldur von Schirach, chief of the Hitler Youth.[74] Without seeming to appear unduly inquisitive, I knew only of the visit, and so I inquired—as the Führer's valet, of course—as to the purpose.

The entire lower half of Hüber's face curved downward. "Search me, Herr Major," he said. "But it must be big, though, because he was talking to himself in English this morning, which he never does, unless it's important."

It wasn't much, but, since any further inquiry might generate suspicion, I thanked the sergeant, rose, and made for the Führer's quarters. If there was additional information to get, better it comes from him. I found him in his nightclothes with Dr. Morell, who was administering him some odd-coloured liquids from a neat row of hypodermic needles.

"Sit down, Linge," the Führer bade me. "While you prepare the outside of me, Morell here prepares the inside." He smiled at his joke. I also smiled. The ugly, sweating physician remained expressionless, said nothing, and went about his business without delay.

---

[74] Though von Schirach's father was a German aristocrat, his mother was American. In 1933 he was made head of the Hitler Youth (*Hitler-Jugend*) and given an SA rank of Gruppenführer.

Once Morell had left and I began the dressing regimen, the Führer waxed euphoric about Morell.

"I must say, Linge, that, while I admired Bloch, this Morell is a true miracle worker. Since he began his treatments, I feel like a new man."

God and Morell only know what the Führer was receiving, but I was forced to confess that it seemed to be working, for, though I couldn't completely agree that the Führer was a "new man," even I could see that he was a much newer man.

I placed the Führer's mail on his desk and began waiting for him to complete his toilette before the dressing marathon began. Once completed, he went over to his desk, placed his hands on the edge, bent over, and gazed down at . . . nothing I could discern. It was as if I didn't exist for him at that moment. I wanted to leave but could not divine his mood or intentions. After what seemed like a lifetime, he raised himself straight.

There was a gentle tap at the study door. "See to that, would you, Linge?" he asked.

"Of course, my Führer," I said and raced to the door to find Dara standing there, clutching some typed papers. I must have retained some feelings, since I felt a slight twinge at the sight of her, but I merely nodded, turned my head back to the Führer, and informed him of her presence.

"Yes, yes," he responded, "come in, Fräulein Daranowski. I assume you have the original and all the copies?"

I stood aside widely as she entered, went over to the Führer, and handed him the papers. "Of course, my Führer" she said.

Just then, Brückner came to the doorway and announced that von Schirach had arrived and was waiting for an audience.

"Have him wait a few minutes, Brückner," the Führer said. "And fetch me Hoffmann."

Without a word, Brückner clicked his heels, heil-Hitlered, turned and left, followed closely by a thanked Dara.

Within no more than ten minutes, Brückner returned with Hoffmann in tow, fully equipped.

"All right, Hoffmann," the Führer said, "we're almost ready for the little ceremony you are to make historic. Set up your machinery for a signing at my desk. Brückner, you can bring in Schirach now."

Though tall, aristocratic, and obviously cultivated, as befitting an SA general from the old Prussian military class, he strode in and saluted with what I considered to be a perfect excess of enthusiasm. The Führer greeted him with his usual limp salute and handshake, told him that the signing of the law-making membership in the Hitler Youth compulsory for all males was an enormous milestone in his master plan for the ultimate militarization of the Reich's male population, and that the signing must be memorialised nationwide by Hoffmann and Goebbels.

Brückner and I stood out of range while Hoffmann "memorialised" the moment. Afterward, as we again cruised the gardens—out of earshot and eavesdropping—Brückner was unusually silent and even sullen. I hesitated to break into his mood, but I've had so few opportunities to converse with such a man that I took a chance. He could always tell me to shut up.

"Is something troubling you, Wilhelm," I ventured.

He stopped and studied his glistening boots intently for a moment, then raised his eye. "You are a relative innocent, Heinz. It would be an injustice to share my misgivings and so spoil your virtue."

"Misgivings? About me?"

"Ah, youth," he chuckled darkly. "Around whom all revolves. No, my fine friend, hardly you."

"Then, please, what?" I entreated. "I won't tattle."

"I know that. It's merely a feeling."

"Then share your feeling, please. I may not be as virtuous as you think."

He smiled thinly, but not without affection. "You are though, Heinz," he said, "you actually are. In any event, I've known of the Führer's plans for our youth for some time, in fact, long before your arrival. I had a sense of unease the first time it came up, and I'm no less discomfited now that it's policy."

"But why, Wilhelm?" I wondered.

He shrugged. "As I said, merely a feeling, so all I can say is this: militarization and maternity[75] seem to me a rather bleak, uninspired, and perilous foundation for the Führer's 'Thousand-Year Reich.'" Then he shrugged, turned, and walked slowly away. I didn't follow.

---

[75] There were also organizations for girls called the *Jungmadelbund* (League of Young Girls), and the *Bund Deutcher Madel* (League of German Girls) to train and indoctrinate German females in the patriotic virtues of homemaking and child bearing.

20 *December* 1936

[The first portion of this entry and certain other sections are missing, I speculate as a result of corruption in the developing process or negative degeneration over time.—Trans.]

. . . of course, but that is for the Führer to decide. I had no option but . . .

[I could locate no legible entries from
20 December to 29 December.—Trans.]

OF LATE, KEMPKA, Schaub, and even that toad Krause have taken pity, I suppose, and have been good enough to pry open their little black books and serve me up a menagerie of willing—some even eager—females to dally with, but unfortunately, they were the sort who would be known by the likes of Kempka, Schaub, and Krause and so were nothing more than accommodating non-entities, coarse coquettes, or vicious vixens, no more desirable or useful than one evening's passing recreation at best, or grinding toleration at worst. Finally, I prevailed upon them to desist—temporarily (for politeness's sake on my part)—and they gladly agreed in jocular frustration, branding me far too particular for them to ever satisfy such an "uppity child" like me. Of course, I took their ribbing all in good spirits, because I believed them to be relatively benign—and they'd never met Emerald or Katrin.

"THAT LOOK ON your face. If you could only see it," she said, exposing a line of perfect teeth and a benign smile. "I told you I'd contact you, didn't I, and so I have done. Incidentally, Happy New Year."

Emerald was perched on my cot as demurely as her costume would allow, the same green gown and accessories she'd worn exactly a year ago, and as otherworldly stunning as I remembered, which, of course, was exact. Brückner had told me long ago that putting a lock on my door was only a matter of courtesy, not privacy, but still and all, how did she manage it? I started to say something, but she shot her long, manicured index finger to her wondrous lips to silence me.

"To answer your unspoken question," she said, "I most certainly possess a far more extensive—and practical—wardrobe. I wore this so you'd recognize me."

She was as clever as I remembered. And as perfect. Her gown was as form fitting as green cellophane, and I could feel a massive stirring under my uniform trousers.

She then lifted herself lithely and moved all her six-foot-one inches over to me, took me gently by the shoulders, leaned her head sideways, and whispered in my ear: "I say, after Heydrich's ever-so-casual remark about your plumbing, might not a nice brisk walk in the gardens be preferable?"

How did she know? I imagined, the same way she got into my room. I slipped back from her grasp and moved slightly away. I could hardly stand to be in the same room with her, much less this close, but I managed to turn my head and whisper back: "But the temperature," I started to caution, but she just smiled, reached over with her long, sleeve-encased arms, cupped my face, and whispered back: "Always the worrier. Endearing but unnecessary."

❧

It was bone-cracking cold, but, amazingly, no snow. We strolled in silence for a time, which I assumed was by her choice. Perhaps she needed me to adjust to her, and she'd have been right. We passed checkpoint after checkpoint, being greeted zealously by the freezing guards with a mixture of awe for me and lust for her. I hoped they might rotate so all could share in the warm festivities inside.

"Over the last year," I finally said to end the silence, "I wondered whether you were real or merely a wishful phantom."

Without missing a mental step, she turned her head slowly towards me. "Of course you did," she replied. "We're far more aware of you than you can imagine. But it doesn't really matter. I'll confess that for a time, we were concerned that you would become so adept at artifice that you would no longer be able to think and act authentically. Then we concluded that being adept merely illustrated aptitude, not attitude, so there you are."

Her enigmatic erudition was far beyond my poor powers to decipher, so I surrendered. "What I meant was whether you were real or just imagined."

My peripheral vision picked up a Cheshire Cat smile. "I

knew what you meant. I'm as real as you are, though not nearly as important."

Not nearly as important? Again, my importance, my uniqueness, my indispensability? I had a fretful feeling about where this conversation was heading, and so I made a feeble attempt to keep it personal—and innocent. "That's a relief. You may find this bizarre, but there actually were times when I even wondered if you were mortal." I meant it as a joke, a poor one, but a joke just the same.

Still the smile. "Well, aside from the lustful attentions of inferior men and women, that's a matter for philosophers, scientists, and ethicists to dwell on. For you, I'm quite mortal—and quite prepared to demonstrate that, when conditions are right."

Conditions are right? It was then that I knew she had more than romance on her mind. We walked farther in silence, then she reached over and held my arm to halt me. She turned me round to face her and removed her arm that I wished remained.

"I say," she remarked in the most casual tone, "do you ever listen to what goes on in those meetings Hitler obliges you to attend?"

My brain suddenly entered the freezer with the rest of me. Why did she want to know? Why was it "Hitler" and not "the Führer"? What did she want? How should I reply?

"Not really," I answered. "Please, Emerald, you need to appreciate that I'm only a valet, a servant, 'below the salt,' as the Führer would say. I'm not his doctor, adjutant, old fighter in the cause, Party official, or guest. My role at meetings is to stand mute and motionless in a corner like an invisible statue and to materialize only to fulfil any menial requests the Führer might make. Usually, he makes none, and so I stand. It's not my job to listen, and so I listen as little as possible. Not terribly active, exciting, or intellectually stimulating, I'm afraid."

Her green gaze bore into me. "You should listen, you know. No one is closer to him than you—literally and figuratively, and his word is destiny for the Reich—and beyond."

I had the distinct feeling that her eyes were seeking something in my expression, in contradiction to my words. What did she expect to see? What did she want to see? What was she getting at? "But what would be the purpose?" I told her. "None of it would have anything whatsoever to do with me or the likes of me. I merely deliver newspapers and his mail, help him dress, and stand by during meals, meetings, and assist when his doctor requires me to render service."

"That's rather passive, I dare say."

"Those are the four corners of the position. Sometimes, I wish the job and I were more exciting." I didn't mean it, but it seemed to be what Emerald wanted to hear.

She paused for a moment, took my arm, and continued walking. "Heinz, you must be aware of Hitler's not-so-gradual seizure of the nation's legal system, the sterilization and euthanasia decrees, the Aryan appropriation measures, the militarization, the alliances, the concentration camps, von Schirach's Hitler Youth, and Lebensborn."[76]

This was certainly not my idea of a date. "I know of them, vaguely, yes. And so?"

---

[76] *Lebensborn* (literally: Fount of Life) was an SS-initiated, state-supported, registered association with the goal of raising the birth rate of Aryan children via extramarital relations of persons classified as "racially pure and healthy" based on Nazi racial hygiene and health ideology. *Lebensborn* encouraged anonymous births by unmarried women and mediated adoption of these children by likewise "racially pure and healthy" parents, particularly SS-members and their families.

"Do you not have an opinion about them? Do you truly have no indication as to where all this monstrousness is headed?"

"Not really," I lied. I'd heard the Führer and his closest associates repeatedly proclaim that such measures were the merest beginnings of a cleansing that would set the Reich apart from all other nations in history and make way for world envy and eventual domination. Yes, I'd heard that much. But talk is talk; the more grandiose, the more fanciful, had been my experience.

"And even if I did," I told her, "so what? Who am I to have an opinion on political matters on the highest level?" The growing bulge in my trousers was becoming truly painful, and I hoped it wasn't visible, but I was afraid to check. And what if a stain on my trouser front should interrupt her interrogation? Why was she wasting such precious sensual possibilities with such perilous and, to me, irrelevant political twaddle?

"Well, my dear Heinz, I certainly meant no offence, but I happen to believe that you do have an opinion, and that right, justice, and basic humanity are not lost on you? Edmund Burke said that 'for evil to flourish, it's only necessary for good men to do nothing.'"

I'd read the passage, but what did it have to do with the price of tea in China? *Good men? Evil? Do nothing? About what?* "Emerald," I cautioned, "don't you realize that all those round me would instantly denounce someone with your notions as a dangerous enemy of the state, despite your obvious gifts and appearance, perhaps even because of them?"

"Oh, yes," she admitted. "I'm quite positive *they* would. The far more important question to me is whether *you* would."

I grabbed a few moments for thought. If she's Himmler's spy, I concluded, I'd already said enough to get Heydrich salivating. "Are you . . . a Communist?" I ventured tentatively.

She laughed. "No, Heinz, I'm not a Communist. I'm not even a Jew. I'm a humanist, albeit, almost as reprehensible to the powers that be, in the times in which we live. I believe in the dignity and worth of all human beings. Don't you?"

I was utterly perplexed and apprehensive from the entire business. "I've begun to feel," I confessed, "that there is a shadow behind me. I move, but it doesn't. That shadow is you, isn't it?"

"No, Heinz, it's *you*, what you *really are* but are compelled to deny, and from which you believe you can escape. But what you feel, you can ignore now, but it will become merely the top layer of an onion of evil that will soon be peeled down to its malignant core. And then, I believe, you'll experience a transforming moment, and all that I've been saying will suddenly become no longer a stationary shadow to you." She shrugged. "But not yet, I'm afraid. Not yet." Then she gazed at me with those lustrous green eyes.

"We've spent much of the little time allotted to us in talk," she said. "It's been a year—exactly, by my calculations. Do you still want me, Heinz? That way?" she murmured. "Because if you do, you can, you know. Tonight."

"That's not why you came."

"What does that matter?"

I took a deep breath. "It matters to me. I realize that I could never have you in the way I'd fantasized all these months, even while we were walking together, earlier. I thought I could, yes. I spent a year thinking, feeling, and believing that I could, and that I'd do anything to have you. Even a nothing like me, wishing that, every day, every night. But now, with you here, actually offering yourself—or at least the part of you that offers—I know that it can't be, that it shouldn't be, rather. It would spoil everything. Your perfection would vanish in an instant of lust, and only used flesh would remain."

Another smile, but thinner. "You sound as if you're quoting from a novel."

"Not surprising. My thoughts are no more profound than those of the authors I've read. Actually, even less, since they at least fully understood what they were writing."

"Not so, Heinz. The words perhaps, but the soul behind the utterances, that's yours and yours alone. A Greek philosopher wrote that 'a man's character is his fate.' I prefer the word 'destiny' to fate. I still believe I was right about you—and your character. One day, my dear Heinz, one day." She touched my cheek with a lightness that a feather would envy, then she raised her arms in mock surrender.

"I can see that you're uncomfortable," she said, "and not merely from the temperature, so I imagine you should be heading back, don't you think, since it's almost midnight?" She turned and walked away into the night, into the freezing night, without a single backward glance.

As I watched her untouchable perfection diminish into the distance, it suddenly struck me like a savage blow from a blunt instrument—the messages, *Julius Caesar*, the conversation in the cold: *She wants me to assassinate the Führer!* Of that, I had no doubt, despite the obfuscation and verbal ballet dancing. Though I could prove nothing—I know that's her intent, clearly.

Well, my friend, another year has ended, and where am I? Perhaps even to ask that question suggests a severe disquiet with my situation. Lao Tzu wrote: "If you do not change direction, you may end up where you are heading." Now as then, it sounds more clever than enlightening. And yet . . . that is to say, *am I heading*, and if so, *where am I heading?*

I shook my head and glanced at my clock. Exactly midnight. "Happy New Year, Heinz," I said aloud—having no idea how I meant it.

1937

1 *January 1937*

CAN ANYTHING BE the same after last night? No sleep, as you would expect after my second encounter with Emerald. But there are far worse things than sleeplessness. Questions, questions! What if someone knows me more than I know yourself? And if I don't know myself, how can I know someone else? My brain aches with questions.

I decided I'd better dress, in this case, merely changing from one uniform to another, when the Führerbuzzer caused my fingers to tear off a shirt button, but luckily, one that my jacket would conceal. In any event, I was long removed from Krause's venomous scrutiny. As I quickly exited my room, I stumbled into Kempka and Baur.

"*Linge*," Kempka blurted, huffing and puffing as if he'd just finished an Olympic sprint, "if you got summoned by the Führer, we can wait, but—"

"No," I assured them, "not to worry. He wants me, yes, but there's some time." I didn't know whether there was or not, but for some reason, I felt the need to hear what the breathless Baur and Kempka had to tell me.

"You're an impossible person to help, Linge," admonished Kempka. "Here, for months, we've been killing ourselves, trying to track down some love goddesses for you, and when we finally find one, you're missing in action."

"Yeah, the Führer gives you leave," said Baur, needlessly, "and you don't see fit to even stay long enough to celebrate with your comrades in arms, and, in this case, if you stayed, you'd actually have had something to celebrate?"

Since I'd been with Emerald, I assumed they were referring to Katrin. If so, how did they accomplish it? "My apologies for not taking advantage of your success," I rejoined. "What did I miss?"

They turned slowly towards each other, then back to me. "I don't know," Kempka teased. "That's some fancy jabber, seeing as how it's coming from an ignorant baby. You know, maybe we should leave you hanging in suspense, and then, maybe next time there's a celebration, you'll make sure to join us peasants before racing off to your monastery, yes?"

"Yeah," Baur joined in, two battle-hardened sergeants joshing a fresh recruit. "Here, you beg us and we go to all this trouble and what for, I say?"

How to deal with these two clowns who mean well but haven't the wits to put on a decent show? But for the Führer, these characters would be swilling cheap beer and picking fights in some seedy beer hall. *Control!* I ordered myself. With luck, maybe they'll soon conclude this infantile nonsense. "But, comrades," I told them, "you can easily take your revenge by telling me what I missed. Make me suffer for my loss, am I right?"

The idiots simulated a furtive glance at each other again, grinned, and turned back to me. "Or maybe we should just let you stew for a while, eh?" said Baur.

"Serve you right, eh?" said Kempka.

Would these characters ever get to the point? Since I felt like an invalid from the previous night and lack of sleep, I was ready to tell both of them to fuck themselves, when Baur finally said: "All right, my young friend, we'll put you out of your misery, right, Erich?" To which Kempka concurred with a reluctant shrug. "We found your Katrin for you at the post-Führer celebration, but you'd already made tracks. She was pretty disappointed, which we find hard to understand, of course, since we know you, but she must see more in you than we do," they kidded.

After a year of searching, then both appear at the celebration at virtually the same time? One tacitly asks me to be an assassin and the other misses me entirely. Quite an evening. Now I felt even more physically and mentally debilitated than before. "How did you happen to come across Katrin?" I asked them.

"We, that is, Baur, Schaub, Bremer,[77] and me, were just standing around, drinking, singing, you know, the usual enjoying-the-festivities stuff, when, from the corner of my eye, I spot this dazzling creature talking with some general. Then she moved away from him and came right over to us and said that we'd been asking about her, in a way, like, you know, as if she knew it was us, and—"

"With a female like that," Baur interrupted, "it's hard to even think, much less answer, you know what I mean? She definitely wasn't like any of the bimbos in my book," he said needlessly. "It's like she was from some other fucking planet, you know?"

"I know," I merely said. "Then what?"

"Anyhow," Kempka resumed, "she asks Karl and I if we had seen you, and we tell her that you left, right after the Führer, and that was that."

"Then what did she do?"

"I'm getting to that," Kempka said with a slight impatient edge to his tone. "Well, she—at least to me—looks really

____

[77] Karl Bremer was one of Hitler's many messengers.

disappointed, God knows why, then she says that after all our efforts, it's a pity that you're unavailable, that her—what did she say?—nemesis, whatever that fucking means, must have got to you first. Oh yeah, and she'd wanted to introduce you to some fellow named, uh, Weis . . . Weis-something-or-other—sounded like a fucking Jew, but she imagined that might have to wait. Hey, kiddie, maybe you're lucky, after all, you know. A Jew of all things at the Führer's New Year's celebration? How would he have got in, you know what I mean? Now how would that look?"

"That's all she said?"

"That's it," Baur said, "except that she said to tell you she would get in touch with you at a more . . . pro, pro, what was that fucking word, Kempka?"

"*Prodidshic*, I think, whatever that means. Something foreign, I think."

I was certain she said *propitious*. I'd never expect them to get it right—but why did she think I would? "Anything else?"

They glanced at each other again. "Nah," Baur said to me. "She just lowers her eyelids like we're shit on her servant's shoes, turns, and glides back to her Jew, and continued jabbering. But real blue-blooded, she was, we could tell. A real dish, but none for the likes of us—except," turning to Kempka, "maybe for our good friend 'von Heinzie' here, the ex-bricklayer's helper, that is, yes?"

I was repelled by their coarseness, but I learnt long ago that from such-like you learn the truth, since they have not the cunning to lie effectively. "My good comrades," I slathered, twisting my lips into the best grin I could summon up for humble indulgence and trusting, with some anxiety, that no one had informed them of my stroll with Emerald, "please believe me when I tell you that after three long, repetitive ceremonies with the Führer, I was so mentally and physically drained that I had to make tracks to my room or I would have collapsed. How the Führer does it is beyond me." I could see that they were warming to my fabrication. "You know that at any other time, I would have been more than happy to celebrate with you, even until the following New Year's Eve if possible, but so it goes." Then, I presented the coup de grâce: "If this Katrin came as a result of your efforts, I'm greatly in your debt. If not, well, let's put the best face on it: if she's that interested in me, she'll do something about it, yes? So, if there's no more you have to tell me, I need to be off to prepare the Führer."

Both shrugged, almost as if rehearsed. "By the look on her face when we told her we didn't know where you'd gone to," Kempka chortled, "she'll be back, you can bet on that."

"And what a fucking dish, at that, Heinzie," Baur murmured. "Man, if I had access to the likes of her, I could have Goebbels burn all my black books with all the others. After you're finished with her, toss her over to me, eh, and I'll be in *your* debt."

After Kempka nodded in vigorous agreement, they both turned and left, the echoes of their mindless sniggering ricocheting off the walls as they walked.

Von Heinzie, the bumbling ex-bricklayer, I muttered to myself. Yes, that's me to them. Another round won.

"She'll be back, you can bet on that," Kempka had snorted yesterday, and the clod was right.

Fortunately, this morning, the Führer had little for me to do after he completed his toilette, had his writing materials and spectacles placed on his desk, and his mail delivered. As was my custom, normally a fruitless enterprise, I wandered over to the Message Centre, Bouhler's little empire, where I discovered an envelope waiting for me with my name on it, followed by "My Vronsky" in parentheses.

Judging from its condition, I was certain that it had been opened and resealed repeatedly and that the dozens of censors, code breakers, and SS-analysts labouring twenty-four hours a day at the Chancellery had experienced a virtual orgasm over the possibilities but hesitated to act because of my unique position. Assuming they had, I tore open the envelope right there and read the typical Katrin no-nonsense message in which she expressed her "deep regret" at missing me on New Year's Eve, expected that we would meet soon, and confirmed that she would send me the date, time, and location by messenger. It was signed: "Your 'Anna.'"

I heaved a sigh of relief; the message appeared harmless enough—even affectionate—for Katrin, that is—unless the snoops were so riddled with paranoia that they automatically assumed sinister meanings in each punctuation mark. I put nothing past these characters. Regardless, to me, it just meant more waiting, something I'd been resigned to ever since she'd abruptly "dismissed me." In all truth, after my last meeting with Emerald, and what I interpreted to be her dreadful intent, I became now more obsessed with Katrin than ever.

I spent most of the day wandering the Berlin streets aimlessly as I waited.

4 *January 1937*

I HADN'T LONG to wait.

As I was walking with Brückner, obeying the Führer's summons for our presence, a man wearing a single-breasted, light-brown Party-leader tunic, approached us. As we walked towards each other, Brückner quickly advised me in a furtive murmur from the corner of his mouth to keep silent, which was no problem, for it was something I'd been well trained to do and had no intention of violating. The man wasn't especially tall, but he had the burly build of a powerful, seasoned wrestler, not unlike a Teutonic Mussolini. His neck was more assumed than real, and his shaved head, sizeable chest, tiny ears, and cliff-like chin completed the picture of the massive beer-hall thugs I'd encountered in my former life—thankfully, at a safe distance. Now, the distance was diminishing rapidly.

Then, with a flurry of heel-clicking and *Heil Hitlers!* I was introduced to the infamous Julius Streicher.[78]

---

[78] Julius Streicher was the founder and publisher of the *Der Stürmer* newspaper, which became a central element of the Nazi propaganda machine. His publishing firm also released three anti-Semitic books for children, including the 1938 *Der Giftpilz* ("The Toadstool" or "The Poison-Mushroom"), one of the most widespread pieces of propaganda, which purported to warn about insidious dangers Jews posed by using the metaphor of an attractive yet deadly mushroom. To protect himself from accountability, Streicher relied on Hitler's protection. Hitler declared that *Der Stürmer* was his favourite newspaper and saw to it that each weekly issue was posted for public reading

"Brückner," Streicher said through a scornful smile, ignoring me completely, "I missed you when I visited the Führer. What are you up to these days, eh?"

"Same as always," he said. "I run errands, see to the Führer's needs, and try to stay out of trouble."

"Mr. Caution as always, eh? Always safe and sound while the Führer advances us to glory, eh?"

"Where he goes, Herr *Gauleiter*, I follow, if that's what you mean."

"Of course, what else could I have meant?" he asked, scorn turning into sneer. "The Führer brings home the meat, and your kind eats it."

"Quite," Brückner responded icily. "What can I do for you?" Brückner asked, his face drained of blood, his eye glazed over.

"You can relieve me of this demeaning task of mail deliverer." He slid his ham hand into his inside pocket and shoved an envelope over to Brückner. "The Reichsführer asked me to deliver it to some Linge fellow, but giving it to you is as far as my dedication goes. He said this Linge works under you."

Brückner took the envelope. "He works *for* the Führer and *with* me, Herr *Gauleiter*," Brückner corrected, "but I can see that he gets it."

Streicher lowered his eyelids and stretched out his flat lips in resignation. "That will be just fine, Brückner, since I'm no fucking postman for Himmler, you, or anyone else."

"Always a pleasure," Brückner said, tonelessly, as Streicher saluted, turned abruptly, and marched away.

As we continued on our way, I ventured to ask him what just happened.

---

in special glassed-in display cases known as *Stürmerkasten*. The newspaper reached a peak circulation of 600,000 in 1935.

"What just happened, my friend, was a collision of two cultures. Streicher represents what some might call the prehistoric Nazi, and I, at least, the next stage in our political evolution."

I knew what he meant. "What do you mean, Wilhelm?" I asked him.

"My apologies, Heinz," he said. "I forgot that even after all this time with us, you're still somewhat naïve about our political history. Streicher ably represents our thuggish origins, when it was deemed necessary to deal with political opponents in alleyways with saps instead of speeches. Most were eliminated, like Röhm and his perverted racist hooligans in the 1934 purge. Some in the SA, like me, were spared, since I'd distanced myself from that mob long before. Some read porn, some read books; I read handwriting on the wall."

"But what about this Streicher?" I asked. "How did he escape?"

"The success of his filthy anti-Semitic shit sheet of a newspaper that the Führer adores. But far more important, Streicher actively participated in the failed Beer Hall Putsch. You know the Führer's addiction to loyalty." His lips curled into a grin. "Also being far from Berlin, he could, as I did, remain separate from Röhm's bunch."

I used to see well-worn copies of *Der Stürmer* on benches in the brickyard locker room and, from time to time, I would glance through some of its virulently anti-Semitic articles and cartoons about all the vile things the Jews were and did that would make the bubonic plague appear like a head cold and Himmler seem like a Rabbi by comparison. At least in Berlin, I'd never seen any of the Jews that Streicher's paper described (and I'd been around), and so I dismissed his hysterical screed as insane rants, though I kept such thoughts to myself, as you would expect, even keeping them from Brückner. But I must tell you that a voice in my head had begun nagging me about a regime that elevated the sort of filth like Streicher—and even Himmler and Heydrich. And what of all those below, who worshipped them and, even if not worshipped, still willingly—even enthusiastically—did their bidding? And the biggest conundrum of them all: How could the Führer countenance such creatures?

"Well, Heinz, since we had to endure that gutter swine of a Streicher, at least we should get the benefit, eh?" he said, as he handed me the envelope. "You don't mind my not having introduced you?"

"To be frank," I answered with a smile, taking the offering and sliding it into my jacket pocket, "I'm eternally in your debt."

"You can read it in front of me," Brückner said cheerily. "I'm certain it's nothing subversive, or Himmler would have delivered it personally."

He was right, of course, nothing was private to me anymore. "You're right, Wilheim," I said. "If Himmler's happy, what's there to fear?" But my real concern was greater than confidentiality: Why didn't Katrin send it directly to me? Why make postmen of the likes of Himmler and Streicher? Who the hell was she? I retrieved the envelope, removed the typewritten contents, and read them to him in hushed tones:

My Dearest H, I may have what you need, but we'll only know that when we meet. I do so hope that you can be with me tomorrow night at the Adlon. I'll be in the Lounge. As I now attract a different kind of attention than I used to, I shan't be able to remain alone for long. I trust that 11:30 p.m. will be not be too inconvenient.

With all my affection. Your B.

Bella!

Brückner pursed his lips. "'My Dearest H?' 'All my affection? Your B?' A late-night assignation at the Adlon? Hmm," he remarked. "Well, if Himmler passed the note on, through a sewer rat like Streicher, it certainly can't be from anyone on his vast list of undesirables. Also, I would guess from the wording, a female."

"I would hope so, Wilhelm. I seldom experience such language from males." We both chuckled at that. "But, Wilhelm," I added for purposes of preserving my ingenuousness, "what is an assignation? Do you think I'm in danger?"

Brückner smiled. "If you're to function effectively in this environment, you must acquire a decent dictionary. Not an assassination. An assignation, old boy, is a lover's secret rendezvous, and that note, well, even though not terribly secret, it has femme fatale written all over it, yes? Best be careful you're not ensnared."

"Ensnared? You're pulling my leg, aren't you?"

He placed his hand on my shoulder. "Of course I am," he assured me. "What male worthy of the name could avoid the advances of a femme fatale? And just consider all the intriguing stories you'll be able to regale Baur and Kempka with, not to mention Fräulein Schroeder? You'll be the talk of the Chancellery."

I laughed half-heartedly. "Something tells me I already am, Wilhelm."

Brückner managed a quizzical look from his one eye, then said: "In any event, let's see what the Führer wants, eh?"

I was only too happily perplexed by the wording of her note and its mode of delivery to even reply, and so I merely nodded and we continued our tiny trek in silence.

∽

The Führer already knew—no longer a great surprise to me—of my "assignation." However, he couldn't have known who—and what—she was. He enquired if I possessed decent formal evening clothes, and when I told him that I didn't even have indecent formal evening clothes, he chuckled and called in Bormann (Albert, that is) and had him take me to the finest tailor in Berlin (a Jew, but one still permitted to operate—for the present) to get me "properly fit out for an elegant liaison."

"Even I," the Führer had said, "the quintessential bohemian artist, was obliged to obtain—which in my case at the time meant rent—a tuxedo in order to socialize with the swells, in order to obtain the funds I needed to continue my mission. Uncomfortable as hell, Linge, but at times, we must all sacrifice our comfort for the greater good," he joked. "Mine was power, yours is romance, but in the end, it's all the same, yes?"

How can I do justice to this night?

I'd passed the Adlon countless times in my aimless travels through the city as well as my—no longer possible—purposeful visits to Adelsheimer's photo shop, but I'd never even glanced over, since I'd felt that actually facing the enormous, magisterial building seemed to be a form of social sacrilege, once my miserable eyes set upon it. And now, I was to enter it as if I were an actual person, bedecked in full dinner dress, driven there in a Mercedes limousine—with two rows of passenger seats, a window separating passengers and driver, and headlights the size of halved watermelons—by Kempka, the Führer's personal chauffeur! In the few seconds of clarity, I hoped that the police who had arrested me countless times for vagrancy or my stalwart compatriots at the brickyard could witness my amazing rise. However, there was one person I hoped to avoid: Katrin. She'd told me that she kept an apartment at the Adlon that I was not to visit, that night at least. It would have been awkward (to say the least) were we to bump into each other on my way to meet Bella.

"Okay," Kempka said, as the hotel doorman approached the car to open my door, as if I couldn't be bothered with such trifles. "You ready to join the upper crust?"

"Take a guess," I answered truthfully.

"Well," Kempka advised, "I'm no fucking Catholic, but they

do have a saying: 'Act as if ye had faith, and faith will be given to you,' or some shit like that. To me, that means if you play the part good enough and long enough, you finally become the part."

I didn't have a chance to respond, for just then the door opened and the man in full hotel doorman's livery declared: "Welcome to the Adlon, sir."[79]

Through my walks around "official Berlin" and my duties at the Chancellery, I'd grown accustomed to grandeur, but nothing had prepared me for the radiant opulence of the Adlon interior. The limitations of my linguistic imagination leave me unfit for descriptions, so the most I can say is that it was like entering an artist's rendering of a foreign potentate's palace.

---

[79] The hotel was built at a cost of 20 million gold marks, 2 million of which were the majority of Adlon's personal fortune. Behind a rather sober façade, the hotel was the most modern in Germany, with hot and cold running water, an on-site laundry, as well as its own power plant to generate electricity. It boasted a huge lobby with enormous square marble columns, a restaurant, a café, a palm court, a ladies' lounge, a library, a music room, a smoking room, a barber shop, a cigar shop, an interior garden with a Japanese-themed elephant fountain, and numerous grand ballrooms. It was located in the heart of the government quarter next to the British Embassy on Wilhelmstrasse, facing the French and American embassies on Pariser Platz and only blocks from the Reich Chancellery and other government ministries farther south on Wilhelmstrasse. During the "Golden Twenties," the Adlon remained one of the most famous hotels in Europe, hosting celebrity guests, including Louise Brooks, Charlie Chaplin, Mary Pickford, Emil Jannings, Albert Einstein, Enrico Caruso, Thomas Mann, Josephine Baker, and Marlene Dietrich, and politicians such as Franklin Roosevelt, Paul von Hindenburg, and Herbert Hoover. The hotel was a favourite hangout of international journalists, including William L. Shirer, who mentions it frequently in his writings. The hotel remained a social centre of the city throughout the Nazi period, though the Nazis themselves preferred the Hotel Kaiserhof a few blocks south and directly across from the Propaganda Ministry and Hitler's Chancellery on Wilhelmplatz. Hitler visited it only once.

Rather than display my ignorance, I wandered round until I saw what had to be the lounge that Bella mentioned in her cryptic note and surveyed the massive yet intimate setting (not a contradiction in a palace like the Adlon). On my way to the long bar, with its glittering kaleidoscope of liquor bottles on multitiered shelving, I passed other formally dressed men (only a few were in uniform, and of those, only generals who could display their red stripe along their collars and trouser legs) and, of course, fashionable women in all their satin-and-jewelled finery. I felt like a butler, which, to a great extent, I was. And the sounds. If there was anything that could be termed an elegant din, the Salon bar had it—almost as if the cacophony itself had sentience, knew where it was, and so possessed a refined sense of decorum in such surroundings.

Frau Bella was seated on a stool in equally imposing apparel, her smooth, bare back to me. All the stools were taken but the one to her right, on which, perched a tiny evening handbag, presumably to ward off the unwanted. I came over, lifted her handbag, and asked her with a smile if the stool was reserved. She took the bag daintily, placed it on her lap, and said: "As a matter of fact, it is."

I sat down.

"Have you ever worn a tux, Heinz?" she asked, with her lips curled up in mischief.

"Is it that obvious?"

"Probably only to me, the Gestapo, and the hotel employees. Observation is basic to our professions—and my so-called race.[80]

---

[80] Setting aside the emotional issues, Jews are clearly not a race. Race is a genetic distinction and refers to people with shared ancestry and shared

Others can afford to merely see what they want or expect to see. In any event, I hope you didn't suffer too many after-effects of your Zombie," she said, lightly. "I wouldn't have wanted to make a boozer out of such purity."

The Führer couldn't have known that my "assignation" was with both a Jew and a journalist to boot, but now, exposed in this exquisite fish tank, would hiding in plain sight still serve?

"I'm hardly that pure," I assured her, without much conviction.

"Yes, you are," she countered. "You really are. And that's both rare and encouraging in such times. I booked us a table, in your name of course, but that can wait, yes? Now, what other exotic elixir can I introduce to you?"

"The Zombie did its work," I said.

"I'm quite certain," she said. "But now, something both new and different, yes? Dare to risk, Heinz."

Could she possibly imagine that being here with the notorious Bella Fromm was not risk enough for a lifetime? Given who I was with, how the meeting was arranged, and who knew of it, I could only question my sanity and smile inwardly at my foolhardiness.

"You're the bartender," I told her, not wishing to spoil her vision of my purity by saying *mixologist*.

"Hmm," she mulled. "I picture you as a decadent adventurer, so I would recommend 'Death in the Afternoon.'"

I only knew the name from having raced through a boring Ernest Hemingway bull-fighting novel, but certainly that fact was not a morsel to be handed to a journalist. "Interesting name.

---

genetic traits. One cannot change one's race; it's in one's DNA. A Caucasian could never become Black or Asian no matter how much he or she might wish to.

You'd think that such a drink would be taken *before* a Zombie, not after."

"I say, you're even more clever than I remember. Your observation's chronologically sound, but that's as far as it goes. One works up to 'Death.' Is it so different in Germany today?"

I let that grenade fly past me. "And so, to you, I'm decadent?"

"Don't fret, Heinz. I was merely poking fun at you. You're anything but decadent, but the drink, well, that's another matter. What could be more decadent than absinthe and Champagne? As I recall, Hemingway's instructions were: 'Pour one jigger of absinthe into a Champagne glass, add iced Champagne until it attains the proper opalescent milkiness, and drink three to five of these slowly.' With you, I'd abstain after one."

"I'll take that as a compliment," I said, bereft of a wittier response.

"Good, for I meant it in no other way. However, I'm rather well known here, so *you* may have to, ah, encourage the bartender to serve us, since I haven't had much luck up to now."

"You mean—?"

"Of course I mean, Heinz. I merely show you the times in which we live."

And of course, I understood what she meant. I called the waiter over. "Two 'Deaths in the Afternoon,' and be quick. The lady has been kept waiting far too long."

The bartender, who wore a Party pin on his white lapel, glanced at me, then slid his beady eyes over to Bella, then back to me. "Sir," he said with a sneer, "with respect, you may not know what she is."

I was forced to employ a will of iron to permit his bared teeth to remain in his mouth. "I know what she is, my friend," I explained, dry ice in my voice, "and I also know what you are." With theatrical deliberation, I took my identity card from my wallet and shoved it in his suddenly bleached-white face. "However, with equal respect, you may not know what *I am*. The Führer knows I'm here with her, as well as Reichsführer Himmler. Would you like me to telephone them to confirm this for you before we can get a drink?"

The "Deaths" arrived in record time, according to Bella, who said with her gloved hand pressing down lightly on my forearm: "See, isn't it delightful being an Aryan?"

"I never thought of it that way."

"Well, my dear Heinz Linge, now you can afford to, but eventually, you'll have to think of it another way, I'm afraid, because what you just experienced is only the merest and most rarefied of beginnings. Berlin and the Adlon are the sheerest tip of an increasingly virulent iceberg." She took a sip without incident. "I say, working in the Chancellery, how in heaven's name have you avoided the issue up to now?"

I thought of the hapless Adolf Adelsheimer and his former photo shop. *How many like him were there in relatively tolerant Berlin, not to mention the far more anti-Semitic sections of the Reich and beyond?* I asked myself but instantly dismissed the question. I didn't wish to discuss race and all that went along with it, but I knew I needed to smooth her way to the topic for our meeting.

I took a small sip of my drink and instantly understood the reason for its name. After I finished coughing, I told her that "I'm hardly an official or foreign guest at the Chancellery" and that my "critical role" at dinner is to "stand mutely at ease at all times, when not needed for some menial task, and especially so when anything is being discussed, including race, which, in all cases, quickly turns into a seemingly endless monologue by the Führer that merely regurgitates his racial pronouncements in *Mein Kampf*. Even Himmler and Heydrich, for whom racial purity is a mania, keep silent and merely listen with almost sexual satisfaction." I took another sip, this time, considerably smaller and with considerably more caution.

"My apologies," she said. "You must think I have race on the brain."

"Actually, you appear to have weathered the racial storm quite well, considering."

She half-smiled. "Barely, as you can see, and temporarily, as you can predict."

I couldn't disagree with her, though I wondered how she'd gotten this far.

"Why don't we transfer our drinks to a table, before we're ordering breakfast?" I suggested.

"A splendid idea," she answered. "I think we were wearing out our welcome here."

∾

When we were seated and my identification card ensured a maximum of service and a minimum of vitriol, I decided to press on for some meaning to all this. Moreover, my "tux," as she called it, felt like body armour constructed of sandpaper, causing me no shortage of discomfort, and the effects of my "Death" were creeping up on me like a predatory lion in the bush. Time was rapidly getting short for any lucidity or comprehension.

"This is all very refined and civilized," I began, trying to keep any severity from my voice, "but I'm dog tired and your note, regardless of its bizarre method of delivery, said you had what I wanted. This might be a good time to give it to me."

She stared at me for a moment with her bottomless brown eyes. While in no way even remotely beautiful, she was truly elegant, no less so than Emerald or Katrin, but with a deep-set sorrow in her face that I assumed was more genetic than anything else. A Jewish variant of the "trail of tears," as I'd read of the forcible removal of the Choctaw Nation from their tribal lands by the Americans in 1831.

"Yes, Heinz, you're right," she said with an odd expression I couldn't interpret. "'A good time.'"

Once seated, we waited until the server had delivered the hors d'oeuvres, then she said: "Through some contacts in high places, who, at least for the present, haven't completely forgotten my name—or remembered it malevolently—I managed to track down this Katrin you were interested in. It seems that she works out of the old Hotel Prinz Albrecht Strasse, the headquarters of the Reich Main Security Office, SD, Gestapo, and SS—in other words, Himmler's hideaway, as I call it. But she doesn't do odd jobs for the Reichsführer directly, they said, but for some rather sinister and secretive SS colonel named Otto Rahn. Have you ever heard of him?"

"No," I replied truthfully.

"Well, this Colonel Rahn works for someone even more sinister and secretive, SS-General Karl Maria Wiligut, alias Weisthor. Ring any bells?"

Weis . . . Weis-something-or-other—sounded like a fucking Jew, Kempka had said. Yes, it rang a bell, but I didn't let on.

"All a mystery to me, I'm afraid," I told her. "Do your . . . contacts know anything about them?"

She shrugged her padded shoulders. "Well, that's the thing. They know nothing. It's as if Weisthor and Rahn inhabit another universe from the other organizations—and they don't advertise."

"Then they probably don't know what she does for these characters?"

"You'd be right. I hate to say this, but I'm assuming as a journalist—even as a frilly society columnist—that only Himmler, probably Heydrich, have such information, and if, with your proximity, you haven't heard anything, it's quite possible they think that you may have no business knowing."

I had no idea what she was talking about. "That's likely," I answered. "If anyone thinks that my so-called position makes me privy to everything that lurks behind the Chancellery curtains, they'd be quite mistaken."

After our main course arrived with almost sickening servility, I asked her: "Frau Bella, do your sources know her full name and how I might contact her?"

She gazed at me again with those intense brown eyes. "Actually," she said, "I was hoping you'd give up your search. I know you're not like the others, and she's only misery for us."

"Who's 'us'?"

"Us? That's easy: the innocents, the vulnerable, the victims."

"And do I fit into any of these categories?"

She hesitated, then stared directly at me. "All of them, I dare say."

It must have been the effects of my "Death."

"I . . . I don't understand you," I confessed, not a little dazed.

She shrugged again. "You will, I trust. Some already know, and some must be shown. In any event, her full name is Reichsgräfin[81] Katrin von Heldenleben, the daughter of Reichsgräf Friedenreich von Heldenleben. She has numerous addresses I'm told, but the only one I have for her is 11 Giesebrechtstrasse."

"She sounds pretty posh."

"Posh hardly describes her, Heinz. Her family traces back

---

[81] Countess of the Empire.

to the days before man's memory runs to the contrary. I didn't ask you at the time, but, given the journalistic imperative, what could possibly be your interest in someone of whom even your exalted Führer doesn't speak?"

I couldn't answer her, since I didn't have the answer, so I chose deflection. "Why did you use such a roundabout method of delivery? Why not send your note directly to me?"

"My source told me that Himmler himself wished you to have, as he called it, 'an appropriate and timely encounter,' and, between him and his boss—and *me* of all people as intermediary—you'd have it. Not a good sign in my book."

Stupid, she wasn't. I shook my head. "I'm confused, to say the least. What is their interest in her in the first place, and why did they want me to have 'an appropriate and timely encounter,' whatever that is, and through you 'of all people,' as you put it?"

"Your guess is as good as mine, Heinz. A mystery. And a mystery is just that. My source is quite reliable, but, unfortunately, not always completely forthcoming in his explanations, and, in my increasingly precarious position, I move gingerly, as you might imagine."

My imagination was fighting the effects of my "Death in the Afternoon" but losing again, as with the "Zombie." Did she ever recommend less-lethal drinks? In any event, it was also well after one thirty, and I had to write to you and also be on call for the Führer.

"You look exhausted," Bella said, reading me with an accuracy I'd come to expect. "But before we part, I'm under an obligation to ask you if you'd accomplished anything for 'Putzi,' I mean—"

"I know what you mean," I replied. "I just hope you'll use the utmost discretion when deciding how to present him with the results. After thoroughly rummaging through the Chancellery gossip factory, I discovered that 'Putzi' is second only to von Neurath on the Führer's 'shit-list,' excuse my language. Goebbels and that crazy Mitford hate his guts and have made every effort to ensure that their view of him prevailed. Personally, I urge you to keep Herr Hanfstaengl dangling on a rope of expectation until he comes to fully appreciate the gravity of his position and concedes defeat, like the elegant gentleman he needs everyone to believe he is."

She merely nodded, as if somehow, she already knew. "Shall we go then? You've been most kind, but I fear I've strained the hotel's tolerance to the breaking point and wish to return, of course, necessarily accompanied by someone who can command the same degree of forbearance."

Perhaps she didn't know, but, as I conclude this entry, I agonize over the fact that during the entire evening at the Adlon, of all places, meeting with an infamous Jew who could boast of a "reli-able" source's connexions with both her and Himmler, with all that, I never once asked her why, in all this craziness, I seemed to possess an immunity to things that, for anyone else, would have proven a catastrophe—and I still don't know why I didn't ask.

Even as a young man in decent physical health, how I survived the "Death in the Afternoon," the hour, and writing to you, I have yet to understand. Given that, this was not the day for what transpired.

The Führerbuzzer summoned me at 1100 hours, and I went there directly, in an understandably addlepated state. When I entered the Führer's quarters, I saw the back of him, already dressed and standing by an undraped window, something he never was or did. Moreover, surrounding him were three SS guards with their pistols drawn and aimed directly at him.

"My Führer," I said, and before I could say more, he turned to me, and I knew instantly that something was wrong. It was the Führer, but it wasn't. Suddenly, the bathroom door opened and another Führer, this time, in a half-opened bathrobe, emerged. I thought I was again hallucinating.

"So, Linge," the bathrobed figure said, "who is the Führer, eh?"

I gazed at both of them for a moment, then turned to the man in the bathrobe. "You are the Führer, of that I'm certain, but—"

"Yes, Linge, you are right, as always," he said, "but isn't this character a marvel? You know that I have six doubles, but none like Weler here. His resemblance to me is so uncanny that I have Bormann conceal him until absolutely necessary, lest he be assassinated or, worse, obeyed."

Even in my debilitated condition, I could easily see the Führer's point. I remember watching an advance copy of the new Hollywood film *Prisoner of Zenda* that Goebbels somehow managed to procure. While the Führer wearied after only a few minutes and retired, he bade me see the entire film. Afterwards, all I could imagine was not the danger of not having a double but quite the opposite.[82] Had he seen it earlier or read the novel?

The Führer then buzzed for Bormann, and he and the SS guards placed a sack over Weler's head and spirited him away. "Amazing likeness, Linge, eh?" the Führer asked. "I still shudder when I think of what he could do if let loose."

"But you need such men, yes, my Führer?" I asked.

"Of course, yes. In my position, unfortunately yes. Do you have any idea how many attempts on my life there have been?"

"No, my Führer," I answered truthfully.

"Well, I can tell you that neither did I, until Himmler had his staff investigate the matter and tabulate the results. Twenty-one times, Linge. Since 1921, *twenty-one times!* If anyone doubted my importance, that should convince even the most rabid sceptic.

---

[82] An English gentleman, Rudolf Rassendyll, takes a fishing vacation in a small middle European country. While there, he meets Colonel Zapt and Captain von Tarlenheim. Zapt introduces him to the soon-to-be-crowned king, Rudolf V, who turns out to be not only his distant relative but also his exact double. Rudolf is astounded and takes a great liking to the Englishman. They celebrate their acquaintance by drinking late into the night. Rudolf is particularly delighted with the bottle of wine sent to him by his half-brother, Duke Michael, so much so that he drinks it all himself. The next morning brings a disastrous discovery: the wine was drugged. Rudolf cannot be awakened, and if he cannot attend his coronation that day, Michael will try to usurp the throne. Zapt convinces a reluctant Rassendyll to impersonate Rudolf for the solemn ceremony.

And can you possibly think for one moment that such attempts will even subside, much less cease? So, a necessary burden."

I watched the Führer shave. He said, while with his razor's edge carefully carved a path through the thick fold of cream as if he were clearing snow on a major road: "As I recall, Linge, you were quite keen on pursuing some fetching female named Katrin, and you thought this meddlesome Jewess Fromm could help. Well then, did she?"

A part of me expected such a request, but another part hoped he'd forget or at least ignore the matter as far too trivial. But what could I say, when he and Himmler had helped facilitate the meeting, it seemed, for purposes not told to me? What was the minimum response I could give to satisfy both of them and at the same time protect myself? My headache returned with a hatchet blow and my stomach was a boiling cauldron.

"Well, my Führer, before I had an opportunity to even have a conversation, she had me order and drink something called 'Death in the Afternoon,' an explosive concoction of absinthe and Champagne that virtually destroyed my senses."

The Führer nodded lightly. "And people constantly make stupid jokes about me abstaining from such foolishness," he said, followed by a snide laugh. "The same with meat. All right, let them destroy their minds and bodies. And now, my young friend, you see the wisdom of what I've been constantly preaching to generally deaf—or drunken and fat-bloated—ears. In any event, even though you were justifiably impaired, do you have any notion of whether your meeting was productive?"

"If I can remember and assemble the fragments of her words, I think I may have gotten the information I came after, my Führer, but only time will tell."

"And did she, by some chance, divulge her source of this information?"

Suddenly, his right hand began to tremble. "Linge," he uttered, far more casually than I would have expected, "help me finish shaving and call for Morell."

❦

I did more than that. I called Brückner, too, and both arrived within less than two minutes of my calls. For some reason that I couldn't articulate, I didn't trust Morell and felt that Brückner's presence would help to soothe my apprehension if not Morell's actions. After a time, seeing nothing untoward, both Brückner and I moved into the hallway, leaving the Führer in Morell's hands.

"Look, Heinz," Brückner said, obviously reading my concern. "I worry about the Führer, too, but if this Morell's a quack, he's a bloody damn good one, and the Führer seems to consider him nothing short of a miracle worker, so what can we do but take what we can get?"

"I suppose you're right," I said without conviction.

"More important, my friend, how did your date fare? I know she's a Jewess, but did it go beyond dinner? Since neither of you is married, you would have been well within the law, at least for the present."[83]

"Wilhelm," I told him truthfully, "after having one 'Death in the Afternoon,' 'it,' as you put it, didn't even get to dessert."

"'Death in the Afternoon'?" he asked. "A drink, perhaps?"

"A drink, definitely. Absinthe and Champagne. Quite a

---

[83] The original Nuremberg Laws only prohibited extramarital sex between Aryans and Jews. Later, the death penalty was applied to *all* interracial sex, under the Law for the Protection of German Blood and Honour section.

devastating contrivance. Perhaps Morell even injects himself with it, to protect him from the Führer's fumes."

Once his laughter has subsided, Brückner led me into the gardens.

"So, you didn't even get a bedroom out of it. Did you at least get what you were actually after?"

I shook my aching head, then thought better of it, but too late. "I think so. Say, is there anyone who didn't know what I was up to?"

"I doubt it," he said. "The Chancellery is one enormous fish tank in which we all both swim and watch each other swim simultaneously. Details and interpretations may vary, but all the fish know the basics, you can be sure."

I was so hung over that I hadn't considered the entire bizarre business, but now, Brückner had forced it into my still-bleary consciousness: that my purely emotional quest for Katrin had been preempted by the Führer and Himmler for reasons unknown to me. Why? Was Frau Bella aware of it? And, of the greatest and most sinister significance: How could a Jewish journalist know what the Reichsführer-SS and the Führer didn't already know?

"I managed to get an address for Katrin," I told him. "11 Giesebrechtstrasse."

At that, Brückner stopped me in my tracks and turned me towards him with a raised eyebrow. "You know that address, don't you?"

"No, but I'm certain I can find it."

"That's not what I meant, my young friend. That address is rather notorious, you know."

An icicle shot through my stomach like a runaway train. "Notorious?"

"You don't know of Salon Kitty?"[84] he exclaimed, though in a hushed tone. "You mean to tell me that Baur, our unofficial Chancellery procurer, never mentioned it?"

"Never," I said truthfully. "All he showed me was his astounding photo collection."

Brückner nodded. "Interesting, since the place is a rather open secret among the upper levels of the Party."

"Well, I must not be 'upper' enough, since I never heard of it."

"Salon Kitty is a brothel, Heinz, but one, of course, catering to only the most illustrious clientele in Berlin, which number more than you'd like to think."

"Have you ever been there?" I asked.

"Better, my friend, if you were to ask why someone like your Katrin would be there."

---

[84] In 1930s Berlin, Salon Kitty was a high-class brothel at 11 Giesebrechtstrasse. Its usual clientele included German dignitaries and foreign diplomats. Its owner was Kitty Schmidt.

[All entries (if any) between 6 January
and 29 January are missing.]

Up early to prepare the Führer for a full day of dictation.

I'd heard him fulminate often about the most "opportune time" to "put the vindictive bastards on notice, both inside and outside the Reich," that a "new Germany," under his inspired leadership, had arrived (if they hadn't noticed), and that "nothing will ever be the same after that." I imagined that today, the "opportune time" had finally arrived when von Ribbentrop entered, followed by three secretaries (Dara was not among them, but Schroeder was, and actually winked at me!). Once the secretaries were settled, and the Führer began his pacing, I stole out, as there was nothing further for me to do, and I already knew what he would be saying in his speech to the Reichstag the next day, celebrating the fourth anniversary of his coming to power.

A few days before, while tidying up the Führer's study, I happened to see Article 231 of the Treaty of Versailles[85] spread across his desk. While called the "War Guilt Clause" by the victorious nations,

---

[85] Article 231, often known as the War Guilt Clause, was the opening article of the reparations section of the Treaty of Versailles, which ended the First World War between the German Empire and the Allied and Associated Powers. The article did not use the word *guilt* but still was designed to serve as a legal basis to compel Germany to pay reparations. Article 231 was one of the most controversial points of the treaty. Substituting "responsibility" for "guilt," it stated:

The Allied and Associated Governments affirm and Germany accepts the responsibility of Germany and her allies for causing all the loss and damage to which the Allied and Associated Governments and their nationals have

in Germany, it was called an abomination, and far worse by the Führer, even though he claimed to harbour a degree of ambivalence towards it. It was the ambivalence that initially confounded me but that ultimately made perfect sense once he explained things.

The "lesson" began while he was screeching obscenities at General Werner von Fritsch, the army commander in chief.

"You strain credulity, Fritsch," he shouted. "Have you no faith in me? *NONE?*"

The general had just told the Führer that, despite the latter's superlative achievements, anything that France and Britain might still view as outright German aggression was utterly and hopelessly premature and so doomed to failure.

"With your pedigree, your medals, your rank, your position, a position, I might add, which I *personally* bestowed upon you," the Führer screamed as he continued his tirade, *"is it possible that you cannot think beyond the battlefields of the last war? Yes? No? WHAT?"*

I had seen cases of shellshock before, and in the face of von Fritsch, I was seeing one again.

"Must I, a mere corporal, become the teacher of generals?" he shouted.

Von Fritsch merely sat at rigid attention, his face a mask of marble.

"All right, if I must," the Führer continued, relaxing his tone a bit, since he was to play one of his favourite roles. "You and all your kind," he began, "are frozen in the last war like insects in amber. You see Germany as one enormous trench in which the German people must hide lest the big bad enemy in the facing trenches, like France and Britain, mow them down. Even as a

---

been subjected as a consequence of the war imposed upon them by the aggression of Germany and her allies.

lowly messenger, I could discern the unnatural imbecility of such a military strategy, though I was hardly positioned to make my knowledge and rage known and, more important, manifest. You see, Fritsch, unlike you, I never saw Germany as a trench, even then, but instead, I saw it as a shark, and a shark never rests, but keeps moving, always searching for prey and, without hesitation, devours anything in its path. He," pointing to the portrait of Frederick the Great, "knew this, instinctively, as I did. 'Always advance,' he said. Yes. Use every means at your disposal to keep advancing—and devour anything in your path. A nation, like a shark, must constantly move and devour, or it will die. You and your kind would have me calculate the international effect of a simple sneeze, and shudder at the prospect. That is your class's hereditary timidity! I will console you: I'll be doing nothing but issuing words, a mere minnow for a shark, and, while the effect on the shark will be a mild and temporary diminution of hunger, the effect on the other sea creatures, I assure you, will go virtually unnoticed. And, my ossified friend, you've seen nothing of what this shark can do. Now do you understand?"

"I understand you perfectly, my Führer," von Fritsch replied, deftly avoiding the answer the Führer was seeking, but the latter appeared to be too much in thrall by his analogy to notice. "May I have your leave to go?" he said, with no more expression than he'd shown before. "I have a staff meeting awaiting my arrival."

"Yes, Fritsch," the Führer answered. "I trust I'll see you at the Rally?" As usual, it wasn't a question.

"Of course, my Führer. After your . . . explanation, I wouldn't miss it for the world." Then he stood, saluted, and left.

The Führer was breathing heavily, hand trembling, as he slumped in to his chair. "*Fools, Linge!*" he shouted. "*Stupid reactionary fools!*" How can I achieve my revolutionary vision with such mummies as these?"

My mind returned for a moment to my hiring "interview," which hadn't been an interview. Was all that happened to me since already known or, at least, predicted? What to say? Anything? Let him rail on? There were questions I wanted to ask him about the entire Katrin matter; for example, if both the Führer and Himmler wished me to locate Katrin for whatever reason, why not tell me straight out and not create the elaborately needless scenario with Frau Bella? But I'd learned that when in doubt (which was most of the time), say nothing, and now was no different.

He rose and paced again. "*Amazing!*" the Führer shouted. "You'd think, by Fritsch's reaction, that I told him I intended to declare war on France instead of making a Reichstag speech repudiating the so-called War Guilt Clause of that excrescence of a Versailles treaty. I certainly had no desire to inform him, one with a mind as inflexible as his, that even that tiny gesture, as modest and internationally inconsequential as it is, was something I hadn't decided on lightly. But be that as it may, what I've done up to now is only the barest of beginnings. As I informed that ambulatory cadaver a few moments ago, the shark must move and devour, and, through you, it will."

Through me? Delivering his mail, timing his toilette? Fixing his bow tie? Standing like a statue behind him at meals? Calling Dr. Morell when he had a seizure of the bowels? What help?

After photographing this, there will be little sleep for me, I fear. So perhaps I'll read about "cabbages and kings."[86] And sharks.

---

[86] From "The Walrus and the Carpenter," by Lewis Carroll (from *Through the Looking-Glass and What Alice Found There*, 1872).

I SPENT THE post-Führer morning in my quarters, chiding myself for failing to follow through on Frau Bella's information and the "encouragement" of the Führer, and even Himmler. Perhaps their involvement is precisely the cause of my procrastination, I told myself, but I wasn't terribly convincing. There had to be more to it, but something in my brain refused to consider what it might be.

My ruminations were cut short by Baur, who burst into my room with a surly truant officer's expression.

"*Shit, Linge!*" he exclaimed. "Have you no regard for us generous souls who broke our backs for you—at no small risk, I might add—and who now sit round with bitten-off nails, ear to the ground, waiting for the next bit of sexual gossip? If you got no mercy for me, at least think of poor Kempka."

I felt he was joshing me, up to a point, but who knew the point? Since everyone seemed to know what I was about—they all required the same fable or there would be suspicion, and I certainly didn't need that. Moreover, since I might need their "services" again, I felt I had to give them something for their pains.

"What can I say, Hans? There's not much to tell, except that this peasant wasn't at all prepared for the lavish magic of the Adlon, especially the drinks."

Baur shook his head. "Heinz, who the fuck cares about the drinks? What about the Jewess? Did anything happen between the two of you, or not?" He raised his lecherous eyebrows and splayed his hands in juicy anticipation.

"She didn't try to circumcise me, if that was worrying you," I kidded to prepare for a subject change, but it was in vain.

"*Aha!*" Baur slobbered, kneading his hands. "So, something *did* happen, you race-defiling hunk. Was this one as fiery as their reputation?"

I decided that they already had an unassailable image of my evening. Since any denial on my part would be pooh-poohed away, I decided to melt into the crowd of their expectations.

"Well, since she was my first Jewess," I guessed, since I'd never felt the need to ask any female I took to bed whether she followed the Hebrew faith, "I don't have any way to measure, but she definitely knew what I wanted, and most certainly delivered."

"All right, then." Baur applauded himself with pursed lips and a nod. "So it was worth all the hazardous efforts Kempka and me put into this, yes?"

"Quite definitely, Hans, and I'm most indebted to you both. Now, my apologies, but the Führer's waiting."

And no more procrastination, I resolved, for I'd also made up my mind to contact Katrin, and soon.

I just hoped it wouldn't require a tuxedo.

I DO BELIEVE that the awkward matter of the piano player has been resolved, my friend, and with no effort or inculpation on my part. It couldn't have come at a better time, since, after a surprising hiatus, my brain-splitting headaches and nightmares have returned with biblical vengeance.

After helping to prepare the Führer to greet the day, I ran into übergossiper Wiedemann.[87] He had the physique of a wrestler: tall, dark, and muscular. With his thick neck, heavy face, friendly eyes, and extremely low forehead, he was considered by most Chancellery females as handsome. Nonetheless, to me, he was a crafty beer hall brute, who combined an uncultivated, primitive mind with the shrewdness and cunning of an animal, completely devoid of delicacy or subtlety.

I usually steered clear of him, since anything said by anyone eventually found its way to everyone. Of course, my being so close to the Führer—literally and figuratively—made me a major target for his insatiable need to gather information to pass on to anyone who'd listen. I believed his craving to be benign but,

---

[87] Fritz Wiedemann and Hitler first came into contact during the First World War when Captain (Hauptmann) Wiedemann, as regimental adjutant, was Corporal Hitler's superior. Wiedemann, no fool, accepted a new offer to link up with his former corporal, initially in the offices of Rudolf Hess, before taking up his post at Hitler's side as one of his adjutants. When Brückner was otherwise unavailable, Wiedemann was a major source of scuttlebutt to the Chancellery staff.

in his position, highly dangerous. Fortunately, his duties kept him away from the Chancellery, and so I seldom had to hide. However, today, with my own needs to satisfy, I took the opportunity to use the user.

"Ah, Linge," he said, before I could open my mouth. "How are you? I hardly get to see you. Taking good care of the Führer? You know, he's more delicate than he lets on. I remember—"

"He's in the best of hands," I interrupted. "Dr. Morell takes care of his delicacy and I take care of his toilette." I studiously refrained from bringing up Brückner, Wiedemann's superior and rival. "I was just thinking, when I saw you. Do you happen to know whatever happened to that piano player, uh, Han-something-or-other? I used to hear him playing all the time, but now, nothing." I knew what had happened, but not the why of it to complete the picture.

At that, Wiedemann's eyes took on a glow. "You mean Hanfstaengl. The Führer didn't tell you? You'll love this," he promised, "so make some time and I'll start from the beginning—and *what a beginning!*" Then, without waiting for me to make time, he began: "The 'Plan for Putzi,'" laughing briefly at his rascally alliteration, "was hatched over lunch. I just happened to be there to give the Führer a report. Goebbels was there, as usual, and you know, with him, no one is safe from his sarcasm. Anyway, Goebbels was in rare form, even for him, and his main victim of the day was that snooty giant Hanfstaengl. He started by attacking Hanfstaengl's character, representing him as a miserly, money-grubbing oaf of highly questionable honesty. But the real death blow was struck when he mentioned the Spanish Civil War and that 'Putzi' had made adverse remarks about the fighting spirit of the German soldiers. The Führer became hysterical with rage at that. You've seen it all before, my friend, and for far lesser transgressions than that. 'This cowardly fellow who has no right to judge the courage of others must be given a lesson!' the Führer said, once he'd calmed down enough.

"And so," Wiedemann continued, smirking at his razor wit, "Project Putzi, as I call it, was put into operation, forthwith. I telephoned Hanfstaengl in Munich to tell him that he was wanted in Berlin at once and that the Führer's personal pilot was to bring him by special plane. Enough for his gorilla-sized ego, eh? So of course he came and met with me, whereupon I told him that the Führer personally wished him to fly to Spain immediately to assist the German journalists who'd gone there to report on the war. Clever of the Führer, yes? I then assured him that, should his mission be successful, he would be instantly reinstated into the Führer's good graces.

"To slather icing on the cake, I told him that his mission was top secret—even from me—and that he must go to Goebbels's ministry to be further briefed. Much to his shock, I imagine, he was greeted with almost slobbering courtesy by one of Goebbels's advisers and given additional details. The next morning, he was further groomed by Göring, who even made a few typical jokes about the medical consequences of sexual encounters with Spanish women."

At this point, though I appeared attentive, I'd actually stopped listening because I already knew this part. Early this morning, I had received a telephone call from Hanfstaengl himself. With not a little fear in his voice and somewhat breathlessly, he thanked me for any efforts I'd made to assist him but said that it was now far too late. He went on to repeat what Wiedemann had told me but added a few morsels the adjutant couldn't have known—that up to the actual flight, Hanfstaengl had been of two minds: one, flattered and encouraged; the other, confused and suspicious. It was only when he boarded the aircraft for

Spain that the latter mind had prevailed. And whatever doubts he may have had about the worth and legitimacy of his "mission" were resolved when the pilot told him he was to fly him over the red lines between Barcelona and Madrid, where he was to parachute down. When he balked, the pilot said his instructions were to fly an "agent" behind enemy lines and drop him, and was he not an agent?

"It dawned on me then and there," Hanfstaengl had said on the phone, "that I'd been a bloody fool. This was a death sentence, pure and not so simple, since there would have been far less elaborate ways of carrying it out." When I pretended to suggest that he might be mistaken, Hanfstaengl laughed sardonically and said: "Herr Linge, always the innocent. Think! What better way to eliminate one of the oldest—but most awkward—of the Führer's associates than with a heroic death on a secret mission?

"But fortune was with me that night, for mechanical trouble caused us to land in a pine forest between Leipzig and Dresden. Once down, I quickly considered my alternatives. If they had thought nothing of killing hundreds of people during the Night of the Long Knives, would they even yawn at the prospect of eliminating me? The question answers itself. So, feigning airsickness, I slipped away and made a couple of calls, one being to you. And so, I'm setting off for neutral Switzerland. Farewell, Linge," he concluded, "and please deliver my regards to Unity and the rest of the gang when you feel able, yes?" Then he laughed again and rang off.

I turned my attention back to Wiedemann, who was now cackling over the beauty of the conspirators' ingenious plan, ignorant of the real fate of Hanfstaengl, sitting in a bistro, chortling with glee at the ineptitude of his enemies. As for me, I merely experienced a wind gush of relief at not having to return a favour I had no intention of returning.

I WAS SUMMONED early to the Führer, where I discovered him in his partially opened bathrobe, "in conference" (meaning a purple-faced, eye-bulging, shrieking lecture) with Goebbels, Himmler, and Göring, his reigning sub-triumvirate. Before I entered, I noticed Cardinal Pacelli, a stick figure, like a spoon balancing precariously on its handle and normally the most stoic prelate I'd ever seen, pacing the anteroom in his lavish Cardinal's robes, apprehensively fingering his ornate rosary. I could hear screaming coming from inside, and, presumably, so could he.

Then, suddenly, the screaming decreased to something vaguely resembling a conversational tone, and I entered, saw the three seated erect in armchairs before the desk that the Führer was standing behind, red-faced, his shaking, white-knuckled fists propping himself up, and so I went immediately to the book-shelves for my superfluous shelving ritual.

"All right," the Führer asked haltingly, "so what do you know now of this, this . . . *shit*?"

"Though it's rather early in the game, my Führer," Himmler began, "I can tell you this: I suspected something, and so, through my informants and others who were . . . persuaded to cooperate, I learnt that the Encyclical[88] was smuggled into

---

[88] *Mit brennender Sorge* (With Burning Anxiety) *on the Church and the German Reich* was an encyclical of Pope Pius XI, issued on 10 March 1937 (but bearing a date of Passion Sunday, 14 March). Written in German, not

the country, where it was secretly printed at twelve different plants. During the weekend of Passion Sunday, it was delivered by courier, mostly boys on foot and on bicycle, many of them travelling to their destinations across fields and through woods in order to avoid public roads. The document was not, at any point, entrusted to the official postal service. In some cases, it was delivered to the parish priest in the confessional. Many priests kept the document locked away. We also know that the document was written in German but addressed not only to the German bishops but also to the Catholic episcopate throughout the world. Despite this, a manageable disaster, if I may say so."

The Führer merely stood there, hunched over his desk, I felt, collecting strength for the next round. "A 'manageable disaster,' you say. All right. Joseph," speaking to Goebbels but gazing at Himmler, "summarise the important parts of this 'manageable disaster' for me."

Goebbels went for some sheets from his lap, cleared his throat, then folded the papers, and slid them into his breast pocket. "It basically states that there is a campaign against the confessional schools, which are guaranteed by the Concordat, and the destruction of free elections."

"He is referring to Germany," Himmler said.

"I'm not an idiot, Heinrich. I know it's Germany. Go on, Joseph."

Goebbels continued, again clearing his throat, at this point to me a nervous gesture rather than a physiological one. "Pius then stated that 'true belief in God could not be reconciled with race, people, or state, raised beyond their standard value to

---

the usual Latin, it was smuggled into Germany for fear of censorship and was read from the pulpits of all German Catholic churches on one of the church's busiest Sundays, Palm Sunday (21 March that year).

idolatrous levels,' that national religion or a national God was rejected as a grave error, and that the Christian God could not be restricted within the frontiers of a single people, within the pedigree of one single race."

Goebbels stopped at this point and looked up at the Führer. "Shall I continue, my Führer?"

The Führer sighed with theatrical patience. "Yes, Joseph, I'll inform you when I've heard enough."

"Pacelli concluded by saying: 'Whoever exalts race, or the people, or the State, or a particular form of State, or the depositories of power, or any other fundamental value of the human community, he is far from the true faith in God and from the concept of life which that faith upholds.'"

"Did your . . . sources have anything to add?"

"Yes, my Führer," he answered with his customary lack of expression. "They were most informative, once they were told, in one way or another, to be in no doubt of the seriousness of their position. We learned of the firms that had collaborated in printing the seditious trash, and they will be shut down, and the individuals involved, dealt with accordingly. Heydrich will order all copies of the document to be confiscated and destroyed. Moreover, I will drastically increase surveillance and infiltration of all Catholic churches and church organizations."

"Hmm. And you, Joseph?" the Führer asked Goebbels.

"Of course, my Führer," he declared passionately, "I will use all the means at my ministry's disposal to counter the pope's pernicious cant with a blizzard of newspaper articles, leaflets, and radio addresses."

Lids at half-mast, the Führer raised his hand slowly, salute-style, to silence Goebbels. "Have you anything to say, Hermann?"

The hillock of uniformed fat shrugged his shoulders to the

accompanying clanging of his medals. "My Führer, my religious beliefs have always resided at the handle of my parachute cord."

"No surprise, Hermann. Regardless, your suggestions?"

The bedecked hippo sat up even straighter, pulling down the tunic that had shifted from the weight of his veneer of medals and decorations. "For my part, my Führer," he said, "beyond what has been proposed, I would recommend reinstating the trials[89] in earnest, and this time, not so limited."

"Hmm, yes, the trials. For the present," the Führer declared, "I want the courts to be so occupied with these cases that they'll have to work day and night, weekends, as well as holidays to deal with this."

The Führer straightened up, lifted his fists from his desk, and began rubbing them, presumably to restore circulation. His face had returned to its normal pallor. For my part, I had shelved and reshelved his books so many times, I was surprised the covers hadn't worn off.

"All right," the Führer concluded, "see to the tasks you've outlined for me, and with all necessary vigour. These treasonous lackeys of a degenerate pope will be taught a valuable lesson in how to deal with me and the Reich. Thank you, gentlemen."

The three rose as one, saluted, and withdrew.

I was not religious in the slightest, only entering a church to escape the police, rain, and snow or to raid the poor box, so I didn't understand what all the fuss was about. I promised myself to ask Brückner about it later, when we next met to sort the mail.

---

[89] Göring was referring to the Morality Trials of 1935–36 in which Catholic religious leaders were accused of sexual abuse of minors and currency misdemeanours. The former allegations were levelled particularly against nuns and clergy responsible for children in orphanages and schools. The latter involved religious congregations financially responsible for missions and communities abroad.

After the door closed behind them, there was a brief period of total silence, then, "Linge," he said, "mark my words: one day we will be rid of the crutch of Catholicism as we will be rid of the Jews. But for the present," he added, "we must keep a low and diplomatic profile for both. In any event, Pacelli must be a straw of sweat by now, so now we let him in."

"Yes, my Führer," I answered, went to the door, and beckoned the pathetic prelate to enter.

The Führer bade Pacelli sit, which he did, prim and deliberate as always, but this time, with a slight tension in his emaciated frame. Then the Führer sat, also, to my mind, somewhat primly, perhaps as a rebuke, perhaps to illustrate the solemnity of the occasion, I knew not which.

"Well, Herr Cardinal," the Führer said with glacial calm, his hands clasped in front of him, "what do you have to say for yourself?"

Pacelli, hands clasped similarly in his purple-robed lap, cleared his throat gently. "Herr Chancellor," he began, "I beg you to understand that under Catholic strictures, a mere cardinal has little authority over a pontiff, save as an adviser. Please know that I strenuously advised His Holiness that he would only be purchasing trouble with his encyclical, but I'm afraid he would not budge."

I tried to imagine this cadaverous creature doing anything strenuous and had to stifle a laugh.

The Führer unclasped his hands. "Are you even dimly aware, my dear Cardinal, that with one stroke of my pen, or even an oblique remark to my ministers, I can instantly transform your precious Concordat into toilet paper?"

"Yes, Herr Chancellor," he answered with a slight waver in his voice. "I am fully aware of the extent of your authority and the delicacy of the instrument. I am merely informing you of my limitations under the circumstances."

"Limitations?" the Führer retorted. "And yet, I have it on the best authority that you were the author of this infamous document."

"With respect, that is not precisely accurate," Pacelli replied. "In point of fact, Archbishop von Faulhaber,[90] no friend of your regime, was the principal author, and I merely edited his work. However, in that capacity, I was able to dilute the most extreme language in the provisions and make certain that it failed to condemn National Socialism and you by name. Given my position, you must appreciate that I could do no more."

The Führer was silent for a pregnant moment, then said: "All right, Herr Cardinal, I accept your explanation and recognize your efforts. However, *you* must now appreciate that, for a time, things will not go well for your church and its practitioners. Despite the Concordat and your best efforts, your pope has insulted and enraged those who serve me and the people I have sworn to serve, and so I cannot take such a grave matter lightly. I am saying this so you will have had ample notice. Nevertheless, you can help your flock by counselling them in the strongest possible terms to take extreme care not to refer in any way to the encyclical in their sermons, writings, or even in their confessionals. However, should they mindlessly and heedlessly bow to that old, deluded, feeble man in the Vatican and ignore your wise and prudent counsel, it will be on their heads and your conscience. Am I sufficiently clear on this?"

Pacelli shrugged his bony shoulders. "You are *abundantly* clear, Herr Chancellor, as always," he said, a whiff of chill

---

[90] Michael von Faulhaber was Archbishop of Munich.

entering his voice. "Please be assured that I will do all within my power to encourage German Catholics to maintain a strict separation of faith and citizenship. However, I operate within a strict hierarchy and no less strict set of rules and so must support your aims with utmost subtlety and caution."

The Führer nodded, I thought, ambiguously, then rose, causing Pacelli to rise as well, bid the Führer goodbye, and depart with a solemn cadence to his steps. When the door closed, I ceased my reshelving, since the need had vanished and my arms were giving out.

As I turned from the books, I saw the Führer shaking his head. "These religious, Linge, even the slithery political ones like Pacelli, can't resist diplomatic obscurantism. He's useful, though, so I tolerate him. He's going places, I can tell, and we'll have need of such a creature when I finally put my plan for the Catholics into operation. As for organized religion generally," he added cryptically, "I will soon rise above and beyond it all, and you will be . . ." His voice trailed off, and he appeared to withdraw to an amorphous realm far away. He'd done this many times, and seemed benign enough, so I took it as a signal to leave.

As I consider the Führer's unfinished reference to me, all I could think of was my own view of religion: a means by which ignorant people explain events, and by which terrified people manage mortality.

It turns out that I didn't need to seek out Katrin, for a note was delivered to me this morning, requesting my presence this evening at the address I'd already been given. No RSVP was requested, so my presence appeared to be something she took for granted.

Since the Führer knew of my desire to meet with Katrin, and had no pressing business that needed my presence, it was relatively easy to get him to agree to free me up by having Krause attend him after dinner. At 2300 hours, as I walked to the main garage to borrow a car from Kempka and get directions from Baur, I mulled over the conversation I'd had with Brückner:

"Well, my bricklaying friend, Salon Kitty is a brothel, but one, of course, catering only to the most illustrious clientele in Berlin, which number more than you'd like to think."

"Have you ever been there?"

"Better, my friend, if you were to ask why someone like your Katrin would be there."

What to make of it? I thought to myself, and came up empty. I didn't know enough to even speculate, so I resolved to temper anticipation with caution, even though I had no idea how. As I'd hoped, I spotted both Kempka and Baur chatting loudly in the former's office about all the possible reprisals the Führer would visit upon the church. When I entered, the subject shifted quickly from religion to lust.

With a leer, Kempka handed me the keys to a sumptuous Mercedes Saloon.

"Need directions?" Baur asked.

"You're quite the comedian," I said. "The shortest route, yes?"

He responded with more a crooked sneer than a smile. "Why of course, Linge. Length is for the customer, not the directions." He then scrawled a series of intersecting lines and street names on a torn-off greasy sheet and handed it to me. "Follow this," he said, "and you'll be in paradise before you know it. I have it on the best of authorities: me. Oh, and a friendly tip: you may notice a lot of highfalutin' characters, some you seen here and on the mountaintop, but they won't . . . recognize you, and you won't recognize them, you understand me? Good form all the way round, eh?"

Good form indeed, I thought. I seriously doubted that any of them would recognize me anyway, and that's exactly the way I wanted it.

&

Following Baur's spare but efficient scribble, I arrived at 11 Giesebrechtstrasse exactly on time. If I had the correct address, Salon Kitty appeared to be just one of a dozen identical, posh, attached, whitewashed apartment buildings, utterly elegant and utterly anonymous, save for the row of magnificent chauffeured limousines and cabriolets that double-lined the quiet street. One would have mistaken it for the embassy of a small nation if not for the lack of an identifying flag. Perhaps, in a sense, it was.

Possessing no chauffeur, I parked a few blocks down to avoid scrutiny and walked purposefully to the large, art nouveau black wooden door (decorated with tasteful rectangles and curves of translucent glass) and buzzed. Almost immediately, a dinner-jacketed person with the beefy physique of a wrestler I assumed was a bouncer[91] opened the door and, without ceremony or speech, ushered me into an enormous, empty, high-ceilinged foyer, as if he knew I was expected. Three tastefully painted walls were bare, but the fourth wall contained a lift, with a door similar to the one that had permitted me entry, but this one contained a large square of translucent glass in the centre. The bouncer waved his burly arm toward it, and I went over and pulled it open, walked in, pushed the inner gate closed, pressed the only button, and up I glided, without a sound.

The lift door opened onto an exquisite little café, not unlike the dining room and bar at the Adlon, but in miniature, and containing only men. All round the room, there were black wooden doors like the ones I'd seen. These contained no glass, but instead had numbers stencilled in the centre. The men in uniform held ranks that only the Führer and his immediate subordinates could possibly outmatch, and the others were in full dinner dress, some with coloured sashes, some with decorations, some with both.

Writhing inside with self-consciousness, I felt like an orderly to the uniformed and a footman to the tuxedoed. But for the purpose of the place, it might have been an English men's club such as I'd read about in so many novels. Some of the men looked foreign, but I assumed they held high positions in their home countries.

Beside the bar, I saw liveried waiters receive plates of food by way of a dumbwaiter not dissimilar to the ones at the Chancellery and the Berghof. In addition to the food and drink on their

---

[91] *Rausschmeißer.*

tables, each man possessed a small plastic card with a number embossed on it. I supposed that the card numbers corresponded to the door numbers, but it was only a guess. No man spoke to another, and I had no intention of calling undue attention to myself.

I sat down at the only empty table, and, not to appear more conspicuous than my uniform rank already announced, I felt the need to order something. In point of fact, I *was* hungry, not having eaten since early morning, but my stomach was churning with anticipation, so I merely ordered a beer and what the waiter recommended in the strongest terms as "Kitty's 'special canapés.'" When the waiter delivered it and left, my concern grew even deeper, and, as I ate, hopefully concealing my nausea at the foul taste, I wondered when, how, and even if I would obtain a plastic card of my own, one that would lead me to Katrin.

Then, as if by some invisible signal, the doors opened, one at a time, and the men with their numbered cards rose and walked through each corresponding door, which instantly closed behind them, leaving only me and the bartender. I looked up at him for some sign of things to come, but he busied himself clearing the tables and didn't once look at me.

After a few minutes, I heard the faint humming sound of machinery, the lift door hissed open, and Katrin emerged, her stature highlighted by a silver lamé, form-encasing gown and matching silver pumps with high, pointed heels. She looked eerily like a mobile ice sculpture. When I stood to greet her at eye level, she held out a kid-gloved hand, which I shook. From her wry expression, I imagined she'd expected a kiss on it instead and was amused by my lack of sophistication. We both sat down and, suddenly bereft of words, I could only stare at her while she ceremoniously removed her gloves.

"Fascinating as ever, Heinz," she said, I expected, to break the silence. "I regret not arranging this meeting sooner, but you know how those things are."

I had no conceivable idea "how those things are," nor did I even know *what* they are, so I remained silent.

"It's still too early for our purposes, but there was someone who eagerly wished to meet you and I was, how shall I say, obliged to arrange it, and so here we are."

So much for romance, I thought, grim with disappointment. *Obliged?* By whom? For what *purpose?* And who comprised the *our?* I had so many questions bombarding my brain that none came out in speech. And, added to that, was her perfect face. Her beautifully sculpted lips were so precise, luminous, red, and smooth, they looked somehow fastened onto her real ones. Her ice-blue eyes, always searching my face for something I knew not what, utterly unnerved me, as I imagined they did many others, not excluding women.

"I have no sense of time, I'm afraid," I replied to her "too early" reference, guessing that what I said was probably not what she'd meant.

"Time isn't everything," she said. "I must keep reminding myself of this. What is meant to be will happen in its own time, and one needs only to be ready, don't you agree?"

I didn't know what the hell she was talking about, but her voice was so seductive, I was compelled to ignore meaning for the pure sound of her. "I imagine so," I replied lamely, for want of wit or understanding.

While I listened to her, I also heard the hum again. The lift door opened and out stepped a middle-aged man of medium height, blond hair parted in the middle and slicked back, small, pinched lips, and the beginnings of a double chin. He wore a brown, double-breasted business suit, perfectly tailored but completely inappropriate for the hour and venue. He gave me one pumping gesture for a handshake, nodded an oddly formal nod to Katrin, and sat down, as did I.

"May I introduce—" Katrin started to say, but the man raised his hand quickly to silence her.

"My name is not important," he declared, "only my purpose." He spoke in a voice somewhat higher than I would have expected. His accent was German, but I couldn't place a specific region.

"Ah, I see you've tried Kitty's 'special canapés,'" he said. "I've heard many good things about them."

"Would you like to try one?" I asked. There were three left on my plate. Three of four. "I wasn't very hungry." Hunger was, of course, hardly the issue: I'd found them utterly loathsome in both taste and texture and couldn't imagine how their reputation could withstand the reality.

He pursed his lips and shook a negative. "Most generous, but I just finished a rather hearty dinner and couldn't possibly ingest more." He patted his stomach to underscore his statement. Just then, the waiter appeared at my side, glanced down at my plate, then up at me, and *tsk-tsked*. "These hors d'oeuvres are a speciality of the house. A pity you couldn't do them justice."

"If Major Linge isn't hungry," Katrin said to him briskly, "then justice is served, yes?"

He snapped his head toward her. "Yes. Of course," he said, without expression, then returned to me. "My apologies, Herr Major. I certainly don't mean to appear insolent."

I was stunned by her formality and his reaction. Shuddering internally with discomfort, I remarked to the waiter: "No insolence, so no apology necessary. All right, justice it shall be. One more then." I forked it into my mouth and forced myself to swallow the repellent thing, struggling not to wince in disgust. "Yes," I lied to the waiter through my teeth, "truly delicious." This appeared to satisfy him and he moved back to the bar as I turned to the guest.

"Katrin said you wanted to meet me?"

"Most definitely," he answered. "You know, you're quite renowned among my associates, so I was curious to see for myself." He reached into his inside jacket pocket, took out a small leather-bound notebook, and flipped some pages. I couldn't see what they contained. He looked down at a page, then looked back up to me.

"A few questions, if I may?"

"Of course," I answered.

"Thank you. Major Linge, are you able to exercise volition in your dreams?"

I was completely flummoxed by the question and the police-station mode of delivery, but I forced myself to appear calm. "Volition?" I asked, as if I'd never heard or read the word.

"He's unschooled, as you must know," Katrin advised, then turned to me. "No offense, Heinz."

"Yes. I overlooked that," the man answered, this time without looking at her, his eyes fixed on me. "My apologies. I'll rephrase the question: When you dream, are you able to exercise control over what you or others do? Also, in your dreams, is there ever a metal object, like a child's top? Two harmless questions, after all, yes?"

Not knowing what was happening, I felt the need to answer as I would a question from the Führer. "I never remember my dreams, so I couldn't really say."

The man nodded ambiguously and put away his notebook.

"Are you satisfied?" Katrin asked him.

"For now, my dear," still not looking at her. "I am most grateful to you, Herr Major, for agreeing to meet with me," he said. Then, without waiting for me to stand, he rose quickly, made for the elevator, entered, closed the door behind him, and I heard the hum.

I shook my head and looked at Katrin. "Can you please explain all this?"

She fixed her gaze on me and shrugged her padded shoulders. "I wish I could, Heinz."

Her expression told me, unmistakably, that pursuing the matter would be futile, so I changed the subject. "All right, but why arrange the meeting at a place like this?"

She smiled. "Why not here?" she answered. "It's private, it's convenient, its reputation is beyond rumour or speculation, and, best of all—" moving her long, slender, gloved arm toward a door beside the bar that had no number, then bringing it back and gently placing her hand on mine. "See that door? It's for me, and tonight, it's for us—if you want it. Does that answer your question?"

It did. I followed her in.

&

Nothing had changed in the café—except Katrin's absence, and the man now standing over my prostrate body. I hadn't seen or felt her departure, or the arrival of the man standing over me. The lights had shut down, so I was sightless.

"Where?" the man asked me. "Only you know where."

I stared up to the voice that I recognized—for who could not know that voice? A voice that stirs millions, a voice that I hear every day. Standing over me in a brothel at Salon Kitty's?

Not even a remote possibility, I told myself. And yet . . . I tried to make sense of the words, but the more I tried to concentrate, the more I felt the edges of my consciousness curl and become fuzzy. Pain now.

"You possess it," the voice declared. Not a question. "Where is it?"

Ahead of me—or perhaps behind—a haze of light that had neither form nor movement. There seemed to be a patch of darkness between those two patches of light, but the pain was too great for me to be sure. I had no certainty of what was happening. Only the certainty of the choking. My choking. No air! Fingers of light reached up into the darkness and quickly disappeared.

"What have you done with it?" the voice repeated, now more strident.

I began to flail, my arms wrenching in their sockets, yearning for surrender. My body burning. I'd thought that it would be ice, not fire—more lies I'd told myself—but oddly, I had no fear of it. Now nothing remained, nothing spurred me on except the choking, and the voice beside me screaming hysterically.

"Where is it?" Then the image of an object, a child's metal top, flickered in my mind like an old, grainy fragment of celluloid grinding through an old projector, and then vanished. The image had cost me. My body stopped and I tried to feel the full weight of my torso pressing down onto the carpet. But I could only feel an object stuck in my throat. Then I seemed to go below the carpet, as if it were dark, placid, oily water. My head swung slowly with the choking sensation. No more lights, no more darkness. The pressing down on the carpet. Legs, arms, no longer there at all. Only the choking.

My past life invading me. Fire. Not intense, a vague, hopeless, infinite longing, to which images—pale and shadowy and unimportant—clung like leeches. I shook my head with superhuman effort, but the top would not dislodge, and panic roared in my ears. The noise of my blood, bidding farewell. The choking, calling me. The carpet filling my nose and throat. Buried alive. A thrust of futility, then a sound chuckled through the fabric, its laughter surrounding me. It was my own laughter. Again and again, spasms in my lungs. My eyes bulged with airlessness, blood-marbled saliva dribbled from the slack corners of my mouth, forming swirls of white and crimson rivulets. I couldn't see it, but I knew it was happening just the same.

"Tell me! Where? What have you done with it? TELL ME!"

FOR THE LAST three days (I was told), I was too infirm to even rise. Nausea, vomiting, and violent, blood-infested diarrhoea, severe abdominal cramps, sweating, dizziness, tearing in the eyes, excessive salivation, mental confusion, partial loss of speech or vision, muscle weakness, difficulty swallowing, dry mouth, and muscle paralysis from the head down through my body. I was thoroughly convinced I was going to die and, my friend, dearly wished for it.

From what I learned later, once Brückner saw my condition, he quickly prevailed on the Führer to send Morell, despite my weak protests that many considered him a dangerous quack and that he would merely replace one form of torture with another. When Morell arrived, he immediately stripped me to total nakedness and performed a series of agonizing procedures that I was too weak, desperate, and terrified to prevent. After syringing me like a pin cushion, he motioned to Brückner and both left my room. Within—I don't know—perhaps just seconds, I glided into a dreamless sleep. No control, no metal tops.

After that, each day was an ordeal, but my condition is now drastically improved, and this morning, I even rose (unsteadily, mind you) and performed some essential tasks in my bathroom to make me appear even remotely human again. I have no idea what Morell put into me, and have no intention of inquiring, but I can now appreciate the Führer's enthusiasm. By the time

Brückner arrived to check on the patient, I was reasonably hygienic and dressed in new pyjamas someone must have secured for me while I recuperated.

"Fear not," Brückner enthused, as he entered and dragged the chair to my cot and sat down. "You'll appear almost alive once we put some meat on those enormous bones. You are beginning to look like a giant Pacelli."

I laughed painfully at the image of me as a cadaverous stick figure in a Cardinal's robes. I patted my stomach gently. "I don't think I'm quite ready for a feast," I told him.

"And no wonder," he told me. "We were all quite concerned about you, despite Morell's fussy assurances—he hardly lacks confidence and ego, I can tell you. The Führer and I looked in on you from time to time, and even Fräulein Schroeder sat vigil for a few hours each night. You've had a true turnaround with her, I must say."

It was too painful to laugh. "It's the Führer's doing, not mine, I'm afraid, but I'll take what I can get."

When I cautioned him that by sitting so close he might catch what I had been stricken with, he told me with a dispassionate voice but with a concerned expression in his one eye, "Heinz, my young friend," he began, hesitatingly, causing me no little unease. "I consulted with both Dr. Morell and the Führer, about your case, and . . ." he paused.

"And?" I pursued. His hesitation was unnerving.

"Morell informed me that you were clearly a victim of food poisoning that might indicate botulism or chemical or toxin food poisoning, such as that from poisonous mushrooms. He said that the symptoms can last from one day up to a couple of months or longer, depending on the type of infection, and can start as early as one hour in the case of staph and as late as ten days in the case of . . . *Campylobacter*, whatever that is. And in either case, the result if not treated immediately is death."

Despite the blow I'd received by what he said, I could see Brückner's lips pucker in thought. "According to Morell," he continued, "it would have to have been the last thing you ingested before your symptoms appeared. Now try to remember, Heinz: Did you have anything to eat at Salon Kitty? Food that is," he bantered, I imagined, to relax me to some extent after seeing my face.

Of course I remembered. "Well," I told him, "the waiter had highly recommended Kitty's 'special canapés,' which, for form's sake, I was obliged to order. I had only one though, but later, at his urging, I had one more. But that was it, since it was utterly vile."

Brückner affected a sinister smile. "I would say, Heinz, that, under the circumstances, 'vile' might be considered an under-statement." Then he abruptly changed the subject. "Just who was this guest of Katrin's?"

"I have no idea, Wilhelm," I answered truthfully.

"Then a description, yes?"

I did the best I could, though descriptions never come easily to me, save for the basics. "I don't know," I concluded.

Brückner nodded solemnly, with his lips pursed in delib-eration. "You mentioned that Katrin does—what was the term you used?—'odd jobs' for Himmler. Unfortunately, your description could fit any number of his characters, both at the top and at the bottom, though I doubt that in this case, it was one of the latter. I know some of them, but our Reichsführer keeps adding more and more such types to his odious stable of fanatical Thoroughbreds. In any event, the Führer asked me to personally initiate an investigation into the matter, and so I asked

SS-Gruppenführer Nebe[92] to become personally involved, and, of course, he accepted. With him in ultimate command of the investigation, the matter should be resolved quickly, and, should he put Müller[93] on the case, decisively as well."

I was shaking to pieces inwardly, both from what I was told had been done to me and now by the fact that my relative invisibility might be severely—and perhaps irrevocably—compromised by the involvement of professional snoopers at the highest levels inquiring in depth into my connexion with Katrin, her "guest," and Salon Kitty. At this point, there appeared to be little I could do, now that the Reich's massive security apparatus had become fully involved. Who tried to do away with me and why were questions I had no possible way of answering satisfactorily and had no means of pursuing my own inquiry. If it happened once, it could happen again and, perhaps, with more lasting results. Schroeder was relatively neutralized by the Führer, so I had no enemies I could think of, except, perhaps, that tumour Krause, who hated my guts from our first encounter and, despite his recent declarations of comradeship, never ceased. But why act now and not earlier? Why that method? Was I to become another Schreck to some other rabidly covetous bastard? Or was it even more ominous than that?

After Brückner left, Morell arrived, examined me fully but innocuously this time, pronounced me recuperated, thanked himself for his timely and efficacious medical diagnosis and regimen, and left, whistling. I merely shook my head and resumed my recuperation under the covers.

---

[92] Arthur Nebe was chief of the *Kriminalpolizei,* the criminal police department for the entire Reich, reporting directly to Heydrich.

[93] Head of the Gestapo, Heinrich Müller was the penultimate policeman. He was even nicknamed "Gestapo Müller."

MY FIRST DAY back on the job, and I was summoned to the
Führer's office at midday. When I entered, I saw, seated, a trim,
salt-and-pepper-haired man with a nose so large and wide, it
almost fully covered his thin upper lip. He looked vaguely like
Streicher's ridiculous cartoons of Jews in *Der Sturmer*—or the
double barrels of a shotgun. The Führer was seated at his desk.
The man rose to greet me in his SS-general's uniform and a broad
smirk-like smile. Without saluting, he stretched out his hand and
I shook it with a slight bow of my head in deference to rank and
fear of his position.

"Why don't you both be comfortable?" asked the Führer,
and we sat down, I, at attention, the other, right leg over left.

"I am *Reichskriminaldirektor*[94] Nebe." He turned to inform
me of this while lifting a leather-bound notebook and pen from
the floor onto his lap. "The Führer, through General Brückner,
has informed me of the egregious attempt on your life and has
requested my personal involvement. Of course, I agreed wholeheartedly. As a result, I'm here, both to introduce myself and to
invite you to visit my headquarters to give as much information
as you can provide regarding all circumstances surrounding the
incident. My resources are quite substantial, and my methods
even more so. Am I right, my Führer?"

---

[94] Chief of the National Police.

The Führer clasped his hands. "Arthur, an attempt has been made on the life of one of my most trusted and valuable employees and, I may say, an indispensable member of my family. You are to spare no resources or expense to uncover this plot and deal with the perpetrators in the harshest possible way."

"Of course, my—"

"But not," the Führer interrupted, "and I repeat, but not before divulging their plot to me in detail, am I understood?"

"Absolutely, my Führer. It shall be done as you have ordered." He turned to me again. "Are you able to accompany me to my office now?"

"Yes, Herr General," I said, turning to a nodding Führer, then back. "At once." As I was about to rise, the Führer raised his hand and lowered it to keep me seated.

"One more thing, Arthur," the Führer added, "and not a small thing at that: from beginning to end, this is to be treated as a matter of state security of the highest order, and so all efforts must be made to keep the investigation both thorough and utterly discreet. All interviews with Linge must never be at your office or at any other government building. No one who does not absolutely need to know, such as General Göring, your superior, General Heydrich, and your subordinate Lieutenant-General Müller, must know all the circumstances—and only personally hand-picked police veterans must be involved. You, and you alone, will collate all findings and report only and directly to me. Any resources I can supply need only be requested. Is that fully understood?"

I noted that Himmler and Heydrich weren't included on the Führer's need-to-know list, but I possessed no way of divining the significance of this fact.

Nebe shrugged, his hands turned, palms upward. "Absolutely,

my Führer," he said. "Though you appreciate that these restrictions might slow the process somewhat, it shall be exactly as you ordered."

The Führer nodded. "Good, Nebe, good. Now be off to your task and keep me informed of any progress. Linge, escort him to your quarters."

Nebe and I click-saluted the Führer, turned, and left.

When we entered my quarters, Nebe asked me if I had an outside line on my phone. When I told him I didn't, he went to it, dialled a number I couldn't make out, spoke to an internal operator. and within seconds, he was speaking to someone in his office. He mentioned several names, presumably of those individuals who would be working with him on my case as per the Führer's directive, and told the person on the other end to have them assembled in his office later that afternoon. Then he hung up and motioned me into my bathroom, moved to the sink, and turned the cold water tap to full.

"Better this way," he said into my ear. "More private."

"I regret to disagree, Herr General," I said into his ear, "but the Reichsführer's deputy came to see me last year, made specific note of what he called my 'plumbing problem,' and wished me to know that it would be taken care of, whatever that meant."

Of course I knew what it meant and, clearly, so did Nebe, who nodded resignedly. Then I thought of Brückner. "A walk in the garden then?" I suggested, trying to imagine how many clandestine conversations had taken place there since the Führer, Himmler, and Heydrich had come to power.

Nebe shook his head no. "It occurs to me that even in the gardens is not such a good idea. It would be better, I think, for

you to not be seen with me here at all. Since we have no connexion that the Führer wants others to know about, the two of
us seen together at the Chancellery might well create awkward
gossip at best and a dangerous suspicion at worst."

I couldn't help but agree. "Then what do you suggest, Herr
Reichskriminaldirektor?" I asked.

"A flat my department maintains for securing and debriefing
high-level confidential informants. I'll have all such activities
switched to another venue so we can employ it as needed."

He placed another call, whispered the address into the
receiver, and we left separately.

Once I provided every single detail of my evening at Salon Kitty,
Nebe nodded, then dismissed me with a caution not to mention
anything concerning the matter to anyone—with the sole exception of the Führer, of course. I returned to the Chancellery and
merely resumed my evening's duties without incident. In my
convalescent state, I required no further excitement, my friend,
so the mundane was more than welcome.

[All entries (if any) between 21 March
and 20 April are missing.]

THIS MORNING, NEBE informed me that "somehow" word of his "discreet" investigation had reached Himmler and Heydrich. To me, this was hardly surprising, but I kept my cynicism to myself, since I believed that there could be only gain from their active involvement. However, up to now, the investigation was, according to Nebe, "still ongoing."

Fortunately, I had no time to bemoan my situation, since this was the Führer's big day. Brückner and I were swamped with household duties all morning. Arrangements for the Führer's forty-eighth birthday had been in preparation for weeks, but today was the execution and, if I may say, the fruition of all that planning. From the highest levels of the Reich's major civilian and military organizations, key individuals were brought in to ensure success. I won't bother to list the obvious names and positions, save that they were highly impressive and quite numerous.

I played no part but was fortunate (as were certain other members on my level, such as Baur, Kempka, Krause, Schroeder, Wolf, Dara, and several others) to witness the main events from a reasonably privileged vantage point (at the very back of the reviewing stand, where I could partake selectively of the festivities—or not at all). Krause made it a point not to stand anywhere near me, and for that I was truly grateful. Moreover, since I was the tallest of my group by far, I had the best view.

Later, Brückner and I flew with the Führer, Goebbels, and Streicher[95] to Munich, where he was to receive gifts (that he would later give to others) and hear a speech in the Bürgerbräukeller,[96] by Hess[97] to the "Old Fighters." Sitting in the very rear of the lengthy and luxurious "Führerplane,"[98] I was approached by Brückner, who had been in the front, conversing with the Führer, Goebbels, and Streicher.

"Deep in your thoughts, Heinz?" he asked in hushed tones. "Do I disturb you?"

"Not in the slightest, Wilhelm. Please join me." He sat down in the seat across, and I proceeded to tell him, also in hushed tones, of my meeting with Nebe.

"Well, my friend," he began, "concerning Nebe's investigation, I'm no less baffled than you. Personally, I would have brought in Himmler and his 'wolfhound,'[99] right from the

---

[95] Hitler usually flew in only one of several identical planes, and never in the same formation twice, to accommodate his inner circle, but mainly, to thwart potential assassination attempts. Baur always piloted Hitler, while Baur's hand-picked pilots flew the others. Hitler always chose his companions, if any, on these flights.

[96] The Bürgerbräukeller is where Hitler's 1923 Beer Hall Putsch originated.

[97] Rudolf Hess studied geopolitics under Karl Haushofer, a proponent of the concept of Lebensraum ("living space"), which later became one of the pillars of Nazi Party ideology. Hess joined the NSDAP (National Socialist German Workers' Party, commonly called the Nazi Party) on 1 July 1920 and was at Hitler's side on 8 November 1923 for the Beer Hall Putsch, which became a foundation of the political platform of the NSDAP. After the Nazi Seizure of Power in 1933, Hess was appointed Deputy Führer and received a post in Hitler's cabinet. He was the third most powerful man in Germany, behind only Hitler and Hermann Göring. He and his friend Albrecht Haushofer shared an interest in astrology, and, more important, Hess also was keen on clairvoyance and the occult.

[98] The name that Linge bestowed on any airplane Hitler occupied.

[99] Brückner was referring to Heydrich. "Wolfhound" was one of the kinder,

beginning, since no secret like that can remain secret from those two for long. That they've come up with nothing after all this time is even more problematic. The suspect list appeared to be short and concentrated enough for a sleuth with the brain of a simian to go through and eliminate, one by one. The why of it is the problem, I'll wager, and perhaps, that's the real reason for Nebe's report to you. I'll also wager there's a good reason for the stall, and it resides with the Führer."

"But, Wilhelm—" I interrupted, stunned by Brückner's words.

"'But Wilhelm' nothing, Heinz. You know as well as I—even better, maybe—that nothing concerning his 'family' is unknown to him. He may be ignorant or oblivious to the details and implications of his decisions, opinions, or actions ostensibly done in his name, but not when it comes to matters concerning you or me, or even the lowliest scullery maid in his household. Sad to say, we're in no position to ask him, but there's no question in my mind that the Führer holds the key to this entire business. Don't ask me how or why, but he does."

I had to speak, or I would burst. "Are you saying . . . I mean, am I to understand . . . that the Führer is behind what happened to me?"

Brückner laughed gently. "No, my dear friend. The Führer wouldn't harm one thinning hair on your precious head. All I'm saying is that he probably knows by now, if not earlier, the who and why of the matter, as well as any course of action to be taken, and has seen fit to keep you in the dark. Why? I have no clue, but it also means that Nebe, Himmler, and Heydrich also know and were sworn to silence."

I was both astonished and confounded, and my face could

---

behind-the-back nicknames for him. It merely referred to his appearance, not his attitudes or actions.

not have signalled otherwise, for Brückner leaned over and patted me lightly on the knee. "Heinz, before you completely surrender to paranoia, look at it this way: now that the entire security apparatus in the Reich is aware of the facts, you should have no further need to worry, yes? I dare say that you may now enjoy a level of protection that before only resided with the Führer himself. Now, don't you feel better?"

I forced a smile that I hoped didn't look forced. "The way you put it, Wilhelm, of course. Perhaps now, the Führer will arrange for *me* to have a few doubles."

Brückner smiled broadly, but I was even more apprehensive and bewildered than before. But that wasn't for Brückner or anyone else to know, either from my face or from my words.

T HE ENTIRE C HANCELLERY was consumed by news of the Führer banning the flight of all hydrogen-filled airships, after the explosion of the *Hindenburg*.[100] It had burst into flames while mooring to a mast in Lakehurst, New Jersey, in America. He was convinced that there was no question of sabotage, though Himmler has his doubts. Himmler always has his doubts. He treats all matters the way a bulldog treats a suspect's throat, making him the perfect policeman, I suppose. As a desperate, wayward youth, I'd run across many third-rate versions, so I always tried to keep a safe distance. Unfortunately, that was now impossible.

The Führer's own secretaries were assigned to write condolence letters to the victims' families, personally signed by the Führer. One hapless soul had even worked as a supervisor in the Chancellery's Message Centre.

The Führer called me to his study in the early evening, something quite unusual for him, ostensibly to help prepare him for a special dinner. Goebbels was bringing Leni Riefenstahl and her technical assistant, Rudolf Schaad, to discuss her idea for promoting the

---

[100] Although German zeppelins had been safe and doing well up until the *Hindenburg* explosion, the disaster signalled the end of passenger travel by dirigible.

unfinished *Olympia*.[101] However, when I arrived, the Führer was already dressed and pacing. Hearing his door close, he stopped and turned towards me.

"I haven't had the opportunity to tell you, but I'm glad you're back to your old self again. We were quite concerned. I, most of all."

It was a truly unexpected sentiment, and I blushed, despite myself. "I'm most grateful, my Führer," I replied. "But it's due to you—and Dr. Morell—that I still *have* an old self to get back to."

The Führer moved to his wall of books and turned.

"Later, Leni Riefenstahl will again be dining with me and Goebbels. A captivating female, totally unlike any of those I met during my time of struggle, or even later, when I'd finally become a person of stature. With her, the closer you get, the more distant she becomes. A blessing, actually. It more than confirms my decision never to become intimately involved with any woman. Tell me about this Katrin of yours. Does she resemble Riefenstahl?"

It was astonishing! Up to that moment, I'd never thought about it, but now that I did, as always, the Führer's instincts were right on the money. "My Führer," I answered, "she's certainly not of mine. Up to now, she's permitted me to know so little of her,

---

[101] In the spring of 1937, Leni Riefenstahl had only just started editing the first part of her magnum opus, and it became clear that the film would not be ready for another year. The German authorities, who were financing the film, began to fear that these delays would have a negative impact on the future commercial success of the two *Olympia* films, and so it was decided to create a promotional film, in English and in French, to maintain public interest for the film. This promotional film was directed by Leni Riefenstahl's technical assistant, Rudolf Schaad, who was aided by her managing director, Walter Traut. They mainly used the material shot by Otto Lantschner, who had been appointed by Riefenstahl to follow her and her cameramen at work during the filming of *Olympia*.

that I can only make the most superficial of guesses, but my guess would be that she could teach Fräulein Riefenstahl a few things."

The Führer laughed. "Then she is truly someone to be feared." He turned towards his bookshelves, slid a pair of reading glasses from his shirt pocket and placed them on the end of his nose, pulled out a volume, and opened it to a particular page that had been bookmarked. "Do you know Rilke?"[102]

A few years before, I'd tried reading something by him, but in vain. Since it was poetry, and never had I been properly introduced to its idiosyncratic ways, though I remembered all the words, I had no means by which to gather any useful meaning. "No, my Führer," I answered, a white lie. "He is a poet, yes?"

The Führer smiled. "Yes, Linge," he replied, "and quite an incisive poet. Here, I want to read you something by him that you will appreciate: 'For beauty is nothing but the beginning of terror which we are barely able to endure, and it amazes us so, because it serenely disdains to destroy us. Every angel is terrible.' So now you know."

Was there anything the Führer didn't know and could summon up without the slightest hesitation? "I have no words, my Führer," was all *I* could summon up. I understood some of it, and what I understood was disquieting in the extreme. Katrin, an angel? Something I couldn't name told me she fell quite short of it. Perhaps that accounted for the terrible. But if that were true of Katrin, what of Emerald and her unspoken request? Where would *she* fall?

The Führer removed his glasses and returned them to his pocket, replaced the book, and continued his silent pacing. I watched him circle the room; he seemed to be moving so fast—a

---

[102] René Karl Wilhelm Johann Josef Maria Rilke is generally considered the German language's greatest poet of the twentieth century.

blur, really—that I began to get lightheaded, and my head felt as if a hammer was pounding a nail through my skull into my brain. The Führer suddenly stopped and fixed his gaze on me. "Linge," he said, faintly, as if from a great distance, "you don't look at all well. Sit down and rest yourself." He went over to the light switch and instantly there was total darkness.

Sitting there, I lost all sense of time and space and sensed an effervescence coursing through my veins, as if my blood were seltzer. But after what seemed to be only a few moments, I heard him, his voice, now closer, now comforting, as if I were under anaesthetic and he was drawing out the nail. "Relax yourself," he said. "You've only just recovered. Perhaps you haven't fully done. In any event, I will console you: for the present, Katrin is unimportant, the why, not to bother with. You know, Linge, I have been called a revolutionary by friend and foe alike. They are all simplistic fools. Revolution is a tactic, not a strategy. Unlike the starched-brained 'vons' in the military and the few 'crazed anarchists' remaining in the Party who would have chaos as a permanent state . . ."

I could see my hands gesticulating to the words but had no control over them, as if they belonged to someone else, impervious to my will.

" . . . revolution must only be the beginning, then, like a wound, it must be cauterised, so as to prevent more."

It was not the words that astonished me but the fact that they were now emanating from *my* mouth and not the Führer's! "Then," I continued, "a new tactic must be employed, in keeping with your strategic design for a Thousand-Year Reich. What I've been witnessing, my Führer, since you chose me to join my fate to yours," my tone now taking on a slight emotional edge, "is *evolution*, a motion, while lacking completion in itself, but, combined with coordinated motions, produces a single action, as with a machine. But always there is movement, and that movement is always forward. There is a pattern to *all* your decisions and actions, and soon, as soon as next year, you must add another forward motion, and then another, all essential, and successful. And through it all, your enemies will be parted like the Red Sea. Once achieved, you will shift the tactic once again to revolution—a final revolution that will end all motion."

Stupefied, I waited anxiously to see if I would say more. I gazed round to see the Führer, sitting behind his desk. Behind me, I heard a door close, but not who closed it. My headache had vanished as well. Then the Führer rose and came over to where I was sitting, and I jumped up to meet him.

"I trust you had a decent nap, Linge," he said with a sly smirk. "And my secretaries continually chide me that I work you too hard."

This . . . whatever it was had happened enough times that I was compelled to ask the question: "My Führer, wasn't I just speaking to you?"

The Führer's little moustache rose with his smile. "No, Linge," he said, "but I must say that your snoring was most eloquent."

As I ENTERED the staff dining room for breakfast, all I heard was a whirl of gossip about the martial nature of Il Duce's visit,[103] during which the Führer introduced Mussolini to massive displays of German military power. They turned to look at me, all, it seemed, with the same concern: "Can the Führer not care that such a glorious display of our military might, might alarm our enemies?" asked the chief housekeeper, to vigorous nods of nervous agreement by the others.

In all political matters, my friend, I have an iron rule that ignorance at best and ambiguity at worst serve to protect me from rumour, scandal, or, far worse, the Führer's displeasure. I also found it interesting that the term *enemies* was used. Regardless of that, in this case, since I attend him every day, ignorance would surely have failed, so it had to be ambiguity.

"Well," I answered blandly, "who among us would deny the Führer's ability to appraise the effect of all his actions—or inactions, for that matter? And as for alarming 'our enemies,' as you put it, I have no special knowledge or wisdom in such matters, but it seems to this humble valet that 'our enemies' become alarmed, no matter what the Führer does, even his sneezes, and yet, their alarms continue to emit no sound." It was a nonsensical

---

[103] Including visits to military equipment factories and demonstrations of weaponry, tanks, and planes, and culminating in several colossal military parades.

statement, but it seemed to satisfy the crowd, bringing forth nods of agreement and gratitude for enlightening them. They also urged me not to convey their concern to the Führer, and I found no difficulty in assuring them of total confidentiality.

❧

After recounting the episode to the Führer, he merely chuckled. Next, *he* recounted something that occurred while I was away on an errand, and he wanted to tell me instead of Brückner.

"During the military review," he began, "the mace bearer was too quick and struck a soldier behind him on the head, and an artillery horse kicked over the traces and bolted right in front of the box. I just laughed and so did Il Duce. Then I turned to him and remarked in his ear in confidence—'*Oy!* as the Jews are so fond of exclaiming, 'I hate to think what will happen to that wretched private. If my experience in the Great War means anything, our perfect German flair for organization will go instantly into motion: the general will go for the colonel; the colonel will go for the major; the major will go for the captain; the captain will go for the lieutenant; the lieutenant will go for the sergeant-major; the sergeant-major for the sergeant; the sergeant for the corporal; and finally, the poor private!'

"I didn't bother to tell him that, by the time it got that far down, the private will have committed suicide in shame."

We both laughed about the poor private—who could have been me.

[Entries between 29 September and 9 October were illegible.]

THE CHANCELLERY WAS a blizzard of bustle, since tomorrow the Duke and Duchess of Windsor are to arrive for a tour of Germany and, ultimately, to meet with the Führer. The planning had been in the works for weeks, and, after several "conferences" (i.e., the Führer issuing directives), Goebbels, Himmler, Kannenberg, and Hoffmann set to work, making the visit into an occasion of historic significance, despite the foreign guests' dubious reputation and want of official status.

⌇

While I arranged and packed his travelling clothes and the selected desk items he'd used up at the Berghof, the Führer was receiving a briefing from Ley,[104] von Ribbentrop, Himmler, Göring, and Goebbels going over the Duke and Duchess's itinerary.

"All right, Ley," the Führer was saying, "give me every detail, leaving out nothing. I'll decide what's important or not."

He struggled up unsteadily. "Yes, my . . . Führer," Ley replied,

---

[104] Enraged by the French occupation of the Ruhr in 1924, Robert Ley became an ultra-nationalist and joined the Nazi Party soon after reading Adolf Hitler's speech at his trial following the Beer Hall Putsch in Munich. When Hitler became chancellor in January 1933, Ley accompanied him to Berlin. In April, when the trade union movement was taken over by the state, Hitler appointed him head of the German Labour Front (*Deutsche Arbeitsfront*, DAF).

with a poorly concealed belch, making the words sound as if Ley harboured doubts about the Führer's position.

I knew that belch—he was intoxicated, as always. All those present knew it as well, but, as I learned from Brückner, because he'd been unwaveringly loyal to the Führer during the "time of struggle," the latter (and, naturally, all those below him) ignored the incessant complaints of the former's arrogance, corruption, incompetence, and drunkenness. Personally, I found the man to be a quite disgusting specimen. A boorish lout, unkempt, even in uniform, and always ready with the filthy joke or anecdote. His hairline began near the top of his head, and, with the shaved sides, he looked like a pallid rendering of an American Mohawk with a Hitler moustache.

"I . . . have it right . . . here," he slurred, then grinned stupidly, patting the right breast of his jacket like the head of a dog, while the others just stared at the Führer. Ley then reached into his inside pocket, fumbled out a wrinkled and greasy folded sheet of paper, and straightened it out. "Aright," he began: "Ah . . . uh . . . the couple will arrive at the Friedrichstrasse station tomorrow morning. As they alight, a . . . brash . . . brass band will play 'God Save the King,' and—"

"Even though he is no longer the king, my Führer?" interrupted Göring, ignorantly. The song was the national anthem and had nothing to do with the Duke's position.

"He's king enough for our purposes, Hermann," the Führer advised, partly in jest, I imagined. "Go on, Ley."

"And after that, the crowd will cry *Heil* Edward! and *Hoch* Windsors! I will greet them, hamb . . . handing" (another, less-concealed belch) "the Dushess . . . a box of chocolates with a card inscribed 'Royal Highness.'[105] As offsshl host," he continued,[106] as Göring's eyes swivelled furtively towards the ceiling, "I will 'scort them to a waiting car, driven and heavly guarded," glancing at the expressionless Himmler who didn't bother to glance back, "by SS, and uh, driven to their hotel. The next day, Dushess will remain at the hotel, while the Duke visits the Deff's-Head Division training school, then . . . ah . . . fly to a Youff Camp where he will perform an 'spection, while the Dushess tours the . . . ah, former imperial palaces at Potsdam." He stopped briefly to steady himself.

I could take no more of Ley's liquor-besotted voice and turned him off in my brain like I would a radio that emitted only distortions and static. I only turned it back on when I heard the Führer ask the group if they had any questions. By Goebbels's and Göring's expressions, I could tell that, in order to prevent a potentially colossal embarrassment, they wished to have the drunken clod removed from his host position but chose wisely not to question the Führer's selection, so they remained silent. Instead, it was Himmler who spoke.

"My Führer," he said, "though all preparations have been made, do you still wish to have them visit a concentration camp?"

Oddly enough, this was the first I'd heard of it and I was startled, being unable to imagine the Führer, on a tour of England, being escorted through a maximum-security prison.

"You put it well, Heinrich," the Führer answered, then faced the others. "All being prepared is the key. You are aware that I've been criticized roundly in the British and American press about the harsh treatment of political prisoners, and especially

---

[105] *Königliche Hoheit.*

[106] The ostensible purpose of the Windsors' visit was to view labour conditions in Germany.

the fucking Jews. Now, we can seize an opportunity to impress our popular guests with our humanity. The 'Potemkin Village'[107] worked wonders for Potemkin, so let it work such wonders for us."

"I'm confident that they will be suitably impressed," Himmler replied blandly, with a slightly wry sneer. "Even Potemkin would marvel at it."

The Führer merely pursed his lips and nodded.

As a final word, Goebbels assured the Führer that the press, both German and foreign, will be moved positively by the entire visit.

Once they'd been dismissed, the Führer bade me sit while he began his pacing ritual. "So, what did you think, Linge?"

I'd grown accustomed to such questions, even though, as always, I could scarcely imagine what I might contribute, or why my opinion would be even remotely worthy of the Führer. "My Führer," I answered, "it seems as if all your expectations will be realized, assuming," I added, "that the Duke and Duchess will respond as hoped." I wanted to add that the Führer's hopes also rested on a depraved drunk, but would never even hint at a criticism of an old comrade.

"Those two effete cartoons?" he spat dismissively. "They will be treated far better in Germany than they have been in England. That harridan runs him like a wind-up toy, and, as

---

[107] The term comes from stories of a fake portable village built solely to impress. According to the story, Grigory Potemkin erected fake settlements along the banks of the Dnieper River in order to fool Empress Catherine II during her journey to Crimea in 1787. The phrase is now used, typically in politics and economics, to describe any construction (literal or figurative) built solely to deceive others into thinking that some situation is better than it really is.

for the once-eminent Duke, he still entertains royal aspirations, though he would never admit to it."

"Yes, my Führer," I coddled. "I'm quite certain you're right. From what I've heard here and there, while the government of England is not particularly fond of the Windsors, the people are still beguiled by their reckless glamour and charm, unlike here, where you and the people are one."

The Führer stopped his pacing, faced me, and clapped his hands excitedly. "*Yes, Linge, exactly so!* In England, if I cannot, ah, influence the government, I can at least get those two jokers to persuade the people of our benign intentions, and, in their idiotic democracy, that may be enough. And who knows? Perhaps, one day, even with that oily Simpson creature by his side," he added cryptically, "he may yet resume the throne."

Was the Führer joking about the Windsors resuming the throne? Knowing his sense of humour, if not irony, I hadn't a clue. As for me, from my reading and furtive conversations furtively overheard, the entire business was ridiculous: the couple were reviled by those who counted in England, and their visit with the Führer would certainly not endear them—and him—further.

I merely shook my head and reached for my camera.

14 *October 1937*

Today, "Much ado about nothing," in my opinion.

The truth is that until I began attending the Führer, I never bothered to consider what "ado" meant, though, in the context of the Shakespeare play, I assumed it meant much excitement. Since then, after countless meetings, visits, speeches, and ceremonies, I'd researched its meaning, and not only was I reasonably on target but also, today, it was amply confirmed.

Ley was both visibly—and audibly—intoxicated most of the time, constantly proclaiming with slurring and stammering abandon his unbridled admiration for the Third Reich and disapproval of the way in which England had treated the couple. Eventually, however, "sourceless" word of his unconscionable behaviour had reached the Führer, and, reluctantly, he replaced Ley with Hess, a more suitable choice all round.

At the appointed time, the Führer dispatched a private train to collect his guests, as well as Hess, who accompanied them. When they reached Berchtesgaden, they were joined by Dr. Schmidt,[108] and the heavily guarded party drove up the mountain to the Berghof. At the entrance, the Führer, dressed in his brown Party jacket, black trousers, and black shoes, stood on the steps, waiting to greet them. Behind him, stood Goebbels, Göring, Himmler, Hess, and von Ribbentrop. Behind them, Schmidt,

---

[108] Hitler's personal translator.

Brückner, the Bormanns, Baur, and Kempka. And behind them, Krause and me. Hoffmann took several photographs of the entire procession, arrival, and, soon, the official greeting.

For a onetime royal head of state, the duke appeared more like a dapper rodent. He was a little, precise man, impeccably dressed in what Brückner termed "bespoke clothing,"[109] which he said was only to be expected of someone with his lineage and wealth and who, according to Brückner, had gone into the Great War with his valet beside him. Brückner asked me, jokingly, if I would have so accompanied the Führer. I replied that I was reasonably certain that very few corporals were permitted to have their valets with them in the trenches. However, I noted that in the place of the duke's own valet was the accursed, equally diminutive Krause, who I wished would go back to England with the duke, permanently.

The duke's dark brown overcoat, covered a light-brown, pin-striped, double-breasted suit with a three-pointed breast-pocket handkerchief, a soft, light-yellow, cuff-linked shirt, and elegantly understated brown brogues. The only personal touches were his reputedly idiosyncratic red-and-brown checkered socks and a large red flower in his lapel buttonhole. Rather rakish.

No less idiosyncratic, the duchess also seemed to have a rakish tendency as well. Having the face of a librarian in a movie, she was anything but handsome, and her clothing did little to alter the fact. Flashy makeup (not a particular favourite with the Führer), obviously expensive jewellery from ear to wrist, dark-blue fitted suit pinched torturously at the waist, medium-heeled pumps, and a soft dark-blue hat with large rose pinned in the

---

[109] *Bespoke* is an adjective for anything commissioned to a particular specification. "Custom-made," "made to order," "made to measure," and sometimes "hand-made" are near synonyms.

centre, she looked like a streetwalker the duke had picked up on his way to the Berghof.

As the royal party reached the stairs, the Führer shook the duke's hand, nodded a bow to the Duchess, then led them into the entrance hall, past the enormous painting of Bismarck, and into an anteroom. There, several tall, well-built young men, personally selected by Himmler, I assumed, stepped forward to remove their coats. They were taken from there through a hallway and down three steps into the even more enormous drawing room, with its entire wall of glass, displaying a breathtaking view of the snow-covered Alps beyond. The Führer told the duke that he would like to speak with him privately in his study, which meant that only Dr. Schmidt and I would accompany him.

Once inside, I could tell that the duke wished to keep the conversation neutral and even banal, but I could also tell that the Führer would have none of it. For the better part of an hour, he repeatedly emphasized his friendly and peaceful intentions towards England, his heartfelt admiration for another Aryan country headed by a royal family with so many ties to Germany,[110] and, finally, that the real enemy of both nations, and even Europe as a whole, was, in fact, Communist Russia, led by the fanatical murderous tyrant Stalin. The Führer did virtually all the talking, with the discreet duke nodding ambiguously at appropriate times and making a few appreciative remarks about Germany's strides in social welfare. As always, I was invisible.

When we exited the study, the entire party repaired to the

---

[110] The House of Windsor is the royal house of the United Kingdom and the other Commonwealth realms. It was founded by King George V by royal proclamation on 17 July 1917, when he changed the name of the British Royal Family from the German Saxe-Coburg and Gotha (a branch of the House of Wettin) to the English Windsor as a result of the anti-German sentiment in the British Empire during World War I.

balcony for afternoon tea, where conversations were more to the duke's liking in that they *were* truly banal, and so not worth recounting here.

After tea, the Führer gave the couple a truly affectionate farewell, shaking the duke's hand vigorously, then taking both hands of the duchess in his own. After that, the Führer stiffened his arm into a rigid Nazi salute that the duke returned. As the car bearing the couple away curved out of sight, the Führer turned to Schmidt and said: "Whorish makeup aside, before this meeting, I must say I had my doubts about the lady, but I can now see that she would have made a decent queen."

⁂

As before, I sat in the rear with Brückner on return trip to Berlin, since the others rode in different aeroplanes, and the Führer was swallowed up by one of his solitary, pensive moods, and so just stared out the window, at what, I couldn't imagine.

"So, my friend," Brückner said, turning from the window, "were you sufficiently awed by a glimpse of real purple?"

"'Real purple' what?" I asked, Brückner being as oblique as always. I knew what he meant, but I held fast to my persona of ignorance, even to Brückner, *especially to Brückner*, because he was so close.

"Royalty, Heinz, the taste of true hereditary decadence." He pursed his lips in thought. "You know, I never felt more patriotic than I did when I considered what Germany would look like governed by a self-obsessed, lazy weasel like Edward. And that desperate, overpainted harridan? God in heaven! And the British criticize us?"

I had to agree with Brückner, even though, from what I'd read, the monarchy in England was merely an expensive formality rather than a real governing entity. They were the face of their nation, no less than the Führer was of his, but truly, the Windsors appeared to be a sorry lot.

"Anyway, we did manage to weather your Bormann and my Krause, a triumph if ever there was one, eh?"

Brückner chuckled with what I could see was a tinge of anxiety. "Like twin cobras curling up to face you."

"Cobras, yes. Perfect," I replied. "I always wonder when they'll strike."

Then he smiled his enigmatic smile. "But I dare say we still have our uses, so the Führer kindly keeps the cobras in their baskets."

Was Brückner right? Were we only as good as our continued usefulness? I spent the rest of the journey wondering how long we would remain useful before the Führer lifted the baskets' lids.

ASSASSINATION DOMINATED THE day, as all the Chancellery were "chatterboxing"[111] over the latest attempt on the Führer's life. An hour previous, one of the Führer's SS guards had confirmed what they'd already read in Goebbels's *Völkischer Beobachter* and Julius Streicher's *Der Stürmer*. Since the former was pure Party propaganda and the latter, a poisonous, anti-Semitic rag, I avoided both with a completely clear conscience, more than content to get my fiction from novels.

According to Wolf, recounting the *V.B.* story to her clerical staff and assorted eavesdroppers, a soldier (unlike the "foul, traitorous Jew-bastard" of Streicher's version) had planted a bomb under a stage where the Führer was to give a speech. Thinking that the speech would go on for hours, the perpetrator decided to relieve himself before detonating the bomb. As luck would have it, the idiot got locked in the toilet and was unable to free himself in time to set off the bomb.

Once the gales of coarse laughter subsided, much of the prattle centred on a disputation over the actual number of assassination attempts. Three? Five? Twenty? The estimates flew round the room raucously, like a flock of crazed birds. Of course, each servant had "absolute knowledge" of a different number. I merely

---

[111] *Schwatzenboxen*, Linge's clever term for meaningless discussion or debate. Presumably, he merely modified *Schattenboxen*, or shadowboxing.

sat there, nibbling on buttered toast and nodding my accord with each guess, since I had no need to guess. There had been eight known attempts, a number related to me by the Führer himself! He had even joked about it at the time.

"You know, Linge," he had said, "life is truly filled with ironies, is it not? In the dark days when I was a poverty-hounded, struggling leader of a tiny outlawed party, I fantasized that one day, I would become important enough so that if I were killed, it would be called an assassination instead of a mere murder. And now look at me. Eight attempts. *Eight!*" he shouted. "So far."

While the disputation over numbers raged, I recalled a statement by Voltaire I'd read, which I would never utter to anyone but you: "The best government is a benevolent tyranny tempered by an occasional assassination." I say this because, as the Führer had informed his guests during one of his many dinner-table lectures: "Pity we must use the messy means of battle to advance an estimable cause. I would much rather demoralize the enemy from within by surprise, terror, sabotage, and assassination. This is the war of the future."

Once Wolf left, they asked me my opinion, and I assured them that the Führer was perfectly safe from harm, owing mainly to the resourceless stupidity of his enemies and the ruthless efficiency of our Security Services, and reminded them of the plot by one Helmut Hirsch, only a year before. While he actually managed to get the bomb into Germany and went to meet his contact, the latter had been arrested three days earlier, and so the hapless Hirsch met a Gestapo agent instead, who promptly arrested him. He was tried in a secret court and beheaded in March of this year.

That appeared to calm the waters, though I felt anything but secure in my assertions. I remembered what I'd been told by a grizzled old cellmate during one of my many incarcerations for vagrancy and petty theft: "Hey, look, my young friend," he'd told me, "if some fuckin' idiot's okay gettin' his own self killed, nobody's safe."

I also thought of Emerald, from whom I'd heard nothing since New Year's Eve. Had she given up on me? Or, considering the latest idiotically botched attempt, would I be hearing from her again?

∾

As I exited the dining room, I narrowly missed colliding with Kannenberg, who, despite his Göring-like girth, was astonishingly lithe. As usual, he was all frenetic bile, bustle, and woe.

"*Clumsy nitwit!*" he spat at me. "*You fucking—*"

I'd learned early in my service that, being in the Fuhrer's good graces, Kannenberg's self-regard had become as massive as his torso and that beneath a benignly servile exterior to those above him resided a merciless tyrant to those below. As a consequence, extreme caution guided my every encounter with him.

"Please forgive my clumsiness, Herr Kannenberg," I said quickly, interrupting his vituperation with an apology, knowing as a certainty that he would not. "Please believe that I had no intention of startling you."

I'd concluded that in his irresponsible haste, the swine must not have, at first, recognized me, for just as quickly, he pulled a wrinkled handkerchief from his trouser pocket, ran it across his forehead, and his tone shifted from a nasty growl to a tolerant twitter.

"Not at all, Linge," he replied with unconcealed disingenuousness, "not at all. I'm made of hardier stuff than that. Didn't recognize you at first, ah, but then, who sees a servant? Such is the way of things, yes? But I have no such luxury, for I *must* see them, or all would be topsy-turvy, and not so good for the Führer. No, not so good for the Führer at all. So, no more chatter, yes? As for me, overburdened as always, no time to spare on frivolities. I just returned from the Berghof, where I finally managed to get those household drudges of mine to function as proper menials. Like you, Linge. I trust the Führer is well."

Of course, health was never the issue. What the vile lummox meant by that last remark was actually a critical issue for him: whether I considered the Führer to be in a receptive mood to meet with him, and, if so, how would he be received. Clearly, I wasn't too "menial" for that. But Kannenberg was far from the only person of rank to grill me on the Führer's "temperature." In point of fact, I still find it not a little disconcerting to actually have field marshals, captains of industry, foreign dignitaries, Party officials, and the like accost me with "humble" requests for a personal weather report on the Führer. Not being a complete idiot with such people, I strive for a delay, at best, or, at worst, a tentative reply of benign ambiguity, while simultaneously gauging whether the Führer actually *would* allow a meeting. It was a clear and dangerous violation of my vow of invisibility.

"Herr Kannenberg," I answered, "I've not yet seen the Führer, but I can say that as of last night, he was reasonably fit. Perhaps, after attending him—" I broke off with a teaser. In actual fact, I had already seen the Führer and felt reasonably confident that a meeting with Kannenberg would have posed no problem, but I wanted that stinking piece of shit to dangle a while, so I lied. That was one of the power perquisites of the job, and I relished every moment of it—as I had with several others.

"Yes, Linge," Kannenberg finally declared. "Of course. Right you are. Splendid idea. Splendid. You're not quite the clod I'd taken you for. Yes, go and attend the Führer," he ordered, as if I were *his* menial, "and report back to me immediately. Now, I must be about some important business." With that, he turned and continued on his way, as if we hadn't met.

❧

Once I'd arrived at the Führer's quarters, I was obliged to wait while Morell ministered to one or more maladies, and, by the odour, I knew that bowels were definitely among them. When the doctor leaned out from the bathroom and ordered me to return in no fewer than two hours, I took this as an opportunity to make some headway into the Führer's mail. On my way to the "mountain," I happened to see the captain (now major) who had kindly and generously assisted me with my missing button when I'd first arrived but whom I hadn't seen since that day.

He appeared somewhat taller than he seemed then, and some fatigue lines had sprung out of the corners of his eyes and round the mouth, but for all that, his SS recruiting-poster face and build hadn't altered. After introducing myself (since he'd displayed no initial signs of recognition), his features seemed to burst open with comradely good fellowship.

I invited him to return to my room, but he demurred, saying that time pressed and, for the purpose, we could converse just as well in the bustling corridor. I shrugged and he smiled, a reasonable simulation of normality.

He told me his name was Siegfried Hausen, "but my friends call me Ziggy," then, "God in heaven," he declared with a metronomic nod of his head, "except for some, ah, minor hair loss, you haven't changed a bit since the day I salvaged your career."

We both laughed at that. "You joke, Ziggy, but, as you well

know, heads roll here on such trivial details. Even heads with thinning hair."

"Believe me, my friend," he replied, "it's no different at 'Chateau Himmler'—perhaps even a little bit worse. Why, do you know that all those with ranks below Heydrich's are measured each month. To make sure we haven't shrunk. Now that sort of obsession wouldn't affect you or me, but it has those on the stature border fearing for their safety. And that's only the least in a host of 'vital' considerations at the top. I won't even get into our daily dependence on Himmler's astrologer's prognostications. It was so much better in the field. The freedom, if nothing else."

"Yes, the freedom," I replied. "None of that here, I'm afraid. But may I ask what exactly was 'the field'?"

It may have been my imagination, but it seemed as if my perfectly innocent question had somehow triggered a subtle alteration in his features: subtle, yes, but to me, obvious all the same.

"Oh, I bounce from one place to another and back again," he said, "from our KZ[112] at Dachau,[113] to our newest and considerably larger one at Buchenwald, then back to Dachau, and so it goes.[114] However," he added, "as the Führer's chief valet,

---

[112] An abbreviation for *Konzentrationslager*, or concentration camp. The term was borrowed from the British "concentration camps" of the Second Anglo-Boer War.

[113] Dachau concentration camp was the first of the Nazi concentration camps opened in Germany, intended to hold political prisoners. It was located on the grounds of an abandoned munitions factory southeast of the medieval town of Dachau, about 16 kilometres northwest of Munich in the state of Bavaria, in southern Germany. Opened in 1933 by Heinrich Himmler, its purpose was quickly enlarged to include forced labour and, eventually, the imprisonment of Jews and ordinary German and Austrian criminals.

[114] Buchenwald concentration camp (literally, in English: beech forest) was a concentration camp established on the Ettersberg (Etter Mountain) near

you must know as much about this as I do, no need to explain my duties."

An expression of pride, perhaps? Or of concern? It galled me that I hadn't the wits to decipher the change. Of course I'd heard of the two KZs, mainly from being "invisible" at meetings between the Führer and Himmler, but, since the subject had no bearing on any interest I might have, I actually heard only disjointed snatches of meaningless chatter. And what I was hearing now seemed a bit too close to a no-explanation-forthcoming-so-don't-inquire-further moat. I could have been dead wrong but decided to follow what I'd understood of Occam's razor[115] and changed the subject. And just as suddenly, his original features returned.

From that conversational dead end, he instead spoke fatalistically of his delicate navigation of "Chateau Himmler," as he jokingly called the RSHA headquarters, the malign idiosyncrasies of Heydrich and those directly below him, details of his home, wife, children, and mistresses—in other words, domestic stuff of no possible interest or relevance to me. In return, I told him of my own navigation, the routineless routine of serving an "ex"-bohemian, my virtual celibacy, and other bloodless tales.

However, despite the perfunctory tedium of our new conversation, I did have—and took—the opportunity to pay him back

---

Weimar in July 1937, one of the first and the largest of the concentration camps on German soil, following Dachau's opening just over four years earlier.

[115] Occam's razor (also written as Ockham's razor and in Latin, *lex parsimoniae*) is a problem-solving principle devised by William of Ockham (c. 1287–1347), an English Franciscan friar and scholastic philosopher and theologian. The principle states that among competing hypotheses, the one with the fewest assumptions should be selected. Other, more complicated solutions may ultimately prove correct, but, in the absence of certainty, the fewer assumptions that are made, the better.

for his moat by constructing one of my own: when he brought up the attempt on my life, and pried for details, I told him in the most humble but definitive fashion that, since he worked for "H & H" as I called them, he must know far more than I, and so relating more would be completely superfluous. I even added a benign smile.

We took leave of each other on a comradely note, vowing to meet again at the earliest opportunity, under much "freer" conditions. He smiled, I nodded, we walked our separate ways, and that was that—up to a point, that is, a point I couldn't explain, for something gnawed at my consciousness. Perhaps it was his reticence to discuss his job.

In any event, I never did get to attend the Führer, since Morell had him sequestered for the rest of the day and night for "intense close observation and treatment."

Kannenberg never returned, so I was spared having to disappoint the bastard.

And one decision I made this night, my friend, before photographing you, was, in future, to listen with more care and attention if and when the subject of KZs arose.

AS I ENTERED the Führer's chambers to help him dress, I saw him sitting at his desk, attired only in his bathrobe, his hair askew, his face unshaven, speaking in an unusually moderate tone to his chief diplomat and principal warriors. The only light source was the Führer's desk lamp so that all but the Führer sat in each other's shadows. Immediately and silently, I moved to the bookshelves behind the oblivious visitors and waited.

"You all," the Führer was saying, "care only about your own tiny little spheres of control, as well you should. This is not a matter of blame. But you must appreciate that I have the ultimate responsibility for all the Reich—and beyond. As a consequence, I must rise above petty, parochial interests."

I noted that the Führer had said almost the very same thing on numerous occasions, both formal and informal. But this was the first time he had added: "and beyond." Was the alteration significant? I was intensely curious to know the what and why of it but, of course, would never ask.

"But, my Führer—" von Neurath started to say, but the Führer cut him off.

"You are all correct," he continued, as if von Neurath had said nothing, "up to a point. Each of your arguments is a single, adequately cut puzzle piece, and I would want or expect no more from you. However," he added, "by focussing only on that, you invariably fail to grasp the ultimate implications of your individual pieces and so are unable to envision the complete picture. Again, no blame can fall on you. But I must—and, of course, do—see that picture. And so now, I will call a conference, to be held in three days, which all of you will attend, to discuss these pieces and to provide me with the opportunity to put the pieces together for you. Rossbach[116] will take and keep the minutes." He turned his head toward the Kriegsmarine commander. "Are you satisfied, Raeder?"

"Yes, my Führer," replied the admiral. "Entirely so."[117]

The Führer then addressed the group as a whole. "Any questions, gentlemen?"

Of course, there were none, all being well versed in the Führer's thinly veiled insults and monologues disguised as exchanges. More important, I knew (and they also knew) from experience that the Führer's "ands," "alsos," and "buts" held far more import than anything he'd said before their appearance. He wanted "an opportunity," and he would take one.

After they'd gone, the Führer remained at his desk in silence. The fewer shadows were replaced by ruminations I could sense but would never dare to interrupt. After a time, he rose slowly and motioned me to follow him into his bathroom. He pointed to his face, and I quickly placed his shaving implements on the ledge above the sink and stood back as he moved to the mirror and gazed into it, but not at himself, behind him, to me.

"You know, Linge," he said, as he lowered his shaving brush into the jar of lather and swirled it round. "And this may

---

[116] Hitler's military adjutant, Colonel Graf (i.e., Count) Friedrich Hossbach, was selected to keep the minutes of the meeting.

[117] Hitler called the conference for 5 November 1937, ostensibly in response to complaints from Admiral Raeder that the navy was not receiving sufficient allocations of steel and other raw materials, and as a result, the entire Kriegsmarine building program was in danger of collapse.

surprise you, that even as a struggling young artist, rejected by the decadent bourgeois art bureaucracy in Austria, even when I was a struggling politician, unjustly attacked and imprisoned by a decadent bourgeois government in Germany, in spite of all that, I believed myself to be blessed with good fortune." He stood there, still gazing at me in the mirror.

I'd listened to the Führer's hardships on several occasions, since he enjoyed continually regaling his employees and guests with tales of his historic rise from the ashes like the phoenix. However, this time, I detached myself from them long enough to consider my own trajectory, from a horrific childhood and miserable adolescence to a major of the SS, observing the Führer of the Third Reich shave, and so considered myself no less fortunate. An amusing, but poignant comparison, I thought at that moment.

"You ask how this can be," the Führer continued, "and I will tell you. It is because I see fortune differently than others do, and so, despite all my battles, I ultimately emerged triumphant, an incontestable fact. It is because, while luck, to others, is nothing but an explanation they give to the good and bad things that happen by chance, I see all things that happen not as chance but as opportunities that must be seized by the throat and strangled into victory. Opportunity and audacity, Linge, employed with ruthless determination—those are the real elements of luck, and never forget it."

"Yes, my Führer," was all I could put in the way of his tidal wave of words. *Strangled into victory?* Eccentric words, even from a man noted for his eccentricities. And troublesome words at that. Then . . .

"Do you know what *autarkic* means?" he asked.

I'd come across that word in my reading but felt the need to again play the ignoramus and made a face to accompany it.

"Of course not, Linge. You would not be expected to," he said with a smile of superiority. "I was merely playing with you. Autarkic is a condition in which a nation is completely self-sufficient, independent, not reliant on others. This is especially with regard to raw materials. Now, would you consider Germany to be autarkic?"

Again, I thought, the Führer must be "playing" with me, for how could I possibly know an answer to that question? "I have no idea, my Führer," I responded feebly.

He nodded, indulgently, I thought, and began to apply the cream to his face and neck.

"When an economy is self-sufficient," he said, "it can theoretically be stronger. When a nation can provide all of the goods and services it needs internally, it is not forced to rely on other nations. This can be a political strength for a nation which does not want to make concessions in order to establish or maintain trade relations. If a country has a closed economy, for example, economic sanctions from other governments which are intended to force that country to address something will have no effect.

"This principle is also valid for military purposes," he continued, while sliding his razor across one cheek, then the other. "A closed economy is desirable, for it can allow a nation to control the supply of technology, goods, and services. For example, Linge, development of weapons systems may be done in an entirely closed economy for the purpose of keeping such systems out of the hands of other nations. A country with a supply of a rare resource can use autarky for political muscle by keeping supplies of that resource out of other countries."

The Führer then began the delicate task of shaving his famous upper lip, and I never ceased to marvel at the deftness with which he did so while speaking.

"In answer to your unspoken question, no, Linge, the Reich is most certainly not autarkic. However, what I'm getting at is this: most would call that bad luck; I call it an opportunity. In such a situation, one must think outside the box, as I have always done. There is a proverb you probably never encountered. It goes: 'If the mountain won't come to Muhammad, then Muhammad must go to the mountain.' These fools who surround me, especially the military men, may have heard it but failed to divine its implications as I have."

Actually, I had come across the statement in my reading of proverbs.[118] I believed at the time that it meant one must bow to the inevitable.

"To me, such a condition of dependence is not bad luck," he continued, "but an opportunity, an opportunity born of necessity—the most potent form of opportunity, I might add. If the resources won't come to the Reich, then the Reich must go to the resources. In other words, the only remedy, and one which might appear to the ordinary as absurd, or worse, revolutionary, merely lies in the acquisition of greater living space—a quest which has at all times been the origin of the formation of states and of the migration of peoples. Yes, Linge, Germany, the very heart of a vastly greater Reich never dreamt of, save by me."

By you, yes, my Führer, I thought to myself—and by any attentive reader of *Mein Kampf.* And yet, how was it that his top military leaders failed to see the picture he'd painted there? That is, unless they had done, but chose not to make reference to it. But if so, why? And why did the Führer not refer to it?

---

[118] The phrase was from chapter 12 of the *Essays of Francis Bacon*, published in 1625. Apparently, Linge was referring to its mention in Schoenmann, *Die Ursprünge der Weisheit* (*The Origins of Wisdom*), to which he would have had more ready access.

"It's all very simple," he concluded, "and so obvious. And yet, my so-called experts believe that going to the mountain means begging, accepting fool's bargains, taking only what's offered, if anything, even going without. Raeder's petty squabble with his comrades-in-mediocrity have provided me with just the forum I need to present my vision, if not my plan. They are all but ghosts, Linge, for I tell you that by next year, they will all have vanished and been replaced by men who, while understandably lacking my unique vision, can and will, at least, assist me fully in achieving it—you not being the least of them," he added, to my utter bafflement.

He'd finished both his speech and his shaving simultaneously, as if he had choreographed the entire activity as ritual, a tableau. Even since my interview with him more than two years before, he (and others) had made such cryptic remarks about me but had never explained, and I'd been obliged to endure the mystery of it, today being the latest instalment of a drama of which I'd read much but knew nothing.

I was given no further duties until dinner, at which I was to assist in serving the Führer, Goebbels, several of his movie actresses, and the championship prize-fighter, "Max" Schmeling.[119]

I cannot recount what transpired there, my friend, because I was enveloped in a fruitless rumination about what he'd written long ago and what the Führer had intended now while he shaved: "Greater Germany"? "Living space"? "By next year"?

And especially: "You not being the least of them"?

---

[119] Maximillian Adolph Otto Siegfried "Max" Schmeling (28 September 1905–2 February 2005) was a German boxer who was heavyweight champion of the world between 1930 and 1932. His first fight with Joe Louis in 1936 ended in a victory for Schmeling.

I DIDN'T ATTEND the Führer's "puzzle-piece" conference since I wasn't asked, and, in my estimation, my presence would have been out of both place and position. But I did obtain the gist from Hossbach, who had taken the minutes, and was now discussing them with Brückner in the latter's office, where I'd gone for my share of the mail.

Hossbach was a smooth, tidy, and precise little chap who exuded both high breeding and utter sterility. I couldn't imagine that he ever perspired or needed to shave. Apparently, he didn't appear to mind my presence, either because he believed I'd overheard the Führer speak previously of the matter to others in the privacy of his rooms, or he didn't believe I had the wherewithal to understand the issues. I infinitely preferred the second interpretation.

I attempted to listen, but all I could concentrate on was the records I would purchase for the new Victrola that Brückner had gotten me as a gift. I'd struggled daily to maintain a professional distance, but I invariably failed, and I understood why: if I couldn't trust Brückner, I was truly alone in the world, and even I needed a friend.

Once Hossbach had finished regaling Brückner, the latter and I strolled round the massive courtyard, savouring the sunny respite from the knife-edge chill that had enveloped Berlin.

"So, Heinz, you were suitably numbed by Hossbach's recitation, yes?"

"I'd heard it all before," I answered with a small shrug.

An equally small chuckle issued from Brückner. "Yes, the Führer has never been exactly timid about announcing his vision and strategy. Pity no one at the conference appeared to take them seriously." He sighed heavily. "I'm afraid that we Germans have a rather unfortunate habit of believing what we want to believe, regardless of any evidence to the contrary. You've read *Mein Kampf*,[120] so you know that the Führer was making the same extreme utterances as early as 1925 but was always able to count on our national capacity for self-delusion."

"Does that mean—" I started to ask, but Brückner cut me off.

"In my poor opinion, yes. But now," he added, "I really think that he's about ready to actually pull it off."

"But what of Great Britain and France?"

"Exactly. The Führer has always had a cultural ambivalence towards the British and a historic hatred of the French. In my estimation, his intention to conquer the East as a prelude to conquering the West is both real and imminent."

Perhaps I was one of those Germans that Brückner chided as self-delusory, but I felt nothing after his prognostication. I merely shook my head and changed the subject.

"I must tell you again of my gratitude for your thoughtfulness. The Führer told me that I was welcome to borrow any of his records, and now, I can oblige him."

Brückner smiled broadly at this. "It was nothing," he replied. "In truth, my motives were not altogether musical. I thought

---

[120] Required reading for anyone training for the SS.

that you might now devote some of your evening to something slightly more highbrow than Salon Kitty's. In point of fact, I think you should get the Iron Cross for bravery, my friend. I would have thought that after that close call, you'd give that place a wide go-by."[121]

My smile was more one of embarrassment than mirth. "I stand rebuked, Wilhelm, but, well, you know how it is. The Chancellery is a poor dating service at best, and, since Emerald and Katrin have failed me and my needs haven't diminished, I go. I just don't do any eating."

"Now *I* stand rebuked," he joked. "Yes, those needs. It appears that I may have to play matchmaker, I think, if only to get you out of harm's way, something a bit less than Emerald and Katrin but far more than Kitty's litter. To look at me now, you wouldn't think I could attract a milk cow, but before my . . . accident, I was quite the rake."

I didn't doubt it. In his quarters stood a framed picture of him taken in 1924, bedecked with medals, an "Aryan God," Goebbels had called him. Divinity aside, even now, he still cuts a dashing figure and, I'm reasonably sure, can procure a decent female companion for his friend, even if that friend has less hair and even less education. I was somewhat startled by his pause before "accident" but was reticent to pursue something that might just have been my perception only.

After leaving for my quarters with my share of the mail, I took some time to consider what Brückner had said concerning the Führer's intentions. From what I'd heard repeatedly over the years from veterans, both firm and infirm, the prospect of virtually endless warfare, even for the best of motives, and with the

---

[121] *Gehen-durch.*

best of materiel, was something truly terrifying to contemplate. Of course, I was never a soldier, but I'd witnessed those at the very apex of the military hierarchy express serious and grave reservations about such a future for Germany. Did the Führer know more than they? He'd worked a wonder with national pride, military might, and industrial and economic growth, more often than not squarely against the advice of so-called experts. So, was this merely one more instance of genius over intelligence and experience?

And yet, why am I now so troubled? Why do Brückner's words pursue me so relentlessly after my initial indifference? Perhaps it was my memory of something I'd read years ago about sharks: that there are some species (including the great white, mako, and whale sharks) that would die from lack of oxygen if they stopped swimming. These sharks were the ones rumoured to have to swim constantly to stay alive. Was the Führer also such a shark? Was Europe merely a vast ocean in which the Führer would swim endlessly?

And feed constantly?

[Possible entries between 5 November and
3 December are missing due to spoilt negatives.]

3 December 1937

THIS MORNING, BEFORE heading to breakfast and the Führer, I once more glanced at the concise little note that Brückner had handed to me yesterday with a knavish grin. Perfumed scent having survived the night, the florid calligraphy welcomed my "interest" (a fabrication from Brückner) and concluded that an evening with me would be "most pleasantly anticipated" (I hoped, not a fabrication from her), and awaited an acknowledgement. It was signed "ZL." I promised myself to write it before bed and send it out the next morning.

After attending the Führer and just as I was to place his reading glasses on his desk, Himmler was announced and, rather than be at the Führer's desk or brush past the Reichsführer, I stayed to tidy up the bathroom, even though it was the task of a chambermaid. The Führer appeared not to notice my change in position.

"Heinrich," the Führer said. "You needed to see me immediately?"

"Yes, my Führer," Himmler replied, as bland and expressionless as ever, but his face appeared to hold a bit more colour than usual. He reached into his narrow briefcase, extracted some papers, and held them up. "Through the efforts of my deputy and his informants, we now have the physical evidence to accompany the narrow and cowardly remarks by Raeder, Blomberg, and Fritsch to you before the conference."

I noted that the Reichsführer-SS had omitted the "vons" and Göring from his announcement, but why, I had no idea.

The Führer nodded, then rummaged round his desk for his spectacles, and I felt the cold stab of an upcoming reproof for not having laid them out earlier. Conceding defeat, the Führer shrugged, said, "That lout of a valet must have mislaid them," and bade Himmler read it to him. I was more terrified than mortified, and so instinctively edged even farther back.

"Of course, my Führer," he replied blandly, and began: "This is a confidential correspondence between General Beck and General von Fritsch in May, to wit: 'The German Army is not prepared to run the risk of war in Central Europe. From the standpoint of materiel, it cannot fight any war at the present time,' etcetera, etcetera, 'therefore, I believe the Army cannot accept the responsibility for preparing an operation against Austria.' It goes on, but you have the essence."

The Führer sat silently for a time, and Himmler placed the document back in his case. Then the former rose and began a slow stroll round the office. Himmler moved not a muscle and stared straight ahead, as if the Führer were still at his desk. The Führer finally returned and sat down, hands clasped on the desktop. "Very good, Heinrich, and congratulate your deputy for me, but the die has already been cast on Blomberg and Fritsch. Raeder, though still far too territorial and timid, still shows promise, that is, once he appreciates the vision behind my strategy, and so he'll remain. At this point, I see no need to employ that document, but do have it available should our two military midgets resist the inevitable. Anything else?"

"Only the latest joke about Göring, my Führer," he said, his eyelids at half-mast.

"What is it?"

"It's stupid," Himmler replied.

"The stupider the better, yes, Heinrich?" the Führer said. "Otherwise, we'd have to take them seriously. Tell it."

"All right: Göring has attached a horizontal arrow below the rows of medals on his tunic. It reads: 'Continued on the back.'"

The Führer snorted. "Obvious, but not in the least harmful. You know that poking fun at power is an honourable German tradition. You should hear the British and Americans go at it."

"Yes, my Führer," Himmler replied. "At least I've remained immune thus far."

The Führer chuckled. "Please don't be offended, Heinrich, but that's because there's nothing even remotely funny about you."

I could see Himmler's lips curl upward ever so slightly. "Yes, my Führer," he said tonelessly, "truly, no one has ever accused me of being humorous."

"You see, Heinrich," the Führer said, "only you could say that being considered humorous is an accusation."

"Will that be all, my Führer?"

"Yes, yes, Heinrich. Definitely. You need time to arrest more comedians."

Without responding, Himmler saluted and left. Immediately, I was summoned from my sanctuary to my fate.

"My apologies, Linge," the Führer said as I approached his desk, "for casting you as the villain in my spectacles search."

"Yes, my Führer," I stammered, "I . . . was just about to place them—"

"I know," he interrupted, "but Himmler hates to wait. Try to understand that sometimes I must do a wrong in order to do an even greater right. In public, to protect you, I must treat you as ordinary, and so susceptible to mistakes. Therefore, when others are present, even when you are completely innocent, I may still have to bawl you out, and do so with sufficient vigour that all will be aware of your fallibility and my lack of favouritism. You do appreciate this."

I swiped at my sweat-dotted brow with the back of my hand and wiped my hand on my trousers. "Yes, my Führer, I do, most definitely," I lied. "I am only human and so make mistakes, and if—"

"Naturally," the Führer cut in, "even you, but also know this: no mistake that would come even close to the extraordinary service you'll provide me at the critical moment. In any event, I hear that Brückner has offered to play cupid. I'm only too aware that the Chancellery can be like a cloistered monastery, so for a normal man, such a service is invaluable. Baur and Kempka mean well, but I must confess that they have a rather squalid approach to sex, so I have confidence that you'll have more success with the likes of Brückner."

I thanked him profusely and left to help his entourage arrange things for the Führer's trip to the Berghof the next day. All the while, I mulled anxiously: "a normal man," the Führer had called me, to provide an "extraordinary service"? What "critical moment"? Whatever the Führer has in mind appears to be encrypted and constantly dangled before me, but its meaning is always out of reach, not unlike the mechanical rabbit in a greyhound race. Tantalizing but futile.

I also puzzled over "operation against Austria," as Himmler's document had stated. The Führer had never mentioned even the possibility in my presence. Or perhaps I hadn't been listening. Was Austria now to be the next morsel for the perpetually moving "shark"?

And, no less important, what would it feed on after that?

4 *December 1937*

EARLY THIS MORNING, and with a shaky and ambivalent hand,
I sent my reply to "ZL" from the *Führerwagen,* in the hope of
getting a positive reply as quickly as possible. While the Führer
and the rest of his entourage still slept, I sat alone in the back
of the luxurious, wood-panelled salon compartment, engulfed
in doubt and fear, recalling Rilke's "dark angel" and Nietzsche's
observation that "the true man wants two things: danger and
play. For that reason he wants woman, as the most dangerous
plaything." After experiencing Emerald and Katrin, did I really
want a "dark angel" or a "dangerous plaything"?

Not knowing what Brückner had told her, my note was a
model of vagueness. I mentioned that, though I was hardly in
Brückner's league, in neither position nor appearance, I was not
exactly a candidate for a circus sideshow. I said nothing about my
lack of education or its substitute and, as for occupation, merely
said that I worked at the Reich Chancellery.

My reasoning was simple: if she already knew who I was,
there was nothing in my note to contradict it, and if she didn't
know, it would give me the air of mystery that I'd been told
women seemed to like in a man. I mentioned that I'd have to be
at the Berghof, and so suggested dinner at the nearby Dietrich
Eckart Lodge.[122]

---

[122] The lodge was built in 1903 by Countess Caroline zu Ortenburg.

To alleviate the obvious inconvenience to her, I told her that, due to Brückner's influence, a first-class train compartment would be arranged, and quarters for her would be provided at the Berghof itself. I could have lied and said that it was due to *my* influence, but I wanted to begin a relationship with reality and see how far that would take me before having to resort to fiction.

But even reality was far from comforting, since the Berghof was the clandestine domain of Eva Braun.[123] I couldn't help but recall the loathing in her eyes during the Führer's dinner party on 18 April of the previous year. Was it for the Führer, who had been railing against marriage for a man in his unique position, or was it for the several females he'd been fawning over—or both? In my situation, it made little difference.

In any event, somehow, regardless of her appearance, I had to persuade Brückner to rescind his generous but perilous offer of the Berghof and have "ZL" secluded at the lodge instead. I prayed that he would awaken first and join me so I could explain my delicate situation in the privacy I felt it demanded.

In 1923, the German poet, mystic, and dabbler in the occult, Dietrich Eckart—a prominent individual in establishing the Nazi party—died in Berchtesgaden on 26 December 1923. In memory of his stay at the house, it was renamed Dietrich Eckart Lodge (*Eckart-Hütte*) after it was enlarged and renovated in 1927.

[123] At twenty-five minutes past two on the morning of 7 February 1912, Eva Anna Paula Braun was born in Munich. She first met Hitler in 1929 while she was assistant to the beer-loving Heinrich Hoffmann, the Third Reich's official photographer. She had twice attempted suicide, the first having been in November 1932 when she was found with a bullet in her neck, and the second, on 28 May 1935. Eva, who often complained of Hitler's neglect, decided to take thirty-five sleeping pills just to "make certain." Late that night, she was found unconscious by her sister Ilse who called a doctor just in time to save her life. It is interesting to note that Eva never became a Nazi Party member. According to Speer's memoirs, Braun never slept in the same room as Hitler and had her own rooms at the Berghof, in Hitler's Berlin residence, and in the Berlin bunker.

As luck would have it, Brückner did arrive before anyone else, but with Baur in tow. When the former saw my eyes widen slightly, he got the hint, sent Baur on a meaningless errand, and we repaired to the dining car for coffee and conversation, where I explained my dilemma, and he displayed the fellow feeling I'd come to expect of him.

"Good point, Heinz," he said with pursed lips and a nod. "I hadn't thought of the Eva factor. All right, as soon as your present arrives, I'll have her spirited to the lodge, and the rest I'll leave to you."

"Is her identity to be a surprise?" I asked him.

"A present should always be a surprise," Brückner answered, as I knew he would. "And this one," he added, "perhaps especially so," which only compounded my eagerness.

My instincts and Brückner's consent coincided perfectly with what greeted us when we arrived at the Berghof. Perhaps to derive some attention by taunting the Führer, Braun had invited her numerous lady friends to stay. They all appeared to be shallow and frivolous types, occasionally even outright offensive in their behaviours (at Braun's suggestion, no doubt), having the manners of the bohemian Munich world that the Führer had left far behind. At table, they spoke openly on the most intimate things, and when an SS batman[124] brought refreshments to their rooms, they pranced round half-naked without a thought. And when a film was shown in the evening, they spoke loudly and lewdly about the actors' physiques and obvious sexual prowess.

That first evening, the Führer scarcely took notice of the tittle-tattle of these "ladies," thinking it only normal that a

---

[124] Personal military servant.

woman should be tedious, stupid, and coarse. It appeared that the only thing that occupied him at the time was Austria—and Munich, only to the extent that they were connected, and nothing beyond that.[125]

Like the Führer, I had only one thing on my mind, but it wasn't Austria or Munich. The moment the film ended, I left quickly to prepare the Führer for bed, then stole away even more quickly to the lodge to "open" Brückner's "present."

Even at that late hour, I appeared to arrive too soon, for the table in a window alcove was vacant. The proprietor, seeing the confusion on my face, raced to inform me in the most deferential tones that "the lady" was fully aware of my presence, apologized for the delay, and would be down momentarily. Nodding him away, I placed my cap on a protrusion jutting out from the ornately carved Tyrolean hat stand, sat down without ordering, and waited.

After no more than five minutes, "the lady" moved elegantly down the stairs without a sound emanating from her stiletto heels on the worn wooden steps and virtually glided to the table. I began to rise in greeting, but she bade me sit, as she herself proceeded to do. Seeing her face up close, my heart began to pound in my ears, for it was Zarah Leander, the celebrated actress and vocalist I'd seen so many times in the Führer's screening rooms and city theatres.[126]

---

[125] According to Brückner, as there were still clashes between National Socialists orchestrated in Berlin, Schuschnigg, the anti-Nazi chancellor of the Federal State of Austria, utterly opposed Hitler's ambitions to absorb Austria into the Third Reich. Many Austrian Nazis had taken refuge in Munich.

[126] Zarah Leander was a Swedish actress and singer. She became particularly famous throughout the German-speaking countries and Scandinavia for

"No ceremony, Heinz, please," she requested with a languid lift of one perfectly manicured hand. "Call me one of those rare artists who is satisfied merely to do a job well, not to bask in mindless adoration. Perhaps that's why Brückner asked me to meet you, and perhaps that's why I agreed."

I nodded once and eased myself down. Though shorter than she appeared in her films, sitting in front of me, she looked even more beautiful than she did on-screen with all the tricks of the trade at her disposal. Her German was nearly perfect, save for a beguiling Scandinavian lilt at the ends of her sentences, and her voice had the male huskiness of Greta Garbo, without the theatrical affectations.

"As a beginning," she said, "perhaps you would tell me a little something about yourself, since General Brückner was rather mysterious. Intriguing, yes, but hardly informative."

"I . . . I'm . . . there's nothing," I stammered, until she took hold of the conversation.

"I have an idea," she said, gently. "Why don't I ask you some innocent questions, at least until you cease being a fan and become a date?"

I merely nodded my grateful assent. After Emerald, Katrin, and Bella, I could hardly believe the depth of my awkwardness and the breadth of my embarrassment. Perhaps, unlike the others, I considered Zarah real.

"I say, a strong drink might do the trick," she remarked. "What do you think?"

I glanced round the room and saw several clusters of high-ranking SS and Wehrmacht men, some in groups, some sitting

her powerful singing voice and moody romantic songs. She is also noted for having been the leading female star of Nazi Germany's film industry.

with jewelled, evening-gowned ladies, and I nodded a yes to the drink.

"See, Heinz," Zarah said, "we merely melt into the crowd. Short of Himmler's headquarters, if one needed to hide in plain sight, this is most certainly a good place for it."

Before I could laugh, she raised a hand and a Tyrolean-attired waiter rushed to our table, towel draped over his arm.

"I think I'll have a—" she started to say, but I cut her off.

"Please, if you have any sense of self-preservation, don't order a Zombie or a Death in the Afternoon."

She gazed at me quizzically. "These are drinks?"

"Weapons of war, more like," I answered.

She laughed lightly. "All right, Heinz, I'm well warned. Can I order a Champagne Cocktail without having it served by a bomb disposal unit?"

"It couldn't be worse. In fact, I'll have one as well."

"Devil may care, eh?" she chuckled. "Two Champagne Cocktails," she told the waiter, "and no fuses," she added, and I laughed heartily.

"You have a delightful sense of humour, Fräulein—"

"It's Frau," she corrected, "but rather more one of form than substance, so no need to reproach yourself for immorality. Please do call me Zarah."

Despite the fact that marriage by such as me to such as her would have been absurd, her reference to *Frau* deflated any expectations I'd fantasized up to then. But, thank God, not the ardour. "Zarah," I mused out loud. "It sounds biblical."

She pressed her lips together into something resembling a grin. "It does, doesn't it?" she said. "My parents must have been in a particularly spiritual frame of mind when they named me. Or ironic. You know, your Reichsminister of Propaganda once asked me: 'Zarah . . . isn't this a Jewish name?' Oh, maybe, I told him, but what about Joseph? That shut the arrogant propagandist up for a second before he replied: 'Hmmm . . . yes, yes, a good answer. We're both cursed, I'm afraid.'"

My Reichsminister of Propaganda? Was this some test? Was she Goebbels's spy? If so, to what purpose? "Why did you agree to meet me, Zarah?" I ventured. "Especially considering the degree of inconvenience."

"Truthfully?" she asked. Our drinks arrived and we *prosit-ed*[127] each other. "Mainly, I owed a favour to Brückner, who, in any case, is a man difficult to refuse. Later, curiosity overtook any other reasons, since he steadfastly refused to tell me anything about you, save that you were tall, worked in the Chancellery, and had thinning hair. I had to believe that there was more to you than that."

I shrugged. "And what if you discovered that those two features were the most interesting things about me?" I jested on the square.

"I would have made you more interesting. Certain women possess that ability."

Another sip.

"I say, if it isn't a state secret, what is it you actually do at the Chancellery?"

A chill moved through me like a river of ice water. "How do I put it? Do you have a lady's maid?" I asked her, rhetorically.

"Of course," she replied. "How else do you think I can look like this?" She rested her folded hands beneath her chin and fluttered her long lashes coquettishly. Beauty and wit; I couldn't believe my good fortune!

---

[127] Used as a toast to wish good health to one's drinking companion.

"Well, Zarah, I'm her equivalent for the Führer."

Her deep blue eyes widened slightly. "You're the Führer's valet?"

"No more, no less. Above-average height, thinning hair—Brückner was dead-on about those—and no formal education. A mere servant, for all that. Now, can you still work your magic and make me more interesting?"

Her lips moved toward a smile, but never quite made it. She finished her drink, set her glass down, and gazed at me for a long moment. "From what you've told me, Heinz," she said, "magic will hardly be necessary. You seem like a kind man, a decent man, a gentle man. Exciting? Not yet so very, but interesting. In these times, and in your unique situation, that's quite interesting enough for me." She rose from her chair, as did I, and she held out her hand for kissing, which I did, and I even threw in a perfect SS heel-click and nod as a gesture for the many onlookers who'd recognized her. "You'll find me in Suite 303," she said, "and no elaborate sequence of knocks will be necessary." She slid her hand back gently, turned, and glided away.

STILL RECUPERATING FROM my evening with Frau Zarah.

As we parted, we promised each other an even more strenuous continuation of what transpired in suite 303. I do believe that she meant it, but I wondered, inexperienced and timid as I still am, could I claim equal sincerity? She had, indeed, at least for that short while, made me an interesting person—and a depleted one as well.

Back at the Berghof, I thanked Brückner exuberantly, who took it all in with his customary opaque nonchalance. I understood none of his prattle but was, nonetheless, most grateful.

Since the Führer had other things to do than speak to me, I spent most of the day in a mindless fog of agonizing sensual euphoria.

But not so mindlessly euphoric that I failed to wonder what favour Zarah was repaying Brückner for, and what any further encounters with her by me would signify. I considered asking him, but perhaps some mysteries are best left unsolved.

THE YEAR OF the British, clearly. First, the Duke and Duchess of Windsor, and today, Lord Halifax.[128] But this visit was different, both in degree and in kind. All round the Berghof, especially among the secretaries and others with access to the Führer's thoughts, the word was Austria, but all I cared about was Zarah. And so, when preparing the Führer's toilette, I pushed most of his pronouncements to a distant place in my brain, only picking up one comment at the end: "That mealy hat rack in brogues is simply a stand-in for that twitchy rodent Chamberlain, and I know that chap's limitations well. But we must all treat this idiot as if he and his master have real meaning, mustn't we?" His voice was all mirth, his eyes all twinkle.

Since I knew the Führer's question to be rhetorical, I nodded, said nothing, and began putting away his toiletries.

As the Führer dictated, Schmidt translated, Halifax grinned and nodded, and von Neurath played statue, I was suddenly jolted by the awareness that I hadn't shaved! It's not that I'd felt my face, since parade rest does not permit such an activity; it was

---

[128] Lord Privy Seal in Chamberlain's cabinet and the man entrusted with the negotiations between Britain and Hitler over the union of Germany and Austria.

merely a sensation of grubbiness difficult to explain but there, just the same.

Approximately one and a half hours later, it was over, whatever it was (since I had no desire to hear the Führer say to Halifax what I already knew), and we all re-emerged, von Neurath still a pillar of elegant ice, but the Führer and Halifax grinning, a tableau of total agreement. After Halifax left, von Neurath, feigning an illness none of us took with even the most remote seriousness, also left. Then the Führer called for Brückner and me, led us back to the study, shut the door, and slapped his thighs in jubilation.

"Well, gentlemen," he beamed, "do I know the British or do I know the British?"

A more rhetorical—if not redundant—question could not have been asked. I said nothing, of course, since Brückner knew far better how to answer such questions.

"I almost felt sorry for the poor Britisher, my Führer," he said. "He might as well have left his teeth and neck with you for future use."

The Führer laughed. "Yes, Brückner, I must say it felt like the old dark days when I was roundly underestimated and dismissed by all, save a few, until the fools could underestimate and dismiss me no longer—a reminiscence I hold to my heart fondly. A pity here, since I still hold the British in some esteem.

"Oh, Brückner," the Führer said as we turned toward the door, "I think that we mustn't work poor Linge so hard that he has no time to shave properly."

"I'll make it a priority, my Führer," he responded with a slight curl of his lips.

℗

"The Führer misses nothing, does he, Wilhelm?" I asked, once we'd taken leave of the Führer.

"Hard to say, Heinz," he said. "With someone like him, you only find out what he's noticed when he tells you. Otherwise, nobody knows. But he means well where you're concerned, never fear. Just don't assume he misses anything, and life with him will be relatively placid."

❧

During their evening discussion, Eva Braun and her friends poked fun at Halifax's gaunt appearance and his upper-class lisp and stutter. For his part, while the Führer agreed with their assessment ("yes, I grant you his looks"), he praised him for his keen insight and his pledge to him that his country would not stand in the way of the latter's Austrian policy. The Führer exclaimed joyfully, "I've always said that the British want to wish me to lead the way, because they make their policy from the same principle as I do: the first priority is the elimination of Bolshevism."

Bolshevism, yes; always the hated and dreaded Bolshevism. I knew a Bolshie in the brickyard. Seemed like a solid chap, all brimming over with fellow feeling and an ardent desire for economic and social justice. He liked his liquor, too, as I recall. I just couldn't see him as an enemy to be "eliminated."

I still can't.

A JOYFUL BUT troublesome day, my friend!

I received a perfumed note from Zarah, apologizing profusely for her lapse of social grace, but that she'd been "on location" and, unfortunately, had no time for "significant correspondence." She then asked if it would be right, proper—and possible—for us to meet again, this time, at the Führer's New Year's celebration, something she'd only heard about, but never attended.

Even after considering the bizarre nature of my previous New Year's Eve experiences, I responded quickly that, while the Chancellery boasted no "Suite 303," I would personally arrange an invitation and looked forward to seeing her again. When I informed Brückner of it, he merely nodded once, winked, and remarked that "conquests are made on even flimsier pretexts."

Conquests? I wasn't sure what he meant, but I knew he meant well, so I thanked him and went about the Führer's business. Then, during the day, a quote from Nietzsche occurred to me: "Pity is the most agreeable feeling among those who have little pride and no prospects of great conquests."[129] For a moment, I asked myself: *What possible sort of "conquest" could a valet hope for from a sagacious, dazzling film star?* Frau Bella had said: "Dare to risk." Zarah was no "Zombie," but I decided that

---

[129] From *The Gay Science: With a Prelude in Rhymes and an Appendix of Songs.*

to ask the question was to answer the question, and so I swatted my insecurities away.

In the early afternoon, I took an enforced stroll with my latter-day confidant, Fräulein Schroeder, recently less and less the converted comrade, and more and more the original adversary, not so much in her words as in her tone. This morning, she was complaining of her "ox-like" workload and my relative leisure, even though she shared duties with Wolf and Dara. Unfortunately, it was difficult to fault her in this matter, for Dara was not the most meticulous of typists, and Wolf was often ill and her work rate was questioned, but nobody could do anything about either one, since they were under the Führer's personal protection—for reasons that escaped the rabidly precise and assiduous Schroeder. Unfortunately, in the matter of the Führer's taste, I could be of no assistance.

Once she got through her obligatory woe-is-me ritual, she proceeded to her main order of business: gossip. This time, it was about Brückner. Either she didn't know of my friendship with him (not possible) or couldn't care less (more likely). She regaled me with ribald tales of his homosexuality while he also engaged in a tumultuous relationship with the noted artist Sophie Storck—a contradiction she appeared quite adept at ignoring. But far more important, she added that his behaviour was "justifiably abhorrent to Herr Bormann (Martin, not Albert) and Herr Kannenberg." Now that was something *I* wasn't quite as capable of ignoring: because it appeared to be none of their business, either professionally or privately, how and why would they know of such things if true, and why would they spread such salacious sewage if not true? The only thing I did know was, true or not, they hadn't done it merely for the entertainment of Fräulein Schroeder.

After enduring a drooling flurry of the latest sex and Jew jokes from Kempka in the Führer's outer office, I managed to escape long enough to locate Brückner and tell him of my latest encounter with Schroeder.

"'Justifiably abhorrent'?" He laughed. "She actually said that?"

"Her very words, Wilhelm," I assured him.

He laughed again, this time somewhat less jocularly. "You know these two characters," he said. "Can you imagine anything they would find 'justifiably abhorrent,' aside from discovering that I was a transsexual Jewish Bolshevik assassin, bent on raping, circumcising, then killing the Führer, that is? And, perhaps, that will be next."

"Wilhelm!" I exclaimed, quite incapable of responding further.

He languidly raised a surrendering hand. "Yes, Heinz, I allow myself to be quite the rascal in your company. This, I admit to you frankly, since you already know. As for that miserable crone Schroeder and her 'Tweedledum and Tweedledee,'[130] I maintain a vigilant disdain for such creatures. Like any other piece of ripe meat, my friend, there will be maggots and vultures ever ready to devour it, and, unfortunately, the Führer is seen as the ripest of meat. Instead of fretting, come with me and we'll drink a toast to the success of your next encounter with Zarah, yes?"

We drank, but I couldn't help considering Brückner's remark about maggots and vultures. I could understand his detached disdain for such as external menace, but I harboured a different image, that of another kind of parasite about which I'd read that

---

[130] The names have become synonymous in Western popular culture slang for any two people who look and act in identical ways; generally used in a derogatory context.

isn't external; instead, it lives in another organism, called the host, and often harms it. As I'd read: "It is dependent on its host for survival and has to be in the host to live, grow and multiply. A parasite cannot live independently. Although a parasite rarely kills the host, in some cases it can happen. The parasite benefits at the expense of the host—the parasite uses the host to gain strength, and the host loses some strength as a result. Parasites, unlike predators, are usually much smaller than their host and reproduce at a faster rate than the host." And I feared, not so much for the Führer but for Brückner, a far more vulnerable "piece of meat."

24 *December 1937*

During my miserable night of pacing, I ruminated on what the Führer told me of his time at Landsberg when I'd first arrived: "As a former prisoner, Linge, I carry not a little insight in the knapsack of memory. And I tell you this: the man who knows he is a prisoner, he adjusts; a man who does not know, he is content. Ah, but the man who is not certain, there is the peril. He knows he is not free, but he does not know why or how. That is a man truly to be pitied. Doubt is the most insidious jailer of all."

Doubt. Yes. But doubt about what? Perhaps that's what the Führer meant by "insidious."

For much of the day, the Führer and Krause sat on the carpet, wrapping presents for the Chancellery staff. It was not the first time, and also not the first time I was told (for morale's sake, I imagine, as if I might actually envy the tiny scorpion) that such a mundane enterprise was both beneath me and a long-standing tradition shared by the Führer and Krause. I accepted it as usual. Can you picture me, Heinz Linge, lying on a carpet with the Führer, wrapping presents? The entire image was otherworldly. But at least I could take a brief vacation, and did, for I had a mission after my "conversation" with Fräulein Schroeder.

I made for Kempka's immense garage, passing the ubiquitous checkpoint tables. I once asked Brückner why tables and not desks, and he chuckled wryly and told me that the entire system was based on Himmler's paranoid worldview: the nature of man is to conceal, and so the ability to conceal must be diminished, if not eliminated entirely. The tables, it followed, allowed for no concealment, as would a desk with drawers. "Tell you the truth," he joked, "if it was up to the Reichsführer, uniforms wouldn't have pockets, and purses would be banned."

The noise of active garage tools and machinery was hardly bearable, so I opened his door without knocking and entered. Kempka was now a lieutenant colonel, as was I, but, unlike me, Kempka acted the part to perfection—and more, as if he'd been elevated to full colonel. As usual, he was wearing a white lab coat open over his uniform, his little torso perched on his "throne," booted legs gleamingly propped on his executive desk, slobbering over the latest banned erotica that he'd securely sequestered within the pages of the *Volkischer Beobachter*.

"Ah, Heinz," he beamed sweatily, closing his newspaper. "What brings you to my humble domain? You need a car? Some, ah, reading material, maybe?" he smirked, tapping his paper. "Just let your Uncle Erich know, and it's yours."

I shook my head no. "Nothing so exciting, 'Uncle Erich,'" I bantered. "I just dropped by to say hello, and to escape routine, I suppose." The lie was entirely plausible, especially to a lazy lowbrow like Kempka.

"Yeah, routine," he sighed. "No routine here. You never know when a car's gonna be needed, and who by and for how many. For example, okay? Your good buddy Krause ordered a car for himself and the Führer to be on standby for late this evening—with me as the driver, naturally. For fucking what, you might ask? Who the fuck knows, but Krause and the Führer? But the right one for the occasion had better be in perfect working order, gassed up, and ready to go, that much is for certain. You see, no routine, that is, unless there's some fucking parade, of course, and even then, routine takes a distant second to security, and that's never known even by me until the last possible moment. Some of the time, I'm not even driving the Führer, but one of his doubles, some Jap mucky-muck, or one of his special friends I can't talk about." He suddenly waved me aside and screamed through the closed door: "*Hey, you goddamn fuckers! Get your asses in gear or guess who'll be reading my report on you, hear me?*" Then he waved me back in place with no discernible change in activity in the massive shop.

"Gotta ride their asses," he told me, "or they'll just stand around scratching their balls. So, what's up, Heinz? You heard about that fucking piano-playing bear, Hanfstaengl?"

I shrugged. "Only what Wiedemann told me, which was not much. He was supposed to be on some secret mission to Spain, but never made it." Not exactly accurate, but I wanted information from Kempka, and being stingy with the facts always helped.

His head performed a metronome of negativity. "Nah," he corrected, "never was a *real* mission, from what I heard. Just an elaborate scheme to finally eliminate a pain in the ass. But the s.o.b. caught on halfway through and skipped to Switzerland. Now he can play his shit for bankers and clockmakers, eh?" A smile to tell me his remark was witty, and I smiled back, a beat too late, but it passed him by. "Hey, whatever happened with them two mystery women of yours? You must be the best fucking keeper of secrets in the Reich, or your charm just fizzled out, which is it?"

I puffed some air from my nostrils. I was tempted to say both but limited it to the fizzle.

"Well, Heinz, hey, you know women. High, low, or in

between, they're gonna fuck with your head, then finally disappoint you." He tapped his newspaper. "But I still got my mags, you know. Amazing pics. Some even doing it with animals, broom handles, enema bags—you name it. More dependable than the real thing, you bet. Anytime you want. Just ask your Uncle Erich."

I could no longer stand the coarse, power-bloated pervert, but one unasked-for mission for Brückner, to make it worthwhile. "I appreciate the offer," I fibbed, "but I'll try the live ones a bit longer, okay? I'll certainly keep you and the enema bags in mind." That part, he could believe. I rose. "Oh, before I run back to the Führer, I meant to ask your opinion of Bormann?"

Kempka buttocked his chair back, lifted his legs from his desk, planted them on the floor, and sat forward, glancing furtively at the wire-mesh-and-glass-panelled door, which was shut tight.

"Which one?" he asked.

"Right. The Reichsleiter," I replied, to fully dry any cement of doubt.

Kempka sat mute for a moment, staring at me, then: "Why do you want to know?"

Careful! I commanded myself. All may rest on his opinion of my reason for asking and, of course, the answer to my question itself—and would he invoke the magic name? "Just curiosity, my friend," I replied in an approximation of Kempka-ese. "He seems to be everywhere and has unlimited access to the big shots, but he's never said even one fucking word to me as long as I've been tending to the Führer. In fact, I never see him outside the Führer's dinners. I just felt it might be useful to know a little about such a chap, know what I mean?"

Kempka tilted his head back, then forward. "'Useful,' you

say?" he remarked with a smear of distaste on his lips. "I'd say essential, more like." He lifted his arm to wave away someone I couldn't see but I assumed was about to enter. "You realize, Linge, that what I tell you goes no further than here, and I'll deny we ever had this conversation, you understand?"

"I was never even here," I answered.

"Right. Well, Bormann's like a lot of the conniving characters round the Führer," he began, "only more so: toadyish ass-kissing above; brutish ass-kicking below. But with Bormann, I tell ya, his one trait—and he's got it in fucking spades—is his way of lookin' like he's working twenty-four hours a day and to make damn sure everyone, especially the Führer, knows it. He started this shit under Hess, not a guy you'd call famous for overworking, and made himself fucking indispensable, to the point where Hess made him his head of staff. But that was nothing," he went on, "compared to when the Berghof was rebuilt. The motherfucker actually had a house built near it so's to give him an excuse to be near the Führer and those mucky-mucks close to him. After that, he starts buying up land on the Obersalzberg, whether the original owners liked it or not. Even the Führer got upset about this, but Bormann the sweet talker convinced him that the owners were beggin' him to buy, and so the Führer was okay with it. And soon Bormann owned the whole fuckin' mountain.

"But that wasn't enough for a crafty s.o.b. who wanted to get ahead. Next, he managed, by schmearing some adjuncts' palms, to get himself invited to the Führer's lunches, and then beg off at the last minute, claiming overwork. Finally, when he did show up, he'd say sorry to the Führer in such a way that he managed to get a reputation as the most tireless fucking worker in the whole Party, and, eventually, you know, he got to be manager of the whole damn Berghof. Now, he was in a position to bury his subordinates and screw his rivals like never before.

"But even that wasn't good enough for the asshole. 'Cause the Führer's a vegetarian, Bormann had to be also, making damn sure that all round him knew how great it was and how it helped him enjoy his superhuman workload more. Same with smoking. But there's more. He also knew the Führer actually read the shit on his shelves, so he secretly hired a team of professional readers to get all the new stuff and give him a summary, so when he ate with the Führer, he could show his book knowledge and the Führer would naturally figure that the books were actually read by him. But you musta seen this shit lotsa times, right?"

I had. "Lotsa times." I'd wondered where somebody with Bormann's workload got the time to do all that reading. I certainly couldn't have done. Now I knew.

"No fucking detail was too small or unimportant for him," said Kempka. "One last example, eh? You know that thousands of people make their way past the Berghof when the Führer's there, hoping to even get a peek. You been there so's you know that he'd stand for hours in the open while people would drive by, right? Okay, so one hot summer's evening, he mentions to Bormann that he found it too much of a strain. So, as if by fucking wizardry, when the Führer comes out of the Berghof next day at the usual hour to greet the crowd, even he was speechless to see this huge leafy tree, which created total shade from the sun. It turns out that the night before, Bormann had the fuckin' thing transported up the Berg and planted there. Impressed, Heinz? Well, the Führer was, I can tell you, and so Bormann got even closer. So, there you are—and mark you, not a word outside this room, yes?"

"Absolutely never," I replied with such a thick veneer of

sincerity that Kempka was truly beguiled. "But one more question, okay?" I said. "Well, maybe two."

Kempka pondered for a moment, then shrugged in surrender.

"Do you, ah, think that I might be one of his rivals?" I asked with strained nonchalance, rhetorically of course.

Just then the telephone rang, but Kempka didn't answer it, didn't even look at it. After what seemed like hours, it stopped and Kempka continued. "You?" He laughed. "Not a chance, my friend. He's heard the Führer call you 'the son he'll never have' far too often for him to dare take you on. He's an ambitious asshole, but he's no dummy."

I was shaking inwardly with relief, but there was one final thing I needed to know, and, fortunately, Kempka happily obliged without prompting.

"No," he said, "not you. But I sure wouldn't want to be in the Führer's adjutants' shoes, especially your pal Brückner's. He's also no fool, but you know, he got a screwy sense of humour and real cheek that a Bormann could use to sway the Führer against him. There's also the Storck matter. But more important, Brückner's in Bormann's way, and he's vulnerable. Like for tonight, Bormann suggested to the Führer that Brückner join him instead of Krause, I'm sure, for nothing good. Just an opinion, mind, but I been around, you know what I mean?"

I knew what he meant—Schreck. No one more than Kempka knew what can happen when someone gets in the way.

Kempka tilted back in his massive chair, which made a garish creak. "Couldn't have the cars sounding like that, eh?"

I shook my head, with lips pursed almost to a pucker.

"Yep, Heinz," he concluded. "You can keep your Himmler, Heydrich, Goebbels, Göring, Hess, the whole military, bankers, and industrialists, even the fucking Jews and Bolshies. Keep 'em all. For my money, Bormann's the most dangerous s.o.b. in the Reich, bar none. Now, I gotta go. Look busy. Like Bormann. You get what you came for?"

I most certainly did get, but nothing I would have him aware of. "I came to escape routine," I reminded him, "and I did. But," looking at my watch, "it's finally found me, I'm afraid." I got up. "Interesting about Hanfstaengl and Bormann," I said, omitting any reference to Brückner. "I do appreciate the information, and please give my regards to Baur."

Kempka nodded. "Anytime, Heinz," he said. "Your Uncle Erich's always happy to relieve boredom of one sort or another—except for tonight, naturally. Tonight, it's my boredom that'll need relieving." The phone rang again, but this time he picked it up while waving me out.

On the way to my quarters, I stopped by the Communications Centre, only to discover that Brückner had been looking for me and had left a message. It appeared, said his note of apology, that he was obliged to postpone our planned evening because Krause had suddenly become indisposed, and so he was to accompany the Führer instead on his little adventuresome jaunt round Berlin this evening. The Führer agreed, and so that was that.

My stomach heaved. *So soon!* I asked myself in astonishment at how events appear to conspire, not only in their nature but in their timing as well. It brought to mind something I'd read some years before in the encyclopaedia, about a Swiss psychiatrist named Carl Jung, and something he called "synchronicity": "the occurrence of two or more events that appear to be meaningfully related but are not causally related." He claimed that such events were "meaningful coincidences" and that "events connected by meaning need not have an explanation in terms of causality." At the time, from what little I understood of anything, it seemed to be just so much contextless supernatural gibberish. However, as I read Brückner's note again, it began to make sense. Now, I believed I'd suddenly discovered both a context and an example. I folded the paper, stuffed it in my pocket, and immediately set off on a search all round the Chancellery for the writer.

I caught him in the gardens, sitting alone on an ornate stone bench, smoking a pungent Gauloise cigarette, stuck into a streaked, yellow-and-white ivory holder, so much the rakish raconteur. He hardly ever smoked, not merely because of his proximity to the Führer, but because, according to him, he needed to secure as much freedom as he could, in what he guardedly called a "gilded political penitentiary." When he'd said that, it reminded me of something else Jung had said: "Every form of addiction is bad, no matter whether the narcotic be alcohol, morphine or idealism." I felt that the last thing about which Brückner needed to worry was idealism. He immediately motioned me to sit with him, which I did with breathless relief, for perhaps there was still time.

"Ah, Heinz," he exclaimed, with what I felt to be a hollow effusiveness. "You're a difficult man to find."

I wanted to tell him that I had the same problem but instead merely told him that I'd been with Kempka.

"Yes, Kempka," he said. "I'll be with him soon myself—with the Führer of course." Then he told me of the change in our plan for the evening. "Up to now, only God and Krause knew what the Führer did on these outings, and I can tell you that I was quite content in my ignorance, but no longer, it would seem. In any event, we can always—"

"It was Bormann's idea."

His eye widened slightly. "Idea? What idea?"

"That you take Krause's place as escort."

"Hmm. You know this?"

"From the highest authority," I joked.

"You mean—"

"Kempka."

"Ah, then it must be true," he joked back through a crooked smile. "But why would Bormann suggest me?"

"He didn't say, but not for any reason that would benefit you," I ventured.

"Well, be that as it may, Heinz," he said, "it seems that—"

"Please don't go," I entreated, then told him of my conversation in the garage. "I see only an orchestrated disaster in this."

"My friend," he replied, "had the Führer not supported Bormann, I could ignore the bastard as I would a flea in the forest." He pulled out the stub of his cigarette, stamped it out, and replaced it with a fresh one, which he lit and took a deep tip-glowing drag off of. "But you do see the difficulty, yes?"

Then something else Kempka said struck me. "Wilhelm, please give me an hour before you make any final arrangements. Will you do that for me?"

Brückner shrugged and blew out a cloud of bluish smoke. "Of course. What difference can an hour make?"

One hell of a lot, I wanted to reply, but merely thanked him, waited a few moments until his puzzled expression evaporated, and left.

The Führer was lecturing von Ribbentrop about his plans for Austria when I arrived. Thankfully, assorted maps, typed and written documents, books, and writing materials were scattered about, so I began discreetly tidying up, while waiting for von Ribbentrop to end his noddings and yes-my-Führers and leave.

When he finally did, I asked the Führer about the success of his gift-wrapping ritual with Krause. He told me that all went well until halfway through, when Krause began complaining of an earache, and so the Führer asked Dara to take his place, a substitution he found to be more than satisfactory. Then I asked him about the effect Krause's "earache" would have on his evening, and he told me that Bormann had arranged for Brückner to take his place. *Now or never,* I concluded.

"My Führer, may . . . may I, ah, ask a favour?"

The Führer smiled. "A favour? Of course, Linge. I'm surprised you don't ask for more, unlike the rest who surround me. What can I do for you?"

"Please take me with you tonight instead of General Brückner," I beseeched him. "I've been eager to take Krause's place, away from official venues, and now, with him . . . indisposed, my curiosity has got the better of me, I suppose."

His eyes narrowed and his tiny moustache lifted with his smile. "You don't see this as an opportunity to spirit me away and hold me for ransom, do you? I'm sad to say I would be worth precious little—so far."

"My Führer!" I exclaimed, "I never . . . such a thing never—"

He held up his hands in mock surrender. "I only joke, Linge. Anything sinister from you would be the furthest thing from my mind." He sat down. "Of course you may accompany me. I can't promise you great excitement, unless you're thrilled sitting next to Kempka for hours at a stretch, but at least your curiosity will be satisfied. You can go and tell Brückner I won't be needing him."

I was shuddering with relief. "I'm most grateful, my Führer," I gushed. "I'll tell the general straight away."

Fuck you, Bormann! I shouted inwardly, as I raced to Brückner's bench with the news.

❧

After sitting for more than an hour beside a silent Kempka, his small four-seater Mercedes parked at the curb on a dark side street directly in front of an apartment building into which the Führer had scurried, the gunshot was like experiencing a sudden thunderclap on a clear day. Yet no one stirred, not even Kempka. No windows opened, no people stopped in the street or ducked for cover. No sirens. No dogs howled or barked. It was as if it had happened in my brain and nowhere else. After a severe flinch, I turned to Kempka, who'd glanced at an upper floor, and asked him what it was. He merely stared at me and said: "The Führer's fine. Get out of the car, Heinz. Go home, and don't look back. You were never here."

As I PICKED at a late breakfast, a Chinese proverb I'd once read rattled round my brain:

> Be careful of your thoughts, for your thoughts become your words. Be careful of your words, for your words become your actions. Be careful of your actions, for your actions become your habits. Be careful of your habits, for your habits become your character. Be careful of your character, for your character becomes your destiny.

What *was* my character, and so my destiny? I splashed ice-cold water on my face, then scalding hot, and shaved. Did I actually have a character? My thoughts becoming my words, said the proverb. Hardly. I laughed darkly to myself. They never have done, even when nothing was at stake, and so you, my friend, must imagine the likelihood now.

My curiosity about last night caused me to visit Kempka before beginning my regular duties, but I was told by his "second in command" that his boss had been summoned to Himmler's headquarters, and predicting a return time from there was problematic at best.

The question of initiating the subject of the previous night dominated my consciousness as I set about my morning routine with the Führer, especially since I noticed what appeared to be a small smear of blood on the back of the Führer's left hand. He was in a mood I can only describe as jolly. He began by wishing me a merry Christmas, joking that he would have to utter and respond all day to that phrase, and he thought he'd practice on me first. Then he had me sit, while he stood behind his desk, leaning over, supported by his arms and splayed hands.

"Gypsies read palms," he began. "I read faces. You're wondering about last night. So now I will confide to you that being the Führer no longer affords me the opportunity to observe our majestic capital as an ordinary citizen, so, from time to time, I take the liberty of sneaking out, in plain clothes. You can appreciate this."

"Of course, my Führer," I answered truthfully. "It must grieve you to isolate yourself from your people in order to do the monumental tasks you've set for yourself and the Reich."

He smiled. "Quite the contrary. My people are the blood that flows in my veins. They are with me so long as I live. No, Linge, if I am 'grieved,' as you put it, I am grieved that my people must be isolated from *me,* while you and I perform the miracle that one day will cleanse and unify the race and transform the Reich into the centre of a new Aryan world. My only regret is that those who serve me at close range, so to say, like Kempka, are obliged to withstand the rigours of Himmler's fanatical demand for ritual."

You and I? What was he talking about? "Rigours, my Führer?"

"A brief and harmless interrogation," he replied with a slight shrug. "A technical rebuke for allowing our little escapade to go forward without officially reporting it to him beforehand. A mere formality, but poor Kempka forgot, having the mind of a mechanic and not of a policeman."

As usual, the Führer then employed the subject to deliver a lecture, one I'd received several times.

"As an old comrade in the Struggle, Linge, you know that

I have the highest regard for Heinrich, though, I must say that fondness eludes me." He lifted his arms from his desk and began pacing. "His relentless insistence that loyalty is mindless obedience is both rigid and wrongheaded, even for those performing the most menial tasks. Obedience takes no courage, no imagination, no will. I knew this as a young soldier and no less as a mature national leader. In my view, Linge, true loyalty requires all these qualities. And poor Heinrich, while a thorough and reliable brother in arms, he is completely bereft of these qualities. In any event, given the protection I afford members of my little family, I'm certain that Kempka will be none the worse for his experience."

I was only partially listening, as I was still in thrall to the gunshot, which the Führer didn't mention—or the blood—and which I had no intention of bringing up. *Be careful of your words,* the proverb warned, *for your words become your actions.*

He sat down with a loud and putrid *pfffffsht* of flatulence. "No need to see to me until dinner, when I give you your Christmas present." Then he waved me out with a tiny smile and a nod before I had a chance to thank him in advance.

I began another hunt for Brückner to relate last night's events and this morning's discoveries, but he seemed to have vanished, until I returned to my quarters and found him sitting in the chair opposite my cot. "Fancy a walk, Heinz," he suggested, with an accompanying head tilt towards the door.

We strolled round the freezing terrace, encased in our black leather greatcoats and woollen mufflers, negotiating interminable checkpoints and innumerable requests from subordinates. After thanking me for my selfless gesture on his behalf, Brückner inquired about my evening as his surrogate. I recounted it all, regardless of sense, even the gunshot I thought I'd heard; Kempka's telling me to exit the automobile and return to the Chancellery by my own devices; his summons to Himmler; the blood on the Führer's hand—all for which I had no explanation. I omitted knowing of Kempka's murder of Schreck. *Be careful of your words, for your words become your actions.*

Brückner stared dead ahead all through my recounting, saying nothing. After a time, he asked, still with his one eye facing forward: "What do you know of Kempka?"

I shrugged. "You knew him before I ever entered the Führer's service. What can I say, except that he drives the Führer and was the one who told me about Bormann. Also, he has an unhealthy appetite for females of a certain appearance and inclination."

"Kempka, then, is a mystery."

"What do you think occurred last night?" I asked.

He halted so quickly that I almost stumbled to hold back. He turned to face me. "Heinz," he said, "be in no doubt of my debt to you for your comradely actions concerning Bormann. Regrettably, with his relentless ambition and ruthless cunning, I'm quite certain he's far from finished with me, and so you merely postponed the inevitable. Given what must be his current frustration, I might even experience a certain compassion for him. However, it's said that in order to afford compassion, one must first be ruthless. Unfortunately, my friend, both are beyond my capacity. So, ultimately, Heinz, he will triumph. As to last night, a dream only. Let it go. I say this to you as a friend."

Yes, a dream. I thought back to that night at Salon Kitty. And that man: *When you dream, are you able to exercise control over what you or others do? Also, in your dreams, is there ever a metal object, like a child's top? Two harmless questions, after all, yes?* What was a harmless question? How would I know? Was that, too, a dream?

"But if it wasn't a dream," I said, "I owe Kempka for taking Himmler's wrath alone. He didn't need to do that."

"Didn't he?" Brückner asked with a slightly lifted eyebrow. Not really a question.

"What are you suggesting?"

"Perhaps he was instructed to," answered Brückner, cryptically. "In any event, I foresee no serious difficulty for him. Go get some rest, my friend," he said, nodding back to the Chancellery. "From the guest list, a busy night ahead, I think. And, as per the Führer's instructions, you're to receive your present then, and he needs you to be in top form."

As always, Brückner was right. Tonight, instead of having dinner first, the Führer had his guests sit in his theatre (without him) and view a new film that Goebbels had, through means known only to him, just procured from America (and had translated into German through subtitles), entitled *Topper*, a fanciful and hectic romantic fable.[131]

It was just before the film began when Brückner entered and escorted Zarah Leander to a vacant seat, right in front of where I was standing. She stole a quick, expressionless gaze at me before gracefully lowering herself into the seat, next to Magda Goebbels. I quaked inwardly with desire, but not so much so that

---

[131] George (Cary Grant) and Marion (Constance Bennett) Kerby are as rich as they are irresponsible. When George wrecks their classy sports car, they wake up from the accident as ghosts. Realizing they aren't in heaven or hell because they've never been responsible enough to do good deeds or bad ones, they decide that freeing their old friend Cosmo Topper (Roland Young) from his regimented lifestyle will be their ticket into heaven.

I didn't see Goebbels's wife visibly shift her body slightly away from Zarah. As Brückner moved to the back, he whispered in my ear: "Your Führer's gift to you, my friend. Merry Christmas."

❧

I watched the film with only that portion of my brain dedicated to memory, for I had no further powers of concentration with Zarah sitting in front of me, the cream-coloured silk of her gown hanging just low enough to display her long, porcelain neck. Every once in a while, Magda's husband would turn his head ever so slightly to glance at Zarah, as did Göring, though with less subtlety as a result of his enormous girth and clattery medals. Of the men, only Himmler appeared indifferent. The women stared so straight ahead, they might as well have been watching the film through a vision-testing device.

As with the film, much of the dinner for me went mentally unattended, for I then had a perfect view of the front of Zarah as well. Sitting among the Reich's luminaries and the Führer's closest circle, it was as if I was seeing her for the first time. Unfortunately, being a universe away from the erudition of writers I'd encountered haphazardly in my ardent but artless attempts at self-education, I hadn't the words to come even close to adequately describing her, save that her features were astonishingly reminiscent of Emerald's and Katrin's: all three were a stunning trinity of Aryan exquisiteness. She may have been the Führer's gift, but it was definitely Brückner's suggestion. I don't believe I'd ever felt more important than I did then, standing along a wall in livery at parade rest. I was fortunate that there was company, for I was bereft of words to express my gratitude for their imaginative—and furtive—thoughtfulness.

Zarah was sitting on the Führer's left, while Eva Braun sat

on his right. It was one of the few times the Führer was seen publicly with the latter, even though she had an apartment in the Chancellery. Fortunately, she and Zarah were seated in such a way that they weren't obliged to face each other. Unfortunately, this was not the case with Magda Goebbels and Emmy Göring, who had no idea that Zarah's presence at table had more to do with me than with the Führer, and their expressions appeared to make no secret of their malevolent envy. On the other hand, the men required no description from me. Even Goebbels, her least ardent fan, appeared star struck. As if to draw women into the occasion, if not the conversation, the Führer waxed eloquently in his usual misogynistic manner.

"The men of the Nordic countries," he said, "have been softened to the point that their most beautiful women suddenly become coy when they have an opportunity of getting their hooks on a man in our part of the world. That's what happened to Göring, here, with his late wife, Karin," he added, despite the fact that his current wife, Emmy, sat beside him. "There's no rebelling against this observation. It's a fact that women love real men. It's their instinct that tells them. Even women accept this."

Normally, I would have switched off the conversation, since I'd heard the Führer go on and on about this at length numerous times, but this time, I was eager to observe the reactions of the women.

"Of course, my Führer," the females immediately concurred, with varying degrees of conviction, the least, I rejoiced, coming from Zarah, who merely lifted her perfect eyebrows slightly.

"In prehistoric times," the Führer continued, "the women looked for the protection of heroes. When two men fight for the possession of a woman, the latter waits to let her heart speak until she knows which of the two will be victorious."

I could have sworn that Zarah frowned at precisely the same time as Magda Goebbels beamed. Eva, I could tell, merely stared into a middle distance, seeing no one.

"Then it's a miracle that the finest example of Aryan womanhood hasn't captured you by now," Goebbels cooed, almost on cue.

The Führer winked back, I thought, theatrically, so all could see. "Not a miracle, Joseph, but firm conviction. It's by design that I'm not married. For me, marriage would have been a disaster." He was facing straight ahead and didn't notice (or wish to notice) Eva Braun's crestfallen expression, subtle but obvious, just the same.

"The bad side of marriage," Göring chimed in, echoing the Führer, as if utterly oblivious to Emmy beside him, "is that it creates rights. In that case, it's far better to have a mistress. The burden is lightened, and everything is placed on the level of a gift."

I immediately thought of Zarah—*my* gift. Would she claim such a role, and, no less important, would I wish her to?

"Now you all must appreciate," the Führer concluded as he always did, "that what I've said applies only to men of a superior sort."

And on that note, dinner ended, the Führer rose (as did the rest), wished all the Merriest of Christmases, and then, apropos of his previous remarks, he told them he still needed to make his annual Christmas speech to the Chancellery staff, oversee the giving out of their presents, and after that return to his office to plan a year none of them, their children, or their children's children would ever forget. He added that they should stay as long as they wished after he'd gone.

Then, as he moved to the double doors that Brückner had

opened, he whispered to me: "Your friend Krause will see to me tonight. You just enjoy your gift." Then he grinned, turned, and left.

After escorting everybody from the dining room, I retrieved Zarah's sable wrap and my greatcoat and walked her to the entrance, where we stood silently in the cold while her Mercedes Cabriolet was fetched, a car remarkably similar to the one I'd been in the previous night but with an infinitely more alluring chauffeur.

Though her appearance was not unlike Katrin's, Zarah's face and voice possessed an expressive warmth that Katrin's couldn't even approximate. Both exhibited a high order of native intelligence and professional polish, but Zarah, for all the theatricality demanded by her profession, appeared to display an authenticity and humanity foreign to Katrin. Perhaps it was merely the one being the consummate actress and the other, bereft of such skills, but I held fast to my need to believe.

As I opened the driver's door for her, she held it back and looked at me with those piercing dark-blue eyes I'd studied all through dinner.

"So good to see you again, but Christ almighty, Heinz, do you really—?" She left the rest unsaid, but I knew what was coming; I'd seen it in her face throughout dinner.

"I'm amazed the snow's let up," I said, attempting to deflect. "This time last year, you couldn't—"

"Yes, I remember," she cut in. "Weather aside, did you actually buy all that bilge your Führer was spewing about women? Can you be honest about that with me?"

She startled me. *My* Führer? *Bilge?* Was this a test? *Trust no one!* I'd always commanded myself, but somehow, I felt differently about her motives and hoped it wasn't because of her fame or my need. *Dare to risk!*

"Not at all," I said, as sincerely as my chattering from the cold would permit. "I didn't . . . 'buy' it, as you say. That's the Führer, not me. And that's the truth, for what it's worth."

She nodded tentatively, waiting.

"You need to understand, Zarah, I'm a valet, not a matinee idol. I'm a menial. My entire role is to be of assistance to the Führer when called upon, and otherwise, stand inconspicuously at ease. A trained monkey could do this without breathing hard. As a consequence, I'm not obliged to listen to the Führer's dinner table monologues, whether agreeable or not, and so I don't. I'm not even obliged to appear interested, since to all, I'm quite invisible." The lie was only partial, but I stated it with as much conviction as the truth.

She reached out and squeezed my arm gently. "In these times, Heinz, truth is worth a great deal, if only for its rarity. So, Christmas morning comes early then. Shall we get in," she suggested, her voice as gentle as her hand, "and go as far away from the cold and misogyny as we can?"

She slid in and fired up the engine. I quickly closed her door, went round to the passenger side, entered, and we were off before I could even close my own door.

We drove, mostly in silence, down the Unter den Linden, past the Hotel Adlon. Zarah had recommended one of the more intimate side-street eateries, mainly, she pointed out, for anonymity, "the kind you claim to enjoy while serving Hitler, that is," she joked, "unless you desire an immense noisy room jammed with nattily dressed toffs and red-striped generals gaping at me instead of their companions." I chuckled at that, more relieved that she was speaking to me, than I was of the humour of her remark. Of course I agreed.

Once we were served our wine (naturally, a name and vintage I'd never heard of), she proposed a toast.

"To truth," she said, staring directly into my eyes, clearly waiting for me to raise my glass and join her.

"Yes," I answered, staring back, "to truth." We both took a sip of the luxurious liquid.

"In my position," she said, "I've encountered many menials, but never one like you—at any age. You know, Heinz," she added, "I almost didn't agree to come. I wish you to know this."

I'd sensed, even at the Chancellery, that she had come with an ulterior motive, and I needed to know what it was before any more "truth" emerged from me. "May I ask why?"

She began swirling her drink. "I thought I knew you from our previous . . . encounter, and so I expected to be merely a dinner guest—no more, no less—after which we would sneak off together. But when General Brückner asked me to be a Christmas gift, I was, of course, offended. I'm no one's gift, even for Hitler's cherished valet. I'm a human being, not one of Göring's pilfered paintings."

Göring? Not the general or even Herr? Pilfered paintings? Then I realized that she was Swedish, despite her perfect fluency in German, and she was certainly not a Party member.

"I never thought of you that way," I said, in an attempt to mollify her. "I'm quite certain it was only a term Brückner used playfully, to represent a date."

"'Playfully,' you say," she retorted. "Do you really mean that?"

"With Brückner, yes. Most definitely."

She said nothing, eyes drilling into my face. She appeared to be considering what I said, so I filled the space. "Since you felt like some holiday-wrapped object, why didn't you just turn Brückner down? I'm certain you were under no compulsion or obligation."

She stopped her swirling. "This may sound worse than it is, but I was eager to see the fascinating human being beneath the anonymous livery. If there even was one, in fact."

Perhaps all the praise for my uniqueness and good nature that I'd received from the Führer and Brückner had gone to my head, but I was hurt by her inference that I was merely some laboratory animal to be studied, albeit a valuable one. At times, I'd felt this about Katrin and Emerald, but I ached not to believe it of Zarah, whom I considered actually real. "This was your plan?" I asked her, my face immobile.

"No plan as such, Heinz. I'm a creature of whimsy and caprice. I don't really know, to be honest. I was improvising. I do it all the time on set, whether the director or other cast members like it or not. It doesn't endear me to them, but it makes them money and so they live with it. In any event, they—and my audience—expect little of a star, except allure and inevitable surrender. I do regret that I may have hurt your feelings."

I desperately wanted to change the subject, but something forced me on, ignoring her regret. "Then what if I had refused the Führer's 'gift'?"

She smiled for the first time, her dazzling face opening up like a rising theatre curtain. "A perplexing question, Heinz. I believe you've told me the truth, so I will tell you the truth: being with you now, I look back and admit that I would have been greatly disappointed." She shrugged. "Now I've said it." She reached forward with her glass, as did I, and we clinked them, I imagined, to celebrate the welcome thaw.

"*Zazdaróvye!*"

"This is Swedish?" I asked.

She smiled gently. "No, Heinz, it's Russian. Like your *prosit* and my *Skål.* Have you ever been to the Soviet Union?"

I laughed. "Except for Berchtesgaden and Munich, I've never been out of Berlin. I'm quite the urban yokel."

"Except for tonight, does your boss permit you any free time, or are you at his constant beck and call?"

Before I could answer, we were interrupted by a short, middle-aged, dapper fellow wearing a double-breasted three-piece bespoke-fitted tweed suit.

"My apologies, Herr Lieutenant Colonel," he said to me while looking at Zarah. "With your permission." He didn't wait for my permission, so I didn't bother to stand, clearly a meaningless male ritual under the circumstances. "You are Zarah Leander?" He was holding a small notebook in a damp hand.

She glanced up. "Yes," she acknowledged casually, as if it was a matter of routine. "And you would like my autograph," she told him, seemingly from habit.

The man removed a sodden handkerchief, swiped his sweaty brow, and reached out with the notebook. "Yes, if you would be so kind. You know, my wife has all of your recordings and sees all your films."

She took the notebook. "You have a pen?"

"I . . . yes, of course," he replied, not a little shy before celebrity. He reached inside his jacket, pulled out a pen, unscrewed the cap, and handed it to her. "My apologies," he said.

"Not to worry. At least you have a pen. Just last week, I was obliged to sign an autograph in ketchup."

We all chortled at that as she signed with a flourish and handed back the pen and notebook. The grateful chap shook her extended hand vigorously and withdrew, almost bumping into a waiter. Never once did he look at me.

"It's for him," she said.

"Him? But he said—"

"Trust me. I know men and I know women. It was for him."

"Did you really sign your name in ketchup?"

"No, Heinz," she laughed lightly. "All for show. Made him feel better, though, didn't it?"

"You treat your fans well," I said.

"It's a small price to pay for what I receive," she said, taking another sip. "In any event, if Hitler can do without you for a while, you really should take some time and visit the Soviet Union. An amazing people doing amazing things—and all without the cultural and technological advantages you Germans had, despite Versailles."

"That's quite a despite," I told her. "At any rate, I warned you I was a yokel." Something was seriously amiss, so I vowed not to drink any more than was prudent. "Just what are you saying?"

She smiled, reached over and took my hand in both of hers. "Nothing sinister or provocative, Heinz. What I'm saying is that it would be a shame if you got all your information about the world from *Mein Kampf* and Goebbels's propaganda machine, as the rest of your countrymen seem to." She slid her hand away. "I say, why don't we have one more toast—this time, your choice— then go back to my apartment, where you can . . . unwrap your gift and enjoy what's inside?"

25 *December 1937*

THE PREVIOUS EVENING had slid by as if I were skating on an oil slick. When I could focus again on anything but my timeless time at Zarah's apartment, I checked the small clock on my dresser: 0145.

Christmas Day.

As always, I incinerated my papers, secreted the bulb, switched off the lights, rewound and removed the negatives, placed them in my hollow shoe heel, placed the empty Leica in my top dresser drawer, flopped down on my cot, and slid imperceptibly . . .

[Portions missing.]

31 December 1937

AFTER ANOTHER FITFUL half sleep, I came to, dreading the day
to come, as I only too often do. Whoever had asked me on that
terrible night at Salon Kitty's whether I exercise any control over
my dreams should follow me into the blazing stairwell and see for
himself. Fireplaces. So many fireplaces in the Chancellery, that I
can never escape. I can no longer even watch a person light his
cigarette, or a waiter, a candle, without . . .

[Portion illegible.]

. . . an insane kaleidoscope of horrific images, like I saw in
a picture book of Hieronymus Bosch's *The Garden of Earthly
Delights* . . .

[Portion illegible.]

. . . impossible to assess or probe. I must attempt to push
it from consciousness, if not from memory, and concentrate
exclusively on the ritualistic chaos of the final day of almost my
third New Year with the Führer.

❧

Omitting to lock my door brought in Kannenberg, who never
considered knocking even a social grace, much less a political
necessity. Even the Führer was subject to Kannenberg's intrusions.

That the former's complaints were only half-hearted indicated the latter's status unmistakably and signalled such to all who might become irritable at his uncultivated sense of entitlement.

"You're late, Linge," he said, not to be bothered with anything as civilized as the customary *Herr* or military rank.

I hated his guts, of which he had more than an ample amount, but, since he and Bormann appeared to hold some mystical sway over the Führer, God knows how or why, I had to be as discreet as humanly possible.

"Late for what, Herr Kannenberg?" I asked, stalling.

"For the Führer, you clod," he declared through a sneer. "Who do you think?"

"Herr Kannenberg," I replied with a forced patience I knew would roar past him like a runaway train, "I believe I am well within the boundaries of the time set forth for me. If you wish to confirm this with the Führer, you are more than welcome to do so."

Perhaps stymied in his attempt to goad me, the loathsome pig plopped down on my freshly sheeted cot, popping out all my squared corners, and generally making of it a wrinkled mess.

"Not necessary, Linge, I'm sure."

I was even more sure, since invoking the Führer's name ended most debates.

"I say, any further rendezvous with that nosy Jew bitch?"

An icicle shot through my bowels. *Trust no one!* "You have me at a disadvantage, Herr Kannenberg," I said in partial mystification. "What 'nosy Jew bitch'? And what 'rendezvous'?" And, more important but unasked: Why did he care?

He wrinkled his red, bulbous, pocked liquor-nose in distaste. "Come now, Linge, you know who I mean. That fucking Fromm creature. Her note."

Her note? How did he know? As if it was any of the gluttonous swine's business. "May I ask, Herr Kannenberg, whether this is an official inquiry or a casual question? If the former, it would naturally have to go through prescribed Security Service channels."

He'd been a tavern owner, now the Führer's Major Domo.[132] If he'd been seconded to Himmler, or even recruited, I needed to know. All I really knew was his friendship of convenience with Bormann, and Bormann's ambitious envy of Brückner, and that, up to now, was more than enough to avoid him like a vile disease.

"My dear chap," Kannenberg suddenly dribbled, obviously feeling his way an inch at a time and encountering a rough path ahead, "only the most casual of questions, I assure you. The Jew Fromm and her Aryan protector were old patrons of my wine tavern, and I merely wondered. Curiosity, no more."

From my perch, there was nothing "merely" in Kannenberg's world. What to say, then, when something's none of his business, and trusting not one single bit of him in any event?

"Herr Kannenberg," I answered, "as you must know, she was . . . *merely* an accompaniment to Herr Hanfstaengl." I could "merely," too, hoping that somehow he was unaware of the second meeting without the pianist. "May I ask what is your interest?"

The fat man shrugged, straining the closed buttons on his costly woollen jacket. "I told you. Curiosity. The bitch and her Aryan were customers only," he said. "No connexion, I assure you. As she was a Jewess, even though a mysteriously privileged one, I was always on my guard, as you would expect."

"Guard against what? An attempted abduction and conversion?" I asked, risking some levity. "Shall I ask Dr. Morell to examine you for a furtive circumcision?"

---

[132] The chief steward of a large household. A house director.

The dangerous buffoon raised his hand in mock surrender and guffawed theatrically. "My error, Linge. You mustn't take things so seriously, you know. In any event, I must be about perfecting today's festivities, so I will bid you a Happy New Year."

"'To err is human,' I once heard someone say. And, of course, a Happy New Year to *you*," I lied.

With that, he heil-Hitlered, turned, and left through the still open door.

❦

The Führer was completely silent through most of our morning ritual, performed somewhat earlier this time because of all the ceremonial activities he'd be forced to engage in on New Year's Eve. However, while I was foraging through the chaos on his desk for his writing materials, spectacles, and certain files, without warning, he sat me down across from him with a gentle push on my shoulders. He moved from me to his desk and eased himself down gingerly with a blast of flatulence, a clear sign that both his haemorrhoids and his bowels were tormenting him again. Experience had taught me that when he could stand no more, I would be told to summon Morell, so I made no offer and merely waited for what he'd planned to say. After a few moments of wincing, he began.

"We have experienced many a New Year's Eve, Linge, but this is an especially auspicious one. We, that is to say, you and I, and a very few select others stand at the threshold of two new eras, one created by might, and the other maintained by—how shall I put it?—extraordinary means. This confounds you, I know. I will tell you that I actually had this self-same conversation with Hess[133] in Landsberg Prison. My thirteen months of imprisonment seemed

---

[133] Now Deputy Führer.

a long time—the more so because I thought I'd be there for six years. Regardless, I was possessed by a frenzy of liberty, for, without the solitude and meditative qualities of my imprisonment, *Mein Kampf* would not have been written. That period gave me the opportunity to deepen and refine various notions for which I then had only an instinctive feeling. It was during my incarceration, too, that I acquired that fearless faith, that optimism, that confidence in my destiny, which nothing could shake thereafter.

"It's from this time that my conviction dates—a thing that many of even my most ardent and loyal supporters failed to understand—that Germany could gain what it required by force but could never maintain it by force. Hess understood this, and we agreed by solemn oath never to reveal this to anyone who was not thoroughly versed in, shall we say, other means."

At first, I thought, as he rhapsodized that his eyes were glassy with pain, but something inside me suspected that it was a glow of supreme, almost superhuman, conviction. Of course, I had no idea what he was talking about—nothing especially remarkable in that—and so my rapt silence throughout was as justified as it was necessary.

"The coming year, Linge," he continued, "will be like no other in our history, of that you can be sure. And your part in this will be pivotal, do you understand?"

From my dictionary and other literary sources, I understood that "pivotal" meant of vital or critical importance, but I understood nothing else of what he was saying. "I don't think so, my Führer," I answered, but by then, his eyes had cleared and his narrow moustache lifted with his smile.

"Good," he replied obliquely, then, "so you've become popular with the ladies," he said, apropos of nothing. "You see, I told you that a handsome, strapping fellow like you would have his day—or should I say night?" He chuckled almost as lewdly as had Kannenberg.

"My Führer," I replied, "I appear to have gained a reputation that quite exceeds reality. I see women, as you know, but haven't nearly the—"

"Nonono," he interrupted. "I didn't intend to suggest that you were a degenerate like Baur, or even a Lothario[134] like Speer. I meant only that you'd finally emerged from that cocoon you were in when you first arrived. Did Kannenberg inform you about the note?"

Up to that moment, I ingenuously imagined that the Führer had placed Brückner and me in sole charge of the mail, but now, suddenly, it seemed as if he hadn't meant *all mail. What else hadn't he meant?* Since when had Kannenberg gone from house manager, a glorified butler, to a not-so-secret agent, a spy? Only for the Führer? Or for Himmler? Or for both?

"Yes, my Führer," I told him honestly. "He even mentioned Fräulein Fromm."

"Ah, yes, that Jewess gossip monger and, naturally, no friend of the Third Reich but, like a select few of her kind, still useful. She is that cowardly traitor Hanfstaengl's crony anyway. The others, well, that's quite another matter." He opened a drawer, removed an envelope, pushed the drawer closed, and handed the paper to me, which I stretched over and took, not daring to stand or ask why he had possession of it in the first place.

"Are you able to handle complexity, Linge," he asked me straight out after one of his excruciatingly pregnant pauses, "or must it all just happen round you?"

---

[134] An unscrupulous rake.

"I . . . don't know what complexity you mean, my Führer," I answered truthfully, "and how I would recognize it?"

The Führer rubbed his hands together vigorously, smiled a teasing smile, rose, as did I, came round the desk to me, and shook my hand with considerable vigour. "You look tired, Linge," he announced, "and so I will relieve you from any further duties today. Krause can do the honours, and you can renew yourself for the wondrous events of the new year to come. Happy New Year, my friend," he said, as he nudged me gently out the door.

Now, I was determined to locate Brückner, come what might. When I finally saw him at the entrance, he was in discussion with one of the adjutants of Count Ciano.[135] I remained out of sight until Brückner was free of him, then I approached.

"Ah, Heinz," Brückner greeted. "I stopped by your quarters earlier, but you'd already gone. My God," he exhaled loudly, "I thought I never be rid of that arrogant fool Vincenzi. He's more elegant but no less stupid and corrupt than Ciano. Well, thankfully, he's on his way back to his boss with the absent Führer's best wishes for the coming year. At any rate, a busy day ahead for us, eh, my friend?"

"This year, not so busy for me, I think. The Führer gave me the rest of the day and night off. You'll be working with Krause, I'm afraid."

"Let's walk, shall we?" he suggested, and we were off.

"Did the Führer give you a reason?"

"For what?"

---

[135] Count Ciano married Benito Mussolini's daughter Edda, with whom he soon left for Shanghai to serve as Italian consul. On his return to Italy in 1935, he became the minister of press and propaganda.

"The little vacation."

"No."

"That's our Führer," Brückner jested. "Makes sense, though. A person in supreme power who gives reasons is never in power for long. A lesson there, my young friend. It's our reasons that do us in, not our desires or even our methods. The Führer understands this instinctively. As with all things, he's made mystery into an art."

It wasn't snowing, but it was freezing cold, and neither of us was wearing his greatcoat. My whole body was trembling and my teeth chattered, but, like Emerald, Brückner appeared utterly untouched by the icy weather.

"In a sense, though," Brückner said, "the Führer did you a favour. That paranoid maniac, Stalin is reputed to have said that any person he trusted completely he'd have to liquidate, for such a person is the most dangerous of all. In my view, he's one man who needn't ever worry, since he trusts no one but has them liquidated anyway."

I smiled grimly. "Sometimes, Wilhelm, I get the feeling that you, too, withhold your reasons for what you do." I was joking, but not entirely.

"Heinz, anyone with brains and an instinct for self-preservation does so," he said with a shrug. "But none so well as you," he added.

I shook my head. What was he implying?

"Me? I don't understand," I said, truthfully. A day of riddles.

"All right, my untutored friend, I'll spell it out for you. A person who doesn't know his reasons is always more mysterious than he who does, even to himself."

"But what is the benefit to him, if he doesn't know?"

"Benefit? Why, innocence of course, one of the most

underrated qualities in the world. Once lost, never regained, and you're changed forever. Few truly appreciate this."

"How?"

"Each to himself." He smiled. "Now what did you want to speak to me about?"

I told him in detail about my morning visit with Kannenberg and what the Führer just told me.

"What do you make of all this?" I asked him. "Interesting how Bormann's name keeps coming up. Now the vulgar lump Kannenberg. Is Hoffmann next?"

He stroked his chin in thought. "Only interesting to Bormann and Kannenberg, which is their aim, I imagine. Bormann's motives are obvious: he wants my job. Badly. As for Kannenberg? Well, somehow, his fortunes are tied to Bormann's. So far, Hoffmann's only interested in making the Führer photogenic, but you never know."

"At least no one seems to want mine, except Krause, but the Führer sorted that out, right and proper."

"Yes, so it would appear—and has done, since you came here. For some reason, you enjoy a special status that even the hyenas surrounding him can't seem to overcome, no matter the sharpness of their teeth or the guilelessness of their prey."

A cold internal disquiet spread through me. Guileless he called me? Artless, ingenuous, naive, unsophisticated? I calmed myself by realizing that my anger arose from the fact that such puerile and even simpleminded characteristics were seen as intentional facets of my carefully manufactured innocence, but real for all that. He was right, and I was angry at his rightness. Why should I be angry with the truth, even when, according to Brückner, it protected me? However, judging Brückner's comments to be gracious rather than malign, I shook off the issue for the moment.

"So, what will you do, Wilhelm?" I asked him. "*These* hyenas appear to be both relentless, tireless, and ruthless."

Brückner stopped and turned to me and smiled thinly. "That's a lot of *-lesses*, my friend. What will I do? I know that you'd like to think that I have contingency plans for any eventuality, and I'm flattered. Unfortunately, I don't—as much to my dismay as it is to yours. However, one thing this old soldier *has* learned is that to negotiate the minefield of the National Socialist political world, one must adapt, adjust, improvise, and overcome. That way, even without a plan, survival is possible, even though unpredictable. I have no better answer than that, I'm afraid. So, we'll have to see what develops." A shrug.

"Now, as for you, as the undisputed Chancellery stud, you should get a date for tonight, eh? I must go and . . . play the game with your pal Krause and my own pals Bormann and Kannenberg to prepare for the festivities to come." He chuckled, shook me gently by the shoulders, turned, and walked back inside.

Please forgive my verbal inability to do my feelings justice, for I haven't the wits to tell you with eloquence of my emotional reaction to Brückner's remarks. How am I to react to the fatalism of one whose friendship and counsel sustain me through my own need to adapt, adjust, improvise, and overcome in an environment completely alien, unpredictable, and mysterious.

Pushing depression aside with no small effort, I returned to my quarters to change uniforms before this "Chancellery stud" made for Salon Kitty's. Once ready, I heard a light scratching at my door, like that of a cat sharpening its nails. As I turned round, I noticed an envelope slide under the door, followed almost instantaneously by the quickly fading tap-tap-tap of a woman's heels on marble, so I didn't waste any time bothering to open the door. I retrieved the envelope from the floor, searching for any identifying markings on it, but saw none, save for some block-printed words: "I hope that you are not rendered anxious by this mode of delivery."

As I mentioned in another entry, it was hardly the first time I'd experienced this "mode of delivery" since entering the Führer's service. But somehow, this time, it felt different, although I couldn't assign a name to the feeling. So, against both my nature and my history, I retrieved the bottle of schnapps I'd received as a Christmas gift from Kempka and downed several shot glass's worth, then, once in a suitable state, locked my door, wobbled to my privy, flopped down on the lid, peeled open the side of the envelope, slid out its contents in two tries (a single sheet of anonymous foolscap, folded three times), and struggled through the tiny-type, single-spaced, edge-to-edge message:

My Dearest Heinz. It's been such a long time and I've missed you terribly. I'm delighted that you and Zarah Leander are keeping company. She's a lovely woman and, like you, trapped by circumstance. However, unlike you, she is fully aware of it and so consciously made her Devil's bargain. She is also quite married, though she didn't care to inform you of that fact. I have the fervent hope that you will not follow her lamentable example. You must have at least a glimmer of realization that you possess special gifts, even though you may be unaware of their nature and extent. But I *do know*, Heinz. Unfortunately, your Führer and a few select others know as well, but with catastrophic motives, so time is precious. Another New Year is beginning, and as Hitler promised, one unlike any before it. Before long, he will call upon you to use your gifts for a purpose that would cause even Satan to shudder. I am just one voice. But there will be other voices, as unlike mine as true humanity is from monstrous brutality. Nietzsche wrote that: "Alas, the time of the most despicable man is coming. Behold, I show you the last man." Please, Heinz, please heed Nietzsche's words, for though it may not have been a warning to him, it is truly a warning to us now. Act, Heinz, act boldly and resolutely before it is too late. I regret not being able to bid you a happy new year, for it will not be. But I can, at least, convey to you all my hope and affection. Your E.

For the moment, my flummoxed brain was too muddled with schnapps to do more than squat in my skull like a mannequin and cause my eyes to stare blankly through the bathroom doorway into my tiny cell. Any critical faculties I might have were fully neutralized. I could only hear a faint hum of semi-consciousness. Then, after a timeless time, a conversation I'd had with the Führer when I'd been with him only a few months broke through the murk:

"I trust my instincts completely, Linge, and so I've given you a position of supreme trust. I know what you are. But I would wish to know from your own lips who you are."

"I am whom you see, my Führer. I am your valet, nothing more."

"Linge, I have spoken to you as I have spoken to no one else,

high or low. Have you drawn nothing from this singular fact? No, Linge, there is far more to you. Infinitely more."

"Then, my Führer, only you are aware of it."

"I hope so, but I suspect not so. But I am being obscure. What I meant was that you didn't just materialize on my doorstep, did you?"

"But, my Führer, in a way, I did materialize on your doorstep, as you put it. I ask you, who was I before I entered your household? A nothing: a vagrant, a transient, a hooligan, a common labourer. That is to say, a cipher. Any meaning I may have achieved has been in your service."

"I hope so, but I suspect not so."

And now, as always, his suspicions have been amply confirmed. From the note, and even more, the sender, I knew what I was being asked—entreated—to do, and I wondered who had seen the note before it was slipped under my door and what they thought it to mean. I couldn't imagine it puzzling them for long. For the moment, I pushed the whole treacherous notion aside. But as I did so, I knew I was sweating away the numbing effects of the liquor, for something else now edged in, a part of a conversation I'd had with the bogus Fräulein Schroeder:

"I am curious, Linge, so indulge me. I mean no offense, but personally, I refuse to believe that you are as simple as you appear. Even you must have some substance, motivation, ambition, something you want, I mean, above and beyond being a mindless servant."

"I want nothing."

"Then need."

"That, even less."

"Ach! A simple question and you run from it."

"No, Fräulein Schroeder, I run from myself."

The last, I'd whispered to her receding back as she strode away. But now, as I sat heavily on my toilet lid, I considered what she'd asked: after all my experiences at the Chancellery since that fateful day in 1935, and after at least one attempt on my life, did I still want nothing? Need nothing? Was I still the same naïve and ignorant greenhorn who accepted the Führer's offer of employment without even considering the way he'd offered it—and perhaps, the reason for that way?

I recalled what an old drunken tramp told me as we both huddled in a slum hallway against the frigid air in the deep winter of 1932. "Old son," he slurred, "there are only two sorts of people: the users and the used. Government don't matter; country don't matter; class don't matter; money don't matter. If you ain't the one, you're t'other. And how that happens? Well, look round you. We're here, freezing our balls off in a fuckin' dump, along with the rest of the garbage, an' we don't even have what it takes to live in it. Check yourself out in five years and see where you are. I'll still be here, you bet; that is, if I'm still breathing. Where will you be, kid?" I thought hard about that, despite the humming in my head. Have I merely traded one frigid hallway for another? The user or the used. Was what that old tramp said as simple as that?

I burned and flushed the note, after joking grimly to myself that I might as well have tacked it to the central Chancellery bulletin board for all the secrecy it still possessed, then sardonically wished myself for the coming 1938, a happy new year.

1938

1 *January 1938*

I PERFORMED MY morning routine slowly as if I were moving through wet cement. Since, after all the festivities of the previous night, the Führer always rose later than usual, I was freed from the Führerbuzzer for a time, but my dreams were occupying so much of my brain that I felt it was suffocating. As I fiddled with my lunch in the officers' mess, all I could see was the dream's distorted stairwell, but this time, there had been no cacophony, no fire, no incinerated bodies—just an Escher-imagined structure, all surrealistic twisted shabbiness, repugnant graffiti, and putrid detritus. And this time, I'd been alone in it all the while, and had no idea why.

It was only later, back in my quarters, that my brain returned to the note. Emerald could have said all that her provocative note contained, and more, and made it all the more striking by actually being with me. Well out of view and earshot, of course. Were we together, I would have asked her why she hated the Führer so much as to crave his assassination—*and at my hands!* Why would she—or anyone—imagine that I would even countenance, much less perform, such an insane—not to say traitorous—act? And what of all those—not least the Führer himself—who routinely intercept my mail? Do they understand and ignore, or search for meaning that eludes them, and so wait for action to interpret it for them?

And yet, despite all this, I still believe in my essential invisibility, for I know that my innermost self is withheld from all, save me. But if they knew that—

My deliberations were disrupted by a soft knock on my door, the clicking turn of a key, and the second entry (to my knowledge) of the fearsome SS-Obergruppenführer und General der Polizei, Reinhard Heydrich. He was accompanied by a man I'd never before seen but whose uniform announced him as a lieutenant colonel. The latter carried a leather briefcase the size of a valise.

I saluted them both enthusiastically, and my salute was returned by both, though with considerably less vigour. Heydrich then proceeded to sit down on my cot, while the other stood at a perfunctory version of attention. Thoughts becoming words, yes, but thoughts generating events? Once, I would have considered the notion absurd. No more.

Heydrich wished me a happy new year with sneering bonhomie, which I returned with a click and nod for emphasis. Creatures like Heydrich know instinctively that fear lies only one thin layer below casualness or bravado. They instinctively know because they instinctively create it.

"Since you failed to engage in last night's festivities," he said, again through his thin, mirthless smile, as if I'd somehow engaged in a disloyal act, "I thought we might enjoy a belated celebration here." He gave an almost imperceptible nod to the colonel and the latter set the case down on my cot, opened it, removed a bottle of expensive-looking wine and three pewter tumblers, opened the bottle, filled each tumbler and handed the first to me, then one to Heydrich, and held onto the third, all rehearsed.

"I'm . . . truly honoured, Herr General," I stammered, bereft of anything more elegant—or strategic—to say.

Heydrich stared at me, his thin lips set in that same ambiguous slit I assumed was a grin. "Not at all, Linge. It is my pleasure. With all my duties and responsibilities, I scarcely have the time to visit my home, much less the Chancellery, and, of course, Reichsführer Himmler prefers to be the exclusive visitor to the Führer from our humble department. And if I don't see the Führer, I don't see you, so there you are. In any event, let's all drink to what promises to be a truly significant year for the Reich." He raised his tumbler and downed the liquid in one swallow. The colonel and I followed suit. I was almost imploding with curiosity about when he would decide to make his true motive known, even obliquely, since I had more than a passing suspicion of what it was.

"Shall we have another?" he said, his tone a galaxy away from inquisitive. The colonel poured and we drank.

"I say, Linge," he said with his usual menacing nonchalance, as he surveyed my surroundings, "has the Führer truly made a voracious reader of you? I see that even the precious space beneath your cot can't contain all the volumes. What's your current project, if I may ask?" His sinister cordiality had me almost vibrating with anxiety—which I assumed was its intent, but he didn't allow me to answer. "Eichmann, fetch me that book peeking out from there," he ordered the colonel, while aiming his long, narrow index finger (not unlike a hunter's pointing dog's stance) towards the area just under my small armoire. He immediately retrieved the book and brought it to Heydrich without even glancing at the cover. The general studied the spine far longer than the short title warranted. "Ah," he finally said, "*The Magic Mountain*. We are quite fortunate to have our own private libraries immune to our minister of Public Enlightenment and Propaganda's flames, yes?"

"This volume is a loan from the Führer's personal library," I responded, feebly-but-accurately.

"Just so," replied Heydrich. "The Führer is, of course, beyond the contamination of such filth. Do you actually understand it? I found it to be rather boring, dense, and obscure—I imagine through the influence of his Jewess wife,[136] don't you find it so?"

"Herr General," I obfuscated, "I have not yet had the opportunity to read it, but if it confounded one such as you, what possible value could it hold for the likes of me?"

I could have been mistaken, but Heydrich's thin lips actually seemed to form as close to a genuine smile as I'd observed up to that moment.

"If nothing else, Linge," he remarked sardonically, "the influence of the Führer has enhanced your degree of sophistication, if nothing else." Then a quick nod to Eichmann. "One last toast, I'm afraid," he said to me, "since we must attend to pressing matters," to which Eichmann obliged instantly and efficiently. "To a new era for the Reich," Heydrich proclaimed, and we all drank to it, I, however, being unsure what the term "new era" meant to such a creature. To me, it had no meaning because I had no substance on which to fasten it.

Heydrich then rose slowly, like a praying mantis simulating a bear, while Eichmann collected the empty tumblers and placed them back in the case. "You may keep the wine," he said to me, "and I do hope you can make more sense of *Magic Mountain* than I did," he said in obvious jest. "Oh yes," he added at the door, "and perhaps you can call me and explain what your . . . heart's

---

[136] Katia Pringsheim, the daughter of a wealthy assimilated Jewish academic.

desire meant by 'Nietzsche's warning,' and what bold act she urged you to perform. In your spare time, naturally." It wasn't a question or even an order. It was Heydrich's warning.

∽

One thing I discovered about this unique environment, my friend, is that the most important things are said as after-thoughts, usually as parting comments, remarks, or questions in doorways. I wanted to ask the general of Security Services and Police whether any progress had been made concerning who had attempted to do me in and why, but I held back because if he had anything he wished me to know, he would have told me, in or out of the doorway. I confess that I was not a little disturbed by this but had nowhere to go with it. What did they all know, and why withhold it from me? And who were the all? These, among others, were questions that would have ever occurred to a bricklayer's apprentice, and certainly not the engineer I'd hoped one day to be while taking shit from all the bricklayers who were senior to me. If I were anyone but myself, how would I have survived in this political world in which mirrors faced each other into infinity? And yet, did the Führer and Emerald know things about me that . . .

[Portions missing.]

AGAIN, I ATTEMPTED to locate Brückner, but no one appeared to know his whereabouts, save that he was "away." Double mail duty for me, then, until further notice.

This morning, I learnt that what the Führer had "predicted" the previous year would come to pass with a vengeance (pun intended). While I was tidying up his study, he was engaged in an "animated" conversation (to say the least) with General Göring and Reichsführer-SS Himmler about General Blomberg and his recent wedding to Erna Gruhn. Schroeder was sitting primly on a small wooden office chair, taking shorthand notes.

"*The blockhead!*" the Führer ranted to Himmler, as he "skated" round his office. "*The fucking numbskull. And he brings Göring and even ME into his stupid mess!*[137] *And this was the man to whom I entrusted my army! A man who thinks with his prick instead of his brain!*"

I couldn't miss the past tense in the sentence. There was also something in the Führer's words and actions that somehow rang off-key.

The medal-laden Luftwaffe chief merely sat there like a wax effigy of a Latin American *Generalissimo*, head down, gazing at his massive belly.

---

[137] Luftwaffe chief Hermann Göring had been Blomberg's best man, and Hitler himself had served as a witness at the wedding.

"Heinrich," the Führer continued, his bombastic tone edging even further upward, "from what you told me, the Berlin police discovered that she had a long criminal record, had posed for pornographic photographs, had been a previously convicted prostitute who had been registered—*registered, Heinrich!*—as a prostitute in the files of seven large German cities; she was in the Berlin criminal files, she had also been sentenced by the Berlin courts for distributing indecent pictures. This, they knew *after the wedding!* Where were they *before the wedding?* Your office investigates anyone who may have had a Jewish neighbour in the fourteenth century, but my army minister is free to marry this notorious trollop?" He moved over to his desk and flopped down heavily.

The Reichsführer-SS stared up at his boss for a few pregnant moments, saying nothing.

"You may leave now, Fräulein Schroeder. Type up your notes, and have them delivered to me as quickly as you can."

Since when did the Führer ever want someone other than the note-taker to deliver sensitive material?

Schroeder shot up. "Yes, my Führer," she said, closed the cover on her stenographer's pad, saluted, and left without even a glance in my direction.

"You have something to say, Heinrich?" asked the Führer.

Himmler's moustache lifted slightly, his most strenuous attempt at mirth. "I would venture that our plan worked out exactly as we'd hoped, my Führer," he said.

The Führer smiled for the first time. "Yes, quite so. You agree, Hermann?"

Göring lifted his head. "Yes, my Führer," he said, "even better than I'd hoped."

The Führer nodded. "Can you imagine the consequences of that fucking tramp's history getting out *before* the wedding?"

Göring splayed his bladder lips. "That idiot of a Blomberg would have cast the bitch to the four winds and still be heading your army, and you'd have to fire him. Now," he sneered, "on the threat of making his wife's past public knowledge, he can resign like a . . . gentleman and your skirts remain pristine.[138] I'd venture that at this very minute, Schroeder is confiding 'secretly' all she heard in here to everyone in the Chancellery," he chortled. "All will expect you to kick Blomberg's ass down the front steps, but he will be spared by a dignified resignation. Pure genius, my Führer."

The Führer pursed his lips and nodded his full acceptance of Göring's assessment. "True," he said, "but the job's not finished. One down and one to go, as they say in sports argot. Yes, Hermann?"

"Most definitely, my Führer," he nodded with such vigour that his medals clanged like cathedral bells.

I knew the what—and who—of it and didn't have to wait long as I redusted the furniture.

"Where is Heydrich's old file?" the Führer asked Himmler.[139] "I happen to know he disobeyed my orders."

Himmler leaned over and reached into his ever-present attaché case, withdrew some typed sheets bearing the imprint

---

[138] Hitler ordered Blomberg to have the marriage annulled to avoid a scandal and to preserve the integrity of the army. Blomberg refused to annul the marriage, but, after Göring threatened to make his wife's past public knowledge, on 27 January 1938, he resigned from his posts.

[139] In 1936, Reinhard Heydrich had prepared a file on Fritsch with allegations of homosexuality and had passed the information on to Hitler, but Hitler had rejected it and ordered Heydrich to destroy the file. However, he did not do so.

of the Interior Ministry, and held them up. "Haste makes waste, my Führer. I judged at the time that you were only half-hearted in your decision, and so I had Heydrich save them on my instructions."

"Ever the pack rat, eh, Heinrich?" the Führer joked. "And a good thing too. Have Heydrich go to Fritsch with the report[140] and give him the same opportunity as that fool of a Blomberg, to take the honourable way out.[141] Then I'll bring in that lapdog Keitel as their replacement, and we'll no longer have honour to impede my progress."

"Is that all, my Führer," asked Himmler, who'd just placed the papers back in his briefcase and locked it.

"Nothing more for you, Heinrich," the Führer answered, "or for you, Hermann. I'm having papers drawn up replacing that limp thorn von Neurath with von Ribbentrop. Always good to have a few 'vons' to display at embassies. Soon, my friends, the transformation will be complete, and those who would impede my vision—and are still breathing—will be walking the unemployment lines. Well done, Heinrich. Now, we immediately proceed to our next objective. I'll call a meeting of all the relevant parties in two days to give them their orders for the task ahead.

---

[140] In the document, Fritsch was again accused of being a homosexual by Himmler and his SS, and, moreover, it claimed that Fritsch had been encouraged by General Ludwig Beck to carry out a military putsch against the Hitler regime.

[141] By all available evidence, Hitler used the situation to transfer the duties of the Ministry of War (*Reichskriegsministerium*) to a new organization—the Supreme Command of the Armed Forces (*Oberkommando der Wehrmacht*, or OKW)—and Wilhelm Keitel, who became the new head of the OKW on 4 February 1938. This weakened the traditional Army High Command (*Oberkommando des Heeres*, or OKH), which was now subordinated to the OKW.

Some will, of course, call me hasty, but I agree with Dante that 'the wisest are the most annoyed at the loss of time.'"

With that, Himmler and Göring rose, saluted, and left me alone with the Führer. I'd read that statement from Dante in Milcher's *Volume of Quotes*, but a footnote also told any interested reader that, ultimately, Dante was condemned to perpetual exile, and if he returned to Florence, he could be burned at the stake. I wondered whether the Führer had read that footnote, but I would never ask him.

I believed that the Führer was about to say something to me, when his face suddenly reddened and his eyes squeezed shut with pain. I ran over to his desk and slammed my hand down on the button that summoned Dr. Morell. I moved back, remaining stationary and mute. Soon, there was a flurry of garbled voices outside, Morell rushed in, ordered me to leave, and moved a doubled-up, groaning Führer to his bathroom. I was more than thankful to Morell, since I had no wish to stay for the "festivities."

I had lunch with the newly returned Brückner at the Romanisches Café, once the hangout of Berlin's scruffy intellectual fringe, now an ocean of Party and military uniforms and pin-striped business suits, the offhanded waiters replaced with military wind-up toys.

"I say, it's as if we'd never left the Chancellery." It was a lame joke of sorts, and, fortunately, Brückner took it as such.

"Undeniable, but it's reasonably close to home, and we have far less of a freezing walk to take and far fewer duties to perform, save eat, drink, and chat. A reasonable trade-off, it seems to me. In any event, I haven't seen you for a while, so I thought you might catch me up on the latest doings."

"You never told me you were going away. I sorely missed you, my friend."

"Much appreciated, Heinz. I too felt the lack."

Brückner pulled the bottle from the ice bucket on the narrow folding table beside us and poured me a glass of wine—expensive, of course—and then one for himself. "You know, it struck me while I was away that we've been working together for a number of years, been through a bit, and yet I know very little about you. Are you so bereft of background, or am I being victimized by my own discretion?"

I dreaded such questions, even from a man I so respected and admired as Brückner—perhaps because I did so respect and admire him—but I had no time to make such analytical distinctions. "You mean Himmler doesn't have it all and more?" I joked.

Brückner laughed, but no more than politeness would dictate. "You know, Heinz," he replied, "'His Himmlership' has information aplenty but only concerning his pet hatreds: Jews, communists, homosexuals, and the intelligentsia."

"To be frank, Wilhelm," I said, "my 'background,' as you called it, *was* bereft, in and of itself. I came from nothing, had done nothing, was nothing, until I began my duties at the Chancellery. Not a matter for pity. It is what it is—no different from a string of losing rolls of the dice, then, finally, and with no warning, getting a jackpot hand at cards. Nevertheless, I always believed that how I got here wasn't important. The fact is: I am here, for what *that's* worth or whatever that may mean." I hoped that humble obfuscation would suffice, since there was nothing else I wished him—or anyone else, for that matter—to know.

"You mean fate or luck?" he asked. "Well, my friend, I don't believe you could be more mistaken, but I won't press, since you're clearly sensitive on the issue."

Not sensitive, Wilhelm, I wanted to say. Damaged and confounded—far more troubling states, but not for even Brückner to know. "Where had you been all this time?" I asked him, to radically change the subject.

His one-eyed gaze illustrated unmistakably both his knowledge of my motives and the idiocy of his activities, of which I had yet to learn.

"Between us only, yes?" he cautioned.

"Between us only. Who else would I tell, save you?"

He laughed again. "*Touché.*"

I squinted with feigned ignorance.

"Forgive me, Heinz. You make me forget at times. *Touché* means a term used as an acknowledgement of a good or clever point made at one's expense by another person."

Having memorized the dictionary, I knew what it meant, but was gratified that Brückner didn't know that I would know. My secret was still secure. And yet I felt a strange and deep sadness, because, once again, I'd forced myself to hide my light under a bushel, even with him, no less than with everyone else. I suddenly experienced a loneliness impossible for me to describe. As I write this, I hated him in my mind and heart for being so important to me, and, perhaps insanely, I couldn't imagine the German people not hating the Führer for the same reason, yet there was only adoration, and I had not the wits to comprehend the difference.

"The Führer, finally succumbing to Himmler's nagging, dispatched me on a secret mission to California, a state in America. They felt that I should meet with a Winona and Norman Stephens, sympathisers of the pro-Nazi Silver Legion of

America,[142] to judge sentiment towards future German assertiveness. I'd never heard of the Stephens or that organization, but Himmler apparently had, so off I went. However, I discovered quickly that to assess American attitudes by talking with the Stephens would be like getting an opinion of reality by interviewing a schizophrenic."

I found Brückner's analogy droll but bewildering, and thoroughly enjoyed it—more because it was a reminder of what I'd missed while he was away than for any informational value. "How did your report fare?"

He waved my question away with a sweep of his hand. "More important, have the authorities made any progress with that attempt on your life at Kitty's?"

Then I saw her. "Look, Wilhelm," I said in lieu of an answer. "Isn't that Bella Fromm sitting in the very rear with that paunchy, merchant-looking chap?"

Brückner turned his head awkwardly so that his only eye would attend to my description.

"That's Frau Bella, all right," he said, with not a little

---

[142] In Reichsführer-SS Himmler's view, Los Angeles was supposed to be the "seat of American fascism," from where Adolf Hitler could rule the United States and restore order. Winona and Norman Stephens were convinced by a German agent named Schmidt, sent by Himmler, that when Germany ultimately won the war, the American government would not be able to stay afloat, thus leading to a time of anarchy in the United States. During that time, they would be able to live in their self-sustaining community and then come out when the opportunity presented itself to help with the German takeover. So, they set out to build a massive area they could use to keep them safe during a war. All in all, it is said that over $4 million was invested in this ranch, and they were able to create an amazing set of structures with that money: a power station, machine shed, fully irrigated hillside for growing food, raised gardens, a massive water tank, and even a place to store diesel fuel. They also built multiple cement stairs up the side of the neighbouring hill to help with the farming and to patrol the area.

snideness in his tone. "If I were any sane mink, chinchilla, or sable, I would run for my life at the very sight of her. I'll wager every Jew in Berlin would give even the little they have left to know her formula for her success. Wonder who the chubby fellow is."

I gazed surreptitiously round the room at all the überofficers' magnificent uniforms, the tedious men in brown and grey bespoke suits and wide-brimmed hats, and the women, dressed with breathtaking stolidity.

"Probably most of the people here know," I responded. "We're probably the only ones who don't."

She must have seen us, for she whispered something to her natty table partner, who proceeded to wave us over.

"What shall we do?" I asked Wilhelm.

"Naturally, we go over and satisfy our curiosity," he replied blithely. "If we're questioned later by Müller's and Heydrich's agents, who appear to be sitting all round, we can always say we're conducting our own investigation."

We got up and went over to Frau Bella's table, bare of all, save a tablecloth. The portly gentleman rose to greet us while Frau Bella sat with her slender hand extended languidly. After all the handshakes, Bella introduced her partner as Herr Lochner,[143] and I introduced Brückner. She invited us to sit with them, and we obliged.

"I'd wager," Bella remarked with a sarcastic smile, "that service will improve tremendously from this moment on." Then she turned to Brückner with those piercing brown eyes. "You see, General, restaurants nowadays run on two kinds of time: Aryan

---

[143] Louis P. Lochner was chief correspondent in Berlin for the Associated Press and president of the Berlin branch of the American Chamber of Commerce.

time, in which service is actually performed within the patron's lifetime; and Jewish time, in which waiters hold back indefinitely until we tire of waiting and leave. It's been quite effective, but my feeling is that they'll rethink their time sense in our favour, don't you, Louis?" Lochner just smiled thinly and shrugged.

Bella was right. An obsequious waiter suddenly raced over to our table, bringing a full set of utensils, glasses, napkins, and menus. "Shall I clear your old table, Herr General?" he asked Brückner, who replied, stone-faced: "Naturally, that is, unless you wish us to return to it." The waiter, clearly understanding Brückner's meaning, but still clearly the rabid Party member, said only to him: "Can I get your party anything to drink, Herr General?" In this, all deferred to Brückner's decision to have the waiter bring the restaurant's most lavish champagne.

After we ordered our food, Bella turned to Brückner.

"I understand that you, too, work for Herr Hitler, yes?"

"You possess a keen understanding, Frau Fromm," he replied. "I have the honour to be the Führer's chief adjutant. Lieutenant Colonel Linge and I share responsibilities at the Chancellery, but I assume you already know that."

Bella looked at me, then back to Brückner. "Yes, I imagine I already did," she riposted. "Has the Chancellery been in a dither over General Blomberg's recent wedding? It's the journalist in me that asks this."

"A dither? Hardly," he lied. "Even generals are permitted some privacy and privileges, save from journalists, of course. Who or what he marries is up to him, not the Führer."

I knew that she was attempting to provoke some indecorous remark from Brückner, and even though I knew he would not permit her to succeed, I felt an obligation to intervene, and so I turned to Lochner. "I say, Herr Lochner, we all know about

Frau Bella and her unique situation, but what is it like to be in your position?"

Lochner took an anxious sip of his champagne and placed his glass down firmly. "I, too, am a journalist, though not quite as successful as Bella here, yet, even as a pacifist, I managed to get two interviews with Herr Hitler, once in 1930 and another in 1933. However, I have serious doubts about ever getting a third." Fromm smiled at that.

I wondered what Lochner's pacifism had to do with interviewing the Führer, but then I thought of that Chinese proverb: "Be careful of your words, for your words become your actions," and so left my wonderings unexpressed.

"And why do you doubt, Herr Lochner?" Brückner asked, puckishly, I imagined, to mask his real curiosity. "The Führer is interviewed constantly."

"Interviews by Reichsminister Goebbels don't count," Bella joked on the square, and we all chuckled to lighten the atmosphere as our food arrived promptly and courteously.

"Ah, then that lessens the number considerably," Brückner told her with a slim smile. "The Führer is building a new Germany, and that leaves little time for chatting with reporters. In any event, he believes in journalists reporting on deeds, not words."

"Admirable," said Lochner. "And so what deeds will he have us reporting on?"

With the assistance of the champagne, I was just beginning to relax, when, beneath the table, Bellas's foot tapped mine and she stealthily placed a folded piece of paper on my lap. I took it with no less furtiveness and slid it gradually into my outside jacket pocket. *What was she up to?* I wondered with disquiet.

"In the month to come," Brückner said, "look to the

southeast. You, Herr Lochner, will be especially pleased, but I'll leave it for you to figure out why." He turned to me and tilted his head towards the entrance. "Heinz, it's time we got back, don't you think?"

Taking what was certainly not a hint, I agreed. "Yes," I told our "hosts," "the general is right. Punctuality is highly prized at the Chancellery—and tardiness is highly noticed," I added.

"Please allow us to pay," Brückner said, moving his palm forward for emphasis. "It's no trouble, since we're not charged. It was a pleasure meeting you, Herr Lochner, and you, Frau Fromm." With that, Brückner and I stood up, heel-clicked, presented a salute with a "Heil Hitler" so that all round could observe, shrugged into our leather greatcoats, and left, neither of us glancing back.

"Oddly, Heinz," Brückner said, as we climbed gratefully into his wonderfully heated two-seater, "I must confess a sense of pity for Frau Bella. She was bitter about poor restaurant service. I predict that soon she and the rest of them will be denied even entry. A pity too. Barring the Jews—even those shabby Orthodox oddities—from active life, will render the Führer's Reich not unlike the Führer's meals: utterly devoid of texture and flavour. Of course, you never heard me say this."

To be frank, I couldn't *believe* I heard him say this. Not that I'd ever heard him rail against the Jews, as had Himmler, Goebbels, Heydrich, and even the Führer, but, as a Party member and a general of the SA, I couldn't imagine that he didn't share their virulent antipathy.

"Of course, Wilhelm," I assured him. "You know how poor my memory is. I've already forgotten it."

Brückner's lips curled upward. "That's the ticket, Heinz. Just out of curiosity, just what did Frau Bella pass to you under the table? I hope it wasn't a love note—for your sake, naturally."

Brückner may have had only one eye, but it was quite a formidable one, and to deny his observation would have been foolishly pointless. "I have no idea," I said in truth. "I just took it and slipped it into my pocket. I agree that a love note from a Jewess would be, to say the least, awkward."

"Yes, to say the least," he echoed, in a far more cautionary tone than before. "I must confess to an unseemly curiosity, but you know that my memory is no better than yours. Perhaps you would read it now, aloud?" As a gesture of finality, he reached over and opened the glove box, removed a small torch and handed it to me.

It seemed oddly disloyal that I would even consider refusing Brückner's intrusion on my privacy to be an act of mean-spiritedness, so I took the paper from my pocket, unfolded it, shone the torch on the crabbed handwriting, and recited:

Herr Linge: Perhaps I am mistaken, but I believe that I got to know you in the short time we shared in my old shop. I solemnly assure you that I would never ask a favour, especially a perilous one, if the situation were not desperate and I did not believe fully that you would, at least, consider my desperate request without reporting me or compromising yourself. If my assessment of you is accurate, and you agree to at least listen, please contact Frau Bella, and she will provide you with a way to contact me. I needn't tell you that time is of the essence, and so please forgive my brazen appeal to what I believe

is your humanity and generosity. With most seriousness
and hope, A. Adelsheimer.

"Adelsheimer. Adelsheimer," Brückner murmured absently
to himself, then said to me: "A Jew? How is it that you know
this Adelsheimer?" His tone was not of malign interrogation but
benign curiosity.

"You know of my hobby, Wilhelm. I wanted no part of
Hoffmann if I could avoid it. This Adelsheimer ran a camera
shop and agreed to teach me to develop film and also to use
his equipment. And, for a time, my presence protected him,
that is, until he was forbidden even to work in his shop, then
I was forced to prevail on Hoffmann for darkroom privileges.
That's all."

Brückner nodded. "And did he get to know you?"

I shrugged. "I don't recall more than photographic lessons
from expert to novice."

Brückner pursed his lips. "Then what could he have been
referring to?"

"Perhaps a relative lack of political zeal on my part? I don't
know. We had so few actual conversations. He may have read my
hesitation as some sort of nonconformity."

"He may well have," Brückner said. "I say this in all friendship, Heinz, but I think you were a babe in the woods."

I knew that; what of the world did I know? But what was
Brückner implying? "What do you mean, Wilhelm?"

"What do I mean?" he asked. "That you wouldn't know what
I mean, for a start. I mean that if you only used his lessons and
equipment, why would this Jew presume to believe, in a million
years, that a high-ranking officer of the SS would help *him of all
people*, and . . . what did he say? . . . that he felt he got to know

you to the point that he could ask you *any* favour, much less a 'perilous favour'? What did he think he got to know? Now, you see what I mean? It could be Heydrich or Müller asking you these questions. And perhaps they *are* asking them—through Adelsheimer. I learned, long ago, my friend, never to underestimate a person just because you don't like him."

I had no way of answering his questions but felt the need to say something to fill the vacuum left by Brückner's practical wisdom. "This must . . . must have been . . . all in his mind," I sputtered. "All in his need to . . . I suppose, believe. Otherwise, why such craziness?"

Brückner took a deep breath and let it out slowly. "Heinz, it's craziness when he writes to you. It's far more than craziness when his message is delivered in public to the Führer's valet by a racial enemy of the Reich. Do you not see the position this puts you in? And me, as well, for being with you when this happened?"

Without warning, Brückner pulled over and stopped. "Has what I've said sunk in, or do you require official proof of your suicidal naïveté?"

I began to tremble, despite the auto's efficient heater. "Do you mean that?" I asked him.

He reached over and banged me gently on the head with his fist. "Heinz, Heinz," he said. "Would we be having this . . . conversation if I meant you harm? On the contrary, I want to save you from yourself. Everyone—and I mean everyone—in the Chancellery managed to learn of that rather provocative 'love note' from your 'green goddess,' and then promptly dismiss it. You think that was magic? Is that what you think? But getting a help-me note from a Jew, delivered by a Jewess, raises the stakes for us all, my friend."

What could I say? "You know that this note will never see the

Chancellery." I tore it into little pieces, rolled down the window, tossed them into the freezing air, and cranked the window back up quickly. "There," I said, "so much for that, yes?" Yet when I said it, I knew Brückner was far from satisfied.

We began moving again. "Heinz," he replied with barely controlled impatience, "so much for what, exactly? No one will see the note from this moment on, true. But how many may have seen it before she slipped it to you, or saw her slip it to you, for that matter? But far more important, because it is far more disastrous in its potential, is her ability to slip it to you in the first place."

I knew where he was going, and I wanted to stop him but had not the means. "We were with her." A statement more lame could not be imagined by me.

He patted me gently on the knee. "Listen to what you just said. You must think things through. All the way through. My friend, just consider the following: How did Frau Fromm know that you would be in that restaurant? Do you think she just walks around Berlin with such a note in the expectation of running into you? Since we're on call at any hour every day, at least twenty key people at the Chancellery knew where and when we would be eating. Now imagine how many *really knew*, once those twenty knew. I believe it's more than reasonable to assume that someone there—or even beyond—tipped off Fromm, for what other possibilities are left to us? Coincidence? Spectacularly good fortune on Fromm's part? What? And, finally, Heinz-the-hapless, what if it *were* just a miraculous coincidence for her to have such a note in her possession at that particular time and place? What if she, as a dangerously well-informed Jewess, were picked up for a friendly chat with Müller or Heydrich for any reason—or for no reason—and they discovered that note? Are the skies clearing up for you now a little?"

He was entirely right, of course. Anyone who lives the clandestine life, prizing underestimation and invisibility, would be shattered by what had happened. *Yes, Wilhelm,* I wanted to tell him, *I asked myself all those questions and more. Yes, Wilhelm, from my first moment in the Chancellery, there appeared to be forces at work that make my situation continually treacherous.* But how could I articulate this even to someone as trustworthy as Brückner, a man I consider the older brother I never had, and still maintain my façade of puerile innocence? And there was also the "simple" fact that, articulate or not, I had no idea what those forces are. Or, for that matter, what my situation is.

So, I merely nodded an agreement and we rode the rest of the way in silence.

[There are no legible entries between
20 January and 9 February.]

I WAS SUMMONED early to prepare the Führer for a day he called "a natural but major step" in realizing his vision.

I stood by while the Führer dictated a letter to the Austrian chancellor saying that he would consent to meet with him at the Berghof on 12 February to "finally settle matters of critical importance." As he was dictating this last part, he chuckled.

The rest of the day and into the evening was consumed with preparations for the trip tomorrow.

AFTER READYING THE Führer for a day of planning for his meeting, I bumped (literally) into Fräulein Wolf, who was on her way to take dictation. I could never understand the Führer's attitude towards her. Breathtakingly ugly, as feminine as a Hamburg stevedore[144] (even to the moustache), a perpetual sourpuss, physically infirm, and a miserably inefficient secretary, her only "positive" features being a hysterical loyalty to the Führer and her role as a major purveyor of gossip to Bormann. She was one of only a select few who could make Fräulein Schroeder seem beguilingly benevolent and alluring. I make every reasonable attempt to avoid her, and, given the vastness of the Chancellery and her staggering consumption of sick leave, I've been reasonably successful. But in the relative confines of the Berghof and with Schroeder's absence, I was trapped.

"Are you this clumsy with the Führer?" she snapped once she'd ostentatiously—and needlessly—adjusted her bulky brown tweed suit to its original pristine sexlessness.

"My apologies, Fräulein Wolf," I replied with fruitless insincerity.

"You're an oaf," she told me by way of establishing her hostility unmistakably. "I trust the Führer is ready?"

I resisted as best I could but finally compromised with my

---

[144] *Hafenarbeiter*, a dock worker.

desire to spoon out her face. "Of course, Fräulein Wolf, or I wouldn't have been here to accost you."

"Your failed attempt at wit is duly noted," she spat.

And will be reported, I was certain, and instantly began considering all the lies I would have to tell to make things right. But she must have seen my face.

"Don't worry, Herr Linge," she said without expression. "I refuse to burden the Führer with such trivialities while he is burdened with the task of expanding the Reich."

I was hardly oblivious to the "while" in her assurance. "I'm most grate—"

Before I could finish my grovelling, she moved past me as if I'd vaporised.

Brückner had been of two minds about coming along: on the one hand, he desperately wished to give a wide berth to his arch enemy, Bormann; and on the other, he feared that, without his constant and active presence, Bormann would have sole access to both the Führer and Wolf, and who knew what nefarious schemes might be hatched to his detriment? So, begrudgingly, he came—much to my delight, I must tell you, because I would now have a companion, and one who would take the pressure and focus away from me, should I require it. To put it bluntly: my relief served to dilute my guilt.

I located him strolling round the gardens, smoking (which he couldn't do in the presence of the Führer), head down.

"I just had a run-in—literally—with Fräulein Wolf," I told him once I'd caught up.

He raised his head and exhaled a cloud of blue smoke in my face. "And you're still here to tell the tale. I congratulate you, my friend. I just hope to be as fortunate with *my* adversary. He appears to have virtually moved into the Führer's rooms, and no one is allowed in but those he chooses. And I'm certainly not one of them."[145]

"So, what are you going to do?"

"There's nothing I can do, here. I just want to get this farcical fait accompli with Schuschnigg over with and get back to Berlin, where I at least have some reasonable opportunity to counter that conniving asshole's manoeuvres."

"Fait accompli?" Always innocence.

"Accomplished fact, Heinz. It's French," he instructed with amused bonhomie. "Perhaps for Schuschnigg, this is a genuine meeting, but for the Führer, it's merely a staged formality, a minor step in his plan to bring his birthplace into the Reich. The Chancellor won't have a chance, so to say."

"So, what's on your agenda, for today?"

"Just a lot of hustle and bustle. The main task is for me to avoid Bormann. Once achieved, I'm to greet von Papen, Keitel,[146] von Reichenau,[147] and Sperle[148] at the airport and deliver them to the Führer for a briefing before they all meet with poor Schuschnigg."

"Why poor?"

"Well, my ingenuous Machiavelli, if the Chancellor doesn't get the Führer's message with *these* 'guests' present, he's too stupid to run Austria anyway."

---

[145] It is well documented that while Hitler was in residence at the Berghof, Bormann was constantly in attendance, acting as Hitler's personal secretary. In this capacity, he began to control the flow of information and access to Hitler.

[146] Chief of the High Command.

[147] Commander of army troops along the German-Austrian border.

[148] Air force general.

Brückner was fortunate; he could avoid Bormann much of the time. But I was less fortunate. I was summoned again to the Führer's office, for reasons I knew not what, and when I arrived at his door, Bormann was standing before it like a gargoyle guarding a cathedral.

"What is it now, Linge?" he barked impatiently, as if I were one of his hapless housekeepers. "If the Führer requires his behind to be wiped, I'll inform you in ample time to ready your tongue."

When such a time should come, Herr Bastard, it'll be your tongue I discover there, I wanted to say. Instead, "Herr Bormann, I merely thought that perhaps the Führer might have an errand for—"

Before I could complete the sentence that told him of the Führer's personal summons, Bormann swung open the door, oozed in, and slammed it in my face.

After another summons from the Führerbuzzer, I stood once again at the door, but this time, Bormann opened the door in the normal manner, and I heard the Führer's melodious "Come in, Linge. Don't be shy." At that, Bormann stepped aside with a scowl, I passed through, and Bormann closed the door behind us. The Führer was standing in front of his vast wall of books.

"Good morning, Linge," the Führer said, then turned to Bormann. "You know, Bormann, you're far too harsh on poor Linge here. He is one of my family, no less than you, and I trust him no less than I do you. One can be protected into impotence."

"Yes, my Führer," Bormann simpered, "I didn't realize you needed him here. Please forgive my presumption."

"Not to unduly concern yourself," the Führer soothed. "I'm always delighted to know that I have so many loyal protectors.

Stalin should feel so lucky. In any event," turning back to me, "when this Austrian rodent arrives, I'll want you to stand by as usual, and fetch anything necessary for our . . . guest—like smelling salts . . ."

Bormann and I chuckled on cue.

" . . . for he'll desperately need them," he added needlessly.

More chuckling, and the Führer turned again to Bormann. "No need for you to be with me, though. With Linge here and my 'welcoming committee,' I'm as well protected as I need to be. It's Schuschnigg who'll need protection when I've done with him. Coordinate with Kannenberg and Hoffmann for his arrival, so he'll think he's important for a few minutes, eh?"

A final chuckle, and with that, Bormann heel-clicked, heil-Hitlered, declared "Of course, my Führer," glared sabres of impotent loathing at me, and withdrew. The Führer then moved to his desk and sat down to the bombastic strains of "unheard" and "unsmelled" flatulence. Again, I resorted to mouth breathing, which, I'm sure, made me appear a moron, but that was not necessarily detrimental.

"A good man, Bormann," he declared. "Pity he's not well liked."

Pity was the least of my emotions about Bormann. "Have you received complaints, my Führer?" I dared to venture.

He shook his head. "Nothing like that. But I know, just as I know many other things not said or done in my presence. I know the fellow has his faults, but they're more than outweighed by his dog-like devotion and machine-like precision and industry. Very few can be like Brückner, who, it seems, is well liked by all, save Bormann, and probably for that very reason. As a former struggling artist, I know envy is a very powerful emotion."

I was deeply saddened that I couldn't correct the Führer by

informing him that, although he was right on target, it was envy of a very different sort and degree. Fortunately for Brückner and me, Bormann would be too occupied for a while to concern himself with us, but, unfortunately, whiles don't last.

Long ago, I'd read in *The Interpretation of Dreams*[149] that dreams were not merely a series of thoughts, images, and sensations occurring in a person's mind during sleep. Because the information in the unconscious is in an unruly and often disturbing form, according to Freud, a "censor" in the preconscious will not allow it to pass unaltered into the conscious. He explained that, during dreams, the preconscious is more lax in this duty than in waking hours but is still attentive, and so the unconscious must distort and warp the meaning of its information to make it through the censorship. As such, images in dreams are often not what they appear to be, according to Freud, and need deeper interpretation if they are to inform on the structures of the unconscious. I consider that frustrating fact as I secretly recount my nightmare to you, aware that it will lack that deeper interpretation:

As I sat naked on the warped stairwell floor impassively watching the silent flames devour my parents, the man sitting beside me whispered in my ear: "It must be you. He cannot accomplish it by himself."

Then the flames disappeared as if doused, and, and as I turned towards him, a sickly light, from no source I could discern, cast an opaque shadow over his features. But I recognized the voice from Salon Kitty's; of that, I was certain.

---

[149] Sigmund Freud, *Die Traumdeutung* (1899).

"But—" I tried to say, but he cut me off.

"I will confide in you that the choice is not yours to make. You will be spared judgment. You will come to appreciate this, but we expect little of you now." Then silence.

I looked down for . . . I didn't know how long, and when I glanced up, Katrin was sitting on the floor that once supported the man. In the dark stairwell, she was a stunning mystery in glowing white satin.

"He had you nailed down, even before we had," she murmured, extending her gloved hand for a kiss I couldn't provide, since she was just beyond my reach. "A dwarf on a giant's shoulders sees farther of the two,"[150] she said, but apropos of what?

"Sees what?" I enquired, calmly, no disquiet, no trepidation, no terror, not even a mild apprehension, even though the acrid filth on which I sat was now rising as if alive and beginning to engulf me.

She gazed at me as I sank beneath the foulness, like a mother would at her heedless infant. "Not yet, my love," she told me, a moist tenderness in her voice I'd never heard from her before. "Not quite yet. The giant has not risen to its full height. Only at that moment can you make the crucial climb that—"

I was jolted awake by the *Führerbuzzer.* My nightly terrors of fire and death had been shoved even more violently aside by another terror of a far different nature, one containing characters who had never before appeared, but I had no time to investigate the significance of this. It was Schuschnigg's nightmare-to-come with the Führer that needed to occupy me totally during waking hours.

It may have been only a dream, but, as I looked for the source of the stench, it was no dream that I'd soiled the sheets. Since the Führer had done the same thing, more times than

---

[150] George Herbert, *Jacula Pudentum* (1651).

merited counting, I decided to save embarrassment by mixing my soiled sheets with his after his next episode and to see to the mattress with carbolic soap myself before retiring.

∾

As done with the Duke and Duchess of Windsor, the Führer himself greeted Schuschnigg as the latter arrived at the Berghof steps. Standing behind him were the three generals. Behind them stood Brückner and Bormann, and behind them, me and *my* Bormann: Krause, all at rigid attention.

We all stood aside as the Führer led Schuschnigg inside and up to the great hall on the second floor, the big room featuring the enormous plate-glass window with its sweeping view of the Alps and, in the far distance, Austria itself. We accompanied him (Krause and I entering last without a sideward glimpse). It was the same a few seconds before, with Brückner and Bormann.

The Führer sat down in a massive armchair and motioned Schuschnigg into a wooden folding chair across from him, like a principal facing his student. Everyone else stood back in a semicircle round them.

I could see that the chancellor was predictably unsettled by this and so attempted to break the ice by engaging in small talk about the view, but the Führer cut him right off.

"Yes," he said. "This vista is impressive, Chancellor. but I didn't summon you here to blabber about weather or the view."

I noted the Führer's use of the word *summon*.

Once their relative positions were established, the Führer "treated" the chancellor to two straight hours of hellish invective in which the soft-spoken Schuschnigg was lambasted without mercy as only the Führer could do.

∾

By the afternoon, my friend, by his face and posture, the forty-one-year-old Schuschnigg had aged at least ten years. As planned, he sat alone in the grand hall, for no lunch had been prepared for him, and, I dare say, he would have had little appetite at any rate. The Führer, with his natural genius for dealing with people, then, with von Papen there for added legitimacy, I imagined, had the chancellor meet privately with that dim, arrogant lackey von Ribbentrop, his new foreign minister, who presented him with a two-page document containing the Führer's demands: all Party members presently jailed in Austria were to be freed; the ban against the Austrian Nazi Party was to be lifted immediately; Austrian lawyer Dr. Arthur Seyss-Inquart, a staunch Nazi supporter, was to become the new minister of the interior with full control of the police, at once. In addition, Nazis were to be appointed as minister of war and minister of finance in preparation for the assimilation of Austria's entire economy into the German Reich. Von Ribbentrop added a postscript to the effect that these were the Führer's final demands and there could be no discussion. The chancellor was to sign immediately, or else.

Regardless, he said he would "consider" signing but first required assurances that there would be no further interference in Austria's internal affairs by the Führer. Von Ribbentrop, joined by von Papen, gave friendly assurances that the Führer would indeed respect Austria's sovereignty once his demands were met fully. As I studied the three in the room, the only expression I could discern was poor Schuschnigg's stricken, pallid face—an expression of defeat.

At this point, Bormann ushered Schuschnigg back in to see the Führer, who underscored his earlier remarks with an unmistakable warning: "You will either sign it as is," he said, his expression a threat in and of itself, "and fulfil my demands within three days, or I will order the march into Austria. Am I perfectly clear, Herr Chancellor?"

"Perfectly," Schuschnigg conceded. "I'll sign. However," he added, "you must realize that, under Austrian law, only Austria's president[151] can ratify such a document and carry out its terms."

At that, the Führer exploded. "*YOU* must guarantee it!" he shouted, only inches from Schuschnigg's face. "*Merciful God! What are you actually thinking of? I am an Austrian by birth and have been sent by providence to create the Greater German State! And you stand in my way? I will crush you!*"

Visibly shaken but oddly still resolute, the Chancellor said he simply could not, for the results would have no legal force and effect within Austria.

The Führer made a fist, clenched to a bloodless white, and shook it in Schuschnigg's face. "*No force?*" he screamed. "*No effect?*" He turned to me: "*Get me Keitel!*"

I rushed to the door, swung it open, and ran to summon the general.

When we arrived, the Führer asked him, "How many divisions are mustered at the border?" And then, "And what does our intelligence say of the opposing army?"

Keitel answered with a scornful smirk. "Not worth mentioning, my Führer."

Then the Führer turned to Schuschnigg and abruptly dismissed him, accompanied by Krause, to a waiting room, which I knew was for the purpose of giving the chancellor a few moments to consider what the Führer would order Keitel to do. When Keitel asked for his orders, the Führer told him there were no orders. "I just wanted to give that mass of drool something

---

[151] Wilhelm Miklas.

to think about. Some bluff with card players," he told Keitel through a cunning grin. "I bluff with world leaders. Now, let's get the chancellor back in here for a 'farewell kiss.'"

A half hour later, a shattered Schuschnigg was ushered back in to see the Führer. He was given three days to take the agreement back to Austria and get it signed by the president—or else. He then left, accompanied again by von Papen back to the border. Once he was gone, the Führer told all to leave the great hall, save me. He sat back down, but I remained standing.

"Do you wish me to prepare you for dinner?" I asked, hopeful to generate some conversation.

He looked up, but his eyes were fixed on a space just beyond my left shoulder for a time. Then his gaze shifted to me.

"No, Linge," he replied. "I'm not hungry, and we have no guests who require my attendance. If I desire a snack later, I'll buzz you."

As I turned to leave, he said: "You know I contrived this entire event. I imagine that Schuschnigg, with the fear-of-Führer drilled into him, can probably get the stubborn fool Miklas to release the imprisoned Party members but never to agree to hand over the police to Seyss-Inquart." He let that settle on me for a few seconds, then he tapped his forefinger on his copy of the demands. "My strategy succeeded. And a good thing, too, for at this time I'm not prepared to deal with a complete acceptance of my terms. Once refused, I'll send Keitel to conduct military manoeuvres near enough to the Austrian border to instil an unmistakable fear in that mulish Miklas to expect an imminent invasion. He'll soon move his ass to accept all my terms. But by then, it'll be too late. The fuse will already have been lit."

"The Führer is masterful as always," I said. "They never had a chance, had they?"

The Führer stopped tapping. "No. Never. But understand, Linge, that all this is a mere sham, a temporary expedient. Yes, this phase was ridiculously simple, but I take no great satisfaction from such a smooth and painless operation. On the most mundane level, as I told the traitor Rauschning years ago, we must be prepared for the hardest struggle that a nation has had to face. If forced upon me, it will be my duty to carry out this war, regardless of losses."

Suddenly, the Führer's stare into my eyes, turned to a gaze over my shoulder, as it had done many times before. "But it will not be that way," he said, in almost a hypnotic monotone, "the mundane is *for* the mundane. Yes. My first war was physical, but my next will be metaphysical, employing a power only understood by me, and only exercised by me. And on that day that will end all days as we know them, I will need no one, not even you."

War? Another war? All the rest I dismissed as just more incoherent arcane twaddle I'd been exposed to since beginning my service. But was the Führer serious about war, or merely posturing? One never fully knew until he acted, but my instinct told me that this was not one of his bluffs.

Then he rose. "However," he said, "this is now. The Reich can wait. It is you who must be tended to first."

"Me, my Führer?"

"Of course you, Linge. I do believe you may be coming down with a cold, with all that sniffing. After he's finished with me, I'll send Morell to your quarters to check you out. Can't be too careful."

Of course, demurring was out of the question.

It's good to be back in Berlin. The labyrinthian vastness of the Chancellery and the opportunities offered by the capital allow Brückner and me the relative anonymity we could never achieve in that giant fishbowl of a Berghof, stuck as in a large lift with the ever-hovering and scheming Bormann and his eager cronies.

The Führer is relentlessly continuing the campaign he began with Schuschnigg. Keitel's manoeuvres appeared to do the trick, and Miklas caved in to all the Führer's demands. Phase one was now over, but that appeared to mean nothing to the Führer, who immediately set out to put phase two into operation, conferring endlessly with Goebbels, Himmler, Keitel, and von Ribbentrop. I wasn't present at most of these "conferences" but managed to secure some scuttlebutt from their adjutants, who informed me that the Führer would continue his provocations to force Austria's leaders into "political quicksand," as Goebbels had supposedly remarked to a delighted Führer.

I gladly left Austria to the Führer while I continued my search for a "conquest" of another order altogether. Baur and Kempka were still shoving their stable of skirts under my nose, and there was always Salon Kitty's palace of prostitutes, but all were oceans away from what I really wanted. I turned to Brückner for assistance, but he said that all the decent females he knew were either happily engaged or happily married. He remarked that the Führer was rather useless in matters of the heart, and Himmler, even more so, but that Göring might be a "gold mine" if approached strategically. This, he gladly agreed to do.

Meanwhile, I'd been following Brückner's advice to the letter and actively ignoring Frau Bella's attempt to enlist me in aiding Adelsheimer. And yet, my irrational sense of unease and betrayal continued to haunt me like a phantom pointing at me through an empty sleeve. However, when I visited the Message Centre, I learned that Reichsführer Himmler wished to see me in his office at 1100 hours. When I mentioned this to the Führer, he told me that it probably had to do with the foiled attempt on my life, though he had no information to substantiate this. "You know our Heinrich," was all he told me, as if I really knew or could ever know such an opaque character. I could think of no other reason, save the incident with Frau Bella, and I tried to push such a calamitous alternative from my mind, lest I dissolve in terror, but it kept returning. So, I sought out Brückner and told him of my "summons."

"Could be nothing," I suggested to Brückner, more a prayer than a guess.

"Keep that thought," Brückner joked darkly. "It will comfort you in the Gestapo cellars."

"Not funny, Wilhelm," I chided him. "The Frau Bella incident keeps stabbing my brain like an ice pick."

"Forgive me, Heinz," he said. "I merely intended to illustrate the silliness of your concern. Believe me, I know 'Uncle Heinrich.' If it concerned Frau Bella and the note, *I* would have been given the 'invitation' first, I can assure you. No, I would guess it involves the assassination attempt, since your other dealings with him are virtually non-existent. He has far bigger fish to fry—literally—than the Führer's prized valet. So, stop fretting, my friend. I'm confident that it's entirely harmless—at least to you."

I'd trusted Brückner's word from the beginning, and there was no tangible reason not to now. Perhaps Brückner was right, and yet, despite that, I was a pulsating mass of unease, for I recalled a conversation I had with the Führer only a few months after I'd been hired. He'd just met with the Reichsführer-SS while I was tidying up, and the latter hadn't acknowledged my presence in any way; I might just as well have been a meaningless book on the Führer's shelf. After he left and I was replacing the used materials on the desk, the Führer spoke to me:

"So, Linge, what do you think of our Uncle Heinrich?"

I'd never met him before, but I'd already learned of his reputation. And in any event, I discerned quickly that the Führer wished to give me his opinion, not receive mine.

"I don't know him, my Führer," I responded.

"You will," he replied, with an odd upward lilt to his words that struck me as more premonition than prediction. "I have a great respect for Heinrich's abilities," he claimed, "but it is quite impossible to be fond of him, I'm afraid. His insistence that service is blind obedience is both rigid and wrong-headed, even for those performing the most menial of tasks. Obedience takes no courage, no imagination, no flexibility, no initiative. In my view, leadership requires all four, don't you agree? Heinrich's life is all in the exterior and allows nothing of the interior. Our Heinrich lives only in details, surface clear through. And utterly ruthless. On the flimsiest of rumours, I daresay he would submit his own mother to hours of rigorous interrogation before having her executed. It pains me to say this, but there you are. Even in such a short amount of time, you sense this, I think."

What sort of answer was he after? Or more to the point,

what sort of answer was I after? "I'm sorry, my Führer," I finally spoke, "but my senses are nowhere near as refined as yours. I am a simple man and reckon people simply, and I can only say that the Herr Reichsführer appears, to the likes of me, to be an able man, though not one to whom humour comes readily."

"Humble as always, Linge, and unknowingly droll. But you needn't concern yourself. Not being a man of words, you amply demonstrate your comprehension through action, the only true test. In that, you might well even outrank our poor humour-less Heinrich."

"Humourless Heinrich," I joked to myself darkly.

Given Himmler's reputation and responsibilities, it would be expected for his headquarters to exude a mysterious, even a sinister and foreboding atmosphere, but such was not the case. It was situated in a stately building containing a veritable rabbit warren of offices. Most required a special pass to enter, but my position afforded me entry with relative ease. A broad stone stairway led me to the outer domain of the Reichsführer-SS, where an adjutant led me through a suite of light, airy, business-like offices, where bustling young uniformed men and women were typing and filing with military efficiency. There was nothing round me that indicated the true nature of the place, certainly nothing police-like, secret, or explicit. There wasn't an overcoat, wide-brim hat, or weapon in sight.

When finally we arrived at Himmler's vast inner sanctum, I was greeted by Heydrich, who relieved the adjutant with a quick tilt of his blond head and bade me sit on a plush leather couch, which I did. He eased his narrow frame down angled towards me.

His berm-like duelling scar glistened whitish red in the brightly lit room.

"Ah, Linge," he said cheerily, "good to see you again. You know, I'll wager you'd forgotten about our solemn promise to get to the bottom of the matter at Salon Kitty's."

I breathed a secret sigh of relief that it had nothing to do with the Jews Bella and Adolf. "Not really, Herr General. The RSHA's reputation for tenacious thoroughness is legendary."

Heydrich lifted his narrow shoulders in a slight shrug. "True," he replied. "Some do forget, though, that is, until the spotlight is in their faces. Then their memory is instantly restored, as if by magic. But sometimes, I will admit to you, a select few zealots stubbornly maintain their amnesia, and so we must rely less on magic and more on—"

Both of us jumped to attention when, just then, Himmler entered, greeted me with surprising cordiality, and had me sit back down while Heydrich remained standing. I'd seen him several times with the Führer, but never in his own realm. Looking at him, it was difficult to believe that he was only forty years old, especially considering that he controlled the entire police force of the Reich, commanded the entire SS, and was in charge of the Reich's vast resettlement program, whereby hundreds of thousands of Germans from several countries are returning to their ancestral homeland. And yet, surprise is considerably diminished when, in his actual presence, you become immediately conscious of indefatigable energy and purpose, unspectacular but unceasing.

"How are you feeling, Linge? I'd heard that you might be coming down with a cold or such-like."

I couldn't help but marvel at his sources of information. "It was nothing, Herr Reichsführer, merely an allergy, I think. It's gone now. Completely."

Himmler's lips pursed. "I'm glad to hear it. We can't have the Führer's chief valet laid up, can we?"

"Absolutely not," I answered needlessly, then added, "and yet, you'd be amazed at how many things the Führer wishes to do himself."

"Not really," he replies with a thin smile. "You must remember that I've known the Führer for many years, and I know him to be anything but one of those Arab potentates who would have a servant even breathe for him, if that were possible. For all his position and power, he remains the bohemian. At any rate, let's get down to the matter at hand." He turned his head towards Heydrich. "Reinhard, please show Herr Linge the reason for his summons."

Heydrich made a lifting motion with his long, narrow manicured hand, and I rose as if on a taut spring. He led me out and away from the bustling business offices, down several flights of stairs to another world, each landing more abject than the one previous, until we arrived at what appeared to be the very bottom of the building, with low-wattage light and pitted and slimy concrete walls, floor, and ceiling, all stained orange and black with rust. The foulest of stenches was close to unbearable. Every few feet of wall contained heavy steel doors, each with a tiny sliding metal portal in the centre. I'd been in enough jails to recognize the basic landmarks. Beside each door sat an SS guard who shot up and saluted as we passed.

When we got to a door marked "18," Heydrich issued the order to open, the guard instantly pushed a heavy bolt aside, swung open the thick metal door, and Heydrich ushered me inside. "Watch your step," he warned, "our . . . guest was regrettably untidy during interrogation." What he meant was that much of the concrete floor was like mounds of wet brown and red sand on a beach, but in this case, the sand was shit and the wetness was urine and blood. I shuddered at the sight and smell.

The door swung shut behind us. Aside from me and my "host," there was a man slumped on a metal chair, a thick leather belt holding him fast to it. He appeared remarkably untouched, save for what I took to be some reddish ooze emanating from his deeply sunken mouth. His eyes were closed and he made no sound, not even a groan.

"Herr Linge, do you recognize his man?" Heydrich asked me, his voice taking on the arid tone of an official inquiry.

"Yes, General," I replied, no less officiously.

"Please place him, with as much precision as possible, Herr Linge."

"He is—was—the waiter at Salon Kitty the evening I almost succumbed."

"Yes, that would coincide with what he eventually told us. He refused to divulge his name but quite readily admitted to having been the one who attempted to poison you. Odd."

"Did he say why?"

A crooked slit of a smile formed on Heydrich's lips. "Do you know how many teeth the average man has, Herr Linge?"

I'd read thirty-two but feigned ignorance. "I have no idea, Herr General."

"Thirty-two. The average male has thirty-two teeth. I asked our guest here why he tried to murder you, thirty-two times, each refusal to answer costing him a tooth. For the most part, he maintained his stubbornness between blood-spurting screams. Quite remarkable, and a sure sign of the importance the answer was to him. Of course, once we were certain he would tell us nothing further, we ripped out his tongue."

Heydrich explained all this horror as if he were informing a subordinate about a new filing system he'd initiated.

"And my role?" I asked him.

"Merely for purposes of identification."

"But what if I didn't recognize him?"

The crooked smile returned. "Even in an organization such as ours, mistakes can occasionally be made. We would have attributed the discrepancy to a mistake and resumed our search. However, that is far from necessary, since we are now convinced that Herr X was part of a heinous, well-planned conspiracy to eliminate you." He looked down at a small piece of notepaper. "At least that's what tooth seventeen and twenty admitted."

"But why me, of all people?" I inquired, with what I thought was justifiable humility.

"Quite," Heydrich said. "But be that as it may, the swine also admitted that his secret society's ultimate mission was to induce you to assassinate the Führer and, in so doing, utterly thwart his vision for the Reich. Insane though that scheme may have been. However, they despaired of accomplishing it and so—"

"He actually admitted this craziness?" I interrupted, mouth agape. My bowels suffered an internal shudder. Was Emerald involved? Did Heydrich know? And what of Katrin, who was there as well? In my panic, I could only joke to myself that if two women were to fight over me, I preferred it to be sexual, not political.

Heydrich glanced at the paper again. "Yes, according to tooth twenty-nine and thirty-one." I could see that the fiend was truly enjoying the telling.

"So, what will become of this fellow?" In my condition, I could conjure up no more than a stupid question.

He shrugged his bony shoulders. "We'll make him a set of dentures, give him a pencil and pad, and send him on his merry way." A joke only a Heydrich could make. "Time we returned to the Reichsführer, eh? He's still deeply concerned about the who and why of your . . . mishap. But he'll sort it out. You can rely absolutely on his patience and dedication."

"I imagine such could also be said of the man in the chair," I quipped, to show my unmistakable nonchalance in the face of horror.

He emitted one hearty laugh. "Quite. It's good to converse, every now and then, with someone who possesses a sense of humour. Despite your admiration, Herr X appeared to lack one. Now, Herr Linge, as long as you're still with me, I would have you make one more identification, yes?"

"If I must."

His eyelids slowly lowered to hooded. "A personal service to me."

I took his eyes seriously. "Then how can I refuse?"

We moved to a cell farther down the corridor, marked "22," and entered. Inside was a man—or what remained of one—slumped in a wooden chair. Most of his head and face above the nose had clearly been smashed in, and below, there was the same sunken, oozing mouth as the man in cell 18. His hands and feet had been hammered through with heavy nails, affixing him to the chair.

I fought like the devil to keep from vomiting.

"Strike a chord?"

Was this sadistic bastard serious? What sort of answer could I risk?

"I'm a valet, not a butcher, Herr General," I replied.

Heydrich smiled thinly again. "Very droll. It was just a wild stab in the dark, so to speak. A Jew I thought you may have encountered in your commercial travels through Berlin. More difficult to encounter one now. Soon, impossible. In any event, we believe he was part of a Jew conspiracy to assassinate key Party officials. While being . . . questioned, my assistant swore that your surname was mentioned, or a name very much like it, so I thought I'd take the off-chance."

"Linge is not an unusual name," I said, not really knowing. "And I imagine he was rather under some stress during questioning and may have slurred between screams."

Heydrich shrugged. "You're probably right. I say, still doing all that reading?"

Careful! "As much as the Führer provides and my schedule allows, Herr General. I fear that soon, I may need a second cot."

His pale, thin lips edged upwards into a sly grin. "Shall we go?" was all he said.

I returned to my quarters utterly depleted, so I apologize for any clumsiness in my recounting. Yet, despite my enervation, a question I'd formed in my mind since that night, and today, accentuated by Heydrich and his "guest," haunted me more than ever: *Why me????* And a thought that rode the back of that question was even more haunting: What possible connexion could exist between me and the Führer's vision for Germany that my life was no less in danger than his? Where could I go for answers?

The dilemma inherent in that question suddenly required resolution. The people surrounding me appear to know far too much and, at the same time, far too little. My grinding

frustration lies in lacking the experience, resources, and knowledge to determine the degree and kind of either.

But more immediate—and more confounding—was my
remorse for having catastrophically failed Adelsheimer.

"*THAT BLASTED FOOL!*" the Führer screamed to Goebbels, von Ribbentrop, Keitel, and . . . me (as I filled his inkwell and replaced the nib he'd smashed into his desk blotter while in an incandescent rage). "Does Schuschnigg think for one instant that I'll stand by like a store-window dummy while he plays an insulting but futile game with my demands?"

"Perhaps in desperation, my Führer," replied Goebbels, "but if I may paraphrase the Englander Dr. John Bridges,[152] 'a fool and his nation are soon parted.'"[153]

The others stared blankly at Goebbels, clearly not knowing the original quote, much less the paraphrase of it. I'd read it some years before but was as confounded then as all, save Goebbels, were now, even the Führer, who squinted with a knitted brow at the Reichsminister, who recognized the signs and rushed quickly to recoup.

"As you well know, my Führer, a fool and his money are soon parted. So it goes with nations."

The explanation appeared to work, for as quickly, the Führer unsquinted, raised his brow, pursed his lips, and nodded.

---

[152] Born in 1536, he became Dean of Salisbury in 1577.

[153] The precise wording of the expression comes from Dr. John Bridges's *Defence of the Government of the Church of England* (1587): "If they pay a penie or two pence more for the reddinesse of them..let them looke to that, a foole and his money is soone parted."

"*Exactly!*" he declared loudly, slapping his thigh with some force. "Does the idiot really believe that I'll play the disinterested spectator while Austria declares its independence by public vote?"

"I'm afraid, my Führer," said von Ribbentrop, "that the plebiscite is the misguided action of a desperate and deluded lackey, who in his desperation believes Austria still has a destiny separate from your Reich."

Goebbels and Keitel gave a "hear-hear" to that.

"Of course, my Führer, you'll have a fitting response for this miserable creature," Colonel-General Keitel said.

The Führer blew a contemptuous blast of air from his nostrils. "That, Keitel, and more," he replied. "Much more."

Lunch ended with the Führer leaving the table alone to plan his "much more." Not seeing Brückner, I decided to stroll the Chancellery grounds by myself to organize what thoughts I'd gathered about my visit to Himmler's headquarters, but my brain was a complete muddle. Fortunately, encountering Dara caused a temporary halt to my useless and frustrating ruminations, and before a thudding headache could rob me of a clear and crisp afternoon. Wearing a business-like brown tweed suit, she was striding to the Führer to take dictation.

Not thinking it a secret for his inner circle, I told her about the Führer's lunchtime ranting and threats, to which she declared that it was "high time" the Führer "put that filthy stinking weasel Schuschnigg in his place—and Austria as well." She rhapsodized on and on about the hideous perfidy of Schuschnigg and his cretinous refusal to understand and appreciate the inherent greatness of National Socialism and the historic mission of the Führer to bring its blessings to a world gone awry. "How dare that Austrian scum attempt to defy the Führer? That Schuschnigg certainly has a comeuppance coming, and I imagine that I'll soon be privy to it." In spewing all this invective, she put even Goebbels to shame.

I was shaken by the stridency of her language and tone of voice, which, from our first encounter, had always been mellow and sultry to the point of seduction. And more than that, for as she spoke, her features, which I'd always found to be so alluring and at times frustratingly irresistible, now began to scrape at my perception like a chisel chipping wood. I claim no explanation for this change, *my* change (for I couldn't believe that she could possibly be the cause), but whatever had attracted me to her and caused my almost murderous envy of Kempka suddenly vanished. Fortunately, she left as quickly as she came, saying that she'd fill me in on her "doings" with Kempka later. Of course, by then, I couldn't have cared less about both of them. I was free, even though at the cost of an illusion.

THE CHANCELLERY WAS jubilant over the Führer's response to Schuschnigg. In a letter to the Austrian leader, and in his radio address, he declared that any referendum would be invariably subject to major fraud and that Germany would not accept it. The Führer also called on the Ministry of Propaganda to issue press reports that riots had broken out in Austria and that large parts of the Austrian population were calling for German troops to restore order.

We in the Führer's inner circle understood fully the significance of these two measures—a foundation being laid for a military incursion into Austria to secure unification. The only thing that concerned me was the slow pace. Why did the Führer not just march into Austria and take it, as he'd done with the Rhineland? I never voiced my concerns, since I was hardly in a position to question the Führer's strategy and was certain that the Führer had good reason for taking his time, even if I had no knowledge of it.

Later, I met with Brückner, who had been on holiday and, thankfully, had just returned.

"Sorry to leave you with all the mail," he apologized, "but I was quite depleted."

"I appreciate your concern, but you needn't bother," I

explained. "The moment you left, your pal Bormann took over all mail duties and I actually had time on my hands, for once."

Brückner merely shook his head resignedly and said: "Indefatigable ambition and energy, Heinz, a formidable combination. Ah well. So, what else happened in my absence?"

I recounted in ghastly detail my visit with Himmler, Heydrich, and their "guest." His first reaction was pure Brückner—he laughed. "So, they finally caught up with your nemesis, a year to the month later. An intriguing delay for such a normally efficient organization, eh, Heinz?"

"More intriguing that they were unable to discover more. They know the why, but didn't seem to know all the who's, like who the leaders of this conspiracy are, for instance. Do you think they know?"

He studied me with his one eye. "It's possible," he said. "Perhaps they just ran out of teeth. But if they do know more, you may find out, but only if and when they wish you to know, and not a second before. Never forget, my friend, that Himmler and Heydrich are not mere flunkeys of the Führer like so many others round him. I have no hard facts, but I assure you that they have plans that go far beyond mere obeisance."

"That's probably how the ambitious get ahead in peacetime, yes?" I joked.

He shook his head. "Peacetime, Heinz? There hasn't been peacetime since '33." He wasn't joking.

WHILE ON MY way to the servants dining room for luncheon, I encountered the loathsome sycophant Major Klaus-Maria von Weisenfeld, General Keitel's adjutant. Through the good offices of the Chancellery gossip factory, I'd learned that he was a genealogist's wet dream, tracing his ancestors all the way back to the time of the Roman emperor Marcus Aurelius, the image of which, to me, merely signified a vulgar, ruthless barbarian, wearing animal skins, possessing more facial hair than a yak, and sporting the temperament of a particularly disgruntled wild boar. However, to those of lower rank and graced with no historical sensibility, his lineage exhibited a provenance worthy of Mount Olympus. If the Führer was beguiled by the man's heritage, he kept it to himself admirably.

Ancestry aside, with Weisenfeld's parade-ground raiment and clumsily effete mannerisms, he looked like a tricked-out circus ape, lampooning the truly old-line aristocrats like von Neurath with tooth-baring, slapstick buffoonery. Truly, it was difficult to be with him face to face and not be physically repelled or straining mightily to repress hysterical laughter. He reminded me of the sort of freak I'd met when I first visited the Chancellery.

"Good morning, Herr Major," I said in as friendly a tone as I could muster without needing to mean it.

He gazed at me with squinty eyes and spread lips, as if he

was studying some particularly disgusting public toilet residue. "What do you want?" he asked, as if my greeting had been a request.

"I was merely issuing a greeting, Herr Major, nothing more."

"Right," he deigned, studiously ignoring the visible fact that I actually outranked him. *Was it worth pointing out?* I asked myself and found the negative to be marginally preferable to satisfying my hatred of him, so I said nothing.

"On your way to wipe the Führer's behind?" He sneered. "Well, you're not to disturb him, for his genius currently requires the most pristine solitude—that is, once I'd provided him with the vital information he sought from General Keitel, along with a few personal observational embellishments of my own," he added with pompous redundancy, followed closely by a theatrical eye fluttering. "And the Führer, he thanked me profusely, and, well, you'll soon see, won't you? All will see." With that, he clicked his heels and marched on.

Not having been summoned, I assumed there was some generic truth in the dandyish cretin's crowing but decided to skip breakfast and visit the Führer anyway, if only to defy the bastard, "pristine solitude" notwithstanding.

When I arrived, the Führer was definitely short on solitude, since his office also contained von Ribbentrop, Göring, and Colonel-General Beck.[154]

"Matters are proceeding as I planned, gentlemen," the Führer, seated at his desk, was saying.

---

[154] Ludwig August Theodor Beck was chief of the German General Staff during the early years of the Nazi regime in Germany before World War II.

Curious as to the "matters," I moved immediately to a corner and stood at parade rest, unseen as usual.

"I was with Dara all night," he continued, "and so today, before you arrived, I sent an ultimatum to Schuschnigg, demanding that he hand over all power to the Austrian Nazis or face an invasion. My ultimatum is set to expire at noon, but I'll allow some grace for their traditionally dithering inefficiency." He looked at Beck. "But, understand me, General, my signed order for you to send troops into Austria will take effect at one o'clock, regardless of Schuschnigg's response."

"I understand, my Führer," Beck answered, "but don't you think that—"

The Führer slapped the desktop with some vigour. "What I *think*, General," he shouted, "is that you are less than enthusiastic about my plan! So, listen well: if you do not issue the appropriate commands at the appropriate time, I will not hesitate to turn the task of invading Austria over to the SA, who, I may add, will be quite jubilant at the opportunity."[155]

Beck shifted in his chair. "Yes, my Führer, your SA will be spared any . . . 'jubilation,' as you put it. I will put your plan into operation exactly as you've ordered."

"Much better, Beck. And to soothe your invisibly furrowed brow, I don't believe for a moment that it will come to violence, so much do I know my former countrymen." Then he faced the entire group. "Any questions?"

Of course there weren't, and so, when the Führer slapped

---

[155] The SA was Hitler's paramilitary organization, the Sturmabteilung. Although there was little doubt that the German Army would win the war with Austria, Beck was appalled by the idea of Germans killing other ethnic Germans. Beck capitulated when told that it would be the army or the SA.

his desk again, lightly this time, as a dismissal, all rose, saluted, and left.

The Führer then motioned for me to sit, and I took the chair that had held General Beck.

"That inconsequential mouse Schuschnigg will balk, Linge, that I know, and he'll race to see if anyone will come to his aid; this I also know. Italy's a washout. Will France cooperate? Never. Britain? Also, never. Both are so afraid of us that they will hide by climbing up their own anuses if needs must. So, what will happen, you ask? Schuschnigg will resign before the day's over, mark my words. My puppet Seyss-Inquart will be named chancellor, and his first act will be to request that German troops enter Austria to help . . . restore order. You ask how I know all this? The same way you know things, and I'll say no more."

He didn't have to; I believed every word. Yet I couldn't help wondering why he was telling me all this. I waited.

"Did you happen to see that conceited pansy of Keitel's, von Weisenfeld? Good God, why he keeps that limp noodle is beyond even *my* powers of understanding. I'm reminded of the Röhm days, and I'd rather not be. I don't know what you think of him, but I'm issuing an order that he deals with me only through you or Brückner, never directly."

"Of course, my Führer." What else could I say?

"By the same token, I know how self-effacing and forbearing you are, Linge, so if I were you, I'd hand him over to Brückner. He'll know how to deal with that pretentious prat."

"An even better idea, my Führer," I exuded gratefully.

"Yes, I thought you'd agree. Now, let's freshen me up for the glorious day ahead, eh?"

12 March 1938

THIS MORNING, MOST of the Chancellery personnel were given leave to sit round their radios and listen to the 8th Army of the Wehrmacht crossing the border into Austria, as per the Führer's plan. We learnt of our troops being greeted hysterically by German Austrians, with Nazi salutes, Nazi flags, and a storm of flowers.

Before that, as I tended to the Führer's morning preparations, he told me that he hadn't really needed troops because no fighting took place, but, regardless, he wished to provide the first big test of the Wehrmacht's machinery. It was a sorry sight, he reported, but provided valuable lessons for the high command, and a first step in getting the rest of Europe accustomed to the sight of advancing German troops. I won't deny some considerable unease at hearing the latter.

I hadn't the luxury of sitting by a radio, since, at nine a.m., the Führer left Berlin by aeroplane. We landed at Oberweisenfeld airport near Munich and from there drove to the staff of Army Group von Bock at Mühldorf on the Austrian border at the same time that our troops marched into Austria. By evening, the Führer was standing on the balcony of the town hall in Linz, announcing the Anschluss of Austria with the German Reich. Next to him stood the new Austrian chancellor, his creature, Seyss-Inquart. I'd accompanied the Führer to many a German rally, but never one this effusive. Below him was a virtual ocean of tear-stained and red-faced hysterics, screaming in a frenzy of adoration, and the Führer basked in it.

When I remarked to Brückner that up to then, I'd never witnessed such an outpouring of idolatry, he laughed.

"Well, Heinz," he said, almost with a straight face, "it's like this: Before even the first soldier crossed the border, 'His Himmlership' and a few hand-picked SS thugs landed in Vienna to arrest prominent representatives of the previous government, namely, Social Democrats and Communists, as well as other potential dissenters, not to mention Jews, to ensure that they would bear silent witness to the Führer's intent from their basement cells."

What more needed to be said on the matter of guaranteed worship?

In all this spontaneity and contrivance, I had nothing to do but sit in one of the Führer's escort automobiles or stand in the background at rallies. The only interesting and unexpected occurrence was being told by him (before he told the rest of his entourage) that he'd initially intended to leave Austria as a puppet state with Seyss-Inquart as head of a pro-Nazi government, but that the tumultuous welcome he received caused him to change course and formally absorb Austria into the Reich. Later, when Keitel inquired about any possible interference from France and Britain, the Führer merely laughed.

From time to time, during the trip, Dara attempted to engage me in animated conversation about the Führer's glorious triumph being merely the beginning of an age of uninterrupted conquest and historic national resplendence, but all I could do was pucker perfunctorily, nod my accord, and leave it at that. I suspected that it was less my reaction to patriotic hysteria and more a way of putting my envy of Kempka to a final rest.

So overwhelming was the reception that little else occupied the Führer's conversations. With Keitel there, there was precious little for von Weisenfeld to do but be actively ignored by Brückner and me. He once attempted an exchange with Goebbels but was unceremoniously rebuffed, because the latter was busy orchestrating with Hoffmann a cinematic exposition of the Führer's astounding triumph, to be shown all over Germany and beyond. He was ultimately relegated to chatting with Dara, who, I could tell, was repelled by him as a person but who shared his fervour.

MY APOLOGIES FOR not returning to you sooner, but the Führer's trip round Austria, which Goebbels, with some accuracy, termed a "triumphal tour," wore me out by day's end. It climaxed today when around two hundred thousand German Austrians gathered round the Heldenplatz Square[156] to hear the Führer say, in front of wildly cheering worshippers, that "when I crossed the former frontier, there met me such a stream of love as I have never experienced. Not as tyrants have we come, but as liberators. You have chosen overwhelmingly to join your fate and fortunes to Germany's, and for that, we most heartedly welcome you. I personally promise you a future that would beggar the imagination of even the most ardent dreamers of greatness. The oldest eastern province of the German people shall be, from this point on, the newest bastion of the German Reich, the barest but vital beginning of a Holy Roman Empire that will eclipse even Rome itself at the height of its power and glory, and an entity far more holy than even the most devout and learned theologians could possibly have conceived." The assembled went virtually insane with rapturous screams, salutes, and cheers.

I must admit that this was one of the most eloquent—and shortest—of the Führer's speeches. And from what Dara was crowing to anyone who would listen, it was exclusively in his

---

[156] Square of Heroes.

own words. Virtually all in our party were visibly moved. Even Goebbels, hardly an amateur with a phrase himself, had a moistness in his eyes while the Führer spoke. The only dry eyes were Brückner's, and I intended to discover the reason.

That evening, on the trip back to Berlin, I had an opportunity to raise the subject, since the big shots sat in the front as usual, except for von Weisenfeld, who was exiled to a lone seat in the centre. In the very rear, I asked Brückner why he didn't seem to share everyone else's unrestrained and impassioned enthusiasm. He remained silent for a time, but finally broke it.

"Discerning as always, Heinz."

"Concerned about Bormann?"

He shrugged a laugh. "That busy beaver? Not quite yet. For him, there's plenty of time. It's early yet. The Führer's just begun. Why try insinuating himself now, needlessly, when he can forbear until all the dirty work's been done? Bormann is now just a fly, buzzing outside a window. He's no fool. He'll wait until someone opens it, then in he comes. No, Heinz, I'm concerned about far more important matters than that assiduous ass licker." He reached into his tunic pocket, drew out a sheet of typed paper, and slipped it to me as did Bella in the restaurant.

"For whatever reason," he whispered, "your 'green goddess' felt me a more receptive mailman than my position would indicate."

I took the sheet no less furtively, held it on my lap, and read the small, cramped type quickly:

My Dear Heinz, If you are reading this, it means we were not mistaken in our judgment of your friend. My sincerest apologies for continuing to involve you in our affairs, but you are the most important of a precious few who can help check the horrors to come. It's vital you

recognize that there are two governments in Germany
and two leaders. And, as it is so often the case, the more
recognized and celebrated is seen to be the sole organ of
national policy, but nothing could be further from the
truth, as circumstances will amply demonstrate. As you
read this, Hitler's plans are already in operation: Jews will
be persecuted in Vienna; they will be driven through
the streets; their homes and shops plundered; and the
process of Aryanisation will begin in earnest, as it has in
Germany itself. And if this is true for the capital of one
of the most urbane cities of Europe, what happens in the
outlying areas will beggar description. You ignored the
desperate plea of Adolf Adelsheimer, and you've witnessed
the grisly result. Yes, he was no more important than
any other innocent human being, but should that not
be enough? Soon, he will be joined by millions, but by
then, it will be too late. We implore you to reconsider
and render assistance to those who, without the good
works of such as you and those whom you trust, will
be at the absolute mercy of a monster who commands
an army of fanatical torturers and executioners. As for
Austria itself, it is now lost to civilization, but it is only
the barest beginnings of a cascading evil that, like lava,
is on a course to destroy and cover all that lies before it.
Should you relent, please contact Bella as quickly as you
can, for her time is borrowed. With my fondest regards
and most impassioned hopes, E.

"Finished?" asked Brückner.

"Yes," I answered. Did I really need more crushing guilt than
I already felt?

"Right. Now fold it up, take it into the toilet, flush the tiny pieces into the anonymity of the sewer, and come right back. We need to talk."

❧

"This is enormously perilous terrain you're traversing," Brückner whispered to me without expression as I sat back down. "And worse yet, it appears as if you booked me on this journey with you."

I felt a sharp pang of responsibility, even though I had nothing to do with Emerald's choice of mail carrier. Somehow, she and her "associates" assumed that Brückner was a most-trusted—and trustworthy—confidante, and it was they who were taking the liberties, not I. Then I recalled what Kierkegaard once wrote about he who dares, losing his footing for a while, but he who does not dare, losing himself.

"Wilhelm," I answered feebly, "I never intended for you to become involved in this. I never even intended for *me* to become involved. It just happened."

"Coincidence, then? You know as well as I do that inside the Chancellery there are no coincidences. And outside of it, there is Himmler."

"So, what will you do?"

"Do you know what a 'Hobson's choice' is?"

"No," I lied. I'd run across the ancient term in my reading, but such was for me alone to know.

"Well, my friend, it's a 'free choice' in which only one option is offered. Since a person may refuse to take that option, the choice is, therefore, between taking the option or not. For example, 'take it or leave it.'[157] That being the case, I'm afraid you've given it to me."

---

[157] The phrase is said to originate with Thomas Hobson (1544–1631), a

I didn't really believe that he had only one choice. "So, what will—"

"I'll give you what assistance I can," he offered. "I'd hate to lose an investment, especially such an expensive one."

I was overcome with gratitude. "Wilhelm . . . I have no words to express—"

He interrupted me with a smile. "Good," he said. "Words can be overheard. Also, being maudlin can be tiresome. With all my other frailties, contracting diabetes would be a most unwelcome development."

"Then what am I to do?" I asked.

He shrugged subtly. "Follow your conscience, my friend, a word not often seen in *Mein Kampf,* I'm afraid, but I can abide it if you can, provided it's exercised with discretion."

"But—"

"But," he finished for me, "whenever possible, please try your best to play on the low swings, so you don't collide with me too often."

He must have seen my eyes moisten, for he said: "Incidentally, poor von Weisenfeld seems so lonely sitting there. Think we should invite him over?"

After our muted chortling subsided, all I could hear was the steady rumble of Baur's perfectly tuned engines and the pounding of blood in my ears. I'd never received love or had even known what it was. But if I could have accurately guessed its nature, I'm certain I loved Brückner at that moment.

---

livery stable owner in Cambridge, England. To rotate the use of his horses, he offered customers the choice of either taking the horse in the stall nearest the door or taking none at all.

Unfortunately, Emerald's note was entirely too accurate. When we returned to Berlin, the Chancellery was vibrant with mirth about Viennese Jews being herded through the streets, being made to scrub the sidewalks with toothbrushes and clean public latrines with their prayer cloths, and being jailed arbitrarily while police stood by as mobs looted Jewish homes, businesses, and places of worship. Only one day after we left Austria, and without a single shot being fired! What the second day would bring, preyed on my mind during all the wicked jubilation surrounding me.[158]

None of this appeared to occupy the Führer, who was totally absorbed with putting final touches on his plan for the Sudetenland. When I asked whether he required of me any services after breakfast, he told me, cryptically, that, save for "essential daily maintenance," for the foreseeable future I was "merely to observe and keep myself in readiness." Of course, I didn't dare ask him what he meant. However, such a regimen would permit me time to consider my degree of commitment to a matter about which I understood so little as well as appreciate the implications for Brückner and me of acting even minimally on Emerald's letter, what actions such a

---

[158] On Himmler's order, and with the ostensible blessing of Hitler, the SS was placed in charge of Jewish affairs in Austria, with Adolf Eichmann establishing an Office for Jewish Emigration in Vienna, extorting countless sums from Jews desperate to escape further persecution.

commitment necessitated, and how many "Hobson's choices" any action would entail.

However, all that needed to be set aside for the moment. Now that Brückner and I had been assigned to keep von Weisenfeld at bay, dealings with the damnable fop will become unavoidable. Brückner was kind enough to take on the major responsibility, but there was no way I could avoid the swine indefinitely. Especially today, for, as I strolled the corridors, I spotted him entering the Chancellery with Fräulein Braun, whom the Führer had kept secreted in an apartment in Munich or tucked away at the Berghof and trotted out only when he felt no pressing need to be seen as the frantically desired mate of *all* Aryan womanhood, and not merely one example.

I knew that she hadn't been sent for, and therefore, it had to be her impatient need for him that prompted her to use the likes of von Weisenfeld to gain access. She had asked the same of me many times, but I used the Führer's strict orders as a shield. How she'd gotten the major to engage in such a reckless and foolhardy adventure was anyone's guess.

Of course, under ordinary circumstances, I would have welcomed their quixotic gesture as a way to eliminate von Weisenfeld from any further excursions into the Chancellery, but I had no desire to humiliate Fräulein Braun or violate the Führer's orders to keep the major away from him and thus bring Brückner and me into disrepute with the Führer. I had to think quickly and decisively. What would Brückner do?

Then it came to me. Speed was essential. I knew that General Kaltenbrunner[159] had just come to see the Führer on the latter's

---

[159] Ernst Kaltenbrunner was born in Ried im Innkreis, Austria. On 18 October 1930, Kaltenbrunner joined the Nazi Party and rose through the ranks. In 1938, acting on orders from Hermann Göring, Kaltenbrunner assisted in the Anschluss with Germany and was thereafter awarded the role of State Secretary for Public Security in the Seyss-Inquart cabinet.

invitation, so I raced to him in the reception room and related the problem. He was no friend of von Weisenfeld and he was also aware of the Führer's "arrangements" for Fräulein Braun, so he grumpily consented to divert the major, while I took her aside and informed her that her "love-mate" had left for Linz to confer with Himmler about security arrangements in the newly absorbed Austria, and that I would see to it that he contact her the very moment he returned.

Fortunately, in this instance, I'd sorted it out, and would continue to do so, provided Brückner and the Führer cooperated when I informed them of my logistical ruse.

But I needn't have worried. After telling the Führer of my midmorning intrigue, he laughed heartily and slapped his thigh in relieved jubilation.

"That confounded, delightful, needy female," he declared jocularly. "I appreciate how frustrating it must be for her, but I ask you, Linge: How many females in the Reich would turn themselves inside-out to be in her position for even one hour?"

"I dare say all, my Führer."

"Yes, Linge, I have to agree with you, but I'm not alone. The men of the Nordic countries have been softened to this point that their most beautiful women buckle their baggage when they have

Controlled from behind the scenes by Himmler, Kaltenbrunner still led, albeit clandestinely, the Austrian SS. On 21 March 1938, he was promoted to SS-Brigadeführer (Major General). He also helped establish the concentration camp at Mauthausen near Linz. On 11 September 1938, Kaltenbrunner was promoted to the rank of SS-Gruppenführer, equivalent to a lieutenant general in the army, while holding the position of Führer of SS-Oberabschnitt Österreich Also in 1938, he was appointed High SS and Police Leader. Sometimes attributed to Göring, but more likely Kaltenbrunner, is the often mistranslated quotation: "When I hear the word 'culture,' that's when I reach for my revolver."

an opportunity of getting their hooks on a man in our part of the world. That's what happened to Göring with his Karin, and now, Emmy. There's no rebelling against this observation. It's a fact that women love real men. As I've said many times before, it's their instinct that tells them. What can I say? Tarts adore poachers."

He sat down at his desk, rummaged through some papers, then glanced up at me, a smile on his lips. "I should also say that I am thoroughly pleased with your part in all this. From a fresh-faced recruit, you've developed into quite the 'palace conspirator.' This situation convinces me that I must be more solicitous of Fräulein Braun's needs, and yet remain steadfast in . . . keeping her out of harm's way, so to speak."

From experience, I knew that "so to speak" meant an even more secure incarceration but with enhanced one-sided visitation rights.

"As for von Weisenfeld," he added, "I'll have a little chat with Keitel and sort it out, once and for all. On your way out, you can send in Kaltenbrunner."

I also knew what the Führer's "little chat" signified. When I recounted all this to Brückner in the afternoon, I also confessed that as much as I detested von Weisenfeld, a part of me felt some pity for him.

Brückner responded: "You're in decent company, my friend. Francis of Assisi said: 'If you have men who will exclude any of God's creatures from the shelter of compassion and pity, you will have men who will deal likewise with their fellow men.' Even our hapless major might qualify. However," he added with a wink, "I'm not quite as certain about Bormann."

[All entries between 16 March and 4 May are corrupted.]

WHEN I ARRIVED at the Führer's rooms, he was in his bath-robe already conferring with Goebbels, von Ribbentrop, General Keitel, and von Brauchitsch concerning his plans for the Sudetenland,[160] which involved nothing short of war with Czechoslovakia. His primary message to all three was simple and direct: muzzle Beck![161]

"That pussyfooting clod must not be permitted to throw his considerable bulk before my onrushing train, you understand me?" the Führer declared stridently, to a chorus of "yes, my Führer."

Standing mute and useless in a corner, I wanted to tell the Führer that his analogy left something to be desired, but, as with all such things, my desire went prudently unmet. The assembled had understood the message and analogies be damned.

---

[160] The Sudetenland is the German name for those northern, southwestern, and western areas of Czechoslovakia that were inhabited primarily by German speakers, specifically the border districts of Bohemia, Moravia, and those parts of Silesia located within Czechoslovakia. Immediately after the Anschluss, Hitler made himself the advocate of ethnic Germans living in Czechoslovakia.

[161] Although most of the generals felt the idea of starting a war in 1938 was highly risky, none of them would confront Hitler with a refusal to carry out orders because the majority opinion was that Beck's arguments against war in 1938 were flawed. From May 1938, Beck had bombarded Hitler, Wilhelm Keitel, and Walther von Brauchitsch with memoranda opposing Fall Grün (Case Green), the plan for a war with Czechoslovakia.

When they'd gone, I began preparing the Führer. Once done, I was about to leave when he sighed deeply and bade me sit, his signal for a lecture to come.

"You know, Linge, before you arrived, Goebbels handed me an article in an English newspaper that referred to me as a 'subversive.' Of course, I took no offence, because, while we share many qualities, the English have never understood me—or Germany, for that matter. And, even though I am roundly misunderstood, I proudly accept the label—but as seen in a different light."

He paused for me to ask the question that would propel him onward—a ritual I learned to perform early in my service. "And what would that light be, my Führer?"

"Linge, I am and always have been a subversive. In another life, I might have been another kind of subversive entirely—an anarchist, perhaps. But destiny set me on a different path." His voice rose with sudden passion. "*I was not to use my genius and position to destroy, but to build. A man not of endings but of beginnings!* Those bourgeois fools who directed the so-called art academies were actually correct, though ruinously misguided. *How could clowns like that even begin to comprehend that my canvas was to be not merely Europe—or even the world—but time and space?*"

Then, just as quickly, his voice dropped to a conversational note, as if nothing had been said before. "Keep my calendar clear. I shall be in conference all day and well into the evening. No disturbances. I'll buzz when I need tucking in."

I already knew that, because earlier I'd sneaked an "innocent" peek at the Führer's personal daybook and saw only one thing: a scrawled initial: "W." I'd seen that initial several times since my service to the Führer began. It always meant one thing, and I was reasonably certain it still did: Weisthor.

5 May 1938

THE FÜHRER WAS possessed by a hysterical frenzy over Beck's memorandum,[162] refusing to dress, eat, give dictation, hold meetings, or allow visits. He even threw Brückner and me out after I handed him the memo and he read it. A force of nature, indeed! I could hardly blame him, since his order to "muzzle Beck" was certainly not carried out with great success. Was it the fault of those he entrusted with the task, or was it the brazenly intransigent nature of the general? I was in no position to know. Even Brückner was puzzled, though he said that he was distressed but hardly surprised. Since the Führer's antechamber was hardly the place to share confidences, we went from there to my quarters.

"You've seen him. Realize, Heinz," he said once we'd arrived, "that Beck is the army chief of staff, not only in the government but in his genes. Unfortunately, there's the inescapable fact that he's also an unimaginative and inflexible product of the nineteenth-century Prussian military tradition. Also, he's not a Party

---

[162] In the first of his memos, dated 5 May, Beck opposed Fall Grün (Case Green), the plan for a war with Czechoslovakia. He argued that the Sino-Japanese War meant Japan would be unable to come to Germany's aid, that the French Army was the best fighting force in Europe, and that Britain was certain to intervene on the side of France should Germany attack Czechoslovakia. Beck ended his memo with the comment: "The military-economic situation of Germany is bad, worse than in 1917–1918. In its current military, military-political, and military-economic condition, Germany cannot expose itself to the risk of a long war."

member, and despises the growing power of the SS and the SA. Remember, my friend, that he opposed the Anschluss for the very same reasons that he now opposes a war with Czechoslovakia, even though he was proven entirely wrong about Austria on every count. I'm quite certain that, once he regains his faculties, the Führer will dispense with his services in short order. Moreover—"

I strained to listen, but my brain began to ache with a horrific vengeance. As I stared at him numbly, Brückner was no longer before me; in his place stood Katrin. Knowing this couldn't be, I shook my head to restore it, but, as always, no restoration occurred. It was now Katrin who spoke to me, her stunning face sternly set, her body encased in shimmering evening finery, while I wore only soiled prison stripes.

"I regret intruding on Brückner's little lecture, Heinz, but all this political prattle holds no significance for you." She then began peeling off her garments, in the manner of a particularly adroit cabaret dancer, until she stood before me completely exposed. But when she reached out, grabbed my shoulders and pulled me toward her and then down with agonizing slowness, all that entered my consciousness was a passage I'd read from the novel *Dracula*:[163]

> The fair girl went on her knees, and bent over me, fairly gloating. There was a deliberate voluptuousness which was both thrilling and repulsive, and as she arched her neck she actually licked her lips like an animal, till I could see in the moonlight the moisture shining on the scarlet lips and on the red tongue as it lapped the white sharp teeth.

[163] Bram Stoker, *Dracula* (1897).

Suddenly flailing in panic, I screamed: "*You're going to kill me!*" but she replied with an ironic smile: "On the contrary, my love. I'm going to make you immortal," but I kept on screaming. Then she added: "But not yet. Not quite yet." When I looked up, she'd vanished and it was Brückner kneeling beside me on the floor, a look of alarm on his face.

"Are you all right, Heinz?" he asked, brow deeply furrowed with concern. "Do you know where you are?"

I was in my quarters. I nodded a yes and discovered that the pain in my head had vanished along with Katrin. "I'm all right, Wilhelm."

"Can you stand?"

"I think so." I eased myself onto one elbow and then used it and a bent leg to lever myself to a standing position, realized that I was completely naked, and was instantly swept away by a crashing wave of embarrassment. "I . . . I don't—"

"Calm yourself, Heinz," he soothed. "I've seen naked men before—and in far more compromised conditions. Clearly, you must have experienced a spell of some sort. We were talking and, suddenly, you began removing your uniform, and when you were down to your . . . 'birthday suit,' you slid slowly to the floor as if you were being guided, then said something about being killed, then you began screaming. My first thought was to call for Morell, but you regained your composure enough to listen to me. And there we are. But if not Morell, then someone who can diagnose this . . . whatever it is, for I ask you: Aside from my concern for your health, what if you underwent an episode like this in front of the Führer or a foreign dignitary?"

What could I say, standing stark naked in front of an SA general in the Führer's intimate circle? "Yes, Wilhelm," I said.

"I fully agree. It would be bad. I promise to make some discreet inquiries."

Brückner nodded resignedly. "At any rate, someone might chance to visit, so, my friend, for the sake of what's left of my reputation, if not your own, you might consider making a quick trip into the bathroom and getting dressed."

[All entries between 5 May and 22 May are corrupted.]

A HARSH BANGING on my door jerked me awake. It was Krause and Bormann, a complete shock because Krause had not visited me since I was first taken on by the Führer three years earlier, and he hated my guts even then as now, especially not for the least of reasons that I now outranked him. All that was etched into the face of the little swine, who glared up at me. Bormann had never visited me on any pretext.

"To what do I owe the pleasure?" I asked with simulated cordiality.

"The Führer has been attempting to summon you," Krause said, "but without success."

Both Krause and I glanced back at the Führerbuzzer on my night table, following the cord down to the floor, where the plug now resided.

"If you didn't wish to be disturbed by the Führer," Krause said, clumsy sarcasm oozing from every syllable, "you should have notified him earlier."

Bulky Bormann just stood to Krause's right, expressionless, save for hooded lids. I suspected that Krause or an underling had sneaked in while I was elsewhere and pulled the plug, but I had no proof.

"Witty as always, Major," I replied, emphasizing the lower rank, then, returning his mockery: "I have no idea which one of the army of housemaids pulled it out while sweeping, but I'll ask the Führer to have the Reichsführer-SS look into the matter immediately. Will that satisfy you and the Reichsleiter?"

At that, Bormann leaned his head to Krause's ear and whispered something I couldn't hear, then the latter stepped aside and Bormann took his place. "I'm certain the matter merely requires a replugging, not an investigation," he said, his tone almost affable. Then he turned to Krause. "I believe I can handle this matter without your assistance."

"Of course, Herr Reichsleiter," Krause said, clearly disappointed that he would miss the thorough dressing-down he was certain I was going to get.

As it was, I harboured less fear than curiosity. Why would a man in Bormann's position bother with a plug that Krause or one of his lackeys had probably pulled? While Krause made an obedient retreat, I waited patiently for the former's motive to be revealed.

"Can I offer you some refreshment, Herr Bormann?" I asked, purposely omitting his rank.

He smiled, I assumed, to acknowledge the omission.

"No, thank you," he said. "Too early, I'm afraid, and I have urgent business elsewhere, so I'll get to the point."

To the point, I thought. Yes, definitely to the point, not to belabour the idiotic matter of the plug.

"You are close with General Brückner, am I right?" he asked needlessly.

"Yes," I responded, "we work closely together."

"Yes," Bormann echoed. "Then I must tell you that the Führer has become increasingly concerned about Brückner's . . . how shall I put it . . . commitment."

"Commitment?" I answered with barely raised eyebrows. "Commitment to what, if I may ask."

Bormann cracked a thin smile. "Let me put it another way: I would take it as a clear sign of your loyalty to the Führer if, as one of Brückner's closest associates, you would inform me as to his movements and activities and the nature of his dealings with other associates. In the most discreet and confidential manner, naturally."

I was exploding with rage but managed to contain it with a lifetime's worth of will and out of necessity. I thought once more to myself—*What sort of vicious scum did the Party allow to join and even rise?* And then, what Brückner had told me years before struck me like a spear: That's precisely what the Party did; that's how the Party began—in the gutter—and it had never quite shook off its origins. That's what it was. That's who they were. But could that be what the Party *is? Now?* Moreover, if the Führer and Bormann believed Brückner to be a security risk, why not bring Himmler and his resources into the equation? Brückner might no longer have all thirty-two teeth but probably had enough for a decent confession. Yes, why not? A creature like Bormann would never hesitate to do just that, so why didn't he? Because I had no answer to these questions, I decided to end this idiotic charade.

"Herr Bormann," I said. "You're quite right, of course. This is most serious and so deserves to be dealt with most seriously— and at the highest level. Therefore, I'll immediately take it up with the Führer and follow his suggestions to the letter."

Bormann quickly raised his hands, palms outward. "I would prefer your keeping this affair between the two of us."

"Doubtless, Herr Reichsleiter, but my personal duty to the Führer is both intimate and direct and so must take precedence over even the most heartfelt and altruistic motives of others, even yours."

Hands still up, he now splayed them in a gesture of involuntary surrender.

"Clearly, Herr Linge. But I believe we can defer our concerns for the time being. No need to involve the Führer while he devotes all his energies to the Sudetenland. There'll be plenty of time later, and what harm could Brückner cause in the short run, I ask you?"

It was as if our roles reversed. "My thoughts exactly, Herr Reichsleiter. What harm, indeed?"

Bormann nodded an ambiguous assent.

"Right. I mustn't keep you from the Führer." He started to leave, then turned round slowly. "Oh, yes, Herr Linge, do remember to reinsert the plug, yes?"

❧

On my way to the Führer, I attempted to reduce my anxiety and confusion over Bormann and Krause's visit, but success eluded me. Despite—or perhaps because of—his backpedalling, did Bormann actually expect me to run to the Führer and, by so doing, cause the latter to wonder even slightly about Brückner's "commitment"? A bizarre strategy at best. And what was Krause's role in it? And to tell me that the Führer was concerned? I'd never heard a word spoken against him. Was all this an attempt by Bormann (with Krause's assistance) to gull me into stirring the pot of suspicion while they remain at a safe distance if confronted?

My questions were as much about me as they were about Brückner, and so icy shivers accompanied me all the way to the Führer's quarters and beyond.

“My deepest apologies, my Führer, for not answering your summons,” I said as I laid out his clothes. “But I had some difficulties with the buzzer plug.”

The Führer pursed his lips.

“Not nearly a problem,” he assured me, “since I hadn’t summoned you. But I trust you remedied the problem.”

So, the shit Krause had lied about that as well. “Absolutely, my Führer. I’ll check constantly to ensure that the plug remains in the socket.”

Then he began his pacing round his office. After a time, he stopped and had me call for a secretary, one I hadn’t seen before, so she presumably was a temporary. Referring to Czech mobilisation, he dictated an order that the Foreign Office assure the Czechoslovaks that he had no demands on their territory, then he turned to me and said with a sneer: “So as to mollify those weak sisters, England and France.”

He stopped pacing and went to his desk and leaned on it, supporting himself with his hands.

“Tonight is to be couples night, it would appear,” he said. “We’ll have Goebbels and his Magda, Henriette and Baldur von Schirach, Emmy and Hermann Göring, Annie Ondra, that Czech actress, and her husband, the superlative prize-fighter Schmeling, and Leni Riefenstahl accompanied by the only person she considers worthy—herself. Come for me round eight.”

At no time did he even hint at a problem with Brückner, nor was Brückner even mentioned.

At dinner, I gave only minor attention to the proceedings, since the Führer was using up all the available air with a theme with which I'd become numbingly familiar: the role of women in the Reich, no less a test of female willpower than the Führer's lung power.

"In no local section of the Party," the Führer concluded, "has a woman ever had the right to hold even the smallest post. It has therefore often been said that we were a party of misogynists who regarded a woman only as a machine for making children, or else as a plaything. That's far from being the case. A man who shouts is not a handsome sight. But if it's a woman, it's terribly shocking. The more she uses her lungs, the more strident her voice becomes. There she is, ready to pull hair out, with all her claws showing. In short, gallantry forbids one to give women an opportunity of putting themselves in situations that do not suit them. Everything that entails combat is exclusively men's business. There are so many other fields in which one must rely upon women. Organizing a house, for example. Few men have Frau Troost's talent in matters concerning interior decoration."

The only moment of note came from the irrepressible Leni, who appeared to take exception to the Führer's declaration.

"But, my Führer," she said, contrived syrup seeping from her tone, and all female heads turned to her, "would you claim that I would be more adept and so more appropriately placed in a kitchen or a nursery than in an editing room or behind a camera?"

All the women then swung their heads to the Führer, who chuckled with mirthful indulgence. "Certainly not you, Fräulein Riefenstahl, but I believe that even you may have failed to grasp my point. Of course, the very last place I would expect—or wish—to see you is in a kitchen or a nursery. However, that doesn't mean that I should or would appoint you to a high military post. A camera, after all, is not a rifle, don't you agree?"

Annie Ondra shifted uncomfortably in her chair. "Regrettably, I must disagree, my Führer," she said, her tone more discreet than her words. "In Fräulein Riefenstahl's hands, a camera *is* a rifle."

The Führer laughed at this, allowing the others to join in the merriment, not the least of whom was enjoying it than Riefenstahl herself, and so the potential storm passed without further incident. The men were in a world apart, and I myself was grateful for the break in blather.

28 *May 1938*

BRÜCKNER IS STILL teasing me about my visit from Bormann and Krause, continuing to deny its seriousness, even though this time I thought I detected an undercurrent of concern amidst the joviality.

"Heinz," he chided, "I'm well told. Knowing Bormann as I do, I'm surprised he didn't ask you to spy on the Führer. Perhaps he has someone else doing that. Old Comrade Stalin would certainly not be surprised. No, if Bormann were poised to strike, he wouldn't have gone to the ridiculous length of trying to enlist you, knowing full well you'd run to me with the news. He merely wants you to shake me up a bit, hoping to panic me into some drastic action he can then use against me. Bormann is a sly and calculating type, and if he does something blatant, you can be sure it's in the service of some more cunning scheme. It's that we should be girded for. By the way, did you hear the one about the Polack fugitive who turned himself in for the reward? Cheer up, my friend, it's not all doom and gloom."

Did I believe him?

⚶

When I arrived at the Führer's office, he was dictating to Wolf an order to all his top officials in the government and military (save Beck) that all preparations should be made to destroy Czechoslovakia by military force and that there should be the immediate mobilisation of ninety-six Wehrmacht divisions. Needlessly engrossed in her shorthand, she was able to avoid acknowledging my presence, which continued clumsily, even after her task had been completed. To be frank, I was thankful for her indifference, even though it was ill intended.

[All entries (if any) between 28 May
and 17 August are missing.]

TODAY, I STOOD in my usual corner and watched Himmler and Heydrich outline a plan with the Führer.

"My Führer," Heydrich was saying, "we can be fairly certain that at the beginning, at least, a measure of guerrilla or partisan warfare will erupt. Therefore, once troops enter Czechoslovakia, the SD[164] and SS must be given leave and be prepared to employ the most extreme measures to establish complete order and absolute obedience to the demands of occupation. Special agents must be trained beforehand to prevent sabotage, by any means necessary, and to be notified *before* any attack, in order to deny them the opportunity to hide themselves, so as to avoid our—"

"Yesyesyes," the Führer interrupted impatiently, ending further discussion with a languid wave of his hand. He turned to Himmler. "How long have we known each other, Heinrich?" And without waiting for a reply: "I'm reasonably confident that you already have a detailed plan and have arranged for all the

---

[164] The SA (*Sicherheitsdienst*), or Security Service, was the intelligence agency of the SS and the Nazi Party. The organization was the first Nazi Party intelligence organization to be established. Between 1933 and 1939, the SD was transferred to the authority of the Reich Main Security Office (*Reichssicherheitshauptamt*, or RSHA), as one of its seven departments/offices. Its first director, Reinhard Heydrich, intended for the SD to bring every single individual within the Third Reich's reach under "continuous supervision."

necessary resources with which to carry it out. And since you have my complete trust, details are superfluous."

I was spared any further chit-chat, for I was sent to fetch a secretary to take the Führer's dictation after the meeting concluded. I wanted to get Schroeder, the least of the evils, but she'd taken a few days of her hitherto untouched vacation time, and Wolf was out ill as usual, and so I was obliged to recruit Dara, whom I recently discovered to be a mean-spirited fanatic, and whom I now found detestable.

"It's about Czechoslovakia, Heinz, yes?" she asked needlessly, since that hapless region was now the only topic currently driving the Chancellery's agendas.

"I don't know, Dara," I told her truthfully. "The Führer is still in conference with Himmler and Heydrich, so it's possible, but you never know. It—"

"I'll bet you that the German-speaking Czechs are only the beginning," she interrupted. "The Führer will know what to do with those filthy Slavs. It gives my stomach the heaves just to have them near us. Doesn't it you?"

"Fortunately, I have a strong stomach," I replied, to avoid her incendiary question.

She laughed, and for the briefest of moments, I could see what had attracted me to her, but then it vanished just as quickly. "Always with the joke, Heinz, but Slavs would put any stomach to the test, even a strong one."

"Give the Führer about fifteen minutes to finish up his meeting, okay?"

"Of course. Fifteen it will be. Oh, and if you see my Erich, say hello for me," she asked.

"Consider it done," I replied amiably, having no intention whatever of doing so.

It was when I went to my quarters that I saw on my cot the envelope bearing my name typed in the centre. For some time, I'd stopped caring about who delivered these messages or who had already seen them, since there was nothing I could do about either. Yet, I still felt the wrench of fear in my gut when first seeing one, but it always dissipated through curiosity about the contents. The message inside was simple and direct:

Dear Heinz, You should be aware by now that Herr A. has been arrested and, if he survives the Gestapo cellars, will be transported to one of your Führer's growing number of "special resorts," where, as a Jew, he will be well taken care of, you can be sure. You might have prevented this but chose to take the coward's way and shove it under your mental rug. I once told you that Germany is going to Hell, but I was wrong: it *is* Hell, and you've chosen to be one of its loyal gatekeepers. I pity you even more than I do Herr A., for his burden will soon be lifted, but yours will continue, whether you recognize it or not. Your Führer will swallow nations and its peoples like a demoniacal glutton at a buffet, and you will be asked to wipe his behind after he excretes the remains. And yet I still ask: Are you able to demonstrate the qualities of humanity that I know you possess? Another choice, so you have my condolences. B.

Several emotions coursed through me, during and after my reading. At first, there was rage, rage that "B" (clearly, Bella) would have the temerity to place the blame for what happened to "A" (clearly Adelsheimer) squarely on my shoulders. *The bitch!*

All I'd wanted was a safe place in which to develop my film, not adopt a Jew! But eventually the rage passed, and I regained the accursed presence of mind to consider what my calculated delay may have cost him as a human being in need, and so came the pity of which Bella wrote. And after that, came a third emotion: self-hatred, no stranger to me. Bella's rebuke only added girth and momentum to the already plummeting snowball of guilt, released by Emerald's last message.

I don't know how long I sat there, but when I finally got up to incinerate and flush the note, I'd resolved to somehow, in a sense, consider their words with a different perspective. If it was too late for Adelsheimer, then perhaps . . .

My first order of business was to acquire an ally—or co-conspirator, as Brückner would call him. And, of course, it had to be Brückner or no one. Another Hobson's choice, but enlisting him was far easier than locating him, which I finally did in one of the smaller reception rooms. He appeared to be engrossed in a book that had no cover.

"*Caught!*" he exclaimed jocularly. "My compliments."

"Doing what?" I inquired. "You seem innocent enough to me. It took me forever to find you."

"Another of my principles for successful Chancellery survival, Heinz, the first, being to always hide in plain sight, and the second, to always be a moving target rather than a stationary one. Served me well up to now, but you never know."

"What are you reading, if I may ask?"

"You may, although you, in turn, must refrain from relating any of this to 'Uncle Heinrich' or Goebbels, our national librarian." We both smiled as he reached up and handed the coverless book to me and I turned to the title: *Der Judenstaat*, by Theodor Herzl.[165]

"My God, one of the most banned books on Goebbels's list!"

---

[165] *The Jewish State*, published in 1896 to immediate acclaim and controversy. In the book, Herzl outlined reasons for the Jewish people to leave Europe, should they desire, either for Argentina or for their historic homeland, Palestine, which he seemed to prefer. Herzl believed that the Jews possessed a nationality and all they were missing was a nation with a political structure of their own. He also believed that the only way to avoid anti-Semitism was

"I dare say, though I find it difficult to understand why our enlightened Reichsminister would object to all Jews leaving Europe for some camel-dung-infested, hostile Arab wasteland. He should make it required reading for all Party members."

"How did you guess that I decided—"

"I delivered the note. And I think I know you a little."

"I still can't believe I'm actually considering—"

"Human nature is always fascinating, my friend," he interrupted. "When helping this Jew of yours would have been relatively possible, you procrastinated, and now, when assistance is moot, and aiding anyone else carries extraordinary peril, you gain a conscience."

"He's not my Jew," I protested weakly.

"Then whose is he?"

I handed back the book. "But why you, Wilhelm?"

"Why *you*, Heinz?"

"I . . . don't know."

"I do. And one fine day, I shall tell you."

I shrugged a concession of defeat. "Then what's to be done?" I asked. "Considering the 'extraordinary peril' you mentioned. Is there anyone we can take into our confidence?"

"No," he said unequivocally. He held up his book.

Then, suddenly, the puzzle pieces began to hint at the eventual picture. The second prisoner Heydrich made me see. Why? I'd wondered at the time in my ingenuousness. But now I knew. I recounted to Brückner my cell tour with Heydrich and the second prisoner he'd shown me.

"But, considering his condition," Brückner asked, "how could you tell?"

---

for Jewish people to have their own state and ability to practice their culture and religion freely.

"Heydrich told me, only I missed his meaning. I was an artless fool. He told me everything but his name and profession. I suppose he hoped I would supply those details that he already knew. Confirmation, perhaps. An admission, possibly. Or a warning, probably."

"With that monstrosity, it could be all three," Brückner said. "But at least now you know that the note was accurate: there *is* nothing you can do for him."

I took that as barren but well-meant consolation, and so I tried to make my next words as soft and harmless as possible. "So, Wilhelm, were you humouring me all along, showing a willingness to assist a young fool whose meagre conscience had just stirred but who would ultimately learn the futility of it all?"

He put his book aside, stood, and clasped me by the shoulders gently. "No, my friend. I was accompanying you on your reluctant journey to the real world. And now, I'm afraid, you've arrived at your destination." He released me and retrieved his book.

"With what I know, should I respond to Bella's note?"

"If you dare," he replied. "I'm fairly certain she already knows what you would tell her, and I doubt she'll thank you for the confirmation. And yet, perhaps it might be the civilized thing to do, even in the real world."

"Then I shall, but, I hope, with your accompaniment, and the utmost stealth and subterfuge."

Brückner smiled his crooked smile. "Well, Heinz, if you've learned nothing else in the Führer's service, it's stealth and subterfuge."

A SLEEPLESS NIGHT, my mind behaving like an upset stomach, heaving and churning over what I should do. Over and over, my brain projected the grotesque image of Adelsheimer nailed to that chair, once a man, now a shredded and mangled casualty of a ravenous hyena named Heydrich. My accursed memory could also smell the acrid stench of faeces, urine, and disinfectant, as well as the burning bile searing my throat. My one opportunity was gone forever. But a line from the nineteenth-century American writer Henry James provided a vague but powerful stimulus: "We work in the dark—we do what we can—we give what we have. Our doubt is our passion and our passion is our task. The rest is the madness of art." Short of the suicidal insanity urged by Emerald, and given all my doubt and passion, I believe I must do *something*, but in the darkness of my imagination and knowledge, I had no idea what.

Perhaps fate, in the form of the Führer, caused a postponement of any notions. When I arrived at his quarters, he told me, between Morell's mysterious injections, that he will be meeting with the British prime minister Chamberlain at the Berghof on the fifteenth, and that all preparations must be made for the journey. A fortuitous interruption? I knew that further discussion with Brückner was also postponed, for he'd been sent on ahead to work with Kannenberg, Hoffmann, and his "friend" Bormann, to have all things prepared for the meeting. Mr. James and I would have to wait.

A DAY OF strategic pageantry, foregone conclusions, and a welcome relief from personal dilemmas.

Baur told me that the Führer had sent his personal chauffeur as a gesture of friendship and respect, but even Kempka knew the truth of the matter, as did I. If Chamberlain knew, he kept his insight well hidden. When the prime minister and his staff landed at Salzburg airport, they were welcomed by von Ribbentrop and Baron von Dörnberg.[166] As with other guests of rank, when they arrived at the Berghof, on the front steps stood the Führer, dressed in full Party uniform. Next to him stood Brückner, Schmundt,[167] Bormann, and the amiable but dim Counsellor Hewel.[168] Behind them, Kannenberg and Hoffmann, and behind them, stood his valets, with Krause as far from me as symmetry and protocol would permit.

The Führer greeted Chamberlain with an outstretched arm, and Chamberlain doffed and waved his hat in a gesture of friendliness. They shook hands, introduced one another to their colleagues, and mounted the broad steps, an umbrella hanging from the prime minister's arm. After some desultory small talk, the Führer led Chamberlain to the cloakroom and then to the

---

[166] Chief of Protocol.

[167] Another of Hitler's many adjutants.

[168] Joachim von Ribbentrop's permanent envoy to Hitler.

study on the first floor, while the rest were conducted to the conservatory. Only the Führer, Chamberlain, the interpreter,[169] and I were present. I was somewhat puzzled that Germany and England were meeting to discuss the fate of Czechoslovakia, yet no Czech was present.

Formalities of friendliness over, the Führer paraded the German grievances, punctuated with several vicious outbursts against President Beneš.[170] For over three hours this went on, Chamberlain listening expressionlessly for most of the Führer's menacing tirades. When he could get a word in, he said that he was prepared to consider any solution to accommodate German interests, so long as force was ruled out. This sparked another storm of invective from the Führer.

Knowing the Führer's method of operation, I wasn't surprised when he appeared to relent, for it was his time-tested strategy. When Chamberlain said that he would have to consult with his ministers, and the Führer assured him that he would take no military action, and both agreed to another meeting, the mood lightened considerably, but then, the Führer stood up and the meeting was over.

After finishing toying with Chamberlain and walking him out to Kempka, the Führer brought in Brückner, Bormann, von Ribbentrop, Hewel, and Weizsäcker[171] and told them what had transpired, buffing his hands with pleasure. He claimed he had manoeuvred Chamberlain into a corner. "In his myopia," he said,

---

[169] Paul Schmidt.

[170] Edvard Beneš was president of Czechoslovakia from 1935 to 1938, and again from 1940 to 1948.

[171] Baron Ernst von Weizsäcker was *Staatssekretär* (State Secretary), the second ranking official after the foreign minister in the German Foreign Office.

"our esteemed mouse failed to grasp that the Czech plebiscite is more important than anything said at the ridiculous meeting today. If the plebiscite goes our way, we take the Sudetenland and go after the rest of Czechoslovakia later. If they refuse a plebiscite, the way will be clear for an invasion. That simpering clod with his umbrella hadn't a prayer, though he didn't seem to know it. This surprises me not one bit." He glanced towards von Ribbentrop. "No writing is to emerge from this visit, you understand. Tactics will settle the matter, not your precious protocol. This little game is far from over, even though the conclusion is foregone."

Soon it was time for dinner, when the two ladies present at the time (the wives of Inspector-General Speer[172] and Bormann) were permitted to leave their rooms and enter into the activities of the Berghof. In the dining hall, the Führer greeted them, then led Frau Speer to the table. They were followed by Bormann and Eva Braun. The rest of the guests came in soon afterwards and very soon the room was a cacophony of table talk. The women, having seen Chamberlain through slits in window curtains, now made fun of the antiquated English gentleman "with the face of a gopher," who was so attached to his umbrella. The Führer put on a stern face and *tsk-tsk*-ed them, saying: "The old man took an aeroplane for the first time to see me, so you need to show

---

[172] Albert Speer joined the Nazi Party in 1931, launching himself on a political and governmental career which lasted fourteen years. His architectural skills made him increasingly prominent within the Party, and he became a member of Hitler's inner circle. Hitler instructed him to design and construct structures, including the Reich Chancellery and the Zeppelinfeld stadium in Nuremberg, where Party rallies were held. Speer also made plans to reconstruct Berlin on a grandiose scale, with huge buildings, wide boulevards, and a reorganized transportation system.

some respect." Clearly, they all knew the Führer to be joking, for they continued their mockery mercilessly.

Standing behind everyone, Brückner and I just turned our heads towards each other with knowing expressions. Later, he told me that "this is just the beginning, my friend; the Führer will play this Chamberlain like an instrument. The British care only about business and don't want war, and the French are still pretending that the Treaty of Versailles is still in force. They dream while the Führer acts."

Since a vile headache and nausea were just beginning to make themselves at home, I said nothing, content to nod as if I gave a wit about Czechoslovakia.

Aside from my pains, I climbed into bed with my entire body aching and suspected it to be the beginning of some dreadful malady.

TODAY, THE CHANCELLERY might as well have closed its doors and gone to bed. All personnel, save the most fanatical workhorses (like Schroeder), were fastened to their radios, awaiting whatever news they could obtain about the final day of the Four-Power Conference taking place in Munich[173] to decide the fate of the Sudetenland. Most of the listeners, high and low, appeared far less concerned about German speakers in Czechoslovakia than they were about the Führer scoring a major diplomatic triumph and humiliating Britain and France.

All of the Führer's inner circle and other top Reich officials are in Munich, while I, on the other hand, am still recuperating from the waning symptoms of the debilitating influenza I'd contracted at the Berghof, and so I was obliged—and happy—to remain in bed.

Far too ill to write yesterday, I can tell you now that Brückner sent a message, telling me that, since the Führer's deadline of 28 September at two o'clock for Czechoslovakia to cede the Sudetenland to Germany or face war had not been met, the British ambassador to Italy, Lord Perth, called Foreign Minister Ciano to request an urgent meeting. Perth informed Ciano that Chamberlain had instructed him to request that Mussolini enter

---

[173] Neville Chamberlain of Britain, Édouard Daladier of France, Benito Mussolini of Italy, and Adolf Hitler.

the negotiations and urge the Führer to delay the ultimatum. At eleven o'clock in the morning, Ciano met with Mussolini and informed him of Chamberlain's proposition; Mussolini agreed with it and responded by telephoning Italy's ambassador to Germany to tell him: "Go to the Fuhrer at once, and tell him that whatever happens, I will be at his side, but that I request a twenty-four-hour delay before hostilities begin. In the meantime, I will study what can be done to solve the problem." The Führer received Mussolini's message while in discussions with the French ambassador, and he told the ambassador, "My good friend Benito Mussolini has asked me to delay for twenty-four hours the marching orders of the German army, and I agreed. Of course, nothing will change except an enhancement of Il Duce's chin-jutting self-importance." As usual, the Führer had these deluded pedestrians in the palm of his hand.

It was good of Brückner to do this, but it was also irksome, for it provided the opportunity for that swine Krause to attend the Führer in his moment of glory.

Even worse, Fräulein Schroeder, with the pretended zeal of the convert, had determined to personally nurse me back to health and pestered Dr. Brandt[174] ceaselessly about my care and treatment. As usual, she was a gossiper's wet dream. During one of her countless visits to my sickbed, she informed me that Himmler believed the Führer to be "far too kind" in his treatment of Czechoslovakia, that he'd urged him to inflict the severest reprisals upon the Czechs for their "Slavic intransigence." However, from her source, she learned that, in order not to alarm Britain and France, the Führer wished to employ a velvet glove rather than an iron fist, since he didn't wish to

---

[174] Another of Hitler's personal physicians. Only Dr. Morell accompanied Hitler to the Four-Power Conference.

appear as a conqueror but as a statesman, and so would accept absorption as a logical next step. I listened to this run-on jabber with my tongue pressed into my cheek, for even I knew that once the Führer had succeeded, Himmler would have ample opportunity to deal with the Czechs as Heydrich had done with Adelsheimer.[175]

---

[175] In the final agreement on the 30th among the four powers, Germany was entirely victorious in its demands regarding the annexation of the Sudetenland. The Czech government had no part in the negotiations and was not a signatory to the agreement. Chamberlain returned home, where he declared: "My good friends, for the second time in our history, a British prime minister has returned from Germany bringing peace with honour. I believe it is peace for our time. We thank you from the bottom of our hearts. Go home and get a nice quiet sleep."

I RECEIVED A message from Frau Bella, surreptitiously delivered, informing me that she'd been urged by her "highly placed" Aryan friend to "read the handwriting on the wall" and finally leave the country. She reluctantly did so, fleeing first to an undisclosed address in Paris and thence by steamer to New York, where she'd be "among her own, in relative peace."

Adelsheimer's fate and my guilt over it overrode any "relative peace" I might have secured from Bella's escape.

[All entries (if any) between 30 September
and 7 November are corrupted.]

In the afternoon, I received a surprise visit by Werner Schrepke, one of my former "brick mates." How he'd gotten in to see me was a mystery I had no intention of solving. He said that when I left to serve the Führer, I was "sorely missed," even though they fully understood that "anyone would fuck his own mother" for the opportunity I'd been given. He joked that when I selfishly abandoned my true calling, the Reich lost one of its finest bricklayers. I joked back that when you walk on eggshells, as all must do in the Führer's service, one mistake and the Reich could quickly regain one of its finest bricklayers. He rhapsodized over that, telling me that my humour was missed even more than my bricklaying skills. I said I didn't doubt that for one moment.

Actually, what I was doing all the while was waiting for the real reason for his visit, since I hadn't had any contact with my former comrades for years. When he finally told me, "in passing," and "by the way," that his cousin would make an excellent servant, and might I prevail on "the powers that be," and so forth, I replied that, although my influence was vastly overrated, I would "see what I could do." In this, I told the truth. He left, happy and hopeful, and I could get on with more urgent matters.

Earlier that morning, I was again tidying the bookshelves while the Führer conferred intensely with Himmler, Goebbels, Göring, von Ribbentrop, and Heydrich over news of the shooting of vom Rath in Paris.[176] Thus far, the "conversation" had been about why Dr. Brandt (an orthopaedic surgeon and my own "personal physician" during my influenza days) needed to be sent to tend him. But the discussion got more serious quickly.

"Brandt aside, my Führer," said Goebbels, "and no matter the relative insignificance of vom Rath, we have been presented with a sterling opportunity to show the Jews that we mean business," at which Göring snorted a laugh (for to him, as expressed on many occasions, he cared far more about Jewish booty than racial pollution). "With all this Czechoslovakia business," he continued, "we've lost valuable momentum on our Jewish policy, and now—"

"Joseph," Göring cut in, "I think we need to have a little perspective here. I believe that we deal far more effectively with the Jewish Question systematically than by a Russian-style pogrom, which will generate hysterical opposition by the foreign Jew-dominated press and their paid government lackeys, who will liken us more to the brutish Cossacks of pre-revolutionary Russia than the enlightened leaders of the Third Reich. What of you, Heinrich?"

With his usual lack of visual or audible expression, Himmler

---

[176] In August 1938 the German authorities announced that residence permits for foreigners were being cancelled and would have to be renewed. This included for German-born Jews of foreign origin. In addition, more than twelve thousand Polish-born Jews were expelled from Germany on 28 October 1938. Among those expelled was the family of Sendel and Riva Grynszpan, Polish Jews who had emigrated to Germany in 1911 and settled in Hanover. Their seventeen-year-old son Herschel was living in Paris with an uncle. On the morning of Monday, 7 November 1938, he purchased a revolver and a box of bullets, then went to the German embassy and asked to see an embassy official. After he was taken to the office of Ernst vom Rath, Grynszpan fired five bullets at vom Rath, two of which hit him in the abdomen. Ironically, the victim was a professional diplomat with the Foreign Office who expressed anti-Nazi sympathies, largely based on the Nazis' treatment of the Jews, and was under Gestapo investigation for being politically unreliable. Three weeks prior to the assassination, Reinhard Heydrich was sent to Paris, the reason, to this day, remains undisclosed.

had been sitting silently with his usual notepad and pen on his lap. Now he answered Göring: "My Führer, I find I must agree with the Luftwaffe commander in chief in this matter. You know that I am no snivelling gradualist—or drooling profiteer," he jabbed at Göring. "Yes, I too counsel restraint in the immediate term but, ultimately, a clean sweep by the SS."

Göring nodded a reluctant assent.

For the briefest of moments, I was taken aback by Himmler and Heydrich's recommendation, that is, until I realized that they only wished to make the reprisals more systematic and widespread, not more benevolent.

As I continued my needless reshelving, I concentrated totally on the Führer's face during this debate, because, unlike him, he hadn't said a word up to now. Through my "invisibility" and the gossip monger Schroeder, I knew that his regard for Goebbels had dwindled of late, mainly because of the latter's extramarital affair with a Czech actress.[177] According to her, Goebbels had even considered divorcing Magda, but the Führer had forbidden him to do so. Not only did Magda Goebbels have a close relationship with the Führer but she was also seen as the quasi–"First Lady" of the Reich. And Baarova was, by far, not the only woman with whom Goebbels was conducting an affair, another fact for which he was criticized. Since all eyes were now aimed at the Führer, clearly a final decision was sought, and it was delivered.

"Much as I dislike having to agree with Joseph," the Führer began, with nothing short of an insult, "I don't believe we have the luxury of time to implement Heinrich's grand scheme or indulge Hermann's lust for loot. The Jews aren't fools. They fully expect a comeuppance right now, and we mustn't disappoint

---

[177] Lida Baarova.

them. Understand, gentlemen, that this was not my intent for the Jews, but that suicidal dupe Grynszpan has forced my hand. Therefore, I believe we need to take a two-step approach: first, an unmistakable warning in advance to key members of the Jewish community in Munich of imminent and severe reprisals; and two, reprisals, consistent with the spirit of the warning. If they fail to heed it, it will be on their heads, not on mine."

Goebbels smiled and Göring nodded. The only one to speak was Himmler, who said: "Of course all shall be consistent with the Führer's wishes."

"Right," the Führer said. "I should not hear of this matter further. Have tomorrow night's preparations been made?"

"Yes, my Führer, completely," Himmler replied, to a sea of ambiguous nods.

"All right. We leave for Munich today, in the late afternoon. Baur's already been informed. After dinner tomorrow night, my friends, I will set events in motion that the whole altered world will long remember. Heinrich, stay for a few moments," he said to Himmler, a sign that the others were dismissed.

Once they were gone, the Führer took a deep breath and unleashed a gas attack of sizeable ferocity. "All right, Heinrich," he said, "you are aware that it will be your task to bring Weisthor and Rahn to the church. All must be in place, you understand."

"I've taken all the necessary steps, my Führer," he replied, then saluted and left.

"*W*," I thought to myself. *Weisthor.* Katrin's companion at Kitty's. My nightmare. I stepped away from the bookshelves and asked if there were any further tasks before I also left.

"Sit, Linge," he bade me. "The time for us to talk has come at last."

Once seated, the Führer unlocked a drawer in his desk,

removed a small, tattered, leather-bound book, and placed it before him.

"I owe the Jews a great deal," he began, still sitting, not answering my question, "for inadvertently helping to bring me to power. And so I must repay them by occasionally throwing some Jewish bones to the German dogs."

"Yes, my Führer," I replied. I'd seen Jewish bones for myself at Heydrich's behest and was hardly comforted by the image.

"But this . . . event just discussed has nothing whatever to do with that," he added. "All will believe it does, and that is what I wish them to believe. But the truth is that the manipulation of Grynszpan, vom Rath's death, and the reprisals to come are all part of a well-planned ritual, essential to setting the stage for those who will play key roles in my transformation. For such a task, any and all the required tools at my disposal must and will be employed. I am telling you this because you are one of them—and always have been. And your role will be performed tomorrow night. As with Nero, we will fiddle while Rome burns. Of all this, you will say nothing to anyone, and that includes Brückner, am I clear?"

What could I tell anyone, Brückner included, even if I were so inclined? I had no idea what he was talking about, but I expect that my understanding was entirely beside the point. "Absolutely clear, my Führer," I replied. Then I left to assist in preparations for the journey to Munich, distracted only by what the Führer might have meant by "transformation."

A MORNING OF numbing routine, an afternoon of shattering revelation, and a night that almost beggared description and utterly defied comprehension.

Virtually the entire inner circle had come to Munich to attend a dinner commemorating the 1923 Beer Hall Putsch. I say *virtually* because, though several women were segments of that circle, none had been invited, thus ensuring the boisterous, monochromatic brutishness that all-male Party events invariably contained.

Since the dignitaries had brought their own personal staffs, the Führer's (Brückner, Schaub, Kempka, Krause, and me) needed only attend to his immediate requirements, which were relatively trivial and handled quickly. I was even able to wander about in the picturesque city. It was when I stopped to take some coffee and was sitting alone, engrossed in a newspaper, that I heard the chair across from me slide back, and bent my neck to see Emerald. She was still a ravishing study in green, but no longer encased in a festive satin gown but turned out in an exquisitely bespoke tweed suit. She'd lost none of the otherworldly allure I remembered, but now, as she rose and moved to the chair before me, her perfect face bore an expression of concern.

"I . . . I never expected—" I stammered.

"You couldn't have done," she interrupted, removing the

paper from my hands and placing it on the floor, then reaching over and taking my hands in hers. "Please listen to me, Heinz. Under ordinary circumstances, I'd love to sit here with you in this pleasant café and exchange romantic inanities, but I'm afraid there's no time. Despite the most careful and ingenious planning, it appears that we're still at the mercy of circumstance. I'll be no less frank than Bella tried to be, and I'll speak to you as I'm sure she would.

"I'm certain that by now you're aware that not all Germans are mindless zealots in hypnotic thrall to your demoniacal 'king' and his court of arch criminals. From your first day with him, we were aware of your . . . unique qualities, and so we sought to enlist you in a most sacred mission: to rid the world of one of the most catastrophically inhuman, savage, and calamitous individuals ever to strut the earth. However, we also understood your inability to perceive what we knew to be a certainty as well as your frightened flight from doing what you know in your heart and mind must be done. Unfortunately, by now, even if we were to succeed with you, millions will perish. But at least the world will be spared a catastrophe of biblical proportions.

"What can I say to you? What can I say to you to make you *see?* What can I say to make you listen to what an American president called 'the better angels of our nature'?[178] What I'm saying to you, Heinz, is that you must choose not to assist them in the fiendishly diabolical scheme they've planned. We—I—implore you to flee Munich. Now. Within the hour—and thence, out of Germany. We can arrange this with relative ease and conceal you until the danger to us all has passed. After that, the two of us can safely resume what we began so long ago."

---

[178] From the closing paragraph of Abraham Lincoln's First Inaugural Address, delivered on 4 March 1861.

She released my hands by sliding hers off slowly and seductively. I'd listened, entranced, ignoring the implications of my even being with her now. It was happening again—I knew I was being seduced, beguiled by her otherworldly beauty, her closeness, her voice, so much so that it took me a while to realize what was happening—and what had happened. My brain suddenly screamed: *Run from this place!*

I made a plausible excuse and left for the lavatory, where, bathed in sweat, I considered that night at Kitty's, during which, I concluded, she, and/or her compatriots (the "we") attempted to eliminate me. Given the fervour inherent in her words and past deeds, I was convinced that my life meant nothing when compared to what they hoped to achieve. What would they stop at, to prevent my meeting with the Führer and Weisthor?

That question accompanied me out the lavatory window and into the alley, where I quickly made for the street and a taxi that would get me safely back to the Führer's temporary residence.

✧

Just before we left in the caravan of limousines to escort Kempka's precious cargo to the beer hall, I was summoned by the Führer to accompany him alone to a quite small, sparsely furnished room on the floor above. When we entered, I noticed the only person there: the man who'd accompanied Katrin to Salon Kitty.

After closing and locking the door to the narrow, windowless rectangle, and without ceremony, he introduced himself as General Karl Maria Weisthor. As before, he wore no uniform and hadn't changed in other ways. He was as tall as I, but considerably frailer, with skin so blanched that his only contact with the sun would have to have been in paintings or behind slatted windows. No facial hair framed his gaunt face, and his deep brown eyes were almost as penetrating as the Führer's. He extended a shiny, black-gloved hand, which I pumped, thinking only of what Emerald had said. But how had she known?

"I've already had the pleasure, Herr General," I told him.

He removed the glove on his left hand and, with a "pardon me," placed his hand across my forehead as if to take my temperature. I flinched involuntarily but recovered swiftly. "I'll be brief. Herr Linge," he began. "I asked you before and I ask you now: In your dreams, are you ever in control?"

"No more than I was when you asked me before, Herr General."

He pursed his lips. "Fair enough. Now I ask you *this* again: Have you ever dreamt of a small top-like metal object with strange symbols etched into it?"

After a pregnant pause. "Yes, Herr General."

"When, Herr Linge?"

"In March of 1937—and last night."

"Do you know what the object is?"

"No, Herr General," I told him truthfully.

"Can you remember that dream?"

For some reason, I didn't want to accommodate him, but something about the warmth of his hand on my forehead seemed to somehow compel me. "It's all chaos round me. I'm in a dilapidated apartment stairwell across from a miserable tenement flat that has burst into flame. All round, a person I can't see for the smoke is screaming. I desperately want to leap over the bannister to a fiery death on the first-floor landing, but instead, I stretch out my arm and reach through the open doorway, through the flames, and, without even getting singed, I pull my hand back out, which is now balled up into a fist and, when I open it, there is the small metal top in my palm. My hand is now throbbing with pain and I scream and drop the object. Another man picks it up."

"Hardly? Can you describe him at all?"

"The fire and smoke . . . hard to see."

"Anything you can pick out will do."

"He seemed to be a small man, blond hair."

"Did he say anything to you?"

"No."

"And you never had this dream before?"

"I've had this dream many times, Herr General, but only twice with the metal object."

Then Weisthor reached into his jacket pocket, drew out a photograph, and handed it to me. "Have you ever seen this man?" he asked.

I stared at it for a few moments to gull them into believing that I was straining to remember. Even as an infant, I'd mastered the duplicitous art of straining to remember when I didn't need to. People wouldn't understand—and I didn't want them to. "Yes," I finally replied, my hand suddenly trembling.

"Where?" Weisthor inquired.

"The . . . blond man . . . in my dream," I stammered.

"Who was he? I mean to say, what part did he play in your dream?"

"When I dropped the top, he was the one who picked it up, but it didn't burn *his* hand."

"And what did he do with it?"

"I don't know. That's when I awoke."

He nodded gravely. "You are aware that there are many who would prevent you from fulfilling your sacred mission."

Where had that come from? "Sacred mission?"

"Nothing less than that. But they will fail as they have all failed. And will pay the price for that failure."

Then two words came to me from a dark place in my brain. "Thirty-two," I said.

His well-padded shoulders lifted slightly. "Thirty-two?"

"Teeth," I replied.

Weisthor shook his head. "Yes, I believe we all have thirty-two teeth."

Not everyone, I said to myself.

Then, just as suddenly, Weisthor's hand was no longer on my forehead, and he was whispering something in the Führer's ear that I couldn't make out. Then the Führer turned to me.

"Excellent, Linge," he said. "Well done. You probably don't remember my mention of the parallel plans of which I spoke some time ago. As to the first, while we play schoolyard games with pygmies like Chamberlain and Deladier, our business tonight will be the beginning of the infinitely more important plan, the one I've been waiting most of my life to set into motion. Come to me just before we leave for the *bierhalle*, to make me ready for the memorable evening to come."

I went back to the tiny hotel room I was forced to share with Krause. Fortunately, he refused to talk to me—or even look at me—not an easy thing to do in a room not much larger than the room I'd just left, but I welcomed the quiet, because I'd begun to consider for the first time what Emerald had told me.

⤸

"Official" word of vom Rath's death reached the Führer while he sat with several key members of the Party at the *bierhalle* commemoration. After a few mouth-to-ear whispered words to Himmler, both nodded an agreement, then they rose, I was motioned to join them, and we left the assembly abruptly without the Führer giving his usual address. I could see the shocked expressions on the faces of the rest of the assembled, but we left too swiftly for me to catch any comments.

After Kempka deposited us at the Frauenkirche,[179] the Führer, Himmler, and I exited the saloon and left our platoon of SS guards behind. Instead of entering through the massive front doors, we moved round to the side, opened a small portal, and descended a set of circular metal stairs down into the bowels of the church, where a long, ancient tunnel, illuminated only by widely spaced thick candles resting in sconces, was situated. No words were spoken all the while.

When we finally got to a weathered wooden door, Himmler reached into his tunic pocket and drew out an enormous rusted key, inserted it, and after a few clanks, we entered a small, narrow, cell-like room, lit by a single candle and furnished only by a heavy wooden table and five wooden high-back chairs. Weisthor and the small blond man in my dream were already seated. The Führer and Himmler joined them while I stood at ease in the corner facing the blond man, who was wearing some ill-fitting suit pants and a shabby corduroy jacket. An absentminded professor's costume.

The blond man shot up, his eyes bulging, mouth gaping, his left hand clutching a schnapps bottle like a just-received trophy, his other hand attached to a forty-five-degree saluting arm. Sensing the man's virtual catatonia, the Führer rose and strode immediately to where the stricken figure was standing, prised the schnapps bottle from his useless hand, placed it back on the tiny table,

---

[179] The Frauenkirche (full name Dom zu Unserer Lieben Frau, "Cathedral of Our Dear Lady") is an enormous church that serves as the cathedral of the Archdiocese of Munich and Freising and the seat of its Archbishop. It is a landmark and is considered a symbol of the Bavarian capital city.

pulled his saluting hand down, nudged him back into his seat, then he returned to his own chair and sat down.

"You know, Rahn," the Führer began, "if I'd had a model with your exact expression when I was a student, I might have stuck to painting. Yes," he said, as if continuing an extended conversation, "this is truly a momentous occasion and . . . you really should close your mouth before you swallow anything flying near you."

The man snapped his mouth shut, his teeth meeting with the click of a Prussian soldier's heels. So, this was Otto Rahn, a name I'd heard before, but, like Weisthor, a name that possessed no significance for me—until now.

"Rahn," the Führer continued, "I am going to tell you a story I have told no one else on Earth, because you are indispensable to my plans for the Fatherland—and infinitely beyond—and it is essential that you know why. Unlike my dealings with others, I shall not be coy, evasive, or disingenuous. I shall not slather you with false charm while contempt glitters in my eyes."

Then he gazed up at the ceiling and clasped his hands so tightly that the skin covering his knuckles stretched into luminescent whiteness.

"Normal man, Rahn, straddles two worlds. But the man who is born to rule, rule completely, is not permitted to remain suspended. He must, through the sheer force of his will, unite those worlds, then go beyond that unification into realms beyond past, present, and future . . . beyond time *itself!*" he shouted, causing Otto's eyes to close and open, though the rest of him remained utterly immobile.

"Instead of driving forward or backward, such a leader must create a world in which direction possesses no meaning. *Will!* That is the only meaning, *the only direction!* Thus, I have taken the fateful step," he continued, judo-chopping the air as he spoke, "and after the mission on which you shall be sent, nothing we have ever known shall ever be the same."

Like a puppet being jerked to attention by a sudden tug on his strings, the Führer shot upright and stared into Rahn's face. He reverted to a monotone, his hands flat and motionless on the tabletop. "It did not come by conscious choice, though as long as I can remember, I have been impelled by dark yearnings for the exquisite moment when power becomes truly absolute, and thereby, unnecessary. Naturally," he asserted matter-of-factly, "to lose humanity in the process is no price at all.

"I will tell you a story now, and listen well. After the War, I was rendered a penniless vagrant. I was sitting in a beer hall, whimpering into my drink like all the others, just another pathetic particle of humanity. I hadn't eaten for days. But as I sat there, a shadow fell across my table.

"I must have fallen into a trance, for I found myself walking endlessly through a mutilated landscape, and as I walked, I came upon a miraculously untouched, pristine, postal card of a village, everything perfect, an artist's dream.

"However, as I walked, it appeared to be empty, not a soul in sight, no sounds, no one walking in the street, no faces in the windows, nothing. Since I was hungry and thirsty, I made first for the beer hall, but, as with the street, there was no one there, and not a single bottle on the shelves. Next, I went to the bakery, but it was the same story. I started knocking on doors, but no one came. I shouted in the street, but no one answered. It was as if every sign of humankind had been obliterated or had never existed in the first place.

"Since by then I was ravenous, I finally went to the butcher shop. And it was there that I found them. In the cavernous deep freezer, hanging upside down from massive rusty hooks jammed into their bare feet. They were all stark naked, and completely skinned!—I will not attempt to describe the indescribable. They were facing each other in pairs, but sightless, for their eyes had been scooped out. Their torsos were blue with cold and the foul death ooze of excrement that covered them like a tattered brown blanket had frozen in place.

"But it was not the sight of them, it was the fact that they were still alive! Their chests heaved with laboured breath. I could actually feel their warmth in the frozen air. As much as I wanted to run from the grotesqueness surrounding me, I remained. Something, I know not what, compelled me to take them down, one by one. But when I attempted to minister to the first one, the one nearest me, the one facing him called to me—*called my name!* It was a woman. The nipples on her skinless breasts were erect and a thin layer of frost coated her pubic hair like new snow on winter scrub, but I could only focus on her words: 'Don't. Too late . . . for us. But not for you. Listen. Listen well . . . and remember: better an end with terror than terror without end.'

"And I listened—and remembered. Rahn, it was *Germany* speaking to me, don't you see? *Crying out!* 'Better an end with terror than terror without end.' *It had been revealed to me! In that vision, in that filthy beer hall, it had been revealed to me!*

"My heart was banging in my chest, and my stomach was churning, as my consciousness returned. But I was no longer alone, for now, across from me sat a man. His eyes were dark and set well back in his skull, and in the winter pallor of his face, they glittered like candles inside a Halloween pumpkin. His face seemed to be an awkward army of features at war with each other, with several bad lapses in anatomical strategy." He smiled at the allusion. "But for all that, attractive in a way I could not decipher.

"I said nothing, too shocked, bewildered, and exhausted to

speak. He then lit a cigar and tilted his head, blowing a stream of smoke almost straight upwards to form a small, wispy cloud. He then reached into his breast pocket and removed a pair of spectacles, hooked them over his ears, and spoke to me: 'I am Weisthor,' he said."

I glanced at Weisthor then, but his eyes were fixed on Rahn's face.

"Weisthor proceeded to consult some arcane symbols on a piece of torn paper he'd extracted from his inside jacket pocket, poured himself a glass of mineral water, tasted some of it, and puckered his lips in disgust. He gazed at the remnants in his glass sadly and pushed it away.

"For reasons I could not then fathom, I knew with electric immediacy that this was to be a crucial moment in my life. Though I started to interrupt him, he made no acknowledgement of my gesture, continuing instead with a marvellous torrent of words which brought me further and further along on the journey that my vision had only begun.

"'If you look under the scabrous Christian exterior, my friend,' he began, 'the old eternal heathendom still lurks and will prevail. Yes, if you but scratch the surface, peel the onion's layers, ancient, inherited beliefs shall be made manifest. That is what you shall build on. That will guide your destiny. Our masses have forgotten their true religion, but that is unimportant. It still lives. Now. Through you, a professor, and a menial close to me that you will come to know. That is all that matters.'

"I must have displayed a look of utter stupefaction," the Führer went on, "for he then bade me not to despair: 'Wagner's Parsifal,' he told me, 'mystically anticipated your perplexity, for his character claimed that he, too, was beset by despair and confusion. He too, believed himself a failure. As you, he also felt the mystic lines surrounding his incapacity to understand the message he was receiving from the ancient talisman of Supreme Power, which you are now hearing in the innermost recesses of your soul. It is a magical medium of revelation, and it is for you and you alone. All you need do is understand its nature, seek the medium and the Chosen One who hold the key to unleashing its power. Then prepare them for their roles, use them at the appointed time, and, ultimately, claim eternity as your own.'

"True," he said, as if addressing unspoken reservations, "I did not at that precise moment fully understand. And Weisthor, my new companion and mentor, also knew this, and so he led me by the hand through these arcane mysteries, carefully and systematically, like a benevolent teacher guiding a witless child. 'Very well then,' he began, 'Nietzsche has told us that man is something that shall be overcome, that man is merely a bridge between the beast and the *superman*,[180] a narrow rope over an abyss. But I tell you here and now that you shall cross it. Without a backward glance.'

"And as he spoke, I slowly became aware of a mighty presence, the same awesome presence which I had experienced inwardly on those rare occasions in my life when, in the midst of grinding poverty, failure, and despair, I had sensed that a great destiny awaited me. And it was confirmed when next he told me of the object, the talisman, 'a bridge between sense and spirit, a vehicle of ultimate revelation and power.'

"*A window was opened up for me!*" he suddenly cried, his hands chopping the air, his face rigidly upturned, "a window through which I saw in a single flash of illumination that through this 'object,' the blood in my veins would, one day, become both the

---

[180] *Übermensch.*

vessel and the essence of my people—but more than that—the essence of all people!"

He paused, his mouth set in grim determination. Then his expression exploded into rapture. "And I knew, *I knew*, that one day, I and I alone would possess that talisman and through it not only fulfil my world-historical role, but *transcend it!* And by transcending it, become all!

"And the man across from me," he continued, "then told me what my instincts had merely suggested to me all my life through insistent whispers: 'There is a kind of power,' he said, 'which broods in those shadowy borderlands of the soul, where darkness covers ordinary conceptions of good and evil, past and future. And this power can be caused to spring up like a wakened beast, to destroy all and create all anew.'"

He brought up his hands in front of his face and began addressing them. "'I am,' the man said, 'speaking of a power which comes with a wonderful and terrible urge to absorb it to the last of its juices, to the last atom of its being, to the last, faint suspiration of its spirit's breath; an ecstasy of omnipotence so complete, so sublime, so irresistible,'" his voice now shaking, "'that it can be taken, only when humanity as we know it dies, and the Superman rises to consume it and spawn a new humanity, more, a new state of being. And you, through your medium and the Chosen One, shall accomplish this sacred task.'"

Rahn flinched again; he appeared to understand what the Führer was saying. I did not.

The Führer then lowered his head and began to stroke the tabletop the way a blind man would read a sheet of braille. "Naturally," he announced with a note of melancholy triumph, "from that moment on, I had no further wish or need for the inane and superfluous comforts of human friendship. I was now a man who stood alone—a man with a mighty and dreadful mission. As my new companion and mentor told me, and as I now tell you: *To rule as I have been chosen to rule, humanity as we know it must be eradicated! Without mercy and without exception, out of which a new, pure humanity will be spawned, a humanity beyond form and so beyond description! And I shall be the vessel which contains that new humanity! The ultimate burden shall be mine and mine alone! I accept it!*"

Then he crashed his palms together, as if a magnificent inspiration had burst full from his consciousness. "*From that moment, in that stinking, glorious beer hall!*" he roared, "*the mere thought of victory, the simultaneous destruction and creation of all we are and know, exalted me to the point of suffocation!*" He fixed his purposeful gaze upon Rahn's pallid face. "I tell you all this, as I have told no one else. During that first encounter, I must confess that I harboured doubts about my worthiness, despite his calm and knowing assurances.

"But before long, something which was inchoate and which took form in my mind, at first no more than an abstract idea, a vagrant thought, insidiously turned to desire, and then, through instruction and initiation, ended in complete awareness and passionate resolve." He pulled himself up again and began tracing and retracing his ovals as he spoke.

"I was told that my rise would begin with small retrogressions, looking toward the past, to the far, deep, Teutonic past, when unquestioning obedience to a leader of the same blood, bone, and spirit offered an ultimate concept of freedom. The *volk* have already witnessed some of the accomplishments of our historic journey into antiquity." He sat down again.

"But, Otto," he informed after an incongruous chuckle, "that was merely the most elemental of beginnings, for my plan goes into another realm, one utterly beyond normal human understanding. *Yes!*" he screamed, his cry thumping lamely, "through my new mentor, a whole concatenation of secret messages began to infiltrate my consciousness, like whispers floating on a breeze, the vague and fleeting movement of shadows down a dark, empty street, a yearning, a stirring of the blood, all the things, my friend, that you could not explain, yet brought you and my . . . medium to this place tonight." He cast a glance at me, then turned back.

Suddenly, the Führer rose again, came over to where I was standing, and told me to sit in the empty chair next to Rahn and to grasp his hand, which I immediately did, saying nothing, as I was as transfixed as my hand mate appeared to be. Despite all the obscure signals I'd received since my service began, all I was hearing was new and disturbingly mystifying.

"Time, Rahn. *Time!*" he screamed, viscous webs of spittle appearing at the corners of his mouth. "That is the ultimate victory! But only by my own transformation can I become the premeditator of eternity!

"It has led me to this," he announced. "I must cast us into an unholy war. *War!*" he shrieked, his hands clawing, chopping, and slicing the air. "*Nothing less!* It is now obvious that my path must lead through rivers of blood, mountains of ashes, and deserts of skulls, a landscape of annihilation. I do not shrink from the task" he shrieked. "*I welcome it!*

"Through Linge and you, I shall cross the threshold of human dissolution and call forth The Beast to prepare the way for my eternal role. Nothing must remain! And when you have succeeded in your mission, we shall be heroes."

Then the Führer tilted his head back and again clasped his hands across his chest, as if someone had laid him out in a casket. Suddenly, he seemed spent, empty. His skin had a dull, waxy, sepulchral pallor, rendered even more ghostly in the candlelight. His hands trembled slightly, and his arms hung limply from his bent shoulders.

Absolute silence; not even the sound of breathing.

Then he rose once again and went over to Rahn, patted him on the back in a gesture of concerned but amused solicitude, then returned to his seat.

"My poor professor, you have had a most disquieting few days," he murmured softly. "But now, perhaps you can begin to glimpse a basic and glorious truth: that while others were living their meaningless lives, and even the most loyal and zealous citizens of the Reich—you, Linge, and I were fulfilling a world-altering destiny.

"All that has happened, my friend, had to happen, for *everything has led us to this moment!* Our lives of struggle and strife were merely the tortuous unfolding of a truly cosmic drama which you have written and I shall perform. The three of us have been shaped by wondrous and terrible forces, both known and unknown to us, and we bear their mark."

I struggled to listen, but, inexplicably—and terrifyingly—an enervating drowsiness had begun to overtake me.

" . . . I shall introduce an order of violence so monumental that only the violence shall remain. And it . . ."

Drowsier, perplexity fading.

" . . . out of the vacuum, you and I . . ."

Eyelids fluttering. *Pinch yourself!*

" . . . inextricably intertwined . . ."

Vision beginning to blur. *Pinch!*

" . . . provide you with a conclusion." The Führer then reached under the table and produced a large volume I hadn't seen until that moment, prised it open with bent fingers to a premarked page, and began to recite. I could make out nothing, and my face registered no shock, because I was too occupied struggling to keep my eyes open.

He slammed the book shut and closed his eyes. "The Chosen . . . your name . . . your journey . . . for . . . it . . . the forces . . ."

Bobbing up and down on gentle waves.

" . . . must . . . deliver it . . . me," he continued, seemingly oblivious to me weaving in my chair, my head lolling, my arms limp at my sides. "Weisthor . . . your instructions . . . leave tonight . . .

" . . . get it . . . name inscribed . . . forever in . . ."

Floating.

" . . . anything . . . you want . . . anything . . ."

Floating, rocking gently on soft waves. Katrin's hair . . .

I AWOKE WITH an odd sense of foreboding. Had I experienced just another nightmare? Of course, I told myself. What else could it have been? Long ago, I'd stopped asking from where the images originated and why.

I was in my Berlin quarters, God knows how, being inundated by Dara with gloriously vengeful tales of limitless brutality towards the Jews of Munich, their persons, homes, and businesses.[181]

"I *knew* you'd enjoy being filled in," she said, her eyes gleaming with racial triumph.

"Very thoughtful of you, Dara, but no need to provide further details." But she seemed determined to go on and on with the grisly lowdown. After a while, nodding as if I were actually listening, but I was only able to focus on Emerald and Katrin, the metal top—and Otto Rahn. Focus, yes. Enlightenment, no.

The horrendous Munich pogrom continued literally unabated

---

[181] The *Kristallnacht* pogrom damaged and, in many cases, destroyed about 200 synagogues (constituting nearly all Germany had), many Jewish cemeteries, more than 7,000 Jewish shops, and 29 department stores. Some Jews were beaten to death while others were forced to watch. More than 30,000 Jewish men were arrested and taken to concentration camps, primarily Dachau, Buchenwald, and Sachsenhausen. The treatment of prisoners in the camps was brutal, but most were released during the following three months on condition that they leave Germany.

and was the sole topic of conversation among the servants at breakfast. In his 1901 autobiography, Charles Stewart remarked that "men and women range themselves into three classes or orders of intelligence; you can tell the lowest class by their habit of always talking about persons; the next, by the fact that their habit is always to converse about things; the highest, by their preference for the discussion of ideas." The only positive aspect I could glean from Kristallnacht is that it temporarily nudged the lower class into the middle.

Saturated with something over which I had no control, I ate quickly and fled. I stopped by the Message Centre to pick up my share of the mail on my way to the Führer, where I discovered a clearly resealed "personal" letter to me from someone I'd never heard of named "Rolf." He informed me that B. was "finally out of harm's way," lamented the "virtual destruction of the Jewish community in Munich," and, according to the letter, believed this to be "merely a further stage" in the Nazis' well-planned program of Jewish annihilation. He concluded by wondering how I could live with such knowledge.

How I could took no great feat of imagination, for I merely remembered what the celebrated writer Gerhard Aegerter said: "I would blame God for this: He gave us sentience, then cursed us with mortality. Fortunately, He also bestowed upon us the priceless gift of denial. Yes, I would blame God for all this, that is, if I believed in God. Then again, what do I believe?"

Then again, what do I believe? Wasting no time seeking an answer, I destroyed the letter in one of the innumerable Chancellery lavatories and made for the Führer's quarters, where he was sequestered with Dara, concocting a draft of a speech, "explaining" (i.e., justifying) the carnage in Munich. Between pauses in dictation, he cursed Goebbels's politically ill-considered actions but placed the entire responsibility upon his own shoulders. "A meddlesome conundrum, I must say." Then he stopped when she appeared to have a problem with the spelling.

"Do you know what a conundrum is, Fräulein Daranowski?" he asked, after spelling it for her.

"No, my Führer."

"It is a confusing and difficult problem or question. My particular conundrum is having to balance the consequences of others' interpretations of *Mein Kampf,* with my own belief in its essence."

As for me, I saw no need whatever to convince the German people of such an action, despite the lowly status of vom Rath, but I reasoned that the speech was actually for international consumption. But there, too, I couldn't imagine that any explanation, even from the Führer himself, would significantly alter any attitudes.[182]

Once Dara left, throwing me a toothy smile on her way out, one that I returned in kind to prevent any possible ill will, I began to tidy up. But the Führer halted my progress by pointing to a plush armchair, into which I sank.

"Glad to see you up and about," he said, a grimace of concern on his face. "When you collapsed at dinner last night, I'm only glad that Morell was handy."

I squinted with perplexity. "Collapsed, my Führer? I have no memory of a collapse. As I recall, we both skipped dinner to meet with Reichsführer Himmler, Weisthor, and someone named Otto Rahn at the Frauenkirche."

---

[182] In an ironic sense, Linge was right. Kristallnacht did not fundamentally alter the international community's response to Hitler. There were many verbal condemnations, but no economic sanctions against Nazi Germany, no severing of diplomatic relations, no easing of immigration quotas, not even a complete opening of the gates to the Jews' own ancient homeland.

The Führer nodded consolingly at me. "Morell was right. Whatever came over you was quite startling and most mysterious. True, we did both leave before dinner, but hardly to visit a church. We took you immediately to your hotel room where I remained to ensure that Morell was tending you thoroughly. The doctor is a wizard, that cannot be doubted, but not always as thorough as he could be. I only left for a few moments to attend to some business, and when I returned, Morell claimed that you were running a high fever and rambling on and on in delirium about a revelation I'd had as a youth, and some . . . mission involving a General Weisthor and someone named Rahn. I was quite concerned. To make certain, we allowed you to remain in bed all day yesterday. Morell still doesn't know what overcame you, but he's confident that you're right as rain now. Am I right?"

I was overcome with confusion. "But the church, my Führer, I—"

"No church, Linge. No meeting. None of it is real. A fever dream only. At any rate, I must deal with that zealous fool Goebbels's debacle, so back to business, eh?"

"Of course, my Führer," I answered, still bewildered over what had taken place (or had not) for the last two days, and was reminded of a passage from Alice in Wonderland:

"Well, it's no use your talking about waking him," said Tweedledum, "when you're only one of the things in his dream. You know very well you're not real."

"I am real!" said Alice and began to cry.

"You won't make yourself a bit realler by crying," Tweedledee remarked: "there's nothing to cry about."

"If I wasn't real," Alice said—half-laughing through her

tears, it all seemed so ridiculous—"I shouldn't be able to cry."

"I hope you don't suppose those are real tears?" Tweedledum interrupted in a tone of great contempt.

"I know they're talking nonsense," Alice thought to herself: "and it's foolish to cry about it." So, she brushed away her tears, and went on as cheerfully as she could."

As did I.

[Any entries between 11 December 1938
and 1 January 1939 are missing.]

1 January–31 August 1939

I ARRIVED AT breakfast, still resentful over the embarrassing advances that Kropp[183] made towards me at the celebration last night. Brückner dropped by and, wise as always, advised me to ignore the entire matter, since the champagne was cascading into glasses like an intoxicating waterfall, and Kropp was merely feeling the effects. He added with a jest that I should be glad that Röhm[184] was long gone, for had I attended any of his all-male "social gatherings," I would never have left with my clothes still on and my member still intact. We both laughed and the matter was settled.

He told me that tonight would be special, for Goebbels had managed (through a passionate admirer of the Führer and the Party, the American automobile manufacturer, Henry Ford) to "secure" a copy of *The Adventures of Robin Hood*, complete with German subtitles. Brückner claimed that even the restless Führer might sit all the way through, because Goebbels had convinced him that, despite the story taking place in England, for all intents and purposes, it might as well be Germany, Hitler being Richard the Lionheart, and the Nazis, Robin Hood. When

---

[183] Robert Kropp was Göring's valet.

[184] Ernst Julius Günther Röhm was a German officer in the Bavarian Army and later an early Nazi leader. He was a cofounder of the Sturmabteilung (SA), the Nazi Party militia, and later was its commander. He was also a notoriously open homosexual. In 1934, as part of the "Night of the Long Knives," he was executed on Adolf Hitler's and Heinrich Himmler's orders as a potential rival.

I told Brückner that Goebbels's ability to twist a story was truly breathtaking, he replied that the real trick would be to get the English to believe it.

⁕

After I arrived at the Führer's rooms with his mail, I joked to myself that if the Führer possessed the heart of a lion, it was definitely not matched by his stomach. I'd caught another furious debate between him and his physicians over the consequences of an all-vegetable diet. I'd seen—and smelled—the debate since my arrival as valet, four years ago, and knew the disputation would continue endlessly.

To me, the Führer's dietary regimen was a gastronomic horror, but I would never say so, even by inference, even though the Führer was unfazed by the fact that this meatless, high-fibre diet was having the opposite effect on his digestion than he intended. Morell even confided to me that after the Führer downed a typical vegetable platter, "constipation and colossal flatulence occurred on a scale I have seldom encountered before." He needn't have, since I was obliged to mouth-breathe in his presence virtually every day. I felt commiserative with his guests, especially those meeting him for the first time, but I assured myself that if it didn't bother the Führer, it had no business bothering me.

⁕

As I passed through the Grand Foyer, a handsome woman, impeccably dressed, came over to me.

"You are Lieutenant Colonel Linge?"

"Yes," I answered with a fraction of hesitation, never having gotten accustomed to being a mere menial holding such an exalted military rank. "What can I do for you, Fräulein?"

"Actually, it's Frau," she corrected, holding up and wiggling her ring finger "as my husband keeps reminding me, and on the contrary, Colonel, it's what I can do for you." She slowly unfurled her hand to display a gold tunic button. "I believe this is yours?"

Her face, while not stunning, was nicely sculpted. The rest of her, though diminutive, was shapely, not like the far loftier Emerald and Katrin, but without their frighteningly dazzling otherworldliness. The only thing that separated her from any other well-appointed European woman of status was the small, red, black, and white, jewel-encrusted enamel Nazi Party pin on her lapel. I'd read that the difference between a beautiful woman and a charming woman is that you notice a beauty, but a charmer notices you. She was truly a charmer. I could feel my face redden. "I had no idea I'd lost one. Where did you find it?"

She smiled coyly. "Now I've embarrassed you."

"It doesn't take much, I'm afraid."

"That's a good quality, you know. At any rate, it was last night. It was late, but I was still dancing, and when my husband twirled me round, I happened to see you standing alone against the wall, fiddling with your jacket, and I noticed your button fall to the ground. You appeared not to notice. I was going to alert you, but you left so abruptly. I placed it in my handbag for safekeeping until I had the opportunity to return it, and, fortunately, today I had the opportunity."

I took the button from her palm and placed it in my pocket. "I'll be frank: You aren't the first to save my reputation though a button, but you're clearly the more charming, if I may say so."

She smiled. "Well, Herr Colonel, it would appear that you did say so, and I'm quite flattered. My husband is a mere captain, and considerably older."

"Might I know of him?" I asked, to prolong the conversation.

She ran her tongue slowly round her glossy red lips, then

pursed them. "I have no idea, but his name is Höss, Rudolf Höss. He was just selected by the Reichsführer to help run the mundane operations of the KZ at Sachsenhausen. Mostly paperwork," she added derisively. "My name is Hedwig. I hope you don't consider me too forward, but I'd like very much to see you again."

I cursed my luck: the first female who interested me who didn't have a fanatic's political agenda like Katrin or Emerald or who wasn't employed as a sex peddler at Salon Kitty, and she's married! "Well, Frau Höss—"

"Hedwig, please."

Initially, I was at a loss, but then it came to me. "Of course. My name is Heinz. Well . . . tonight, if I can prevail on the Führer, would you—and your husband, of course—like to see the American film *The Adventures of Robin Hood* that Reichsminister Goebbels secured for us?"

She looked at me with just a whiff of coquettishness. "Actually, my husband will be stuck in Sachsenhausen for several weeks, God knows why, but *I'd* love to see the film—if etiquette permits."

"I'm reasonably certain it will permit. I'll try to arrange it and call you."

She unclasped and reached into her handbag, drew out a small, stiff calling card embossed with the initials "HH" and a telephone number, and handed it to me. "I'll look forward to hearing from you," she said as she pivoted on her high, narrow heels and walked away, turning once at the entrance to lift her hand in farewell before vanishing.

When I approached the Führer about inviting Hedwig to the

"cinema," he was all chortles and smirks. Clearly, Morell had worked another of his left-handed "miracles."

"A button indeed!" he declared. "I confess that if your uniforms contained zippers instead, romance would come to a complete halt. Of course invite her. Ah, Linge," he sighed, "for quite a while, you've had me deeply concerned. Someone like you, frequenting the likes of a Salon Kitty! When I was a soldier, the saying was that in a market, the buyer is more concerned with securing a bargain than with the quality of the purchase. Thankfully, my singular position now places me beyond such gross physical concerns. But I tell you, Linge, what lovely women there are in the world! I remember one time long ago, some old cronies and I were sitting in the Ratskeller at Bremen. A woman came in. One would truly have thought that Olympus had opened its gates. Radiant, dazzling. The diners unanimously put down their knives and forks, and all eyes were fixed on her, yet she noticed me instantly, despite the number of eligible males seated there. I had other matters to attend to, so I looked away. Later I was told that my avoidance made her even more eager to meet me.

"Another time, at Brunswick—I was a person of note by then—a young girl rushed towards my car to offer me a bouquet. She was blonde, dashing, wonderful. Everyone round me was amazed, but not one of these idiots had the idea of asking the girl for her address so that I could send her a word of thanks. I've always reproached myself most bitterly. On yet another occasion, I was at a reception at the Bayrischer Hof. There were splendid women there, elegant and covered with jewels. A woman entered who was so beautiful that all the others were eclipsed. She wore no jewels. It was Frau Hanfstaengl. I saw her again just once, with Mary Stuck at Erna Hanfstaengl's. Three women together, one more beautiful than the others. What a picture!"

The Führer sighed again, this time, more deeply. "And now, just who is this button-finder of yours?"

"Her name is Hedwig, my Führer, Hedwig Höss, the wife of a captain at Sachsenhausen, Rudolf Höss."

The Führer shrugged. "The name means nothing, but that's not important. Even I can't know everyone, can I? A KZ? That's Himmler's area, anyway. Aren't you perhaps concerned about whispers of infidelity?"

"My Führer, I merely asked her to see a film."

The Führer nodded with knowingly pursed lips. "Of course. A film. And do you expect to, ah, discuss it afterwards?"

"Only if she wishes to, my Führer."

"My sense of it is that she will wish to discuss it—and in some detail."

Even I had serious qualms about dealing so with a married woman, but I dressed it away through the disguise of harmless intrigue. "Will it be all right if—?"

He laughed. "Of course, Linge. It'll be fine. Our guest list is hardly a dangerous one concerning such matters. Compared to Himmler, Göring, and Goebbels, you will be like a protective brother escorting his sister to church. It's just that the two of you won't be able to sit together, with you standing behind me and then running the projector. We don't wish to provide more gossip than is absolutely necessary, eh?"

"That will not be a problem, my Führer. She knows my position and I can even warn her, well ahead of time."

"Right then, let's get to my mail, so we'll both be free tonight. I've been told that I look vaguely like Errol Flynn, did you know that?"

Looking at the Führer, the word *vaguely* took on increased meaning. *I'm certain you have. And I look vaguely like Clark Gable,* I so wanted to say, but merely nodded and said, "I hope he does you justice, my Führer."

He smiled mischievously. "Taking from the rich through violent means, and giving it to the poor? This Robin Hood is actually a National Socialist at heart. Pity I can't convince the English of this."

↶

The screening appeared to go extraordinarily well, considering that my "date" was obliged to sit unescorted while being microscopically appraised by Emmy Göring, Margarete Himmler, and Magda Goebbels, hardly amateurs in the female art of negative reviews. Standing beside the projector, I was—literally—in no position to engage her in conversation, but afterwards, when our driver parked in front of her flat, she became quite the chatterbox.

"You must have thought me quite brazen to be so forward, Heinz, but once people know I have a husband, well, I needn't explain it. And yet, for all intents and purposes, I might as well be single or a widow, yes, perhaps that's what I am—a widow, the widow of a petty bureaucrat. I did tell you that he's only a captain, while those considerably younger, like you, play occupational leapfrog with him and win every time."

She placed her gloved hand on my upper cheek and slid it down with erotic gentleness. "Please don't misunderstand me, Heinz. I do love my husband, after a fashion. But I'd also like to admire him, you know what I'm saying? Tonight, actually meeting our Führer and sitting with the wives of the most powerful men in the entire Reich, an honour to be sure, I felt like a servant—no offence meant—who'd sneaked in while no one was looking. I know they all wondered who this lowly intruder was, that is, if they thought of me at all, since none chose to speak to me. My poor Rudolf, I'm sad to say, he's not in the real military, or even at the Reichsführer's headquarters, where promotions can be won, even in peacetime, but is merely a petty paper-pusher in a KZ. And," pressing my arm slightly, "his appearance, well, unfortunately, he looks more like a common wrestler than an officer of the SS." She removed her hand. "Now please don't think me an ingrate, Heinz. He provides me with a comfortable house and this nice flat, and he does serve the Führer in his own way. It's only that—"

I couldn't take any more of her damnation by faint praise and interrupted with a change of subject. "But what did you think of the film?"

She shrugged her thickly padded shoulders. "I usually don't like subtitled films," she declared. "A character prattles a paragraph of gibberish, but only one or two words appear at the bottom of the screen. It's like reading every twentieth word of a novel and trying to make sense of it. I will say it was a busy film, but one fitted more to men, wouldn't you agree? Except for a few moments of chaste romance between this Robin Hood and Maid Marian, it's all shooting arrows and dancing round with swords. If I'm to suffer through subtitles, I much prefer films like Anna Karenina. You will come up for a nightcap, yes?"

2 *January 1939*

THE FÜHRER BEGAN the day in a most foul frame of mind this morning. While I made his bathroom ready for his toilette, he was shouting, red-faced, at Keitel,[185] who stood stoically against the onslaught. "My God, Keitel, are you completely incapable of reining in that fool Canaris?[186] Who put him up to this? You think it was his own idea? *To put me in such a position when relations between Germany and Britain hang by the slenderest of threads!* I'd have him taken out and shot if not for his powerful friends, whom I must abide—for the present—*but I will brook no repetition of this, you understand me?"*

"It shall be as you order, my Führer," was all he said, but I could see that his hands were trembling, then he saluted and left. I remained in the bathroom for a time, to allow the fire to wane,

---

[185] In 1937, Keitel was promoted to the rank of full general (*Generaloberst*). In the following year, after the Blomberg-Fritsch Affair, the War Ministry was replaced by the Supreme Command of the Armed Forces (Oberkommando der Wehrmacht), and Keitel was appointed as its chief. This effectively made him Germany's war minister, and accordingly, he was appointed to the Hitler cabinet.

[186] In January 1939, Canaris, without informing Hitler, manufactured the "Dutch War Scare," that Germany intended to invade the Netherlands in February 1939. All this information was false, intended by Canaris to achieve a change in British foreign policy. In this, Canaris was "successful," since it played a major role in causing Chamberlain to make the "continental commitment" (i.e., sending a large British ground force to the defence of France) in February 1939.

then slowly entered the bedroom and fished out my stopwatch to time the Führer's dressing, but he went into his "speed-skating" mode, circling and circling the room with his hands clasped behind his back, muttering: "Fool or traitor, Canaris will be dealt with, I can assure you. Be in no doubt of that." I didn't imagine for a moment that he was speaking to me, so I merely stood there, watch in hand, and waited.

Suddenly, the Führer stopped at an armchair, lowered himself into it with a sizeable blast of flatulence, and motioned me to the chair next to his. "And so, Linge," he asked with a sly wink, as if I'd been imagining the scene with Keitel, "how did your . . . liaison with Frau Höss go, eh?"

I'd been close to the Führer since 1935, yet I was still amazed at the way he could shift moods and topics with the speed and precision of a finely calibrated automobile transmission (Kempka's analogy, naturally). And more than that, I never ceased to be astounded at his interest in anything, both substantial and trivial, regarding his "family."

"The truth, my Führer," I replied, "is that I took her back to her flat, went up with her, had a drink, claimed to have a severe headache, and left."

"Linge, Linge," the Führer joked, "headaches are excuses for women, not for men. Was she not even suitable for an evening's . . . relaxation?"

"Her appearance was more than suitable, my Führer, but her personality was far from alluring. In fact, I found her rather sour, discontented, and generally unpleasant. How her poor husband deals with her is to me a mystery, except that she says that he's away much of the time, so perhaps—"

"Absence makes the heart grow fonder, eh?"

"Exactly so, my Führer," I replied, though not entirely convinced that the saying actually applied to her.

"I discovered this sad fact quite early on in my dealings with women," the Führer commiserated. "It's as if they are told at birth to find and marry the most important man they can stomach, or at least the most promising. But when the important man falls, or that promise is unfulfilled, well, I needn't draw you a picture."

"No, my Führer, quite unnecessary," I replied.

THIS MORNING, AFTER a tour of the new Chancellery building, the Führer was virtually shuddering with joy over his chief architect, Speer, who'd just informed him, once we'd landed, that the New Chancellery was ready, two days ahead of schedule! Speer admitted that he'd padded the completion date, so as not to disappoint, but the Führer waved away the admission, shouting: *"This is genius!* Now, when people ask me what genius is, I will no longer have need to boast, for now, I can show them your masterpiece as well as my own, which is Germany itself."

We'd just returned from a short trip to Munich in the early morning and immediately drove to the construction site. The Führer was in a mood of high suspense, expecting mountains of debris and an army of workmen and cleaners scurrying about, but all he saw was a fully completed testament to German planning, industry, and accomplishment. He especially appreciated the long trek that state guests and diplomats would have to make before reaching the reception hall. When Speer told him of the dangers of a polished marble floor without runners, he replied: "No, Speer, that's exactly right. Diplomats should have practice in moving on a slippery surface."

The Führer's only misgiving was over the size of the reception hall, which he considered too small, and he immediately ordered it tripled. At that moment, I looked away from Speer out of courtesy and diplomacy—my own "slippery surface." However, the Führer waxed rhapsodic over his enormous study, especially his desk, which contained an inlay representing a half-drawn sword. He almost sang: "Good, good. When the diplomats sitting before me at this desk see that, they'll learn to shiver and shake, a valuable lesson they've been able to avoid up to now."

However, the Führer's joy was bittersweet, I knew, for he'd ordered haste because of his ever-present fear of an early death. Many times since I joined his staff, the Führer would say to me that if his "destined path" were irrevocably blocked, he would be obliged to employ the "traditional measures of ordinary mortals—as a mortal, and so would never live to see the fruition of his Thousand-Year Reich.

Not having the incalculable benefit of formal schooling, I had great difficulty reconciling "destined" with failure but refused to dwell on the apparent contradiction, leaving such weighty philosophical matters for the Führer. Fortunately, this morning, his mortality was temporarily nudged aside, as he luxuriated in Speer's announcement.

The only tense moment for me was when Speer, a man seemingly of exceptional sensitivity and cultivation, condemned the events in Munich in November of the previous year. He said it reminded him of the "gutter tactics" of the Party's origins, perhaps essential at the time but entirely unworthy of the miracle the Führer had made of the Reich since taking power. Few if any but Speer could have gotten away with such a damning critique, but it must be that, for the Führer, Speer is clearly exceptional, perhaps, and, if I dare mention, a symbol of how the Führer had seen himself as a youth. Naturally, I see him differently. For me, Speer is everything I am not and could never be: movie-idol handsome, wealthy, elegant, worldly, classically educated, artistic, and virtually fearless. By comparison, I'm so inferior, I cannot even envy him.

The Führer merely answered Speer's audacious remark with a shrug: "Even the most loyal dog demands a bone now and then."

I'd never thought of Germans as "dogs" or Jews as "bones," but I'd also never thought of myself as the Führer. Still and all, the remark torments me.

[Entries between 7 January and 13 March are corrupted.]

AGAIN, MY APOLOGIES for appearing to neglect you, but, for reasons not disclosed to me, that imperious oaf Hoffmann temporarily curtailed my use of his photographic facilities. With uncharacteristic refinement, he assured me that it was not personal but that he needed "unfettered access" for a time, as he put it, which to me meant unshared access. So, no writings until film could be safely sent.

Tonight, the Chancellery dining room had the aura of a courtroom in a restaurant. Several major figures in the judiciary were present as well as Goebbels and Himmler. But in this case, the judges seemed to be in the dock. As Brückner and I stood behind the Führer, I couldn't help but consider that my only contact with judges had been on the lowest level. Before the brickyard, being sentenced by some lowly magistrate to a relatively short period of time in gaol had become almost an occupation in itself. At least it was a place where I would receive regular meals and be temporarily shielded from the elements and hungrier hooligans. And yet, since I had no contact with organized religion or the military, prior to joining the Führer's service, even more so than the police, and definitely more so than the clergy, these gentlemen represented the only symbols of absolute power and prestige (even worship) with which I could identify, and, as a result, I stood in awe and terror of them, until the Führer disabused me of such false idolatry. But he could never rid me of the terror.

The Führer was in rare form, even for him, on the subject of lawyers and judges, for whom it appeared most clearly that he had no respect or great liking as a "species," as he called them.

"A father fresh from another irrational court ruling comes into a bar," he began. "Angrily he shouts, '*I think all judges are assholes!* A slurred response from the back of the bar is heard: '*I resent that!* The father peers into the back and asks, 'Why, are you a judge?' 'No,' the voice slurs, 'I'm an asshole.'"

Goebbels roared with laughter, Himmler moved his lips slightly upwards, and the judges tittered uneasily.

"I can tell you," the Führer continued, "that I have the German jurists to thank for only one thing: I was sentenced to a term in Landsberg Prison, which provided me with the time and peace I required to write *Mein Kampf.* I suggest in principle that it's impossible for a normal intelligence to understand any part of the edifices built up by the jurists, and I can explain this mental distortion only by the influence of the Jews. In a nutshell, I regard the whole of our present jurisprudence as a systematisation of the method that consists in saddling other people with one's own obligations.

"Therefore, I shall do everything in my power to make the study of law utterly contemptible if it is to be guided by such notions. I'll see to it that the administration of justice shall be cleared of all judges who don't constitute a genuine elite. Let their number be reduced to a tenth if necessary! The comedy of courts with a jury must come to an end. I wish once and for all to prevent a judge from being able to shake off this responsibility by claiming that he has been outvoted by the jurymen or by invoking other excuses of that nature. I desire only judges who have the requisite personality, but in that case they must be very generously reimbursed. I need men for judges who are deeply convinced that the law ought not to guarantee the interests of the individual against those of the state, that their duty is to see to it, above all, that Germany does not perish."

He turned his head towards his minister of justice. "Gürtner, here, has not succeeded in forming judges of this type. He has himself had difficulty in ridding himself of his legal superstitions. Threatened by some and despised by others, he has succeeded only slowly in adopting more reasonable attitudes, spurred by the necessity of bringing justice into harmony with the imperatives of action. If anyone were to think I chose Gürtner as Minister of Justice because once upon a time, in his capacity as judge, he must have treated me with particular understanding, that wouldn't at all correspond to the facts. It was I who had to make an effort of objectivity—and a great effort, too—to call to the Ministry of Justice the man who had me imprisoned. But when I had to choose amongst the men who were in the running, I couldn't find anyone better. Freissler was nothing but a Bolshevik. As for the other (Schlegelberger), his face could not deceive me. It was enough to have seen him once.[187]

"Thus," he concluded, "today, I can declare without circumlocution that every jurist must be regarded as a man deficient by nature or else deformed by usage.

"And as for lawyers, no one stands closer in mentality to the criminal than the lawyer. And if you can see much difference between them, I can't. The only way to clean up this profession

---

[187] From *Hitler's Table Talk 1941–1944: His Private Conversations*, edited by Gerhard L. Weinberg, preface and essay by H. R. Trevor-Roper, translated by Norman Cameron and R. H. Stevens (New York; Enigma Books, 2000–2008), 284.

is to nationalise it. Incidentally, it is scandalous that these people should be entitled to call themselves 'doctor.'

"But don't think for a moment, gentlemen, that I won't sort all this out, right and proper." The Führer then raised his hand slightly, so I called for a housekeeper to clear away his plate. He paused while his plate was removed, his customary signal that others could now enter the "conversation."

There was only silence from the legal community.

"My Führer." It was Goebbels. "I see your point clearly. I believe that the future of law in the Reich must soon rest totally with the Peoples' and Special Courts, especially now that justice must be swift as well as sure." A crooked smile sliced across his cadaver-like face. "Going forward, men like Freissler and Rothaug, here, will be the future of your judicial system."

The Führer nodded. "Perhaps," he said, then turned his head towards Himmler. "But perhaps our Reichsführer will be its future instead."

"All shall be done in accordance with your wishes, my Führer," was all Himmler said.

As usual, no expression appeared on Himmler's face, but I could have sworn that the barest hint of a stricken look appeared on Gürtner's. I had no understanding of Goebbels's use of "swift," but I saw in my mind, the two hapless prisoners in Himmler's cellars and wondered what justice would look like in his "court."

Considering what the Führer's reference to "our Reichsführer" might foreshadow, I felt something glide down the small of my back. It was perspiration.

I've BEEN RECEIVING several furtive calls from Frau Höss, I imagine, to get to see more of the Führer's films (I jest), but I have remained steadfast in my decision to maintain some semblance of cordiality while avoiding any actual contact. For someone as unsophisticated and shy as I am, this has proven to be a delicate and dangerous balancing act, but a necessary one, and I believe I've achieved sufficient success. However, only time will confirm or deny this.

I made a few tentative overtures to a quite personable and comely member of the housekeeping staff, but she told me she was warned not to become involved romantically with anyone who answered directly to the Führer. When I questioned her about this, asking her who would give such preposterous advice, and told her that, logically, it was far better for her to be involved with someone in my unique position than with anyone who answers to a person lower (and so more insecure) in the pecking order, she froze up, merely saying that she needed to keep our relationship purely professional. She is either a coward or an idiot, and I can live without either. The secretaries are far too homely and/or politically fanatical to be worthy of effort, Kempka and Baur are too sordid to rely on, and the chance of my meeting anyone outside the cloistered confines of the Chancellery or the Berghof is extraordinarily slim. And Zarah, even Zarah, for whom I still ache despite her marital duplicity, has seen fit to remain incommunicado since our last assignation. The result: Salon Kitty or my own devices, namely, Brückner.

By now, only a moron in a coma would fail to grasp that the Führer has decided to put what he called the "traditional measures of ordinary mortals" into operation, which to me is unmistakable proof that war on a large scale was imminent and that his other plan, whatever that could possibly be (immortal?) has not yet achieved fruition. For weeks, the halls have buzzed with generals, diplomats, industrialists, and other top Reich officials and leaders of every description.

But today, there was an even livelier atmosphere in the Chancellery if that can be imagined. Keitel, Brückner, Göring, Goebbels, Himmler, officers of the General Staff, and I disappeared into the conservatory, where they spread out their plans for the invasion of Czechoslovakia!

"That paper president Hácha[188] will be here tomorrow," the Führer announced. "This time, I shan't need a conference. In Munich they said A, now they'll have to say B."

All laughed, but with all, save G., G., and H., I detected a somewhat guarded quality in their laughter.

The "paper president" arrived with his foreign minister. By the Führer's specific design, the hapless men were escorted first all round the new Chancellery by a company of SS Leibstandarte[189] Adolf Hitler, as a means to unmistakably illustrate the power

---

[188] President of Czechoslovakia.

[189] The term *Leibstandarte* was derived partly from *Leibgarde,* a somewhat archaic German translation of "Guard of Corps," or personal bodyguard of a military leader (*Leib,* i.e., literally "body, torso"; and *Standarte*: the Schutzstaffel (SS) or Sturmabteilung (SA) term for a regiment-sized unit).

and might of Germany and more than hint at what they were up against. At last, with Brückner and me posted at either side of the study door, they were brought before their "host," who stood before them with the calculated demeanour of the greatest ruler of all time. For a moment, I thought of Il Duce, with his puffed-out-chest-and-chin haughtiness.

After a frosty greeting, the Führer told them to sit at the table where Göring and von Ribbentrop were already seated. Without pleasantries or preliminaries, the Führer demanded that Hácha and his minister immediately sign a prepared document which rendered Czechoslovakia a protectorate of Germany. I noticed that with Hácha, the Führer dispensed with all the theatrics he'd employed with Chancellor Schuschnigg of Austria and merely told the Czech that the Wehrmacht was ready to occupy the entire territory.

Much to my surprise, Hácha refused to sign the document, and so the atmosphere instantly switched from ice to fire. I was somewhat jolted when von Ribbentrop jumped up, hovered over Hácha and ordered him to sign, then resumed his seat. Pure theatre.

The Führer then said, in a tone of pure foregone conclusion: "I give you two options: cooperate with Germany, in which case the entry of German troops will take place in a tolerable manner and permit Czechoslovakia a generous life of her own, autonomy, and a degree of national freedom, or face a scenario in which resistance will be broken by overwhelming force of arms, using all means at our disposal. I tell you this: Refuse to sign, my friends, and before you arrive back at your homes, German bombers will have reduced Prague to ruins! Do you doubt me for a single moment?"

At that, poor Hácha swooned, and Morell was called in to

minister to him. SS men carried Hácha to a neighbouring room, where the physician gave him one of his mysterious injections and managed to revive him.

He was instantly taken back to the Führer, a fountain pen pushed into his hand, and the Führer repeated the illusory consoling statement that he had no intention to "Germanise" the territory and that it would be "allowed" complete independence. Brückner and I glanced at each other knowingly and marvelled once again at the audacious brilliance of the Führer's style. It had its desired effect: Hácha signed. But (as Brückner explained to me afterwards) the Führer recognized that for appearance's sake, his brutal victory required soft edges, and so he called in Schroeder and dictated a formal request from Hácha to Germany that the latter (Germany) take the former (Czechoslovakia) under its military wing and, thereby, "liberate it from inner disturbances and pressure on its borders." This was typed up on the spot, handed to Hácha, and he signed that as well.

Hácha, panting and clearly out of breath, informed the government in Prague of the documents he had signed, the Czech military received orders to lay down their arms, which they reluctantly did, and German troops entered the former Czechoslovakia. Again, the Führer's victory was total and complete!

I'D INTENDED TO visit Kitty's this evening, but that plan evaporated quickly. A mere half hour after Hácha departed, the Führer, Keitel, Himmler, Brückner, Kempka, Bormann, and I boarded the train at Anhalt station, aimed on a direct route for Prague, and we left when the Führer was certain that Wehrmacht troops had "pacified" the area.

As the train made its way south, Brückner and I sat separate from the rest, who were busy conferring about plans for the Führer's newest conquest. I welcomed this opportunity to talk to Brückner since I felt that, aside from obligatory meetings with the Führer, he'd been avoiding me, and I couldn't imagine why. Paranoia, perhaps? At least that's what I hoped.

"Heinz, just look at our exalted Reichsführer," Brückner whispered, "the Reich's new 'Chief Justice, without portfolio,' you might say, so eager to . . . execute the Führer's innovative judicial system. My God, you can actually see it for once—the man can literally taste the delight of passing summary sentence and administering the inevitable punishment through the tender mercies of his ever-assiduous henchmen, Heydrich and Eichmann."

Just before, the Reichsführer-SS had been attempting to regale the Führer with his "pacification measures," as he called them, but the Führer had quashed it, saying: "No need, Heinrich.

I trust that you'll act in full accordance with my wishes," to which Himmler replied: "Of course, my Führer. That goes without saying," to which the Führer responded: "Then it's fitting that no more be said."

"Himmler does appear more animated than usual, I must admit," I told Brückner.

He tilted his head slightly to the right where it almost met his raised shoulder. "Never lose that sense of humour, my friend," he remarked. "'More animated?' The bloody fiend is positively twitching with impatience to personally direct the liquidation of Czech patriots. And this is only the barest of beginnings, I can assure you."

He sank back in his seat and sipped his Riesling. "You know, Heinz," he said, "I've been with the Führer since 1930, and it still fascinates me how he deals with unpleasantness."

"What do you mean?" I asked, intrigued.

"Well, just now, for example. Himmler was longing to reveal to the Führer all the . . . diversions he and Heydrich planned for those poor Czechs who managed to survive the Wehrmacht's pitiless onslaught, but the Führer would hear none of it. The measures, yes, but not the mention. I've always been fascinated by the difference between the Führer's pronouncements and his practice. An undisputed master of bombast, he employs rhapsodically ruthless terms with his subordinates like 'crush,' 'annihilate,' 'exterminate,' 'destroy,' 'eradicate,' and 'obliterate,' among others—while providing no details, of course. And yet, when these same subordinates attempt to report on how they carried out such terms, the Führer covers his ears, so to speak. Curious, no?"

"Curious, yes," I replied. I'd witnessed this apparent contradiction in the Führer's character many times, but never thought about it, much less analysed it. "But his 'underlings,' as you put it, appear to know what to do, regardless of specifics. It's as if the Führer draws the outlines with a broad brush, leaves it to others to choose and fill in the colours, and wishes only to see the final painting. It gives those underlings considerable freedom."

"And the Führer, too, I think."

"What do you mean?" I asked, suddenly confused.

"For another time," was all he replied, then smiled: "So what's new with you? With all this Czech business, I haven't had a chance to catch up with your whirlwind sex life."

"As usual, Wilhelm," I kidded, "you flatter me." I swallowed my embarrassment and filled him in on my dealings with Frau Höss, Kitty's, and the housekeeper. As I spoke, I summoned up the courage to ask him for some possible candidates.

"Let me think about it and I'll let you know. A young, decent-looking, tall, strapping fellow in your position, even with your thinning hair, shouldn't have to make bored *frauen*[190] feel wanted, frequent the likes of a Salon Kitty, or immerse yourself in grotesque debaucheries with Kempka's stable of sluts."

"I'd be most grateful, Wilhelm." *Risk!* I ordered myself. "I've missed you, you know."

Brückner took another sip. He appeared almost diffident, unusual for him.

"Yes," he answered. "My apologies, but this Czech matter has taken up so much of my time, that—"

No, I thought to myself. He'd been in even more complex circumstances before, but always had time for a chat. "Please, Wilhelm, tell me—and without the gloves on, eh?"

There was utter silence, except for the Czech chat of the

---

[190] Married women.

pack in front. I was becoming increasingly apprehensive, with no outlet for my anxiety.

Finally, Brückner nodded an assent. "All right, Heinz, gloves off. Let's move to the vestibule, yes?"

We got up casually, Brückner fished out his cigarette case and ivory holder, and we headed out. Once out of others' sight and hearing, Brückner turned to face the flying scenery, slowly lit a Gauloise with cupped hands, and drew on it for a few moments while I sweated with anticipation. Then he turned to me.

"Iago."

"Iago?" I replied, my eyelids fluttering in confusion.

Brückner smiled. "I don't imagine for a moment that you've read *Othello*—or even know who Shakespeare is, for that matter—and so I wouldn't imagine that you'd recognize the character of Iago. A pity in this case."

I had and I did, though that was not for Brückner to know. A pity in my case? "You're right, Wilhelm, as usual," I said. "What are Shakespeare and Iago, and what do they have to do with you avoiding me?"

"My God, Heinz, we have to get you some schooling before you die of ignorance. Shakespeare was an English poet, playwright, and actor, widely regarded as the greatest writer in the English language and the world's preeminent dramatist. But, as the Führer is so fond of pointing out, only the Germans can truly appreciate him. With me, the jury's still out. At any rate, in *Othello*, Iago is a soldier who has fought beside Othello for several years, and has become his trusted adviser. At the beginning of the play, Iago claims to have been unfairly passed over for promotion to the rank of Othello's lieutenant in favour of a fellow named Cassio.

"Not content with this state of affairs," he went on, "Iago

plots to manipulate Othello into demoting Cassio, and thereafter, to bring about the downfall of Othello himself. After Iago engineers a drunken brawl to ensure Cassio's demotion, he sets to work on his second scheme: leading Othello to believe that his wife, Desdemona, is having an affair with Cassio. Iago's plan appears to succeed when Othello kills Desdemona, and then kills himself. Iago is one of Shakespeare's most sinister villains, often considered such because of the unique trust that Othello places in him, which he betrays while maintaining his reputation of honesty and dedication. Now, Heinz, does this Iago remind you of anyone we know?"

I'd read the play years ago and, of course, knew it word for word, but understood none of it, since, even in German, the words and their presentation were completely obscure to me. But now, with Brückner's summary, it finally took on some meaning.

"Again with your tests and riddles, Wilhelm?" I said in mock umbrage. "I'm no Othello. Nobody could possibly envy me enough to plot against me—even that little pile of shit Krause. And I certainly don't have a Desdemona, as you well know."

"Forget Krause and Desdemona," he said. "And while we're about it, forget yourself. Find an Othello and go from there. *Now* do you know?"

The train noise in the corridor bombarded my brain, but I struggled to concentrate, and finally I ventured. "He would go that far?"

Brückner grabbed my arm tightly in a gesture of appreciation. "Thank you. Yes, Heinz, he would go that far—even further. He has been doing it, and is probably doing it now, as we speak. All Iago's motives: jealousy, ambition, envy, want of self-esteem—they're all there. In this cunning bulldog. I have it on good authority that, because he can't get to me on political grounds, he's scouring the countryside of my past to find some social . . . irregularities. And, since my past will reveal no shortage of irregularities, one day this bulldog will succeed as Iago did; of that, I'm fairly certain—you know how puritanical the Führer is about propriety. And I didn't wish you to join me in this inevitability."

Now I knew about Iago. "So, by avoiding me, you thought you were protecting me?"

"In a word, yes."

I won't deny the mixture of affection and anger coursing through me like a lava stream at that moment. "Did you feel me incapable of appreciating your concern but making my own decision?"

He shrugged. "My sincerest apologies, Heinz, but what if I had done? What would you have decided?"

"Can't you guess?" Now I gave tests.

"Of course I can. That's why I alone made the decision."

I tried to prevent my eyes from welling up, but I was singularly unsuccessful.

"And you truly believed that by avoiding me, you would be 'the bulldog's' sole victim? I commend your motives, but not your knowledge of me. You must understand that you've become a fa . . . an older brother to me, a most-revered older brother, and that it would be utterly unfair and even disrespectful of you not to allow me to shoulder a burden of this magnitude with you. Do you not see this?"

Just then, the door swung open and "the bulldog" was standing there. We both turned to face him.

"Yes?" asked Brückner.

"The Führer wishes to have you rejoin the discussion, Herr General."

"Tell the Führer that I'll be right along. Thank you, Herr Bormann."

"As you wish," Bormann replied, with no more expression than Himmler, save the barest trace of a silky smirk, and left.

Brückner turned back to me. "My apologies, Heinz. I meant no offence to you. But I take your point. It should have been your decision, not mine."

"Thank you, Wilhelm," I said. "I'm perfectly willing to take my chances with Bormann. I haven't burnt my bridge to the brickyard."

Brückner laughed. "Good for you, Heinz. But it wasn't only Bormann I was trying to protect you from."

"Who then?"

"The Führer," he answered, then, before I could respond, patted me on the shoulder, turned, and went to join the others, leaving me shaking my head in bewilderment.

16 March 1939

Around midnight, our caravan sped from Reichenberg in the Sudetenland and on to and through the capital. Night lights glowed in the shop windows, and the streets appeared empty of soldiers and police. After a wrong turning, we finally arrived at the historic castle on the hill above Prague,[191] the residence of the former president of Czechoslovakia. The Führer climbed out, moved to the massive doors that opened as if on a timed machine, and he went through to the room that Bormann had ordered to be made up for him and settled in with his entire entourage.

The Führer wished to feed all present, but there was nothing prepared for him to offer (a rare slip by the up-to-then-infallible Bormann). This drove him to a fury at a stroke, and he commanded, in the most unmistakable terms, that all food and drink be brought to him with all deliberate speed and placed on the table—which was done, with my frantically determined assistance. And the now-satisfied Führer spent almost all night in lively conversation in the residence's enormous, ornate library concerning plans for the next day. Only Heydrich was absent, supervising his SS and Gestapo men, who were methodically rushing round making mass arrests.

The Führer explained to Himmler, Goebbels, and Keitel his

---

[191] The Hradschin.

plans for dealing with the Slavs: "This is only the beginning, you understand," he was saying as I entered, "but a beginning that history will note. This is a battle for civilization itself. As such, whoever fails to heed the German as the prime emblem of the master race must reckon with certain, rigorous, and uncompromising punishment."

I thought of what Brückner told me about the Führer's generic bombast, and I had to agree. I hadn't considered it before, but now I was forced to, for once the toothpaste of information was free of the tube, there was no shoving it back in. He went on and on like this for hours, while I stood mute, along with Brückner and "the bulldog."

Once Himmler arrived to report on his triumphant "tour" of Prague, and the soldiers had returned to the castle, the Führer gleefully announced the occupation as complete, philosophizing about the "relentless accretion of 'living space'" and the true symbolic meaning of his taking of Czechoslovakia.

AFTER A HEARTY lunch (by then, the kitchen staff knew better than to be unprepared), Kempka drove the Führer through the Prague streets. As in any German city, he stood up straight in his car so that, as Himmler put it, "the Czechs could see their new master." On the way back to Berlin, the Führer said that "marching into Prague pleased me far more than all that stupid shilly-shallying in Munich."

I couldn't see it in his face, but I knew from his expression that Brückner was troubled by the Führer's earlier use of "as such" in his attitude towards the Slavic peoples. I imagined that my friend had the frightful words "certain, rigorous, and uncompromising punishment" churning in his brain, and what those words would mean for the Czechs. To the Führer, bombast; to the Reichsführer-SS, license. So, to Brückner, and now perhaps to me, it was as much a triumph for Himmler as for the Führer—perhaps even more so. If Brückner did anything more than grimace, it would be just the political "irregularity" Bormann needed.

19 March 1939

I URGE YOU to overlook my scrawl, for my hands are still trembling.

Compelled by some force from within, I recount what occurred while arranging the Führer's desk. At the time, the Führer was speaking sharply to Göring about some military matter of no interest to me, when I heard an impatient rapping on the door. I raced over to see who would dare disturb the Führer without an appointment. It was Morell, who drifted by me as if his feet had no contact with the floor—astonishingly unnoticed by the Führer or Göring. He proceeded to the Führer's desk and, with force, swept all I'd arranged onto the carpet without the slightest sound. He then bade me undress, which I did, and by a disembodied command I climbed up and positioned my naked body on the desktop, facing upwards. Morell then shouted some words in a language I didn't know, and the man from Salon Kitty, also apparently unseen by the Führer and Göring, strode in and moved to the desk where I lay naked, arms and legs splayed.

After some soundless words, he began stroking my forehead with his long, narrow, translucent fingers, and suddenly the desk vanished, and I was now lying on the squalid stairwell landing of my nightmares, to which I was now strapped. This time there was no fire or even smoke. Above me hung suspended two glaring mercury vapour lamps, with their greenish light bearing down on my immobile nakedness. The man from Kitty's stood over me, gazing at a space just below my midsection, viscous drool descending in oozing drops onto my chest. "Is he prepared," said the man to Morell, and the doctor replied: "He has the article, of this I'm certain." Then the man gazed down at me, and it was no longer the man from Kitty's but a toothless Adelsheimer, his broken mouth a red and purple toothless void.

The former shopkeeper stated clinically with not a trace of warmth: "I will develop you like film, Linge. As a man of hidden intelligence, you will have the procedure explained as I go. You are fortunate to have no need for anaesthesia or sutures, and the risk of permanent damage is minimal." He then pulled on rubber surgical gloves, snapped the ends to his wrists, and held up an exotic metal device I'd never encountered.

"You're curious, Linge," he said without expression, his eyes dead. "Good. I show you a Gomko clamp. It is made up of four parts: a plate, a bell, a yoke, and a nut to tighten the clamp. The nut and the yoke can be common to several sizes. Only the bell and the plate need to be selected to fit the patient. Careful pairing of these is, of course, required.

"I now introduce the bell over the glans and under the foreskin, and the prepuce is drawn over it."

Glans! I remember seeing the word, but I was so benumbed with terror that I was unable to move or scream, much less think. I craned my neck but could only see the movement of his arms and nothing else, as if they were disembodied. Then, suddenly it struck me as if a bolt of lightning had shot through my body: *My penis! A dead photography shop proprietor is circumcising my penis!* I squeezed my eyes shut and just listened to the Yiddish-accented voice.

"Now," he said, "I'm making a dorsal slit in the foreskin to separate the foreskin from the glans. I'm taking the bell of the clamp and placing it over the glans and pulling the foreskin over the bell. That done, I place the base of the clamp over the bell, and fit the clamp's arm. Good. Now I'm confirming the correct fitting and placement and the amount to be excised. I'm tightening the nut on the clamp, thus causing the clamping of nerves and blood flow to the foreskin. Done. Now, I'm leaving the clamp in place to the count of ten to allow clotting of blood to occur. All right, now I remove the foreskin with a scalpel, and remove the base and bell of the clamp, condition and bandage the penis. Well done."

I counted to one hundred and when I opened my eyes, I was back in the Führer's study in full uniform, standing at ease. The desk was as I'd organized it. The only change was the Führer and Göring standing before me with concerned expressions creasing their features.

"Linge, are you all right," the Führer asked.

Unnerved, I could only stammer: "Yes, my Führer, I . . . I'm fine. W . . . why do you ask?"

"Why do I ask? First, I catch you in my bathroom stark naked, holding your member over my sink, and then you were organizing my desktop when suddenly you're waving your arms like a crazy man and screaming about your penis being mutilated."

Göring burst into spasms of fat-flailing laughter.

"I . . . I have no explanation, my Führer," I squeaked, mortified.

"Well, Linge," the Führer said in his lightest tone, "perhaps you should return to your quarters and perform a thorough inspection of your lower realm, eh? And then, find a suitable female to deal with your . . . preoccupation." The Führer smiled indulgently, and Göring resumed his boisterous laughter, which followed me all the way out.

I did return to my quarters and stripped, shuddering with relief that there were no alterations to my member—save for a slight tingling sensation and three brain-grinding questions:

What was the significance of this episode?

Why was the Führer so nonchalant about something so bizarre and potentially disastrous to him publicly?

Am I going mad??!!?

[Entries between 19 March and 1 April were unreadable.]

THE FÜHRER, POSSESSED of a jocular mood, declared a holiday for all nonessential Chancellery personnel (excluding Brückner, myself, and one secretary). When I asked him why, he chuckled and told me that it came to him during the night, when he was pondering his "masterful dealings with world leaders," that April Fool's Day was a more-than-apt holiday, though not so much so that he would declare it for the Reich as a whole.

"We can't squander the unlimited energies of the German people who are preparing the Reich for a holy crusade merely to satisfy a personal whim," he explained. He pointed out that the day had a "pivotal significance" for him, since it was on 1 April 1923 that he was sentenced to prison for his role in the Beer Hall Putsch of 8 November the year previous.

"*High treason, Linge!*" he shouted, then resumed his conversational tone. "That was the charge. However, I must confess that, to a great extent, they were right to so label it. But they were also complete fools, and sentencing me on April first was a brilliant metaphor for that foolishness.

"My trial brought me more attention and publicity than ever before. With a crowd of thousands—including press from around the world—watching the proceedings, I made the most of this opportunity by going on the offensive. While the trial dragged on, I took every opportunity to turn the subject away from the putsch itself and onto the malignancies that were destroying Germany. On and on, day after day, I made speech after speech about the Jews, Marxism, and France and the urgent need for a national resurgence. In a million years, I couldn't have paid for such exposure. My imprisonment was a classic example of losing the battle but winning the war. I never forgot the lessons of that experience, even though the rest of the world has done."

With that, he slapped his thigh as he always did in moments of triumph. I'd heard this story many times, but it always fascinated me how he could retell it and retell it with no loss of fervour, as if he were telling it for the first time. And I had to admit that the tale held true. Those judges and prosecutors were long gone, from an age long gone. He'd lectured me continually about the great leaders of the past, their virtues, and their fallibilities, but today, I felt—no, I knew—that the Führer, unlike the others, possessed the singular virtue of recognizing others' weaknesses and exploiting them to his advantage. No, not a mere virtue. *A genius!*

∽

Brückner was as good as his word. No more was he the absentee mentor but a constant friend. He told me again that he's still searching for the "perfect match" for me and that, in the meantime, I should avoid Kitty's. I finally asked him why it was so difficult for him, considering who and what he knows me to be, and he merely replied, as befitting Brückner the abstruse: "To ask the question is to answer it."

I didn't pursue the matter, but my patience (and other things) can withstand just so many delays.

2 *April 1939*

AGAIN, THE FÜHRER was with Morell all morning, complaining of a variety of ailments that required the doctor's complete attention and speedy remedies. This allowed me—forced me, rather—the time to consider some matters I'd been avoiding up to now with some success. As you probably guessed, I left some unfinished business in my entry of 24 January,[192] the fourth anniversary of my entry into the Führer's household. I believe now that I must come to terms with the changes that have taken place in me in the last four years.

The first is the irony of reading far less (even with total access to the Führer's vast and diverse Goebbels-proof library)[193] and comprehending far more. Moreover, this comprehension is not merely existential but retroactive, and this has altered my feelings about several things, both fresh and venerable. I remain a greenhorn when it comes to phraseology and the implications of those things I now understand, but even this is diminishing rapidly, as if each word were feeding on the others. This I also found to be occurring in my writing, for I'd never put pen to paper before entering the Führer's service. Even though I had no editors to inform or correct me, I do believe that there has

---

[192] The entry is missing.

[193] See Timothy W. Ryback, *Hitler's Private Library: The Books That Shaped His Life*, Vintage Books (January 2010).

been emerging, geometrically, a far greater connexion between my reading and my writing, both in content and in style, not remotely original, mind you, but a far more accurate imitation.

As important as this is to my ego as a sign of personal growth, I'm also growing more and more concerned about my ability to maintain my persona of artlessness and invisibility in the face of this growth, and the increasing temptations such growth creates. After four years and innumerable experiences that would astonish and perplex the brightest of common labourers, I suddenly feel the urgency of assessing the benefits and costs of revealing my emerging nature. Along those lines, I have harboured the suspicion that Brückner long ago penetrated my shield and rendered me just as naked as his own needs and ability to conceal would permit. This is how I'm interpreting many of our recent conversations, and I'm quite troubled by the significance. Even more troubling is the question of how many others may have also passed through my defences—and who. And, no less important, do I dare confide all this in Brückner in order to confirm or disprove my suspicions?

The second is my interest in affairs of state. I joined the Party in 1933 when all my brickyard mates were joining (with an unfortunate few exceptions). Perhaps, considering my "workplace," I never had, nor do I have even now, any fervent interest in politics and government, being content to improve my mind, not the lot of the German people. Of course, Brückner would probably say that, no offense intended, nobody really cares about the brain of a valet, especially my boss and everybody else. Loyalty and efficiency, definitely, political indifference, maybe, but for the rest—? It could be argued that at this point, does it really matter if everyone knows of my "gifts"? To that, I have no answer except an instinct—not so different from the Führer's—that whispers

to me that there is safety in underestimation. No, again as with
the Führer, more than safety—power.

And what to make of my most recent hallucination?

I was roused from my ruminations by the Führerbuzzer,
thank God.

When I entered, Morell was nowhere to be seen, and Baur was
busy entertaining the Führer with an anecdote about Göring.
Since Baur was an excellent storyteller and Göring was an excellent subject, I listened while sorting the already-sorted mail and
arranging the immaculate desk.

"Then a storm loomed up ahead," he was saying about
Göring's flight to Rome. "I suggested that we should fly through
it, which meant instrument flying, and of course the 'air ace'[194]
was forced to agree." The Führer just shook his head. "You'll love
this, my Führer," he continued. "Once he agreed, the, ah, general
immediately vacated his seat next to me, because he knew nothing about blind flying and didn't want to betray his ignorance.
Naturally, such flying was nothing new to me, so I flew through
the storm without any incident, save some turbulence, while
the Luftwaffe chief sat in the back, hunched over with his head
in his hands, moaning. After making a perfect landing. The first
thing Balbo[195] did was to congratulate Göring on the expert way
he'd landed the plane—by then, of course, he'd taken his seat
up front with me again. Göring graciously accepted the praise,

---

[194] In World War I, Göring finished the war with twenty-two victories. A
thorough postwar examination of Allied loss records showed that only two of
his claimed victories were doubtful. Three were possible, and seventeen were
certain, or highly likely.

[195] The Italian air marshal.

and just winked at me when no one was looking. I, of course, said nothing."

The Führer laughed heartily and patted Baur on the shoulder. "Well, Baur," the Führer replied, "it appears that we must face the sad fact that our bemedalled Commander in Chief of the Luftwaffe is now more adept at flying a plane from a couch than from a cockpit."

Story aside, I continue to be amazed at the medical miracles Morell performs. The Führer never looked sprightlier. Before leaving, Baur told the Führer about his fruitless attempts to secure me fitting female companionship. "I do my best, my Führer, but our friend Linge, here," he said, "is far too exclusive for my recommendations."

The Führer *tsk-tsk*-ed and turned to me as I was rearranging his profusion of coloured pencils, then back to Baur. "My friend," he said, "have you no sympathy for poor Linge? You don't care if the female you cavort with is a sheep, so long as it's female. The lad, here, is more particular, and so he rejects the barnyard. In these matters, I can be of no assistance, so you must try to secure him more exalted creatures."

"Right, my Führer," he said. "Whatever you say. I'll toss my notebooks aside and scour the society pages instead." It was clearly a joke, and the Führer took it as such.

After Baur left, the Führer asked me to organize his elaborate military maps for the following day. I had no idea what he wanted them for, and would never ask, but, after Austria, the Sudetenland, and Czechoslovakia, I had a general idea.

A PIVOTAL DAY for the Führer—and for me.

Brückner and I were present (as literal bystanders) at a top-level military meeting in the Führer's conference room. Along with the Führer were Chief of Staff Keitel, Chief of Operation Staff Jodl, Chief of Plans Warlimont, Chief of Foreign and Counter-Intelligence Canaris, OKH head von Brauchitsch, OKM head Raeder, and Foreign Minister von Ribbentrop. They were all hunched over an enormous Art Deco oval table that was strewn with the maps I'd arranged yesterday. The Führer was speaking down to the map.

"Knowing Chamberlain for what he is, and knowing the French in general, I'm convinced that we have a free hand concerning Danzig. Opinions, gentlemen?"

In that I'd learned to call such questions "Führer-speak," that meant confirmation.

I was right. All stood up straight and sang in unison: "Yes, my Führer, a free hand."

In my peripheral vision, I saw the Führer also straighten and swivel his head round the oval, with what I interpreted as a gaze of barely masked contempt. *Of course, yes,* his eyes said.

"But free hands are not why I gathered you here," he said. "That moustachioed mouse Chamberlain and his supporters believe that war can be avoided and hope that Germany will agree to leave the rest of Poland alone. And, of course, even if we do agree, it will have no meaning—"

"But what of France, my Führer?" interrupted von Ribbentrop.

I just waited for the explosion.

"*FRANCE?*" The Führer screamed, his pounding fist rearranging the maps. "Ribbentrop, are you serious? Those fools want war even less than the British. They only wish to be left alone to grow their grapes, promenade through their parks, and visit their museums. *Forget both of them!*" he declared with Führer-like finality. "Now, gentlemen," he continued, "'Fall White'[196] has been hovering over us for years like a stalled dirigible. Now, it's time to put it into motion. My secretary has typed up a thorough summary of the plan and the roles each of you will play. I also prepared a separate set for our industrialists and bankers, who require a slightly different slant on the matter. Any questions?"

Of course there were none. There began a long silence while the military men stared down at the maps and von Ribbentrop appeared to be anxiously seeking a way to mollify the Führer after an uncharacteristically independent remark. I had the feeling that they'd known about this plan for some time, and little more needed to be said, save "yes, my Führer," which they all did before saluting and filing out.

In the afternoon, Brückner summoned me for a stroll-round-the-gardens chat. "I haven't given up on my offer to find suitable female companionship," he said. "In fact, I think I may have

---

[196] *Fall Weiß* called for a start of hostilities before the declaration of war. German units were to invade Poland from three directions. All three assaults were to converge on Warsaw, while the main Polish army was to be encircled and destroyed west of the Vistula River.

found a candidate, provided we can raise your level of sophistication beyond your years and background."

"You mean go back to school?" I joked.

"Not all that drastic a transformation. Just a bit more social polish and academic erudition."

"My God, Wilhelm, is she some university professor with a von before her surname?"

Brückner laughed. "Well, I can tell you that she comes reasonably close. An acquaintance of Sophie's,[197] though we met on the job, you might say."

He'd said "on the job" before, and for a long time, I wondered without asking just what it could mean. Knowing Brückner as I did, this hadn't surprised me, even his reticence, for Brückner was not the sort who would donate to a charity and place his name on the gift. But I suspected that there was somehow more to his "on the job." Again, only intuition.

But my faux friend Schroeder the gossip monger once mentioned something that had surprised me and gave me no dearth of disquiet but also something I resolved never to raise with him. She'd told me that his one-time girlfriend, the artist Sophie Storck (who'd also been in the car accident that cost Brückner his eye, receiving numerous injuries of her own), was a favourite of the Führer and a frequent guest at the Berghof. She was also intensely jealous and, eventually, had been supplanted by Magda Quandt, who later married Goebbels. Brückner had always remained mum concerning his own social life, and I never pressed him on it, even as a tease, but I now saw something that Bormann could employ to set the Führer against him and that might go to explain Brückner's pessimism.

---

[197] Brückner's fiancés, a highly talented artist and a good friend of Eva Braun.

"Not that I'm anxious, mind you," I said, "but when do you think I'll be . . . worthy of this find of yours?"

Brückner laughed so hard that the army of sentries turned their heads towards us. "I see I hit a nerve. I was only pulling your leg about your qualities. Actually, I think she'll find you most charming and even witty. The rest, she'll have to decide for herself. Unfortunately, the lady is currently on holiday, but the moment she returns to Berlin, I'll arrange a meeting, how would that be?"

"When is she to return?"

"Within a fortnight, I should think. If sooner, I'll—"

A fortnight! "Can you tell me anything about her, to make the time go faster?"

"You create a nonwinnable scenario, my friend. If I tell you of her virtues, you'll gain in impatience. If I tell you of her vices, the time will quicken, but you'll dread the meeting. Misery attends both, I'm afraid. Best if we ignore time in this case, eh?"

He was right, as usual. "You're the devil's logician, Wilhelm," I joked, though concerned that I'd gone out of character.

Brückner paused, as I feared he might do. "Yes," he said, "fortnight be damned. She might be just the woman for you."

4 *April* 1939

My crushing migraines returned this morning with such ferocity after months of relief that I even asked the Führer for access to
Morell, which he promptly gave with eager concern. All morning
and into the night, the doctor plied me with nostrums which
accomplished nothing. The magic he was able to perform on the
Führer was utterly lost on me. Finally, in frustration—which he
attributed to my body's apparent unwillingness to respond to
his quackery—he injected me with a potion, the only effect of
which was to merely transport me back to the nightly nightmare
of flames—though this time, with the addition of the small,
mysterious metal top.

And yet, insane as it may seem, in a way, a part of me actually
welcomes these migraines, for they occupy a space that would be
bursting with feelings of loneliness, isolation, and foreboding.
No family, no peers with whom to confide, no female companionship, and with only Brückner to replace them. Not enough,
I'm afraid. Not nearly enough. I confess to you that, to a great
extent, my chosen persona and its need for invisibility have
amply contributed to this dismal state of affairs, but the result
remains, aided and abetted by Brückner's fucking fortnight!

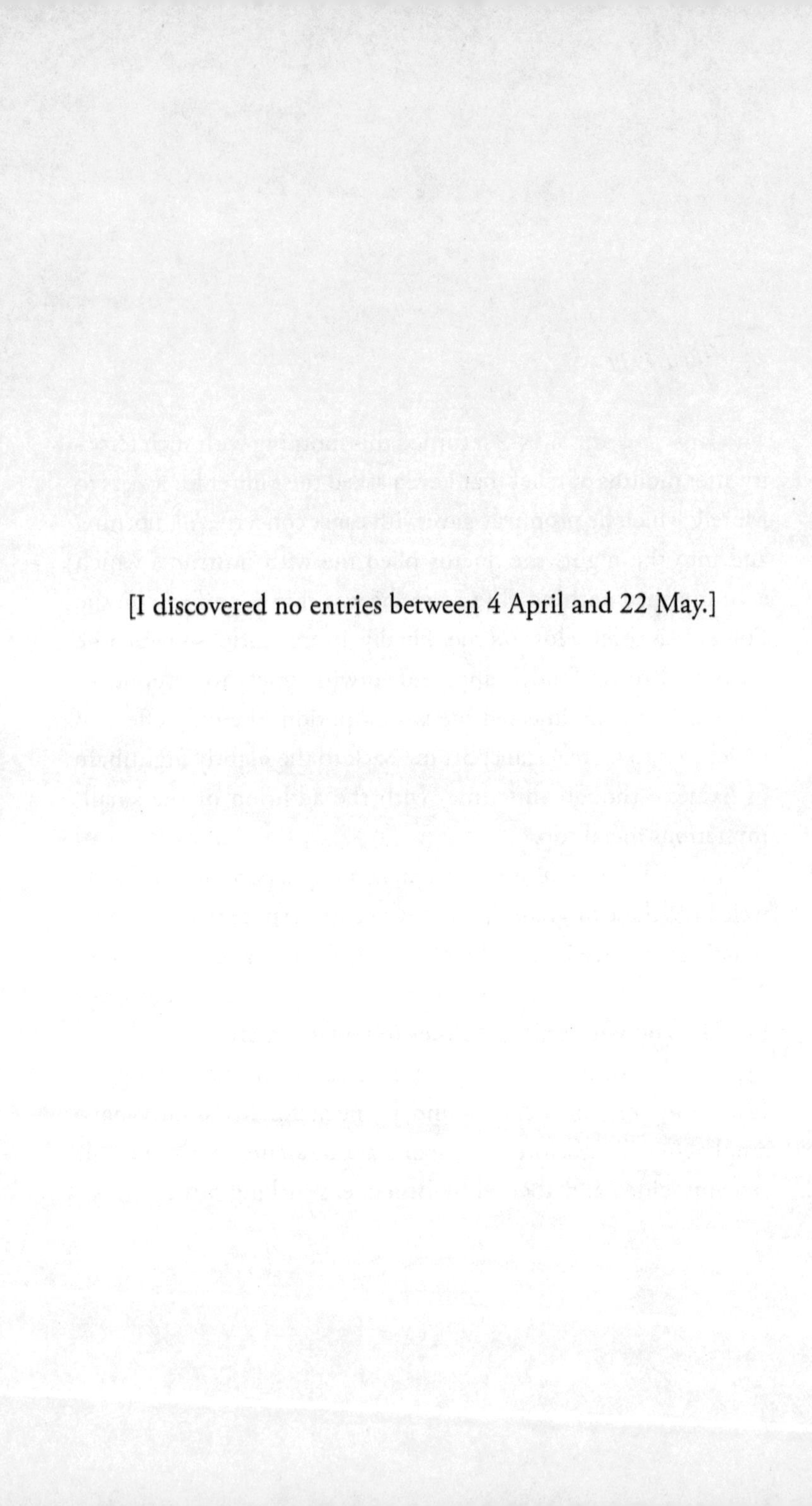

[I discovered no entries between 4 April and 22 May.]

A WAKE ALL NIGHT *again!*

I showered and torturously changed from my sweat-drenched pyjamas into a freshly laundered SS colonel's uniform. While I'm determined to lose the past, the past is even more determined to find me. Am I more now than I was then (the orphan, the urchin, the ignoramus, the roustabout, the bricklayer's apprentice)? Adelsheimer, Bella, Katrin, and Emerald might say: Perhaps, but more *what?* Coward? Procrastinator? Political naïf? Moral cripple? Perhaps then, *more* is the wrong term. Different, then? I'm certainly different from what I was, I know that. But does the difference hold any positive significance? I dare say that at least the four I mentioned above would shout an emphatic negative.

Since I arrived at my current position, I'd met only three men, good, bad, or indifferent, whom I would classify as naturally cultivated: Brückner, Heydrich, and Speer; the rest, as varying degrees of coarse. Naturally, the Führer is in a class entirely by himself and so defies categorization.

As if he'd been listening to my brain by magical means, Speer actually arrived at my door, asking for a "few moments of my valuable time." This was the first time the Führer's architect even acknowledged my existence, much less asked for an "audience." I believe I've described him adequately in an earlier entry, so there's no further need to do so here, since he hadn't even remotely deteriorated in the interim.

I hoped that my face didn't betray my surprise as I ushered him to my only chair and I sat on the edge of my sweat-soiled cot and waited. And waited. Clearly, he was discomfited, whether by being with me or by some other matter he intended to relate when he'd become emotionally available—or both. I needed him to get to the point before the Führerbuzzer dictated a postponement.

"Herr Linge," he finally began, "I'm here on a most delicate and, I hope, discreet matter."

"Yes?" I answered, bereft of a better response.

"This is very difficult for me, so I will be grateful for some patience. I speak to you because, unlike the others who hover round, you are a particularly privileged intimate of the Führer, even more so than Fräulein Braun, I dare say. As such, you cannot be unaware of the shift in the mood of the German people, that is to say, a . . . drooping morale. Now such a state of affairs is nothing new and, in all probability, a mere passing tremor of national malaise. My concern is, however, the Führer's morale. You are aware of how close the Führer and I have been, as we planned and executed the architectural beginnings of a new Berlin. And yet, of late, I've found the Führer to be increasingly withdrawn, angry, and impatient with all things, both significant and trivial.

"As only one example, you may recall that only two years before, the Führer had often stepped out on the 'historic balcony,' but no longer. In fact, he told me to have it raised even further from the crowds that hardly see him now, and when they do, they now receive orchestration in place of the former spontaneity. Now, he snaps at his adjutants, even General Brückner, when they come to him with the request that he show himself. *Stop bothering me with that!* is a typical refrain. You would know better than I that the Führer is betraying a—how shall I call it?—an . . . uneasiness he had not shown before. Not long before, in a meeting, the Führer said to me: 'You know, Speer, considering the current state of some of my affairs, of which you should know nothing, it's not out of the question that I shall someday be forced to take unpopular measures. These might possibly lead to riots. We must, therefore, provide for that eventuality.' He then ordered that all the buildings in the square be fitted with doors of steel and heavy iron gates to close off the square when necessary. He also ordered that his bodyguard grow into a fully motorised regiment and armed with only the latest equipment. In all, I detected the beginnings of a . . . cruelty, you might say, in his approach to architecture, that didn't exist before. I could relate more, but you can see what I'm getting at, yes?"

I had seen and heard the things which Speer described—and much more—but had no intention of sharing my own misgivings with him. And, to be frank, I hadn't a clue to what he was "getting at."

"And how can I be of service, Herr Speer?" was all I said.

My offer appeared to bewilder him, as if he expected a prolonged explanation of the Führer's mental processes at best, or at least, some confided rationale, both of which I could not provide, even if I wished to.

Speer just shrugged and pursed his lips, a sign, I hoped, that he expected little from me.

"Well, Colonel," he answered, "I hoped you might possess a clue to the change in the Führer, or, if not, you might agree to make some quiet inquiries along those lines."

"A most reasonable request, Herr Speer. To be frank, I have no idea what has caused this change you say you noticed in the Führer, since I have not the training, competence, or position to notice such things, much less analyse them. Moreover, the Führer, as you must know, keeps his thoughts well to himself. However," I lied, "I agree to make, as you say, discreet inquiries—if and when the right moment presents itself. Will that be sufficient?"

Speer, not a demonstrative sort, merely smiled (I thought, genuinely), told me that he would be most grateful for anything I could relate to him, thanked me for my valuable time, and left without saluting. Since the Führerbuzzer was temporarily silent, and despite the merciless pounding in my brain, I sat down on the toilet lid and grabbed a few moments to consider Speer's observations and request.

I hadn't overheard the related conversation the Führer had with Speer, but it didn't completely surprise me. In many a vocal rumination, the Führer, even with his genius and historical perspective, had repeated severe misgivings about "mortal abilities," as he mysteriously put it, to surmount the ultimately doomed achievements of previous "warlords." But, unlike the "uneasiness" of which Speer spoke, I would substitute the word *impatience*. But impatience for what?

In any event, I had no intention of bringing up the matter in any form to the Führer. I'd learned, years before, that for safety's sake, one must promise anything and then stretch it out until the promisee either loses interest or gives up in frustration. And what I wouldn't do for my colleague Kempka or for the hapless Adelsheimer, I certainly won't do for the arrogant Speer. A clandestine life necessitates lies, and with this particular liar, it seems, inaction as well.

However, I cannot deny the guilt that attends such a life. Safety and security aren't free to such a man. And what sort of man is he? A coward, to be sure. But perhaps, beneath it all, a humanist as well, despite the apparent contradiction.

Unfortunately, the problem may go even deeper. Dostoevsky wrote that "lying to ourselves is more deeply ingrained than lying to others." If so, to what extent and of what concerns have I lied to myself? About my cowardice? About my humanity? My need for safety and security? All these issues and questions collide with each other as spirals within spirals, inside a battered brain that's resumed its aching.

§

When I arrived, the Führer was loudly reprimanding one of his "army" of clerks about some hearsay he'd been told by the clerk's immediate superior (the chinless man I wrote about on my first day at the Chancellery). I'd seen the Führer do this often, especially recently, and, aside from wondering how he could fit so many trivial matters into his day, I also wondered why he would do so. In many ways, especially concerning his staff, the Führer was a petty engine that ran on rumours. How I've escaped such a scolding thus far is just one more unsolvable mystery I shove to the back of my brain.

"*Linge,*" the Führer shouted while I laid out his clothes, "*fetch a pen and pad!*"

I knew what was coming: the "judge" had rendered a verdict, and I was to record the "sentence." I dropped what I was doing, raced to his desk, and picked up the two items. I also knew the sentence.

"Linge, what's his name?"

"Schucke, my Führer," I told him. "Horst Schucke."

"Yes, Schucke. Write: This Schucke is to be immediately eliminated from my service, and transferred to the Wehrmacht, and given the lowliest position they can find." He turned to the miserable shaking creature before him. "Perhaps some front-line latrine duty will inject some loyalty and discipline into you, eh?"

"Y . . . yes . . . my Führer," he croaked, then saluted, pivoted, and exited quickly.

Once squeezed from the tube, I thought to myself. That is to say, once sensitised by Speer, I cannot shake my awareness that he was right: the Führer *had* changed. There was a time when a mere reprimand would have done, but now, he was meting out punishments as well. This was not strength but something that a merciless Himmler would officiously pass onto a gleeful Heydrich, and it concerned me greatly.

My thoughts were interrupted by a jubilant Goebbels, who burst in with Brückner to announce that the agreement had just been signed by Foreign Minister Ciano of Italy and von Ribbentrop.[198] While Goebbels was clearly elated, his mood was not shared by the Führer, who merely shrugged, moved over to his chair, and farted his way down to a landing.

Since the Führer remained silent, Goebbels, never one to suffer silence when it could be supplanted by words, congratu- lated the Führer on yet another triumph. Brückner moved over to where I'd resumed the deliberately slow laying out of clothes and stood expressionlessly at ease. I wanted to lean over and ask him if he'd arranged a meeting with his "mystery woman" but

---

[198] Known formally as the Pact of Friendship and Alliance between Germany and Italy, it was a military and political alliance between the Kingdom of Italy and Germany. The pact was initially drafted as a tripartite military alliance of Japan, Italy, and Germany. Whereas Japan wanted the focus of the pact to be aimed at the Soviet Union, Italy and Germany wanted it aimed at Britain and France. Because of this disagreement, the pact was signed without Japan and became an agreement between Fascist Italy and Nazi Germany.

laughed the nonsense away without a sound. As before, it would have to wait.

"A triumph, you say," the Führer finally replied. "Yes, Joseph, in a manner of speaking, you're right. Unfortunately, it's what I need just now, though it might have been better with Japanese involvement, but as I think about it, we needn't disturb Comrade Stalin more than is necessary. 'Pact of Steel' has a strong ring to it, even though it will probably mean little when the going gets rough."

I caught the "unfortunately" but could do nothing with it. I could tell that Goebbels caught it too.

"Naturally," Goebbels said, "only Great Britain and France will react, and I cannot imagine that you are disturbed by that."

"I'm not," was all he said, highly unusual for him.

Goebbels also caught the "even though."

"Then why will the pact mean little?" he asked.

"Joseph," the Führer said, with patient indulgence in his voice, "you know that I have only the highest regard for Il Duce. This pact was a commitment that to some extent I wanted, but I must confess that my admiration for Il Duce does not extend to the Italians, generally. Also, Italian Fascism is but a pale ghost of our National Socialism, and Il Duce can do only so much within it, and no more. But don't think for a moment that I won't test its limits."

I could tell that Goebbels was disappointed in the Führer's reaction but could do little to alter it.

"I fully understand, my Führer," said Goebbels. "My ministry will handle the matter with a light touch." Then he saluted and withdrew.

After a few moments, the Führer rose and moved silently

to his bathroom and, within seconds, the familiar thunderclaps reverberated throughout.

Brückner remained at ease, his eye at half-mast, while I finished with the Führer's clothes and began arranging his desk. When the Führer returned, he sent Brückner on an errand and sat back down heavily at his desk, reached for his phone, pressed two buttons that I knew would summon Himmler, and replaced the receiver.

"Poor Joseph," he said to me with a heavy sigh. "He wanted so much to trumpet the pact to the world as one more victory for his Führer and the Reich. However, even he knows that Il Duce is only lukewarm on the issue[199] and wants the whole business to be kept secret. So, we must meet in the middle. At any rate, a far more crucial matter occupies me and requires my fullest attention. Brückner is fetching Ribbentrop so we can proceed swiftly. Go and tell Schroeder to come, in case dictation is required, and make certain that my clerk has Weisthor and Himmler pencilled into my calendar for this evening."

I would never ask, but, as I left for Schroeder, I believed I knew what the "crucial matter" was: Stalin. I'd overheard the Führer discoursing on him innumerable times since I became valet and, most recently, on Stalin's foreign minister, Molotov, Litvinov's replacement. "A pity about Litvinov," the Führer once remarked to von Ribbentrop with some regret, "a rare Soviet statesman of wit and intelligence, forcibly replaced with an unimaginative, plodding bureaucrat, but it had to be done. Can't be seen negotiating with a Jew, after all, and his ties to Britain and France are too well known and inconvenient."

---

[199] Mussolini even dubbed the agreement the "Pact of Steel" (German: *Stahlpakt;* Italian: *Patto d'Acciaio)*, after being told that the original name, "Pact of Blood," would most likely be poorly received in Italy.

In my amateur's estimation, von Ribbentrop couldn't have cared less about the ethnicity of Litvinov, except to the extent the Führer cared, which also seemed to me questionable. The former was just relieved that now he'd be facing an inferior.

⁂

After I secured Schroeder—and endured an obligatory gossip session in which she had to know all that had transpired before I arrived—I sat alone on a marble bench in the Grand Hallway, mulling over Brückner's endlessly delayed matchmaking. One would have thought that he was Cardinal Woolsey attempting to arrange a marriage for King Henry.

I also ruminated over what Speer had told me this morning. And, looking round, the realization washed over me that the Chancellery had also changed. Truly, it looked more like photographs I'd seen of military garrisons, and it had become so, without my even registering it, so used to seeing a river of uniforms as I was. But now, with Speer's words rattling round in my brain, I could see that the river had been slowly transformed into a sea. I had to admit that Speer was onto something. But what was it? And why hadn't I noticed it before?

As if by telepathy, it was just when I'd determined to visit Salon Kitty after dinner that Brückner returned. He strode over to me with a broad smile bisecting his face and sat beside me.

"Speer visited me this morning," I told him.

A grimace of surprise. "You mean to tell me that the Führer's artistic surrogate deigned to venture below stairs?"

"He asked me about the change in the Führer's mood."

"So, the fellow actually got out of himself long enough to notice someone else. It must be serious."

I shrugged. "Is it?" I asked, refraining from telling him what Speer wanted of me.

Brückner nodded and sighed. "Speer is no more sensitive than I am. From my vantage point—and yours—" he said, "I see the ominous signs all round me, and they all point to one thing: very soon, the military as we know it will be rendered obsolete, and all Germans, men, women, and children, will be soldiers, one way or another. When we have an ex-corporal in charge of the greatest military machine in history, what implications need to be spelled out?"

"None," I replied, bereft of a response that wouldn't be outrageously speculative. "I'll take your word." I decided not to pursue the Führer's mood, or why he appeared so dissatisfied with events that looked to me like triumphs for his foreign policy.

"Right," Brückner said, and after a quizzical pause: "Ah, Heinz," he announced in a jesting tone, "When I came up just now, it's as if you knew I was the bearer of good tidings."

"Good tidings?"

"Well, for one as wholesome, sexually repressed, and impatient as you, I'd say so."

"So Katrin, Emerald, Hedwig, and the fair maidens of Salon Kitty don't count? My record's expunged retroactively? Saint Heinz, then and now?"

He laughed. "Well, 'Saint Heinz' is going a bit far, but as for the rest, well . . ." He let the "rest" trail away.

Normally, I dislike—and so benumb myself to—obligatory inconsequential banter before the true subject eventually emerges, but Brückner is so beguiling that I forbore it with good cheer.

"So, Wilhelm, what are these good tidings?"

"She's consented to meet you."

Who the hell *was* this creature? "Should I be aroused or honoured?" I asked him with just a hint of annoyance-generated, yawning indifference in my voice.

Brückner exhaled loudly. "Neither, I dare say, but that will be up to you to judge. She expects a call from you 'at your convenience,' as she put it to me."

"Sounds like a job application," I joked.

"Some relationships are," he joked back, then added, "but, then, some jobs are worth it."

"And this one is?"

"Apply, and judge for yourself, my friend."

As usual with Brückner, I conceded defeat. "All right, Wilhelm, again you win. But from what you've said—and haven't said—I hope I'm worthy."

"Heinz, would I have made the effort if I thought otherwise?"

I was forced to agree, since, with me, his humour never even descended to parody, much less cruelty.

"At least tell me something about her."

"I'd rather you discovered that by yourself."

"I'll wager she knows about me."

A comradely clap on the shoulder and a wink. "Heinz," he said, "even *I* don't know about you. Do *you*?"

EVEN IN THE brickyard I'd been mistrustful of the "blind dates" that a few well-meaning (and not so well-meaning) "colleagues" arranged for me from time to time, as they—with no little justification—considered me to be utterly inept at securing a date for myself. Even the cruel can be accurate. With several subsequent opportunities to accumulate evidence, I'm now quite convinced that in such matters, even after contact (such as it was) with the likes of an Emerald and Katrin, and even a Hedwig (not to mention the corrupt confections at Salon Kitty), I have not notably improved, and so the efforts of Brückner were as welcome as they were terrifying.

But before I could demonstrate my boudoir prowess, I was obliged to tend the Führer while he queried, lectured, paced, muttered, shouted, and otherwise "conferred" with his military and political bigwigs. The subject seemed to be Poland, but much of his topsy-turvy recitations glided through my ears as if nothing within blocked their progress. I surmised that his late-night meeting with Himmler and Weisthor must not have gone well, for his mood alternated between rage and depression with no discernible cause or warning, creating no little consternation in his "guests."

For my part, I shuddered with fearful impatience over the phone call I had to make once I left the Führer's rooms. *What's wrong with you, Heinz?* I chided. *It's only a date; it's only a female; it was arranged by Brückner. What could be amiss?* And yet I trembled. Just a feeling, but it had me sweating. He'd asked me not to make the call from the Chancellery. I couldn't deny some perplexity. I refrained from questioning his request, but it hardly allayed my anxiety.

As the Führer ranted and ruminated, I questioned Brückner's furtiveness, even to the point of the fanciful. Was the lady married? Was she the mistress of a high-ranking official? Was she a fugitive, and if so, from what? Was she even a German? What did I really know about Brückner and his life outside the Chancellery. And what did I actually feel? Perhaps a malaise, lurking beneath fear and a feverish anticipation: that there was to be an end of something—or a beginning.

"My God, Linge, these fools play me like a ball in a tennis match," the Führer said, and his words brought me back to his study. "Back and forth, back and forth, we can, we can't, it's too early, it's too late, they'll object, they'll stand mute. *Shit! All shit!* It's bad enough that I alone must make the hard decisions without having to endure from those idiots pledged to assist me this carnival of contradictions!"

I glanced round and there was only me and the Führer. How did I miss the rest leaving? Unfortunately, there was no time for strategy. "Are you not fortunate, my Führer," I finally answered. "You are able to hear both sides of an issue, and then you can choose which makes the greater sense of your intentions. Only you can know this. If I may say so, your greatest burden is also your greatest benefit." Inwardly, I shuddered at my gross breach of persona, but I was truly possessed by my impending phone call.

The Führer pursed his lips. "I can see that your time with

me was not wasted. My influence has borne fruit. I wish I could say the same for the others. You asked for the rest of the day. As a reward, done. Just tell Krause."

I hadn't recalled asking, and it perplexed me. "Thank you, my Führer," I said, and walked out the door.

∽

My phone call:

"Yes?" The voice was old and phlegmy.

"Hello, is this Christiane?"

"Of course not." A snarl.

"Right. May I speak to her?"

"Wait," the voice said, not a command, but a grumpy, perfunctory instruction.

I waited while two female voices I couldn't make out whispered angrily to each other.

The old, phlegmy voice returned. "Who are you?"

"I'm a personal friend of General Brückner. He gave me this number for Christiane Glöckner. Have I the correct number?"

"Where are you calling from?"

"A telephone kiosk."

A pregnant pause, then: "Tiergarten, secluded restaurant table. She will know you."

Click.

∽

I love the Tiergarten, and always have done, even when I used to hide there from the police and the more predatory urchins, employing the many of its urban/rural nooks and crannies for safe but frigid shelter. Sometimes, weather permitting, while I hid, I could overhear the grand Berlin Philharmonic Orchestra performing outdoors for ardent listeners and even more ardent daters. I never knew what they were playing, but it was pleasant to the ear, the only negative element being the hearty applause that would invariably—and rudely—awaken me.

Weather being ideal, the Tiergarten was overflowing with romantic couples, tourists, native sightseers, men and women in uniform and suits, strolling alone or in packs. I headed for the restaurant and, there, to as much of a quiet corner as possible. I'd thought to bring a copy of the *Volkischer Beobachter*, a useless pile of propaganda, but good for the appearance of reading when furtively searching for someone. I couldn't have been there for more than five minutes when I heard a voice behind me that I recognized.

"Heinz!" the voice exclaimed. "So you actually get into the sunlight once in a while."

I turned casually to see Gerhard Baumgärtner, a Hauptsturmführer[200] in Himmler's Interior Ministry, Department of Criminal Investigation, and a liaison between Heydrich and the Führer—by way of Brückner (did Brückner's duties ever end?).

I stood, we exchanged salutes, and he sat down without my invitation. True to type, he was above-average height, quite fit, sported an impassive, chiselled face with green eyes, thin lips, and recruiting-poster nose.

"Good to see you in daylight and outdoors," Baumgärtner repeated. "We all thought you might be a vampire." He chucked mirthlessly at that.

As surreptitious as the lady appeared to be, she will hardly show herself when the only free chair is held by an SS policeman. "This is, of course, a possibility, Gerhard," I replied, with even

---

[200] The equivalent of a captain in the Wehrmacht.

less mirth. "But the Führer keeps me so much at hand that I have no time to lurk in the shadows, seeking a ripe neck." *I leave such activities to Heydrich*, I thought.

"I don't doubt it," he said. "'His Reinhardship' is no less the taskmaster, I can tell you, and soon, he'll be even more so, with this Polish thing coming up. No promotions in peacetime, you know. That is," he joked, "unless you're at the Chancellery. But we'll be getting them soon, and lickety-split, you bet, once we get our hands on those Polacks."

I hadn't been paying much attention to the Führer's discourses and plans, so I needed to disguise my ignorance. "I don't believe the Führer anticipates any trouble."

Baumgärtner laughed. "These are Polacks," Heinz. "They're not Jews, after all. Polacks are stupid enough to resist. That's when we'll have our promotion parties. 'Uncle Heinrich' says that the Führer has left such matters in his and Heydrich's hands. The rest, I leave to your imagination."

After my "guided tour" of Heydrich's basement, nothing further needed to be imagined. "Gerhard," I said, "My apologies, but you see, I'm waiting for a lady, and . . ."

"Ah, Herr Obersturmbannführer, a date, yes? And you don't wish to introduce her to me? Of course not. We policemen have a habit of taking the bloom off the rose, don't we? Well then, I'll leave with all due discretion."

I doubted he'd leave the Poles that way, but anything to rid myself of the sadistic swine.

"I'm much obliged," I said. "And good to see you once again," I lied.

With that, we rose as one, saluted with gusto, he withdrew, and I continued waiting—and hoping that Baumgärtner the policeman wouldn't be lurking round to watch.

Frustrated, I actually began to read the rag, when again, I heard a voice, this time a female's, and far more welcome. I glanced round and shot up as if the Führer had just entered. My brain searched desperately for a name to accompany her glorious face and elegant stature, and what film or films in which I'd seen her, but came up short, which meant that either she wasn't a film star or I'd never seen her on the screen. Instantly, Katrin and Emerald vanished from my pantheon.

"May I sit?" she enquired, a warm lilt in her voice.

I stifled a laugh. "Of course." I raced round to pull back her chair, but by then, she'd already sat down, and I was left standing beside her like a waiter.

She gazed up at me. "I say, would *you* like to sit?" she asked with a twinkle in her marvellously mischievous hazel eyes.

Without a sound, I moved back to my chair and sat down. From that one embarrassing moment, I already knew something about her, and what I knew made me eager to know more— which I believe she also desired. It also made me apprehensive.

I stole a moment to study her while appearing to peruse the menu. She was a woman of crisp angles: the arch of her brows, the precipitous cheekbones, the turn of her padded shoulders, the long, graceful line of her perfectly tailored tweed suit. But there was a softness, too: the thick waves of auburn hair, the feline eyes, the full lips (the lower one, pugnaciously plump), and a voice almost as husky as a man's, yet sultry and strangely soothing. I harboured no doubts that she knew what I was doing and was herself doing the same. It was so comic, we laughed simultaneously.

I removed my cap awkwardly and set it atop the table. I must have been staring at her, for she said, "You needn't feel self-conscious. I'm flattered, actually."

I forced myself not to stammer. "You must have become accustomed to such attention."

She smiled. "The genteel kind, never, I hope. The lascivious kind, I've learned to abide. You have considerably more hair than General Brückner claimed you had."

Clearly, I hadn't escaped her scrutiny. "In some matters, Brückner tends to exaggerate, especially when it concerns my thinning thatch. I only fear that soon, he'll be right."

"*Heil Hitler!* Your order, sir?" sang the young waiter who just arrived, perfect teeth gleaming, a towel neatly draped over his black-liveried forearm. He merely glanced at my uniform but gave Christiane a thorough inspection. She ordered some J. J. Prüm Riesling. I ordered a Beck's.

"Beer?" she exclaimed gently with a slight jocularity. "Brückner caused me to expect a bit more exotica from you."

"Really?" I exclaimed. "I don't know what Brückner told you, but he should also have mentioned that I've tried exotica—and paid for it dearly. Once bitten, twice shy, don't they say?" I couldn't get myself to say *burnt*.

"I think you mean burnt," she corrected with gentleness. "Well, Heinz—may I call you Heinz?—at least you risked a bite. Few do nowadays."

We shifted to silence when the waiter returned with our drinks and asked if we wished some food. We said no simultaneously (generating another concurrent laugh), and he left, eyebrow raised fractionally.

"It appears that we're on the same vessel," she quipped, and raised her glass. "To a fortuitous journey," she toasted, and I followed suit, not knowing what she meant by journey, short of a beginning.

After a few sips, I told her I was enormously pleased that

Brückner had taken the trouble to arrange our meeting. I left out the strange conversation with the foul hag on the telephone.

"Yes," she said. "Wilhelm is a dear man. A rare man. He has a keen eye (no pun intended) for people of unique worth. He claimed you were one of them."

She was as witty as she was beautiful. Yes, Brückner was a truly rare man. "How does he know you?" I ventured.

"His family and mine have known each other for many years. He's a sort of godfather to me, you might say."

I could say almost the same thing—without the family connexion, of course. "Do you work?" I asked her, "or are you a homebody?"

Her lips turned up slightly. "Both, you might say. But that's confusing, I know. I love being home, but I work outside."

"What sort of work, if I may ask?"

She finished her drink, and I ordered her another. "Oh, I . . . coordinate things for the soon-to-be director of the Reich Main Security Office."

Heydrich! She'd said it so matter-of-factly, as if she were claiming to be a receptionist for a bank manager. *Coordinate things?* She was also a master of the nondescript. I wondered whether she knew Hauptsturmführer Baumgärtner. "Ah, I see," I responded in character.

She gave me an appraising look. "And what is it like to work directly for the Führer?"

Careful, my friend! I warned myself. I shrugged. "To be frank, a high honour, to be sure, but quite routine. It isn't as if I consult, propose policy, or implement political directives. I do what you'd expect any valet to do, and no more. I lay out clothes, sort and deliver mail, keep his desk and bookshelves neat and tidy, screen some potential guests, and occasionally run a movie projector. But most of the time, I just stand at ease while the Führer performs his tasks. An exalted rank for such duties, you might think, and you'd be right. However, the rank goes with my venue, not my value."

She laughed huskily and took another sip. "Wilhelm said you had a . . . what did he call it? . . . a 'highly articulate but almost arrogantly self-deprecating sense of humour,' and I now believe him to be right on the mark." She stared, her perfect eyebrows slightly lifted at the empty beer glass I'd been holding. "I say, aren't you having another?"

Instead, I ordered a glass of what she was having. *Arrogantly self-deprecating?* I certainly had Brückner fooled all this time, I chided myself with grim sarcasm. I noticed that the sun was descending, and I knew she saw me noticing it.

"Yes, it's getting late," she said. "Shall I see you again?" she asked. "Perhaps with food, this time, yes? Dinner at my apartment?"

I had to laugh.

"This to you is humorous?" There was a slight flash of emotion in her eyes.

I apologized abjectly, then: "No, no. I was just going to ask if that woman who answered the phone would be there?"

She chuckled. "Of course, Heinz. 'That woman' is my mother—being protective, you understand. The next time, she'll be most complimentary, I promise."

I chuckled. The thought of such a response was not especially enticing to me, which I knew she could tell. "I don't mean that she'll slobber all over you. She's definitely not a slobberer. What I meant was that she'll merely be entirely cordial and hospitable—as well she should be. I'm sure you can appreciate that, aside from those characters working in the Interior Ministry, most men run for their lives once they know whom I work for. I applaud your bravery."

I didn't know how to respond, and she must have sensed this. "Now I've embarrassed you," she said, her sensuous voice suddenly taking on an incongruously contrite quality. "My apologies, Heinz. I only meant it as a joke, but I can see how it might be received."

Then she rose before I could pull out her chair. "I must remember to give thanks to Wilhelm," was all she said. She held out her hand, I pumped it gently, and she strolled away, leaving me delightfully bedevilled, for all I could think of was that I, too, had to thank Brückner.

I MET BRÜCKNER next to the enormous, over-embellished fountain the Führer had Speer design and build. It was gaudy and hideous but, thankfully, noisy.

"Thank you, Wilhelm, I think."

"So, my friend, it went well?"

"I have no real way of telling. I think so. But why her?" I asked, not a little touch of disquiet in my voice.

Brückner frowned. "Why not her? Not your sort?"

"Not her, Wilhelm, her boss."

"Forget her boss."

"Why?" I wanted to ask how but left it at why.

"You met her, so you know why."

"She wants to see me again."

"Of course she does. I know a perfect match when I arrange one. Let her."

HIMMLER AND HIS minions must be having a racial orgasm. According to Brückner's contact at "Himmlerville," last month, SS authorities established Ravensbrück, the largest concentration camp for women (mostly Jewesses), north of Berlin, and now, his ministry just established the "Reich Association of Jews in Germany" (with leadership handpicked by the German Security Police), as the sole legal Jewish organization in Germany. Not content with that, in addition, by fiat, the last remaining Jewish enterprises in the Reich were closed. When Goebbels mentioned it to the Führer as a possible "public relations thorn in Germany's side," the Führer merely said: "I have no idea what Heinrich's up to. But when I trust, I delegate. If he feels such measures are necessary for security and order, that's his job, and the matter's closed."

The entire Chancellery seemed to know more about this than I, for there was no end of congratulatory toasts, "Jew jokes," and a general spirit of coarse conviviality. For the most part, I performed my hail-fellow-well-met to all I knew and managed to escape, but I couldn't erase Adelsheimer from my consciousness—as if he were the embodiment of all Jews. Fortunately, I was so eager to see Christiane at her apartment this very evening that any other concerns were shoved to the side.

The Führer has become increasingly anxious in recent weeks, and, since his anxieties appeared to have found a home in his bowels, more and more was required of Dr. Morell. Seldom in recent weeks did I come at the Führer's command not to find Morell in attendance, and today was no exception.

As I entered the Führer's conference room to straighten up the chaos of maps, diagrams, documents, and implements, a virtual platoon of military and diplomatic officials was leaving hurriedly, at their heels the Führer's screams:

"*Imbeciles!*" he was shouting, his face glowing red. "*I'm surrounded by imbeciles! I blame myself. If there is a decision to be made, I alone must make it!*"

It was another instance of the Führer meaning more than he intended to mean. Of course, by definition, he had to make all the decisions he decided he must make. That's why he chose the people he had round him in the first place. *However,* I thought to myself as I rolled up his maps of Eastern Europe, *how many decisions does he leave to others?*

He shook his head with mock exasperation. "They're upset with me because I intend to negotiate with Stalin. They say that it violates all of my principles and pronouncements about the 'Red Peril.' They are, of course, right—in a myopic way—but I must go where the best options lead. You understand me, Linge?"

I didn't of course, but I knew he'd provide more detail, so I merely shrugged. He continued his breathless rant, and I thought only of my dinner with Christiane—and her mother(!).

It seemed strange to me that Christiane's third-floor apartment was located in the Scheunenviertel,[201] although, after my experience

---

[201] The *Scheunenviertel,* or Barn Quarter, is a historic district. The odd name

with the pitiable Adelsheimer, I had accepted such things as a fact of Berlin life: Aryans would appropriate Jewish dwellings as well as their businesses. After negotiating the labyrinth of crooked lanes that I hadn't travelled since those terrible days when I sought shelter in doorways and received no more than an occasional philanthropic blanket and cup of warm borscht from the Jewish residents, I arrived at 24 Orienenburgerstraße Number 3.

When I knocked on her door, I noticed a small, faded vertical rectangle on the right side of the jamb that had once accommodated a metal Jewish prayer holder they called a *mezuzah*.[202] Before my second knock, the door opened sharply, and I stared down at the tiny, gaunt, age-spotted figure before me. Her face was a complex web of deep wrinkles, her once-blue eyes were faded into virtual transparence, her jowls hung listlessly from the sides of a skeletal chin, and her hair was a clotted cluster of salt-and-pepper braids. She took a step back and narrowed her eyes, pulling her thin lips into a frown as she sized me up.

"You must be most dedicated, Herr Obersturmbannführer, to wear your SS uniform to an apartment dinner?" she said, with no little rebuke in the voice I recognized from the phone.

"I regret that I have no civilian clothes, Frau Glöckner," I

---

harkens back centuries to when the area was home to highly flammable hay barns. It later became Berlin's main Jewish quarter (although Jewish cultural and commercial life was centred on the neighbouring *Spandauer Vorstadt*, where the New Synagogue and other Jewish establishments are located).

[202] The *mezuzah* is a small piece of parchment (often contained in a decorative metal case) inscribed with specified Hebrew verses from the Torah. These verses compose the Jewish prayer "*Shema Yisrael*." A *mezuzah* is affixed to the doorframe in Jewish homes to fulfil the *mitzvah* (Biblical commandment) to inscribe the words of the *Shema* "on the doorposts of your house."

replied with a slight head tilt and shrug of exaggerated innocence. "May I come in?"

Without a word, she moved aside and I entered, far enough
in to allow her to close the door, but not so far in as to assume
a welcome. "And do please call me Heinz. I'm in uniform, yes,
but I'm not on duty."

She stared up at me from the door like a hag in a Flemish
painting. "Christiane will be with you shortly." She aimed her
long, skinny index finger as she would a pistol, towards a once-
plush, well-worn, velvet sofa. "You would sit?" Then she turned
and went down a long hallway, and a moment later, I could hear
a door shut.

It was an old person's apartment, with its claustrophobi-
cally massive, dark, intricate, dust-welcoming furniture, long
sideboard with several faded areas on the surface that hinted
at the multiple rows of family photographs it must once have
supported, a long, dark hallway, and a swinging door to the
kitchen. Oddly, there were no domestic odours: kitchen, boudoir, powder room, or pantry. As a place of hospitality, warmth,
and conviviality, it was even more austere than my monastic cell
at the Chancellery, save for the considerable number of paintings
and photographs of the Führer that lined all four of the living
room walls. I doubted that even Christiane's boss, Himmler,
could boast of such walls.

Eventually, Christiane emerged, greeting me with all the
warmth that her apartment (and her mother) lacked. She was
as exquisite as when I first met her. She wore a simple but fitted
print dress and medium-heel pumps. Her shoulder-length hair
was combed somewhat flat across the top and front and wavy at
the sides—as the latest fashion dictated. She wore no jewellery,
and if she'd applied makeup, it was far too subtle for me to

detect (I knew that the Party disdained the wearing of jewellery and makeup, branding them as non-Aryan signs of female decadence).

After a robust hug and a puckered kiss on both my cheeks, she told me that her mother was not feeling well and so it would be better if we went to a restaurant. Desperately wishing to flee that sterile, Führer shrine with its frigid sentinel, I agreed with no little relief and gratitude, and we were off.

❧

At Christiane's suggestion, we went to the Gründlhaus, a relatively new restaurant that she told me had once contained a Jewish orphanage. From the outside, it looked like an orphanage, Jewish or otherwise, with all the expected icy bleakness, but once inside, I was quite dazzled by the warmth, energy, and opulence surrounding us—and the mob of military and civilian patrons energetically enjoying the food and song. An orphanage no more.

"You see," Christiane chided, once we'd been seated, "I told you that you mustn't be ruled by first impressions."

I nodded reluctantly in agreement. I'd striven to avoid orphanages as a child (at no small risk) and had no intention of attending one now. "But I did agree, didn't I?" I defended weakly.

She just smiled and suggested that I call for a waiter, no simple matter in a place so bustling, but I eventually succeeded, and, at Christiane's suggestion, I ordered a bottle of J. J. Prüm Riesling Trockenbeerenauslese. I'd overheard Speer rhapsodize about its qualities in a manner that suggested a connoisseur's knowledge. He'd also said that it was one of the most expensive wines in the world. When I informed Christiane that my valet's salary would hardly cover the cork, she merely said: "When you order, dear Heinz, just make sure the waiter knows who you are and whom you serve." Again, she was right. It was something a Baur, a Kempka, or a Krause would do instinctively, but even now, I felt as if I were stealing.

Speer was also right; the wine was superb, and, while gazing at each other, we made our first glass a toast to Brückner the matchmaker.

After several minutes of soaking in the revelry round us, she said: "A pity you didn't have the opportunity to meet my mother at her best."

After the phone call and the doorway greeting, I thought I had done. "I hope she feels better soon," was all I said.

"Her name is Clotilda. It means 'famous battle maid,' you know."

I didn't know, but it made perfect sense. "I'll remember that if we're ever positioned to do battle."

She laughed heartily and took a sip of her Riesling. "Please forgive my presumption, but even considering whom you serve, you're wasted as a valet," she declared. "You don't mind me saying this?"

"You'd be amazed how well I take compliments," I answered in my usual ambiguous manner.

"You should have been in the diplomatic service," she said. "You're quite the natural."

I thought about this for a moment, as I sipped. Unfortunately, incessant diplomacy rules out any sort of intimacy—only the illusion of it, an abstract, unspoken tissue of agreed-upon ritual. "I'd have to differ, Christiane. In my humble opinion, a valet must be the most adept diplomat there is, and especially so if he attends a man like the Führer."

She reached over and took my hand in hers, gripping it. "Brückner is truly a magician, and I stand—or sit, rather—corrected." She took her hand back, returned it to her glass, and emptied it. I took only another sip but filled her glass, knowing that I'd better order some food.

"I like you, Heinz Linge," she said, "diplomat, thinning hair, and all. I like you very much. When you're with someone, and you're already looking forward to being with that person again, you can savour two gifts at the same time. I hope you don't consider me too brash."

Just then our first course arrived, a perfect camouflage for escape, and I made the most of it. She was no less a mystery than Emerald or Katrin, but at least Christiane resembled a human, and I wanted to know more without giving more, and all the while, wondering what she saw in the likes of me. "I wouldn't know what brash is," I admitted truthfully, realizing that true escape is futile when the pursuer's sitting right in front of you—and you desperately want her there. "You appear to know a lot about me," I said, "but I know nothing about you. Since 'coordinate things' is a rather vague activity, what kind of work do you actually do?"

She shifted in her seat, reached for the bottle, and filled her glass, her fourth thus far.

"I . . . minimise inconvenience, the same as you, in your own way."

That answer was no more enlightening than "coordinating things," only more erudite, and more sinister. But she'd made it clear that any further questions would be met with more generalities and evasions. "Yes," I said, "no boss relishes inconvenience." My tone suggested levity, in spite of the fact that she would, in any event, know that I'd reconciled myself to accepting a meaningless job description. After all, I'm merely an autodidactic menial with thinning hair, yes? No mystery to someone like her—with Brückner's able assistance, of course. I'd only had two glasses, but at that moment, as I gazed into the seductive hazel pools above her flawless nose, I ached to leap across the table, tear off her clothes, and ravage her then and there, all to the obliviousness of the other Aryan revellers in the former Jewish orphanage.

And now, as I sit in my quarters writing to you, in an odd sense, a part of me believes that the less I know, the better—a beautiful enigma that won't vanish like the other two. Or will she?

AFTER I GOT him dressed and otherwise prepared for the day, the Führer ordered me out while he conferred with this Weisthor character and Himmler. This provided the opportunity to seek out Brückner, who I found dallying in the Communications Centre. I drew him into the gardens, where I attempted to extract some information about Christiane.

"Heinz," he said, as we strolled, "you have that inquiring gaze, and it can be about only one thing. Did she herself not give you the information you sought?"

"No, Wilhelm," I replied. "She did anything but. Her ability to make simple matters obscure is both breathtaking and frustrating. Since you steadfastly refused to tell me anything about her, save her phone number, why must the two of you make her such a mystery?"

"Well, then, perhaps matters are not so simple. Ah, Heinz," he said, "she's not a mystery. Whether there is life after death is a mystery, why we are who we are and not someone else may be a mystery. No, my friend, what are freely called mysteries are, in reality, puzzles, and each encounter should supply at least one or more pieces of that puzzle. And, as with any puzzle worth anything, it requires patience and imagination to fit the pieces together and appreciate the final result. The only question for you should be whether she's worth the effort."

Remembering last night at dinner and later, at the hotel, I answered: "I believe her to be worth the effort."

Brückner shrugged. "So, there it is," he said. "To the simpleminded, everything is a mystery. Recognising puzzles and solving them demonstrate our intelligence. When is your next encounter?"

"It depends on the Führer," I told him. "Fortunately, she understands my situation and agreed to accommodate it. Incidentally, we both expressed our gratitude to you with a toast."

"Then I'm well gratified, but Heinz, consider this: perhaps there are some puzzles that should remain incomplete."

WHILE I OVERHEARD nothing but unbridled praise for the Führer's diplomatic genius in general, many (even on the highest levels) hinted gingerly at misgivings about the Molotov–Von Ribbentrop pact signed today.

The Führer seemed to be affected by this, though I couldn't imagine why.

"*Have they no faith in me? In my judgment?*" he screamed at the portrait of Frederick the Great. Then he returned to his chair and plopped down heavily. "I weary of this, Linge. Whenever I ask them anything of import, I seem to receive only two responses: what they think I want to hear—useless; or dissension—even more useless. How can I conduct the most consequential affairs of state under such conditions?"

I knew his question possessed the usual rhetorical flourishes, and so I had to give him what he was really asking for—his answer: "Then perhaps you shouldn't ask them, my Führer."

"*Exactly so!*" he shouted, after a theatrical pause to simulate thought. "You've gained great wisdom in my service, Linge. I should replace them all with you."

No, I thought, *you should replace them all with you.*

It was my fourth date with Christiane, and not since that first night has she invited me back to her apartment—for which I was both grateful and perplexed. Her claim that her mother was still not well enough to receive visitors was an impenetrable excuse, and so required acquiescence if not belief. After several abortive attempts to finesse some details about her role at "Himmlerville," I did, during our last assignation, manage to wheedle a few paltry personal details from her: that her father was a Lutheran pastor; her mother tended the females of his flock, "the only proper function for a pastor's wife," Christiane told me; and that he passed away, some years before, from an "ailment of the heart," and from that moment forward, her mother began to "wither away in morbid solitude." Anything deeper, Christiane's life at home, her growing up, her friends, her education, her other— and there had to have been other—men in her life, her joining Himmler's staff, her duties, were all foreclosed to me. Brückner was of no assistance, and I dared not make inquiries elsewhere. And yet I abided—and more than I dare admit to you—such was her sensual and "puzzling" spell over me. My thoughts of—and desire for—her, though unbidden, pursued me through the days and nights. An addiction, to be sure, that even being with her wouldn't abate.

At least on a most superficial level, I could treat her to the finest that Berlin has to offer, for the Führer pays his closest staff handsomely, and for the most strategic of reasons, short of generosity. "My people," he remarked once, "have a standard of living with me which I consider the correct one. Working at my side, they should have an adequate income. Nobody should have to succumb to temptation, allow themselves to be corrupted, or engage in unfair practices for need of money. If they do, I reserve the right in such cases to punish harshly and pitilessly." And he did so. For example, when two orderlies I won't name stole paintings and artistic models from his display of birthday presents, they were immediately given over to Himmler, and from thence, to a concentration camp. He occasionally threatened others openly with imminent transfer to a camp, and this always had the desired effect.

IT WAS ONLY a matter of time—and a short amount of time at that—before Poland would be subjected to the entire might of the Reich's formidable military machine, and that not even the possibility of intervention by the Americans would slow the Führer's advance.

A few days ago, he'd received a telegram from their President Roosevelt, entreating him to desist from an attack on Poland in exchange for efforts to achieve general disarmament and equal access by Germany to raw materials in the world market. This, of course, sent the Führer into one of his calculatedly hysterical rages.

"*That cripple Roosevelt's lily-livered arrogance!*" he screamed, his face crimson. "Those isolationist fools went to slumberland after Versailles, while we regained our military primacy. And now they justifiably shake in their boots. *Well, that's all they'll do!* They have an army worthy of Africa, a navy worthy of Switzerland, and an air force worthy of Carnivals. *Just let them try to stop me with their ridiculous Keystone Cops military machine!*"

All round him at the time laughed themselves silly at the imagery, but the Führer was far from finished, and made one of his emotionally dazzling speeches to the Reichstag and (through Goebbels's control of radio broadcasts) the entire nation, bringing his audience to roars of derision and guffaws. The Führer returned to the Chancellery in sweaty elation, ready for the hot bath I'd prepared for him.

However, I knew that beneath all the bluster and merriment, the Führer, irrespective of the arguments of all his "advisers" (save the maverick, Canaris), and even after several severe provocations, was hoping for a first strike from Poland. But it never came.

The remarkable thing, the mysterious thing about the entire affair, was what I sensed lay just below the surface of the Führer's demeanour. Despite the clamorous invective, what I also sensed was a resignation, frustration, and futility, as if war was being forced upon him because other means were just out of reach.

Why the Führer believed for one moment that a nation and a people he's mocked for years would dare risk annihilation by attacking Germany was beyond my poor powers of analysis, but the Führer, in private, claimed to desire it all the same. This morning, he must have seen the puzzlement on my face, despite my attempt at otherwise-occupied blankness.

"You're perplexed, I know," he said, studying his desk blotter. "So are they. But understand, Linge, that after dealing with Czechoslovakia as I did, I cannot now be too harsh with those who mistakenly believe that they know me, and so strenuously advise another *blitzkrieg*,[203] and then be astonished at my reticence. But you know that when it comes to conventional means of waging a conventional war, I've always been of two minds, and with so much at stake with this Polish business, even more so. However, after last night, I may be forced to satisfy my critics and make the decisive move."

Actually, I didn't understand. What was the unconventional

---

[203] Lightning War.

way? "Yes, my Führer," I said, having no idea what the "decisive move" might be, short of that *blitzkrieg*.

He continued gazing down at his blotter, then rose with a grunt of capitulation, turned, said, "Good day, Linge," and shuffled into his bathroom, closing the door quietly behind him.

While attempting to straighten out the chaos on the Führer's desk, I happened upon a telegram from SS Colonel Otto Rahn to Himmler, which he must have presented to the Führer last night. It said: "Objects remain elusive. Believe one still in Germany. Other here in Montségur. Am confident can secure latter. Securing former, must be Reichsführer-SS."

[Caveat: In this entry, Linge's handwriting, typically rendered in the autodidact's self-conscious calligraphy, degenerated into a chaotic scribble, rendering many passages unreadable and the remainder requiring several subjective liberties. However, I believe that ample justification for its inclusion will be readily apparent from the content.]

I SPEAK TO you tonight through a force of will worthy of a Hercules.[204] I pray not to falter before setting it down.

⤝

This morning, all the Chancellery appear delirious with anticipation. That is, all, save the Führer, who awoke early, having slept calmly and deeply, despite all the excitation round him. To a stranger he would give the impression that it was just another day, though I knew he was in turmoil. As I tended him, his vegetarian's breath, never very sweet, was particularly foul—to the point of completely masking his incessant toxic flatulence. When I'd dried him off from his bath, he went to his phone and called Großadmiral Raeder, ordering him to order all German-flagged ships to head at once to German ports. It was the final item on his agenda.

Later, on a brief garden stroll, Brückner predicted a major triumph for the Führer but added that "triumph dispels doubts and becomes an addiction, and the craving can only be satisfied by more and more triumphs." I had no reason to doubt my friend—and it filled me with a dark foreboding that I hoped lunch with Christiane would overcome.

⤝

---

[204] Hercules was the son of Zeus. In classical mythology, Hercules is famous for his strength.

I waited for two hours in the tucked-away Café Rix, normally alive with chatter, laughter, the clinking of glasses, and general lunchtime big-city bustle, but today, as subdued and expectant as a father-to-be chain-smoking in a hospital waiting room. When Christiane failed to appear, and a call to her apartment wasn't answered, I reluctantly telephoned Himmler's ministry to get a reason for her absence. Instead, I was told that they never even heard of a Christiane Glöckner, much less knew where she might be!

Now, even more anxious than the people surrounding me, I paid my coffee bill despite the waiter's obsequious protestations, and left, determined to visit her apartment and see what I could learn.

The streets still wore a moist sheen from the night before. As I walked, I could hear all the sounds of a wet street: the galumphing of rubber-clad feet, the hissing spray of tram wheels, and the swishing and whooshing of car and bicycle tyres.

I negotiated the tangle of streets, slotting into the homebound flood of clerks and shop girls who normally sauntered with their usual minimum of conscious effort but who now moved with a purposeful stride. Tonight, instead of sitting down to a long supper or dressing for a date, they would eat hurriedly and sit, clustered around their radios, waiting for the Führer's fateful move. As would all of Germany, save me, since I already knew and had lost interest days before.

It was nothing tangible at first, just an animal sense that something wasn't right. I told myself to ignore the sudden anxiety, but trying to ignore what I sensed was as futile as trying not to close one's eyes when sneezing. Brückner once told me that "shutting your mind to something locks it in, not out."

Something inchoate was gnawing through my nerves like a rat through cheese. It was only when I turned slightly that my peripheral vision caught the two figures in leather coats and fedoras hastily pivot round and unfurl their newspapers with all the subtlety of a military parade. Imagination? Coincidence? Perhaps, but the rat continued to gnaw.

Suddenly, the sky trembled and umbrellas snapped to, as though an entire parachute battalion had opened up simultaneously in midfall. Having left my umbrella at the Chancellery, when the rain began plummeting with waterfall ferocity, my immaculate uniform transmuted into a shapeless, sodden rag in a matter of seconds. However, instead of seeking immediate shelter, I moved forward to justify or negate my anxiety.

I crossed the street, then abruptly stopped in front of a large department store window, attempting to use it as a mirror while pedestrians swirled round me with expressions of puzzlement or irritation. There they were, standing at the kerb, again at left face, casually reading their now-soaked and useless newspapers. Himmler's "Keystone Cops," as Brückner called the cloddish Gestapo flatfeet.

A wet gust smacked against my neck, but it felt like breath, warm against my skin as I moved out at a brisk pace, turned a corner, and stopped abruptly to turn up my collar. Again, my line of sight picked up the leather coats and fedoras standing in the street, arms raised as if summoning a taxi. With a snort of derision, I made for the next corner and looked round, as if deciding whether to cross or not, gazed down at my soppy feet, and shook my head. I purposely missed a break in the traffic and let my shoulders drop, my body go limp—an act of resignation I felt worthy of the finest actor.

A slight flap of the arms, self-evident theatrical impatience, and I set off again, shoulders bowed against the horizontally slanted rain, eyes on the pavement. My uniform had long since given up any resemblance to clothing, and so I stopped worrying about it. Two young women approaching and passed, staring at me oddly and exchanging unkind giggles behind my back. I barely noticed them.

Negotiating the rain-battered swarm, my heart pounding, I struggled to compose myself, to think, but I gave that up since I had no idea of my followers' purpose. However, suspecting the worst and temporarily bereft of alternatives, I recalled some advice in *The Secret Agent* by Joseph Conrad: Don't worry about who or why. Elude! Now alert, not just to the leather coats and fedoras but to everything around me, it was as if all my nerves stretched along the surface of my skin, finely tuned for the first indication of danger. Then it dawned on me that all the elaborate strategizing, the prize-winning acting, the evasion itself—was patently ridiculous. In this weather, the only thing I should be evading was the rain.

As I penetrated deeper into Berlin's slowing heart, the crowds thinned dangerously, and I slowed to a crawl, forcing the followers to hang back. But when I turned my head slightly at a corner, they were nowhere to be seen. Had they given up? Were they more adroit than I thought? Was the entire business the product of an overwrought imagination? These questions were colliding with each other like bumper cars at a carnival funhouse, when a uniformed man came towards me, his face concealed by an umbrella.

"Herr Obersturmbannführer!" a familiar voice exclaimed beneath the umbrella. "You look like a drowned dog." When he raised his umbrella slightly, I could see it was Hauptsturmführer Schlegl, one of the Chancellery's legion of sentries. A head shorter but built like a bulldog, he'd come on board at the same time as I, and continually ribbed me for my rapid advancement as opposed to his "sentry stagnation," as he called it. Normally, he was pedestrian and tiresome, but now, I welcomed the company.

"Then it's good of you to offer your umbrella, Horst," I joked. Horst Schlegl was not one of life's sharers.

"That'll be the day," he grumped, "what you need is to get to shelter till the rain stops. Here," he said, raising his umbrella, "you're the giant. You hold it over both of us and we'll hunt for some covered space."

In answer, I took the handle and we were off like Mutt and Jeff.[205] Within a few awkward minutes, Schlegl pointed to a partially covered alleyway and, turning, we pushed through the swarm and entered.

"Sure glad you came along," I said as Schlegl shook out his umbrella.

"Not to worry," he answered with a smirk. "The least I could do for a superior officer. But why were you out there in the first place? There are plenty of taxis in Berlin, you know. And for us," he added, "they're free."

"You'll think me paranoid, Horst, but I thought I was being followed by some lamebrained Gestapo types."

Schlegl shook his head. "Ach! Now why would they do that? Surely, you'd be the last person under any kind of suspicion."

I'd never told him about the attempt on my life, but I knew how such secrets fly around the Chancellery. "I agree. Just jumpy about tomorrow, I suppose."

"Hardly necessary, my friend. Should those idiots in England

---

[205] *Mutt and Jeff* was a long-running and widely popular American newspaper comic strip created by cartoonist Bud Fisher in 1907 about two mismatched characters. Jeff was short, bald as a billiard ball, and wore mutton-chop sideburns; Mutt was tall and lanky.

and France rattle their sabres, the Führer will shove them up their arses. As for the Polacks, you hear this? How do you stop a Polish army on horseback? Turn off the carousel."

I faked a chuckle, as the pounding roar of rain suddenly subsided to a light sprinkle.

Shlegl shrugged his massive shoulders. "But, if you're so worried, go and sneak a check and see if you spot them."

I shrugged. "Not necessary, Horst. I probably imagined the whole thing."

"Yeah, probably," said Schlegl. "But since you're a worrier, you can't be too careful, so check it out and then you'll be sure."

"If you think so," I said without conviction.

"Right," he replied, "go to it."

I moved to the alleyway's edge and peered out in all directions but one, and saw no leather greatcoats or fedoras, only ordinary pedestrians hastily sloshing along the puddled street.

When I turned back, I saw the dagger in Shlegl's hand swing upward, just in time for me to sidestep. Fortunately, even more than my brain, the senses never forget, and in a fraction of an instant I was the streetwise criminal again, all instinct, anticipation, and reaction.

I pivoted and the blade slid past me. As I spun back, he charged like the mindless bear he was, but despite my size, I was far more nimble. Slipping to the side, I pushed Shlegl's elbow down and away, grabbed his head, and threw him onto the sodden ground, causing the dagger to fly out of his reach.

But before I could seize the advantage, he was on his feet. Head hunched down into his massive shoulders, he threw his bulk into my chest, ramming me against a wall. Now apparently heedless of the noise and seeing me temporarily breathless, he moved back slightly and pulled out his pistol.

Adrenalin replaced breath. I grabbed his wrist, drove his arm over his shoulder, and pulled him backward and down. I had the gun even before the Hauptsturmführer landed. I bent over and smashed him on the forehead with it. That would have done for anyone else, but not this bulldog.

Still on the ground, the now-bloody Shlegl gripped my ankle with his feet, twisted it, and sent me reeling back to the wall. This gave him time to pull himself up, rush towards me, and put out a stiff right.

I shoved myself to the left to avoid it, then reached out, pulled his head forward, and smashed his nose with my knee. Now the bulldog was a bleeding, groaning hulk, but like any wounded animal, still dangerous, so I shoved my other hand into his crotch, put my shoulder into him, lifted him off the ground, and slammed him down on the cement.

One last grunt and he went limp, his mouth and eyes gaping. The animal still in control, I lifted my booted leg and brought it down like a piston, crushing his head as if it were a ripe melon.

Then, without delay and oblivious to my sodden, bloody, and bruised appearance, I made it to the street, hailed a taxi, and commanded the alarmed driver to take me to the Adlon. I intended to book a room, have my uniform sponged and pressed, perform some emergency cosmetic repair on my face and hands, race back to my quarters, and hope that my position and rank would stifle in the womb the inevitable alarm over my ravaged appearance.

However, once I'd been delivered to the Chancellery, it took no prodigious feat of imagination to grasp the perils of using the main entrance, with its myriad checkpoints, stunned stares, robotic demands for my "papers," and only too human appeals for an explanation of my ragged state.

So, with a shudder so violent that it drove all my wounds to erupt in agony, I moved stealthily to the relatively little-known, and so relatively eremitic, side entrance to the main garage, where, I expected, there would be far fewer gapes and only one interrogation.

"Scheisse!" Kempka cried out, wide-eyeing up and down my battered condition. "Man, I sure hope to hell you gave as good as you got."

Even after viewing the wreckage in the Adlon's bathroom mirror, I hadn't fully acknowledged the brutal extent of my facial injuries until I attempted to answer him, and an electric pain in my jaw permitted only a wincing, tearful mumble.

Seeing my distress, the little chauffeur reached out, took me gingerly by the elbow, turned me round, guided me into his tiny, wire-glass-surrounded office, and sat me down, then switched off all the lights, save for a small desk lamp whose sepulchral shadows must have made me resemble Frankenstein's monster.

"Don't talk!" he commanded needlessly. "You can fill me in on all the juicy details when the Führer has Morell make you resemble a human again." He moved a few steps over to his desk, pulled open a drawer, produced a bottle of brandy and two water glasses, and returned to me. "Take heart," he joked as he poured, "you won't be alone. After tomorrow, all of Poland will look like you—and maybe even worse." He handed me a glass, full to the meniscus point, and I took it gingerly with my slightly less bruised and trembling left hand, held it up in a feeble toasting gesture, moved it to my battered lips, and downed the whole thing in one long, painful swig.

"Smart lad," he said, shaking his head with an accompanying

smile. "You knew better than to go through the main entrance like that. I know the feeling. Just your good luck I was still here." He drained his glass. "I'm pretty sure we're alone down here, but I'll just check to be positive. Last thing we need are any nosy parkers running round making mischief, now, do we? You can stay here tonight on that," nodding toward his battered leather sofa with its discoloured stuffing oozing through the fissures.

When he returned a few minutes later, he dropped down on his dilapidated swivel chair with a creaking crash. "Just as I thought," he sighed. "We're it. I imagine everybody else is glued to their radios, waiting for the second shoe to drop—on Warsaw." He chuckled at that, then nodded to the tiny sink in the corner. "Okay, my son, let's get you cleaned up a little, then I'll sneak up to your quarters and fetch you a clean uniform. Later, you can tell everybody you were tangling with a professional wrestler over some beer hall bitch." The smile again, this time, a little broader and joined by a wink.

I did nothing to disabuse him of the notion.

✑

"Have you ever killed anyone," Brückner once asked me.

I said I hadn't but I lied. Why would someone ask me something like that when Germany was awash in violence from top to bottom, side to side? And until I had some answers to what took place after I left Café Rix, I would lie again.

So, I join all the others in the Reich, who, for their own reasons, would not sleep this night.

The End of Volume One